The Brin Archives

Jim Cronin

ALL RIGHTS RESERVED

Publisher's Note:

This is a work of fiction. All names, characters, places, and
events are the work of the author's imagination.

Any resemblance to real persons, places, or events is
coincidental.

Solstice Publishing - www.solsticepublishing.com

The Brin Archives

Jim Cronin

The Brin Archives is dedicated to everyone in my family, past, present and future. Those of you from my past provided the foundation of a shared history my life is built on. Those of you here in the present have helped to refine and improve me as an individual. Your guidance has molded my strengths and weaknesses to make me the person I am today. And to those yet to come, you are my inspiration, and my hope. It is for you that I have worked to do my little part to improve this fragile world and make it worthy of your arrival.

Hegira

Preface

"Come in, Latonia Base…come in Latonia Base. This is Starship Hegira, repeat, this is Hegira. Come in, Latonia."

Static crackled from the speaker. The lieutenant, bleeding and dying from the injuries he received during the mutiny trembled feebly as he gripped the microphone. Blood soaked his crest feathers; his talons broken and jagged from the hand-to-hand combat in the spaceship's passageways. He knew his wounds were fatal, but his duty was clear: to report back to base about the failure of the mission. His body tensed as the next wave of pain shot through him.

"Latonia Base, this is Hegira. Come in. Priority clearance Falcon, Delta. Come in Base. Damn you to hell!" the soldier shouted in desperation. "Somebody answer! Come in, Latonia!" The microphone dropped from his talons, clattering on the control panel before falling to the metal plated floor. The lieutenant slumped back into the chair, pressing a blood soaked rag to his shoulder. Staring out the view port he watched the star-filled blackness and wondered at the cruel turn fate had taken over the past few days.

A pounding on the hatch caused the lieutenant to reach for his sidearm. "Lieutenant Yardef! It's Vedak. Let me in, sir!"

The lieutenant pulled himself up in the chair and reached out with a fractured, bloodstained talon to press the door release circuit. With a sharp hiss, the door slid open and in hobbled Sergeant Vedak, one of his few remaining platoon members.

"It worked, sir," the soldier said, crashing into the second chair in the room.

Yardef surveyed his subordinate's injuries, noting several which would prove to be fatal. "You okay, Sarge? You don't look so good."

"Look who's talking," said the young soldier. He tugged at his uniform, checking his wounds.

"We got most of them sealed in the lower decks and opened the cargo hatches to space. They didn't stand a chance once we decompressed decks one through ten. They're all dead now. Just a few survivors are holed up one deck above us." Ripping a piece from his ruined shirt he wrapped the makeshift bandage around the laser shot in his arm.

"Good. Were you able to get the hatches closed again?"

The sergeant looked his superior in the eyes and shook his head. "Negative. All the controls are fried."

"I need you to go find the engineer. See if he can do anything."

"He's dead, sir. He bought it down in cargo bay C during the first assault."

The two sat in silence for several long minutes before either could speak. "That looks pretty bad, sir. Want me to look at it?" Vedak pointed at the lieutenant's shoulder, still bleeding heavily despite the thick bandage he pressed against it.

"Don't waste your time." The officer coughed and winced as the pain gripped him again. "At least I won't have to wait around to starve to death. Are those vials secured?"

"Yes, sir. We were able to pull them from cryogenics before those clerics overran us. I locked them up in the high security bay. No one can get to them now. What's so important about those two samples, sir? Out of the thousands of samples, why just those two?"

Lieutenant Yardef shrugged his shoulders, his face contorting at the new stab of pain. "Don't ask me, Sarge. All I know is the orders specified keeping those two samples out of fundamentalist hands at all cost. When the mutiny began, the Captain ordered me to make them our top priority. Way above my pay grade to ask why."

"I hope they're worth the lives they cost us," said the sergeant. "Any luck with communications?"

The older man shook his head in silence. "Nothing but static so far. I'll ..." He coughed again and dropped to the floor.

"Lieutenant!" Vedak jumped out of his chair and fell to his knees, lifting the lifeless body of the officer.

The sound of sporadic energy blasts tore his attention away from the dead lieutenant. He checked the monitor and stumbled to the intercom controls. "What's going on out there, soldier?" he demanded of the man he saw on the camera. The bright orange flash of a laser blast missed the soldier's head by inches.

"The fundie rebels, Sarge," called out the soldier as he fired several rounds down the corridor behind him. "They broke out of their makeshift fortress on deck twelve and forced us to regroup here. We got most of them, but it cost us. Only a few of us left now."

The sergeant quickly appraised the situation and made his decision. "Stand your ground, soldier. Nobody gets through you into this room. I've got to try to reach Latonia Base. Kill anything in a robe that's still breathing."

"Those fucking fundies are as good as dead, Sarge."

Another flash lit up the monitor and blood splattered the camera lens before he could acknowledge. As the sergeant stepped back into the ether wave room he heard the speakers come to life. "Hegira, this is Latonia Base. Do you read us, Hegira? Come in."

The sergeant lunged to the floor, grabbing the microphone in his shaking hand; the last remnants of his self-control dissolving rapidly. "Latonia Base, this is Hegira. I read you," he responded. "Praise The Eternal! You can hear me. Please help. They're killing each other. Only a few of us are left and badly wounded. Help us!"

Part One

Chapter One

Location: Deep Space, Catalan Sector

Alarms echoed throughout the ship.

"Alert code Delta...Alert code Delta," the ship-wide communications blared. "This is no drill...Repeat, this is no drill."

The *Helven* was the first of her kind. Built by the Skae Space Command to explore the farthest regions of space, she had traveled farther than any other vessel in the fleet. While designed for exploration, the *Helven* came equipped with the most advanced technology for both scientific and military encounters. The Skae had few rivals in exploration of the galaxy, but recently, the Gorvin had begun to challenge them in nearby sectors. After a year in Sector Beta 14, this was the Helven's first live action.

Captain Pok entered the bridge from his private briefing room. Senior commander of the fleet with twenty-seven years' experience, he was the natural choice for command of the Helven on such a mission. A jagged scar cut through the deep blue skin of his left temple, the result of action he saw during the Gorvin Wars. He scanned the banks of computer screens to read the ship's condition and to see if the sensors detected any threats.

"So what do we have?"

"Our communications buoys have picked up a ship distress signal. It appears to be from an alien vessel about three parsecs from our current position. The signal appears automated and we have not been able to raise anything in response. We are not close enough for sensors to pick up life signs or weapons status."

"Any sign of hostile activity?" Recent intel didn't mention any Gorvin activity out this far, but information about this sector was sketchy at best.

"No, sir," replied the first officer. "No enemy energy signatures within range of our sensors."

"Very well then, take us to the ship, Ensign Tagol. Keep weapons on alert status and sensors on full range. Engines at point eight."

It took only a few moments for the flight crew to set their instruments to the assigned coordinates and flight pattern. The ship responded without sound or any apparent change in acceleration, but the control panels all indicated their new trajectory toward the source of the distress signal. "How long till arrival, Ensign?"

"We should arrive at the coordinates in three days, Captain."

"Very well. Notify me if there are any changes or if sensors pick up anything unusual." Pok left the bridge after a glance and a nod to his second in command. He left for his quarters to catch up on the endless flow of reports and, hopefully, get at least a few hours of sleep before his duty watch arrived.

Seventy-five hours later, in the Captain's briefing room, the ensign of the watch reported on the latest updates regarding the alien vessel.

Captain Pok's brow furrowed as he raised his hand to interrupt the report. "Just this automated distress signal and no signs of life? What about weapons?"

"The ship contains only a minimum of weaponry and those are only standard lasers, no threat to our vessel. Their propulsion system is ionic thruster based. Power levels are barely registering. There are only faint life sign readings. Sensors show it to be a cargo vessel, probably fully automated and it seems to have had a mechanical malfunction of some sort."

"Any threat to a survey team?" asked the second in command.

"No, sir, no threat detected. Radiation levels are minimal. Sensors detect no evidence of active security measures on board. However, temperature and atmospheric conditions will require the use of environmental suits."

"Very well then. Dismissed, Ensign." The officer turned back to the Captain. Tagol saluted smartly and marched out of the briefing room.

"First contact with a new species is always a delicate business," said the Captain. "Let's do this one strictly by the book until we learn more."

On the main view screen a silvery space ship, shaped like a flattened ovoid approximately one hundred meters long, fifty meters wide and forty meters thick and bifurcated at the stern, showed numerous portholes indicating at least six decks. Three thrust manifolds protruded from aft, apparently inoperative, as the ship drifted aimlessly against the immensity of space. No lights or energy emissions of any sort were to be seen. Years of micro-meteorite impacts pitted the derelict ship's skin, as if some demented space demon had used it as a chew toy. There were a few small breeches in the hull originating from the ship's interior, but otherwise it seemed to be intact.

In the Captain's briefing room, the command crew sat around the oblong table.

"Those breeches came from some sort of small arms fire," said the chief weapons officer as he pointed at the holes in the vessel. "They could have been defending themselves from something."

The science officer examined the data on his screen. "Whatever happened occurred a long time ago. Sensor readings indicate the ship has been adrift for over twenty years."

Captain Pok leaned back in his chair, examining the faces of his officers. "Very well then. Have a survey team ready to board, but with caution and in full protective measures in place. If there was a crew, no telling what might have killed them, so we don't want any alien infections brought back here. Level ten decontamination upon return as well, just to be safe. And let's go in on full alert. If this was the result of hostile action we don't want to be caught with our drawers down."

Once they arrived, Pok dispatched several teams to check out the disabled vessel. "Explore Team One here, sir. We have entered the ship and are heading toward the bridge."

"Very good Team One, proceed with caution."

"Team Two here. The corridors are a bit short; we definitely need to be careful getting through these hatchways. Strange design, pointed archways on top, the bulkheads are slightly concave and the rooms are circular. Whoever they were, they didn't like straight lines or corners. No sign of any survivors. All we have here are the remains of the crew. There appears to have been some sort of battle among the crew. Bodies are scattered everywhere, some still frozen in their final struggle."

"Can you describe them, Ensign?" the Captain asked.

Tagol shined his light over the bodies floating in the room to his left. "Yes, sir, they are humanoid, but more avian in appearance. They are short, only around six feet tall. I can see colorful feather-like crests on the tops of their heads covering a portion of their skulls, shorter feathers covering the rest of their heads, except for their faces. They have four fingers on each hand with talons instead of fingernails. At least one of the fingers appears to be opposable. Their skin appears smooth, but there is a very faint texture of scales. Not visible unless the light hits them just right. No external ears are visible."

"Okay, Ensign, continue your search. Bag up a few of them for examination by medical. Stay in constant communication."

"Team Three here, we have found what appears to be the main bridge. More signs of a struggle here, too. Some of the crew had a small hand-held energy weapon. Others are armed with knives or metal pipes. This looks more like a mutiny than outside hostilities, Captain. We're commencing to download their data logs."

"Very good, Team Three. Return to base once you have the data collected. We will begin translation and analysis once you get back."

"Captain! Team Two here. We have found what scanners indicate to be a vast collection of DNA samples in one of the cargo bays. Thousands of them! Power is off so they've degraded significantly, but sensors show that two still seem to be viable. We will retrieve these and return."

***

Six hours later, Captain Pok called all department chiefs to a conference.

The young Ensign Tagol turned on his recording device and stood at attention behind the Captain as the officers filed into the briefing room. "All department seniors present and accounted for, Captain."

Pok surveyed the faces around the rectangular briefing table. "Let's get this over with quickly. I want to get on with our mission as soon as possible. Engineering…"

"Just as we suspected, sir," said the senior chief, reading his notes, scanning over the details. "The ship was a primitive design, ion impulse engines, no external weaponry, flowing electron operating systems throughout the vessel. Nothing worth salvaging, unless you want to stay an extra month to carve it up into scrap metal for reworking.

"Not likely," the Captain replied, shaking his head and signaling for the next officer to begin. "Security…"

"No threats, biological or weapons, sir. The ship lacked any external armament, the only sign of weapons were obsolete hand-held plasma beam in design. No survivors."

"Navigation, do we know where the ship came from?"

"We did locate the star system, Captain, but bad news there. The central star went supernova about twenty years ago. No chance of anything surviving anywhere in the system."

Captain Pok rocked back in his chair, and rubbed his chin. "Could this ship have been some sort of attempt to preserve some remnant of their world?"

"A distinct possibility, sir," replied the bioscience officer. "All those DNA samples and machinery were very likely some last ditch effort to find a new home for themselves. It looks like—"

"With that ship?" cut in the chief engineer, shaking his head, his hands raised with elbows on the table. "It never stood a chance of getting to another star system. Those engines weren't nearly enough for the task. If this was their best effort at saving themselves they must have been incredibly desperate."

"The data banks are still in pretty bad shape, Captain," said the communications chief. "We will know more once we finish reconstruction from the mirrored files."

Pok nodded, ending the topic for the moment and looked to the next officer for her report.

Moving from one to the next, each officer stated his or her findings, nothing unexpected or surprising, until…

"Bioscience, let's finish this up."

"We have a Red Dart indicator, sir," replied the chief after clearing her throat. All eyes turned to the chief, backs stiff, muscles tensed. Red Dart alerts were something mentioned only in the academy as part of their history courses. "While the specimens are ordinary carbon based life forms, similar to everything we have encountered so far, except for the avian features, the indicators popped up once we began to analyze their DNA. Whatever the computers saw to trigger the alarm is something way beyond my pay grade, Captain."

"Damn!" said Pok, slapping his hand on the table amidst a general groan from the officers assembled. "Alright everyone, this briefing is over. Red Dart protocols are in effect. Encrypt all reports at level omega and have them delivered to me within the hour. Get comfortable, everyone, we aren't going anywhere until High Command has a look at this."

* * *

At the appointed time, Captain Pok keyed in the series of codes to enable the Eyes Only Security Net and punched the communications connection. The image of High Commander Tobuk appeared on the screen, flanked by Admiral Contu, chief medical advisor to the Emperor.

"Captain Pok, your discovery of this alien DNA has created an immediate Red Dart Alpha priority revision of your mission." The high commander's imperious tone and stiff demeanor warned Pok to hold his tongue for now. "Until further notice you and your crew will consider yourself outside the regular command structure and under the sole command of Admiral Contu. No outside communications by any crewmember, including yourself, are permitted without clearance by the admiral himself."

Pok stiffened in his chair, his mind racing with a thousand questions, but duty and training restrained him... barely. "Understood, sir."

"Thank you, Commander," said Admiral Contu dismissing the man, silently waiting until he was alone. "Captain Pok," he said, eyes burning into the screen, his face held firm as if made of granite. "There has not been a Red Dart alert for over fifteen hundred years. Not since the loss of the Kolandi and the rise of the Gorvins. We've been searching for ways to eradicate the Kolandi infection and return them to their former strength alongside us in the Galactic Forces ever since. Without success as you know."

"Yes, sir," replied Pok. The Skae learned this horrific history lesson in their earliest school days, and tales of the Gorvin monsters permeated many of the stories parents told their children when they misbehaved. It was the darkest moment of their generally glorious past. The Gorvin effectively eliminated the Kolandi with a genetic plague and nearly conquered the galaxy. Only extreme daring and chance brought the war to a standoff, with occasional minor wars breaking out over the following centuries. Pok absently brought a finger to his facial scar as he remembered his own close call during the latest of these encounters.

"This new DNA you discovered contains sequences we believe will finally provide the solution we have searched for. In the next few days you will receive orders containing instructions on how to proceed, including details on what you are authorized to reveal to your crew and which of them, due to their specialized skills, will be cleared to proceed with the reanimation of the DNA."

"Excuse me, sir," said Pok, unable to restrain himself any longer. "Reanimate the DNA? Are you talking about cloning, sir?"

"That is only the beginning, Captain. Your orders will tell you as much as we dare allow, and will undoubtedly sound incredible, but we are desperate, Captain."

"Understood, sir," Pok said as he saluted the monitor.

"And, Captain," said the Admiral returning the salute. "Do not fail. The future of the galaxy may very well rest on the success of this mission."

***

A week later, Captain Pok stepped through the bridge entryway, assumed his place in the command chair and pressed the ship-wide communications switch.

"All sector chiefs report to the briefing room immediately, repeat, immediately. Captain out."

The assembled chiefs questioned each other as they sat around the table awaiting the Captain, who entered through his private passage only a minute later, going directly to his place at the head of the table.

"Alright, everyone, settle down. We are about to receive a priority Delta communication from High Command." He pressed a switch on the table and seconds later, a ghostly holographic image began to form.

Captain Pok hesitated briefly, his jaw dropping almost imperceptibly as he recognized the personage before them. Lifting two fingers of his left hand to his temple in salute, he stood to attention. "Your Highness, this is truly unexpected."

"Yes, Captain," replied the image of the supreme ruler of all Skae. "High Command analyzed the data you transmitted and relayed their conclusions to me personally." The officers remained speechless, only able to gape incredulously at each other and the hologram before them as it paused. "By now, Captain, you have received your orders from Admiral Contu. You are the finest crew ever assembled and we have the utmost faith in your ability to carry out these orders. We know all too well the extreme hardship our restrictions will cause, but they are necessary and the rewards of success are too great to risk. Good luck gentlemen. All of our hopes go with you."

The officers shared stunned looks across the table as the image vanished. Captain Pok keyed in the commands to bring up images on the main screen.

"This, gentlemen, is our new mission…"

***

A month later, deep in the bowels of the *Helven*, specialists in the sterile science labs wore the high-level protective wardrobe required by protocols when dealing with foreign materials. Computer banks blinked as they processed the information fed to them, and several screens displayed the information as it became available. Line after line of genetic code appeared on the main screen.

"Can you imagine, the entire crew gone…all fifty-eight killed off, and by each other's hand," said Zem, lab specialist level four.

"Yeah, deciphering their computer logs is taking some time to translate due to the high levels of corruption, but it appears to have been the result of some political struggle between crew members over their cargo," Bolt, chief of the labs, replied.

"Yep, nothing but completely degenerated vials of DNA and the equipment to reanimate them once they had reached their destination is what we figure."

Bolt continued to examine the specimens at his station, then glanced over his shoulder to see if anyone was close enough to overhear him. "Know anything about the other two vials? The ones the rumors are about?"

The conversation between the two technicians was brought to an immediate halt by the entrance of the principal science officer. "You two know the regulations regarding discussion of any matters dealing with the alien ship. All such information is limited to officers and those directly involved. We have enough rumors and matters of policy to deal with without you two adding to the list of difficulties. You know your duties, get back to work, and leave these other matters alone until the Captain sees fit to fill everyone in on what is happening."

"Yes, sir, but you would think that after a month of communication blackout and sections of the ship being placed on top level security clearance, somebody would tell us something, sir," said Bolt.

"Well, when you reach the rank of admiral and want to walk right up to the Captain and demand an answer, feel free to go right ahead, Specialist Bolt, but until then, I suggest you stick to your usual duties."

"Yes, sir, no harm or disrespect intended, sir. Just a lot of scientific curiosity, sir."

"Okay, okay, lighten up with the 'sirs', Bolt. You know what I mean. We are all just as anxious as you are to know what is going on. The Captain will inform us just as soon as he can straighten out all of the political crap. Got me?"

Chapter Two

Bolt mind wandered fitfully over the past two decades as he monitored his student's progress. He startled back to the present as his pupil interrupted once again with more questions.

"So this cosmic string is going to take us back in time so I can take control and avoid the situations which caused the destruction of the Brin ship...my ship?" asked Karm, running his talons through his long crest feathers.

"That is correct," replied his mentor Bolt. The Skae's nimble blue hands danced over the control panel to display more images. "Most cosmic strings allow us to travel quickly through the vast distances of space. However, we have learned there are some strings, which, if approached using extremely precise calculations, allow us to travel through time as well as space. Unfortunately, these time-traveling strings are not as precise as the others, and much more dangerous. We have located a string to send you back in time to your home planet, but we can only approximate, with a fair degree of certainty, when you will arrive. This particular string does seem to be far enough in the past to allow for reasonable error and still provide you with sufficient time to complete your mission, within the twelve percent margin of error. Your case is unique and has thus received approval, despite the inherent dangers."

"Won't my going back in time change things?"

Bolt nodded. "The planet will not survive long enough for most changes to the timeline to matter. In addition, that is why we have provided you with this biocomputer. It will provide you with precisely the information you need to prevent you from doing too much damage to the timeline. It took a bit of skillful plastic surgery and some minor changes to your anatomy to accommodate the device, but your appearance is still well within the norm for a Brin, according to the databanks retrieved from your ship. Listen to me, Karm," said Bolt as he looked into Karm's eyes. "You cannot allow the timeline to change beyond the parameters we have given you. There are some events, which, if altered even in the short term remaining, could have far-reaching effects for our plan. Events in time are like ripples in a pond. Your biocomputer should help keep you in the outer, less vital ripples, far from the central events, but beware, the data we collected from your ship was corrupted. There are many gaps in the records where we could only extrapolate probabilities for occurrence. There is still a danger if you change things too much."

Bolt had been the junior officer in charge of analyzing the DNA sequence data downloaded from the derelict ship after its discovery 21 years ago. After receiving a highly classified reply to his Red Dart Emergency communication, the Captain held an immediate briefing in his ready room for the command staff. The result of that meeting was a quarantining of three decks and Bolt's promotion to what became known as the Brin department. He was ordered to grow a clone from one of the surviving DNA samples so long as strict isolation and secrecy protocols were implemented. Bolt was restricted to the quarantined section of the ship for the duration of the project. He named the clone Karm, after a favorite character in a novel he read as a child. He was now the senior officer in charge of Karm's instruction and training.

Learning the Brin language was the toughest part of all, but if Karm was to save his people, he had to be taught how to communicate in proper Brin-speak. Fortunately, the Brin ship contained enough verbal data to manage the task reasonably well. To be fluent, Karm would simply have to be careful and learn the nuances of the language once he arrived.

"But can't you give me anything more?" asked Karm, pacing nervously, his talons fidgeting with the hem of his sleeve. "I feel as if I'm going in blind. I wish you would tell me everything you know."

Bolt raised his long, blue index finger and wagged it in Karm's direction. "You know we cannot do that. We have been over this many times, Karm."

"Yes, I know," Karm said as he sat back in his chair and recited his first lesson again. "Unless there is a direct and imminent threat of destruction to our vessel and its crew, all alien races must be allowed to progress without interference. In the event direct contact is unavoidable, contact must be minimal for the safety and protection of all concerned."

"But what happens if I die in some unforeseen accident?"

"We have contingencies in place. Besides, you won't have that much longer to worry about it. Soon enough you will be on your way back to your planet's past and your mission will begin. Want to test your holoprojection system and biocomputer connections again? Practicing with the holograms always seems to get your mind off things."

Karm held out his left hand, palm up, and thought about the projector. *Activate!* Instantly, a light glowed in his palm and a three dimensional projection appeared a few inches above his hand. As he thought again about information regarding Dyan'ta, its image appeared in fine detail. The entire Brin ship's database, along with vital knowledge possessed by the Skae regarding the destruction of the Brin's home planet had been downloaded into the biocomputer. This information, which was integrated into his body at formation, provided Karm with certain advantages. Even with the corruption gaps Karm could access enough data to ensure at least ninety two percent accuracy of historical events on Dyan'ta. At least this was Bolt's theory. After years of training, he had learned how to access almost every part of the databanks at will. Learning how to manipulate the biocomputer was never an easy task, requiring both concentration and focus, neither of which Karm possessed at first. Recalling his early days often became a source of merriment for Bolt and the others during mealtime, much to Karm's chagrin. The conversations usually started with: "Do you remember the first time he ever attempted to…?"

This was followed with a detailed description of how Karm nearly killed himself with a feedback loop, wiped out an entire circuit board, collapsed in spasms from an excessive overload, or simply received information regarding worms when he tried to study interdimensional worm holes. Karm always felt his muscles tense and his crest feathers prickle at these good-natured jabs as he tried to laugh along with his instructors, but he became determined to master the biocomputer and end the jests.

After years of practice Karm learned to manipulate the image with great precision so now, when called on, the device provided exactly the information requested in the detail required. Karm was able to see the oceans, land masses, and all the geography he might desire. He zoomed in to such a tiny scale, he could pick out individual Brin and identify them by the names he had invented, or their actual names if they were important enough to have their information on file in the ship's computers. He could even bring up printed data about any aspect of the planet, and the Brin civilization, he wanted, going back thousands of years.

"When will you trust me enough to allow me access to the entire database?" asked Karm.

"You know it is not a matter of trust, Karm," replied Bolt as he placed his long blue arm gently around Karm's shoulder. "Too much information might cause you to change events too soon and you know the data was corrupted so, in certain circumstances, it can provide only statistical probabilities of events, some with errors of up to thirty-four percent possibility. You will be provided access to the data you need when the time is right for you to have it, but there will be times when you will need to rely on your own instincts and intelligence." Bolt took Karm by the elbow and looked directly into his eyes. "Even the wisest might be sorely tempted to misuse that much information about the future. This is too important of a mission to risk failure due to greed or overconfidence."

Karm ran a frustrated hand through his top crest, clenching the feathers in a tight fist, and turned away. "I know…I know. I just get frustrated being cooped up in here for so long. I want to get started."

"Karm," Bolt said, softly raising his hand toward him.

Karm turned back to Bolt and reached up to touch Bolt's hand. A soft glow enveloped them both and Karm felt a sense of serenity flow through him, limited mind alteration links being one of the added advantages of his biocomputer. He relaxed and returned to his training.

Time passed slowly, but eventually they arrived at the cosmic string that would take Karm back in time. Passing through the long hallways, he began to reminisce.

Twenty years of training for this, and now it's finally here. The fate of so many rests in my hands. Am I ready for this? Karm lifted his head and squared his shoulders. *It's now or never. No more doubts, too much is at stake. Focus on the job and get it done.*

The two crew members accompanying him along the time curve were equally silent, but seemed more reflective. Karm did not want to intrude on his companions. He did not fully comprehend their sense of loss at leaving the ship, but he respected them and kept to himself.

They soon arrived at the hatchway leading to the small transport vessel. Reaching up to slap his hand on the bulkhead high above his head, Karm entered the ship and found his seat. The others entered as well, ducking slightly to avoid hitting their heads, and each settled into their places and prepared for departure.

"Docking clamps released…Engines at stand-by… All hatches secure. Ready for departure." They went through the familiar pre-launch checklist and prepared themselves for the journey ahead.

"Karm, hit the ignition switch."

Karm reached for the switch, but hesitated. A look of grave concern crossed his face.

"What's the matter?"

"Nothing, just a flashback to the Kreldig incident." Karm hit the switch and sat back, checking the security of his shoulder straps.

"I thought you were over that," said Bolt, his brows furrowing. "After all, everyone did survive…eventually."

In moments, the holding clamps released with a slight jolt, maneuvering thrusters gently steered the shuttle free. Its engines engaged and they set coordinates toward the string. Karm watched out his porthole as the *Helven* silently slipped away above him. Their sensors registered the position of the string and automatically aligned the ship for entry.

"String augmenter to full strength," Bolt said as he manipulated the dials on his console. "Curve directional controls set and aligned to target time dimensions."

"Entering cosmic string now," said Bolt as the ship lurched to one side. "Singularity compensators engaged. Hull stresses well within parameters."

Karm closed his eyes and white-knuckled the armrests of his seat. A faint odor of ozone filled the cabin.

The passage was jarring as the ship buffeted around, but uneventful until his companions began some unexpected activity.

"Countdown to biopod launch," announced Bolt.

"What's going on?" asked Karm, turning his head as best he could while under restraint, but they ignored him.

"Launch countdown confirmed for ten seconds," replied Zem. "Target branch in range and launch sequence is steady."

A slight shudder ran through the ship as the biopod launched. The shaking and noise ended abruptly as they completed their passage along the cosmic string and found themselves in the vicinity of Dyan'ta. Karm looked in amazement at the first planet he had ever seen without the aid of his holoprojector. *It looks so much less real than my projections somehow.*

Rousing himself from his fascination with the planet, he turned to Bolt. "I don't suppose you want to tell me what that biopod stuff is all about, do you?"

"Not now, Karm." Bolt glanced at Zem with a wink then returned his attention to the displays at his console. "Your biocomputer will let you know what to do about the pod when the proper time arrives. For now, trust us and your computer system to provide you with the appropriate information when you most require it."

Karm's neck feathers always ruffled a bit when Bolt said this. He preferred knowing more up front, but he trusted Bolt, accepted what his mentor told him, and focused on his mission. Always the mission. The ship's sensors confirmed they had arrived three years ahead of the mark, the moment in history calculated as the precise tipping point he had trained for. Bolt entered the coordinates to take them to their destination and they soon landed in a remote area of the planet.

Karm and Bolt left the tight confines of the ship together. They faced each other and Bolt smiled. "Even after all this time, you still struggle with personal connections."

The two companions stood together silently, breathing deeply, admiring the beauty of this world, enjoying the freedom after their long confinement aboard ship.

Karm dug his hands into his pockets and looked off into the distance. The tall buildings of a city rose in the distance, the setting sun reflecting flashes of orange off their windows. The blue tinged leaves of the nearby forest shimmered in the breeze, the branches rustled with the darting movements of brightly colored flying creatures Karm's biocomputer identified as Mutons, their leathery wings contrasting with the feathers covering the rest of their bodies. Small furry, six legged animals with dark eyes and long ears, identified as Dinters, swung from branch to branch using their prehensile tails. A herd of large, golden colored, six-legged animals with a single horn protruding from their heads grazed in the distance, unconcerned with the appearance of the visitors from above.

"It's difficult, but I'm getting better at it."

"Have you taken your medication, yet?"

Karm reached into his pocket and pulled out a large red pill. Swallowing it, he grimaced.

"First thing I need to do is find a way to improve the taste of these awful things."

Bolt smiled at his student and they stood a while longer looking across the scene stretching out before them. When the two could no longer delay the inevitable, they raised their hands and touched palms. The familiar tingle raced up their arms and the faint green glow surrounded their connected hands. Breaking the connection, Bolt turned toward the ship.

"What will you do now?" Karm asked his friend, knowing that cosmic string time travel followed a closed time curve and only worked in one direction.

"What we must."

Karm nodded and watched as Bolt left and climbed back up the ramp. As the ship rose into the sky, gradually diminishing into a barely visible speck, and then vanish beyond his sight. He looked down, picked up a few blades of grass at his feet and brought them to his nose. "Huh...I thought it would smell differently."

***

"Can you repeat that, stranger? Not quite sure I caught your meaning, what with your accent and all." The young man wearing the yellow smock held his pen over the notepad, confusion written all over his face.

Karm composed himself and attempted as genuine a smile as he tried again. His first attempt at communication with a living Brin proved to be more difficult than he had hoped.

"I request food...for consumption to eat...please... fruit with leaves of salad...and water liquid. Bring now here to me?" He pointed to a picture of what he hoped he was asking for on the menu cards.

"You want some fruit, a salad and some water?" repeated the serving man, also pointing to the items Karm indicated. "I swear, mister, no offense, but I haven't heard an accent like yours ever before. Where are you from?"

Swallowing hard and continuing to smile, the talons of his left hand clenched tight, Karm replied, "I from ocean...other side. Grepwon Island...town small."

The serving man, Karm's biocomputer now identified the profession as waiter, shook his head and ran the talons of one hand through his crest. "If you say so, mister. I'll be right back with your food." He hesitated, a frown growing on his brow. "You can pay for the food, can't you, mister?"

Karm reached into his pocket and pulled out several of the coins the Skae fabricated for him.

"Huh," he said taking one of the coins, turning it in his fingers, feeling its weight. "Must be another new one of them coins from the capital."

The young man turned and walked briskly toward the kitchen, glancing back over his shoulder at Karm as he pushed through the shiny metallic doors.

To avoid the embarrassment and frustration of similar encounters in the future, Karm devised his plan of visiting a busy section of town for several hours each day. He sat quietly on a bench or walked slowly through the crowds of Brin, listening to their conversations. The biocomputer recording each one for future reference. At night, alone in his small rented room with the yellowing wallpaper, thin brown rug and windows so dirty there was no need for curtains, he listened to the flow of the words, learning the syntax and nuances of the Brin language. He could not afford to stand out. His destiny required anonymity.

Chapter Three

"**F**eathers and Quills!" shouted Karm into the receiver, throwing his arms in the air, letting the stack of papers fly, his crest feathers turning crimson with rage. "How could this happen? How could I have lost everything so fast?"

In only five years, Karm found himself the master of a small fortune, the result of his biocomputer's suggestions for speculation in the money exchange market, judicious buying and selling of several land acquisitions, shares purchased in a number of small, but successful business ventures, and careful management of his growing estate. His greed also grew in proportion to his wealth to the point where he started ignoring the advice of his biocomputer and bankers, trusting instead his own ego driven wishes.

"Sir," replied the voice over the speaker, "we tried to warn you about investing in such marginal markets. Our data indicated, as we informed you last month, the strong possibility of collapse. Had you listened to us you would not be facing bankruptcy today. You will need to divest your holdings and—"

"Don't lecture me, sir." Karm drew out and emphasized the 'sir' mocking the banker's formality. "If I always listened to your timid advice I would never have accumulated enough to worry about losing in the first place! Just sell off whatever you need to and resolve this mess. I'll call later to make final arrangements and assess the damages. Save as much as you can." Karm hit the off switch with a shaking talon, rubbed his face and slumped heavily back in his chair. Breathing deeply to gather his emotions, he swiveled around, jumped to his feet and strode quickly out of the room, feeling the need for a drive into the countryside.

With the mag-lev's dome retracted, the air blew briskly through his crest, sending a chill down his spine. He loved driving, especially this time of year when he could set the controls to automatically follow the magnetic propulsion system buried beneath the roadbed and enjoy the new colors of the season. The crisp autumn air always helped clear his mind. Thick dark clouds gathered over the taller mountains in the distance, giving the ominous appearance of a building storm. He pulled off into the red dirt trailhead parking lot, one of his favorite places to escape and think, turned off the electromagnetic drive, and found the bench by the stream he always found soothing. There was something about the sound of water tumbling over the rocks and listening to the creek of the trunks as the wind gently blew through the yellow flowering Tark trees, their fragrant leaves smelling of fresh mint that calmed his mind, allowing him to think clearly. Downstream, a nearly silent Hodak waded into the flowing water, its single spiral horn sending out v-shaped ripples as the gentle creature bent its head for a drink.

"How could I have gotten so careless?" he muttered aloud to himself. His head hung low, resting in his hands, his elbows perched on his knees. Holding out his hand and thinking the activation command, he reviewed the biocomputer's analysis of his recent, and most disastrous, investments. "Negative ratings across the board. The machine was right all along. Bolt warned me about ignoring this thing." An hour later, Karm leaned over, picked up a grey flat rock and sent it skipping across the stream. "Never again," he growled at himself. He stood, straightening his shoulders and lifting his chin, having made the necessary decisions. Back in the city, he pulled into the first used mag-lev sales lot he found, haggled with the man in charge, and fed in the commands to transfer ownership. Turning up the collar of his overcoat to ward off the chill in the air, he walked home, determined to never fall prey to arrogance again. Wealth and authority over others were essential ingredients to accomplish his task. They were not his personal toys to play with as he wished. The mission is too important.

***

"I don't care what you think. You are an advisor, while I am the one spending the money here. You are paid, and rather well, I might add, regardless of whether my investments go bust or not. I expect you to carry out my instructions and not question them. If you cannot conduct business under these terms, let me know now so that I can stop wasting my time and go elsewhere." *I'm making this dinter-brain a fortune with my investments. It would take an army of accountants to unravel all of my dummy corporations, off-shore accounts and legal entities. I know the man's just doing his job, but the wrong question from a brainless broker could send up a red flag that sends an investigation my way. I can't allow sentiment to interfere with the mission. Maybe it is time to move on before he starts to wonder just where my information is coming from.*

Karm knew he could not afford to linger too long in any one location, yet he did enjoy being here in this small mountain town. People here were friendly. After the factory shut down most of the townspeople had moved on to the larger cities to find work, but enough remained to take advantage of the tourists. The town itself was like something out of a tourist bureau poster. The blue-leafed trees produced flowers of so many colors, they rivaled the rainbows. The highest peaks of distant mountains usually maintained at least some snow, no matter the season. A small stream flowing through town sparkled and held a number of great fishing spots within walking distance of his home here. Families of thick-furred Petzels using their tusks to root in the fields for their dinner made for great sport with youngsters learning to hunt. *Never expected I would get so addicted to standing in cold water trying to convince some fish to sacrifice itself for my enjoyment.*

Karm sat on his porch, enjoying the solitude and scenery before getting back to business. A pair of flightless Quol hunted in a nearby grove of trees. Their long legs and bulk made their graceful movements all the more beautiful. *Maybe just a couple more years? No. Not worth the risk. Five years of following the plan I cannot get off track again. It is nice here, though. Maybe I'll get lucky again.*

Activate Accounts. And, holding out his hand, the soft glow of his palm presented a detailed and beautifully displayed holographic graph of the required information.

Total Assets §160,926,462.34. Good diversification in all the necessary areas as well. Construction, Pharmaceuticals, Engineering, R & D, all falling into place as planned.

Alright, everything seems in order and on schedule so far. Nothing like a bit of historical perspective to enhance one's portfolio. Activate Calendar: Appointments for the week.

With a satisfied nod, Karm surveyed the holographic calendar, noting the dates and times of upcoming meetings with executives of soon to be acquired additions to his growing empire, as well as the precious time he always set aside to indulge his beloved fly fishing habit.

Fifteen years of pursuing the plan and, despite the setbacks I created, everything's on schedule. Still so much to do before everything is ready. Still a few hours of daylight left though. Deactivate.

The hologram vanished and the glow in his palm faded. Karm got up from the bench, crossed the porch, and grabbed his favorite fly rod and a box of flies. *That big fella is out there in those riffles and it's just about his dinner time.*

As he stood in the stream that evening watching the pool for rises, an idea struck him. *As the head of a financial empire, I am going to need someplace to bring potential clients and partners for meetings; someplace to impress them as they are wined and dined. This area offers some spectacular advantages for just such an enterprise. Lots of available land and a people starved for employment. I think this might work.* He cast his line one final time and watched as it floated downstream without taking a hit. He shrugged and reeled in the line absentmindedly as he considered his next move.

The following weeks were a blur of activity. Karm described his vision to a local architect whom he hired to create the blueprints and architectural drawings. Once everything was completed to his satisfaction he called together the local real estate broker, the banker, the mayor, and the town council. He explained his idea for the purchase of a large parcel of land and the development he envisioned.

"I want to build an estate home on several hundred acres back beyond those forested hills to the west," he told them. "This will be a type of resort home where I will be able to bring clients and entertain dignitaries in high style." He unveiled the series of artistic and architectural designs as he described the project. The drawings illustrated a large castle-like building surrounded by well-preserved natural settings. "Your town needs a strong financial base now that your factory is gone. And the quarry and masons could certainly use a boost to their business. This project will provide employment for everyone. I'll need hundreds of construction workers over the next decade. Once finished, there will be steady employment for many more. Staff will be needed to run the facility, cooks, maintenance and security personnel, grounds keepers, all hired locally."

The mayor looked over at the council members and stood to take the lead. "Now, just hold on a minute here, Karm. We like our nice quiet little town just the way it is. What you're talking about sounds like you want to turn our fine town into some sort of amusement park."

Karm shook his head in response. "Not at all, Mr. Mayor, quite the opposite I assure you. This will be a strictly private operation. The general public will not be allowed on the grounds. My plan is for the estate to be used for my private business affairs. The only people who come here will be at my invitation. Our town will not be changed in any way, except to be put on a much more permanent economic footing." He smiled at them and leaned in closer as if to bring them into his little conspiracy. "Of course exclusive contracts for all of my needs in the facility will be made only with your townspeople. No outside involvement. Imagine the boost to local business."

"Give us just a moment, Karm." The mayor and council members walked over to a corner of the room and whispered among themselves for a few minutes. When they returned, the mayor grabbed Karm's hand and shook it vigorously. "I think we have a deal."

"Wonderful! I'll have my people draw up some contracts right away." Karm picked up a glass of red valum, sniffed the fruity scent, and toasted his new partners.

The room buzzed with animated talk over the opportunities and potential this proposal had for the town. Council members drank and smiled as they considered their future. Then one of the council members called out to Karm over the noise. "What do you intend to call this project?"

He pointed to the central architectural drawing of the front façade of the castle and beamed, "I call it, The Citadel."

***

The noise was deafening. Heavy lifters roared in protest as they placed stone blocks into position in the walls of The Citadel.

Excavators plowed up vast tracts of land for the landscaping. Construction supervisors shouting instructions to hundreds of workers who continued to pound, saw, drill and yell back in response all contributed to the organized chaos of the site. Karm sat in the manager's hut going over the blueprints with the architects.

"What is so difficult about this?" he asked the supervisor. "Your job is to see my wishes are carried out exactly as directed. Money is not your concern. No more alterations to any part of this design or the materials specified without my direct orders. Is that understood?"

The supervisor gathered up the diagrams and placed them back into their folders. "Yes, sir," he replied. "I wouldn't be doing my job if I didn't try to bring this job on time and under budget for you. Many of these specifications require materials and artisans that are nearly impossible to find. The locals are skilled, but would benefit from the guidance and training of a master guildsman. We're only six months into construction and delays are starting to build up."

Karm collected himself with a deep breath, then leaned forward, hands clasped on the table. His eyes fixed firmly on the supervisor. "There are reasons why these provisions are necessary. I am not worried about delays, just make sure the plans are followed exactly as required. I can provide you any extra help you need to find the specialists and rare materials."

At that moment the door to the small hut opened. Karm and the supervisor turned to see who was interrupting their meeting. A large man wearing a dark suit, carrying a valise entered the cramped quarters and closed the door behind him.

"I was told I would find Karm in here," he said, leveling his eyes at the two men inside.

"I'm Karm. Who let you in here and what do you mean by barging in here like this?"

"My name is Darkon." He held out a business disk to Karm. "I'm with the Securities and Exchange Division. We need to talk."

Karm's left palm itched and his eyes looked off as if distracted for a brief moment. "Excuse us for a bit," he said to the supervisor. "I'll be back tomorrow to discuss this further with you." He placed a hand on Darkon's shoulder and gave the government agent his most ingratiating smile. "It's such a nice day today, why don't we discuss this down by the river, away from all this noise. I have a nice pergola down there where we can order some lunch and talk in private."

Twenty minutes later they were seated in comfortable chairs listening to the sound of the flowing river. "So, what can I do for you, Darkon?"

Darkon opened his valise and brought out a thick folder, which he set on the table in front of him. "About three months ago we started receiving some very disturbing information about some of your operations, Karm. I was assigned to investigate the matter. I need to ask you some very serious questions about your finances."

Karm leaned back in his chair and took a sip of his tea. "What exactly is your concern, Darkon? I can assure you all of my finances are quite legitimate and above board. I've hired an army of lawyers and tax experts to make sure everything is double checked and completely legal."

"That is not precisely our concern," said Darkon as he opened the file and turned a few pages. "It is you yourself that is the real mystery here. You seem to be quite the financial genius, Karm. You always manage to invest in just the right companies at the exact moment of maximum value for your efforts. How do you manage that? Dozens of investments over the past ten years, all without fail. That is unprecedented and very suspect."

Karm's palm tingled again and he paused before replying, then smiled. "Come now, Darkon. I'm sure your investigation was very thorough and showed no illicit or illegal activity on any transactions. Surely it's no crime to be smarter than the other investors. What are you really after here?"

Darkon sat up straight and closed the folder. He looked Karm directly in the eye, studying him for a moment. "Very well, then. As I said, it is you that is the real mystery here. My investigation led me to look further into your background. Of course, all of the paperwork was in perfect order. Birth certificate, census and school records, all seemingly normal. Until I took it upon myself to take a more personal approach."

"And what did you turn up?" asked Karm, seemingly unconcerned and relaxed.

"I went to the university to talk with some of the professors in the economics department, which is your declared major according to the documents. I also visited your old neighborhoods listed in the census records, your old primary schools, even your parent's gravesite. It seems nobody has any personal recollection of you or your family. Nothing at all."

"It was a long time ago, Darkon. We were a very quiet family, nothing remarkable. I'm not surprised nobody remembers us."

"I am," said Darkon. "I've never experienced such a complete anonymity as yours. What are you hiding, Karm? Who are you?"

"Is there anything illegal, immoral, or unethical in anything you found?"

"No, nothing like that. In fact, I have already filed my report to my superiors clearing you of any suspicions. My job was to try to discover anything illegal in your dealings. Your mysterious history is not illegal and therefore not their concern. As far as the Securities and Exchange Division is concerned, you are clean as a whistle. This was something I did on my own. I don't like unanswered questions."

"Come walk with me." Karm stood and headed down to the path next to the river. Darkon followed. A few minutes later, under the teal leaves of the trees overhanging the path and the gentle gurgling of the river in their ears, Karm placed his left hand on Darkon's shoulder. A faint blue glow surrounded the two men. "So what are your intentions now? Is it blackmail you're after?"

"Not at all," said Darkon. "as I said, I don't like unanswered questions. The more I dug, the less I found. Nobody is that well hidden, but you have managed it. I want to know how and why. I can offer you something valuable in return."

Karm removed his arm from Darkon's shoulder, turning to face him with narrowed eyes. "And what would that be? What can you possibly have that I would be interested in?"

Darkon stopped and turned to face Karm. "I'm not sure why, but I trust you, Karm. Anybody else who would go through all of this effort to hide their past would have done it for some nefarious purpose. You didn't. In my experience, you are a rarity, Karm. Despite my personal convictions to the contrary, I have been unable to uncover so much as a single shred of evidence of any wrongdoing. Oh, there were the normal bits of devious business acumen, perfectly reasonable for anyone in your position, but nothing to indicate subversive or other scandalous intent. And believe me, I have looked." He looked hard into Karm's eyes and held them for a moment. "You must have some powerful reasons for hiding yourself like this. If I discovered as much as I have about you, others may be able to as well. I can help you with the mistakes you made that roused my curiosity so much. Your trail was good, but not perfect. I can help you fix that…if you'll hire me as head of your security group."

"That is quite a bold statement, Darkon. Why should I trust you?"

Darkon held his ground. He opened his valise and took out the files inside, holding them out for Karm. "There are no copies of these, they are now yours. I came to you with this information when I could just as easily gone to the authorities. While your past is not illegal, it is very unusual. Something that would quickly get noticed by the monarch's security people." Darkon thought briefly before continuing, "I'll be honest. I first came here to get a sense of you in person. I wasn't sure what I wanted to do with what I discovered. I really don't like mysteries, but I do have a gut instinct about you now that we have talked. Maybe someday, if I prove my value to you, I will find the answers."

Karm smiled and reached out to shake talons with Darkon. "I won't promise you anything other than a job, Darkon. In fact, I can pretty well guarantee your questions will remain unanswered. I can, however, promise some very interesting times ahead. If you can live with that, we have a deal."

Darkon smiled in return and grasped Karm's talons in return. A faint blue nimbus again surrounded both men, then faded as quickly as it came.

"Do you like to fish, Mr. Darkon?" asked Karm, smiling as they headed off in the direction of the stream.

***

A tingling sensation in his left arm startled Karm awake. *Must have dozed off for a bit. What's going on now?* Shaking his head and running his fingers through his crest to help clear his mind, he looked down at his arm and saw the soft glow emanating from his palm. *Activate.* An image of Dyan'ta hovered above his outstretched hand and rotated to the northern hemisphere. Data filled his mind as if long suppressed memories suddenly awakened. Karm stared blankly as the images and details sorted themselves into understanding. Looking down at the image of Dyan'ta he saw that it zoomed to a particular location. A set of coordinates blazed in crimson. He took a deep breath, stood, and walked to his desk. Still rubbing his eyes, Karm pressed the video-intercom button for his secretary.

"Kirta, I need you to clear my schedule for the next four days."

"Yes, sir," she replied. "Is there a specific reason that I can provide?"

"No, use your best judgment on how to handle that, but don't get too creative."

"Yes, sir, right away. Shall I notify Krell to prepare your bags?"

He stopped his pacing and thought for a moment. "No, I'll handle that myself. Under no circumstances is anyone to contact me for anything. I don't care if The Eternal stops by for afternoon tea. No calls."

"Yes, sir. No calls." Kirta looked at Karm, studying him. "I do hope everything is alright, sir."

"Everything is fine. Thank you for your concern. Just tell Krell to have the levicoach ready. And call the airport. I want the jet ready in two hours."

"Alright, sir. Be well. See you in four days." She returned her attention to the papers on her desk.

"Thank you, Kirta." Karm went to his private quarters to pack.

Twenty-four hours later Karm found himself in the middle of the Latonian Desert, hundreds of miles from the nearest town. He sat by his campfire trying to eat the meal he had just burned. "What was he thinking?" Karm muttered aloud to himself, grimacing at the unpleasant taste of his attempt to cook. "Building and managing a financial empire I can deal with, but this?" He threw down his unfinished meat and stared at the night sky. *Bolt, my old friend, wherever you are now, I hope I'm making you proud. Our plans are going well. I just hope that I'm up for what's ahead.* He turned to look at the lopsided tent he had attempted to set up, checked the biocomputer for any signs of rebel activity in the vicinity, and decided it would be safer to sleep under the stars.

In the morning, he awoke to the familiar tingling in his left arm. The soft glow in his palm had taken on a greenish hue now. *Activate.* A two-hour countdown projected above his hand. *Good. Time for a bit of breakfast first. Let's see if I can avoid poisoning myself today.*

He dug through his pack and located a tin of eggs and some sort of breakfast meat. Setting it on some flat rocks surrounding the fire, he returned to the pack and found a bottle of fruit juice.

As the countdown neared zero, he stood at the edge of his camp looking up at the sky. He noticed a small light growing larger as it headed straight toward him. The bright object left a vapor trail in its wake as it streaked through the atmosphere. At an altitude of 100 meters, the object stopped and hovered for a moment. Karm's palm tingled in a rhythmic pattern. The floating object turned and headed in his direction. Two hundred yards from the camp, the object stopped and settled gently onto the ground.

Karm stared at the craft, then at his palm. With a shrug of his shoulders, he headed in the direction of the craft.

Karm recognized the biopod that Bolt had launched from their ship the day he arrived at Dyan'ta. It was no more than two meters long and only slightly scarred by the heat of passing through the atmosphere. There were no visible signs of a hatch. He reached out his left hand and placed it on the hull. A rectangular outline appeared. The hatch dropped down and slid to the side revealing the interior. He stood for a moment, examining the contents of the craft. His palm glowed in changing hues of orange, blue and red, reflecting the turmoil he felt within, but the glow soon settled into a pleasant shade of soft green.

Karm reached down, hands trembling slightly, and picked up the infant inside. He passed his left hand over the child and his glowing palm registered strong vital signs.

"Hello, Maripa," he said in a voice he hoped was soothing, but came out a bit too shaky and high-pitched. "You don't seem to be any worse for wear after your journey."

Karm then reached inside, pressed a series of switches on the control panel and walked away. An energy field shimmered around the vessel. In a few seconds, the ship collapsed into dust. Karm looked back making sure no traces remained.

Back in camp, Karm sat stiffly with his new charge sleeping peacefully in his lap. *Activate: Infant Care: Female.* The data required to care for this child, and additional data concerning the most probable course for her future, raced through his mind.

"Well, young lady," Karm said. "Welcome to Dyan'ta. My name is Karm. Not sure I'm up to this particular challenge, but you are apparently a vital cog to this mission's success. I'll figure it out somehow."

Chapter Four

The stream flowed fast and cold. The air was crisp, the sky slightly overcast and the trees displayed their brilliant orange and red of the season. It was quiet as the sun rose above the horizon. Karm gazed fixedly as he studied a deep pool on the opposite bank. *I know he's hiding in there somewhere. Just need the right incentive to get him to rise.* He turned over a few rocks, identified the insect larvae hiding there, and made his choice. *Yes, just the thing. Now all I need is to land it gently and see if he's hungry.* Karm cast his line out and watched the indicator closely for a strike.

"Sir, important call for you," called out Karm's driver.

"Jetu, Matto, and Jopa!" cursed Karm. "Not now! Tell them I'm in a meeting."

"Sorry, sir, it's Bandu Pharmaceuticals. You said to notify you right away if a call came in about it."

Kak! Forgot about the time zone difference. "Tell the early bird bastards I'm wrapping up another meeting." As he reeled in his line, Karm saw a set of concentric circles form in the center of the pool. "Would have gotten you this time. Don't go anywhere, I'll be back!" he yelled.

Karm climbed up the stream bank, handed his gear to the driver, and slammed himself into his limousine.

Karm's assistant sat inside the levicoach examining some papers. "The Bandu group wants to alter the contract again, sir," he said as Karm grabbed a breakfast bar and juice from the limo's refrigerator.

"What good does it do to own a private river, if I can't ever enjoy it? I've worked for 20 years, I have more money than The Eternal, and I can't convince anyone to let me catch that quetzal down there!" He grumbled, bit off a chunk of the bar and guzzled half the bottle of juice.

The limousine drove through the security gate of Karm's mountain retreat. The iron arch above the gate spelled out The Citadel. The mansion sat in the center of a 300-acre forested estate. A thousand years ago this structure served as the summer castle of the Eastern continent's ruling family. Karm commissioned it to be moved and restored to its original glory by an army of resident artisans. Stonemasons from the local quarry expertly reconstructed those portions proving impossible to transport. The walls were hand carved stone three stories tall, curving magnificently and seamlessly into the floors and ceiling and displayed large stained glass windows. Rounded turrets stood at each corner, complete with conical roofs and flags. The archway into the main courtyard held a functioning drawbridge rising after the limo drove toward the main entrance. There were even a dozen or so gargoyles haunting the parapet.

Karm and his assistant exited the mag-lev and briskly headed into The Citadel. Karm's personal valet took his jacket as soon as he entered the foyer. The stoic manservant then cleared his throat and pointed to the antechamber before his employer took another step in his muddy boots. As he sat and changed into a comfortable pair of house shoes, another servant brought Karm a tray of food and morning cocktails. He grabbed a roll and a glass of juice, talons fitting precisely into the holes in the handle measured by expert craftsmen for him alone, then motioned for her to follow him to his second floor office.

The interior was even more of a museum than the outside. Imported marble floors reflected the light of the large crystal chandeliers hanging from the ceiling. Original paintings from several of the great masters hung prominently on every wall. Outrageously expensive antique furniture, hand-woven rugs, and rare collections adorned every room.

"Thank you, Brill," Karm said as the girl set her tray on the table by the fireplace.

"Will you need anything else, sir?"

"Not for now, thank you. I'll ring you if I need something."

"Very well then, sir. Have a good day." Brill left the room, gently closing the door behind her.

Karm sat behind his desk, glanced through the papers left for him there, and hit the intercom button on his phone. "Kirta, get Bandu on the line."

"I dialed them as you arrived, sir. Video conference is set up on line one."

Karm punched the top button. The view screen on the wall lit up to display five men surrounding a conference table. They looked up from their conversations as the call connected.

"What is it you want, gentlemen?"

The elderly man seated in the chair at the far end of the table spoke. "Yes, Karm. We wanted to discuss several of the provisions in the contract. Our board is not completely satisfied with some of them and we want to negotiate better terms." Their heads all nodded in agreement.

"And what gives you the idea that I am inclined to offer anything more than we have already discussed? With the death of the monarch and the uncertainties regarding his son's qualifications, you should be pleased I am offering this much."

The men turned to look at the one who sat at the end of the table. He shot a quick glance at them before focusing on Karm's image. "Some of the board believes the buyout you are offering is below market value and —"

"Have you had any better offers?"

The appointed speaker shuffled in his seat, then pointed at Karm's image in an attempt to take charge of the conversation. "That is completely beside the point..."

"I repeat, sir, have you had any better offers?" Karm sipped at the drink in his hand.

"No, sir, not yet," the man replied, dropping his hands to the table. A general confusion of discussions erupted among the other men, each trying to be heard above the others. Karm sipped his drink and waited until they quieted. "And you won't. I have controlling interest in all of the other companies that could possibly be in a position to do so and I have vetoed any efforts in that direction. You have no bargaining strength here, and I have no desire to pay you any more than the §43 billion I have set out already."

"Sir, that is hardly what this company is worth," the others all murmured in agreement.

"Your company's value is no more or less than what I say it is. Or would you rather let it go into corporate collapse where I can simply offer to take it off of the government's hands for taxes owed? You have no options left, gentlemen. My lawyers will bring you the papers to sign in the morning." Karm hung up, sat back, closed his eyes and rubbed his temples. He got up, walked across to the large world map on the wall and placed a red pin on the coast of the major continent. *Three more acquisitions and everything will be ready. Probably within the next three years.* Karm sat at the small table, kicked off his shoes, picked up a sandwich and turned on the ballgame. Nothing happened. He tried another button, then another. He flopped back into the sofa, sighed, tossed the remote aside and held out his palm. *Catalog* and the holographic image appeared above his glowing hand showing the latest in handcrafted fishing equipment.

***

Maripa's tenth birthday celebration was everything a young girl could want. All of her classmates attended. Her uncle spared no expense decorating the lavish mansion in the hills in her favorite colors. Music from a live band filled the air. Even life-size paper geldrigs (her favorite mythological creatures), complete with the long flowing, rainbow colored manes, six legs, hooves sparkling as they ran, hanging from strings as if they were guardian sentinels sent from The Eternal, a stable of Tals for riding, and plenty of servants with unending trays of food and drink for all. Why, then, did Karm find her drying tears from her face, alone in the library?

"What is the matter, child? Why aren't you out there with your friends enjoying your party?" He stood at a distance, hands clasped behind his back, eyes wandering from bookshelf to desktop, only briefly settling on his niece.

Wiping her nose on her sleeve, Maripa looked up at Karm, fighting back more tears. "Those are not my friends," she began. "I don't have any real friends, those are just my classmates. Why couldn't we just go somewhere, just you and me, instead? You never make any time just for me. That is what I really wanted."

Karm stiffened at her question, his shoulders fell slightly, but otherwise remained as he was. "I thought you would enjoy all of this. I consulted with the finest party managers in town. They assured me you would…"

"Why didn't you ask me? You never ask me what I want. Darkon would have known exactly what I wanted. He always knows." She stood her ground, refusing to look away or show any further weakness in front of him.

Karm strode to his desk and sat in the heavy padded chair. He leaned forward, supporting his chin with one hand, examining the young girl. "You are right, my dear. I should have discussed this with you. You are not a youngling any more, something I have a difficult time realizing."

Maripa smiled at this and approached the desk, but remained across the massive wooden fixture, not daring to come closer, fearing the appearance of weakness in his eyes. She stood facing Karm, unable to say what she so desperately longed for.

"If spending time together is what you would enjoy, then we shall do so," Karm said, leaning back in his chair, smiling broadly, his hands now folding behind his head. "How about next weekend?"

Maripa's heart leaped in her chest, her crest feathers flushed a brilliant combination of blue and green, but she resisted the impulse to rush into his arms, knowing the crushing result of any attempt at such familiarity. "I would like that, uncle," she replied with a smile. "Very much."

"It's settled then," he slapped the desk with his palm and brought two talons to his chest, tapping it three times to signal the promise. "Run along now and try to enjoy the rest of your party. We will discuss this later in the week. I have some business to deal with now, but I will see you for the blessing cheer later. We can discuss your acceptance as a cadet into The Academy, too. I'm very proud of you for that, you know."

"Thank you, uncle," Maripa said as she turned to leave. "Please don't forget again."

"Don't worry, my dear. We have a date next weekend."

As she opened the door, she saw Darkon approaching with the local newspaper in hand.

"Hello, Squirt," he said, ruffling her top crest with his hand.

"I hate that name, you know." She strained a lopsided grin at the man.

The big man flashed a huge smile at her. "I know, Squirt. Join me for a game of tuttles later?"

Maripa nodded non-committedly as Darkon continued into the elliptical office, tossing the paper onto Karm's desk. The headline read:

MONARCH PRO-TEM DIES IN TRAGIC BOATING ACCIDENT. BRACH TO ASSUME THRONE.

Watching from the doorway, Maripa saw Karm reach for the phone and knew that once again, all plans were off. She silently closed the door behind her and headed off to her room.

Chapter Five

Brach, second son of Tallett, the ruling monarch of Dyan'ta, and First Chancellor to the Supreme Council, sat among the many family members and functionaries at his father's deathbed. He was tall for a Brin, slightly over six feet, and broad chested, with a thick and colorful head feathering. The crest feathers, long and well preened at all times, served to optimize a display of confidence and strength. To an outsider, the somber scene gave every appearance of a family grieving the passing of a beloved elder. The royal bedchambers were dark, lit only dimly by a few candles. Heavy velvet curtains blocked the many tall windows. A dozen heavy chairs surrounded the large canopied bed, each occupied by family members of various levels. Martek, the eldest son and heir to the throne sat slumped, his head bowed, shoulders shaking as he wept silently, ignoring the constant flow of dignitaries maneuvering for position once the dynasty changed hands. The queen mother stood behind Martek, one hand firmly on his shoulder, trying desperately to will some backbone into her hopeless son. Sitting opposite these two, Lerit, two years younger than Brach, remained impassive, eyes darting everywhere as he maintained the appropriate mask of sorrow and reflection. Everyone dressed in the violet hues of mourning. If anyone spoke, it was brief and hushed so as not to disturb the carefully maintained pose of others in the tableau. A half dozen servants lined the walls of the room awaiting the merest signal calling for their immediate attention. Everyone listened carefully to the erratically rasping breath of the pale, skeletal figure lying in the bed.

Unable to tolerate the charade any longer, Brach rose silently from his chair and approached his mother. Laying a hand gently on her shoulder he leaned in to whisper in her ear coverts. "I will return soon, mother, There are some important matters of state that cannot wait." He gave her a tender peck on top of her grey, sparsely feathered head, and turned to weave his way through the gathering.

"Wine! Now!" yelled Brach, bursting through the heavy doors of his personal chambers. Servants scrambled while his aides jumped to attention. The young royal grabbed the glass offered and slammed the contents down his throat in one sudden jerk. "If I have to sit one more second with those hypocrites I'm going to explode!" He held out the glass for the servant to refill. "They can't wait for that old bird to die so they can start fawning over my idiot brother and gain his favors. And if I don't play the game better than all of them then I'll be their first target." Brach downed the second glass just as quickly as the first and set it on the small table next to the chair he slumped into.

"Your Highness," Brach's senior aide, the Colonel, remained at attention, or at least always looked as though he was at attention as he spoke. "You are well protected and have no need to fear any plots against you. Our informant network will provide ample warning if anyone tries to subvert your position."

Brach stared at the Colonel. The man always dressed in his red and gold Royal Guard uniform, complete with the vast array of medals, ribbons and decorations he had earned throughout his long service to the monarch. The three silver tridents that signified his rank, prominently displayed on his cap and epaulets, reflected brilliantly the sunlight streaming through the tall windows. *How long have I known this man? I can't remember ever not knowing him.* The Colonel had always been an impressive figure, marked for rapid advancement by the heads of state even while he was still a student in the academy so long ago. Brach thought it odd that the Colonel was the only person who nobody ever seemed to address by name, only by his rank. Not even his father, the monarch, called him anything other than Colonel. *I may not know his name, but he is the only person whose loyalty to me is beyond reproach, at least so far. I would hate to have to eliminate such a valuable asset.*

Waving his talons dismissively, Brach brushed away the Colonel's statement. "Yes, yes, don't pay me any mind, Colonel. I'm just irritated right now." He stopped himself before continuing as he noticed the servants still in attendance. "All of you are dismissed now," Brach said. "I will ring if I need anything. Secure the door behind you and see that we are not disturbed."

"Why won't that old bird just get it over with and die already?" Brach said once the doors were closed. "He's been at it for over a week now. I never imagined anyone, even him, could hang on so long."

"Be patient, Your Highness. It cannot be much longer. Even your father must succumb eventually."

Brach pushed himself up from the chair and stomped across the circular room to refill his glass with more wine. "And to name Martek as his successor. That's the real feather twister." Brach swallowed the wine in another quick gulp. "Martek wouldn't know which talon to scratch his crest with if I wasn't there to remind him every day."

The Colonel stiffened, his face even more stone-like than normal. "It is customary for the eldest son to be successor to the throne."

Brach threw his empty glass against the wall, shattered shards danced as they scattered across the floor. "Well that custom is going to doom the kingdom! Those sycophant toadies will have him signing over all of the authority and power of the monarchy within a year. All Martek really cares about are his boats. He'll agree to anything if it will allow him to go race his sailing yacht. Something has to be done."

The Colonel shifted his stance slightly as he thought. "Tradition dictates six months of mourning before a successor can assume the throne, Your Highness. The senate cannot conduct anything more than the most basic of services until then. There is time. In the meantime, there are pressing matters needing your approval."

Two hours later, Brach sat at his desk reading the stack of official documents he had allowed to pile up while sitting by his father's bedside. The doors to his chambers creaked quietly as they opened. "I told you not to disturb me," he said without stopping his efforts.

"I am sorry, brother," said Lerit, waving a careless dismissal to the Colonel. "I must not have heard you amid all of the wailing down the hall."

"What do you want, Lerit?" Brach asked, rubbing his eyes with the palms of his hands. "I don't have time for visiting, or did you want to pour out your heart about dear old father?"

Lerit snorted, slipped his talons through the ornate holes in one of the goblets on the table, poured himself a drink and fell into the chair across the desk from Brach. "We have business to discuss, dear brother."

"We have nothing to—"

"Yes, we do. Neither of us believes for one second Martek is capable of being monarch."

"He will make a decent showing if I guide him; help him negotiate the flocks of sycophants bound to surround him."

Lerit took another long sip from his goblet, raised his eyes toward the high, arched ceiling, and sighed. "I hope you are right. Nevertheless, you know Martek as well as I do. He is weak and will inevitably fall prey to those who tell him what he wants to hear. We need to be prepared for this future, and I need you to know I have no aspirations for the throne and am no threat to you."

Brach set his pen aside, placed both hands on the table, drumming his talons rhythmically, narrowing his eyes as he studied his younger brother. "Explain yourself."

Lerit stood and leaned on Brach's desk, lowering his voice conspiratorially. "I sincerely hope your efforts to control Martek succeed, but I hold out little hope. I believe his incompetence will force you to remove him from the throne, preferably, but not necessarily preserving his life. When that happens, I plan to renounce all claims to the succession and take up the robes of a cleric."

Shaking his head, Brach chuckled in disbelief, and ran his talons through his crest. "Now why would you want to do such a fool thing? You are no more a cleric than I am. You would never..."

Lerit held up a hand, pointing a talon at his brother. "When you succeed poor Martek as our monarch, I would be next in line. You would never be free of my potential to usurp you unless I was legally bound to the church rather than the palace. We both know you are the one with the talent, ambition, and desire to rule. Neither of us will need to keep looking over our shoulders. I may not be a born cleric, but better that life than none at all. Besides, have you ever considered how completely pervasive and eternal the church is? Many ruling families have come and gone under the watchful eye of the church. I believe any thoughts of authority I may conceive will be amply fulfilled within their ranks."

"Would you be willing to state this intention in writing with the Grand Elder as witness?"

"With the understanding my joining the ranks of the bishops, my preferred rank to start with, would be delayed so long as Martek is monarch. After all, he will need both of us to guide him in this difficult role he is assuming."

Brach eyed his sibling up and down, searching for any trace of guile or deception. "I can find no fault with your plan," he replied after leaning back in his chair, arms folded across his chest. "We can have the papers drawn up in a day or two." He reached forward again, picked up his pen and returned to the stack of papers in front of him. Lerit smiled, raised his goblet in salute and strolled back to the table with the crystal decanters to refill his glass.

A knock on the heavy wooden doors broke the silence. The hinges creaked as the doors swung slowly open, light from the antechamber spilling into the room. "I am sorry, brothers, but father has died." Brach froze in mid signature and looked up to see Martek, eyes red and swollen, standing in the doorway. "Mother has asked me to come bring you both back to pay your respects." Martek used his sleeve to wipe his nose and dry his eyes.

Our future monarch. Brach hung his head and made his choice. *This, I cannot allow.* Crossing the room to join his elder brother, Brach embraced the now sobbing young man. "Be strong, brother," said Brach in his most reassuring manner. "You are our monarch now. You must be strong for the rest of us."

"I cannot replace Father," Martek continued to sob. "I don't know how to be monarch. Will you help me, brother?"

Brach took his brother by the shoulders and looked him in the eyes. "You know you can always count on me." Brach straightened his brother's collar, his talons deftly re-knotting the cravat. "I will be right by your side for as long as you need me." *Or at least as long as I let you live.* "Now go use my wash basin to rinse yourself off and we will go pay our respects to Father together."

***

Two months later, life was starting to return to normal in the palace. The royal funeral had been the grand affair people continued to talk about during the many state dinners. Brach resumed his duties as First Chancellor to the Supreme Council, but now with the added responsibility of guiding Martek through the intricacies of ruling as the new monarch. Martek tried hard to be a good monarch, but had the uncanny ability to surround himself with the worst possible sort of advisors. All of them were conniving in one way or another to undermine the monarchy in favor of their own interests. Despite Brach's best efforts, Martek continued to appoint individuals who appealed to his sensibilities and who whispered false praises in his ear whenever Brach was not around to intercede.

"But why shouldn't the mining guilders be exempt from the land use fee?" Martek's face twisted in confused concentration during one of his rare private moments with Brach. The two had managed to sneak away from the palace for a ride in the countryside. Their powerful Tals effortlessly galloped over the hilly terrain. Blooming wildflowers filled the air with invigorating aromas. The ever present royal guards maintained a discrete distance behind. "It is such a small fee, only three duckets per acre, and it will allow them enough of a profit margin to upgrade their equipment to make mining more efficient."

Brach fought to control his anger as he shook his head in dismay. Reigning in his Tal, he turned in his saddle to face his elder brother. "You still aren't seeing the long term effects," he explained. "The mining guilders pay that fee on tens of millions of acres across all of Dyan'ta. That would make a very significant reduction in the royal budget."

"Yes, but—"

"Wait, there's more. Those millions of duckets, even if they did go into upgrading equipment instead of lining the pockets of the head guilders, would eliminate the need for thousands of miners."

Martek squirmed, feigning interest in a flock of smats flying overhead. "Of course they will go towards equipment. Don't you think I asked about that already?"

"I'm sure you did. Did you get their promises written into the contracts and legislation?"

"Not yet, but they assure me it will all be there in the end."

"And you trust them? Are you still that naïve, brother?" Brach reigned in beside his brother, grabbed one arm and fixed him with a stern gaze. "What do you think will happen to all those miners who lose their jobs? They will join the ranks of so many others on government welfare, costing the royal treasury millions more every month. Even with government assistance, many will lose their homes, reducing our income even further without the income from those taxes. Can you see where this eventually leads? Do you want to reignite the terrorist movement out there after father fought so long to defeat them?"

Martek looked defeated as he faced his brother and slumped in his saddle. "I am trying, Brach, I really am trying to understand all of this. It's just so difficult to see everything the way you do."

"I know you are, Martek." Brach rubbed his temple with the knuckles of one hand, trying to drive out the frustration he felt building there. "You just need to remember that everyone is out for their own interests and you are in charge of protecting ours. You cannot afford to believe anything they tell you."

"But they're my friends. How can I —"

"No! They are NOT your friends!" Brach shouted, pounding his fist on his leg, startling his Tal. "The monarch has no friends. Those people only want to influence you so they will gain an advantage over their competitors, probably even over you and the rest of the government. They don't care about you, or anything else for that matter, except what will improve their own interests."

The two rode on in silence for a while. "I'll try harder, Brach. I won't let them fool me again," Martek said in a barely audible whisper.

"You must. You can't afford to do any less. I cannot watch over you all twenty six hours every day."

"I am so glad you are here to help me through all of this, brother. I don't know what I would do without you."

Brach nudged his Tal closer to Martek and reached out, taking his sibling's four-fingered hand in his. "You can always rely on me, brother," he said gently. "Why don't you head back home now. I have some pressing business to discuss with the Colonel that can't wait."

"Thank you, brother," said Martek, tears welling up in his eyes. He pulled on the reigns to head back the way they had come.

***

"I have tried, Colonel," Brach said as the two men slowly walked their mounts under the overhanging branches of a forested trail. "I have done everything I can to try to teach Martek how to be the monarch. He is simply not up to the task. If I had not been forcing him to bring me every piece of proposed legislation before he signed it we would be bankrupt and at the mercy of every guild on the planet as soon as the mourning period was over."

The Colonel stood at attention, talons clasped firmly behind his back. "There is no time to lose then. You must give approval to our plans to eliminate him before he does something you cannot prevent."

"I am afraid you are right, Colonel. I cannot allow Martek to be crowned monarch. How long will it take to set everything in motion once I give final approval?"

"The Darthon Cup Regatta is next week, Your Highness. It will be difficult to arrange in only ten days, but we can be ready by then."

"Alright. Just make certain nobody can possibly believe it is anything but a tragic accident."

"Of course, Highness. It will be as we discussed." The Colonel nodded and the two conspirators increased their pace to a canter, returning to the castle in time for the dinner hour.

***

The sky was a crisp and clear teal with a strong wind out of the west—perfect conditions for the premier regatta of the season. Martek's crew efficiently raced from one set of ropes to another, maintaining perfect tension on the sails and positioning themselves expertly for the next tack. It was in mid tack, as they cut through the eye of the wind and salt spray that the main halyard snapped. Martek gaped helplessly as the mainsail collapsed heavily around him. A sudden gust caught the loose fabric, tearing it from the boom as well. Now flying free in the wind, the sail wrapped itself around Martek and two other crew members, dragging them overboard. The water soaked fabric of the sail held the not yet coronated monarch under the waves for fifteen minutes. By the time rescue boats arrived, it was too late. Martek had drowned, unable to extricate himself from the tangle of sail and ropes.

Brach, now the new monarch-to-be, was grief stricken. He gave orders for his closest advisor, the Colonel, to lead an investigation into the tragic accident that took the life of his beloved brother. Once more, the nation was plunged into mourning at the passing of another leader. Once again, the state funeral was a grand event with all of the pomp and circumstance due such a young and promising monarch. And, after the appropriate six months of mourning, Brach assumed the throne. The day following the coronation, official statements from the palace announced not only the promotion of The Colonel to Volery General, but also the election of Lerit, youngest of the ruling house, to the bishopric of Elnon, the central authority of the clergy. Millions of faithful Brin viewed Lerit's consecration across the continent. The Grand Elder himself presided over the ceremony, accepting the newly ordained bishop's renunciation of all worldly claims, including those to the royal throne.

***

Before Brach even had an opportunity to settle comfortably on the throne, Dr. Malek, the aging curator of astronomy at the royal observatory, asked for an audience. The grandly curving and elevated bench of the science academy's governing board ascended high above the gallery. The dais normally accommodated a dozen members of the Science Academy. Only Dalvet, the president of the board, Clavarn, the chairman of the review committee and, due to the special invitation, Brach, His Highness the monarch, were in attendance. The thick maroon carpeting, padded chairs surrounding the room and heavy tapestries hanging on the walls of this oval-shaped chamber quieted the nearly empty room, giving it a tomb-like quality. Of course, the royal guards posted at every entrance also ensured the absence of prying ears and eyes. The glass-covered oculus provided only a dim light to the room. Holographic projections of the documents hung in the air before the only occupants today.

"These figures have been verified?" asked Dalvet. "There is no mistake?"

"None," Malek replied, sorting through the virtual images until he found the charts he was looking for. "As you can see in the supporting documents everything has been carefully examined by two outside sources, completely independent of each other. Our conclusions are accurate and reliable. Our sun is going supernova. I sincerely wish I could say otherwise."

A dreadful silence filled the room as everyone present absorbed this statement.

"I have spoken with both of the corroborating scientists, your Highness," said Clavarn, nervously clearing his throat. "There can be no doubt as to the correctness of the data, or the accuracy of the conclusions."

Brach cleared his throat and leaned forward as he folded his hands on the table in front of him. "So what you are saying is that our world is about to die, but you have no clear idea as to when?"

"Yes, Your Majesty," said Malek.

"And there is nothing anyone can do about it?"

"That is correct, Your Majesty."

Brach turned to the others at the bench beside him. "So what are your recommendations, gentlemen?"

After a brief silence, Dalvet responded. "After careful consideration of the possible consequences, Your Majesty, we believe it would be in everyone's best interest to reveal the truth of the matter to the world. News like this will inevitably leak out sooner or later. If we control the press releases we can manage the situation more effectively."

The monarch stared into his hands as he replied, "And just how trustworthy is your plan for building a fleet of spaceships to rescue the population of the planet? Sounds like feather fluff to me."

"Of course the technology does not exist at this time, Your Majesty," said Clavarn. "However, the knowledge that we most likely have a thousand years, give or take a few hundred, to develop the fleet will keep panic at bay. We can reassure everyone that they are completely safe here on Dyan'ta for many generations to come, and we are hard at work developing the plan to rescue those who are alive at some distant time in the future."

"But you said it may explode tomorrow. Why bother with all of this at all?"

The life of an average star spans roughly ten billion years. A few thousand years may seem like forever to us, but it is merely the blink of an eye to a star. In all probability we still have time to —"

Brach shoved the report away, scattering the loose papers on the floor. "I am not comfortable with that date," "It seems to me we lose all sense of urgency with something so far into the future. The people will need something a bit more concrete to wrap their brains around. What if we told them one hundred years instead?"

Dalvert and Clavarn glanced at each other for a moment and nodded their agreement. "That would be acceptable, Your Majesty," said Dalvert. "Still a couple of generations to come, but easier to grasp while still providing time to develop the technology. Yes, that should serve nicely. And it may even be accurate."

"Do you really believe we can find a way to get us all off Dyan'ta before the sun explodes?"

"I believe so, Your Majesty, but it will require a tremendous financial and political commitment from the government unprecedented in our history. Any wavering or political maneuvering would be a disastrous blow to public support."

"Good then. We are agreed." Brach rose and shook hands with the two scientists. His four-digit grip, well-practiced during his political career, was firm, but brief. His talons were heavy and sharp, always meticulously manicured. The translucent scales on the back of his hands and arms were slightly pearlescent in the dim light of the room. He looked directly at Malek. "Thank you, Dr. Malek. You handled this well so far. My office will call you soon to arrange the dates and times for you to make your public announcements. This is, after all, your discovery, but we must wait for the right moment. Once the people are mollified with the prosperity of the new work programs we are going to develop, only then will they be ready to handle the knowledge of what is to come. Even then there will be trouble, but not the total loss of control we would face otherwise. We might even arrange to give you the Prelim Award for your role in helping save our race from extinction."

Malek stood to leave. "Thank you, Your Majesty." He pushed his chair back under the table, gathered his papers, and walked up the sloping aisle toward the large double doors.

Once the doors shut behind Malek, Brach motioned for the two heads of the Science Academy to come closer. "Do you actually believe any of this will work?" he asked them in a hushed, conspiratorial voice. "I mean, is there honestly any hope of developing the technology to build spaceships large enough, and fast enough, to take so many Brin to another planet?"

Neither man responded for a minute, each hoping the other would speak. "In science, we never say anything is impossible, Your Majesty," said Dalvert nervously grasping his talons behind his back, his eyes shifting nervously to his colleague. "But in all honesty, I cannot see how it will be possible. Our current state of technology and the best minds in the field of rocket propulsion are far from any ability to accomplish something of this magnitude. With enough time and resources though, anything is possible."

"That then is our problem. How much time do we really have?"

"That is up to The Eternal, Your Majesty," said Clavarn. "We cannot say exactly when, although we do know with absolute certainty it will happen."

"Well then, my friends, let us hope future generations of Brin have the opportunity to solve this problem, and that they are more capable than we are." Brach walked around the bench, down the stairs and up the aisle. His guards snapped to attention as the giant doors opened and followed him back to the palace.

***

The monarch smiled as he inspected the newly dedicated mine. Crowds of miners cheered him as he passed by, demonstrating their appreciation of his efforts to increase employment throughout the realm. "What a difference from my father's constant battles with those insurgent uprisings centered here all those years ago. Prosperity finally accomplished what military might never could," said Brach as he waved to the gathered crowds. The immense hauling vehicles, processing and refining facilities, accommodations for the miners and their families, his gaze took in every detail, his ears rejoiced in the cheers of the workers as he passed by in the royal mag-lev limousine. "Only four years into the plan, and we are ready to start the controlled release of news about the supernova. Are the scientists and press prepared to handle this, General?"

"Yes, Your Majesty. I have seen to the briefings personally. Everyone is well aware of the consequences for any dissention or breaking ranks. There will be no trouble we are not ready to deal with."

"Very good. We cannot afford to overlook anything if this is going to succeed."

***

"Police departments throughout the continent tell us of sporadic looting and there are unconfirmed stories of minor rioting in some cities." Karm sat silently in his study watching the news reports on his monitors. "While some have resorted to violence in the aftermath of yesterday's news about our dying sun, churches everywhere show signs of unprecedented attendance during services." Scenes of violence interspersed with those of churches filled to capacity flashed on the screen as the reporter read his script. Interviews of individuals on the street ranged from those angrily accusing the government of vast conspiracies to others pleading for calm and a return to normalcy. Karm touched his talon to the remote, turning off the monitors.

"And so it begins." He poured himself a glass of orange colored Gorbett Ale and downed it in one swift shot. Karm grimaced as the too sweet draught flowed down his throat and wished the hour was late enough for a stronger bitter ale. It wasn't the first time he regretted instructing his staff to make sure he adhered to the social conventions, but his status required him to play this role so he would play the game. He held out his palm and called for it to activate. A brief perusal of the data reassured him everything was in place and on schedule. Setting his glass on the desk, Karm took in a deep breath, exhaled forcefully to release any lingering tensions, and reached for his communicator pad. "Time to get to work."

***

"I'm sorry, Lerit, but I cannot agree to your transfer out of the treasury." Corab, Elder of the church's treasury, peered over the top of his spectacles at the young bishop seated before him. "You are too valuable to me here. Your expertise has been invaluable in reorganizing our accounts."

Lerit kept his head bowed respectfully, his talons folded on the table. "If I may speak on my own behalf, Elder Corab. My education excelled in languages and I believe I can be of even greater value in the library translating ancient texts. It is as if The Eternal has led me to this goal my entire life. I feel his calling."

The Elder smiled and leaned forward as if to bestow some pearl of grandfatherly wisdom. "Patience Lerit. You are still young. There is plenty of time to learn the Eternal's plans for you. For now, you are to remain here with us."

"But Elder Corab, if I may…"

"My decision is final, Lerit." He hesitated, eyes searching the ceiling as he considered how to proceed. "I had not wished to discuss this with you until I had all of the facts, but there have been suspicious rumors regarding you and some apparent efforts to influence a number of the other bishops and clergy. Mind you these are unconfirmed, and, frankly, I consider them nothing more than jealousy over your rapid rise among us, but I must clear your name before your future can be discussed."

Lerit tensed, but quickly brought himself under control. "I am ashamed that my name has been brought under suspicion, Elder." Lerit bowed his head, covering his face with his hands. "I pray you will see there is nothing to these rumors. I am in your service. You have my blessings, Bishop Lerit. Go in the grace of The Eternal. I am sure my investigation will be brief and you may yet have your wish to work in the library."

"Thank you elder," Lerit said as he bowed and left the old cleric's chamber. Back in his own sparse room he slammed a fist into the stone wall. "No, Elder Corab, you will not get in my way. I will make you the sacrifice here. Your name will go down in shame once I am through with you.

Chapter Six

"Mother! Where are you?" screamed Maripa. She strained to see through the mist. "I can't see you!"

"I'm here, darling," called her mother's voice, "I'm right here."

"Mother, I'm lost, help me!"

"I'm here, Maripa, sweetheart. I'm here."

Her mother's voice grew fainter as the mist thickened. Maripa could barely see her hand stretched out in front of her now. She ran after the fading voice into the mist.

Maripa bolted upright in her bed. Her heart raced and she gasped for breath in the darkness. "Mother! Don't leave me!"

"Ripa!" shouted Tessen as she leapt up from her bed across the room and turned on the lights. "What's wrong? Wake up!" She grabbed Maripa by the shoulders and shook her gently.

Maripa's eyes began to focus. "Tessen? What are you doing? What happened?"

What do you mean 'What happened?' You scared the mutes out of me, girl! You just started screaming. Something about your mother. That must have been one strix of a nightmare. I thought you were an orphan or something."

"It was nothing," said Maripa as she wiped her forehead with her nightgown sleeve. "Just a stupid dream. Go back to sleep."

"Oh no, not now. Something like that just doesn't come out of nowhere. Especially for someone like you. You aren't afraid of anything, honey. And you never talk about your family." Tessen pulled her feet up under her on the bed and turned Maripa to face her. "We've been friends and roommates here at the academy for two years now. I've been your sparring partner and your cadet unit second for over a year. We're graduating tomorrow. Talk to me." She reached under the mattress and removed a metallic flask. After pouring two small cups she handed one to Maripa. "Here, take a swig of this. It'll help."

"Thanks." Maripa took the glass and shot back the drink in one swift motion.

Maripa's shaking gradually subsided and her breathing became more regular. "There's nothing to tell. I used to have them all the time as a kid. It has been years though. Just turn off the light and go back to bed."

Tessen took Maripa's hands in hers and looked her straight in the eyes. "I said talk to me."

Maripa paused for a moment and then decided. "What the strix. You might as well know." She looked up at the ceiling shut her eyes as she spoke. "Did I ever tell you how my parents died?"

"Something about a levicoach wreck, I think."

"That's right. I was just an infant when it happened. They were both killed, but somehow I survived the accident. I don't remember them or the accident at all. I've been with my uncle ever since."

"Is he the rich uncle you go stay with during breaks?"

"Yeah, my father's brother. He was the only family I had left so he took me in and raised me the best he could. He wasn't really prepared to be a parent though. He was too busy with all of his financial dealings. He set me up with an army of nannies so he could leave town to take care of business."

Tessen flicked her lower lip with one talon in disgust. "What a quetzal!"

"Not really. I mean, I used to think so, but now I'm not so sure. I barely remember him when I lived with him as a child. He was always off to some part of the globe on business trips for weeks at a time. The nannies were great, and he always spent time with me when he got back, but he always had to leave again just as I was getting comfortable with him." Maripa leaned back against the wall and tucked her knees up under her chin. "Once I was old enough, he sent me off to boarding school. Straden Military Academy was the best so this is where I have been ever since."

"Like I said. A real quetzal. He didn't have time to waste on you so he just shipped you off while he got rich." Tessen spit into the trash can at the foot of the bed.

"Maybe," Maripa said, frowning as she stared at wall. "But he was so nice to me when I came home on breaks. He always seemed interested to hear about my school work and training. He often suggested courses that he thought I might be good at. It was Karm who got me interested in business administration as a career. He was even very supportive when I started showing some promise in combat skills."

"You are good at all of it, too. Not only are you at the top of your class, but you can whoop up on anyone twice your size. And your records on the shooting range may stand until the next century. Who would have thought such a tiny thing like you could be so bad ass?" Tessen refilled their cups and reached out, tipping her drink in salute.

Maripa smiled bit and shot a sideways glance at her roommate. "It is really fun sometimes. Darkon, his security chief, was always there for me. He's the one who taught me to play tuttle." She smiled briefly at the memories of Darkon and all of his small kindnesses toward her, even now. "And I love the look on Uncle Karm's face when I bring home a new trophy to put in my display case. He's always taken care of me so I do want him to be proud of me."

"Has he ever come to visit you here? I never see him at cadet reviews or when you receive an award. What's up with him?"

"He's just so busy all the time. It's like he's on some sort of mission. The corporation always comes first. He always made sure that I got the best of everything."

Tessen snorted and rolled her eyes at Maripa. "The best of everything except himself! That must have been a very lonely childhood for you. All by yourself up there at that castle of his with only the servants and nannies around. Did you ever have any friends to play with?"

"Oh, yes. There were always children around the place. The servants would bring their children to play with me most of the time. I had lots of friends."

"Friends? Sounds more like companions for hire." Tessen mimed spitting on the floor.

Maripa lowered her head. Her voice softened to a whisper. "I always thought they were friends, at least until I got older and heard one of them being scolded by her mother for playing too rough with me. I'll never forget the look of anger on the girl's face when she yelled back at her mother saying she never wanted to come here in the first place and ask why she couldn't stay home and play with her real friends."

"Ouch! That sucks."

"It was right after that when Karm sent me to boarding school. Misery loves company so I did make a few friends there. At least with some of the other girls who were in the same boat as me. Absentee parents and all." Maripa shook herself trying to regain her composure. "Don't get me wrong, Tessen, times weren't all rough like that. There were plenty of great times as well. Karm never forgot my birthdays, and most holidays he carved out at least one day to spend completely with me doing whatever I wanted. We had some great adventures together."

Tessen managed a dismal smile while shaking her head. "Still sounds like a rough way to grow up. I used to envy you when we first met, but now...I wouldn't trade my life for yours at all."

Maripa shook her head. "It made me strong. I learned how to cope with it all and take life as it came. I devoted myself to my studies and learned to defend myself. But that's all in the past now. Did you know he wants me to work for him after graduation? Some sort of personal assistant from the way he talks about it."

"Are you going to take the job?"

Maripa let her eyes and thoughts rise toward the high ceiling as she pondered a moment. "I think so. It sounds exciting. He travels all over Dyan'ta on business and I would accompany him. It might finally give us a chance to get to know each other. And I could start to repay him for everything he's done for me."

"I'm sure you would be great at it. Strix, you're great at everything you try. Is there anything you can't do?" Tessen laughed and punched Maripa on the arm.

Maripa threw off the covers and stomped over to the bathroom sink. She splashed cold water on her face, trying to regain her composure. "Kak! One little bad dream and I start blubbering like some freshman away from home for the first time. I've never told anyone that mutes before."

"Don't worry, your secret is safe with me, Ripa," Tessen said as she slid off the bed.

"It better be, Lieutenant. Or I'll have your ass in the ring in two shakes of a flea's tits."

"Now, that's the Cadet Captain Maripa that I know and love. Here, have one more for the road." Tessen poured another drink from her flask. They tapped glasses and downed their drinks in another single gulp. "Now go back to sleep. We don't want our class valedictorian to fall asleep in the middle of her commencement address."

***

Bishop Lerit, assistant to Zelph, Elder of church records, entered the Grand Elder's office carrying an ancient scroll and a packet of papers. "Holy Pater, I have momentous news." He genuflected before approaching the pale and wrinkled leader of the church.

Squinting through thick lenses, the Grand Elder smiled in recognition. "Ah, Lerit, my trusted friend, what has you so worked up today?"

"I believe I have found something in the holy scrolls of incredible import." He spread the papers in front of the Grand Elder. "Something that could possibly change the entire future of our beloved church."

"Lerit, my son," The elderly man, frail and bald, patted Lerit on the hand. Always so full of zeal. Ever since you uncovered the unfortunate Corab's betrayals, your services to this office have been invaluable. I do miss the days of my youth. I, too, saw great import in nearly everything. Let me take a look at your latest discovery."

His head shaking slightly, the Elder adjusted his glasses and leaned forward, pulling the papers to within inches of his failing eyes. As he read the pages, the Elder's hands began to tremble violently. His smile faded into an open-mouthed gape, and he dropped the packet back onto the table, grasping unsteadily at his glasses, dropping them on top of the table as he rubbed his eyes. "Have you verified these translations? How could something of this magnitude have escaped us for so long?"

With a look of sincere shock on his face, Lerit rose and stepped quickly to a cabinet along one wall of the office and withdrew a vial of yellow, oily liquid. "Pater," he said with a nervous tremor in his voice, "let me get you your medicine. Then we can discuss my findings."

"Thank The Eternal for you, my boy," the trembling old cleric said as he swallowed the bitter tasting dosage. "If your translations are correct then we must waste no time in informing the High Council of Elders. There must be verification of this and plans drawn up to bring this new revelation to the people."

Lerit waited a moment as the Elder read through the information again, noticing the tremors subsiding. "Is the medicine helping, Grand Elder?"

The infirmed head of the church dropped the papers, some falling to the floor. His eyes lost their focus and his words slurred as he looked up toward Lerit. "Yes my son. I feel better now. Thank you. What were you about to say?"

Lerit relaxed visibly as he returned to his chair. "I was saying we should not rush into anything just yet, Grand Elder. What with the unrest everywhere now due to the news of our impending doom, is it really the wisest course to upset the people even further? Maybe you should let me handle this quietly."

Staring blankly ahead, face contorted in great effort the Grand Elder slumped, waved his hand and let his chin fall to his chest. "Yes, yes, Lerit. Of course, you are right, as always. So wise for your young years. I place this matter in your hands."

Chapter Seven

Banners proclaiming the grand elevation flew across every major thoroughfare. Although the public was not participating in the event itself, there were parades, concerts, public speeches, sporting events and pyrotechnic displays enough to satiate everyone. Booths serving foods of all descriptions, roast Quol in Tequel sauce, Petzel eggs cooked inside their brown and orange speckled shells, sweet boiled pudding, along with cart after cart of fresh vegetables and homemade treats for sale. The mixing of aromas in the air watered mouths from one end of the grounds to the other. Colorful costumed characters on stilts portrayed the many heroes from the Book of The Eternal, tossing coins, food packages, and toys to the children. Lerit, the Bishop of Elnon, ranking bishop of the order, was celebrating the tenth anniversary of his installation. Having passed the initiation period, his installation as an Elder, and the traditional vote of the Elders to select their leader, as was proper whenever a new Elder joined the ranks, was a grand celebration. The election, a mere formality reaffirming the current Grand Elder's office, held little interest for anyone, but traditions must be upheld, no matter the added length to an already overly full schedule. Dignitaries, high officials, government and business leaders from all corners of Dyan'ta attended the gala.

The brothers stood together behind the screen of tall gold and silver curtains serving as a backdrop for the main stage. In the Grand Courtyard before the stage, a troop of elite dancers performed the ancient dance of the joining. A row of drums beat a steady rhythm, copied by the stamping feet of the dancers as pairs, male and female, circled each other. For several beats, the dancers hunched forward, shoulders rolled; arms extended and curled in front, heads bowed. They hooted and made guttural sounds in counterpoint to the drums. Suddenly, they jumped high, raised their faces to the sky, reaching high and wide, emitting a haunting, yet piercing shriek. At this moment, the audience joined in the cacophony, waving their arms in the air. This pattern repeated, with minor variations, for several minutes, until the pairs embraced each other, and began a new, more balletic portion of the dance.

"Well, brother," said Lerit to his oldest surviving sibling, "are you satisfied I have upheld my end of our agreement?"

Brach adjusted the ornate silver and gold robe of office on his brother's shoulders and slapped him on the back. "I never doubted you, Lerit. Our collaboration has succeeded beyond my wildest dreams. I am very proud of you. Are you ready to assume your new role?"

"I have been preparing for this day as long as I can remember. It will be a day nobody will ever forget." Lerit smiled at Brach, turned, and took his place behind the senior Elders as they formed the V-shaped procession, led by the Grand Elder, into the grand hall of the cathedral. Brach smiled and bowed his head in respect as the Grand Elder passed by, but the high priest only stared ahead, eyes glazed, his steps shaky, as if he was in a trance. Brach tilted his head, his crest ruffled and flushed; a sense of unease rose in his mind as he followed the procession and took his place on the royal throne to the left of the dais.

Three hours of speeches in the increasingly uncomfortable hall finally ended and the moment of election arrived. One by one, the elders rose from their wooden high backed chairs, vaguely reminiscent of a throne, took a small stone from a clay vessel, moved behind a translucent screen, made the mark of their selection, and deposited the stone into a gold, jewel encrusted vessel with the words: "This is my choice. May The Eternal grant him wisdom."

When all of the votes were cast, the Grand Elder rose, walked behind the screen and counted the votes. As he counted each stone, the Grand Elder dropped it into a grinder where it was pulverized. At the conclusion, he returned to the center of the dais, removed his sash of office and hung it on the central chair. Turning to the audience, his face and arms raised in beatific rapture, he announced the name of the elected.

"By the guiding hand of The Eternal and all the Prophets, all honor and praise go to Lerit, Elder of Elnon, on his elevation as our Grand Elder."

The gathered crowd sat silently for a moment before erupting into a clamor of shouting and disorder. Brach maintained his control by the slimmest of margins. Turning to the General, seated slightly behind and to his left, he commanded, "Find out what my idiot brother thinks he is doing! No novice has ever assumed the office of Grand Elder. I can't even recall the last time a new Grand Elder was elected before the death of his predecessor. Has he lost his mind?"

Amid the uproar and confusion, Lerit seated himself on the central chair while the former Grand Elder fitted the sash of office on his shoulders. Lerit rose and held his arms high, signaling for order and attention. "Today marks the opening of a new era. The Eternal himself foretold my election to this esteemed position to me. My prayers and studies have revealed to me many wrongdoings and shortcomings of this order. I have spent the past few years teaching these revelations to my fellow brothers and The Eternal has opened their eyes to the truth."

The crowd murmured, heads turning left and right to verify they were hearing everything correctly. Lerit paused for the commotion to subside before continuing.

"Henceforth, by the authority now invested in me by The Eternal and his clergy here in this realm, I am abolishing the old covenants. A new order, one known as The Faith, will follow in its place. Our new mission, as revealed to me by The Eternal, will be to guide us away from the deceptions of our misplaced trust in government and science and into a life of purity and peace, led by His teachings. As a sign to all of our commitment to a new order, I take the name, and title of Pareth, Prior of Dregor, the noblest of our prophets. May his example be a shining light for us all."

He turned, arms wide, encompassing the gathered Elders behind him and continued, an orange glow appearing to enfold the holy men assembled on the stage, taking the form of a great flaming bird as it grew in size and intensity. The form then broke into smaller individual flames, one for each of the brothers on stage, appearing to absorb into their bodies. "In accordance with the dictates of The Eternal, as revealed to me, the Elders are no more. Instead, they are henceforth to be known as The Brothers of The Convocation, and I, as their chosen leader, will be known

as the Prior. May the blessings of The Eternal be on you all."
The assembly of Brothers approached their new leader, removed
the ornate robe of the former office, and wrapped him instead
with a plain, homespun cloth.

Pareth bowed, signaled to the brothers, turned and led
the procession offstage. Brach rushed after them, his face no
longer able to contain the rage in his mind. The assembled
dignitaries, confused and dismayed, shoved their way to the
exits. Hundreds of those gathered in the hushed crowd burst into
awed proclamations of faith, arms raised up to the sky, tears
streaming down their faces.

***

Brach slammed his fist into the wall of his carriage, upsetting
the balance of the candlesticks mounted there, which toppled to
the floor in response. "He refuses to see me!" He roared. "Me!
His monarch! Not to mention his only surviving brother!"
Grabbing the nearest object at hand, a crystal goblet awarded
him by the merchants in honor of his newest tax relief measures,
he hurled it across the carriage, shattering it into a thousand
pieces against the wall next to the General's head.

The General sat, impassive as ever, waiting for Brach's
temper to run its course. The clatter of the Tal's hooves, and the
rumble of the carriage wheels on the cobblestones as they sped
through the city drowned the monarch's continuing rants from
outside ears. In due time, he poured his sovereign another drink,
this time in a pewter goblet, and placed it in the holder next to
him. "Your Majesty," he began cautiously, "While it is
disturbing, and worth serious investigation, your brother's
elevation to leadership of this new religion of his does not appear
to be any immediate threat to your position. He did, after all,
publicly renounce any claims to the throne."

"You know my brother," Brach said, downing the goblet
in one swift gulp, falling heavily against the back of his padded
seat. "He is intelligent and devious. How else do you explain his
being able to hide this plot of his from me, and everyone else?"
Brach ripped off his formal coat, tossing it aside and raked the
wall again, his talons leaving deep gouges in the ornate
woodwork as he continued to shout. "I don't fear his taking over

the throne, but he is certainly in a position to wield sufficient power to influence, if not control a great many events."

"Unfortunately, there is very little you can do about it now, except to consolidate your base and limit the damage the new Prior can do."

"I had one brother killed, why not another? He surely has made some powerful enemies we could lay the blame on."

Shaking his head, the General leaned forward, placing himself directly in front of Brach, forcing him to listen. "That would be most unwise, Your Majesty. There are far more subtle ways of controlling the situation. The risks are far too great. And you certainly do not want to turn him into a martyr for their new cause."

Brach glared at his advisor, his body shaking in anger. "I don't just want him killed, I want him flayed alive and then his head stuck on a pike on the castle parapets."

The General remained impervious to Brach's rage.

"Perhaps you are right," said Brach, his shoulders slumping as he exhaled loudly. "We will need to set up an immediate surveillance team, infiltrate this new Brothers of The Convocation, and keep a close eye on my dear brother from now on. I don't want any more surprises. And find out how he pulled off that theatrical stunt with the lights!"

"I will see it done immediately, Your Majesty."

The royal carriage pulled into the palace courtyard, stopping in front of the massive doorway. Brach stormed out of the carriage before any of the footmen had a chance to assist him. Flailing his arms and shouting to nobody in particular, mostly in a variations of creative and most un-royal curses, Brach bulled his way to his private chambers.

***

A week later, the General walked into the monarch's office and waited to be recognized.

"Did you get what I wanted, General?" asked the monarch, still focused on the papers he was examining.

"Your suspicions were correct, Your Majesty. Almost all of the Elders, except the former Grand Elder, the doddering old fool, was connected to some sort of impropriety, some even criminal in nature, but your brother intervened on their behalf and their names were cleared. While there is no hard evidence, he appears to be directly connected to their elevation to the hierarchy. Your brother appears to have been very busy these past ten years."

Brach flipped through the papers, stopping occasionally to focus on some point of interest. "How are your efforts to infiltrate The Brotherhood proceeding?

"Not as well as expected, Your Majesty. They are extremely cautious and suspicious of anyone outside their organization. It will take some time to work our associates into their confidence."

"Very well. Keep at it. I need to know what Lerit... excuse me, Prior Pareth, is up to.

Chapter Eight

"**Y**ou worry too much, Maripa," Karm said. "This is just a dinner supporting my friend Noldar for a seat in Parliament."

Karm stood in front of the world map in his office, contemplating the dozens of various colored pins on every continent. Each color represented a different category of holding under his control. Reds indicated pharmaceutical companies; aerospace engineering firms were green. Yellow showed manufacturing plants. Blue pins for computer facilities. Other colors showed the locations of the many companies, universities, banks and other organizations he maintained interest in as either a board member or major stockholder. He pulled out one additional pin. A gold one. This he placed in the middle of the Latonian Desert.

Maripa tapped her foot rapidly, fists clenching at her side. "Yes, sir, but you have been attending a lot of these functions lately. You are becoming a celebrity. Are you sure all of the publicity is wise?" She sat at her small desk and began sorting through several files accumulating there.

"Nothing to concern yourself with. Just take care of these files and have my levicoach ready in an hour." Karm looked at Maripa, appraising her from head-to-toe. "Pick out something suitable to wear yourself. I think it is time you started accompanying me at these functions. You never know when I might need your special talents."

"As you wish, sir," said Maripa. She stood, organized the folders into neat stacks, with perhaps a bit too much force, and walked toward the door. "It is part of my job though to let you know when I believe there is a security risk. I haven't spent all these years training just to let you take unnecessary risks."

He sighed and turned to look at her. "I appreciate that, Maripa, but this is just a fundraiser. How much of a security risk can it be?"

"Not just this dinner, sir. It's all of the events you have been attending in the past few months. The more recognized you become, the bigger the target you make."

"Nothing I can't handle. I've been doing this for a long time, now. I know what I'm doing. Now, go get ready and meet me in an hour." He placed his hand on her shoulder. "Trust me."

"Yes, sir," she said, shutting the door behind her as she left.

The fundraiser was a lavish §10,000 a plate affair; all of the leading party representatives, corporate heads and celebrities received invitations. The men wore their dark tuxedos while the women dazzled the onlookers with their shimmering gowns in an incredible variety of colors. Internationally renowned chefs who flew in the week before prepared the food and the symphony orchestra hired for the evening performed from their alcove. Security personnel kept the news media, paparazzi, and protesters at a distance, but the flashes popped everywhere as each vehicle arrived.

Karm stepped out of his levicoach and extended a hand to Maripa. He was dressed in his finest tuxedo. She wore an iridescent jade gown she had specially made for ease of movement. She refused to wear heels despite Karm's protests.

"Heels will only get in the way if I have to act quickly," she told him. He decided not to press the matter any further.

He presented his arm to Maripa and they paraded down the walkway.

"Over here!"

"Look this way!"

"Who is your companion, Karm?"

Karm waved at the photographers and reporters as they called to him, but continued to walk toward the door. Maripa scanned the crowd for potential threats. Servants took their cloaks as they entered the foyer. Karm grabbed a drink from one of the trays circulating the room and walked toward a small group he recognized. Maripa followed at a respectful distance. She observed the crowd warily as they entered the gathering.

"Good evening, Prime Minister," Karm said as he approached the leading member of Parliament and shook his hand. "Looks like the money is pouring in for Noldar. What do you think of his chances?"

"With you on his side, how can he fail?" said the official, continuing to grasp Karm's hand. "Thanks to you we can pay for twice the campaign ads as any of his opponents. The polls show Noldar in a comfortable lead."

"Wonderful. And how is the little matter of the Anti-Cloning legislation coming? I hope there have been no difficulties."

"None at all. We've managed to tie up the bill in committee so deep it has no chance of surfacing for a vote." The Prime Minister leaned in closer to Karm and surveyed the room. "We have managed to counter every tactic mounted by the clergy and their people, so far. However, they are gaining in strength in some districts, particularly Elnon. We may not be able to contain them much longer."

"We need to keep clone research alive, Dolmak. I don't need to remind you of the consequences of failure here."

"Yes, we are in agreement there, Karm, but the monarch is not as solid as he was a couple of years ago. He may be starting to sympathize with the church and their ideology. I think he believes they have grown too powerful already, or perhaps he simply feels more secure with his own brother as the bishop. He may be courting them for support."

"That is concerning. Keep me informed if anything develops there." Karm raised his glass of champagne and tilted it toward the Prime Minister before taking a sip.

"Of course. Now, if you will excuse me, I have other matters to attend to." The Prime Minister walked off and found another group of dignitaries to engage.

There were many other officials with whom Karm met and discussed a wide assortment of issues. The dignitaries frequently pressed him into posing with them for photos by the official event photographers. Maripa, somehow, always managed to be at least partially hidden in each photo.

The tower clock struck midnight as Karm led Maripa out to their waiting levicoach. While they waited for traffic to pass at the end of the private driveway, a series of blinding flashes erupted from outside to their left.

"Maripa!" Karm shouted as he raised his hand to shield his eyes from the flashes. Before he could turn, he heard the coach door open. Maripa sprang into action.

The photographer retreated a few steps before Maripa seized his camera. "No, stay back! You can't do that!"

Maripa twisted the camera and easily relieved the man of his equipment. She dropped the camera on the ground, picked up a large rock, and smashed it.

"No pictures," she told the man. Reaching into her pocket, she pulled out §300 and tossed it on the ground. "For the damages." She turned, got back in the mag-lev, and closed the door. The driver accelerated onto the road, leaving the photographer behind.

"Did you get all that?" the paparazzo called to the bushes behind him.

A second man stood up from his concealment. "Yeah, got it. Who was that?"

"That is what we are getting paid to find out. Let's go." The two men walked to the levicoach they had hidden on a side road.

Karm returned to his office. "Kirta, please get me the Chancellor at the university now. No video this time." He grabbed a goblet and poured himself a drink, downing it in one quick shot. He reached into the top left desk drawer and pulled out a small silver box. From inside he removed a large violet capsule and swallowed it. He poured another drink and sat at his desk. *No more distractions. From here on, I stick to the plan. Keep focused on the priorities. Play time is over.*

"The Chancellor is on line two," said Kirta over the intercom.

Karm hit the second button and turned on the speaker phone. "Good morning, Chancellor."

"Karm, delighted to hear from you. I wasn't expecting your call until later though; what can I do for you?"

"I have been looking over the list of candidates for that associate Professor of genetics position you are trying to fill. I think I have a candidate for you."

"Wonderful, who did you have in mind?"

"A brilliant young man with some very novel ideas. He just got his appointment, recently married, very eager to get started."

"Sounds like someone we would be interested in. What is his name?"

"Dr. Jontar Rocker."

The Chancellor hesitated before speaking. "Oh, that one. We eliminated him from consideration. The background check revealed some information leading us to believe he did not fit in with our philosophy."

"Nonsense, Chancellor. I think he would be a perfect addition to the faculty."

"There are many other fine candidates, Karm. Surely we can find someone better suited to our needs."

"You don't understand, Chancellor. Jontar Rocker is my choice for the position. You will hire Dr. Rocker and convince the other board members of the wisdom in this decision. Or do I need to rethink my support for the new engineering building?"

There was a longer hesitation this time. "No, sir, that will not be necessary. I am sure Dr. Rocker will work out just fine."

"Thank you, Chancellor. I am glad you agree. We'll talk again soon."

Karm disconnected the line and sat back in his chair. He held out his hand. *Activate: Rocker.* His palm glowed and the image of Jontar Rocker, along with a detailed biography appeared, hovering above his hand. He grabbed his goblet and downed the drink in one shot as he read the dossier. *Dr. Rocker, this should be a very interesting meeting.*

Part Two

Chapter Nine

Campus police charged around the corner wearing full protective gear and with shock rods raised, ready for a confrontation. Rocker raced through the growing crowd toward the protection of the police. "Holy mutes!" he cried as he ducked, a rock grazing his head. Now protecting his skull with his tattered case as he dodged more missiles, he shoved through the angry crowd, their placards waving in the air: *The Eternal Hates Clones! You Can't Clone A Soul! Clones Are Brin Too! We Are All Brin!* Both factions exploded violently around him, their shouts seething with irrational hatred. A glass bottle exploded on the sidewalk after narrowly missing his head. *Shit! That was too close. I've gotta get the* strix *out of here, and fast.* As he closed in on the barricades, an officer the size of a small house raised his shock rod and took aim at Rocker's noggin. Rocker held up his faculty ID badge with his talons and waved it as he ran closer. "I'm Professor Rocker, Head of Genetics!" he shouted.

The constable hesitated, and then lowered his weapon, but only slightly. Rocker noted that he still held it at the ready. "Good thing you ran into me instead of one of the rookies out here, Professor." Rocker slowed to catch his breath, bent over, leaning heavily on his knees. The officer frowned, holding the electrically charged baton tightly in his opposable talons. "You might have gotten your head bashed in if I hadn't recognized that faculty badge. Now get going before all strix breaks loose. This is going to get bad." The officer pointed the weapon in the direction of the nearest building behind him and shoved Rocker out of his way.

Rocker made it to the safety of his building just as the mob smashed through the barricades, trampling the officers in their path just before they attacked each other with signs and fists. The police let loose with repel-gas canisters and bystanders scrambled for safety. The scene before Rocker as he stared out at the chaos from behind the protective glass of the vestibule blurred slightly as his inner eyelids closed instinctively against the noxious fumes drifting toward the building.

"You okay, Jontar?" Rocker looked up to see one of the secretaries from the pool approaching.

"Yeah, I got caught in the middle of that mess out there. Nothing too serious."

"It's disgraceful," she replied. "Even when faced with our planet's destruction, we still fight amongst ourselves."

His head was starting to ache where the rock had hit him. He felt among his feathers and discovered a large bump beginning to form, but no blood. He winced as he pressed against the lump. "I would have thought everyone would be more afraid of the end of the world than clones. Honestly, we are only barely able to grow a few replacement organs, we're nowhere near being capable of accomplishing what they are accusing us of. I guess extinction is just too big to deal with right now." Rocker watched the chaotic scene a bit longer, then squared his shoulders and headed toward his classroom, waving goodbye to the woman as she turned to continue her duties.

Rocker nodded to the half-empty circular lecture hall and dropped his bag on the lectern. "Alright then, any questions from yesterday's lesson?"

"Professor?" Called out a student as she stood to address the class. She was tall, dressed in the colorful fashions of the well-to-do. Her impeccably preened red and yellow head feathers perfectly matched her painted talons. "I just don't get all this stuff about clones. I mean, they're just a bunch of animals the Progressives want to turn into a class of slaves, right? At least that is what my boyfriend says." She ran her talons through her crest, eyes rolling upward, as if searching her mind for further details before continuing. "Even some of the readings you have assigned us, and many of the recent news broadcasts seem to support this belief, but it doesn't feel right to me."

"And let the games begin," muttered Rocker softly as hands flew up. "Go ahead, Lokem," he said, pointing to a student in the third row.

"Your position appears to be grounded in research and verifiable data," stated the young man, "but I am not sure that your conclusions are a direct result of that data. Can you clarify your position?"

The girl squirmed at the lectern and scrunched her face as she searched through her papers. "I am just saying, if we ever do discover how to make clones, it seems like they will be our slaves and not free individuals."

"Your statements are not supported by scientific data," called out another student from the back of the room. "What you are saying is more personal opinion than evidence."

So far, so good, thought Rocker. The students were keeping the discussion to the ground rules, and after a few more questions, he almost started to relax. Then the inevitable happened.

"But doesn't The Faith tell us that a cloned individual, because it is manufactured by us and not created by The Eternal and therefore is without a soul, cannot be a true Brin?" the girl continued. Her comment opened the floodgates and the rules of discussion were as forgotten as yesterday's lecture. Students shouted out accusations and recriminations at will.

"You cannot be serious!" Hands flailing and voices raised, Rocker's students argued their perspective on the basic nature of clones. "How can you possibly believe clones are not true Brin?"

"Have you ever met one? Of course not, they don't exist, at least not yet," argued some students.

"So we just sit back and wait for these atrocities to exist? Not me." a second orated.

"Well, who appointed you the final judge of who is True Brin and who is not?" called out another student. "The Eternal loves all Brin, cloned or not."

Professor Rocker decided enough was enough and raked his talons across the chalk board to get their attention. Everyone suddenly cringed and covered their auricular as the spine wrenching screech filled the room. He then turned to the board and wrote in huge bold letters:

FOLLOW THE EVIDENCE!
FACTS NOT FEELINGS!

"Does everyone remember our discussion regarding the most basic rules of science?" he asked the class. "If you cannot maintain this sort of mental discipline, then may I suggest you change your major to Comparative Religions, or Philosophy?" Rocker replaced the chalk in its tray and turned to face the class. "This subject is not for everyone. I, too, struggle to keep my own personal beliefs out of my research. However, it is precisely this sort of discipline science requires. Especially now that our world is threatened and we search for ways to save ourselves." Rocker lowered his eyes and took a deep breath. "If we're lucky."

A student in the first row raised his hand. "Well, yes sir, what you say is true, but can you give us your perspective on this matter?" Rocker looked up and saw his top student, who also happened to be the son of the university's Chancellor, asked the question. The same Chancellor who was looking for any excuse to fire Rocker. A few months ago, Rocker openly ridiculed his boss for introducing a proposal to include "Life, as designed by the Eternal" to the science curriculum. Rocker forced a smile and said, "Now, what good would it do you if I were to tell you my personal beliefs? I wouldn't be very good at this job if I influenced my students with my own personal biases, whatever they may be." Rocker winked at the class. His crest feathers ruffled and flashed just a bit of red.

"Feather Fluff!" the young man called out. He stood and waved his arms to emphasize his frustration. "That's a cop-out! Why don't you tell us what you think?"

Students turned, mouths open and eyes wide, first at the student, then at the Professor, holding their breath.

Rocker held himself in check and said, "Remember, a genetics classroom is for science, and is not the place for politics or philosophy. If you must debate philosophical matters then stick to the realities of technological advancement." Rocker studied the room for a moment before continuing. "What is the real fear of scientists with any new discovery or advancement?"

A shout from the back of the room answered. "Being ignored or dismissed as lunacy by our peers."

"No. While that does happen I am referring to something much more sinister." The lecture hall became silent except for the nervous shuffling of papers. Everyone tried to become invisible out of fear they would be called on to respond. "What I am talking about is the appropriation and misuse of our theories by the government or the military for their own destructive purposes. Think back through our history. How many times has the government taken scientific theories, originally intended for the benefit and advancement of society, then distorted and weaponized them?"

"Mag-lev technology," came a quiet voice from the audience. "It was first developed to improve transportation by making it safer for everyone. The military found a way to make their plasma weapons out of it."

"Precisely! Instead of worrying about whether clones have souls or not, imagine what the military could do if they chose to take over cloning technology to design the perfect soldier. Stick to the science, people. There are enough nightmares out there without inventing new ones to lose sleep over." Your first research paper is due in two days. I have extended my office hours today and tomorrow for any of you who need extra help. Class dismissed."

Dr. Rocker gathered his valise and mug and headed out the door. He turned left at the next hallway instead of heading to his office to stop off in the lab first He noticed the yellow "Experiment In Progress" light flashing above the doorway as he entered the room.

The lab, brightly lit by the solar panels in the ceiling, illuminated several rows of long tables filled the room. Shelves of ceramic containers and equipment lined the almost imperceptibly concave walls. Experiments conducted by the graduate students were in various stages of progress on each of the tables. *Now, this is where I belong.* Rocker smiled as he inhaled the scent of chemical reactions permeating the lab.

"Good morning, Professor," said Gardet, one of his lab assistants this semester. "Crebot asked me to remind you to talk to him when you arrived."

"Good morning, Gardet. That's why I'm here. How's the new technique working out?"

"Much better than what I was doing before. Thanks for the articles. They really helped." She beamed at him, pointed toward the intricate set of glassware gently percolating on the table, and handed him her notebook. "You can see the new data is very promising. Of course, the results are only preliminary, but I am hopeful."

Rocker perused the data tables and scribbled notes. "Yes…yes, I agree. Much more encouraging than before. Your alterations to the design show a great deal of promise. You made sure to account for the new density variants?"

"Of course, Professor. You can see it right here." She turned a few pages of her notes and pointed to a set of calculations. "I should be ready for live tests on the eukaryotic cells in a few days, if everything turns out well."

Dr. Rocker leaned over, examining the set-up. He nodded his approval and patted her on the back. "Yes, looks much better. I have to run now, but I'll check in with you later. Keep up the good work, Gardet."

"Thank you, professor." Her voice was soft as it quavered. She wiped a hand over her eyes.

"Is anything wrong, Gardet?" asked Rocker, noticing the redness in her eyes and the slight trembling of her hands.

"It's nothing, professor, really. I'm just tired and overreacting to all the news about the supernova lately and all the terrible things happing." She hesitated, wiping her eyes again and grabbed for a tissue to blow her nose. "Don't mind me, I'm fine. That mob outside today just sort of got to me is all."

Rocker placed a hand gently on her shoulder and sat on the stool next to her. "Not all the news is bad, Gardet. Most individuals are taking it all in stride and just trying to get on with their lives. Many are even going out of their way to be better, kinder. The reporters just seem to get better ratings when they sensationalize the horrible things."

"I know, professor, I know. And I'm fine…really. It all just sort of ganged up on me for some reason. I know we will find a way to survive, after all, a hundred years is a long time to figure it all out."

"Those idiots out there haven't shaken your faith in our research have they?"

"Feathers no!" She replied, sitting up straighter and turning to face him. "Those crazies haven't got a clue about what they are saying so I usually don't pay them any mind at all. I don't know what got into me today. Just one of those things I guess. Thanks for talking to me about it though. It helped, but I better get back to work now."

Rocker stood up to leave, patting her on the shoulder as she picked up another tissue and blew out her sinuses again. "Good girl."

He turned and headed to the back of the room where Crebot, his most senior graduate assistant maintained his domain. The young man was huddled over his notebooks, writing furiously as he muttered to himself.

"Good morning, Crebot. How's your cervical vertebra cloning process going?"

Crebot startled and slammed shut his notebook. He jumped to his feet and spun to face the Professor. "I have some new ideas on that, Professor. I think I have a better approach."

Dr. Rocker shook his head. "Alright, slow down, let's not jump to conclusions. Show me what you have."

Crebot's eyes gleamed as he spoke. "As you know, one of the most common orthopedic injuries is to the cervical vertebrae. Sixteen small bones supporting our skulls is just not a practical arrangement."

Dr. Rocker nodded. "That's why I have you working on cloning replacement vertebrae."

"But why simply replace such an inefficient system? Why not improve it? This is what I am proposing." He opened his notebook to the calculations and diagrams of his latest theory.

Rocker twisted his mouth to one side and shook his head as he examined the notebook. "This looks like you want to reduce the number of vertebrae from sixteen to seven,"

Not noticing the negative reaction, Crebot continued his excited elucidation. "Exactly! Mammals have a much more efficient vertebral column. The cervical bones are thicker and less vulnerable. Instead of simply repairing the problem, why not fix it permanently? We have the ability to change our species. Why shouldn't we strive to improve ourselves?"

Dr. Rocker flipped through the pages of formulae and illustrations. His frown deepened as he read the young man's writings. "I admire your enthusiasm, Crebot," he said as he closed the manual, "but I have to tell you that, while this is an excellent exercise in the theoretical possibilities of genetics, I cannot allow you to proceed in this area. Stick to the original problem of cloning replacement vertebrae. We are not The Eternal. It's not our place to redesign our anatomy. We have no idea what the repercussions might be, or how such things might be misused."

Crebot's face and crest reddened and he fought to control his voice as he responded to the criticism. "Engineers improve their designs all the time. The world rewards them for developing new concepts that improve the efficiency and performance of our technology. We, on the other hand, are suppressed and vilified for any attempt to improve ourselves."

Dr. Rocker maintained his composure and tried to assume a more reassuring tone as he replied. "We've been over this before, Crebot. There are people out there suffering from spinal cord injuries. Your work here can provide them with real hope for a cure, if you don't allow yourself to get sidetracked. Do you want them to continue their struggles and live on in pain while you pursue some grand ideal of your own? They need relief now. Focus on the immediate concern before you go off on some flight of fancy. And, as we have already discussed, you know that society is just not ready for such extreme applications of our theories. Are you ready to accept the responsibility if some secret government program appropriates your work to create an invincible army of artificially created soldiers? You've got to learn more restraint. Your passions do you credit, but you let yourself get carried away by them too often. Wasn't it just last month that you wanted to reroute the arterial pathways instead of simply cloning the replacement blood vessels? And last year you proposed a strategy for developing retractable talons."

Crebot refused to back down. "Science is the pursuit of truth. We should not be constrained by the small minds of outsiders who cannot comprehend what we are doing."

Rocker shook his head again. "Science has nothing to do with truth, Crebot. It is simply the discovery and analysis of facts and evidence. Truth is an abstract concept. We deal in the concrete."

"What good is the evidence if it doesn't lead us to the truth, Professor?"

"Stick to the process. Let others worry about truth. I have to get back to my office now, but think about what we've discussed. Stop by my office later if you need to talk further. You have the makings of a great geneticist. Just learn to control your passions."

"Yes, sir," Crebot replied. He started to say something else, but stopped and returned to his notebooks.

Dr. Rocker stood watching for a moment, then left the lab, and walked toward his office. *That boy is brilliant, but he's becoming too concerned over truth.*

Dr. Rocker strode through the hallways of the building lost in concern over Crebot until he rounded the corner that held his office. The usual gaggle of students was already lining up outside his door with questions, concerns and a few brilliant insights that every geneticist in history had apparently missed.

"Give me ten minutes to get myself organized before you send in the first one," Rocker told his secretary. He went into his office and shut the door behind him.

Rocker sloughed into his uncomfortable chair behind his desk, deposited the notes in a random pile, took a long drink from his mug, and buried his head in his hands. Looking up between his talons, his eyes wandered among the framed certificates hanging on the wall and his most recent trophy from the Individual Rings Championship last semester, and settled on a photo of a younger self in his new Special Forces uniform surrounded by some friends from his unit. He held up the mug and took another drink in salute to the long lost comrades. He unconsciously felt for the gold ring hanging on its silver chain under his shirt and lingered there for only a moment.

Running his talons through his crest feathers and giving his head a shake, he got his mind back onto the matters at hand and he readied himself for the inevitable onslaught of students.

"Okay, Marique," he buzzed over the intercom on his desk, "you can let them in now."

"Yes, sir," came the slightly fuzzy, electronic reply.

All the usual complaints filled the next two hours, requests for deadline extensions and cries for help with understanding the latest set of lecture notes. Thankfully, the last of the supplicants concluded the afternoon's session with plenty of time left for a quick set of Rings before heading home. Rocker gathered his bags and turned out the lights as he left.

"Oh, Professor," called his secretary as he reached her desk. "This just came for you." She handed him a note. The official seal of the Chancellor was stamped on the front.

Rocker opened the note and read its contents:

"Your presence is required in my office no later than eight o'clock tomorrow morning. Urgent matters concerning your most recent lecture will need to be discussed."

He refolded the note and placed it in his pocket. *Now what in Dyan'ta does that molting old buzzard want now? Hasn't anyone preened his tail enough today?*

"Okay, tell him I'll be there first thing in the morning." Rocker knew this could not be good. The Chancellor never wanted to talk to anybody who was not donating large sums of cash, or presenting him with some honorific. The mere mention of the Chancellor aroused vivid and unpleasant memories of the old man. Rocker shuddered as he recalled the summons he received only a month before. "Politicians should never be in charge of education," he muttered to himself.

Shaking his head to ward off the memories, Rocker rejoined the present. *Guess I better get going. No sense prolonging the inevitable.* Rocker grabbed his mug and downed the last of the tea. His gaze returned to the old photo. *I've survived worse than this. If Alpha Unit didn't kill me this certainly won't.* Rocker started to walk out of the office, but stopped and called back to his secretary. "Marique, after you contact the Chancellor could you please call Professor Barl and let him know I'm on my way to our Rings match. I'll just be a couple of minutes late. I want to stop by the cafeteria on my way."

"Will do, sir," he heard her reply just as the door closed behind him.

Chapter Ten

The room smelled of disinfectant, sterile and cold. The machines quietly beeped and displayed her vital signs in numbers and graphs that were meaningless to the uninitiated. Jontar Rocker sat silently holding his wife's hand as she lay comatose and dying in the hospital bed. Her body pale and gaunt from the ravages of bronchocilliary diskinesia, a rare genetic disorder. The late onset of her symptoms made the disease particularly virulent. A nurse, wearing the powder blue uniform of the night shift quietly entered the room and checked the monitors, recording a few notes on her pad. Her crest was long and flowing with a streak of green amid the yellow feathers.

"We don't normally see this sort of thing in adults. Children can usually survive, even with the disabilities. Tragic, but at least they live." She took a damp cloth from the basin and wiped her patient's forehead and arms to relieve some of the fever.

"No adult has ever survived this disease though," said Rocker. "At least nobody else will have to go through this." He lowered his head as tears welled up in his eyes.

"May I get you anything, Professor?" She asked, laying a gentle hand on his shoulder.

"I'm okay thank you," he replied hoarsely.

"Alright, then. You be sure to ring if you need anything." The young woman patted his shoulder and lingered at the door only a moment, holding back her own tears.

Professor Rocker wiped the tears falling down his cheeks with a single talon of his left hand. "I am so sorry, Betha. I should have worked harder. If only I had been smarter. It's just too late now. I should have seen the answer sooner. Our cure would only increase your suffering now. I am so sorry." His shoulders shook with the deep fits of sobbing overtaking him again.

Struggling to regain his composure, Dr. Rocker recalled all of his fondest memories of the years he and Betha had spent together before her illness stole her away. "Remember the weekend up at the cabin we rented for our second anniversary? How hard we tried to make a baby then? You were so disappointed when you didn't get pregnant." He entwined his four talons with hers and squeezed tightly. "We did keep trying though. It just wasn't in the stars for us I guess. You were so beautiful. Why didn't I try harder? If only the kaking university had parted with some more of their precious grant money to allow me some better equipment and more assistants."

As Rocker continued to speak and reminisce better times with his unconscious wife her breathing became shallow and rasping. The monitors sent a warning signal to the nurse's station down the hallway, summoning the head nurse within seconds.

"Are you sure you won't change your mind and allow us to take any further measures, Professor?" she asked after a brief check of the displays.

"I'm sure. We discussed this and she was adamant about not sustaining her life artificially when there was no longer any hope. Is this it?" Tears streamed down his face as the realization hit him.

The nurse struggled to maintain her own emotions as she turned to stand by her patient's husband, gently laying a hand on his arm. "I'm afraid so, Professor. It's only a matter of moments now. She is a strong woman though."

Rocker leaned in close and kissed his wife, then spoke quietly to her. "It's okay to go now, my love. You need to let go. I will always love and miss you, but your time here is over now. Go...be at peace." He kissed her again and sat back in his chair, still holding her hand.

Another minute passed and Betha's face seemed to relax. Her chest rose and fell one final time, and then she was gone.

Dr. Rocker awoke screaming. The nightmare had returned. He sat up, heart pounding and sweat soaking his sheets. "Holy strix!" He gasped, reaching for the light switch. "Been a long time since I had that one. What time is it?" Glancing toward the clock he saw the numbers read four twenty seven in the morning. His heart and breathing slowly returned to normal as he sat. "Feathers! Thought I was finally getting over her death. Guess I still have a few ghosts to deal with." He rubbed his eyes and stood, walking to the bathroom to splash some water on his face. "No sense trying to go back to sleep now. Might as well get up and face the day. Maybe I can get in a little practice before seeing the old bird this morning."

***

"Good morning, Professor," the Chancellor's secretary greeted Rocker as he entered the office. Gert was a fixture in the Chancellor's office. She was one of those indispensable personnel who each of the previous three Chancellors depended on to keep the office running seamlessly. Her crest was starting to grey now, but her eyes were bright and she had the reputation of knowing where all the bodies were buried.

"Hello, Gert. Do I need to ask what His Lordship's mood is today?"

She gave him a sly smile and her eyes sparkled with mischief. "I would have thought he made that clear already. You did bring your spare ass with you, didn't you?"

"My spare ass?" Rocker cocked his head and hesitated as he began to sit.

"Yeah, you know, to replace the one he is going to chew off." Her eyes twinkled as she looked at Rocker.

"So just a normal inquisition then, okay," replied Rocker as he relaxed and continued to sit in the wobbly chair reserved for supplicants to the office.

"How do you put up with His Eminence? You could work for any department you wanted to with a fraction of the hassles you get here."

Gert tilted her head and smiled, "Now, Professor, you know these Chancellors couldn't tie their own shoes without me to help them. I am the sole force keeping this place functioning."

Just then a light flashed on the secretary's desk and she ushered him into the Chancellor's private office.

The office Rocker entered was plush, in the manner of most high officials. Large leather chairs populated several locations about the room. An ornate and highly polished wooden desk with an even grander throne of a chair behind it left no doubt as to who was in charge. Photos lined the wall of the Chancellor posing and shaking hands with all manner of government, religious and other immediately recognizable aristocrats testifying to the immense importance of the occupant of this office. A large embossed certificate announcing the Chancellor's nomination to the rank of High Director of The Faith hung prominently behind the desk.

The Chancellor stood looking out of the large window behind his desk. The morning sun glowed deep orange as it rose above the horizon, its light casting a vibrant glow to the room. Tall and broad in the chest he wore brilliant silver and gold rings on each of the four fingers on his large, strong hands. His eyes were a penetrating deep brown. Even his top crest was artfully greyed just enough to give the impression of the wisdom of age, but still with eternal reserves of vitality. His suit, meticulously tailored in the fashion of a wealthy power broker. A large diamond graced the center of his university logo tie clasp. He stood, gazing out the window for a moment longer, forcing Rocker to remain standing.

"Good morning, Professor," he said, waving a hand to indicate a chair and permission to sit.

Sitting down at his desk, the Chancellor picked up his cigar and a small glass of translucent crimson liqueur. "Nothing like a fine Drasnian wine and an imported Pakish cigar, is there, Professor?" he said as he swirled the liquid in his glass and blew a cloud of smoke into the air above his head.

Rocker tensed, his hands clutched the arms of the chair and his crest reddened slightly. Then, fighting down the reaction he leaned back into the chair. "I'm a tea man myself, Chancellor, but with times the way they are, even that is getting out of financial reach now."

"Professor," said the Chancellor, ignoring Rocker's remark. "Are you aware of what keeps this university alive?"

Rocker locked eyes with the Chancellor. "The students and our research are our primary functions here, sir."

"No, Professor, in fact, they are not. It is money and the good will of those providing it is our primary responsibility. If I know about the inexcusable riot in your classroom today then rest assured others on the board know about it too, and so will a great many of our benefactors. I can guarantee you many of them will not like what they are hearing about you." He took a sip of his drink and another puff on the cigar to let his message sink in. Would you care to explain what happened yesterday?"

"To what are you referring, sir?"

"Don't be coy with me, Professor. I am not in the mood for games." The Chancellor looked as if he had eaten a dozen lemons right off the tree. "You know very well about the near riot you started among your students. Your new line of research is under a great deal of scrutiny and far from a second committee review. The probability of extending your grant in this area is highly doubtful at best. You have made some very impressive breakthroughs in your field, but your increasingly radical work and increasingly questionable teaching methods are bringing a great deal of negative scrutiny on yourself and this university. I am already under pressure to revoke your tenure. It won't take much to..."

The door to his office opened and in walked two very lethal-looking men in identical dark suits. They stood to either side of the doorway, admitting a small woman dressed impeccably in the latest designer fashions, but cut for functionality, not style. Her green eyes bore the look of a predator; her feathers and crest were preened short.

Rocker instinctively reached for the sidearm he had not worn for nearly ten years.

"What...who...what is the meaning of this?" sputtered the completely flummoxed Chancellor. He reached for the phone on his desk.

"Sit down, sir," commanded the young woman as she walked toward the Chancellor's desk. "This is official government business and we are in need of Professor Rocker." She effortlessly removed the phone from his grip and replaced it on the cradle.

"Who do you think you are, barging in here like this? I'm —"

The woman cut off the Chancellor's response. "Who we are is not important and is none of your concern. The only thing you need to know is that we need your office and you need to leave now, Chancellor."

"I will not stand for this, young lady. You need to leave before I call security."

"Answer your phone, Chancellor," she commanded.

"What do you mean, answer my…" The phone on the Chancellor's desk rang. He stared at it, then back at the implacable woman and her escorts. The Chancellor slumped back in his chair and answered the phone. "This is the Chancellor; who is this?" His eyes widened and his attempts to respond to the speaker at the other end instantly silenced. "Yes, sir, I understand," was all he could manage before hanging up. With an angry glare at the professor, and giving the woman a wide berth, he left his office. One of the escorts, stepping to the other side, closed the door behind him.

Rocker remained in his chair as the woman moved behind the large desk, placed a thick folder on its surface and sat in the Chancellor's chair. "Hello, Professor. Nice to finally meet you."

Rocker nodded, taking inventory of possible weapons at his disposal.

"Well, first of all, we are not exactly from the government, Professor," she continued. "More precisely, we represent a private organization that is working independently on a project attempting to find a solution to the situation our world is facing, and we need your help."

Rocker kept his voice level and strong when he replied, "I'm an associate Professor at a level two university. What makes you think I can help you?"

The woman opened the folder she had placed on the desk and sorted through the papers it held. "Professor Jontar Rocker, only son of Gret and Martak Rocker?"

"Yes."

"Recipient of the Regent's award at age fifteen, graduated High School at age sixteen?"

"Yes."

"After your father's death in a levicoach wreck the night after your graduation there were several arrests for minor offenses, and then a felony charge that forced you into the military?"

Rocker tensed and glanced over his shoulder at the man who still stood at the door. "From where are you getting all of this information? Those are sealed juvenile records. Even the university could not gain access to those files when they hired me."

The woman glanced up at him, then back down and turned to the next page in the folder.

"Several field promotions for valor, Alpha Corp. Commander then promoted to Captain at the Galantar Marine training facilities. Married eight years ago, current status: widower."

The word "widower" stung, causing Rocker to jump out of his chair. The guard behind him reached out to grab his shoulder, but Rocker reacted. Grabbing the big man's wrist and twisting violently, he kicked the man in his knee, and brought his own elbow down to break the man's arm. There was a loud crack as the guard shouted out in pain, his arm bent at an unnatural angle. Before he could do any further damage, he heard a distinctive buzzing and felt the cold barrel of the second guard's energy pistol at his temple. He froze for a moment, picked up the chair and sat down again.

"Leave her out of this. You have no right…" The words strangled in his throat.

"Thank you, Professor," said the woman as if nothing had happened. "Let's proceed now." She turned to the next page of the dossier.

Rocker watched as the second guard removed the injured man from the office.

"Shortly after marrying you retired from military service and earned a degree in genetic engineering. You then gained employment in this university upon graduation. Currently involved in research developing new strategies to use chemical means to find a more stable process for the Somatic Cell Nuclear Transfer, more commonly known by its acronym, SCNT. Your research is being stonewalled due to political pressures trying to prevent publication of your theories."

"Now, just stop right there. How do you know all of this and why are you so interested in my life? What gives you the right to invade my privacy like this?"

"Isn't it obvious? We have been following your career for some time now, Professor. Your work has the potential to solve some of the problems that have recently stalled our own progress. We are trying to save our society, Professor. And we're running out of time. The current political situation is threatening our future and we need your help."

We are also aware that you have publicly expressed concerns over the potential ramifications of your work, however, you have no strong political convictions. Science is your true religion. We need you on our team. At this university your work is considered radical, even subversive. It's only a matter of time before the board of directors decides to let you go. Our facilities at GenCore are state of the art. We hire only the brightest and most innovative thinkers. We encourage our people to take their ideas as far as they can. GenCore will not pressure you or interfere with your research. You have become one of the leading authorities in cloning technology. With our team you will be surrounded by the personnel, equipment, and ideology that recognize and appreciate your genius."

Rocker's crest rose slightly, his eyes narrowed. "So why haven't I ever heard of GenCore? If it's everything you claim it to be, surely I would have heard something."

"GenCore is a new division of a much larger conglomerate of corporations. We see real potential in your work, Professor, and think there is a future in cloning technology. Our director believes your theories hold the most promise for a lucrative investment."

The professor scratched at his auricles and leaned forward in his chair. This proposition was just too good to be true. "Let me get this straight. You want to hire me so that I can continue my research on cloning technology without restrictions? What's the catch here? Are you looking to enhance your profits with some new military contracts or looking to cash in on the new advancements we're making in cloned organs?"

Nothing of the sort, Professor," she said, closing the file and leaned forward, folding her hands on the desk. "We assiduously avoid anything to do with the military, and our interests go far beyond the cloning of a few organs. You will have full publishing rights to anything you develop and you will lead a team of the finest geneticists on the planet. Think of it, Professor, an entire facility devoted to seeing your theories realized. Of course we would retain any patents on the technology resulting from your work, for which you will be generously compensated," said the woman as she smiled, sliding a contract across the table for him, "and did we mention full benefits at triple your current salary?"

Professor Rocker's letter of resignation was on the Chancellor's desk within the hour.

Chapter Eleven

Brach was unsettled. He was not used to being unsettled, which troubled him even more. He had been hearing rumors of some unidentified organization that was apparently manipulating recent legislation in a manner he did not appreciate. As monarch, he was supposed to control the passage or rejection of any act of Parliament that he desired. Current events were proving this assumption to be in error. He pressed the button on his desk.

The door opened and his chamberlain silently entered the private quarters. "Yes, Your Majesty?"

"Has the General arrived yet?"

"Only minutes ago, Sire. I was on my way to announce him when you rang."

"Admit him at once, then."

"Yes, sire." The chamberlain retreated two precise steps, turned, and left the room.

The General entered the royal chambers, and the doors automatically closed and locked behind him with a solid thump. His formal gold and red uniform shone brilliantly in the sunlight streaming through the tall windows. Dozens of ribbons and medals decorated the sash across his chest. His trousers, crisply pressed, displayed a gold stripe down the side. His black boots, impeccably polished, resounded sharply as he marched across the stone floor.

Tapestries depicting fierce battle scenes hung from gently curved stone walls which flowed perfectly into the floor. Immense paintings of a long line of monarchs produced by the current dynasty hung among the tapestries. Suits of armor and chainmail stood against the walls. Several cabinets displayed a wide variety of weapons of both current and past ages. A large, intricately carved stone rectangular table occupied the center of the room. The surface of the table was inlaid with panels of richly stained wood in elaborate geometric patterns, surrounded by a dozen richly upholstered chairs. The one at the end sat on a raised platform and had a tall back, decorated with all the symbols of the royal family. Tall windows filled the space between the bookshelves, providing ample light for study. The upper portions of each window contained historic scenes depicted in brightly colored stained glass. A menagerie of maps and documents, scattered in no particular arrangement covered the table. The monarch, in his usual attire of blue shirt and black slacks when in private, sat at his desk on the far side of the room rummaging through more papers. His gold and silver crown sat squarely on his head.

"Have you seen these reports, General?" the monarch asked, still studying the papers before him. "Somebody, possibly several somebodies, is attempting to influence members of Parliament. Many of the votes we use to consider solidly in our control have begun to stray."

"Yes, Sire. While the votes have predominantly been on minor matters of commerce, they are most troubling in their implications."

"This news is very disturbing, General. Why wasn't I informed about this activity before now?"

The General snapped to attention as he replied. "We have only just now discovered the information, sire. They hid their tracks very skillfully. The efforts appear to focus on reducing regulations concerning corporate mergers, elimination of penalties on certain monopolies, and land acquisitions. The name GenCore has come to our attention, but we haven't been able to verify anything. It's all just speculation so far."

"I need to find out what is going on and who's behind it all. We can't afford any interference with our plans now. Get to the bottom of it and report back to me within the week."

"Yes, Sire. Whoever is responsible for these matters is meticulous at covering their tracks. We are lucky to have noticed the disturbances at all. I am continuing to work on the problem and have set several of our best agents into the field to see what they can learn."

Brach thought about this for a bit while the General remained at attention, his uniform glowing in the sunlit room.

"Have you been able to determine how long this has been going on?"

"Not precisely, Sire, but it does appear that the trend has been occurring with increasing frequency for several years at least."

Brach threw the papers on the table and slammed his fist on top of them. "Keep on it, General. We cannot afford to be caught unprepared if this turns out to be more than just an innocent set of coincidences. Matters are much too fragile right now and a slight alteration could bring all of my efforts crashing down around us."

"Yes, Sire," the General turned and marched out of the room.

Once the door closed behind the General, a curtain opened on the opposite side of the room and a figure emerged from the hidden alcove. The man wore a short, simple, brown hooded robe and trousers with a homespun shirt. The only visible ornamentation being the iron Eye of The Eternal, symbol of The Faith, hanging from a leather necklace.

"This news is most disturbing, Your Majesty," said the man. "We hope this meddler is not going to interfere with our arrangements."

"Not at all, Bishop," said Brach. He bowed to the clergyman and kissed the ring on his raised hand. "The Faith has nothing to be worried about. Our cooperation will ensure enough placement of your faithful to control Parliament in just a few years. We can handle this inconvenience."

The Bishop was a tall man so thin and pale that he appeared almost cadaverous with dark, sunken eyes and protruding cheek bones. Being second in command of The Faith, and one of the few true believers, he commanded unquestioning obedience of his followers, but the monarch was of special interest as a potential convert and had to be treated carefully.

"We hope you are correct, Your majesty. The Eternal commands us in this task and we cannot fail. We need to be confident that our alliance with you is no error. Your own brother cautions us to be wary around even you with constant reminders of how politicians are swayed as easily as leaves in the breeze." He watched the monarch closely for any sign of infidelity.

"Do not concern yourself, Your Grace. I have been playing this game all my life. I know how to control Parliament. We will not fail."

"Very good then, Your Majesty. I will leave you to handle matters. Here is The Prior's latest proclamation and his wishes for Parliament's next session." He handed a sealed case to Brach and turned to leave.

"Thank you, Your Grace," Brach said, accepting the case. "Give my regards to my brother."

Brach tossed the case negligently on his desk once the Bishop left. His crest flared red as he yanked on the cord summoning the General.

"Yes, Your Majesty?"

"I want you to set up and train a special division within our spy network," Brach said, leaning heavily on his desk, drumming his talons sharply on the wooden surface. "This will be a particularly dangerous task and you must take extra care in choosing only those whose loyalty is beyond question."

"Yes, Your Majesty. May I ask who will be the target of such men?"

"My brother.

Chapter Twelve

"Is everything satisfactory, Dr. Rocker?" asked Dr. Contor, the lead geneticist.

Rocker could only nod. Entering the laboratory felt like the first time he saw the Eternity Festival celebrations since childhood. He saw his guide shift his feet and glance toward the door. Dr. Rocker cleared his throat.

"Yes, this will do very well," he said, and motioned for his new colleague to continue the tour. *Feathers! I hope I didn't sound like a pompous ass. I'm going to need all the help I can get here if I want to hit the ground running.*

GenCore's facilities proved to be without equal and a far cry from the dingy basement make-shift lab he was accustomed to at the university. Rocker marveled at the equipment that he now commanded. Sterile biohazard rooms glistened behind large windows. Four long lab tables filled the center of the room under banks of lights, providing near daylight conditions. State of the art equipment occupied the surface of the lab tables, some of which Rocker read about only recently in the journals. Liquid nitrogen storage tanks, electrophoresis gels by the score, digital microscopes, two electron microscopes, and computers at each lab station. Everything a cutting edge laboratory required. *Back at the university I had to beg for every petri dish and test tube. I must have died and gone to...*

"If there is anything you require, just tell your administrative assistant. We are here to make sure that you lack for nothing."

"I see," Rocker replied, gesturing around the room. "I can't imagine anything has been forgotten here, but I will keep your offer in mind. This is incredible. It must have cost a fortune. Even your Rings courts in the gymnasium are high tech. Worthy of any pro team."

Dr. Contor smiled, nodding in agreement. "It's nice having a fairy godmother. Seriously though, our benefactor, The Director, has very deep pockets and takes pride in his facilities being the finest anywhere."

The older geneticist grabbed Rocker's elbow and guided him toward a group all dressed in lab coats. "Our staff geneticists and lab techs have been recruited from the finest facilities in the world. We have been steadily raiding corporations, labs, and universities for a couple of years now."

Rocker hooked talons with the men as they were introduced.

"This is Dr. Kintar Rishman and Dr. Ponan Shigmer," said Contar. "They're the geniuses who developed everything we have accomplished so far here at GenCore."

After exchanging a few pleasantries, Rocker pulled Contar aside so they could speak privately. "Are you sure I'm the right guy to tell them what to do? I'm just an associate professor of genetics. Will they accept me as their department leader?"

"Oh, yes, sir. Everyone here has read your work and we are excited about how it has expanded our thinking into areas nobody had anticipated. You are, without doubt, the right man to lead us to the next level in clone animation."

"How have you read my work? The university only published my more mundane research. Certainly nothing that would inspire the likes of these geniuses."

"As I said, Dr. Rocker, the director has very deep pockets and a great deal of influence. I don't think anything is beyond his reach if he puts his mind to it."

Before Rocker could respond, the door to the lab swung open and a young man entered, handed the guide a paper, and left.

Dr. Contor's eyes darted over the note and pursed his lips. "Hmm. It appears that the boss wants to see you before we continue our tour. Follow me, Doctor."

"Okay, I guess I do need to meet him at some point or another. Can you tell me anything about him that might help make a good first impression?"

"Oh, this won't be his first impression of you. The director personally directed your vetting process." Contor pointed up at the ceiling. "I'm sure he's been observing you as we have toured the facilities."

Rocker looked up and noticed the security cameras at regular, strategic intervals along the hallway, feeling *his neck feathers prickle realizing he was under constant surveillance.* He turned to Contor and said, "Man, you guys take your security measures pretty seriously."

"Yes, we have a great deal of proprietary work going on here a lot of people would love to get their hands on. Access codes are changed weekly. ID badges are encoded and updated monthly and a number of other precautions nobody but those who need to know can actually confirm." He got a conspiratorial grin on his face and leaned in close to Rocker. "We even heard rumors that they are going to install a moat, complete with flesh-eating sarts, next month."

Rocker laughed and clapped Dr. Contor on the back. "Lead on, then," Rocker said. With a flourish of his hand and a slight bow to his guide, they headed to the executive offices on the top floor of the building. All along the way, Rocker looked for signs of hidden security measures. He noticed the smooth narrow ceiling length panels in the wall curving gently into the walls and thought they might be metal or electronic detectors of some sort. *Bet there's plenty more I'm not seeing. Oh well, with what they are paying me, I guess a lack of privacy just comes with the territory.*

"Welcome to GenCore, Dr. Rocker," said Kirta as the two geneticists entered the outer office, "he's waiting for you. Go right in." She pointed toward the doorway on her right. Emblazoned on the door was a bronze plate that read:

> Karm
> Director
> GenCore Inc.

The only decoration was a large map of Dyan'ta, lit by two sconces on either side. Dozens of multicolored pins decorated various locations on every continent. The long table in the center of the room was stacked with books and littered with folders and loose papers. A desk sat by the window, small, wooden, also piled high with additional papers and books. A tan-shaded lamp sat precariously on top of one of the stacks. A large monitor hung on the wall nearest the desk. It displayed multiple images from numerous locations within the building. Rocker looked more closely at the monitors and recognized some of the hallways they passed through on their way to the Director's office.

The man who sat reading through a folder at the desk appeared elderly, but still gave the impression of great vitality. Though not physically impressive, his presence commanded respect. The office was not the typical setting of a man in such a position of authority. Other than the large wall map it displayed none of the expected symbols of power and authority Rocker had grown accustomed to in the military and at the university.

"Good afternoon, Doctor," the director said as he stood and reached out his hand to hook talons with Rocker.

"Good afternoon, Director," a strange sense of familiarity struck Rocker as he hooked talons with his employer. "May I first express my gratitude in your selection of me to head up GenCore's clone research department? It's a great honor."

The director waved off Rocker's modesty as he advanced. "Nonsense, I only hire the best, and everyone here tells me you have already surpassed all others in the field of cloning research." He continued shaking Rocker's hand without saying anything and then broke off the contact with a nervous laugh. "I make it a point to welcome all of my department heads, but I must admit I was exceptionally excited to meet you in person. After all, your work is charting a new course for our future."

Rocker wanted to ask the director what he meant by "our future", but a concealed door opened and in walked the small woman he met in the Chancellor's office. She wore a stylish business suit, but her efficient movements across the room made it look more like a uniform. After handing the director a binder marked, CONFIDENTIAL she took a position next to the secret doorway.

Rocker smiled at her and said, "I want to thank you for rescuing me from the Chancellor the other day. That was quite some achievement. I've never seen him take orders from a..."

"From a what?" she asked, shifting her feet a shoulder's width apart, clenching her left fist. "A woman?" The crest feathers on her head changed color to a threatening red.

"From ahhh…from anyone," Rocker laughed and put his hands up to surrender. "Sorry, I meant no offense. I was just expressing my gratitude." Despite the initial impression, his chest gave a slight flutter, reminiscent of the ones he felt when watching his wife approach. A rush of guilt surged through him.

The director looked up absently from the binder and said, "Dr. Rocker, may I introduce Maripa, my personal assistant. Maripa, of course, already knows you."

Rocker took a step forward with his hand extended, but Maripa's scrutiny discouraged him from proceeding. He stepped back and placed his hand to his shoulder in mock salute. "Nice to see you again, Maripa is it?"

"You will have to excuse Maripa, Doctor," the Director continued when Maripa did not reply. "She is not one for pleasantries, but, as you have witnessed, she is very effective at what she does."

"That I have, sir. The likes of which I have never seen before. But, as I said, I appreciate the rescue," Rocker said with a sideways glance at Maripa. "And I am also very pleased to see the quality of the labs you have provided for my research. Your staff and your facilities here are unmatched anywhere on Dyan'ta."

"Anything worth doing, Professor," the Director responded before drawing his attention back to the confidential binder.

Rocker could not hold back any longer. "Excuse me, sir, but have we ever met before? I cannot get over the sensation of familiarity I am feeling here. I do not mean to be impertinent, but I just have to ask."

A dark cloud shadowed the director's face, but it quickly vanished behind a polished smile and dead eyes. "If I had a dorket for every time I hear that, I would be a rich man. Wait… I am a rich man!" He laughed at his own joke and smacked his hand on the binder. "I guess I just have one of those faces that blends into a crowd and looks like everyone's favorite old uncle or something."

"That is probably it then. I am sorry, Director. Again. I meant no disrespect or undue familiarity."

"None taken, Doctor," the director responded as he closed the binder and set it aside. "Now let's get down to business. Maripa has brought in all of the necessary paper work: security codes, medical forms, stock option opportunities, and your official clearance badge and employee handbook. Everything you need to get off on the right foot here at GenCore." He passed the binder over to Rocker who looked inside and took out his holographic photo ID badge. He winced at the hologram, and clipped it to his shirt pocket.

"Now, I know you've had a busy day and I don't want to keep you any longer. I just wanted to welcome you personally and assure you that everything you need will be provided. After all, we do have a vital job to accomplish here and not much time to do it in."

"And just what is that vital job, sir?" Rocker asked, tilting his head, crest feathers lifting in confusion. "Why is there not much time? My work is theoretical. There's nothing time sensitive about any of it. With the growing influence of The Faith, I doubt seriously the government will allow any research that results in producing a viable clone. Not when they have more pressing research dedicated to preventing our extinction."

"I thought you understood, Doctor, we are going to save our world," the director said, and slapped Rocker on the back. He escorted the silent professor to the lobby outside his office and shook his hand again. "I have to rush off to another meeting, Professor, and I'm sure you're anxious to get started in the lab."

Rocker robotically shook the director's hand with an unsteady, "Of course, sir." He watched as Karm strode back into his office. Before the door closed completely, he saw Maripa and the director exchange worried glances.

Inside the office, the director sat behind his desk and laced his fingers behind his head. "No need to fret, Maripa. Dr. Rocker knows nothing more than he did when we hired him. He's an insightful and intuitive man who is gifted at analytical reasoning, but he will only know what we allow him to know."

"If you say so, Karm, but I intend to keep an even closer eye on him for a while. He is still not out of danger and we need him."

"Yes, yes, of course you are right. He has already begun to notice and ask about our normal security measures. Just don't let him discover your team's surveillance of him. We don't want to scare him off at this delicate time."

"I know how to conduct a discrete surveillance, Karm," Maripa glowered and returned to her office to make the necessary calls.

As the door closed, Karm pressed the intercom button on his phone. "Is that call to the Prime Minister ready, Kirta?"

"Yes, sir. On video line two."

Karm pressed the button and an image of the Prime Minister appeared on the screen.

"Hello, Karm," said the Prime Minister putting on his most diplomatic smile, "What can I do for you today?"

"I want to know why that pharmaceutical bill is being stalled," said Karm. "You know how important that piece of legislation is to my interests. I have put too much time and effort into it for anything to go wrong now."

"Don't worry, Karm. We had a bit of trouble with some of the new members of the ministry, who were attempting to block it, but we have that solved now and there should be no further delays."

"What happened? There wasn't supposed to be any opposition." Karm sat up straighter and furrowed his brows in concern at this news.

"It seems The Faith has been able to influence a number of new ministers. They have been coerced into signing some sort of anti-cloning pledge and they were refusing to compromise on the issue. We were able to get enough votes in spite of them and get the bill moving."

"Send me some more information about this pledge and who is signing it. I may need to take steps to counteract The Faith if they start gaining more strength." He hung up and sat back in his chair rubbing his eyes as he contemplated his options.

***

On his way home, Rocker reflected on the events of the long day. The drive was not much longer than from his old job at the university, but instead of bumper to bumper traffic, he now commuted along a tree lined countryside dotted with small farms. The levicoach maintained a constant ten centimeter suspension above the pavement regardless of speed and conditions. He appreciated not having the brightness in his eyes during the drive home. The annoying glare from the dying orange sun had been a daily reminder of the impending end.

Rocker wondered how his clone research could possibly be anything so vital to the current situation. The experts were saying the planet still had about 100 years before the sun goes nova. Too much just didn't add up. Turning absently into his driveway, he barely registered the dark blue coupe parked across the street. As he got out of his levicoach, a reflection from the driver's side of the unfamiliar vehicle caught his attention. His heart skipped a beat and he quickly surveyed his surroundings. *Okay, big fella, slow down, now. You're not in the desert anymore. It's just someone waiting for the neighbor to go out to dinner or something. GenCore's excessive security paranoia just has you spooked.* He closed the front door behind him, turned on the porch light, and a few more lights than necessary inside the house. After one quick glance out the front window, he proceeded to look for something to eat.

While nibbling distractedly on his meal, Rocker absentmindedly began twirling the ring on his finger and gazed at the worn photo he still carried. *I wish you were here to help me figure this out, my love. This Karm character seems just too good to be true. I should have done this before accepting the job, but a bit of recon on Karm and his assistant are definitely in order.*

The large man down the street, hidden in the shadows, returned his energy pistol to its holster as his talon pressed the contact to disarm the weapon. He noted the arrival of Dr. Rocker in his log book, as well as the departure of the unrecognized blue vehicle and its two occupants, shortly after the doctor's arrival home.

"I need a check on a dark blue Alpha Dotson, registration ID 822BL4. Possible security risk to Gen One."

"Roger that, Gen One Eyes," came the response over the earphones. "Next check in four hours."

"Roger that. Out." And he settled down for his watch.

***

In the middle of the third triad the game was still too close to call. Rocker had joined the company Rings club at GenCore and in just a few days was earning the reputation as a leading contender for the individual championship trophy. Standing at mid court he flicked the hard rubber coated ceramic ball in his net. A quick double juke and a hard slam of his shoulder into his opponent gave him the open lane to the small center ring on the back wall. Rocker leaped high, extending his net as high as he could reach and deftly tossed the ball through the ring. An orange light lit up above the ring adding five points to Rocker's score on the electronic board.

"Good move, Jontar," said Dr. Contar, his regular Rings partner. "See if you can stop this one."

Contar scooped up the ball from the floor and bounced it hard so it ricocheted off of the corner and back to mid court behind Rocker. Using the foot long stick of his net to knock Rocker's net aside, Contar drove his shoulder into Rocker and circled around him just in time to catch the ball in his net as it descended.

"Cute move," said Rocker as he raced up behind Contar, then darted around him with a body block to cut off his lane. "Got ya now!"

"Nice try, but not in time to stop this," taunted Contar. He spun quickly to his left and stepped into the bonus area where he jumped and shot his ball into the larger left side ring. "Yes! Double points!" He shouted as the orange light, plus a blue one next to it both lit up, increasing his score another six points.

Back and forth they went over the next seven minutes, each taking over the lead as they made shots that drew appreciative cheers and applause from the small after-work crowd watching them. When the final buzzer sounded, Rocker won by only three points.

Both men stood, breathing hard with hands on their knees dripping sweat. "Good game," Rocker said as he reached out to shake talons with Contar.

"Almost had you there," Contar smiled back. "Where did you learn those moves? I've never seen anything like it outside the pros."

"Join me for a drink after we get cleaned up and I'll tell you."

Half an hour later, doctors Rocker and Contar sat at a table in the local tavern sipping their drinks. Sitting at the bar had become nearly impossible since the news of the supernova. At least this crowd seemed more peaceful than in other regions. Their conversation drifted from Rings strategy and techniques to the office and briefly onto family before Rocker broached the topic he planned for this evening. Taking a long sip on his brew, he looked Contar in the eyes and lowered his voice.

"So what's the story behind Karm?" He asked conspiratorially, his eyes glancing around the room. "I've never heard of him before that Maripa showed up at the university and recruited me."

Dr. Contar placed his mug on the table, leaned in and lowered his voice. "Not much to tell, actually. What I hear is that he made his fortune as some big wheeler dealer buying and selling companies and real estate. He saw the market for research opportunities in genetics and built GenCore as a new division in his empire. He recruited the best and brightest minds on the planet and the rest is history."

Rocker frowned and shifted in his seat. "Is he connected to the military or the government in any way? Aren't you nervous about what might come of all this new technology we are developing?"

"Not at all. That's exactly why I left my previous employer. I found out he was looking for ways to earn some new military contracts. Haven't you read your employment agreement?"

"I skimmed it through. Probably not as thoroughly as I should have," said Rocker lowering his eyes toward his mug feeling a little embarrassed to admit this oversight.

"Well, if you had, you would have seen a clause stating that any individuals having any connections with the government or military, even responding to interview requests without notifying GenCore management immediately will be terminated on the spot and all of their research confiscated and reassigned. Karm is absolutely adamant about this facility, and all of his holdings, being absolutely under his, and only his control. He is almost paranoid about that sort of interference. We had one lab assistant who failed to put down on her application form an uncle who is some minor official for the roads and transportation division over in the capital. When security found out, she was interrogated by Karm himself, as they all are, and escorted off the grounds before anyone even knew what was happening."

Rocker frowned, his crest twitched nervously. "That does sound extreme. I'm not so sure it reassures me though. He sounds like some sort of control freak. Does he ever interfere with your research?"

Dr. Contar shook his head in response. "Absolutely not. The old man gives us the freedom to take our research in any direction we think is necessary. He always says that those who know most about the work should determine the process and procedures. All he demands is regular reports on our progress."

Rocker sat quietly for a while, contemplating this new information. *Nobody is that altruistic. There must be something he's hiding. I'm going to need to keep my eyes open on this one. I don't want to be remembered as the father of some genetically enhanced group of super soldiers.* A loud uproar from the bar interrupted his internal reflections.

"Looks like the Raptors just clinched the division title," Contar said, pointing to the monitor. "Kak, I was hoping the Nationals would go farther this year."

"Not a chance," replied Rocker as he recovered his wits. "The Raptors have too good a defense. So you're sure about Karm and his intentions?"

"Absolutely. I wouldn't be here if I wasn't. You're not the only one who hates to have his work controlled by some bureaucrat with delusions of godhood. As long as he leaves me alone to do my research and isn't looking for government contracts I'm happy."

Rocker smiled and lifted his mug in salute. "OK, thanks. Being the new guy on the block I was just looking for some insight into the boss and what he's like. Sounds like a pretty sweet deal here. It helps to know more about the company's history." *But it still doesn't sit right. I need to keep digging.*

In the back of the room, seated at a small wooden table, sat a small woman, her head covered in a plain brown scarf. Her rough clothing and quiet demeanor gave the impression of a mid-grade working girl, probably a seamstress or clerk in some office, just stopping in for her evening meal. Her head turned as Rocker stood to leave. She quickly placed a few coins on the table, waited for him to exit out the front door, and headed out through the kitchen.

Chapter Thirteen

The clear night sky sparkled with stars winking on and off in the blackness. A beautiful evening for a stroll to clear one's mind. Rocker often used these quiet moments to organize his thoughts and ponder new combinations of the chemicals he knew were the key to stabilizing the somatic cell nuclear transfer, commonly called the SCNT. *We've made more progress in the past few months than I made over two years of research at the university.*

Rocker walked with a bounce to his steps these days. He no longer felt concern about the unusually high levels of security, chalking it up to private industry concerns over patents. He rarely even noticed the ever present cameras and guards in the labs. Even so, he always seemed to be aware of Maripa's presence whenever she was around. His crest always gave a slight twitch when he noticed her nearby. The security measures never interfered with his work, so he, in turn, ignored them.

*It's only a matter of developing the correct proportions and dosages to fully stabilize the process. It may be just a matter of…*and then everything went black.

The pain in his head was something he had not felt since being wounded in Alpha Corp's fire fight against the Latonian desert rebels. He tried sitting up and opening his eyes, but the vertigo proved to be overwhelming. *Better not try that just yet.* He laid still to let the world stop spinning. *What the strix happened?*

"Dr. Rocker, I see you are awake now," an unfamiliar voice commented, as if no more concerned than asking about the weather. "You probably have a concussion, so you don't want to move around too quickly yet."

Rocker tried to speak, but his throat was too dry. He swallowed and tried again. "Where am I, and what the hell happened? Was I in an accident?"

"No, Doctor. No accident," the voice answered. "We…invited you here for a polite conversation."

Rocker opened his eyes a bit more carefully this time. Everything blurred, but at least the spinning was subsiding and his eyes slowly regained their focus. The room sounded spacious, like the inside of a warehouse. Voices and machinery echoed through the space. As his vision cleared, Rocker noticed aisles of metal shelves filled with various containers and boxes filled the large room. He lay on a cot with a blanket covering him and he felt a bandage around his head. He winced as he touched the large knot beginning to grow underneath it. The voice speaking to him came from a man behind a small wooden desk. There was a light behind the man, shining in Rocker's direction so he could not make out any features, only a shadow against the light.

"And a simple 'Please come with us' was out of the question, I suppose?" Rocker sat up slowly and placed his feet on the concrete floor. He stretched and rubbed his neck as he tried to survey the room, but it was too dark to see anything, and the throbbing in his head made it impossible to focus on anything else.

"I'm afraid not, Professor."

"Okay then, suppose you tell me why I am here. And can you get me an aspirin or something? My head is killing me."

"Certainly, Doctor." The shadow picked up a phone, spoke into it quietly and hung up. Before long there was a knock at the door. A woman in a blue uniform walked in with a tray, placed it on the shadow's desk, and left. The shadow brought the glass of water and pills to Rocker, then returned to his desk.

Once Rocker swallowed the pills, the shadow continued. "How is your work progressing, Doctor? Have you solved the imbalance problems yet?"

Rocker paused and looked toward the shadow. His back straightened as he brought his hand to feel the knot on his head. "You know I can't answer that."

"Yes, we know, and it really doesn't matter anyway. We just need you to stop what you are doing and end this line of research. You are here so we can discuss this matter."

"Sorry, I don't believe we have anything to discuss. I never have taken kindly to bullies." He placed his feet more firmly on the floor, and tried to stand. Off to one side, back in the darkness, he heard a brief shuffle of feet and the electric hum of an energy weapon being armed.

"Now, Doctor Rocker, please stay seated. It should be clear to you by now that we are willing to go to extremes to get what we want. This is merely a polite warning. Next time, well...no need to discuss those messy matters, now is there?" The shadow never moved or changed the matter-of-fact manner of his voice. There was a cold deadliness to him. Rocker became nervous.

"And just how am I to manage this?" Rocker asked. "There will be a lot of tough questions if I suddenly stop everything, especially after..." He stopped before going any further, cursing himself for almost revealing too much.

"You are an intelligent man, Doctor. I am sure you can come up with some clever method of convincing your superiors that your research has hit a dead end."

"Not very likely," Rocker said as he looked around the room, trying to locate a weapon and the exits.

"Oh, I think you..." The shadow gave a sudden jerk and reached for his neck. He stiffened, and slumped over onto the desk without further sound. A small, hooded figure appeared from nowhere, spun and tossed a silvery object into the darkness. Rocker heard the thump as another body hit the ground.

"Are you alright, Dr. Rocker?" a feminine voice laced with steel asked. A definite contrast to the caress of a soft hand on his forehead.

"What's going on? Who the hell are you?"

"It's Maripa, Dr. Rocker. Sorry it took me a while to get here. I was across town when word came in that you had been taken. Can you walk?"

"I can damn well run to get out of this place. Let's go."

The young woman made no sound as she crept ahead of Dr. Rocker through the aisles. One hand held beneath her cloak, eyes aware of everything. Near the door they were approaching lounged two workmen. Rocker noticed, however, they did not appear to be doing much work, only watching.

"Wait here," She turned and scurried up the shelves as easily as a six legged dinter up a tree. Rocker watched as she effortlessly lifted herself into the rafters. He marveled at her grace and skill as she ran along the narrow beams. Upon reaching a point directly above the two workmen by the door, she dropped from her perch, landing a solid kick to the head of the one on the left. She rolled to one side, leaped, and landed another kick to the face of the second man. Neither had a chance to raise an alarm. She signaled for Rocker to come along. "Help me move these two out of sight."

They hid the unconscious men behind some boxes and opened the door.

"Drem, that you?" came a voice from outside.

Before Rocker could even think, the woman reached inside her cloak, and tossed a small dart at the man in the doorway. The man fell to the ground before he could say or do anything. Maripa grabbed the unconscious man by his wrists and dragged him toward where they hid the other two. Rocker leaned against the wall to steady himself. As he watched Maripa, he noticed another man appear in the doorway aiming a weapon at Maripa's back. Rocker reached down to a pile of bricks and hefted one of them. He struck at the man's head with the brick, but missed and hit him in the shoulder instead. The man dropped his weapon and swore as he turned to face Rocker.

"Oh, mutes!" muttered Rocker as the man approached.

Gathering all of his strength, Rocker hit the man square in the face with a second shot. The man's face exploded in a spray of blood and he collapsed to the floor just as Maripa returned.

"Nice work, Doctor," she said looking at the man on the floor and the gun beside him.

"Let's just get out of here," He dropped the brick and they ran through the doorway.

Rocker stumbled after the woman toward the security fence. She led him to an opening. They escaped into a waiting levicoach just as an alarm rang out.

"GO!" she commanded to the driver. She reached into the small refrigerator and pulled out a bottle of water. She then retrieved some pills from another compartment.

"Here, Dr. Rocker," Maripa said as they settled into their seats. "This will help reduce the swelling and dizziness." Her voice seemed somehow softer, and more anxious than usual.

"Maripa," he began as he swallowed the tablets and took a drink of the water. "What are you doing here?"

"I thought that would be obvious by now, Dr. Rocker."

Feeling a bit chagrined, he avoided her gaze by examining the interior of the mag-lev. "Thank you. I was beginning to think I might not get out of there in one piece. Nice getaway coach."

"Karm will want to talk to you right away," was her only response as she removed the hood of her cloak. She preened her crest to settle it comfortably, her eyes never leaving the road behind them.

"You were pretty remarkable back there. Ex-Military?"

Her look was uncompromising. Conversation was not part of the rescue. Her demeanor returned abruptly to her more familiar detached persona.

Rocker sat back, took in a deep breath and gave a long, relaxing exhale. Then he drifted off.

Only then did the man next to the driver speak. "Are you okay?" he asked Maripa, gentle concern in his voice.

She looked up at Darkon, unable to contain a brief smile. "Always worried about me. Yes, I'm fine. Nothing we couldn't handle."

"We?"

"Yeah," Maripa said, pointing at Rocker. "Turns out he's pretty good in a fight."

The debriefing with Karm and Darkon proved to be relatively painless, but Rocker was not about to let this slide by. "I don't like being kept in the dark, Karm. You need to tell me why my project is worth somebody kidnapping and threatening me." He paced back and forth pointing his finger at Karm.

"We don't know for certain who kidnapped you yet," said Darkon. "Our best bet is on some faction of The Faith, but we haven't ruled out government interference yet."

"Maripa is investigating it as we speak," added Karm.

"Those people certainly acted like some para-military organization," Rocker said, still pacing angrily. "Much too good for a bunch of down-heads. If you have any ambitions about weaponizing my research, turning clones into some sort of super soldiers, think again. I'll be out of here and talking to everyone I can find so fast it'll make your head spin."

"Calm down, Doctor." Karm stood now and walked around to stand in front of his desk as he spoke. "I promise you, I have nothing of that sort in mind. I am as opposed to using clone research for something as unthinkable as that as you are. This is precisely why I am working so hard to keep the government out of our crests and in the dark as to our true purpose."

"And just what might our true purpose be? It obviously isn't anything as simple as clone research."

"All in due time, I assure you. Surely, you can appreciate the need for tight security. For now, you will have to be satisfied with my guarantee nothing immoral or unethical is going on."

Rocker paced again, but felt his anger fading. He stopped in front of Karm and faced him, pointing a talon at his chest. "There better not be."

"You have my word," replied Karm. "And one more thing, Professor. Your research may be closer than you think to becoming not only practical, but in all likelihood the most important scientific development in history."

An hour later, Rocker reached up and rubbed the painful lump on his skull. His head continued to throb as he tried to adjust his pillow to a more comfortable position. He still could not shake the odd feeling of familiarity whenever he met with Karm. The lab nurse assured him there was no permanent damage and that he could return to work after a couple of days rest. For security reasons they were relocating him to a new house on the grounds of the GenCore campus. He understood the need for security, but objected to being watched 26-10. Although having Maripa as his new babysitter was not altogether unpleasant. She was a very pretty young thing, at least when she didn't scowl at him. She definitely was not one for conversation, but he could tolerate her shadowing him everywhere so long as she did not interfere with his work. Still, there was something about her that he couldn't shake. He finally drifted off to a disturbingly erotic dream involving himself, Maripa, and a deserted warehouse.

***

The General stood in the warehouse, watching the man struggle back to consciousness lifting his head from the desktop. As his eyes began to focus, he saw his prisoner had escaped. Then he saw the General.

"Care to explain what happened here?" the General asked. His gaze never wavered, and only his inner eyelids blinked.

"I can't, sir. One minute I was interrogating the prisoner, then nothing until now." The man sweated profusely and looked toward the body of his partner by the doorway.

"I see." The General raised his hand. His talon pressed the firing contact twice. A beam of charged ions split the air with an orange beam. The man fell over onto the floor, a pool of blood spread out from under the body.

The General pulled a communicator from his pocket and hit the first button. "No, sir, the incompetents we hired let him escape." He listened impassively to the irate response on the other end.

"Yes, Your Majesty, I know. That makes things more difficult now."

***

After double checking her security patrols around Dr. Rocker's house, Maripa returned to her private quarters. She ate a few leftovers she scrounged from the refrigerator, gave up on the book she tried to read, but couldn't quite focus on and headed off for a shower and bed. She tossed and turned, unable to turn off her brain. For some inexplicable reason, thoughts of Dr. Rocker prevented her from drifting off to sleep. She kept revisiting her surveillance of his Rings games. Watching his agility and skill at the game always impressed her. *What the strix am I doing? Knock it off, girl. You have a job to do. Focus on the job.* She fluffed the covers around her and gave her pillow another thrashing, then began her meditation routine to settle her mind and purge Rocker from her thoughts.

Chapter Fourteen

A few days later, Maripa sat at her desk when the computer screen flashed a warning box.

SECURITY BREACH. LEVEL FIVE FIREWALL ATTACKED.

She picked up the phone and dialed the number for security. "Darkon, what's happened?"

"Someone attempted to break into level five secure files. The firewall appears to have held so only some of the lower level files were compromised."

"Are you tracking it?"

"The tracers kicked in automatically. We should have something for you in a couple of hours."

"Good. Keep me informed." She hung up and went to the door allowing her direct access to Karm's private office.

"We have a security breach, sir. Someone just tried to break the level five files. Security protocols held up and we are investigating the problem."

Karm dropped the papers he was reading onto his desk and lifted his gaze to Maripa. "This is serious. Level five is supposed to be unbreakable."

"Yes, sir. The higher level files are still secure, but some non-critical information was accessed. We need to find out who has the ability to get as far as they did."

"Do what you need to do. Keep me informed."

"Yes, sir," she said, turning to leave. "I may need to use the unregistered coach tonight."

Later that evening Maripa sat in the back seat of the levicoach with Darkon. She wore dark, tight fitting apparel, soft soled shoes and a dark hooded cloak. She pulled the hood forward to completely hide her face in its shadows.

The name UNIVERSAL CHARITY shined brightly above the main entrance. "You sure this is it?" she asked her companion.

Darkon nodded in the darkness of the vehicle's interior. "No doubt about it. They attempted to cover their trail, but we were able to trace the signal to this location. Examination of the building blueprints indicate the most probable location is on the top floor."

"Wait for me here. I won't be too long." She slid silently out of the transport and disappeared into the night.

The night watchman was not a problem. She pulled out the hollow metal tube from a hidden pocket in her cloak and loaded it with the small dart. With perfect aim, the dart hit the guard in the neck. He dropped his cigarette, grabbed for the dart, and slumped to the ground. Relieving the guard of his keys and pass card, she dragged the man around to the back of the building. Slipping on a pair of gloves equipped with razor sharp metallic talon tips, she scaled the side of the building and pulled herself onto the roof. Tossing a small metal star, she knocked out the solitary light plunging the roof into blackness. She glided noiselessly across the roof to the access door and used the keys to enter the stairwell.

Upon reaching the fifth floor, she pulled out a small disk, unlocked the door, and cracked it open. She pressed the button on the disk and tossed it inside. *Let's see how their cameras handle a magnetic pulse.* A bright flash shone through the crack in the doorway. Maripa entered the hall and saw the cameras had gone dark. *Now for the fun part.* Sticking to the shadows, she moved silently down the hallway and used the guard's pass card to enter the nearest office.

Once inside, Maripa went straight to the computer and turned it on. She plugged in the security bypass drive and watched the screen as the proper passwords and codes were deciphered and input. She pressed a few keys and bypassed the local security network, allowing her access to everything the organization had on file. *Now let's find out why Universal Charity is so interested in us.* Ten minutes later she found the incriminating files showing someone in the organization was gathering information about Karm's empire and his work with the adult DNA cloning process. Maripa downloaded the information, then inserted a second drive and downloaded the virus. She watched as the files vanished from the screen. *That should take care of their system for some time now.* She removed the card, shut off the machine, and left the office.

An orange light flashed in the hallway and a sharp pain erupted in her shoulder. Maripa was thrown to the ground from the impact of the beam. She spun as she hit the floor and reached into her cloak. She tossed three metal stars at her assailant and watched him fall back, firing once more, harmlessly into the ceiling. "Kak!" she swore as she reached down to examine her leg. "Feathers!" *Should have checked more closely for another guard. I'm getting as careless as Karm.* She could not lift her arm and she saw blood flowing freely from the wound. Using her cloak, she pressed against the hole to staunch the bleeding. Her head was spinning and her eyes were unfocused as she stood. Leaning on the wall for support, she headed to the stairwell and down to the main floor. Locating the loading dock doors, she exited the building and returned, limping heavily, to the waiting levicoach.

"What happened?" asked Darkon. "We heard shots."

"I got careless. There was a second guard. I never saw him until he shot me." It was hard to focus now, her mind drifting. She forced herself to stay conscious.

Darkon's face paled when he saw her wound. "We need to get you to a hospital."

"No, no hospitals. Get me back to the house. Call Karm and have him get the doctor. He can handle this. Just help me stop the worst of the bleeding until we get there."

"Alright, lie down and let me get a look at it, Squirt." Forcing himself to sound calmer than he felt, Darkon grabbed the first aid kit from its compartment and pulled out his knife. Quickly slicing up the leg of her pants, he revealed a deep gash, scorched at the edges. He used one portion of the torn clothing to wipe away the pooling blood.

Maripa gripped the edge of the seat, inhaling sharply through gritted teeth. "Careful! That hurts like a quetzel! Is this your way of getting back at me for all the times I beat you at tuttles, old man?"

"Don't be such a baby," Darkon said as he ripped open several gauze pads, placing them on the wound. "You know I let you win most of those games." he said, giving a wink.

Maripa laughed, but tensed suddenly as new waves of pain shot through her leg.

"Here, press down on this hard so I can get it wrapped." He grabbed her hand, placing it on the reddening pads. Pausing briefly, he looked up to see her face contorted in attempts to control her pain.

"Nothing to worry about, Squirt." He bound her leg with more gauze wrapping, pulling it tight. "I've seen you with injuries worse than this before. Just lost a bit of blood is all." He forced himself to smile as he continued to wrap her leg. "Remember that time you fell out of that Tark tree? We thought you broke your neck for sure. I knew you would try climbing that damned tree as soon as you were able, so I ordered the gardener to cut it down. Karm reamed me good for it, but I couldn't risk another fall like that one again. There! All patched up and ready to go. Let's get you to the doc."

He looked up and saw Maripa had slipped into unconsciousness. A quick touch to her wrist confirmed a steady, but weak pulse. "You'll be fine, Squirt," he said gently squeezing her hand. Sleep is what you need now. I'll get you home safe."

Darkon released his grip on Maripa's hand and, securing her to the seat, hurried to the driver's seat and gunned the engine.

***

Karm paced the hall outside Maripa's quarters. He wore a long blue robe and leather slippers, both covered in blood from when he carried Maripa to her room. The doctor was waiting for her and had ordered Karm out of the room. An hour later, the doctor opened the door and quietly closed it behind him.

"She is out of danger now. I've given her a transfusion and a few stitches. She'll be fine in a few days. She does need to rest, so keep her in bed for at least a couple of days."

Karm exhaled in relief and grabbed the doctor's hands. "Thank you, doctor. Can I see her now?"

"Yes, but only for a few minutes. The sedative will be taking effect soon and she needs sleep more than anything right now. I'll send a nurse over to sit with her and take care of the I.V."

"Thank you again, doctor," Karm said as he released the doctor's hands and turned to open the door to Maripa's room. As he entered, he saw the pile of bloody clothes on the floor. With an effort, he averted his eyes from them and looked toward the bed. Maripa lay there, leaning back on her pillow. Her leg, bound with bandages but otherwise uncovered, sat propped up on several large pillows. She opened her eyes and watched as he approached.

"Well, that was a royal cluster kak," she said weakly, trying to fight the effects of the sedative.

"Don't worry about that now. Darkon tells me you got the information we needed and destroyed their entire system. I'm just glad you weren't more seriously injured."

"We're both getting sloppy," she said, wincing as she adjusted her position on the pillows.

Karm lowered his head and sat gently on the foot of the bed, placing one hand on her leg. "I know. You tried to tell me, but I wouldn't listen. Now look what I've done. You could have been killed." He carefully squeezed Maripa's leg and stood to leave. "Get some sleep now. We'll talk later."

"Karm," Maripa called after him. "This was not your fault, but we do need to talk."

Karm nodded and left the room. Darkon stood waiting in the hall. He had not changed out of the blood soaked clothes he'd arrived in. "She's a tough little gal, sir; she'll pull through in no time," he said.

"I know. Nevertheless, I never should have let things go this far. There are going to be a few changes around here, Darkon. Come to my office first thing in the morning."

"It is morning, sir."

"It is?" Karm looked out one of the hallway windows into the soft light of dawn. "Well, go get yourself cleaned up, get some breakfast and come see me in a couple of hours."

"Yes, sir." He turned and left for his own room in the north wing.

***

The monarch leaned on the table in front of him, fists clenched, gritting his teeth.

"Anything new on that break in yet?"

"No, sir," responded the General, snapping to attention. "They managed to trace our connection. Everything at Universal

Charity was destroyed before we could analyze it and one of our people was killed."

"How did this happen?"

"We don't know, sir. All security cameras were disabled and the other guard rendered unconscious. He never saw anything. They discovered a virus planted into their system wiping out all references to Karm and his interests. Any proof we may have had is gone."

"Our friends in The Faith will not be pleased with this. They think Karm has been the one responsible for blocking their attempts at enacting certain legislations they have been supporting."

"Yes, Your Majesty." The General stood at full attention. "There is one small matter needing investigate though."

The monarch waited.

"We have a photograph of Karm leaving a fundraiser a few weeks ago. The photographer was attacked, and his camera destroyed by someone who was with Karm. The photographer was smart enough to have a partner with him who caught the entire incident on film."

"And...?"

"The assailant was a young woman. We cannot find any record of her prior to a few years back when she attended The Academy. She seems to be his personal assistant, but there are some anomalies warranting further investigation."

"Find out everything you can. We need to know more about Karm, his plans, and this mystery woman."

Chapter Fifteen

Maripa felt the tension in the lab immediately. Rocker sat with two of his staff geneticists examining the data on one of the view screens.

"Another failure, gentlemen," Rocker said. He arched his back and rubbed his eyes. "It's still falling apart at the amino group bond. We need to rethink our entire approach."

"Perhaps, if we attempted something out of the heavier Halogens…"

Rocker shook his head. "No, too volatile, the reaction would be too rapid,"

"We seemed to be so close… but now?" The younger man looked to his boss for encouragement.

"We were wrong, gentlemen. The data doesn't lie. We just need to rethink what the data is showing us and see where it leads us."

"That could take months, maybe years."

Rocker pounded his fist on the table and stood up. "It will take what it takes. It isn't helping anything sitting here wallowing around in frustration. Let's just drop all of this, start acting like scientists, and get back to work." He pushed past the men and headed toward his office. He grabbed a folder off the top of a precariously balanced stack, flipped it open and rifled through the pages, examining the series of calculations it contained. With an angry growl, he threw the folder across the room, scattering the papers like confetti fired from a popper. Not satisfied with this small bit of chaos, Rocker kicked at his desk, toppling the remaining folders to the ground, adding to the debris field. Standing in the midst of this bedlam, Rocker grabbed his top crest with both hands, closed his eyes, forcing himself to regain his composure. After a few moments, he began to feel himself again and attempted to gather the papers into some resemblance of order again, only to surrender in defeat almost immediately. Returning to the doorway, he leaned his head against the frame and hesitated before opening it. "Sorry, gentlemen. I'm just frustrated and tired. You're doing a great job. This is just a difficult nut to crack." He turned to face them. "Go home, it's late. See you in the morning."

He noticed Maripa at the door and waved to her. "Be right there."

The slightly rounded hallway echoed their footsteps as Rocker and Maripa walked toward the exit. "I could use a drink," said Rocker, turning to Maripa. "Looks as if you could use one, too. Let's get away from here for a bit. How does Barto's sound?"

She stopped and looked at him, narrowing her eyes suspiciously.

"What, after all these months you think I don't know you, at least a little?" He smiled. "C'mon, we both need to get out of here and kick back a little."

She continued to scrutinize him a bit longer and then her face relaxed. "What the strix, I do need a drink tonight. But it's too dangerous to leave the compound. Let's just go to your place."

"Alright. I think I can rustle us up something to take our minds off our troubles."

Maripa was surprised to find her heart suddenly thumping somewhat harder in her chest.

A couple of hours, a little food and a few drinks later, they both started to relax.

"You know, Dr. Rocker, your actions with Alpha Corp during the Latonian uprisings were admirable," Maripa said, taking another bite of her sandwich as she nursed her third glass and brought her bare feet up under her on the sofa.

"Admirable enough to get me discharged," Rocker said swirling the ice in his drink. He was on his fourth Golden Talon, savoring the thick fruity taste of the intoxicating liquid sliding down his throat, and picked at the remaining crumbs on the plate in his lap, and caught himself noticing how green her eyes were.

"You saved the lives of one third of your unit under conditions nobody should have survived. You deserved the Royal Medal of Honor instead of your CO. If it were me, I would have fragged him when no one was looking." She finished her drink and held it out to Rocker, shaking it for a refill.

He took her glass and filled it from the pitcher. He poured another for himself and said, "That's not quite how the court martial court saw it." He sat in the chair across from her, watching as she finished her sandwich, and kicked off his shoes. The drinks relaxed him and Rocker noted how pretty she was. A sudden feeling of guilt rushed over him and he hoped it did not show on his face, fearing another relationship might destroy him.

"There really is much more to you than one sees at first glance, Doctor."

"I do have a name, you know. Do we have to be so formal here...now?"

"No, I guess we don't. Jontar it is, then." She raised her glass to him and took a drink. "What I mean is how many Special Forces soldiers can even spell geneticist, let alone even dream of the ground-breaking research you are doing here?"

Rocker took a long drink and sat back closing his eyes. "Thanks, but if we don't start getting results soon, Karm may want to get somebody to replace me. With all of the recent set-backs, and The Faith putting more and more pressure on Parliament to cancel our permits, I can't imagine him being patient much longer." He reached up with one hand and rubbed his neck.

Maripa looked at him for a moment; she seemed to be trying to come to a decision. After a brief hesitation she stood and walked around behind him. She reached down and began to massage his temples. "Trust me, Karm will not replace you. He has faith in your abilities. How's that?"

"Mmmmm, feels good. Thanks. I hope you are right. I know we are close. All we need is just one break." His mind drifted and the nerves unknotted. *I could really get used to this. Wonder what other talents she is hiding. Oh feathers! What am I doing? It's only been a few years since her death, but why don't I want to stop?*

"And don't you worry about The Faith, Parliament, or any of the rest of the nonsense going on out there. Karm has more than enough resources to handle them." She worked her way down to Rocker's shoulders, and began to dig into a particularly large knot she found there.

"Even Karm can't stand against the world forever." Rocker winced as her knuckles dug into the knot. "There's a lot of pressure to pass some very restrictive legislation on our work. The politicians won't stay loyal when the voters turn against them." He hesitated before continuing. "This is precisely why I am so concerned about Karm's intentions. Everyone I have talked to reassures me of his grand ideals and altruism, but I can't shake the feeling that something here is just too good to be true." He took another sip from his glass. "Can you honestly tell me he has no ulterior motives in all of this?"

"No wonder you are stuck. You worry too much. I have known Karm all my life. He may not be perfect, and he is probably the most secretive and mysterious person on the planet, but I have never known him to be cruel or have any ambitions beyond this grand scheme of his. Trust Karm to deal with those matters and focus on the lab. He is the perfect SOB to handle all of them." She gave one final twist into the knot and ruffled his crest.

She hopped back into her place on the sofa and sat on her knees. She took another long drink and smiled. "What you need Doctor, I mean Jontar, is a good workout every morning. It's just the thing to get the blood flowing and the mind charged. You haven't played a good game of rings in months. How about you join me at the gym starting tomorrow?"

"You play Rings?" Rocker eyed the tiny girl up and down, trying to judge her ability. "I've never seen you on the court."

"I usually practice when you are in the labs. Not much chance of anything happening to you there, so I can grab a quick work out then."

"But against me? I must be twice your weight and a good foot taller. Wouldn't be much of a game."

Maripa's eyes narrowed dangerously. "You're probably right, but I'll try to take it easy on you,"

Rocker noticed her glare and swallowed his laugh before it escaped his lips. His actual response was more nonchalant, or at least he hoped it was. "Sure, why not? I'll try anything at this point. My workouts have been pretty sporadic ever since I moved on campus. If you're sure I won't get in your way or anything."

"No problem at all. I'll reserve a court for us. How's six sound?"

"Great. Looking forward to it."

"It's settled then. I'll see you there." She set her glass in the sink and grabbed her valise. "Don't be late," she said as she opened the door.

Rocker stood to lock the door behind her. "Good night, and thanks, Maripa," he said as she walked down the path to the waiting levicoach.

He watched as she turned to wave, and then tripped on a loose stone in the path, catching herself quickly despite her slight intoxication. He laughed quietly as she slapped herself on the forehead, increasing her speed toward the waiting mag-lev.

As Rocker closed the door, he unconsciously reached up with his left hand and held the ring still hanging under his shirt. He shut the door, locked it and then headed up to bed, realizing he was looking forward to seeing her in the tight fitting Rings attire.

The game proved to be as one sided as Rocker had thought it would be…just not in the direction he had thought. Maripa's speed and agility outmatched him at every encounter. Even by the second period after he decided to forget she was a girl and half his size she always outmaneuvered him and avoided his attempts at any blocks or slams. During one of his attempted blocks she landed an elbow into his sternum. The blow was not particularly hard, but an electric shock shot up his chest, paralyzing his breath for a second or two. Streaming sweat and breathing hard at the end of the game he leaned against one wall downing a bottle of water.

"Okay, I surrender and admit defeat. Where did you learn to play like this, and why don't you own every trophy the company games give out?"

Maripa smiled up at him as she slowly sipped from her own water bottle, not showing any signs of having given him one of the toughest games of his life. "Oh, I don't compete. I use this game as one of my workouts to stay sharp." She took another sip and gave a sly wink. "You're good, though. I normally have to train against two or three others to make it competitive.

"Thanks. And on behalf of all my fellow male players, we appreciate your concern for our fragile egos. He performed an elegant bow in mock respect.

Maripa smiled again and walked off to the locker room. "See you out front. The car should be here by now."

Rocker finished his water as he watched Maripa walk away. She definitely looked good in Rings gear.

As the next several weeks passed, their games of Rings continued to end mostly in Maripa's favor, but Rocker found his own skills improving and the scores were not so embarrassing lately. They began to spend more time together, mostly having lunch or an occasional dinner.

***

Rocker leaned back in his chair, stretched, rubbed his eyes, and ran his talons through his crest. The data on his monitor continued to be a frustrating mass of seemingly conflicting information. "Enough is enough," he said aloud to himself as he rose to his feet. Grabbing the jacket off its hook on the wall, he opened his office door and called out to Dr. Contar. "I need to get out of here for a while and clear my head. Be back in a couple of hours." Dr. Contar raised a hand, waving, without looking up, intently peering into a microscope.

He borrowed the keys to a mag-lev from the motor pool and headed into town. Finding a parking spot next to the town square, he locked the vehicle and paid a street vendor for a sack of Tormund and a bottle of Kral juice. The sticky-sweet mixture, his go-to guilty pleasure, contrasted well with the sour drink. As he walked along the path, an angry voice intruded into his thoughts. Looking around, he noticed a crowd surrounding a young, grey-robed cleric. The man was gesturing wildly as he berated the onlookers. Just as he was about to turn and walk the other way, he recognized something familiar about the speaker and continued to approach.

"You are all witness to The Eternal's wrath!" shouted the cleric, wide eyed, pointing manically at those gathered around him. "He has condemned this world to oblivion because of your heresies!"

Rocker's eyes shot wide open as recognition flooded his awareness. *Crebot? Yes, of course. Feathers he's changed. By The Eternal what happened to him?*

"You have closed your eyes to the TRUTH!" Crebot continued to shout. Some in the crowd began calling back in agreement, others in disgust. "I know! I was once a sinner like you! Worse than that. I was a willing participant in the heresy of clones. My wickedness helped lead us all into damnation!" Crebot's eyes suddenly locked onto Rocker, recognizing his former professor on the edges of his audience. "And there, among you, is one of the unrepentant! Beware of his false teachings!" Crebot leveled his gaze and both arms, palms upward, toward Rocker. All eyes turned to see him, some just stared, mouths open, as though they were seeing the cursed one himself. Others took on a more menacing posture. Responding to the mob, Crebot continued. "No, my flock, do not harm this poor deceived wretch. Vengeance and retribution belongs to The Eternal. Pray instead for his salvation that he may turn from his wickedness and come to see the TRUTH."

Not waiting for any further development, Rocker turned and walked quickly back to his vehicle and returned to the lab. Shaken by the experience, he sat in the garage for a few moments, trying to reconcile the Crebot he once knew with the fanatic he witnessed today. Combing talons through his crest, Rocker exited the mag-lev, returned the keys and calling in to inform Dr. Contar he was taking the rest of the day off, and walked home.

Chapter Sixteen

"Hurry up you two," called Darkon from the mag-lev, checking his pocket timepiece for the third time. "Karm is expecting us at the new sampling facility and we are late already and this storm is only going to get worse."

Rocker and Maripa hurried down the path from his main lab huddled together under an umbrella and climbed into the vehicle.

"Relax, old man," chided Maripa. "We have plenty of time. Just sit back and enjoy the ride in the mountains." She flashed a smile at the security chief who grunted excessively before turning around to face the front of the transport, barely concealing his own smile.

The new facility was located three hours away in a secluded valley in the Montar range, some of the highest peaks on the planet and a favorite vacation spot for the famous and ridiculously wealthy. Rocker sat, hand-in-hand, with Maripa gazing out the window as the car wound its way next to a shimmering creek. The grey sky, spitting bits of snow, contrasted beautifully with the orange foliage of the trees. Grey mountain dintars climbed and swung among the branches over the heads of grazing, spiral horned Quol. Dense flocks of colorful winged insects hovered above the flowering bushes. Occasional views of snow-capped peaks in the distance added their majesty to the scene.

Their inspection of the facility, a beautiful building constructed of native stone and designed to blend into the surroundings, proceeded as expected. The personnel proved to be highly skilled and only minor alterations to a few components and procedures were ordered.

"I think I hear a stream calling me. It won't be long before the river freezes over so I want to get in a few casts while I still can," Karm said stretching his long arms above his head, gazing longingly down the hill and the sound of rushing water. "I'll catch up with you back at The Citadel tomorrow."

Maripa laughed gently and rolled her eyes. "Alright, Karm. It's not too late for us to head back now and I have some work piling up back in my office."

"Sure you don't want to stay and rest a bit?" asked Rocker as he surveyed the surrounding mountains. "I could stand a few more hours relaxing up here, maybe spend the night if this weather gets any worse."

"Wish I could," she replied turning to walk back to the corporate mag-lev. "But there are some time sensitive matters I need to attend to. Go collect Darkon so we can get started will you?"

The drive back down the twisting road proved almost as beautiful as the ride up, even if the increasing snow did hide some of the trees. Out of the corner of his eye, Rocker caught a glimpse of something large and brown leaping in front of their vehicle, and everything vanished into a chaos of noise, flashing light, and then darkness.

As the darkness slowly grew into brighter shades of grey and the sound of running water became recognizable in his ears, Rocker opened his eyes to a world turned upside down, and an uncomfortable pressure on his hips and shoulders, not to mention the ache in his head and left leg.

"Maripa, are you okay? I think we hit something."

He heard a soft moan from somewhere nearby and, turning to locate Maripa, he realized the mag-lev was upside down, its front end dug into the creek. Maripa hung suspended next to him by her safety restraints, her crest hanging over her face, as her hands searched her body for injuries.

"I'm okay. How about you?"

"I think I cracked my head and knee a bit, but nothing too bad. Let me see if I can get out of these restraints." He struggled with the clasp, finally releasing it, allowing him to crash head first into the crumpled roof. Twisting himself around, he worked to free Maripa, catching her as she fell free. Kicking out the remains of the window, they crawled out of the wreck and fell onto their backs on the rocks of the streambed.

"Darkon!" Maripa, sat up suddenly, looking for the security chief. "Jontar, where is Darkon? Help me find him!"

Jontar fought to stand up and began searching the area. "The driver seems alright," he called out, feeling for his pulse and listening for breathing. "Just unconscious." Then he noticed the figure lying face down in the water just beyond the sandbar a few yards away.

"Maripa! Over there!" He pointed in the direction of the still form as he ran toward it.

Maripa arrived, splashing the freezing water as she ran, just as Rocker pulled Darkon's body onto the sandbar. Looking up at the frantic face of the girl, he saw panic rising inside her.

"I don't feel a pulse."

Maripa shoved Rocker aside, gathered Darkon's head into her lap, running her hands over his face and chest. Without warning, she began to scream.

"No! Not like this, old man! Not like this!" She grabbed one of Darkon's hands and held it to her face, her eyes welling up in tears she fought to keep in check. "Not some senseless accident! You were supposed to grow old and play with my children! You promised me!"

Rocker knelt behind her, gently rubbing her back as she held the body, her eyes and wordless expressions a confusion of anger and loss. He dug the communicator from his pocket, and called GenCore's emergency number.

Hours later, after the doctor's cleared them, dressed in the dry clothes one of the nurses located for them, Rocker escorted Maripa, his arm securely around her waist supporting her, up the walk to her house. Once inside, he helped her upstairs to her bedroom and, after removing her shoes and jacket, gently helped her lay down, the doctor's sedatives beginning to take effect.

"Don't leave me," she pleaded quietly. "I don't want to be alone."

"I'm not going anywhere. As long as you need me, I'm right here."

Maripa curled up next to Rocker, her head resting in his lap as sat on the bed beside her.

"Why did he have to die like that? Why him?"

"Only The Eternal knows. Sometimes there is no sense to make of it."

Maripa shivered in his arms as silent tears fell down her cheeks. "Did you know, when I was a little girl, it was Darkon who I was most comfortable with? He always seemed to have time for me. Karm was always too busy." She shifted her position to bring Rocker closer, tightening her grip. "I even discovered it was he who actually bought my birthday presents and reminded Karm of the date. He was always there for me."

Rocker softly preened her feathers with his talons as her breathing gradually subsided into the soft, regular rhythm of sleep.

The morning sun glowed warm in her room as she stirred. A sudden awareness of not being alone shocked her into full alert mode. "Feathers and Quills!" She bolted upright from her sleep, knocking Rocker off the bed. "Why are you still here?" She jumped to the other side of the bed, eyes searching for something sturdy to swing.

Struggling up from the floor, he raised his hands, palms out defensively. "Easy, Maripa," he said calmly. "Nothing happened. You needed me to stay, so I stayed. That's all."

Noticing for the first time they were both fully clothed, and the bed was still made up, she relaxed her posture and tilted her head as she studied him, memories of yesterday's tragedy returned.

"Okay, good," he said, also starting to recover his wits. "You were so distraught over Darkon I couldn't leave you alone. I know what it's like to lose someone close, so I wanted to be here for you." He rubbed his eyes to remove some of the sleep still left over. "You want some narl tea?"

Maripa sat back down on the bed, still studying Rocker, trying to understand. "Yes, please," she said quietly, leaning back onto one elbow. "I definitely need some caffeine this morning. And thank you. I was just startled to find you here when I woke up. Sorry."

Rocker laughed, shaking his head as he left to start breakfast. "I'm just glad you didn't break my neck."

After a shower and putting on her most comfortable sweatshirt and leggings, Maripa stood quietly in the doorway to the kitchen, watching Rocker as he puttered about the room. He looked up to see her standing there, an unfamiliar expression on her face. "I was just about to call you," he said, smiling and handed her a steaming cup of the pink tea. "Breakfast is served."

"You are a puzzle, Dr. Rocker. A very curious puzzle."

"Is that good?"

"Only time will tell."

***

In the months following Darkon's funeral, Maripa became a regular visitor in the lab, this time casually leaning on Rocker's shoulder as they viewed some new data on the screen.

"Thank you for dinner last night," she whispered in his ear. "I do enjoy our talks."

"Me too," replied Rocker squeezing her hand briefly.

She watched the monitor as Rocker fed data into the computer. "I still don't completely understand what you are looking for, Jontar," she said.

"Here, let me show you something," he said, reaching for a device on the counter.

He took her hand and brought the device up to her fingers. "What are you doing?" Maripa jerked her hand away.

"Trust me," he said, holding out his hand for her.

"I don't like needles," she said, hesitantly placing her hand back in his.

"This isn't a needle, just a sampling probe. All I need is one drop of blood. You won't feel a thing." He pressed the probe against her finger and pressed the button. "All done."

"That's it?" she examined her finger. "Now what?"

"I just set the probe into the slot here and the computers do the rest. Let's take a look at your DNA." He typed in a few commands and the computer screen flashed a series of responses. After a brief exchange of prompts and commands, the screen displayed a long sequence of letters, the representation of Maripa's genetic code.

A-A-G-T-C-C-G-T-T-A-C-C-C-T-T-G-A-A-G-G-T-G-T-C-C-A-G-T-A-A-C-

Page after page of code flashed by. Millions of purines and pyrimidines, or organic compounds which make up all DNA linked together in the code representing the individual.

As Rocker watched the screen, he explained how the DNA strand worked to code for the proteins which are responsible for life.

"The sequence is the key," he told her. "Any changes to the sequence result in completely different organisms, mutations, or any number of genetic diseases. The wrong mutations in the sequence can be fatal. The problem is in the replication process. Traditional methods have relied on electricity to stimulate the mitotic processes. I believe that the electric shock is responsible for the degradation of the amino bond to the nitrogenous bases, all those letters you see here on the screen." He looked up to see if Maripa was following.

"So far so good. Keep going," she said, looking back at him and then up at the screen.

"My theories involve combinations of certain chemicals instead of electricity to stimulate mitosis and preserve the forces linking the compounds."

"Is this the Somatic Cell Nuclear Transfer process you've mentioned before? That SCNT thing?"

"Yes, exactly, very good," he said, smiling as she leaned in closer. "The problem is we haven't been able to isolate the right combination of chemicals to do the job. Every time we get close, the bonds just fall apart. Not as catastrophically as with electricity, but they still fall to pieces. It's driving us all crazy."

"And what is this here?" She pointed to a blinking portion of the sequence on the monitor.

"What?" Rocker asked as he looked where she was pointing. "Wait, that's impossible!" He grabbed the keyboard and typed in a command, watching as the monitor gave a new view, showing much more of the gene sequence at once.

"Now there are several parts blinking. What does that mean, Jontar?"

"This is just impossible." Rocker continued to feed commands to the computer and examine the data displayed on the monitor. "It can't be." He turned to face Maripa, his eyes wide with astonishment.

"You're starting to scare me, Jontar. Tell me." She sat down in the chair next to his.

Rocker took her hands in his, leaned forward and looked deep into her eyes. "You are a clone, Maripa." He paused for her to register that information. "The indicators are undeniable. I rechecked every parameter and there are no mistakes. You are a clone. How is that possible?" He let go of her hands and pulled back realizing the magnitude of what he had just said, his fears suddenly re-emerging in full force.

Maripa's mouth dropped open. He saw the confusion in her eyes.

"You're the great geneticist, you tell me!" She reached out to him, but he pulled back further.

"What's the matter, Jontar?" She hesitated, and then reached for him again. "Don't you dare do this to me...not now!"

"Maripa, you're a clone," was all he could manage.

Maripa jumped up, knocking her chair over. Her crest flamed red and her eyes hardened. *How could I have been so stupid! I knew this was a mistake!*

"Karm!" she whispered. Turning to leave she felt Rocker grab her arm.

"I'm going with you."

"Oh, no, you stay right here. I need to deal with that old man myself."

"Not on your life. I need to find out what's going on here as much as you. I'm going."

She held up her hand, blocking him. Rocker did not flinch.

"Suit yourself," she said as she turned and marched from the room. Rocker stayed just out of arm's reach as he followed her to the executive offices.

Maripa slammed open the office door, storming into the room ready for battle. "Alright, Karm, we need to talk,"

"Sit down, Maripa," Karm said as he stood looking out his window. "We do indeed need to talk."

Rocker entered the office behind her and saw the two of them locked in place. As he surveyed the room, he noticed the monitors were all showing his station in the lab. The central monitor displayed a close up of his terminal s flashing bits of genetic code.

"Is it true, Karm?" Maripa asked as stood toe-to-toe glaring up at her uncle, her fists clenched.

Karm looked at them both as he considered his options. "Yes," he replied. "Sit down, both of you. This will take some time and probably several drinks." He motioned to the chairs by the window. Shot glasses and an open bottle were already set out on the offices mini-bar.

"Well?" asked Maripa. Her eyes never left Karm's face as she sat. "I'm waiting."

"It all began about seventy-five years ago..." As he began his tale, Karm held out his left arm. His palm began to glow and an image began to form in the air above his hand.

Chapter Seventeen

Karm poured Rocker and Maripa a drink and brought them their glasses as they sat speechless.

"You can probably use this about now," he said, looking at the two of them. They took the glasses, but did not drink.

Dr. Rocker looked at Maripa, then back at Karm. He was a scientist. He knew none of this was possible. Rocker took a drink from his glass without moving his eyes from Karm's face.

"What is that device there?" asked Rocker pointing wide eyed to Karm's palm. "Are you some sort of living computer or something? What are you?"

"I told you, this is merely an implant given to me by the Skae…"

"And who, exactly, are the Skae?" asked Maripa, curling her feet underneath her as she sat.

Karm smiled patiently as he explained again about how the Skae found his DNA in the lost ship. "I realize this is difficult to take in. I will answer whatever questions I can."

"How does that device of yours work?" asked Rocker, peering at the images projected and the glow from Karm's hand.

"It's called a biocomputer and is connected to my central nervous system. I operate it by thought."

"And Bolt is what…your mentor or something?" asked Maripa.

"Much more than a mentor," said Karm smiling fondly at his memories. "He was my friend."

"This is ridiculous, Karm. How can she be a clone? The technology doesn't exist yet. And if it does, why do you need me? If you already have clones working for you, then you don't need my research. What is your game here? I've seen what Maripa can do. Are you trying to build yourself an army of super soldiers? Is she one of your prototypes? By The Eternal, Karm, what are you up to?"

"You are correct, Dr. Rocker," said Karm as he sat in a nearby chair facing them. "The technology does not exist. At least not in this time."

"Rocker shook his head and held his hands out in front of him. "What do you mean, 'not in this time.'? Either it exists or it doesn't."

"The Skae cloned Maripa, just as they cloned me, from our surviving DNA. I realize this is confusing, but some of my past is actually still far into your future."

Rocker opened his mouth to respond, but then closed it and simply stared at Karm.

"So these Skae," Maripa interrupted, eyes downcast, "have the ability to make clones. Then why didn't they just tell you how to do it instead of going through all of this?"

"They didn't invent the technology. Bolt told me they learned how after going through the wrecked ship's databanks. I don't really understand this either, but he explained that since we, actually you Dr. Rocker, are the ones who developed the technology in the first place, we are the ones who have to do it, but here in the past so they can discover it in the future. As a result, I was not allowed to bring any of the cloning technology with me and my biocomputer will not access any meaningful information on the topic. We need you to develop the technology for us now. Not for building armies, but to save our species."

Rocker dug his knuckles hard into his temples. "Do you really expect us to believe this nonsense about time travel?"

"For now, yes. Can you really offer a better explanation for all of this, other than what I have revealed? There is only so much I can disclose without changing the future to irreparable proportions. I know this is a lot to ask, but you do need to trust me on this."

Maripa dropped her glass on the floor, its contents spilling over her shoes. She stood and hit Karm with a right cross knocking him back a few steps.

"How could you? How could you not tell me any of this before now?"

She ran from the room.

Rocker stood to go after her, but stopped halfway to his feet and fell back into his chair. He took another drink and stared at the door.

"We need to talk, Jontar," said Karm as he rubbed his chin and returned to the chair behind his desk.

"Haven't you said enough?" Rocker turned to face Karm, his crest streaked with red.

"Not yet. You have a lot to think about right now. Take a few days to process it all. I will be here to answer as many of your questions as I can. "

"And what if I decide this is all some sort of colossal hoax?"

"I've read your files, Jontar. I have followed your life and your career very closely. It's no accident you wound up at the university when you did." He paused and took another sip of his drink. "I know about your mistrust of the government and your fears about the potential exploitation of your research, and I know what you have just learned has set you reeling. You and Maripa have gotten very close over the past months and now you learn the truth about her. Anyone would be conflicted and confused over it all."

"You think so, Mr. Time Traveler?" Rocker stiffened and stared threateningly at Karm.

"There is a lot you still don't know, Doctor; there is still a great deal I cannot tell you yet. Don't be too quick to judge. I am well aware of your hesitance to become involved in another relationship since the tragic death of your wife. I can't imagine how difficult it is for you to risk starting over again with Maripa, only to discover this, especially given your fears. Please believe me when I say I never anticipated you testing her blood and discovering this secret. Now you know. But what you know is only part of the truth."

"Then tell me the rest."

"Not now," said Karm. "When the time is right, but not now. You will just have to trust me for the time being."

Rocker leaned forward and the two men locked eyes. "That's asking a lot, Karm."

"I know, but you have to believe my intentions are for the best. Not only for you and Maripa, but for the entire Brin species."

"Go on."

"You're a scientist, Dr. Rocker. You believe in the evidence of your research, despite what your personal prejudices may tell you. You have a unique ability to suspend your personal beliefs and accept the data you collect. Can you do that now?" He sat on the edge of his desk and looked at Rocker, raising his brows in question.

"What do you mean? What evidence? What data?"

I know you have been asking questions about me and what people think about me and my intentions. Doesn't everything you learned from your investigations convince you of my goals for your work? I am not the monster you fear, and neither is she."

Rocker slumped, his eyes glazed over. "I just don't know."

"Trust the evidence, Doctor. Trust your instincts and I think you will discover the answer. Take a few days to think it over, then get back to the labs and continue your work. We are too close to stop now. I know you will come to the right conclusions."

"Alright, Karm, I'll admit I wasn't able to find anything wrong with what you are doing here, and I was beginning to trust you, but your story is a bit much to swallow. Do you really expect me to accept all of this?"

Karm stood, placed his hand on Rocker's shoulder. "For now, yes. There will come a time when I can tell you more, but right now I am asking for your trust. But I am probably not your biggest concern, Maripa does not give her trust easily. I doubt she has ever opened herself up to anyone as she has to you. Your reaction has been quite a blow to her, one I hope the two of you can overcome." He patted Rocker's shoulder and left him alone in the office.

The trail of destruction preceded Karm through the halls to Maripa's quarters. Overturned tables, statues, and glassware littered the carpet with the occasional tapestry ripped from its moorings. Several servants peered cautiously from behind half opened doorways. The sound of breaking glass, shattering furniture, and swearing grew louder as he approached her rooms.

Karm took a deep breath before turning the knob and entering Maripa's quarters. He saw her sitting on the floor amid the rubble staring blankly. "Care for round two?"

"Get out of here, old man, before I decide to take you up on your offer." She pulled her knees up tight, her head buried in her chest.

Karm waited silently, closing the door behind him.

"What the hell am I? Did you make me from spare parts just to be your personal assassin squad? Who are my 'parents'? And who the strix are you? You're obviously not my uncle." She stood and shook her talon at him as she faced Karm. "What gave you the right to play The Eternal with my life? Do I even have any rights, or am I just something for you to use and toss aside when you are done with me like one of your companies?"

Karm looked directly into Maripa's eyes. "I have never thought of you as anything less than my own daughter. Yes, you were brought up and trained with some very unique skills, but that was necessary. I wish it could have been different, but I am bound by history and the future and I cannot always do as I wish."

"You're not making any sense. Just go away before I decide to use some of those skills you created me to use."

"Not until I know you aren't going to do anything stupid. You know there are a great many things I cannot reveal yet. I cannot risk that, even for you. I've been saying this a lot lately, but you need to find some way to trust me."

"Ha! What gives you the right to tell me I have to trust you? You have betrayed me and everything I thought I knew." She turned her back to Karm walked to her window. "You know as well as I do about his anxiety over his work being used to create Brin with precisely my skills and abilities, not to mention his nervousness about being in a new relationship. Things were going so well. Did you see the look on his face? How can anything ever be the same again?"

"Don't underestimate him. I think he will prove to be more than his dossier. I know this has been quite a shock for you. Take a few days and think things through. If you want to continue then come back and we can pick up where we left off. It would be a terrible shame to give up on him without giving him a chance." He reached over and rubbed her shaking back.

"I saw the look in his eyes. Do you honestly believe he can get passed his beliefs on this or ever be able to feel the same way about me again?" She looked up at Karm, her eyes wide and pleading.

"I do," he said. "You just need to give him a chance. I think I know Dr. Rocker a little better than most and I trust him. Don't judge him based on his immediate reaction to such shattering news. Give him time to adjust and think things through. He will probably surprise you."

Maripa turned to face Karm, leveling her deadliest glare on him. "I do hope you are right, but don't get any ideas that I will ever trust you again, old man. I have a lot to think about and I'm not even sure I want to be part of this anymore. Just try not to get yourself killed while I am gone. Now get out of here." She shut the door behind him and went to pack her bags.

Chapter Eighteen

In the months following her time away, Maripa continued her duties as Rocker's body guard. They saw each other daily in the labs. Their conversations, polite at first, gradually grew more comfortable and they began to relax around each other again. While still far from their previous closeness, a mutual, but carefully guarded friendship grew in strength as they helped each other face the facts of their new realities. Then the results for Batch 821-b4 came in.

Batch 821-b4 began as just another promising variation of the chemical soup their current research had guided them toward. They applied it to the prepared cells the day before and left it to incubate overnight. In the morning, the lab tech recovered the petri dish from the incubator and set it into the microscopic analyzer. She then went about the rest of her work to prepare the lab for the day. An hour later, Dr. Rocker entered with Maripa close behind. She took up her post by the door.

Rocker went to his office and read the seemingly endless string of emails that had accumulated since yesterday. He watched as the rest of the staff arrived and got to work.

"Are the results from the last batch in yet?" Dr. Contor asked the lab tech.

"Yes, Doctor. I set them in the analyzer first thing. You should be able to see the analysis on your screen by now."

Dr. Contor turned on his monitor and clicked on the file labeled Batch 821-4b results. His excitement grew as he read the analysis. As soon as he finished reading, Dr. Contor leapt out of his chair and ran to Rocker's office. "Dr. Rocker, you need to see this," he blurted out as he swung open the door.

"What's up?" asked Rocker.

"Come and take a look for yourself."

Rocker got up and followed his department chief to his station.

"Sit down and read this," said Contor, pointing to the monitor.

What Rocker saw on the screen took a moment to fully register in his brain.

METABOLIC PROCESSES: STABLE
CELL GROWTH PARAMETERS: STABLE
SCNT: STABLE
MITOTIC RATE: STABLE
DNA EQUILIBRIUM: STABLE

"Has this been verified?" Rocker asked the chief.

"Starting verification now, sir," said Dr. Contor, already on his way to the incubator to get a second sample.

An hour later, the results of the second sample confirmed the original readings. The room erupted into cheers and shouts, the geneticists hugged each other, and threw papers in the air. Tears streamed from a few eyes. Maripa could not contain herself any longer and she approached the celebrating group.

"What just happened?"

Dr. Rocker turned, saw Maripa and grabbed her up in a twirling bear hug. "We did it! It worked!"

"What worked?" she asked as he landed her on the ground again.

"Batch 821-b4. It worked; the process is stable and growing normally. There is no sign of degeneration."

"Your process works? Does Karm know?"

Rocker stopped dancing and kissed her. "Guess I better tell him." He pulled out his pocket communicator to make the call.

Maripa stood, mouth open in shock, staring after him. A smile gradually appeared, but she shook her head to help gather her thoughts.

Karm burst through the door out of breath after running all the way from his offices on the top floor. "Show me the results!" he called over the bedlam in the lab.

"Over here, Karm!" shouted Rocker.

Back in Rocker's office, they shared a bottle of Ophlam, brown and very strong, Rocker had been saving for this moment. "Of course, we need to retest an entirely new batch and send out the results for internal review, we can't risk letting the world know just yet, but the data is solid. We did it." He held up his glass to the others and they all toasted their success.

"Congratulations, Dr. Rocker. Dr. Contor, please extend my gratitude to your entire team. You might also let them know I intend to see they get a healthy bonus this month." Karm raised his glass in salute noting that Rocker and Maripa were sitting next to each other.

"I will leave you all to your celebrations now, Dr. Rocker. But will you and Maripa please meet with me in my office tomorrow morning at 10:00?"

"Yes, sir," they said in unison.

That night, as Maripa again escorted Rocker to his home, he turned to her before getting out of the levicoach. "I know things have been rough for you these past few months, and I haven't been helping matters much, but I am trying to work through it all."

She shifted her position to face him. "I know you have been and I appreciate that."

"Would you like to come in and talk?" He looked into her eyes, searching for something.

"Not just yet. Let's just take this slowly and see how it all develops."

"Alright, see you in the morning then?"

"Nine-thirty sharp." She smiled at him, took his hand and held it for a moment, but then turned away.

Rocker got out of the coach and entered his house. When the door shut, he set the alarm system and watched through the front window as Maripa drove off, his fingers absently reaching once again for the ring still hanging under his shirt. He headed off to bed, feeling a little unsteady from the celebrations and too exhausted to stay awake any longer.

The next morning at exactly ten, Maripa led Dr. Rocker into Karm's office.

Kirta looked up from the computer screen as they entered. "I understand congratulations are in order, Dr. Rocker."

"Thank you, Kirta," said Rocker, smiling through a slight headache.

"There's been a slight change in plans. He's waiting for you on the roof on the executive patio." She smiled and returned to her work.

They took the elevator to the top floor and headed down the hallway toward a large glass wall. Using her pass card Maripa unlocked the door and the two of them stepped out into the fresh air. Karm was standing by the rail looking out over the grounds of his headquarters. Nearby stood a table containing an assortment of fruits, breads, and breakfast sweets, along with three choices of juice.

"Come join me. I hope you haven't eaten yet."

"Just some juice, sir," said Rocker. "And a little food might be good, thank you."

"Maripa?" Karm looked toward his assistant. "Join us, please."

"Thank you, sir. I could use a bit of food, too."

They both sat at the table and loaded their plates with several items from the tray. After further congratulations and small talk about the cloning process, Karm cleared his throat and began to talk more seriously.

"I think it is now time to let you both in on the rest of my plans." He picked up the remote and aimed it at the glass wall of the building. The partition turned opaque, but remained blank. He pressed a couple of the other buttons, but the wall remained blank.

Maripa reached for the controller. "Let me, sir." She pressed the top button and the view came to life. "Just use the arrow keys now, sir," she told Karm, returning the device to him. The interior of a vast factory appeared. In the center of the view, the framework of a large oblong metallic vessel came into view.

Rocker stared at the image, his hand frozen halfway between his plate and mouth. "What is that?"

Karm beamed broadly. "This is the Hegira. Isn't she beautiful?"

"Hegira? Isn't that the name of the mountain where Tokal supposedly brought all those animals and a number of the ancients deep into the caverns there to save them from the comet that wiped out almost all life back then?"

Karm laughed appreciatively. "Very good, Jontar. Yes, the Brothers teach that story from the Book of the Eternal. The name is appropriate, don't you think?"

"I don't understand, sir," Rocker said, his face still contorted, trying to work out the puzzle.

Maripa's face lit up in sudden realization. "It's a rescue ship."

"Good girl, Maripa. Yes, it is! This is how we are going to save the Brin from total annihilation."

Rocker shook his head, not sure he was getting the full implication of what he was hearing. "Maybe you better start from the beginning, sir. I'm still not quite following you."

Karm stood and started to pace around the patio as he spoke; his hands waving and pointing to emphasize specific details.

"This whole planet and everything on it is doomed. We have known this for some time now, but have been unable to get Parliament to support any one strategy to save us. They believe the next one hundred years before the sun goes nova is plenty of time. They hope to pass the dilemma along to future generations. I've decided to venture out on my own to build this ship and equip it with the resources necessary to at least save our species and as many other species as we can manage."

"Keep going," said Rocker.

"A number of years ago, astronomers located a planet in a relatively nearby system so similar to Dyan'ta they think it could support life. Spectral analysis indicates an oxygen and nitrogen atmosphere as well as the presence of water."

Rocker frowned and shook his head. "What good is that? You're talking about something requiring thousands of years to reach. It would necessitate generations and a ship far larger than what you are showing us here."

"Your lab is not my only investment. While you have been trying to solve your problems, others have been developing a new method of propulsion. They call it Hyper-Ionic Drive. This new drive can get a vessel from Dyan'ta to the new planet in only eighteen years."

Rocker waved a hand toward the projection, shaking his head dismissively. "That's great, but your ship can't possibly hold all the supplies and equipment for more than a few dozen people at best. It's just not enough people to ensure enough genetic variability for long term survival."

"And that is where your cloning process comes into the picture. I don't intend to send more than sixty people on this voyage. In addition to the crew, there will be DNA samples for tens of thousands of individuals placed into storage. Once the ship lands on the new world, we named it Raince'to, those sixty can use your technique to awaken the samples and grow whole cities of people. The sixty will act as surrogate parents, educators, and government for the developing civilization. Even the crops and animals they'll need can be sent as DNA samples."

Rocker and Maripa just looked at each other in silence, unable to move as they absorbed everything they just heard.

Finally, Rocker shook himself out of his stupor. "Are you sure this will work?"

"Some of the greatest minds on the planet assure me it will. And what alternative do we have? Even if the engines fail or the planet turns out to be uninhabitable nothing is lost that wasn't doomed already."

Maripa stared wide-eyed at her 'uncle'. "It's amazing, Karm. How soon will it all be ready?"

"There is still a lot of work left to do. We still have some final testing of the engines before they are installed. There are all those DNA samples to collect and you, Dr. Rocker, need to work on reducing the size and weight of your equipment so they can be carried in the Hegira. Then we have to notify Parliament and allow them to help select the crew so we can get the launch permits. And let's not forget logistics and loading all of the supplies the crew will need during the flight. I anticipate at least three more years before we can launch."

Maripa's eyes scrunched in thought, one hand cupping her chin, a taloned finger tapping her cheek. "Eighteen years is still a long time. How will the crew stay sane being stuck inside such a confined space for so long?"

"I have one of my engineering and pharmaceutical divisions working on a cryogenic suspended animation process. The entire crew of sixty will not be needed to operate the ship en route so most of them can sleep in rotating shifts of a year or so."

"Looks as though you have thought of everything," said Rocker. "I'm speechless."

"Not quite everything, Doctor. I haven't been able to stem the growth of The Faith, and their growing influence poses a real threat to the project. That is why I have been operating under such tight security all this time." Karm stopped pacing and looked at them both directly. "You are now my co-conspirators. Nobody else knows what the others are doing, and each group is operating under the impression their work is for something entirely different. If anything were to happen to me, it will be up to the two of you to see this thing through. Are you with me?"

Rocker and Maripa looked across the table at each other. They each gave a nod in silent agreement. "We're in," they said together. "Just tell us what we need to do."

Chapter Nineteen

"Welcome, gentlemen." Dressed in the more casual outdoorsman attire he preferred when staying at The Citadel, Karm greeted the members of Parliament as they arrived. He kept this castle as a place to impress people when he called them to meetings he considered particularly vital.

"I am sure you are all tired from your journey, so I have had rooms prepared for each of you. We will not meet until tomorrow, so make yourselves comfortable and enjoy the facilities here."

Maripa met Karm as he re-entered the castle. She dressed in her usual business suit and flat shoes. "Scans completed, sir," she said. "There weren't any weapons, but a couple of them did have hidden recording devices. We neutralized them so everything is secure."

"Thank you, Maripa. Shut down the cell tower to eliminate phone connections to the outside and we will be ready to begin. And have your investigations completed by tomorrow afternoon. I will want to meet with you once our guests leave."

"Already done, sir." Maripa proceeded to walk the guest wing of the castle ostensibly to check on the welfare of the guests, but always alert for security risks.

At the evening gatherings, she took up her station in her office and monitored the cameras. Seeing nothing more than the usual small talk and occasional Parliamentary maneuverings, she called the security chief. "All yours now, chief. Call me if anything happens."

"Yes, ma'am," he replied. She retired for the evening.

The new day dawned warm and clear. The grounds behind The Citadel, what Karm referred to as the backyard, was filled with large white canopies. Servants carried dozens of trays of food to the waiting steam tables under two of the awnings. Folding chairs, good enough to be used in most homes as fine furniture, were assembled under the main shelter, ten to a table. A podium stood at the front, flanked by loudspeakers. Microphones placed on each table allowed anyone wishing to speak to be heard by all in attendance. A large screen hung from the ceiling behind the podium. The support poles all contained electronic dampening devices guaranteed to prevent any discussions held inside the main tent could not be overheard even a few feet away on the outside. Nevertheless, storm clouds brewed as the meeting started.

Karm strode to the lectern and raised his arms as he addressed the assembly. "Welcome again, gentlemen. We have vital business to discuss today so let's get to it."

Gardak, the Prime Minister, stood, approached the podium, and addressed the gathering, "It has come time to address the threat we are all facing from The Faith and their constituency."

There was a general buzz of agreement, but a few members sat silently. One of the elder statesmen present rose to speak.

"We have never encountered anything like this, Karm. Only four years ago The Faith was a back country fringe group with no real organization. Three years ago, after the announcement of new brain cloning technology, they suddenly gained a following. Pareth was able to unite people behind the belief that science, cloning in particular, was threatening to destroy belief in The Eternal. He was able to have enough of their followers elected to office so they could disrupt the progress of some our bills."

"Yes," Karm interrupted, "but that was only a minor inconvenience. We were able to control those who opposed us"

"That was then, Karm, but no longer. The movement has grown in popularity among the people and a significant number of Parliament is being swayed by it. There is even a new effort to have members of parliament sign a loyalty oath obligating anyone who The Faith supports to oppose all legislation not approved by them."

Karm waved his hand in dismissal. "A loyalty oath? Nonsense!"

"Not at all, sir," continued the elder statesman. "If they don't sign the oath, and follow through with their votes, The Faith will remove their support and replace the uncooperative representatives in the next election. Many of our members have discovered just how powerful The Faith's followers can be. We lost a dozen members to them in the last election with several dozen more threatened next year. Some of us have been around long enough to resist them, but we will be powerless before long if The Faith is allowed to continue."

Karm surveyed the room and saw most of those present nodding in agreement. "So, you all feel this way? I will have to call in some of these junior members and assure them of my support so that they won't have to fear re-election."

Another representative stood to speak. "That won't work. The Faith controls voters in too many districts now. The masses are afraid for their souls. Since we released word of the supernova, many Brin who never put much stock in such beliefs have found solace in rediscovering religion. The Faith has convinced them that joining is the only way to gain the protection of The Eternal when the end comes. All of your money and power cannot overcome the blind belief of these individuals."

"So it is their way or nothing? What do they want so we might be able to come to a compromise with them? There must be something they need that we can use to gain the upper hand."

"No, sir. Nothing," replied the first statesman. "We are dealing with matters of faith here. They are so convinced they are guided by The Eternal, that any compromise is seen as a denial of their beliefs. This is a sort of holy war for them and they intend to win at all costs." He spread his arms, palms upward, in a helpless gesture, and sat down.

"Rather than allow for any other opinions or values, they would risk a holy war which threatens the extinction of the entire Brin race? Karm slammed his fist on the table. "That is insane."

"Not to them, sir. It is strictly a matter of faith. The security of their souls being with The Eternal in the afterlife trumps any losses here in the physical world. Besides, time is on their side. Dyan'ta's destruction is not likely for another one hundred years. All of us will be long gone by then."

Karm walked to the podium and pressed a button on the control panel. Kirta retrieved a stack of papers from her table at the back of the tent. She distributed these to each of the legislators in attendance and left. As each man read the information before him they turned to Karm in disbelief.

The Prime Ministers hands trembled as he read the document. "What is this? Where did you get this material?"

"My people have access to much more accurate equipment than any government facility, gentlemen. I have employed the best minds on Brin for many years now and given them essentially unlimited resources. They are developing some amazing devices. What you see is the end result of an exhaustive study I initiated two years ago. We don't have a century. There are only ten years left before our sun explodes and destroys everything. I can provide the raw data for you and your own experts to examine if you wish."

The assembly erupted in confused and angry shouts. Many of the dignitaries reached for their communicators, only to discover all communications cut off. Their offices, loved ones, bankers, whomever they attempted to contact, impossible to reach. Others gathered in small groups, arguing over the best means of dealing with this now imminent disaster. He let them process the shock and then continued to address them. "This information does not leave these grounds, gentlemen."

The Prime Minister raised his hands and asked for quiet. "Of course, we will want to examine the data more thoroughly, but let's suppose for now that your analysis is correct. Wouldn't it be better to openly enlist the resources of the entire planet to try to find a solution?"

"You know how the public would react," replied Karm, scowling and grasping the lectern with both hands. "If news of this were to ever leak out the resulting panic would be global and devastating. We cannot allow that to happen."

"But the populace has a right to know!" shouted one of the officials.

"No, actually, they do not," said Karm. "The public cannot be allowed to know any of this. Think about it. Do you really want to live out the last ten years of your lives with global rioting and chaos? Why should anyone follow the laws if the consequences no longer matter? Look at what happened in the aftermath of the revelation we had a hundred years left. However, I do have a plan. Now if you will all sit down and listen, I will tell you what I've been preparing." He pressed another button on the control panel and the screen behind him lit up with a series of images detailing each point as he spoke.

"As you know, Dr. Rocker has solved the problem of cloning individuals so there is no longer the trouble with DNA degradation."

"Releasing that information was foolish," shouted another of the council members. "The protests against cloning were bad enough before, but now we may all lose our jobs. I've had to hire extra security to protect my home from the mobs."

"The next elections are the least of our concerns now. As I was saying, Dr. Rocker is now perfecting the equipment for that process to make it more portable. Once this is accomplished, we will collect DNA samples from as many Brin as possible in the next five years."

"And just what good will collecting DNA samples do us?" asked one of the representatives. "The DNA will be destroyed along with everything else. The whole damn planet is going to be incinerated."

"Not if they are no longer on the planet. My engineers and manufacturing plants have been constructing a spaceship to take the samples to Raince'to. You all remember the news a couple of years back, about the planet that was discovered only twenty light years away? We will send the DNA samples there, to be reanimated and the Brin will survive."

"And just who would reanimate them?" asked one of the legislators.

"I propose we choose a group of sixty individuals based on the requirements for developing a colony. The ship can only carry so many together with the supplies and equipment they will need. We will enlist construction workers, farmers, ranchers, engineers, medical personnel, teachers, and scientists…all those who would be essential for organizing and building colonies on the new world. The only individual I must insist on is Dr. Rocker. Nobody understands his process better than he does. If anything were to go wrong then he will be the only one able to fix it. Otherwise the entire operation will be a waste."

"Lies!" Came a shrill cry from one of the tables near the front. "The Prior is right! We cannot listen to the scientists and their supporters any longer!"

The delegates erupted in pandemonium. "Sit down, sir!" "Who let this maniac in?" "What is he talking about?" Some tried to restrain the legate, but he shoved them away and continued to yell. Security pushed their way through the crowd attempting to reach the deranged individual before he could disrupt the gathering any further.

"Only The Faith tells us the truth of things!" The wild-eyed representative reached inside his belt and brought out a long thin blade. He raised his arm as if to throw the weapon at Karm, who stood less than fifteen feet away. There was a quick flicker of reflection and the would-be assassin screamed, grabbing his hand and dropping the blade. A silvery metal star protruded from his bleeding wrist. Maripa appeared as if from nowhere, subduing the maniac onto the ground. As soon as the other guards reached them, she handed the offender over and helped escort him from the area. The entire incident was over almost as quickly as it began.

Karm called out to his panicking guests. "Please! Everyone, please listen to me!" A faint blue glow radiated out from Karm, encompassing the entire gathering, and then fading before anyone could notice. The delegates slowly calmed and listened. "Everything is under control now. You can all resume your seats now. It's all over and nobody is hurt."

"You expect us to stay here after what just happened?" asked one of the dignitaries when his composure returned.

"Yes, I do," Karm said as calmly as he could manage. "The matter before us is too important to allow a brief incident to bring us to a halt." He looked over his audience and reassured them as best he could. "We have all faced dangerous situations before. That is the nature of our jobs. Let's all remain calm, take a moment to take a deep breath, and continue."

The Prime Minister rose to speak. "I agree. If what we have just learned is true then we cannot waste another second." His look dared any of those gathered to contradict him before continuing. "You seem to have been at this for quite some time already, Karm. How do we know you can accomplish all of this in time?"

Karm tilted his head, touched one talon to his temple and smiled. "We are ahead of schedule actually. The ship will be ready for launch in four years if necessary."

"Be that as it may, how can we possibly keep all of this under wraps for so long? And how can we hold off The Faith long enough to accomplish everything in time? You know how strong they will become in the next election. You may have bottomless pockets, but even you are not above the law. They will see to it that all of your work on cloning is stopped and destroyed."

"Leave The Faith to me," Karm said, pointing his finger at each of the men in turn. "All you need to do is overlook what you now know about the sun. Keep the government running and keep those anti-cloners out of mischief as long as you can. The survival of our species depends on this."

"What do you plan to do, Karm?" asked the Prime Minister.

"Nothing you need to worry about, Gardak. Everything is strictly legal, but the less you know the more you can deny later." Karm gave the head of Parliament his most politically correct smile, and then addressed the entire assembly. "Gentlemen, I think we have covered everything we needed to. You all know your jobs. You are welcome to stay for the dinner being prepared. However, your bags have been packed and brought out to vehicles that will take you back to the airport after you have eaten. Unfortunately, I will not be joining you. I have another pressing engagement to attend to. Please return the information sheet to my secretary as you head out." Karm left the room and servants entered to direct the guests to the awaiting meal in the adjoining canopies. A few moments later, Karm joined Maripa in the security office where she was watching as his guests talked over their meal. "We will discuss the attack later," he said. "In the meantime, how's it going out there?"

"They are understandably disturbed, but I don't think we will have any trouble with them. They definitely do not want worldwide anarchy erupting so they are clamping down on anyone who they think might leak the information." She pointed to a small group on the monitor huddled together in a heated discussion.

"Good. Monitor them until they leave and then join me in my office." He satisfied himself with one more look at the monitors and then left.

Two hours later, Maripa caught up to Karm in his third floor office. "All of the guests have left. I don't think we will have any trouble with them. The Prime Minister had private words with each of them to reinforce everything you told them. He also made sure nobody will gossip about the incident either. The last thing he wants is for more rumors about The Faith to get out."

"Alright then, what do you have for me? How could that idiot have gotten past you?"

Maripa stiffened and refused to lower her eyes. "I have no idea. He must have been keeping his alignment with The Faith a secret. It may even be something he has been only on the fringe of, until he broke under the strain of what you told him today."

What about the knife? People just don't walk around carrying concealed weapons."

Maripa let out a quick smirk. "You'd be surprised. Many in power carry just that sort of thing in case of an attack, especially with the turmoil on the streets these days."

"If this is such a common thing, then how did he evade your security searches?"

Her scowl deepened and her voice grew strained. "I take full responsibility for that breech, sir. It would seem my staff needs a refresher course in their technique and a long talk about diligence in their duties."

Taking a deep breath, Karm let the tension ease from his body. "No matter now. At least nobody got hurt. Is he still here on the grounds?"

"He's being held under guard and in restraints in the cellar. I didn't want to call the police until we had a chance to talk. I know how sensitive the information he now has is and I didn't think you wanted to lose custody of him just yet."

"Good. I can arrange it so he forgets everything that happened to him over the past two days. He'll simply wake up in the hospital and have no idea why he is there, or how he got there." He held up his hand and a deep orange glow hovered in the air above it.

"One more item though, sir." Maripa place a folder on his desk. "It is much worse than we had thought, sir." She began to pace the floor as she talked. "It appears His Majesty is being recruited by The Faith."

"Are you sure about him? If they join forces they could upset things badly."

"Yes, sir. We have confirmation from several of our insiders indicating one of The Faith's bishops visited the Monarch and is a frequent guest at many of their functions since that initial encounter. Brach and Lerit, sorry, Pareth, have also met privately on at least two occasions we know of. The Faith's bank accounts have substantially increased in value since this meeting as well."

"Brach is not the most religious man on the planet, Maripa. He and the Prior are still brothers after all."

"Possibly, he's being very accommodating to them so the two of them could be collaborating. They are accomplished politicians and very intelligent so it would be hard to tell their real motives. I will want to maintain surveillance of His Majesty just to be sure."

"Of course. Do what you need to do to find out what they are up to. We need to know if this is just a ruse or a real alliance." Karm flipped absentmindedly through the report Maripa gave him. "What is this about a possible military faction?"

Maripa stopped her pacing and approached Karm's desk. "That's the most disturbing part of it all. It appears the Monarch's 'conversion' has had a profound effect on the military. Entire regiments are, under direct orders, joining The Faith. Some, however, appear to be joining willingly. No indications yet if The Faith's leaders intend to use them as enforcers, but why else would they recruit so many so quickly? We need to keep a very close eye on this."

"Well, so much for my little vacation down by the stream." He sighed and threw his arms up in disgust.

***

His Majesty sat at his desk stamping the royal seal to a series of documents he had just signed when his seneschal entered the room.

"The General has arrived as you commanded, Your Majesty."

"Good, good, send him in," replied Brach as he continued to press the stamp into the soft wax.

The General, in the red and gold uniform he always wore for an audience with the monarch, marched into the room, clicked his heels to attention, and saluted. "Your Majesty. "You summoned me?"

"Yes, General. I have a rather unique request of you."

The General's eyebrows rose slightly, "Request, Sire?"

"Command actually."

"Yes, Sire."

"You will need to resign your commission immediately, General." Brach looked up from his documents and watched the General's reaction.

He hesitated only a moment, his stance wavered slightly, and then he recovered. "Of course, Sire. May I be permitted to ask why, Sire?"

"You are going to join The Faith, General." Brach paused to allow the impact of this statement to take full effect. "The prior and I need to keep open our lines of communication and you will serve that need as our liaison. To convince my brother of your neutrality, you will need to sever all official ties to me. You can tell him your honor requires you to be completely neutral if you are to perform your new duties to the best of your abilities. After some time has passed, you can begin to develop an interest in The Faith and eventually become a devout follower."

The General frowned as he thought this over. "I believe your brother would accept my honorable decision to sever ties to you in deference to my duties as a liaison, but I sincerely doubt he would ever believe my conversion to his religion."

"A lot of Brin are doing many things out of character these days, my old friend. You could always claim to succumb to the inevitability of our fate and a desire for peace at the end."

"I suppose that would be at least reasonable, Sire, but I still have my reservations."

"I have complete faith in your ability to be convincing," Brach replied with a dismissive wave of his hand. "Within the next year or so you will fully convert to The Faith, join the ranks of the clergy and, in time, become the cause of my final conversion and rise to the rank of Archbishop." Brach watched the General's face carefully as he said this.

"Forgive me, Sire, but I am a military man. I have no interest in religion. I would make a very poor follower and unlikely to rise at all in their ranks." He maintained a stance of rigid attention, but his eyes mirrored the questions in his mind.

Brach smiled and gave a laugh. "Don't worry General, this is a special assignment and I believe only you can pull it off. All of my other attempts have failed, but I don't think they will be able to resist having you as a convert. Especially when you tell them that you have my ear and should be able to complete my conversion as well."

The General paused briefly to consider the matter. "I would be more inclined to believe your brother would see me as too great a risk."

"True, but his bishop's might be persuaded and, if we are lucky, they might not be able to resist the publicity of me becoming one of the faithful, despite his reservations. And we really do need your services as our go-between. You are the one person we both can trust to be honorable and trustworthy in this position."

"Of course, Sire. I would never betray such a confidence."

"There is no doubt of the extreme danger in this ruse, so while this is officially a command, I would feel better knowing you are willing to put yourself in such a position."

The General's eyes brightened and he stood at full attention again. "I see, Sire. I understand. When do I begin this campaign?"

"I will let my brother know immediately, General," said Brach. "But, give it a few weeks, then start spreading some rumors about your growing interest in The Faith. Maybe you should start having a few religious visions and hear some voices compelling you to convert. Let one of them approach you first and then you can begin. In the meantime, we will need to work out a way to communicate secretly while you are among them. Any further questions?"

"No, Sire." The General snapped another salute, turned on his heel and marched out of the room.

Chapter Twenty

Rocker and Maripa stared dumfounded at Karm. "What do you mean you are going to meet with The Faith?" asked Rocker. "You can't seriously want to surrender yourself to them like this." The sound of the river flowing by was the only disturbance as the three accomplices sat under one of the pergolas Karm had built near his favorite fishing holes. The lunch prepared for them remained only partially eaten as they argued.

"At least demand that the meeting be held at some neutral site, not in the palace," said Maripa. She stalked around the structure flailing her arms in frustration. She bent down, picked up a stone and hurled it into the water. The plunk startled several birds downstream sending them noisily into the air.

"You both know how powerful The Faith has become in the past year," said Karm. He sat calmly chewing his sandwich, as he watched the pair vent at him. "My support has become inconsequential in the past year. Those fools have the power to demand whatever they want now. And once the elections are over they will be in a position to severely threaten our project. We need to switch strategies."

Rocker leaned up against one of the support posts and shrugged. "What strategies do we have left? They know they have us by the crests. Why even bother calling you in for this meeting?"

Maripa moved next where Rocker stood, took his hand, and leaned against him. "They are probably just waiting to arrest you on some trumped up charges. Or worse yet, have you assassinated. I need to go with you."

"Oh, you are going with me," said Karm, "but not for the reasons you think. You're simply going as my personal aide. I still have appearances to maintain." He gave them both a wide grin and winked. "Besides, I might still have a trick or two up my sleeve."

"What are you planning, Karm?" asked Maripa.

Karm grinned from one auricular to the other. "Patience, my dear."

He stood and walked over to join his co-conspirators. "I wouldn't want to spoil the surprise." He turned to watch the river. A slight breeze rustled the leaves of the trees above them.

"I hate surprises." She frowned and tensed her grip on Rocker's hand.

"Dr. Rocker, I believe you have some important work to get back to in your lab. I would not want to keep you from it any longer." He shook Rocker's hand, and slapped him on the back. "Don't look so glum. We have them right where we want them."

Rocker shook his head and tried to smile. "Whatever you say. Just don't get yourselves killed with whatever you've cooked up."

"You just go back to your lab and get that equipment down to size in time. You let me worry about the politicians." He turned to Maripa. "Shall we head into the bertal's den?" He helped them pick up the remains of their lunch and led them back across the open field to The Citadel.

In a matter of hours, Karm and Maripa arrived at the palace. The sun beat down from overhead in a clear teal sky, casting only the shortest of shadows. The white marble exterior of the palace gleamed in the bright daylight. The beauty went unnoticed by Maripa as she stepped out of the levicoach. Her attention was riveted on the crowd gathered in the plaza before them. "Oh, strix," she muttered. "We don't need this right now. Where are the palace guards? Why don't they clear these idiots away?"

"Clones are an abomination to The Eternal!"

"The Faith is the only way to salvation!"

Several dozen individuals marched back and forth on the plaza shouting and waving their signs while dozens more watched the spectacle from afar, including, as Maripa now noticed, five of the palace guards.

"I don't like this," she warned, taking Karm by the elbow. "We need to get out of here right now."

"Don't be so worried, my dear," said Karm. "I don't think we are in any real danger here and I absolutely must attend this meeting. I have no doubt you will keep me perfectly safe if the need arises."

Maripa stared at Karm, unable to think of anything to say as he started toward the protesters. The crowd grew louder and closer as they approached, but only continued to shout their slogans. She led the way through them, occasionally needing to elbow a pathway through the mob. They soon exited the throng without incident and continued to cross the plaza leaving the protest behind them.

"You see," beamed Karm. "I told you there was nothing to worry about. That was just a show put on for our benefit by our hosts."

Maripa rolled her eyes and stalked on ahead, muttering a great number of curses under her breath.

As she and Karm mounted the stairs, guards opened the massive doors to allow them entry. Servants took their cloaks and showed the visitors to a waiting room. Karm helped himself to a plate of fruit from the table already prepared with a variety of drinks and foods for them. Maripa was not hungry.

He sank into one of the large overstuffed chairs and ate silently as they waited to be summoned. She sat in her chair watching the doorways.

An hour later, the door to the back of the room opened and a retainer dressed in the red and gold silks of the palace officials, walked in. "His Majesty will see you now."

Karm and Maripa rose, straightened their clothes, and followed the functionary down a long hallway. He stopped before a door about two thirds of the way down the hall and opened it for them. Karm squared his shoulders, put on his best politician's expression, and entered the room. Maripa followed, scanning every face and corner in the room.

A large rectangular conference table dominated the room. A dozen men dressed in plain brown and grey robes sat around the table with the Monarch at its head. All eyes turned to watch the pair as they took their seats at the foot of the long table.

"Thank you for the opportunity to meet with you today, Your Majesty," said Karm as he sat.

"Silence, heretic!" shouted one of the younger robed figures. "We have summoned you here. This is no opportunity for you to exploit." He shook his pointing finger at Karm.

Pareth raised his head and turned to the young man. He said nothing, but all those present grew deathly quiet. The young man sniffed and lowered his hand.

"No need to be disrespectful, brothers," Brach said as he turned to look directly at the young enthusiast. "Civility is the hallmark of intelligence and breeding. I am sure we can all agree to handle matters without shouting and insults."

Karm nodded his head in agreement and waved for the Monarch to continue.

"As you know, we of The Faith disapprove of what you are doing in your work with cloning." Several of the robed men murmured and thumped the table in agreement. "We have called you here to ask you to stop this unethical and immoral experimentation."

Karm's eyes widened in perfect innocence, his arms spread in supplication. "I am a bit confused here, Your Majesty. Have I broken any laws? Mine is a privately run corporation. I take no government money. I have no bank loans. The way I see it I can do as I wish with my money and my businesses."

Another of the robed men jumped to his feet and pounded his fist on the table. "You have broken The Eternal's laws, heretic! The laws of decency and Brinality! You are creating abominations in His eyes and will burn for it unless you repent and cease immediately."

"That will be all, brother Crebot," said Pareth with deadly calm. His grey eyes burned into the zealot.

"I apologize, Prior," he said between clenched teeth as he sat back down. His crest continued to blaze red.

The monarch allowed a moment of quiet and then proceeded, "No laws have been broken as of yet, Karm. However, once the next elections occur, The Faith will control a majority in Parliament. With my support we will pass legislation that will outlaw cloning of anything other than replacement organs. If you do not cease immediately, you will find yourself in front of a magistrate."

"Do you realize how many Brin I employ? Hundreds of thousands would be out of work if you pass those laws. How long do you think you can remain in control with that many angry voters?"

"Acceptable losses," said one of the robed men. "As more of the masses join The Faith, the more they will see the necessity of eliminating this abomination. We will stand behind those who support us."

"I see," said Karm. "I guess I have no choice then." He looked at each of the men at the table and lowered his eyes. He placed his hands in his lap and his left palm began to glow.

"No, you do not. We will give you two months to dismantle your operations that deal with the cloning of individuals and…"

Karm's voice was calm and quiet, yet reverberated with authority. "You misunderstand me, Your Majesty. I mean that you have left me no choice but to do this the hard way." He turned to Maripa who opened a blue folder and handed the papers inside to each of the men at the table.

The monarch bolted upright in his chair, sputtering in astonishment. "What is this?"

"Information you need to know before you pass final sentence on my work." Karm gave the men a few moments to read the paper.

"This is heresy! Scientific trickery!" shouted Crebot, the young zealot. "I was once deceived by the spell of science. I understand their treachery. Only the Eternal can reveal the truth to us, not the unbeliever scientists. We cannot trust them."

"Abomination!" shouted others as they tore the paper into pieces.

"Brothers," said Pareth in a calm, but firm voice. He looked directly at Crebot. "We will listen to all voices here. Be still."

The young zealot did not reply, but his face contorted in anger as he returned the Prior's stare.

"I assure you it is not a trick. You are welcome to share the data with any of your scientists if you wish. Our sun is going nova is less than ten years, not the one hundred or so as we had previously believed." Karm stood and leaned on the table in front of him. "I caution you, however, be careful what you do with this knowledge. Revealing this to the world will cause nothing but panic and rioting. Nobody will have any control over anything."

The monarch looked up from his paper. "How is it you have discovered this when our best scientists have not?"

"My equipment is much better than anything the government has access to. All of your funding cuts to scientific research have left you far behind recent developments in the private sector. You are welcome to send some of your best men to my facilities to check the validity of the data."

Pareth then raised his hand for quiet and spoke. "Then it appears your experiments with cloning are a wasted effort after all, Karm. Why continue with them now? Why not join us and save what is left of your soul?"

"I have no intention of discontinuing my work, Pareth. I have nothing better to do in the years we have left and I think it is better to keep everything as normal as possible. As long as the people are kept busy they're less likely to lose control."

"Then if, as you claim, we only have ten years left, I believe our time is best spent fulfilling the wishes of The Eternal. Our duty requires us to stop your experiments. The people are sure to turn to us out of need for comfort in their final years. We will provide for their souls. You have nothing they want."

"I was afraid you might come up with something along those lines," Karm handed a red folder to Maripa and she passed out the documents it contained.

"Now what?" asked the monarch. He picked up the paper and began to read.

As the figures at the table absorbed the incriminating facts in front of them, many began to stir and shift their gaze from one to another.

"My staff has been busy for the past several months collecting data on The Faith. We have gathered quite a bit of information about your finances, political connections, investments, even background on your entire leadership. It appears many of you are in for a great deal of explaining about your personal finances. Not to mention the lesser known doctrines of your so-called religion regarding concubines, tax advantages and special privileges allowed your leadership." He paused to look at each of the robed men around him; none of them returned his scrutiny. "This is only a sample of what I possess, gentlemen. Do you really think the society will turn to you once this is leaked?"

"This is blackmail!" said the young zealot, but he remained seated and did not look up at Karm.

"Yes, it is, young man. Have no doubts about my intentions or willingness to follow through with it if I am interfered with in any way. Moreover, that includes any threats on my life, or the life of anyone in my employment. Any attempt to disrupt my efforts in any manner will result in the automatic and immediate release of everything you see before you. All of your hypocrisies will come crashing down right on top of your heads."

"Come now, Karm," said the monarch. "A simple pre-emptive public act of contrition and purging of the ranks of The Faith will only instill greater admiration in the masses for our cause. We can lay the blame on a few sacrificial scapegoats, revealed by our own efforts. The people will love us even more for keeping our own house clean. What else do you have, Karm? We are shepherds of the sheep and you are the wolf. Who will they believe?"

"Perhaps," said Karm. "That might work for some, but what if your charade leaves shadows of doubt in the rest? I'll take my chances and go right on with my work, Your Majesty, but I will let you in on a little secret." He smiled and sat back down in his chair. "Maripa, are you ready?"

"Just a moment, sir." Maripa opened her case and removed a small holoprojector. She pressed a few buttons and the machine beamed the image of a silvery spaceship to the center of the table.

"This is why I cannot allow you to interfere with my work, gentlemen. I am going to save the Brin." Karm proceeded to outline his plans for the spaceship and the clones. He told them of the sixty crew members required to man the ship and set up the colony on Raince'to. He explained about the new type of propulsion system powering the ship and how it could reach another planet in a matter of four decades rather than centuries. The holoprojector flashed images and data related to each of the areas he discussed. Then the images dissipated.

"In summary, gentlemen, if left unmolested, I can complete this project and be ready to launch in four or five years. If you try to stop me, you condemn our race to extinction."

The young zealot looked up at Karm. "What you propose is not salvation. You want to send abominations to the new world and not True Brin."

"That is your doctrine, not mine, and certainly not one belonging to most of Brin. Especially if I release the information I just showed you."

Pareth turned to Karm and raised his hands spreading his arms wide. "If what you say is true, then what is in it for us? What is our incentive to agree to your plans? Why should we not take our chances and see just how strong our influence over the populace is rooted?"

Karm smiled as he leaned back in his chair. "I am prepared to make one small concession, Pareth. If I am allowed to continue my efforts without interference of any kind then I will set aside one twentieth of the crew slots for members of your clergy. You will have the opportunity to be the only religion on the planet."

"A planet of soulless abominations," said the zealot.

"Now, brother," said Pareth, waving his hand at the younger man, his eyes narrowing, studying Karm. "Let us not be so blinded by doctrine. We are open to new instruction from The Eternal. If we do not attend to the needs of this new flock then who will? Perhaps by our ministrations we can bring souls to the soulless. But I do not see how we could possibly manage such a feat with such a small percentage of the crew. I believe one third to be a more acceptable number for our holy work."

Karm raised an eyebrow and brought his hand to his chin. "A third of the crew seems a bit presumptuous to me. I will agree to ten percent."

The Prior folded his hands, clacking two talons together, and surveyed his brethren with a glance. "Yes, ten percent would be acceptable to me as well."

Karm smiled at the men around the table and raised hands to the monarch. "You see? New opportunities for everybody. Are we in agreement then, gentlemen?"

"I think we have no choice, Karm," said the monarch. "You will keep us informed of your progress and allow periodic inspections of the ship and supplies?"

"Of course, Your Majesty, but on my terms alone. This is, after all, still my money and my organization. Let's not forget that I also control the largest manufacturers of military hardware and software. Do you think for one minute that I would forget to put in place a means of controlling all of your forces? With one call I can either shut down or take complete control of your entire army."

"Very well. We are in accord." The monarch rose and left through his private entrance followed by his brother. The others remained in their seats as Karm and Maripa exited the room.

The sun cast much longer shadows now as it sunk lower in the sky. The protesters confronting their arrival were gone. Karm and Maripa walked down the stairs outside the main palace entrance. The melodies of songbirds competed with the cacophony of those carrying out the affairs of state. Karm stopped as he reached the levicoach waiting for them and looked around.

"My, what a beautiful day," he said as the chauffeur opened the door for them.

"How does it feel to be the canary who ate the cat?" Maripa said once they were on their way.

Karm smiled at Maripa and reached into the refrigerator for a bottle of Champagne and two glasses. "You didn't think I was going into that den of thieves to surrender, did you? I thought you knew me better than that." He popped the cork and poured them each a drink.

"You planned all this?"

"Of course. I have been five moves ahead of them for the past two years. Go ahead and call your boyfriend and tell him to stop worrying." He reached into his pocket to pull out one of his violet pills and downed it with a quick gulp.

"Boyfriend? We're getting along at this point, but I'm not so sure I am ready for anything more just yet. I know he is still trying to come to grips with his feelings for me while dealing with the guilt he feels over the death of his wife." She took a long drink and looked out the window.

"Give him time, Maripa. He'll come around. Have a little faith." He winked as she looked back at him.

"And what makes you so sure they won't double cross you?"

"You forget my advantage." He held out his glowing palm. "I tapped into their brainwaves and electronics. If any of them makes the slightest move to cause us problems I can make sure he is removed and kept quiet. The Brothers of The Convocation do not want to risk their positions so they will keep everyone in line."

"You can do that? Access their thoughts?"

"Yes. I only did it as a last resort, but it was necessary. Now, make that call."

***

Back in his offices Brach could release the seething hatred he forced himself to control during the meeting.

"How dare that insolent, egotistical, blackmailer! How dare he threaten me!"

Rampaging through his private office, waving his arms, shouting at the portraits of his esteemed predecessors, sweeping everything from the surface of his desk, he raged on.

"How could you let Karm gain the advantage like that?" demanded Pareth, grabbing his brother by the shoulders, bringing them nose to nose.

"This is not over. I will see Karm rotting in the deepest dungeon I can find."

"Don't let stupidity compound the mistake," said Pareth, disgustedly shoving Brach away. "So long as Karm holds the upper hand, we must at least appear to go along, while we search for a weakness we can use to our own advantage."

Brach stormed over to the decanter nearby, poured himself a goblet of wine, and downed it in one swift gulp, spilling large portions on his shirt in the process. "I know that, you idiot," he grumbled, wiping the excess wine from his chin. "It galls me to have to play this role in the game. Rest assured I will find his shell's thin point and crush him with it."

Pareth studied his brother for a moment before coming to a decision. "Just don't let your emotions get the better of you again, brother. Karm is a dangerous adversary. We cannot afford any more blunders. Let him have his moment for now. His fall will be that much more satisfying in the end."

Three hours later, their plan to bring down Karm was complete. Brach went to his desk and pulled the cord to summon The General. "Alright, Karm," he muttered to himself. "You threw the gauntlet and have the first blow. We will see who is still standing at the end."

Chapter Twenty-One

*This is ridiculous. I can't keep going back and forth like this. I love her, but...*Rocker shook his head and rubbed his eyes again. The clock told him it was three in the morning and he was staring into the refrigerator. He grabbed a juice carton and a container of two-day-old left-overs. Drinking from the carton he stumbled to the kitchen table and sat looking out into the darkness. He was startled by a loud knock at the door.

"Good, you're still up," said Karm as he walked past Rocker into the kitchen.

"What the strix are you doing here? It's the middle of the night!"

"And we're both wide awake. We need to talk," Karm said as he produced two bottles of whiskey. "Where are the glasses?"

Rocker opened a cabinet and pulled out two large tumblers and added some ice from the freezer. Karm filled both glasses with an unsteady hand and handed the one with less to Rocker as he sat himself down in the rickety chair.

Karm took a long sip. He spilled some of the drink onto the table as he set it down. "I'm getting tired of waiting for you to grow up, Jontar. What is wrong with you? Don't you realize this was an even greater shock to her than it was to you? She's been trying to get her life in order but keeps stumbling over you and your damn issues with clones."

Rocker's eyes widened and he took a deep gulp of the amber liquid. "I don't see what business this is of yours. You may be the boss, but this is personal."

"The strix it is. Things are starting to move faster now and I need Maripa back at her job without all these idiotic distractions. I can't afford to have her wondering about what you think about her in some critical situation. One mistake at the wrong time could get us all killed." He refilled both of their tumblers, spilling even more in the attempt.

Rocker swallowed half of his drink in one quick gulp and, BANG! Slammed his glass back onto the table. "So, that's it. You don't really care about her, or me, or anybody. It's always just the mission and the plan. I've finally accepted the fact that you aren't going to use my research for some nefarious plot to take over the planet, but you're just a clone so maybe you can't really feel anything for others, at least not the way us non-clones do. But I'm flesh and blood, a TRUE Brin. I can't just ignore my feelings."

"Alright then, explain those feelings to me," said Karm, tightening his grip on his glass as he took another drink and topped off the glasses again.

"What do we really know about clones? Do they love or feel commitment to others the same as the rest of us? How long will they live? How resistant are they to disease? Can they mate with a true Bin and have children or are they sterile? You two are the only samples in existence. We don't know anything about your kind at all."

Karm leveled a steady glare at Rocker, as if measuring him. "Come now, Professor, you don't expect me to buy that, do you? You're too good a scientist for that to be what's really bothering you. Out with it! The truth this time!"

Rocker jumped out of his chair, knocking it to the floor behind him as he stalked off to the other side of the room. He stood shaking and silent before making his final decision. "Alright," he shouted. "If you really need to know…I'm afraid!"

Karm studied him a bit longer, then softened his tone and replied. "Afraid of what?"

"You know how she is," said Rocker waving his arms around him. "Always jumping out of one fire into another. She's already been shot once from what I've heard. What if she gets killed trying to protect one of us next time? How do I live with that? I don't know if I would survive another loss like that."

He gripped the edge of the sink and stared out the window into the dark night.

"What if she wakes up one morning and decides she is no longer interested in this little 'experiment' with a real person and leaves? How could I survive being rejected like that again?" He stopped suddenly and stared at Karm, his body shaking.

Karm reached out and gently placed his hand on Rocker's shoulder. "Your wife didn't reject you, Jontar. She died. There's nothing you could have done. Your research has saved hundreds of lives from a terrible disease, but it came just too late to save her. It's a horrible reality of medicine. You cannot keep condemning yourself for it."

"I should have worked harder. We were so close to the cure."

"Nobody could have worked harder. You may be the finest geneticist on the planet, but you're not omnipotent, Dr. Rocker. We both know your difficulties over her being a clone are just a cover-up for the real issue. You lost one love to disease. Do you want to lose another to ignorance and fear?"

Rocker covered his face with his hands and leaned on the table. "No, I don't."

Karm finished his drink and stood to leave. "Maybe you should consider that as well during your self-examination." He closed the door and left Rocker alone with his thoughts.

The sun was just starting to light up the horizon as he sat pondering this dilemma. Unable to settle his mind on the issue, he stood up and went upstairs to shower and dress for the day. At the mirror he noticed the gold ring hanging on the chain from his neck. He held the band in his fist for a moment, then removed the chain from around his neck. He laid the ring inside his top drawer, patted it gently, and slowly closed the drawer. He finished dressing and met Maripa at the waiting levicoach out front. She smiled as he walked up to her.

"Good morning. Sleep well?"

"Yep, the full four hours. Pretty good these days." He bent down to give her a kiss and got into the coach. "You're looking lovely today."

Maripa rolled her eyes and laughed as she got in behind him. Then she looked closely at him and noticed the missing necklace. "Did something happen last night?" She asked, pointing to his neck.

"Karm paid me a visit," he said, nodding his head. "He helped me come to grips with a few things I've been struggling with and I think I've come to some decisions… about us…and a great many other things. We need to talk."

She hesitated before continuing, knowing this was shaky territory. "I know you have been struggling with your feelings for me and the guilt over your wife's death. All your agitation over me being a clone was just a convenient excuse. I've been willing to wait for you to figure it out, but I was starting to worry about you." She patted his arm and waited as he gathered his thoughts.

"I need to exorcise some old ghosts before I commit to anything more. Can you be patient with me while I do this? He sighed and turned to face her. "It may take a while."

"I know, and yes. I believe you will work it out. At least Brach and Pareth are keeping their side of the bargain and have left us alone." She turned away to look out the window and sighed. "Just don't take forever. We really don't have much longer, you know."

Later that afternoon, Rocker visited the engineering labs to check on the progress of their latest designs for the miniaturized electrophoresis equipment. The lab was a typical engineer's playground. Several lab benches were scattered with electronic gizmos that flashed and made all kinds of noises. Other benches held robotic arms of various sizes and designs being tested to grab, lift, turn, drill, and virtually any other motion imaginable. One had to watch their step in the lab because of the various robotic vehicles skittering across the floor performing their intricate pirouettes.

Rocker scanned the room and located the lead engineer. "Nebitt, hello!" he called out as he crossed the room carefully, stepping over one of the maneuvering robotic carts. "Looks like you have a few new toys here to play with."

Dek Nebitt was monitoring one of the electronic devices, adjusting some dials to alter the read out, which Rocker saw only as lines on a wiggling graph. He quickly looked up and waved, but returned his focus to the screen and dials.

"I suppose you want to see the latest designs on your gel things?"

Rocker knew better than to correct Nebitt concerning the name of his equipment. He purposely said such things just to annoy others. It was one of the engineer's joys in life. Nebitt was a genius and had multiple advanced degrees in Chemistry, Physics, and Electronics. Engineering allowed him to put his genius to practical use. It was what he often referred to as "The only game worth playing."

"Yep. How are we on the Mark 5? Did you solve the connectivity issue?"

"We'll know in a minute," replied Nebitt. He set down his gadget and turned it off. "Let's go take a look." He led the way to another bench where other engineers were stationed. As usual Nebitt was frequently distracted and veered off in random directions to check on several other projects under way. "You can see the progress with our coolant system here," he said, adjusting a handle to reduce the cloud of vapor escaping from one of the containers. "Watch yourself here, that stuff is pretty cold."

"You've overcome the timeframe problem? We can keep the samples cold for the duration of the journey?"

"Absolutely!" Nebitt replied. "Solved that one a few days ago. I was going to send you a report today."

A loud whistle and a mechanical clang caused both men to jump. "Feathers and Quills! Not again!" cried Nebitt. "I thought we had it this time."

"Should I ask?"

"Just a problem with stabilizing the water purification system. As you know, we're trying to shrink it down another thirty percent. There's still a few technical glitches to work through, but nothing we can't handle." They watched as two other technicians ran over to the offending equipment and began flipping switches to turn off the mechanism.

After making inspections at a few other locations they finally arrived at their original destination. Nebitt approached one of the men at the bench and asked, "Are you finished testing the Mark 5 yet?"

"Just now, boss," said the man. "Everything looks good. Moving the connections to quadrant 4 solved the problem as we thought. We should be good to go on the final reduction now."

"That's great. How about the pressure tanks?"

Nebitt waved his arm indicating another corner of the lab. "Oh, we figured them out yesterday. We got them down to specs and they're holding just fine."

"Wonderful! Looks like we will make it after all. I should have known better than to worry. You are the miracle man."

"Tell that to Karm and get me a raise," replied Nebitt, "I could really use another lab and a dozen more engineers. "Oh, mutes!" he shouted. He took off running back to his bench and grabbed his machine, madly turning dials.

"Just send me the prototypes when they are ready for field testing," Rocker called out to Nebitt as he left the lab.

Rocker had to hurry. He was nearly late to his weekly briefing with Karm. At least the jog across the commons helped clear his head. He bounded up the stairs to the administrative offices and headed to the elevators. He reached the top floor and Karm's office with five minutes to spare.

"Welcome, Dr. Rocker. You're just in time." Karm waved him over to the mini bar and poured them both a cup of tea. "How's your work coming?"

"Just fine. We've solved the connectivity problem and the coolant tanks are ready for final trials. Those were the main difficulties left to overcome so we should be ready in plenty of time."

"Good…good. Exactly what I wanted to hear. Come over here and sit down." Karm led the way to the fireplace and sat on the sofa. Rocker followed and settled into the heavy chair. Karm pressed a button on the control panel in the arm of the sofa and Maripa entered through the connecting door to her office.

"Good afternoon, Jontar," she said as she handed Karm a folder.

"Hi, Maripa." The two exchanged smiles and then she turned to return to her office.

Karm smiled as he observed the not-so-subtle body language between the two of them and started to comment, but changed his mind and opened the folder instead. "Good news on all fronts. The ship is a week ahead of schedule and the collection of DNA is gaining steam across the globe." He tossed the folder down onto the sofa next to him and reached for his tea.

"I just had my DNA collected a couple of days ago," said Rocker. "I told them mine wouldn't be necessary since I was going to be on the ship in person, but they said something about wanting to use my DNA to help calibrate their system. I'm not an engineer, but that makes sense, I guess. The CAT scan surprised me though. Since when are scans part of DNA sample collection?" Rocker sipped at tea and watched Karm for any reaction.

Karm waved his hand as if brushing away flies in front of his face. "Just taking precautions, Doctor. We need to be sure we don't miss any genetic defects that could cause problems later on. The scan is set to look for flaws in the neuro-pathways indicating potential genetic diseases of the nervous system. It is an experimental device cooked up by one of the divisions so we are field testing it."

"Why wasn't I informed of this? I will want to see the specs on it as soon as possible."

"Of course, Doctor, I will have them sent to your office. No need to worry about it, though. It is a harmless procedure and we just want to see if it can be of any practical benefit."

"I still want to see the specs."

"You will have them on your desk tomorrow. Now, about those coolant tanks..."

Chapter Twenty-Two

The monarch had little time to indulge in falconry these days, but this particular morning he woke up with a complete apathy toward paper work and a burning desire for fresh air. He pulled the cord by his bedside summoning his seneschal.

"Yes, sire," said the servant upon entering the room. "How may I serve you this morning?"

"Cancel my morning appointments and have my Tal readied. Tell the royal falconer to meet me in the stables immediately after breakfast and tell the cook to prepare a traveling lunch for us."

"Shall I notify the Captain of the royal guard as well, Your Majesty?"

"Yes, but tell him to join me without any additional guards. I need to get away from all of this for a while. The last thing I want is a crowd of noisy guards blocking the view and scaring off any prey."

The servant bowed and left the royal bedchambers. Two hours later Brach was pounding through the forest on the back of his prized Tal, a large black animal specially bred for hunting. The beast covered miles of terrain without tiring, using long, powerful strides, claws on all four legs chopped at the hard-packed dirt of the path they followed. Its scales shone bright in the morning sun, golden eyes with the deep red vertical slit irises, a sign of champion breeding lines, flashing brightly as he ran.

"I had almost forgotten what this felt like," he said happily to the royal falconer who rode beside him. "I can almost feel the pressures melting away." Brach held a large hooded grey and black striped bird with a broad speckled tail on his heavily gloved left arm. "Let's see what we can stir up over the next rise." He spurred his mount into a lunging gallop, removed the hood and launched his raptor into the air. The Captain following behind at a discrete distance.

As they rode, Brach and the royal falconer discussed various techniques of training different species of birds of prey for the hunt, new trends in the sport, and pros and cons of different styles of equipment. The monarch particularly enjoyed the heated discussions of their preferred species of birds, and his own ideas for new breeding combinations, most of which the older, more traditional falconer discounted with something approaching derision.

As the morning drew on and approached the lunch hour the trio found a clearing to make camp and prepare lunch.

"A good hunt, Your Majesty," said the falconer. He pulled this morning's catches out of the sack he carried them in and laid them out on the grass.

"Yes," agreed Brach admiring the day's catch as he rubbed down his Tal. Six Blue-Frilled Smats, the four winged birds that migrated through this region every year, three Mot-Mots, a common yellow striped burrowing rodent with dark grey fur, and even one large Red-Tongued Grek, prized for its iridescent scales and savory meat.

"They'll make a fine supper for tonight." With great skill, he skinned and gutted the game, cutting off several small pieces for the falcons who had done the actual work.

As they sat eating their lunch, the Captain abruptly jumped to his feet and grabbed his sword. "Men approaching, Your Majesty."

"How many?"

"I count three, Your Majesty. Looks like the new Archbishop."

"Well, there goes a beautiful day," Brach sighed. He stood up and brushed off the grass sticking to his trousers and shirt, trying to make himself at least somewhat presentable.

The Archbishop arrived astride an only slightly less magnificent Tal, most likely bred from the same stock as those in the royal stables. He wore the red and gold colors appropriate to his station. Somehow, even the muted colors and simple fabric looked regal on the man. He always reveled in the ribbons and medals decorating the uniform he wore when he was known as The General, so he contrived to have the garments fitted in such a way that they displayed subtle refinements, yet conformed to the rules of The Faith.

"Good afternoon, Your Majesty," he said as he dismounted, handing the reins to his companion.

"Congratulations, Archbishop," he called out as his co-conspirator reigned in beside him under the trees. "I never doubted for a minute you could do this." They dismounted to stretch their legs and walk the animals a while. Come, tell me what our 'friends' in The Faith are up to."

"Thank you, Your Majesty. I think you will be pleased by what I have been able to learn."

Brach removed the hood from the bird of prey on his gloved hand and launched it into the air. "Tell me, then, are our partners in crime really behaving themselves after Karm's ultimatum?"

"For the most part they are, Your Majesty." The new Archbishop adjusted his riding habit and removed the golden skullcap signifying his rank. "Even with the majority in Parliament since the last elections they are too afraid of Karm. They definitely will not propose any legislation that interferes with his endeavors. They do keep discussing strategies for increasing the number of their followers on Karm's escape vessel. And there is still the matter of a small group of extremists within the organization trying to push for legislation outlawing cloning in any form, even organ replacement."

"Should we worry about them?"

"No, Your Majesty. We should probably keep a close watch on the young zealot named Crebot. He seems to be the most radical and outspoken of the group. But the Brothers have been able to curtail him so far."

"As long as they are still under control and just sit around discussing ideas we have nothing to worry about. We should speed up our own efforts to get our people on Karm's ship in greater numbers. Maybe we can..." The arrival of a messenger diverted his attention. The courier handed an envelope to the Captain of the guards, their only companion.

"Sire," the guardsman rode up beside them and reached out to hand Brach a sealed packet. "I am sorry to interrupt, but you told me to let you know as soon as the messenger you were expecting arrived."

"Send him over here right away." Brach said, examining the papers. "You probably want to see this, Archbishop. This might be just what we have been waiting for."

"Are you sure it is wise for this man to see us together, Your Majesty? What if word of the true purpose behind our hunts leaks out?"

"Don't worry, my friend. This is no mere messenger. He is one of my most secret agents and knows his life is forfeit is he reveals anything."

After looking through the stack of photos and other papers the messenger delivered, the monarch passed them over to The Archbishop. "Are you sure this is accurate?" he asked the messenger.

"Without a doubt, sire. My men have been using the new QK4300 system to recover the data and enhance the images from cameras surrounding the Universal Charity buildings. This is unquestionably what we suspected all along."

"Excellent. Leave these with me and go pick up your voucher from the seneschal before you return to your assignment." He picked up several of the papers and tossed them in the air. "We have him, General! We finally have him!"

"Is this who I think it is, Your Majesty?"

"Karm's mysterious young attendant caught in the act!" He whistled, summoning his falcon to return. Once the bird was safely hooded and tethered again the party returned to the palace. Once back in his quarters Brach summoned his seneschal. "Get Karm in here first thing in the morning." When the servant departed, Brach poured himself a large goblet of wine, sat behind his desk and smiled as he swirled the golden liquid in the glass. "Now it's my turn to make him squirm."

Chapter Twenty-Three

"His Majesty will see you now," the doorman said and stood beside the door that led into the monarch's most impressive reception hall.

The palace reception hall was a showcase for all of the trappings of royal status. Clear crystal cases displayed numerous jeweled ornaments worn only during the highest of ceremonial affairs. Grand portraits of the past seven hundred years of the royal lineage hung on the walls, appearing to judge all who passed before them. Tall windows of intricately designed colored glass depicted the great historical moments of the monarchy. Karm strode nonchalantly down the passage, apparently unimpressed by the show of opulence. Maripa followed close behind, watching warily for any sign of threat. A thick, heavily embroidered carpet muffled their footsteps. At the far end of the room sat the royal monarch on a tall back chair, reminiscent of the throne, behind a grand wooden desk, heavily carved with the symbols of his office, all raised on a two tiered marble dais. Two small simple chairs sat empty in front of the desk. Brach himself wore a military uniform with a deep green and gold-bordered sash showing off perfectly the multi-colored ribbons and jeweled badges displayed there.

He motioned for them to sit.

"What can I do for you, Your Majesty?" asked Karm.

"Do you remember the break-in and murder at Universal Charities a few years back? Terrible thing. One guard injured and another killed. All of their files sabotaged." He watched Maripa for any sign of nervousness, but she remained cool and reserved.

Karm rubbed his chin with two talons, his eyes searched the ceiling as he appeared to think. Maripa sat motionless. "I seem to recall something about it. But, as you said, it was a few years back."

"I think you should look at these." The monarch handed Karm a folder filled with papers and photographs.

One of the photos Karm examined showed images of Maripa pulling a man's body alongside the Universal Charities building. Another showed her on top of the roof next to the roof access door. The images were highly pixelated and dark, but her face was unmistakable. The papers provided time notations and code references linked to the various photos. Karm closed up the folder and placed it back onto the monarch's desk. He looked up at the monarch, but there was no defiance in his eyes.

"So now what?" Are you prepared to shut down our last hope for survival?"

"Nothing so dramatic, Karm. After all, since our scientists confirmed your findings I have no choice but to accept our fate. I do not, however, need to accept your choice of who travels on your rescue ship."

"What do you want, Brach?"

"It's really very simple. I want total control over the sixty members of the crew. I decide who goes and who stays behind." Brach placed both hands on the desk and leaned forward. His face was hard and his eyes cold.

"And just what is your plan? Have you let your brother, the Prior, in on your discovery?" Karm dropped his hands into his lap. His left palm glowed.

Brach smiled conspiratorially. "No, Karm, why don't we keep Pareth out of this for now. You and I are in agreement as to how dangerous too many members of his phony sect could be to this mission. So I want half of the crew to be my people. My name will top the list as will several of my family. The remaining half, other than a small handful of representatives of The Faith, will be the necessary scientists and technicians. You will supply me with the dossiers of your top people and I might even be persuaded to accept some of them." Brach paused for a moment and sat back, crossing his arms. "You, this young lady here, and your Dr. Rocker will definitely not be going anywhere."

"And what is to stop me from halting all work on the ship?"

Brach pointed at Maripa. "Any delays or falling behind schedule will result in this saboteur's immediate arrest, trial, and execution for murder. I will also expose your complicity in the matter ensuring that the public's trust in you vanishes." Maripa sat rigidly in her chair. Her face held under strict control. Her eyes bored straight into the monarch.

"You will allow my inspectors on site and they will have access to all of your data. Any interference or attempts at subterfuge and she suffers the same fate."

"We're going to all die anyway. What difference does it make if she, or any of us, die now or in a couple of years? You're going to have to give me more than this if you want my cooperation."

"And what will it take for you to play along?" The monarch's jaw stiffened, his crest bristling at the affront to his ultimatum.

"You need to agree that the three of us get on the ship."

Brach considered the options before him, then a cat-like grin grew as he extended his hand. "All right. If I allow you and your friends on board, I control the entire operation. Agreed?"

"Agreed. How do you intend to keep this from the Convocation?"

"You let me deal with them. They have been valuable pawns, but they are losing their usefulness lately. I am still the monarch here and even they are not immune from my royal decrees."

"So it was a scam after all? Another one of your political maneuverings?"

"As they will soon find out to their displeasure. I think this session is over. I will send my people in a few days. Be certain they are well informed and supplied. I will send for you if I need you again." He reached for the cord and summoned the seneschal.

Back in their coach Maripa finally spoke. "I fouled up. I not only got myself shot, but I endangered the entire operation." She sighed and turned to look out the window. "I trusted you, Karm. You told me you had them all under your control. I thought you could see their plots and protect us. Guess I was wrong."

"Don't be so melodramatic." Karm was smiling. "I am amazed that this took so long. I had to practically spoon feed them everything."

"What?" Maripa jerked upright and snapped to face Karm in the seat next to her. "You planned this? You wanted them to know what I did." Her jaw dropped.

"Of course. You don't think those cretins could actually outmaneuver me at this point, do you? Everything is going exactly as planned. I need them to feel in control so they won't snoop around too much." He reached out and took her chin in his hand, turning her face to his. "As long as they feel they have won, they won't be plotting anything too extreme. This was always part of the plan."

"All right," she said, raising her hands to rub her face, then turning again to stare out the window. "But remember, you're pushing the limits with all of us."

Chapter Twenty-Four

Two months later, Rocker decided he was ready for their talk. "Do you think Karm will give us a few days at The Citadel?"

Tilting her head, Maripa greeted him with one raised, questioning eyebrow. "Good morning to you, too, Dr. Rocker."

"Sorry, my thoughts are pretty scattered today. Good morning," he leaned over and gave her a hug and kiss. "What do you think? Can you get away? Is The Citadel booked for anything the next few days?"

"I don't think there would be a problem. What's going on?"

Rocker turned and held her small hands in his. "Not here. Talk to Karm and see if we can get out there tonight. We need to escape and be alone for the things I need to say."

Maripa felt a cold chill run up her spine and she shivered. "Is everything okay? You're making me nervous here."

"No, it's all good. I just think we need to talk in private and The Citadel is about the most secluded place in the world. Is that all right?"

"Fine, I'll play along. I can arrange it for the rest of the week. Have your bags packed and ready to go by six tonight."

"Good. See you then." Rocker gave her a quick kiss and jumped out of the levicoach as it stopped in front of his labs. He turned to wave as he entered the building and then disappeared inside.

Maripa raised her hand and touched the cheek where Rocker's lips had been. Her brows furrowed, her head tilted, as if trying to decide something. She exited the coach as it arrived in front of the executive building.

Later that day, Rocker left the lab early so he would have time to pack and prepare himself to finally vanquish the last of his demons. Maripa grabbed a quick bite to eat and packed her own bags before calling for a driver to take them to the airport. She had one last drink to settle her nerves.

"You sure everything is good between us?" she asked as Rocker climbed into the mag-lev. "You're killing me with all this secrecy."

"Absolutely. Don't worry. I just really want us to be alone when we talk." He put his arm around her shoulders and tried to reassure her.

When they landed on The Citadel's airfield Maripa saw a levicoach waiting for them. The mansion windows glowed warmly in the night and servants appeared at the door as they arrived. A dinner was prepared and ready for them in the smaller dining room often reserved for intimate meals. Their conversation remained on the safe topics, a recent Rings match, progress in the lab, the weather, anything to avoid what they both wanted most desperately to discuss; their current relationship status.

"Would you join me for a walk?" Rocker asked when they finished eating.

"It's a nice night. Why not?" She searched his face for some clue to the mystery of what he was thinking.

Rocker and Maripa walked along the path that led back into the woods along the stream. They paused in a small meadow, enjoyed the warm air, and watched as the full moon rose over the tree tops. "I want to apologize to you for being a first class quetzal," said Rocker as he looked up into the night sky. "I got so paralyzed by my own fears I ...I don't know how exactly to explain it, but every time I tried to talk with you, all I could think about was how hard it would be to lose somebody I cared about again. I know it was all in my head ..."

Rocker hung his head, shoulders slumped, hands stuffed inside his pockets, "I know you have every right to walk away, but can you ever forgive me?"

Maripa stopped and faced Rocker. "You hurt me, Jontar. You abandoned me when I needed you most. It's not easy to get over something like that. It took me a long time before I even felt comfortable being in the same room with you. But now I have come to grips with the situation and I think I can."

He turned his back to her as he spoke. "Her death nearly killed me and I didn't know if ...well, let's face it; your job here is not exactly the normal routine of a personal secretary. I guess I used the clone thing as an excuse and took it out on you."

She walked around to face him and looked into his down-turned eyes. "Tell me what you want to say."

He hesitated for a moment, arguing with his own thoughts, then with a deep sigh, made his decision. "I love you." He grabbed her hands and looked back into her eyes. "It took me far too long to finally…oh, feathers! Can you forgive me? Do you still want me?"

Maripa threw both arms around his neck, pulled him tight and kissed him, tears welling in her eyes, her heart pounding in her chest, nearly toppling both of them to the ground.

Breaking the kiss, Maripa gave him a straight right to the shoulder sending Rocker off balance. "You had me scared shitless!" she yelled at him. "I convinced myself you wanted to try to end it all between us. I wasted hours trying to come up with all sorts of arguments to convince you how wrong you were." She moved slowly into his arms and planted another long deep kiss lasting for several minutes, then stepping back, punched him in the shoulder. "Does that answer your stupid question?"

Rocker grabbed Maripa and lifted her off her feet in a bear hug, returning the kiss. They fell to the ground still in their embrace.

"I have been waiting for this for a long time, Jontar," she said as she gasped for air. "I do love you. I have for a long time now. I don't know what I would have done if you decided to leave me. I am a trained killer, you know."

They continued to kiss and slowly worked the buttons on each other's shirts. Rocker's hands gently explored her naked breasts. He leaned down and took her areoles into his mouth. His hands squeezed her to him. He reached down and pulled off her pants.

Maripa's crest ranged through an array of colors, mirroring her unfamiliar jumble of emotions. She shivered at his touch as she removed his trousers.

The two lovers reveled in each other as they became one. Their bodies intertwined and moved in harmony exchanging soft moans and expressions of love. Together, their bodies shook in a final expression of ecstasy and they settled into a quiet embrace.

"That was worth waiting for," Maripa said as she gazed into his eyes. Her fingers played in his crest which turned a deep blue. The cool night air washed over them, distant sounds of the night creatures echoed in the forest around them.

They spent the next few days at The Citadel exploring all of the ways the two lovers could enjoy the many different rooms of the mansion.

The time soon came, however, when they needed to return to the real world of the labs and their duties. When the plane landed back at the airport they saw Karm waiting for them standing by the coach.

"Welcome back," Karm said as they approached. "Just looking at the two of you I don't think I need to ask how things went." He smiled and shook Rocker's hand then placed his hand on Maripa's shoulder.

"Everything went just splendidly," Maripa said as she slid into the levicoach.

"So, you two solved your problem?"

She smiled at her surrogate father, taking one of his hands in hers. "Yes, we did. You don't have to worry about us any longer."

Karm gave Maripa a hug. "I never doubted you for a moment. I'm just glad everything worked out. I may be your boss, but I'm also your 'uncle' and, though it may not always seem like it, I do want you to be happy."

She simply smiled in response and took Rocker's hand.

Maripa suddenly wrinkled her brow and, with squinted eyes, turned to Karm. "Why are you meeting us out here at this late hour? Is everything alright?"

"Oh, yes, everything is just fine. You two aren't the only ones who can take time off now and then. I just flew in about a half hour ago and decided to wait for you to arrive and give you a ride home."

"Where did you go?" asked Rocker.

"Back out to the desert. I can completely get away from it all out there."

"How do you stand it? I would go crazy out in the middle of that miserable sand pit with nothing to do and no place to go. What's the attraction?"

"I enjoy the solitude. The land is beautiful."

"To each his own, I guess," replied Rocker and he turned his attention to Maripa.

His face took on its more normal stern and business-like demeanor as he changed the subject. "This may be a bad time to ask, but is everything ready for an inspection? The monarch sent a message telling us his team of inspectors will arrive here tomorrow morning. We want to impress them, but not allow them to see anything we don't intend for them to see."

"Everything should be fine, Karm," Maripa replied. "I've been anticipating an inspection for some time now and directed our people to set up the networks to hide anything of real importance. Fake files and menus are in place and populated with a heavy mix of reality and imagination. Security measures are set to prevent any intrusions, but without looking as if they are blocking anything. Some of the software the network people came up with is phenomenal. Far superior to anything the inspectors could possibly anticipate. Everything should look absolutely real to the monarch's men. I will check with my people as soon as we get back just as a final precaution."

"Excellent," Karm said, relaxing back into his seat.

Maripa turned her attention back to Rocker. "It's late. The labs are probably shutting down now so why don't we drop you off at home and I will join you for dinner after I check in with the office. It shouldn't take long."

They spent the night together for the first time without fears or doubts about their future. However long remained for them would be spent together.

The next morning, Karm waited in his office. He watched through his window as the inspection team arrived. "Time to begin the games," he muttered aloud while downing the last of his juice. "Let's see who blinks first." Grabbing another pastry, he went to the wall map of his empire and removed the gold pin from the Latonian Desert just as the intercom lit up.

"Your ten o'clock appointment is here, sir."

"Send them in, Kirta." He stood to greet the inspectors as the five of them walked in. Each was dressed in the latest business fashion and carried a briefcase.

"Welcome gentlemen. It's a pleasure to have you here. How would you like to proceed? We are at your service today." Karm shook their hands and directed them to waiting chairs.

"Thank you, Karm," said the lead man. "My name is Belcor. I have an agenda here that lists everything the monarch wishes us to see today."

Karm accepted the paper and read it carefully. "This is quite a lot for one day, gentlemen. We should probably get started." He pushed the intercom button on his phone again. "Kirta, send in the guides for our guests."

The door opened and in walked five more men dressed in somewhat more expensive, impeccably tailored suits. Each was wearing badges identifying them as GenCore security personnel.

Karm directed his attention to the guides. "Gentlemen, you are to answer any and all questions these men have for you. Please conduct them to wherever they wish to go and grant them access to anything they need. I have provided you with all the necessary passcodes and access cards. Withhold nothing, interfere with nothing. Do I make myself clear?"

"Yes, sir," each of the men replied in unison.

"I hope that is satisfactory," he said turning his attention to Belcor. "My staff is preparing lunch for you back in this office at 1:00 so you may ask me anything you want at that time. If you need me before then, simply tell your guide and I will be contacted immediately. Have a good day, gentlemen. I know you will find everything in order."

Karm shook their hands again and opened the door for them as they left. He returned to his desk and activated the monitors on the wall. Maripa entered through the door to her connecting office. She set her computer on one of the tables and started up the security scan programs.

"We can watch them and keep a record of everything they access from here," she said as she settled down into her cushioned chair. "The IT people are in the security office just in case anything needs to be fixed on the fly."

"Everything will be just fine. Just relax and enjoy the show." Karm settled back into his favorite chair, set his hands on top of his desk, and turned his left palm up as it began to glow.

***

The monarch bounced in his saddle as his Tal galloped over the top of the hill. The falcon hunts had proven to be highly successful as a means of conducting clandestine business with the former General. They could easily discuss matters far from prying ears and eyes. Their common interest in the hobby was well known and served well as a cover to disguise the true nature of their regular excursions.

After exchanging a few pleasantries Brach asked his entourage to leave them alone for a while to eat their lunch and discuss their secret agenda.

"How did the inspection go?" asked the Archbishop once the others departed to a reasonable distance. "Anything we can use to hang that arrogant quetzal with?"

"No, Your Grace, nothing at all. The inspectors report everything went smoothly. They were able to access everything we told them to look for. Our best people cannot find any discrepancies or faults with the information they brought back." The monarch sat down on the grass and stretched out his legs comfortably as he spoke. "It appears our 'friend' is cooperating. We will of course continue to watch him and send in surprise inspectors from time to time."

"I still don't trust the man," said the Archbishop as he continued to stand. He would never presume to sit next to his monarch on the ground, even if asked.

"Neither do I, my good man, but so far we have been unable to find anything wrong with any of his operations. We accessed thousands of terabytes of documents and data covering every aspect of his operations. Everything is exactly the way we expected. There were the usual tax issues and attempts to hide large corporate assets, which they wanted us to find. However, after some high level digging with our new decryption software we did locate a few concealed files leading us to some illegal title transfers involving several mining facilities and banking operations in the eastern province. The security people became most unhappy when we discovered those hidden attempts to deceive us."

The monarch grinned as he lay back to watch the clouds pass overhead. "I am sure they did not expect us to have access to such sophisticated technology. We will have to deal with Karm on this matter, certainly. Enough of this, though. How are things over at The Faith? Are our people keeping matters under control?"

"So far, Your Majesty. There are still a few hotheads wanting to publicly condemn Karm and announce to the world the new date of Armageddon, but The Convocation still seems to be on top of things."

The monarch's brow furrowed as he leaned toward the Archbishop. "Make sure they do. We can't afford to lose control to a bunch of idiotic fanatics at this stage of the game. If they gain the upper hand there's no telling how far the panic will spread. This is one area I think Karm underestimated: the capacity of the people to wreak havoc."

"I agree, Your Majesty. There would not be enough time for faith to overcome the terror. A terrified populace may not stop long enough to worry about their souls."

"Has the Convocation fully accepted you into their inner circles yet?"

"I am starting to gain some headway in that regard. The few who do not fully trust me yet are protesting on grounds of age and years of service. None of them suspect my true purpose there."

"I knew you were the right man for the job, Your Grace."

"There is one further matter, Sire. Your brother requests a personal audience."

"What does he want now?"

"He would not tell me his reasons, Sire, only to bring you this urgent request."

Brach sighed, scanning the skies for his falcon, but only heard its plaintive screeching reverberating off the hillsides. "Very well. Tell him I will receive him tomorrow morning."

***

"Don't think you have me fooled for a minute," Pareth said as he slid regally into his chair opposite Brach. His assistant remained standing by the door. "Your spy, The General, may have fooled some of my bishops, but did you really believe I would be deceived by this charade? Do you truly consider me such a dullard?"

Brach raised his hands in supplication, eyes wide in mock sincerity. "Not at all, dear brother. Nevertheless, I must have my little games. And you certainly have profited by the public's acceptance of his conversion, not to mention my own." He plucked a red berry from a bowl, wincing at its tartness as he bit into it.

"And that is the only reason I have put up with his presence in our order," Pareth said pointing a talon at Brach. "And, since I have been so understanding, I feel it is only right to expect some recompense for the inconveniences you and your spy have caused me."

Brach sat up straight, narrowing his eyes as he inspected his brown robed visitor. "Just what do you mean, 'recompense'?" his voice lowered dangerously.

"Oh, come now, brother. You know you cannot intimidate me. All I ask for is an increase of twenty-five percent to my share of the personnel onboard the ship, plus a guarantee that whatever new world we find will be ruled as a theocracy."

Brach laughed as he responded. "You can't be serious! What makes you think I would ever let you take the throne anywhere? Have you lost your mind?"

"Oh, you would still retain your position as monarch, but subject to my authority as the representative of The Eternal. Surely, you understand by now the power of my influence over the people. I thought I was being..."

"Have you gone mad? You don't believe in The Eternal any more than I do. I will not surrender the throne to the likes of you."

Pareth sighed and leaned back, folding his hands in his lap. "I thought not, but we did need a starting point for our negotiations, didn't we?"

"I wasn't aware we were negotiating anything. Now if you'll excuse me..."

"Sit down, brother. If we are to succeed in this little gamble to take control from Karm, we need to work together. And, since you have so obviously tried to deceive me, I require something to convince me you will not be so foolish in the future. We must have absolute trust in each other...or at least as much trust as we can both agree on." Pareth paused as he appeared to think over his demands. "It occurs to me, dear brother, you still do not understand the nature of true power and who controls it. Perhaps a small demonstration is required."

Pareth sighed, rose to his feet and strode nonchalantly to whisper in his assistant's ear. The man paled, but a look of ecstasy grew on his face. As Pareth returned to his seat, the man reached into a pocket, pulled out a small round case, opened it, removed a red capsule and swallowed it. Within seconds his eyes rolled back in his head, he began to spasm, and then dropped to the floor, lifeless eyes raised to the heavens.

Brach jumped to his feet and pulled the cord calling for his aides. "What have you done?" He sputtered in amazement, unable to turn away from the body. The door opened and he signaled for his servants to remove the inert figure.

"Merely a demonstration of true power, brother dear. I simply told him of a recent vision in which The Eternal called his name, showed me the place reserved for him, and told him it was his time to join The Eternal. Would your soldiers be so willing to do the same for you?"

The monarch, unable to find words, sat dumbly, finally turning his gaze back to his brother.

"Don't worry, though. I am willing to be reasonable about this. If you insist on resisting a complete rule by theocracy, then it occurs to me the planet is bound to have more than one continent. What would you say to sharing the new world?"

"You mean we each control our own continents?" Brach, emerging from his shock, stroked his chin as he considered the suggestion. "We would need a treaty on non-aggression between us. After all, it would be several generations before we could even begin to civilize an entire continent, much less a planet. Our descendants could deal with the issue in their own time. But, how do I know you won't be back in a month with more demands?"

"You don't," Pareth said rising from his chair, extending his hand. "For the same reasons I am compelled to trust that you won't send your soldiers to block us from boarding the ship at the last minute. I have taken precautions against that, by the way."

"What do you mean, precautions?"

"Now, Brach," chided the Prior, waggling a talon at his brother, "you don't suppose the Latonian peace treaty has been maintained through the military alone, do you? It really is amazing how tractable some fanatics can be when you take care to fill their souls along with their bellies. So long as we are in agreement that our shared enemy is Karm and we must work together to remove him from the equation as soon as possible."

Brach hesitated, deeply troubled about how he could have so greatly misjudged his sibling's ruthlessness. When at last he pulled his mind out of its depths, he stood and extended a hand to his brother. "Agreed."

Chapter Twenty-Five

Karm enjoyed his dinner as he watched the snow falling outside his window. The first snow of the season always signaled a special treat for him. *Time to dig out the winter waders and fingerless mittens. Those fish are getting hungry now.* His fingers twitched at the thought of a wet line humming through his reel with a hooked trout on the other end. *I hope our trout DNA takes to the water of the new world. I can't imagine...*

"What the...?" The alarm tingled through his left arm as a holographic image appeared of a young cleric, robed in purple, standing on the steps of The Faith's central church. The man, Karm recognized him as Crebot, was gesturing at a crowd gathering in the plaza before him, visibly angry at the reporter shoving a microphone in his face.

"Yes, you heard me! You only have eight years to save your souls and join The Eternal when our world ends." The young cleric's eyes were wild and his voice trembled with righteousness as he shouted into the camera. "You are listening to lies and heresies. Your worldly leaders have kept the truth from you. Only by renouncing them and joining with us can you be saved." He returned his icy glare to the reporter. "You and your smug condemnation of our teachings will be the first to suffer the wrath of The Eternal. You mock our beliefs, but have none of your own. Well, hear me now. This world is about to die and all of you with it. Heed my warning and tend to your souls or perish for all eternity."

Karm was on his video phone and in direct contact with the Prior of The Faith within seconds. "What the strix happened? What do you think you are doing letting that idiot expose us all?" *And how did he evade my mind probe?* He watched the image in his hologram as other ministers tried to grab the young fanatic's arms and take him away from the cameras. Pareth, the Prior, disheveled and his eyes bleary, came into focus on the video screen.

"I don't know, Karm. We certainly did not authorize this. Crebot has always been a lead figure among the more fundamentalist clerics, but we have been watching him carefully. I already sent some of the Brothers to bring him in."

"I will be there as soon as possible. Get the fool in seclusion and shut him up until we can determine the extent of the damages." Karm punched the off button. "Kak!" He growled out loud to himself, pounding a fist on his desk in frustration. "How did this happen?" He held out his palm, waited for the faint glow, and ordered a system check of all the brain wave monitor links. Within seconds, the change to a green hue indicated all connections were still in effect and at full strength.

The phone lit up on all lines. Karm hit the monarch's line and watched as Brach's image appeared on screen.

"What's happening, Karm? Have you seen what some insane extremist is doing on camera?" The monarch pointed at a view screen behind him showing the chaotic scene as he spoke. "I just spoke to Lerit, or Pareth, or whatever the damnation he calls himself, and he claims to have no knowledge of what happened."

"Calm down, Brach. I spoke to the Prior, too. I'm going over there right now. You probably will want to join us. We need to coordinate our efforts to squash this as quickly and permanently as possible." He hung up on the monarch and called Maripa's line.

He swore into the phone as soon as he heard her pick up. "Have you seen what this religious fanatic is doing on the news?"

"Yes, sir. Who let him get in front of a news camera?"

"I don't know, but we are going to find out. Be ready in five minutes." Karm hit the off button and disconnected all of his lines. At that moment, the door burst open and Dr. Rocker ran into the room, breathless and sweating, stopping in mid thought as he saw Karm's dark visage behind the desk.

"Not now, Jontar. I have an emergency to deal with."

"I was going to ask if you saw Crebot on the monitors, but I can see you did. I need to talk to you about him." He moved, still breathing heavily, to pour himself a glass of water, drank it in one gulp, refilled the glass and sat heavily into the chair opposite Karm.

"You know this down-headed fool?" Karm asked, his brows raised in surprise.

"He was a former graduate student of mine at the university. Brilliant, but unstable, always reaching beyond acceptable limits of his research when he believed he knew what was right."

Karm leaned forward, focused, concerned. "You say he is unstable?"

"He was always trying to discover what he considered to be 'Truth'. The chancellors eventually had to remove him from the program when his research went far beyond the parameters he was given. Years later, I saw him standing on a street corner addressing a small crowd. When he recognized me, he berated me for my 'misplaced faith in science' and how we all needed to 'seek the truth in The Eternal'. To me, at least, he seemed to have lost himself in some sort of religious conversion fervor."

"So he is nothing more than a fanatic?"

Rocker frowned, placing both hands on Karm's desk as he leaned in. "No, far from it. He had a brilliant mind, one of the best I had ever worked with, and knows many of the details of my theories on cloning. He could be very dangerous if he is under control of The Faith and has turned his genius against us."

Karm clenched some papers in his fist and snarled. "I'm going to have them all filleted and served up on a platter!" He stormed out of his office and down to a waiting levicoach.

The lower levels of the Church of The Faith were dark and damp. The foundation, being built from large blocks of basalt, gave the appearance and feel of a medieval dungeon straight out of the movies. An elder escorted Karm and Maripa down to the third level. At the end of a long chilly hallway stood a heavy wooden door with two palace guards blocking their path. They raised their energy rifles as the group approached.

The elder raised his hands. "We are expected."

The guards unlocked the door and admitted them. The glare of a single bare bulb hanging by its cord from the ceiling dimly lit the small room. A table stood in the center of the small cell. Karm barely recognized the skeletal young man seated at the table. Disrobed and wearing only his loose undergarments, Crebot was haggard, but still defiant. He sat alone on one side of the table with another guard standing behind him. He scowled and his unblinking eyes stared at the Prior and the monarch who sat across from him. An empty chair waited for Karm.

"Alright," Karm said as he took the chair. "What have you learned so far?" Maripa stood to one side of the table and watched the zealot closely.

The Prior spoke first. "It appears this young fool simply lost his temper at a reporter and let his religious fervor get the better of him. The reporter is a well-known agnostic and critic of our beliefs and he was attempting to goad him into a reaction he could use on the evening broadcast."

"So this was a spontaneous outburst? Not something planned or pre-determined?" Karm rubbed his left forearm absently. *Certainly explains how he evaded my mind monitors.*

"It would appear so," said the monarch. "He simply lost his temper and his ardent radicalism took over what few brains he initially possessed."

The extremist raised his head and glared at each of them. "You still think you can manipulate the truth? The Eternal cannot be controlled or hidden. His truth will always be known."

"Silence, Crebot," commanded the Prior. "You will speak only when told to speak. You are defrocked and no longer hold any authority here."

"My authority comes from The Eternal, not from anyone on this world. I speak His Truth." Crebot raised his hand and pointed in judgment at the others in the room. "I am not concerned with your secrets. The souls of the people are my province. The Eternal commands that we bring all souls to Him and in this I shall not fail. Your dealings in worldly matters corrupt you and condemned you to damnation. Your plan to deliver soulless abominations to a holy new world proclaims your departure from His glorious teachings."

The young man rose to his feet, every limb trembling with the effort. He reached inside his shirt and scratched himself nervously. Maripa was suddenly alert, watching the deranged youth for the slightest sign danger.

"The Eternal has spoken to me. He tells me of your treasons and your plots against Him. He instructs me in the ways of His new church, which I am destined to lead."

"This man has obviously lost his mind," said the monarch. "Guard, return him to his seat and keep him quiet."

The guard stepped forward and placed one hand on the trembling fanatic's shoulder. Crebot screamed and struck the guard in the chest with a long thin knife he had kept hidden under his clothing. Blood sprayed and covered both of the men in red splotches. He yanked the blade free and turned to face the three leaders across from him. In an instant, Maripa sprang into action.

"Now you all will pay the price for your—."The rest of the sentence died in his throat as Maripa landed on him. She had leaped onto the table and bounded high above the others in the room. Her heel crushed heavily into Crebot's temple sending him flying backwards. Before he could recover, she grabbed the knife from his hand and thrust it into his neck severing the arteries. With another kick she sent the dying man flying into the wall. He collapsed gurgling into a pool of his own blood. She stood over the body for a moment to be sure he was dead, then turned to face the others. The two guards from the hallway burst into the room brandishing their weapons.

She glared at the men around the table. "Didn't any of you think to search him?"

"Weapons of any kind are forbidden," said the Prior. "He should not have had a knife. Ours is a faith of peace."

"Maybe you ought to investigate compliance with your doctrines a bit more closely, Prior," said the monarch. "We wouldn't want to take a chance Crebot had recruited others to his holy cause."

"We will certainly be more cautious in the future," said the Prior. He faced Maripa for the first time. "I want to thank you, young lady, for saving our lives. The Eternal certainly provided you with some useful gifts."

"You're welcome, but your Eternal had nothing to do with it. I was protecting Karm. Saving you and the monarch was an unfortunate byproduct."

"That's enough, Maripa," said Karm. "We don't need to make any more enemies than we already have. Why don't you go get yourself cleaned up?"

"Yes, sir," She followed the guards out of the room as they removed Crebot's body.

Karm, Brach, and the Prior sat quietly at the table.

After a brief moment to gather his thoughts, Karm stood and paced the room. "We need to assess the damage and take immediate measures to quell any thoughts that Crebot was rational or even remotely plausible. We cannot leave anyone to wonder if what he said bore any measure of truth to it. What are our best options?"

Brach sat upright as he regained his composure. "I can call in the media and state unequivocally there is no value in the claims he made to that reporter. Our best scientists will back me up and denounce everything supporting his statements. People must believe he was no more than a raving lunatic."

The Prior joined in. "I can tell our followers the poor man had been given too many responsibilities and he suffered a nervous breakdown. I'll use the fact that he was a well-known zealot against him. We can blame his rants on dementia intensifying his fears to the point where he became delusional. The press release can state he is recovering from his illness secluded in a remote monastery. His few followers will be dispersed to a monastic life where vows of silence and isolation in some very small locked cells will keep them from ever communicating with anyone in the foreseeable future."

Karm thought for a moment before speaking. "Agreed. And I think it would be best if I played no role at all in any of this. My position is too well known and might be construed as suspect. I don't want any rumors of collusion developing so I need to be out of the public eye on this one."

"One more thing," said the monarch. "I think we need to reevaluate our launch date. Given this new development I am not so sure we can keep everything under wraps for another three years. We need to launch by the end of next year."

Karm ran the talons of one hand through his crest, shaking his head. "Impossible. We are already on double shifts to meet the current deadlines. I don't have enough people to move the date up so far."

"Find them. I am not asking you, I'm ordering you. As an incentive I will allow you to provide a small number of your people with credentials as crewmembers, but only on the provision you can launch before the end of next year. I don't think we can keep the lid on this any longer."

Considering his options, Karm stopped his pacing and faced the monarch and his brother. "I'm going to need some sort of cover story to hide the reason for the sudden increase in manpower I'll be taking on. Thousands of new employees are certain to raise a few questions out there."

The monarch smiled and winked at Karm. "You're a very creative man. I'm sure you'll come up with something. Are we in agreement?"

"I want those credentials on my desk tomorrow if I am going to go along with this."

"Absolutely. First thing in the morning. Do we all agree on our cover story for why we are all headed into space?"

"Yes, yes," Karm replied. "As far as my staff and the press are concerned, this is just a publicity stunt to promote a new alternative to regular flights around the planet. A rocket large enough to take passengers up into orbit and land safely on the other side of the world in only a matter of an hour or so will revolutionize the airline industry. You and the Prior are going on the inaugural flight to emphasize the safety and reliability of the rocket.

Pareth took over the narrative. "Then a computer malfunction will prevent us from shutting down the engines so we are hurtled out into space. A tragic accident, certain to cause an upheaval, but not the worldwide panic any knowledge of our true mission would cause."

Brach nodded in agreement as he turned to address Karm. "Excellent. You can tell the press how construction and testing exceeded your expectations and you are ready to proceed ahead of schedule. The 'accident' will explain why we don't return."

"Alright then, let's get going. We all have a very busy day ahead of us."

The three men stood to leave, but Pareth grabbed his brother's sleeve. "Pardon me, Your Majesty. Might I have a moment? We should probably coordinate the timing of our broadcasts."

"Certainly, Your Grace. Until next time, Karm."

Karm left the room. Before the doors closed he noticed the two leaders deep in conversation.

"You should have discussed your plan to offer him additional credentials, Your Majesty. A quarter of the passengers belong to me. Do you intend giving up some of your seats to them?"

"I have no intention of giving up anything, Your Grace. I had to offer him something to get him to agree to the new launch date. We will ensure he and his friends miss their boarding time when it comes."

The Prior lowered his voice and held up a single finger in warning. "It occurs to me I will need to be extra vigilant to ensure none of my flock misses their departure times. I don't mean to appear lacking in faith, but prudence demands I take steps to protect their interests."

"You are welcome to take whatever steps you deem necessary," said the monarch. "Karm is our common enemy here. He would love us to tear each other apart in mutual distrust. I assure you, neither you nor your flock have anything to fear from me."

"This is good to hear, Your Majesty. Just the same, I will be cautious." The Prior stood and gestured toward the closed door. "After you, Your Majesty."

The next day, Karm monitored the news broadcasts on the screens across from his desk. The monarch was speaking on the main network channels.

"… and I guarantee you, all the ravings of the poor deranged individual have not even a speck of truth in them. The man was suffering from delusions and hearing voices. The Prior informs me he is currently being treated at an undisclosed location by members of his order."

The reporter turned his attention to the scientists who sat alongside the monarch. "Can you gentlemen spread any light on some of the claims the cleric made about the sun?"

"Rest assured there is absolutely no truth to his claims," said the scientist seated next to the monarch. "Every astronomer on the planet has been monitoring the sun for the past decade. Not one single bit of data suggests anything other than what we are telling you. The sun will continue to degrade and it will eventually go nova, but not for another one hundred years, at least. There is more than enough time to work on solutions. Nobody alive today or in the near future needs to fear being swallowed up by an exploding star."

"What about the claims of Dr. Bladett confirming what was said yesterday?"

Brach leaned into his microphone as he responded. "Dr. Bladett is an old and respected member of the scientific community, but he is retired and no longer privy to the most accurate information. His connections to The Faith and its most radical factions contribute to his misinterpretation of the old data he still works with." He raised his hands to quiet the reporters. "All of the data will be released and you all will have free access to our best scientists. I hope our transparency in this matter will quiet any concerns that have unfortunately arisen as a result of the ravings of one individual. I guarantee all of you are safe for the duration of your lifetime. Dyan'ta will continue to remain safe for the lives of your children." He stood and left the table. The scientists remained to continue answering questions.

Karm turned off his monitors and took a long drink. He stared at the ceiling for a moment before reaching for the phone.

Activate secure line and his palm glowed. When he heard the line change tones he punched lines three, five, and nine together.

"Yes, sir?"

"We need to step up production. Can everything be ready a year from now?"

"No problem, sir. We are well ahead of schedule so there is no problem kicking it up a notch. I'll send you the adjusted schedule and supply requirements in a couple of days."

"Very good. Proceed as usual." *Deactivate secure line* and the glow in his palm faded.

***

Maripa awoke warm and naked under the heavy blankets of the room she shared with Rocker whenever they could escape. She stretched and turned over, reaching for her lover only to discover his absence. A crash of metal resounded up from the lower floor. "Oh, no," she sighed. "He's trying to cook again. I've got to tell him the truth before he poisons us." Groaning, she grabbed her robe and headed down to the kitchen, the smell of burnt smat eggs and grek sausage rising to meet her on the stairs.

"There are reasons why we have cooks and other servants here," she reminded Rocker again. "As much as I appreciate the effort, you don't really have to do this." She walked barefoot over the tiled floor and embraced him tightly, standing on her toes to kiss him good morning.

"I know," he said once she released him and he could breathe again. "I wanted to surprise you with something new I came up with for breakfast. You might actually like this one." He smiled down at her and kissed her again before turning back to the cabinets.

"Oh, no, you don't," she said, grabbing him by the hand and pulling him out of the kitchen. "I hate to tell you this, but you can't cook. Let the chef do his job."

"Now you're starting to sound just like Betha. She didn't like my cooking either."

Maripa felt her stomach lurch a bit. "I'm sorry, Jontar… I didn't mean to…"

"Hush!" he said, pulling her into his arms. "I'm okay with that now. She will always hold a special place in my heart, but I know she approves of us…and I love you."

Maripa's heart soared and she sunk even deeper into his embrace. "I love you, too, Jontar."

The air was cold, but the sun shone bright orange in the sky as they strolled the grounds that afternoon. The snow crunched under their feet, their breath formed clouds before them as they walked.

Taking Maripa's hand, Rocker stared off into the woods, not really noticing any of the beauty. "Do you really believe Karm can pull this off?"

Maripa hesitated for only the briefest moment before responding. "Without a doubt. I've known him my entire life and he has never once failed to accomplish what he set out to do."

"Even with the secrets he still hides from us?"

"Listen to me." She stopped and took both of his gloved hands in hers. "I trust him with every fiber in my body. I may not like his secrets any more than you do, but I know he has his reasons."

"The timeline and all that?"

"I'm not saying I understand it all, but he has managed to stay two steps ahead of everyone else all this time. I believe him even if I don't understand him."

Rocker thought about this and then came to his decision. "The scientist in me has a hard time accepting his claims of time travel and aliens, but he does seem to genuinely care about saving all of us." He stepped closer to Maripa, searching for something in her eyes. "Okay, if you trust him, then I'm all in, too. For better or worse."

Chapter Twenty-Six

"Are you sure this is the wisest move?" asked the Archbishop. "There are only a few months left before we launch. Karm is not causing any difficulties now that we are in control. Siege tactics might be more prudent than an attack at this time."

"No. I mean to squash Karm, not just control him. He has been a thorn in my side for far too long and I cannot escape the feeling that he is taking his defeat too calmly." The monarch shoved the food on his plate around with his fork as he spoke. The reports he read sat open beside him. He was feeling petulant. With so much at stake now, he could no longer afford to escape on another falcon hunt. Staying on top of Karm's maneuverings and keeping Pareth at bay trapped him in the palace. He missed the fresh air and relief from the constant pressures of the office.

The Archbishop set down his utensil and folded his hands on the table. "You have already won, Sire. There is no need for this show of force. Karm will never board the ship, so he will perish here with everyone else. This attempt may only serve to renew his determination to regain some measure of control. Who knows what trouble he might cause if he is pushed too far?"

"No. I will show him what true power is. He will know he lost and it was I who destroyed him. I want to see the look of defeat in his eyes before we leave this world. Now, go set your men to their task at the mines. I want this operation underway before the day is over."

"Very well, Your Majesty. As you command." He pushed his chair back, bowed to the monarch, and left the room.

Back at The Citadel a few days later Karm, Rocker, and Maripa enjoyed a rare weekend together. Karm rose early and sorted through his fly boxes as he finished breakfast.

"Off to try and catch your finned adversary again, Karm?" Rocker shuffled into the study and grabbed a cup of narl tea from the buffet table.

"What else? Who knows how many opportunities I have left? Time is growing short and we don't have any more free weekends as the launch approaches. I mean to get that quetzal of a fish before we go."

"Good Luck. Don't forget our lunch date in town later."

"I won't. By the way, I want you to keep an eye on Brach and the Archbishop." Karm held up his left hand and scratched at his palm. "I've been getting some indications that they might be up to something, but I can't quite pinpoint anything specific, yet. Brach has been raging for a few days now, which usually means he is up to some sort of mischief."

"Alright. I'll tell Maripa you want her to look into it. We'll let you know what she finds at lunch. She should be getting up soon."

"Alright. See you then." Karm grabbed his vest and rod, and then clomped out the back door wearing his waders.

An hour later, Maripa joined Rocker in the study. She was dressed in jeans, t-shirt, and a light sweater, crest feathers not yet preened. Her bare feet silently crossed the polished stone floor. She grunted as she sat in one of the upholstered chairs near the fireplace.

"Good Morning," Rocker said as he poured her some narl tea. He handed her the mug and kissed her lightly on the top of her head.

"Not until at least my second cup," she mumbled, sipping at the steaming brew.

One of the servants entered the room and placed a pile of papers on the table next to Maripa. "The morning reports, ma'am."

Maripa muttered a barely audible, "Mm...Hmmm...thanks," and sorted through the stack as she drank.

"Anything important?" Rocker joined her by the fireplace with a plate of smat eggs, grek bacon and sausage, and fruit from the assortment left by the cooks.

"Nothing out of the ordinary. Wait, here is something from one of the mining facilities up north. Someone out there is stirring up the miners, causing some strikes and a few delays to their deliveries."

"You don't sound too worried about it," Rocker said as he gnawed absently on some bacon.

"Not really. Nothing more than a few days, a week or two at most in delays to our time table. I'll send some people down there to settle the matter and we should be fine. Maybe only a short delay to the launch date. Nothing really." She finished her mug in a quick gulp and hoisted herself up out of the chair to get another.

"Karm was worried that The monarch might be up to something. We should let him know about this."

"Maybe. But right now I need to go for a run. Want to come along?" She stood and stretched her arms toward the ceiling.

"Sure. I could go for chasing you around in the woods again. Who knows? Maybe I'll catch you today."

Maripa smiled, pecked him on the cheek, and gave him a sly wink. "You can always try. I suppose there's a first time for everything."

It was one o'clock by the time Karm showed up to their lunch meeting. He still wore the waders and vest, with his fishing rod in one hand. He pulled up an empty chair to join them at the table in the sidewalk café. A waiter took their order and left a pitcher of water on the table.

Noticing the empty fish bag, Rocker couldn't resist provoking the old angler. "No luck today?"

"Not a nibble," Karm said, frowning as he scratched at his left palm again. "This darn thing kept distracting me all morning, but all I keep getting is Brach's anger. He is so focused on me and because of his hatred, I can't get a clear handle on his ultimate plan." He poured himself a glass of water and turned to Maripa. "What did you find?"

Maripa took another bite of her fruit as she gave her report. "Nothing out of the ordinary. At least nothing of any significance. The only thing going on is some disturbance at one of the northern mining facilities."

Karm bolted upright and his jaw dropped open, his eyes lost focus as if his mind was in some far off world. An angry red glow lit his palm. "What sort of disturbance? What mines?"

Maripa's eyes narrowed and she handed Karm the notices. "Some clerics are stirring up the workers at one of the copper mines, causing some strikes and other slight delays, but nothing too serious. I already sent a group down there to handle the matter. There shouldn't be any more than a day or two delay to the launch."

"That down-head! What does that mutes-brained quetzal think he is doing?" Karm jumped up and ran to the waiting levicoach. Rocker and Maripa ran after him and barely seated themselves before it took off.

Maripa sat across from Karm in the coach. "What's the matter, Karm? What's so important about some remote copper mine? What are you keeping from us this time?"

"That mine is a critical focal point in our timeline. We cannot allow Brach to interfere there. The repercussions could be catastrophic. This could destroy everything we have worked for," Karm clenched the report in his fist.

"Rocker sat next to Maripa and shook his head. "It's only a day or two at the most, Karm. We still have plenty of time to launch and escape."

Karm turned his anger on the scientist. "No. We don't have any time to spare at all. You just don't understand. Everything is proceeding according to a pre-determined and precise time schedule." He punctuated each point with sharp gestures as if stacking the events in order. "It all has to happen exactly as it did before. Any alterations or delays, even for a few hours could cause irreparable damage to the timeline and set everything to total chaos. Brach thinks he is showing me once and for all who is in charge, the feather fluffed idiot. In reality, he's unwittingly setting in motion events I may not be able to salvage." For the remainder of their journey, Karm sat rigidly staring out the window, occasionally erupting with vile epithets directed at the monarchs intelligence and heritage.

As soon as the levicoach arrived back at The Citadel, Karm jumped out and ran to his office. He hit the button for The monarch's private line and tried to remove his waders and vest while he waited for Brach to pick up.

"What in The Eternal's name do you think you are doing?" shouted Karm as soon as he heard the monarch's voice. "What could you possibly hope to accomplish by such childish games as a miners' strike?"

The monarch paused before he responded. His image in the view screen showed him sitting at his desk, smiling. "Ah, Karm. I see you received my message."

"Your message? Is that what this is all about? You're still obsessed with who's in control here? Is this nothing more than a game of power to you?"

"Yes, Karm. That is all anything is ever about. Power and who controls it. I wanted you to know once and for all your smug self-assurance and money are useless when those with real power choose to utilize it. I want you to understand I am in charge of the situation here, not you. I control the populace and the resources you need for your so-called empire. I want you to realize I can cut you off any time I choose. This is power, Karm. For now, my point has been made with just a small demonstration at one mine. Tomorrow, it could be hundreds of mines or factories. I could bring this entire project to its knees with just a few simple commands."

Karm stared at The monarch's image and slumped back into his chair. "You have no idea what you are doing, Brach. This is no contest of power. A contest would require that both sides have a reasonable chance of winning. You are completely out of your league here. Stop now before you force my hand. I cannot allow this action to continue."

The monarch's eyes widened in surprise at Karm's continued defiance. "You cannot allow? You are defeated, Karm. None of your bullying or posturing will help you now. Surrender and I may see fit to allow the workers to return to their jobs in a few days. The launch will happen, but according to my schedule, not yours."

"A few days is unacceptable, Brach." He sat up and stared directly into the eyes of The monarch's image. "The launch must take place as planned. If you persist in this you force me to take measures I have no wish to take. Thousands of lives are at stake here, Brach. Stop now before you learn what true power is."

The monarch shifted his glance a bit, but then returned his gaze to his monitor. "Forget it, Karm. No empty threats will help you now. You have until tonight to submit."

Karm closed his eyes, and sunk back into his chair. "You give me no choice, then. Contact your bevy at those mines and see what they tell you. Call me tomorrow if you want to discuss power again." He hit the off switch and The monarch's image vanished.

Karm tapped another button on his phone and activated the security features of his biocomputer. His left hand glowed red. "I am sending you the coordinates now," he told the voice on the other end of the line. "Launch the missiles immediately." He hung up and his palm returned to normal. Karm went to his liquor cabinet and poured himself a tall drink from the first bottle he saw and downed it in one long gulp. He then collapsed into a nearby chair and called for Maripa and Rocker to join him. *They'll hate me for this, but I had no choice.* He poured another drink and downed it just as quickly as the first. *How much longer before I can just disappear and no longer be such a monster?*

Karm sat with Maripa and Rocker in his office as they watched the wall of monitors relaying news of the disaster. The evening news broadcasted the breaking story of the catastrophe at the mines.

"Thirty-three thousand dead," reported the man on one of the video screens in Karm's office.

"Apparently the result of a military accident. Some sort of missile test gone horribly wrong," said the journalist on another screen.

"All attempts to reach the palace for comment have gone unanswered so far," said another reporter on another display.

"He left me with no choice," Karm said as he hit the remote control and turned off the monitors. "I cannot allow any delays. Not at this late date. New workers will arrive in the morning and production will be brought back on schedule by tomorrow evening."

"Thousands of innocents!" Maripa, wiping tears from her cheeks, could not bring herself to turn away from the grizzly scenes on the monitors. "Why? Just to show The monarch you were still in control? I've killed before, but only when there was no other recourse. I would never have believed you capable of such horrors."

"Do you honestly believe I wanted this? You still don't understand." Karm downed another in a long succession of drinks. "Our entire future hangs by a thread. By sacrificing those few, millions more will live. If I had done nothing, everyone on the planet would die. The future timeline must be maintained no matter what the cost."

"The future? All I can see is more secrets. You still won't let us in. And yet you still demand our trust in you. It doesn't work this way. How can we help if you won't tell us your plans?" Tears streamed down her face as she turned to face him.

"There is no other way. This is my burden and mine alone. I accepted this task with all it implied. You can either accept the fact or not. I will continue to do what I must."

Rocker stood and approached Maripa, placing his arm around her shoulder. "You know we will not desert you, Karm, but you need to know you have severely damaged our faith in you. You have just committed an atrocity, even if it was for some greater good in your view. Until you are willing to include us in this view of yours, we cannot condone or even understand what you have done."

They turned and left Karm alone in his office. In the darkness, Karm picked up the remote again and turned on the monitors. He took another long drink as he watched the reports of his destruction.

Chapter Twenty-Seven

The orange sun rose bright in the clear morning sky. Karm stood looking out his window at The Citadel, already dressed in his waders and vest. *Go ahead and do your worst now, you big ball of gas. We beat you. We are going to survive your assassination plans.* He stuck out his tongue and flicked it with the second talon of his right hand in defiance at the dying star, then clomped downstairs to eat some breakfast. He grabbed the sack with his usual hard-boiled smat egg, slice of grek ham and carton of hodak milk from the kitchen table. The butler handed him his rod and hat as headed toward his favorite spot along the stream.

"Send the others down to pick me up when they arrive," he called back over his shoulder and bounded down the steps.

On the flight to The Citadel, Maripa snuggled next to Rocker as they looked out the window at the world passing below them. "Will the new planet be as beautiful?"

"We can't say exactly what it looks like, but it will be livable. Everything we have been able to gather tells us there must be plant life of some sort. An oxygen atmosphere would require that. The temperature ranges indicate a dynamic ecosystem with enough liquid water to moderate any real extremes—"

Maripa jabbed her elbow into his side. "You down-head. You may be one of the smartest people on the planet, but sometimes you can be so dense." She wormed her way closer to him, pulling his arm around her. "Just tell me everything will be alright."

"Our new home will be beautiful, just like you." He held her tight, delighting in her warmth and the scent of her crest.

The plane landed and taxied to the waiting levicoach. The staff removed their luggage and stored it in the vehicle's trunk before they set foot on the tarmac. The Citadel shone bright in the morning sun. The trees had shed their leaves long ago and the grass had turned to a dormant brown for the winter. There was a stark beauty to the sight.

"Is he down at the river?"

The driver laughed. "Where else, sir? He wants us to retrieve him there and head directly to the launch pad."

Maripa rolled her eyes skyward. "Well let's hope he caught a few this morning. He'd just fuss all the way into space if he had to leave without at least one."

They found Karm in his usual spot by the deep pool. His rod bent sharply and he frantically pulled in the line. They heard him laughing and reveling in his triumph as they exited the coach.

Rocker cupped one hand beside his mouth as he called out. "Looks like a big one!"

"The son of an old quetzal who always taunted me!" Karm shouted back as he played out some line. "I may never have caught him, but I got his offspring!"

Just as Karm reached out to land the silvery beast in his net, the creature gave one last burst of desperation and snapped the line. Karm lost his balance and fell waist deep into the stream.

"Kak!" Karm yelled as he slammed his rod into the water. He struggled to stand with his waders full of the icy water. "You may have won this round, but I got your DNA. This isn't over yet." He shook his fist and rod at the large wake cutting across the stream to the opposite bank.

Maripa reached out to help him onto the bank. "Are you okay?"

"I'm fine," Karm grumbled back as he climbed the bank of the stream. "Just soaked. Get the heaters going in the coach."

Karm changed into drier clothes and joined his companions in the mag-lev. "Mutes, almost had him that time. Would have loved to actually land him just once before taking off. You two all set?"

Rocker and Maripa nodded. "All packed and ready to go." The levicoach accelerated down the dirt road, spraying gravel in its wake.

"Good. I sent my belongings on ahead yesterday so looks like we are good to go." He pulled a small silver case out of his pocket and removed a violet capsule. Karm tossed the pill into his mouth and chased it down with a swallow of water.

An hour later they arrived at the launch pad facilities. Guards checked their IDs at the gate while security officers searched the vehicle inside and out.

The guard snapped a crisp salute. "Welcome to Pad One, sir. You may proceed to the main hangar." He waved the vehicle on and the gate slid closed behind them. They were accustomed to the high level of security measures during the past year. Their frequent trips to supervise the installation of the equipment and DNA samples required regular trips to the site.

The levicoach pulled up to the main entrance of the hangar and more security personnel surrounded them. After a final inspection of all luggage and passing through security detectors they entered the facility itself. Once inside, they saw members of the monarch's staff and clerics of various ranks of The Faith, which embodied the rest of the crew. Each group was outfitted in their flight suits, but kept to themselves. Karm located the launch control room and headed in.

"The countdown is proceeding normally, sir," reported the flight director. "Crew insertion in one hour."

"Thank you, Captain. We'll be in the prep room getting ready." He left the control room and walked back to Maripa and Rocker.

"Time to suit up."

They followed him into the suit-up area and sat on the contoured chairs as the technicians helped them into their bulky pressurized suits. In thirty minutes, they finished dressing and headed out. They carried their helmets and coolant cases back to the waiting area joining the rest of the crew.

A tall soldier with rows of ribbons and medals on his chest entered the room with two armed soldiers in attendance. "Time to get you folks to the launch pad," he said in a booming voice that echoed throughout the room. "Follow me to the transport." He turned on his heels and led the way down the starkly lit hallway. The two armed soldiers stood guard as the crew followed. Three additional guards trailed behind them, weapons at the ready.

Loading the transport proved to be tricky while they struggled to maneuver in their pressurized suits. With the help of several technicians, everyone soon found themselves safely deposited into their seats and buckled in for the short drive to the ship. Three towers surrounded the gleaming vessel, each with a large freight elevator leading to different levels. The crew divided into three groups, each assigned to separate towers. Karm, Maripa, and Rocker were collected with The monarch's group. Security guards, led the way and accompanied each elevator to the designated level. When the elevator stopped, a guard raised the gate and the group began to board the ship in single file crossing the gantry to the open hatch.

As Karm began to exit the elevator the guards blocked his way and lowered their weapons, the red light of the firing contact indicating the weapons were fully charged and armed.

"What is the meaning of this?" Karm demanded of the soldiers.

Maripa found herself unable to act. She was blocked by both Karm and Rocker. Her pressurized suit proved too stiff and bulky for her to move effectively on the narrow gantry. She was definitely not in any position to attack trained soldiers with plasma beam rifles aimed at the group. The guards lowered the gate between them, trapping the three in the elevator.

"So now we say goodbye at last, Karm." The monarch walked back out across the gantry and stood behind the guards.

"This is outrageous, Brach. Let us through. The ship will launch in just a few minutes. We don't have time for any games."

Brach smiled at Karm's frustration. "I quite agree. I am done playing your games. You are no longer in charge here, and you certainly will not be boarding this vessel."

Rocker finally found his voice. "What if something goes wrong with the regeneration equipment? How will you fix it without us on board? I'm the one who designed the systems and I know them better than anyone."

"We have plenty of very smart people with us, Dr. Rocker and they are all well briefed in your designs and specs. My people assure me they learned your systems well enough to do just fine without you to hold their hands... but thank you for all your hard work. None of this would have been possible without you."

He turned to walk back into the ship. "Take them to the bunker and don't let them out until after launch. After that you can release them unharmed. They cannot do anything once we reach space. I think I'm going to enjoy the thought of your prolonged suffering over the next few years." He stopped and faced the small group of prisoners. "I want you to remember who finally outwitted you and condemned you and your friends to die here on this world while we survive to colonize a new world."

"Don't do this, Brach. You'll never make it without us."

"Still defiant? You still think you have the upper hand?" the monarch reached into a pocket in his spacesuit and pulled out a small beam pistol. "Come to think of it, I would rather see the look in your eyes as you die at my own hand." He pressed the firing contact.

At the first sight of the monarch's weapon, Maripa shoved her way forward and slammed the full weight of her body into Karm, knocking him to one side. As he fell to the ground, the orange beam grazed Karm's shoulder instead of burning into his heart. Rocker landed a sidekick to one of the guards who fell screaming over the railing of the gangway one hundred feet above the concrete below. He grabbed the second guard before the man could raise his weapon.

"Get down!" yelled Maripa as she ripped the metallic emblem from her portable oxygen tank and hurled it toward the monarch. The object embedded itself in his arm causing him to drop his gun.

"Now you die," she said to the monarch as he gripped his wound, her body coiled in the manner of a predator preparing to launch into its prey, her eyes firmly fixed on Brach as she sprang.

Maripa swore as she got caught in the struggle between Rocker and the remaining guard. She broke free just as Brach escaped into the ship and closed the hatch. She approached the porthole in the door and the two eyed each other. She punched the window with such force, The monarch jumped back in fear. She turned to see Rocker finishing off the remaining guard with a powerful twist, breaking his neck.

"Two minutes to launch," called out the loudspeaker from the elevator.

Karm sat up holding his shoulder. "Maripa, get back here now! We need to get down to the emergency bunker before this thing launches!"

She ran back to the tower as Rocker shoved the guard's body out of the way. He closed the gate and hit the emergency escape button. The elevator dropped at an alarming rate, braking only at the last possible moment, crashing them all to the floor.

Rocker helped Karm to his feet. "Maripa, Hurry! Get the bunker door open. I'll help him."

"One minute to launch," called the loudspeaker.

Maripa sprinted the twenty yards to the emergency shelter and keyed in the access code. The lock clicked and she pulled the door open just as Rocker and Karm arrived. She slammed the hatch shut behind them as they stumbled inside.

Karm sat silently on a chair in a corner. Maripa located the first aid kit and began to dress his shoulder. Rocker stood stunned in the center of the room.

"I should have killed him," Maripa said as she applied the bandages. "Is there a phone in here? Maybe there's still time to stop the launch."

Suddenly the ground shook and a deep rumble sounded through the bunker. The sound grew to a roar as the entire room quaked and then faded to silence.

"No! No! No!" Maripa ran to the door, but Rocker caught her before she could open it. "They can't launch! It can't end like this!"

Rocker took her by the shoulders and held her tight. "We're together and that's all that matters, my love," he whispered in her ear as she trembled.

The rumbling gradually subsided. Karm stood and walked over to Rocker and Maripa, still holding each other. "Alright, what's done is done. Let's get out of here and back to the control room."

"What's the point?" Rocker asked, cradling Maripa in his arms. "We lost. Shouldn't we go home and make the best of the time left to us?"

"Don't give up yet. You never know what the fickle future holds for us." He walked over to his friends, placing his free hand on Rocker's shoulder.

After a few moments they walked over to the transport and drove back to mission control.

"Karm! What are you doing here? Why didn't you board the ship?" The startled Captain sprang from his chair as the bedraggled trio entered the room.

"Apparently, the monarch had other plans and we weren't invited. He infiltrated some of our security forces with his own men and they prevented us from boarding the ship."

"I'll round up those men and court martial them!"

"No need. They're dead. Brach tried to kill us and these two," he said pointing to Maripa and Rocker, "were more than a match for them. You might find a few charred pieces of bone at the launch pad, but I doubt it."

A man at one of the computer banks suddenly interrupted. "Captain, I think we have a problem here. You need to take a look at these trajectory numbers."

The Captain looked over the engineer's shoulder at the screen. "This can't be right. These coordinates show them heading off into space. They were supposed to do a couple of orbits and reenter. What happened?"

"I'm not sure, sir, but it looks as though their computer changed the coordinates and ignited the engines. The new trajectory is taking them into deep space. We can't override it. They cut us out." The engineer frantically typed instructions to his console and reset switches. "Nothing is working. They're leaving orbit now."

The Captain turned to Karm and shook his head. "Looks like you were the lucky ones after all, sir. If we can't re-establish communications and telemetry control, the ship is lost and everyone on board will die out there." He stared helplessly at the monitors and the engineers. "This was supposed to be a simple demonstration. The monarch is aboard that ship."

Karm place a reassuring hand on the officer's shoulder. "I know, Captain. There will of course be a full investigation and every system will be torn apart and analyzed until we find out what went wrong. If you can't restore communications or control in the next hour they will be lost for good . Keep at it until then. I will start preparing for the worst, though. I'll check back with you soon." He signaled for Maripa and Rocker to follow him as he left toward one of the nearby offices.

Karm quietly closed the door behind them and turned to face Rocker and Maripa. "We need to maintain the cover story and protect our people at all costs, especially now. We don't want to live on a world in total panic if the true condition of that ship ever leaks out." He walked over to one of the chairs and sat down. "We need to let everyone believe the ship became lost in a freak accident in space. There will be some turmoil until the government stabilizes again, but we can't risk the public finding out the truth."

Rocker nodded in agreement. "We agree with you, Karm. As long as we are stuck here, we will want to live in peace until the end. How would you like some company back at The Citadel?"

He smiled and took Maripa's face in his hands. "We could find worse places to celebrate the end of the world."

Without warning, the door opened and in walked The General dressed in his finest military uniform.

Karm stood and eyed the intruder. "You seem to have had a relapse in your devotion to The Faith, General. Why are you here and not on board with your friends?"

"I am sure you knew my role as a spy, Karm. You are too good a strategist to have been fooled for long. An unfortunate heart condition prevents me from joining His Majesty on this journey, but I still serve as required. His Majesty's final instructions were for me to deliver this message to you." The General pulled an envelope out of his jacket and handed it to Karm. He saluted and left as quickly as he arrived.

Maripa scowled at the closing door, every fiber of her being screamed to give chase and kill the monster. "What does that traitor have to say?"

Karm opened the envelope and read the message aloud.

My Dear Karm,

By now you are coming to grips with the fact that you have finally been outwitted. My companions and I are leaving orbit and on our way to Raince'to. I want you to know I have always considered you a most worthy adversary. I had almost given up hope of defeating you.

You should also know I will ensure your name and Dr. Rocker's live on in the colonies we build. You and your people will be given full credit for your genius and for saving our people. I give you my royal and solemn oath.

I also wanted to assure you that neither of us want The Faith to have any authority whatsoever in our new society. I have taken steps to eliminate the threat once and for all. If, somehow, you find a way to follow us to the new world you will probably find the path marked by the bodies of a few dozen clergy.

Farewell my old friend.

Brach

"He must have written this in one of his saner moments before he became obsessed with killing me." Karm folded the letter and stuck it in his pocket. "Let's go home. I need a drink."

Chapter Twenty-Eight

"Set course for Latonia base," said Karm to the pilot as they boarded the jet.

"Yes, sir. Estimated arrival time - four hours."

Maripa snapped to attention at the mention of the desert base. "What the strix are you doing, Karm? Why in the world would we want to go into the middle of that wasteland during a crisis like this?"

Karm looked at Maripa with wide innocent eyes while sporting a mischievous grin. "Now, you wouldn't want me to spoil the surprise, would you?"

"Don't play games with us, Karm. You don't want me getting angry right now."

Karm somehow maintained his virtuous expression.

"Me? I would never play games with you. Not in a million years."

Rocker straightened himself in his seat and scowled at Karm. "We don't have a million years."

Karm gave them a mischievous wink. "Oh, I wouldn't be too sure about that. Just sit back and enjoy the scenery for the next few hours. I promise, all your questions will be answered when we arrive." He waved a dismissive hand and buckled himself into his seat.

Rocker turned to Maripa, seeking guidance in her equally confused face. "Do we trust him once more?"

She shrugged her shoulders and took his hand in hers. "He's almost never let us down, so I guess one more time won't kill us. Not that it matters anymore." They buckled in and leaned on each other as the plane accelerated down the runway.

"Good. I'm glad that's settled. Wake me when we arrive. I need a nap." Karm pulled a blanket over himself and closed his eyes.

Four hours later the pilot's voice broke the silence in the cabin. "Beginning our descent to Latonia Base. Wheels down in fifteen minutes."

Maripa startled awake. "Have a nice rest?" Rocker asked as he brushed one stray crest feather from her face.

"Must have been more tired than I thought." She stretched, sat up and tousled her crest. "Did you sleep?"

"Not really. I've been trying to calculate how long it would take to build another rescue ship and replace all of our equipment. I don't think it's possible. Not with how little time we have."

Maripa held his hand and leaned over to kiss him. Her eye caught the view outside the plane. "What the strix? Why are we landing? Take a look."

Rocker turned to look out his window. "There's nothing down there. No town, no roads, only a broken down old runway." He turned back into the cabin, unbuckled his seatbelt, and stepped across the aisle. "Karm, wake up. You need to tell us what's going on. Why are we landing in the middle of nowhere?"

Karm looked out of his window. "Ah, Latonia Base. We're here."

"What do you mean 'we're here'? We aren't anywhere except the most desolate part of the most isolated desert on the planet. There's nothing out there." Rocker jabbed a finger toward the window.

"Sit down and buckle in before we land. I'll explain everything once we are on the ground."

Rocker and Maripa watched through their window as the plane lost altitude. They saw nothing except rock and dirt from one horizon to the next. The jet shook with the rumble of machinery as the landing gear lowered and locked into place. Then a single bounce and the plane taxied to the lone building next to the runway. It was a small adobe shack with a uniformed guard standing outside awaiting their arrival. The plane rolled to a stop in front of the weather-beaten shed. The pilot opened the doorway and lowered the steps. A wall of oppressive heat slammed into the three passengers as they departed. An intense sunlight forced them to shield their eyes until they reached the small bit of shade provided by the rickety structure. The sentry snapped to attention.

"Welcome to Latonia Base, sir. May I see your identifications, please?" He held out his left hand to receive the documents while his right hand rested on his sidearm. The soldier gave the papers a quick examination and returned them. "You may enter now, sir. They are waiting for you on level four."

"Thank you, Lieutenant." He waved to the others to follow him inside.

The interior of the shack proved no more revealing than the outside. Some broken wooden crates in one corner and an antique refrigerator hummed and rattled in another. The open window allowed a thin tattered curtain to flutter in the slight breeze. A single table occupied the center of the room, surrounded by four chairs looking as though they might collapse should a fly land on them.

Rocker pulled out one chair for Maripa, and sat himself in the one next to her. "Having fun, Karm? Care to let us in on your little secret now? And what did he mean by 'level four'? This place barely has one level. One good kick would bring the whole building down around us."

"Yes, I'm ready to explain everything. You two sit down. This will take a while."

They sat cautiously in the suspect chairs and waited.

"Ready for descent to level four." Karm said in a voice too loud for such close quarters. The floor shook and started to drop into the ground. They were surrounded by metallic walls on all sides. The square of light receded into the distance far above them. Maripa and Rocker both grabbed the table to steady themselves as the elevator took them deep underground. A few moments later, their descent slowed and they came to a gentle stop. A doorway to their left slid open with a hiss.

Karm spread his arms as he stood and walked out into an enormous underground facility. "Welcome to my little secret,"

Rocker and Maripa followed and their jaws dropped as they looked around the space. A large silver spaceship shaped like a somewhat flattened sphere occupied the center of the hangar. Scaffolding surrounded the vessel and hundreds of men and robotic machines operated in a perpetual buzz of activity. Dozens of motorized carts delivered supplies to the men, then vanished down ramps along the walls. Cranes hoisted sheets of metal to men who welded them onto the ship's frame. Announcements of various schedules and orders were broadcast throughout the area.

Karm stood, hands on hips, gazing up at the vessel. "This is Hegira II; our real mission." He allowed his stunned companions a moment to realize what he had just said. "Follow me and I will explain everything." He led them through a doorway and into a control room where dozens of computer screens fed information to the men seated at the stations before them.

"Taket," he called out to the mission control officer, "have you been able to raise them yet?"

"Yes, sir. We have them located and we are ready for you to contact them whenever you give the order."

"No time like the present. Give me the microphone and hail them."

The man handed Karm the microphone and rotated a couple of dials, listening to the changing frequencies, nodding when he recognized correct signals. "Go ahead, sir."

"Hegira, this is Karm. Are you reading me? This is a secure channel."

"This is Brach, Karm. I see you survived despite all my efforts to the contrary. I'm glad, really. It might be even more satisfying thinking of you, stranded and helpless, watching the sun explode. Oh, did you receive my message?"

"I got your message. You do as you see fit. I was just checking our communication link. Nothing more to talk about at this time. Out." Karm handed the microphone back to the radioman and returned to Rocker and Maripa.

Karm opened the door and motioned for his companions to follow him. "Let's go into a more private room to talk."

"Will you please tell us what's going on, now?" Maripa asked as the door to the conference room shut behind them. "No more games or delays. Out with it."

"Absolutely, my dear. Where do I begin? I always knew neither the monarch nor any of The Faith could be trusted as allies. Each of us concocted an agenda that could not survive so long as the others existed. Therefore, I ordered the construction of this entire facility as an emergency back-up. Everything we need is here. All of the equipment built for the Hegira was duplicated in this facility for the Hegira II with a few special modifications, of course."

Rocker cocked his head, suspicion rising again in his thoughts. "What do you mean by special modifications?"

"None of the genetic equipment onboard the original Hegira will function for more than two minutes once it is turned on. Everything looks normal during the testing phase, but the circuits will blow under actual field conditions. The ship itself is also a fake."

"How can it be a fake?" asked Maripa. "We saw it launch, or at least its trail, and you just spoke to the monarch out in space."

"Oh, it's real enough for that. But the HyperIonic drive we constructed cannot achieve anywhere near the speeds required to reach Raince'to within three generations. All of the test data and specs were lies from the start. The monitoring equipment was falsely calibrated so all of the data looked exactly like it was supposed to. None of Brach's people could possibly have known any better."

Rocker's face scrunched as he considered the implications. "You sent them out there to die?"

"If you remember, they did everything they could to force their way onto the ship."

"And you let them prevent us from getting on board." He nodded his head. "Good. Let them rot out there in space."

"Yes. I had several contingency plans ensuring we would be left behind, but Brach was very accommodating." He looked at his companions and saw their confusion. "I am sorry I had to keep this a secret from you. The monarch's men are actually very good. Once again, events forced me to make sure that your reactions were genuine so he would be convinced he was in control."

Maripa's eyes lit up in anticipation. "Wait, you said the other ship's engines cannot get them to the new world, but this one can?"

"I assure you, this ship will bring us there faster than you ever imagined. We are still a few months away from our launch date, but everything is on schedule and nobody is the wiser. Even if they do become suspicious, you saw how well we disguised this base. We will need to stay here while the ship is completed so that our cover story is maintained. As far as the rest of the world is concerned, we are on that ship with the monarch. Those who saw us after the launch have been reassigned here to keep them in isolation. I took the liberty of having all of your belongings brought to your quarters here on the base. Let me show you to your new home."

The next two months passed uneventfully. Karm visited the communications center regularly to check on the Hegira, but nothing had been heard from them in weeks. Rocker objected strenuously upon discovering his credentials allowed only brief access to the genetic equipment he helped design, but he understood the deadline pressures and did not interfere. He and Maripa kept busy helping with supervision of loading supplies and equipment onto the ship. There appeared to be a few minor design changes, but nothing drastic enough to cause alarm. Then came judgment day.

The speaker on his desk suddenly crackled to life. "Karm, come to the communications room immediately."

Karm hit the talk button. "What's going on?"

"We have an emergency transmission from the Hegira. You need to come to the C-R right away."

"On my way. Call Dr. Rocker and Maripa and tell them to join us."

The speakers broadcast an unfamiliar voice as Karm entered the room.

"Over here, sir," said the lieutenant in charge. Karm noticed that Rocker and Maripa huddled with the lieutenant around the loudspeaker listening to the voice on the other end. He listened as he approached.

"Is any one there? Please answer. They're killing each other. Is anyone there?" The voice sounded weak and barely audible through the static.

Karm grabbed the microphone. "This is Karm. Who are you? What do you mean 'they're killing each other'?"

The voice was barely audible through the static. "Can you hear me? Is anyone there? This is Sergeant Vedak. Please, can anyone hear me? We need help."

The radio man adjusted the dials attempting to strengthen the signal. "That's the best I can do, sir. Try again."

Karm pressed the talk button again. "Sergeant Vedak, do you read me? What is going on up there?"

"Praise The Eternal! You can hear me. Please help. They're killing each other. Only a few of us are left. Most are badly wounded. Help us!"

"We can't help you unless you tell us what's going on, Sergeant. Talk to me."

"Yes, sir. The monarch ordered us to round up all of the clerics and confine them to their quarters, but they were armed and resisted. How did they get weapons, sir? Nobody but the soldiers were supposed to be issued weapons."

"Keep talking Sergeant."

"Yes, sir. As I said, sir, the clerics brought weapons onboard somehow and began firing as we approached. Our guys started firing back. A lot of us died in the first attack, sir. We set up barricades and tried to hold them off. We contained them in the lower decks around medical and some of the barracks, but they broke through our lines. They had knives too, sir. A lot of our guys got cut up pretty bad, sir. Once they gained access to the weapons lockers, they were able to fight their way up through the rest of the ship." The sergeant's voice broke off in a fit of violent coughing. "I'm hit bad, sir. You've got to send help."

"Sergeant, you know the situation. We can't send help, but finish your report...keep talking. Tell us what happened."

"Yes, sir. Some of our weapons fire penetrated the hull. We had to seal off most of the lower decks. A lot of people got trapped down there. They're probably all dead now from decompression. Some of us are left in the command deck. Our cartridges are almost empty. The enemy's going to break through soon, sir. Are you sure there's no way to send reinforcements?"

"No, soldier. There is no way to send help." Karm put his hand over the microphone and looked up at the others in the room.

"Yes, sir. I know, sir," said the sergeant. "It was a quetzal of a mission though. Wish I could say goodbye to my mother…before the end and all."

"I'll see what we can do, soldier. Hang in there, son." Karm looked up at the control room supervisor. "There must be some way we can contact this man's mother and get her on the line for him?"

"I'm not sure, sir. I'll find out right away."

After a few minutes of searching the databases, the supervisor pointed at his screen. "I found her, sir. Turns out she's also stationed here as a machinist. We can bring her here in ten minutes."

"Make it five minutes."

A few minutes later the control room door opened and in walked a woman dressed in grease covered overalls guided by a lieutenant.

Karm reached out to the woman as he stood to provide her with his chair by the microphone. "Over here, ma'am. Did they tell you what's going on?"

The woman looked fearfully around the room, then approached Karm to take the seat he offered her. "Yes, sir, they did," Her eyes were red and she wiped her nose on her dirty sleeve, but she remained calm. "Is he still up there? Can I talk to him?"

"Yes, ma'am. Right here. Just press this button when you want to talk." Karm stood back as she reached out for the mike and pressed the button.

"Kellend, are you there, honey?"

"Mom! Is that you?" came the sergeant's reply. "What are you doing there?"

Karm looked around the room and spread his arms, ushering everyone out of the room. "Let's give them some privacy."

Twenty minutes later the woman exited the room. Her cheeks were streaked with tears. "Thank you, sir…thank you."

The lieutenant took her by the shoulders, supporting her as he gently led her down the corridor. The others re-entered the control room.

"Just like it happened before," Karm said quietly. "Cut off all communication links. There's nothing we can do for them."

"Yes, sir." The radioman pressed a button and all lights on the panel went out.

Karm turned and walked slowly back to his office followed by Rocker and Maripa.

Maripa placed her hands gently on Karm's shoulders as he slumped in a chair. "What do you mean 'just like before'?"

Karm's head bowed and he kept his back to Maripa as he responded. "You remember I told you how my DNA was reconstructed by the aliens from a dead ship. Well, the Hegira is that ship. They trained me and sent me back to complete the failed mission from that crew. It has always been my responsibility…my destiny to ensure that everything happened in exactly the same way it had before so history would unfold in the manner it was supposed to."

"So you knew all this was going to happen?" She looked from Karm to Rocker and back to Karm. "I guess I never quite believed your story about coming from the future." She reached out and took Rocker's hand.

"Yes, it's all true. I am sorry about keeping you both in the dark so much. I could not risk anything happening to change the timeline. I had to make sure everything occurred not only the way it did before, but at the exact same time as before." He looked up at Maripa and Rocker, then down at the floor. "This is why those miners had to die. The delays caused by a strike would have caused irreparable damage to the timeline. There was no other choice."

Rocker reached out to Karm with his free hand, and placed it on his shaking back. "I know, Karm. I understand, now, what a terrible burden you've been carrying for all of us. I'm not sure I would have had the strength to do the same."

Maripa released her grip on Rocker's hand, and gathered both of her men in a warm embrace.

"In my timeline, those people on the Hegira died many decades ago and our entire race died with them. It was my task to keep us from extinction. The Hegira II launches in one month just after the new year dawns. This mission will succeed."

Chapter Twenty-Nine

Everything was ready for launch. All of the supplies and equipment were securely stored away. The DNA samples were safely locked in dormant hibernation. Maripa, Karm, and Rocker were in the suit-up room getting stuffed into their pressurized suits.

"Hope this goes better than the last launch," laughed Rocker as he struggled with his left boot.

"Don't remind me," Maripa said connecting her coolant hoses.

With the final checks of their suits completed, one of the engineers led them to the main hangar. The roof had been opened over the past hour and they looked up into a starlit night. They continued on to the ramp leading up to the ship's main hatchway and on to the bridge. Karm took the Captain's chair on the left. Maripa sat in the center chair and Rocker on the right. Each of them had practiced with the controls in front of them and were familiar with their duties for the flight.

Karm flipped the communications switch at his side. "Command crew buckled in and secure for launch."

Maripa and Rocker turned dials and set their controls just as they rehearsed during training drills.

"Drive motors at max. Coolant flow nominal," called out Maripa.

"Stabilizers balanced. Internal environmental controls show five by five," said Rocker.

Karm examined the control panel and nodded. "Ready to close and seal hatches."

Maripa and Rocker jumped at his command. "Wait Karm, not yet. What about the rest of the crew? They haven't boarded yet. We still have another hour before we need to close the hatches."

Karm stared at the main view screen. "Sorry guys. another one of those vital secrets I had to hide from you. There is no crew for this voyage, only the DNA and equipment we are transporting. Launch is in one minute. No time to explain now. I can fill you in once we are in space. Oh, and don't worry about hitting any wrong switches. I'm in full control of the ship." He held out his left arm. The glow of his palm could be seen even through the heavy glove. In fact, his entire body seemed to shine.

The electronic crackle of mission control sounded in their headphones. "T minus 10...9...8...7...6... ignition sequence start...5...4...3...2...1... all systems go. You are go for lift off."

There was no vibration, nor any sound. But through the view screen Rocker and Maripa could see the shrinking shadow of the ship as they shot high above the desert floor. In no time, they saw the curve of the planet's horizon in the distance backlit by the dying sun. They could feel gravity diminishing as they reached orbit.

"Standard orbit achieved." Karm reached up and removed his helmet, then took off his gloves and placed them inside the helmet as it floated in free fall in front of him. Rocker and Maripa removed their helmets and gloves as well. Rocker took all of their unneeded equipment and stowed them in the bay next to his seat.

Karm unbuckled himself and floated free of his chair. "Don't start with the inquisition, you two. I can finally tell you the entire story, so follow me to the command crew quarters and listen."

Maripa and Rocker looked at each other, unfastened their restraints and drifted down the passageway after Karm.

Maripa gasped at the sensation of weightlessness. "This is fun!" She performed effortless somersaults and various combat maneuvers as she propelled herself toward the meeting room.

Rocker, in contrast, turned a ghastly green. "I don't feel so good." He barely managed opening the bag attached to his belt before retching violently into it.

They struggled a bit at first trying to match the fastening strips on their suits to those in the chairs, but did manage to secure themselves.

Maripa glared at Karm. "This better be good."

"Trust me. Once you hear the entire tale you will understand why I kept you and everyone else in the dark. You remember I told you about the alien ship that discovered the original Hegira and my DNA among the thousands of destroyed samples? Yours too, Maripa. Ours were the only survivors."

They both nodded in agreement.

"Those aliens, as I have told you, were from a civilization who call themselves the Skae. Technologically far beyond anything you can imagine. They only let me see a small part of their ship so I would be as free from contamination and knowledge of the future as possible. Their principal edict forbids them from interfering with the development of other races. Ours turned out to be a special case, but they never did tell me why. I always assumed they decided in our favor since an entire species, ours, was on the brink of extinction. After recovering the ship's logs and data bases they formulated a plan to save us. The key was finding the two surviving DNA samples. Once the DNA was grown, they could train one of our own species to carry out the plan. They could not directly take steps to interfere on their own, but apparently two members of the destroyed species, when specially trained and equipped, was permissible."

"You still haven't explained why we don't have a crew."

"I'm getting there. The Skae provided me with this biocomputer implant you both have seen me put to good use. However, it only provides me certain information and only allows me to tap into a fraction of what it is capable of doing. It always tells me just enough to succeed, but never so much that I might endanger the future. They also provided me with enough information to build this ship. As you have already seen, none of the bridge stations are functional. My biocomputer is the true control mechanism. Our engines are only powerful enough to lift us into orbit. My friends out there will help us with the rest."

"You mean the Skae are out here waiting for us?" Maripa searched outside her window for some sign of a ship.

As she scanned the sky, she noticed a tiny light moving across the star field in their view screen. The light grew and took the shape of a small spaceship. The speakers crackled as communication channels opened.

A gentle voice sounded over the speaker. "Hello Karm. Congratulations on the success of your mission."

"Bolt, my old friend. It has been too long. Thank you for all you have done to help us."

"We could not allow your species to die. We did what we had to do. Are you ready for the jump?"

"Yes, we are. Is Zem with you, now?"

A second, somewhat more nasal voice sounded over the speaker. "I am here. I am pleased to hear you again. I will send the tow beam now."

"Thank you, Zem. I read a steady connection. Please take us to the string."

"The Skae are here? They really exist?" Maripa and Rocker said in unison as they watched the view screen.

"Yes, and now I should continue with my story. Our current technology does not have the ability to power a ship to even the nearest stars, unless we are prepared to build a ship of immense size capable of carrying generations of people. We are incapable of such an undertaking, so my friends out there devised this entire deception to hide themselves from us. They are about to connect us to a cosmic string and tow us to our new home. That's how they brought the two of us here," he said as he looked at Maripa. "cosmic strings can be influenced by their advanced technology to not only allow travel across space at incredible speeds, but also through time. Manipulating the time stream is how I arrived here decades before Maripa. Since I am from the future I knew most of what was supposed to happen and how to control it to my advantage."

Rocker ruffled his crest as he tried to assimilate what he was hearing. "But, didn't your manipulation of events on Dyan'ta disrupt the time continuum?"

"Those events stayed isolated to Dyan'ta, and when it is destroyed, there's no potential for those events to radiate out to the universe and interfere with the existing time continuum."

"This is unbelievable."

"Just wait until you hear the rest of the story. Despite all of their advances, the Skae were not able to reanimate me without some difficulty. My DNA started to spontaneously decay at an alarming rate. To keep me alive long enough to complete the mission, their scientists developed the pills I take to stabilize the decay and, hopefully, will allow me to live a long and productive life." He held up one of the violet capsules and swallowed it. "Fortunately, they improved their techniques enough to solve the problem before animating Maripa's DNA. That is why you don't need the pills. I just wish they had figured it out sooner. These things taste terrible.

Karm turned to face Rocker, pointing a talon at his companion. "Your discovery did something even they could not do. You learned how to reanimate the DNA without the degradation problems. Only now, having seen your designs and calculations, the Skae invented ways to greatly improve them. Our new equipment can grow a new clone to maturity in only one week!"

"Oh, great! So we have a batch of fully grown week-old babies on our hands." Rocker threw his hands up in exasperation. "Won't that be fun!"

"Not at all. You remember those CAT scans you questioned me about? We added a few alien enhancements. The scans were much more than an examination for genetic defects. Those probes collected the entire body of knowledge from each individual. We can implant their knowledge and grow fully developed and educated adults in one week. We don't need to bring along a large crew, only the thousands of DNA samples."

Maripa rubbed her temple. "So you kept us in the dark to preserve the alien's prime directive and the future timeline. They could help us, but nobody could know about it."

Karm applauded her and smiled. "Absolutely correct. Even now they cannot reveal the technology connecting us to the cosmic string or the location of our new home. We will need to learn these things on our own. Our isolation on the new planet will ensure secrecy for generations to come."

Rocker shook his head. "That still doesn't explain why we didn't bring anyone else with us. We aren't leaving all those workers behind to die are we?"

"Not at all. As I said, the cosmic strings can also manipulate time, so, after we left, the Skae sent another ship down to Latonia Base and gathered up enough of them to help us start a settlement on the new world. They should actually already be there working to build the new community. Unfortunately, we cannot save all of them, but we devised a lottery for those with the skills we will require, and remember, with the CAT scan pathways implanted, the clones will wake up with all the memories and thought patterns of their originals. They may actually believe they are the original and not a clone."

"Alright, Karm. I guess you're forgiven. You sure that's everything? No more secrets?"

"Well, maybe just one more, but that can wait until we arrive on the new planet and settle in. It's more of a present for you than a secret."

"Wonderful. You can't help yourself, can you? There always has to be one more trick up your sleeve." Rocker chuckled as he turned back to Maripa.

Maripa interrupted and pointed at the view screen. "Is that what I think it is?"

A bright ribbon appeared on their sensors and resolved on the main screen. It moved sinuously across the sky, reminiscent of a living thing.

"Looks like it extends on forever," she said, glued to the image on the screen. "It's incredible."

"That is our ride. It's a cosmic string. We better hurry back up to the bridge. This is going to be bumpy."

The journey along the string took only a few minutes. Their ship shuddered violently as it tossed about, but it was well built and everything survived, mostly in one piece. As the shaking subsided the ship slowly rotated to reveal a brightly lit blue planet ahead of them. Approaching closer to the shining orb revealed clouds in the atmosphere. Several large land masses grew in size with their descent.

"Adjust to coordinates 2268.910 by 427.336," Zem's voice directed them over the speaker.

"Heading in now. See you there in five minutes."

Karm's body glowed again as it took over control of the ship. Maripa and Rocker watched the view screen as the continent below them expanded. Forests and grasslands came into view. Large rivers and lakes crossed the landscape.

Maripa stared in amazement at the scene below. "Everything is so green. Not quite like home, but very pretty."

Rocker watched at her side, equally astonished. "And did you get a look at that sun? It's yellow, not orange. It must be a few billion years younger than our old star. That is a comforting thought."

The Hegira II set down on a grassy meadow not far from a meandering river. Karm stopped glowing as he shut down the ship's controls and opened the hatchway.

"Looks as though our friends have been busy," Karm said as he left the ship.

They stepped off the ship onto their new home and saw a small village waiting for them. Several homes sat along a winding dirt road. As the three travelers approached, they saw several large buildings, their construction almost complete, near the center of town. To one side of the village fenced pastures sat peaceful and green, waiting for the animals to fill them. The hum of electricity could be heard in the distance. A number of Brin could be seen busy with the new construction.

Karm pointed toward a rise in the distance. "They must have built the power plant on the other side of those hills. The much smaller spaceship that towed them along the cosmic string landed almost silently nearby. The hatch opened and two figures, dressed in flowing colorful attire, walked toward them. They stood about eight feet tall on long thin legs. Their arms were equally long and spindly with five fingers on each hand. Their wavy brown hair accentuated the deep blue of their smooth skin.

Karm ran to greet them. "Bolt! Zem! I am so glad to see you again." He caught himself suddenly and stopped in front of them. He raised his fist to his chest and bowed remembering the customary greeting he had learned many years ago.

The two smiled as they returned his greeting. Bolt extended his arms to embrace his old friend. "It is good to see you again as well. We can stay for a brief time to help you adjust and confirm everything is operating properly, but then we must leave you again."

"I understand. Let me introduce you to my friends."

Bolt grinned down at Karm. "Ahhh, friends…so, you did learn after all. I am glad."

***

Five months later, the three administrators sat at the kitchen table eating breakfast before starting their day.

"Looks as if the neighbors are getting an early start," Maripa said as she looked out the window. "How many more are scheduled for release today?"

Rocker looked up at the ceiling as he did a few calculations. "Twelve this morning and another ten this afternoon." He took a bite from his muffin. "We should be able to expand and speed up production once the new facilities are finished in another week. The new seeds are ready for planting just as soon as the additional fields are plowed."

Maripa grimaced as she shifted in her seat uncomfortably. "How long before we need a new town? This one is getting a bit crowded now. What is our current population? It must be over a thousand."

"One thousand and ninety eight healthy productive adults."

Karm strolled down the stairs dressed in his waders and vest, his new rod and reel in hand. "Gotta run now. I want to see how those fish we spawned last month are doing." He waved at the two of them as he opened the door, then paused and looked back. "I almost forgot. Here, Jontar. I want you to take a look at this." He reached in his pocket and handed Rocker a small glass vial with a yellow liquid inside.

"What is this?"

"Just a sample of my DNA, and the present I promised you when we left Dyan'ta. I'm off now. Have fun you two!" Karm whistled as he walked down the road to the river. He waved at some of the people he passed along the way.

Maripa took the sample from her husband, examining it closely in the morning light. "Why did he give you his DNA sample now? He never let us have it before. Do you think he's experiencing symptoms again?"

"No, the new treatments we developed cured his degeneration problem. He hasn't had to take any of those pills in a month now." He took the sample back, held up the vial to the light and swirled the liquid as he peered into it. "Maybe I better take a look at this." He went back into his private office and set the small bottle into the reader. A few moments later the monitor displayed row after row of base pair sequences.

Maripa was cleaning up in the kitchen when she heard his shouts.

"Maripa! Get in here! You're not going to believe this!"

She draped the towel over the back of a chair, stretched her back, and went down the hall to Rocker's office.

"What now?" she asked as she entered the room.

"That old conniving Quetzal. He did it again. One last present he called it. Look at these results." Rocker laughed as he pulled Maripa into his arms.

She looked at the screen and saw the flashing message above the images of Karm and Rocker.

DNA MATCH 98% certainty Karm / Dr. Jontar Rocker.

"That old coot is my clone! It was my DNA the Skae recovered from the dead ship." He shook his head and placed his hand on his wife's swollen belly. "This is going to be some story to tell you when you are born." He felt the tiny movement inside his wife and looked up into her eyes.

She looked lovingly into her husband's eyes, a wistful smile on her face. "Do you really need to go in to work today?"

"I'm the boss and father, at least according to the new clones we are raising. I can stay home any time I want." He stood and gathered her to him in a gentle embrace.

"Good," she said, pulling him closer.

Recusant

Book 2 of the Brin Archives

Prologue

(Approximately 1,200 years ago)

"Skae High Command, this is Kolandi Raj Ansus, please respond, Skae High Command."

Static echoed in the Raj's ears as she gripped the com link in a white-knuckled desperation. Her royal robes and long brown hair showed the neglect of long hours in the war room. Ansus rose only recently to the position of High Raj. She fervently hoped it was not her destiny to be the last Raj.

Her nose became insensitive to the stench of bodies during her confinement in the dim bunker long ago. The deep space images on the screen before her revealed the devastation of their fleet in their encounter with the Gorvin. Two hundred top-of-the-line war cruisers had been completely destroyed, another three hundred fighters were out of commission. She watched as the overwhelming forces of the Gorvin plowed through their defenses like an energy blade through a cloud, and were now aimed straight at Kodut, their home world.

On the displays, a second line of vessels, the laser launch ships, took up their attack formation. A cloud began to grow ahead of the ships as they deployed their weapons.

"Raj Ansus, Raj Ansus, this is Skae High Command. We are receiving you."

"Praise the gods." Ansus let out a sigh of relief, realizing she had been holding her breath in anticipation. The Skae had their own difficulties with the Gorvin and communications were unreliable at best. "High Command, we need your help. Our fleet is gone. The Gorvin are preparing to attack Kodut. Their light sail probes will enter our atmosphere in a matter of hours. Our planetary defense satellites cannot handle so many small devices traveling at those speeds. Please, we need help."

Technicians monitoring the long range sensors continued to report the enemy's progress. "Probe light sails are open, launch ships are powering up their laser cannons." In moments, tens of thousands of light sail devices, each a package no more than ten centimeters across, and filled with millions of microscopic nanobots and micro-encapsulated genetically enhanced viruses, leapt forward toward Kodut at half the speed of light, powered by photons fired from hundreds of laser cannons on the launch ships.

Static filled the room for what seemed an eternity. Ansus heard quiet sobbing from one of the attendants huddled behind her. Her own mind filled with rising panic as time passed without a response.

"Skae High Command, come in. Are you receiving us? We need your help. Come in, please."

A deep, resonant voice answered. "Raj Ansus, this is Imperial Commander Tac. I regret to inform you that we have nothing in your sector to send to your aid. All of our forces were sent to the Keldon sector in response to Gorvin threats there. It will be three days at best before our ships can reach you."

"We won't survive three days, commander Tac. You must send immediate help."

"I'm sorry, Raj Ansus. There is nothing we can do. We simply do not have the resources to send you until then. Take shelter as best you can, preferably deep underground in well-filtered bunkers. The Gorvin weapons are biological and technological. Your people will survive, but you must shield your technology from the attack. We will send our fleet as soon as we can, but we are too far away to reach you at this time."

"There is no *time*, commander. We don't have the time to shield our systems. We barely have time to get ourselves into shelters. Are you certain the filters will keep out the virus?"

"They are the best we have. Far superior to previous versions, but test results are marginal. I wish you the best. Have faith. Get your people to safety. We will come as quickly as we can. Commander Tac out."

Four hours later, deep underground in the royal bunker beneath the capitol city, Raj Ansus, her court, and many of the government officials sat in tense silence as monitors revealed the sky ablaze with streaks of fire as the Gorvin probes entered the atmosphere. Similar reports of the attack came from outposts across the planet. The light sails, each one a meter in diameter and manufactured from enhanced graphene nanotubes now acted as atmospheric brakes. Heat and drag forces broke open the probes, releasing the viral and nanobot weapons into the atmosphere.

"Our only hope now is the filters." General Dorn, leader of the Kolandi military forces, nodded as he assessed the dispersal patterns. "If they fail, the nanobots will seek out and shut down all our technology, down to the simplest devices."

Raj Ansus nodded in agreement. She sat in her padded chair, hands folded in her lap as she conferred with her military experts. "How severe will the damage be, General? How soon will we be able to rebuild?"

"Without our tech, life in the cities will be unsustainable. We must be prepared for planetwide pandemics, starvation, rebellion, in other words, the end of our civilization. Save those we can, but then the virus will infect us all."

"But all the reports say it isn't lethal. The Gorvin weapons rarely cause death."

"Yes, but in cases like ours, when they have attacked the closest allies of the Skae, those races are trapped on their planets. The virus alters their physiology setting up a biological resonance with a planet's natural gravitational field. Any attempt to return to space and rejoin the Skae as an ally results in their death. No cure has ever been found, despite all the efforts of the Skae and other allies."

The lights began to flicker and static filled the monitors. Technicians fought to maintain their panels. "All systems are failing, communications are down in sectors twelve, twenty-six, and twenty-nine. Massive overloads are building across the globe."

Raj Ansus started to ask another question, her mouth opened to begin, but she could not find the words. The horror of her people's future was too great to comprehend. She gathered her will in an attempt to project courage to those around her.

Four days later, the Skae fleet arrived. The first unmanned scout ships lost all power as they attempted to enter Kordut's atmosphere. The majority of the fleet held back and orbited Kodut between the twin moons. Early attempts to communicate with the Kolandi proved useless. The Gorvin nanobots had nearly eliminated all electronic wavelengths planetwide. Only when a very high intensity beam pierced the barrier could communications with the surface take place.

"Yes, Commander Tac, we can read you, but barely." Raj Ansus stood outside the entrance to the royal bunker. The communications officer worked furiously at a panel of knobs and switches trying to eek the last bit of power from a rapidly draining battery pack. "The filters were unsuccessful against the virus. We regained consciousness yesterday with only minimal fatalities, but medical tests show we are definitely infected. The Gorvins have destroyed all electronics. Can you provide any information on the expected life of these devices?"

"Our best estimates, you must realize these are only preliminary, indicate the devices are replicating and will remain active for a minimum of five hundred years. Our readings also show the virus has established itself in your biosphere and shows signs of growth. We cannot assist you without risking ourselves."

Ansus felt her heart sink. She slumped into a nearby chair, her mind desperate for any sign of hope. "There must be something you can do. You can't abandon us. We have supported you for generations. We have bled and died for you. Help us."

The silence which followed lasted long enough to convince the Raj communications had been lost until a crackle from the speaker broke the stillness and commander Tac's voice, barely audible now, pronounced their sentence. "My most profound apologies, Raj Ansus. There is nothing we can do. Rest assured, though, our scientists will never stop looking for a cure to the virus, and our technicians will find a way to break through the dampening field. We will not abandon you. One day we…"

The communications officer checked his instruments, looked up at his Raj, threw his hands up in defeat, and shook his head. "That's it. The battery is gone. We're on our own for now. Those blue-skinned devils are going to let us die aren't they?"

"There is nothing they can do for us. We must survive, or die as best we can. Gather the rest of the officers. We must begin preparations for evacuation of the city and learn to become farmers." Raj turned and strode off to be alone and gather her thoughts. *We must survive. We will survive.* A tear ran down her brown cheek as she straightened her shoulders and lifted her face toward the sky. *This will not be the end of us.*

Chapter One

The desert sun beat down on Maliche Rocker's prostrate body like a microwaver set to rapid bake a Tirpit roast. Lying down on his belly as he gingerly laser-picked the matrix away, one grain at a time, from a new discovery of some engraved metallic shards among some ancient pottery had his heart racing. The life of an archaeologist was ninety-nine percent drudgery spent in a damp cellar or lecturing in a broken down classroom, but the one percent times like this were thrilling and made the rest, as well as the ridicule of his family, all worth it.

"I can't be sure, but if my suspicions are correct, we have just made the discovery of the century, Aras. Take a look at these engravings." He adjusted the settings on his laser-pick so a broader beam swept away dust from the surface.

Aras, the enthusiastic grad student scooted in closer to get a better look. She held her broad-brimmed hat above them to help shade the artifact and give them a glare-free view. The thin epidermal scales of her bare arms glinted in the sunlight. "I don't recognize the language, professor. What are they?"

Maliche laughed, puffing up a bit of dust in the process. "If my memory is correct, nobody has seen anything like this in over two hundred years. This may be an artifact of the Kolandi."

Aras's eyes shot open as she rolled onto one side looking at her mentor. "Wait, the Kolandi? What makes you say that? All Kolandi artifacts recovered so far are pottery, some rough metal farming implements and such. These are too advanced to be Kolandi."

"Most others would probably agree with you. But you forget my ancestry. Being a direct descendant of the original Rockers gives me a few advantages. I know I've seen these markings before, and on something similar. I just can't place it right now, but when we get back I'll be able to confirm my suspicions."

After clearing away enough of the matrix, Maliche reached out to pull the fragment free. "Ouch! What the phalk?" He pulled back his hand and sat up to examine his fingers, certain to find a bad burn. "Huh, not a scratch. It felt like I stuck my hand in a power generator when I touched it."

"Let me try, professor." Aras pulled on her gloves and slowly extended her hand toward the artifact, wincing in anticipation, as her fingers got closer. At her touch, she relaxed. "It seems okay now, professor. I'm not feeling anything." As Maliche watched, she pulled off her glove and carefully touched it again. "Nothing. It feels fine. Hold out the box for me and I'll pull it free."

Examining the engraved shard in the container, Maliche again attempted touching it, but pulled back, shaking his hand in pain as he absorbed another shock. "How can you not feel that? It wasn't as bad as the first time, but still stings like a quetzal." He handed the box to one of the nearby laborers. "Put this thing on the artifact table in the tent. And be careful with it. I'll be there in a minute."

The worker accepted the container and headed toward the tent. Out of curiosity, he tried touching the piece of metal with one gentle talon, only detecting the warmth of metal sitting in the sun. He glanced back over his shoulder, shrugged, and carried the object to the artifact tent, handing it to one of the preparers.

The research assistant sitting at the long wooden table dropped his pen when he saw the engravings. He jumped up, grabbed the laborer by his sleeve, and pulled him to a far corner of the tent. "Where did you get this?"

"The boss found it over there." He pointed in the direction of Maliche and Aras, still focused on the remaining pieces of pottery in the new site. "He told me to bring it to you."

He pulled the smaller man close, whispering nose-to-nose. "All right, go about your business, but don't tell anyone about this. Understand?"

The man glanced around nervously, but nodded in agreement. "No problem, sir. It's just a piece of metal out of the desert. No need to get so upset. I'm simply here to do my job and get paid."

The preparer glared at the man for a moment, tossed him loose, and waved him off. He examined the artifact again, glanced around the room quickly to make sure he was not being observed, and stashed the metal in his pocket.

Later that evening, the camp was in an uproar once Maliche discovered his potentially historic discovery was missing. None of the workers had seen or heard anything, and the one he entrusted it to swore he did exactly as told and turned the item over to the preparers in the tent.

Aras burst into the tent, breathless from her running. "It's true. One of the research assistants took a shuttle a few hours ago. Probably the one we thought was the supply ship heading back home. No flight plan was filed, so we have no way to track where they actually went."

"Phalk. Get on the communicator and alert the authorities that we have a stolen shuttle. Maybe they can track it down for us."

Aras approached Maliche, placing one hand on his shoulder. "Don't worry, professor. We'll find the artifact. It can't be too difficult to trace. There's nothing else like it, so our people will know the minute it shows up on the black market."

Maliche leaned heavily on the table, his head hung low. "I hope you're right. That piece was the discovery of a lifetime. We need to close up camp early and get back to try to find it. The rest of this site was pretty common anyway. We can come back next year if we need to."

"I'll see to it, professor. Keep your hopes up. It's bound to turn up soon. You'll see."

***

A week later, back at First Town, the capital of Brin civilization on Raince'to, the streets radiated out from the center of the city where the Savior's Memorial stood. Maliche set his mag-lev to auto pilot so he could gather his thoughts. The sight of the Savior Memorial always stirred deep and reflective emotions within Maliche Rocker. *I've spent my life chasing after their memory. This new artifact may have answered all my questions. How could I have been so careless? I never should have left it out of my sight. Dr. Neywa certainly seemed anxious about the sketches I made when we talked last night. Maybe he found the key to the writing on them. Could it finally be proof of the Kolandi?* He slammed his fist on his knee. *Maybe this will be the discovery to*

wake up those feather-fluffed quetzals in The Assembly and force
them to listen to someone other than the guilds and provide some
decent funding for our research.

The vehicle came to rest in his reserved parking spot,
and Maliche stepped out to wander among the familiar story of
his ancestors. The imposing structure with its polished pink
granite exterior and tall columns housed a museum as well as the
ancient tombs of Jontar Rocker, Maripa, and Karm; The Saviors.
A shuffling of feet and hushed whispers disturbed his thoughts.

"Can anyone tell me the significance of these
holographs?" The teacher smiled as dozens of eager hands shot
into the air. "Marita, what can you tell us about them?"

The girl, her school uniform immaculately pressed for
this trip, and bursting with pride, proceeded to describe the
scenes before the class. "This one shows our ancestors
transporting the DNA samples across the galaxy in the Hegira II.
And these others show how Jontar and Maripa Rocker built first
town and saved the early colonists from starvation."

Maliche smiled as he strode passed the group. Elsewhere
in the shrine, endlessly smiling docents, dressed in period
accurate attire, told the stories to hushed and reverent groups.

The security guard at the entrance to the holy of holies
smiled and nodded at Maliche as he passed.

"Good morning, Professor Rocker. Nice to see you
again."

Karm's Obelisk stood in the very center of the rotunda.
Flanking the obelisk to the left, Maripa's simple marble
headstone and inscription only added to her mythological status
as The Mother Savior. Of course, Jontar Rocker's marker stood
over an empty grave, but that mattered little to those who stood
silently, often wiping back tears paying their respects. These
were the ultimate ancestors of Maliche and Selan, eight
generations removed. This accident of birth gave rise to the
exalted position of all direct descendants of The Saviors, each
one taking the name of Rocker once their genetic markers tested
at the accepted level of relatedness.

A while later, back in his mag-lev, Maliche sat in
another ground traffic jam. He watched wistfully at the free
flowing commute of the air vehicles traveling in six separate

layers above him. *One of these days I'm going to give in and let Selan buy me one of those. The mag-lev ground lanes are always the worst. Good thing my classes don't start until the afternoon.*

A light drizzle began as Maliche finally pulled into his parking spot on the outskirts of the university campus an hour later. *Maybe I should have stuck with genetics instead of the desolate backwaters of archaeology. A spot in the parking garage would almost be worth it on days like this.* He set the controls to lower the support pads, turned off the magnetics, and gathered his gear as the vehicle settled onto its extended landing legs. Maliche lifted his jacket over his head and jogged the quarter mile to his office.

Cutting through the main genetics department building allowed him to get out of the rain momentarily. There were five other buildings devoted to the study of anything and everything to do with DNA, but this four story building stood as the crown jewel of the school. Maliche paused to listen in to a counselor talking to a batch of new students as they gazed at the murals of his ancestors on the high stone walls.

"Each of you will play an important role in the eventual discovery of a cure for our desperate situation. You will soon take a battery of aptitude tests to determine which field of research you are best suited for. Each of the five buildings devoted to this worthy profession is dedicated to a different area of research. When you receive your results, you will be assigned to a lab in one of these buildings." She paused for a moment, slowly gazing at each of her charges and breaking into a broad smile. "Who knows, but one of you may go down in history along with the revered Rockers as a new savior."

Due to a mysterious set of circumstances related to this planet's environment, The Brin faced a desperate situation. Each succeeding generation's life span was becoming shorter than the previous generation. As a result, the study of genetics was the most noble and vital profession any Brin could aspire to, especially if one's name was Rocker. Maliche's choice of archaeology proved to be an embarrassment to his family, and a never ending source of ridicule from his father and brother.

A guard scowled at Maliche as his wet shoes squeaked on the granite floor. The rainwater dripping from his jacket marked a long trail behind him. Maliche simply smiled at the guard as he passed by the desk, flashing his ID badge. The blue and green border with gold helix declared his rank as a pure Rocker.

The guard snapped to attention. "Sorry, sir. I'm new to this building. Haven't seen you here before."

Maliche waved off any concerns, reading the name off the man's badge. "No problem, Officer Tagut. I've been away doing some field research for a few weeks. Just got back in town. Keep up the good work."

Taking the corridor to his left, Maliche maneuvered through crowds of students on their way to classes, eventually reaching the exit door at the other end.

After using two more buildings as temporary shelters, Maliche arrived at the entry to the archaeology department. Actually, the building belonged to the music department. Archaeology rented out the basement and a couple of classrooms on the second floor. As he passed the displays of various artifacts in the hall, Maliche slowed his pace, eventually stopping completely to examine the specimens contained within the glass cases. Small cards with his name on them as the discoverer flanked several of the pieces. He grinned as his thoughts danced over memories of past expeditions to remote regions of the planet. He tapped the glass and sped down the hall toward his office.

"Hello, Professor," called out Maliche as he opened the door at the bottom of the stairwell. He wove his way through one of the narrow, dimly lit aisles amid the tall metal shelves. Half of the ceiling panels either flickered randomly, or were completely black. Hundreds of boxes and assorted pieces of pottery, fabric, utensils, and other artifacts filled the dozens of shelves. The smell of dust and mildew permeated the air. In the back of the room hunched the figure of Professor Neywa, peering through a hand lens as he read one of the books piled around him, a threadbare shawl covered his shoulders. Maliche heard the steady plink of water dripping into a puddle from one of the overhead pipes. A small service robot hovered nearby with suction tubes trying to deal with the mess.

"Haven't they come to fix that leak yet?"

"Sometime next week, they tell me," answered the elderly head of the department without looking up from his reading. "Better go check the service bot before it overflows. That thing is so old, its sensors don't always register when it is full."

"Maintenance has been saying that for two weeks now. You'd think they could spare us an hour." Maliche hung his jacket on the wall hook and set his valise on the floor by his chair at the only other desk in the room. He tapped the controls on the rusted robot, checking the panel readout. "It looks okay to me, but I'm going to call maintenance again and tell them to get out here today."

The old man chuckled as he looked up from his work. "Now don't go and do something foolish like that. If we make too big a stink over a dripping pipe, the board may decide we're not worth the expense after all. Then where would you be?"

"You mean without this fine office and the prestige of a professorship at this outstanding university?" Maliche dropped heavily into his chair and nearly toppled over backward, catching himself at the last second. "Kak mag-supports again! I'm surprised they keep us around at all. If they got their way, the board would require two courses of genetics instead of one every semester and dump us, along with history, philosophy, art, and a few other less than prime departments to make room. It's probably only a matter of time before they start calling it the theology department and make my phalking ancestor's stories their book of holies."

"My, aren't we in a grand mood today," the old professor said, placing his hand lens carefully on the book. "What's happened this time?"

Maliche opened his mouth to start his rant, but changed his mind when he looked into the calm, wrinkled, gentle face of his mentor. He rubbed his talons through his disheveled crest in an attempt to preen and straighten some of the rain-soaked feathers back into shape. "Nothing, professor, just another argument with my brother over my work here. I wish he would, at least, be a bit more understanding and helpful. You would think he might be able to use his influence on The Assembly to help his brother a little, instead of treating me like an embarrassment to the family."

"Don't waste your time wishing for the impossible. I learned long ago to keep my crest feathers down and my opinions to myself. The more we can fly under their radar, the better off we are. We may be the only ones who truly appreciate the importance of our work, but one day, others will see it as well."

"And what am I then... chopped grendel bait?" Aras stood a few feet away with feet firmly planted and arms folded across her chest. Her knee length dress, worn over torn canvas pants and high black boots, hung gracefully on her curves. A faded and well used pack slung negligently from one shoulder.

Dr. Neywa never noticed her approach and jumped at the sound of her voice. "Sorry, Aras. I should have said the three of us. Can you forgive an old man his inexcusable forgetfulness?" He bowed his head and reached out with upturned hands to the pretty graduate student.

She held her stance and maintained her reproachful stare. Maliche suppressed a smile.

"This department, and myself especially, would crumble and wither into oblivion without your invaluable assistance, my dear. We are eternally indebted to you and your tireless efforts." He gave Aras the most pitiful look of remorse he could muster.

"And don't either of you ever forget it!" Aras smacked one of the flickering wall light panels shocking it back to life, smiled, and grabbed her microelectronic reader pad, stylus and hover-desk pane from the nearby shelf. She tossed her pack onto a dry section of floor and sat gracefully in her chair under the now functioning light panel.

"Are your notes for next week's labs ready for me to look over yet?" asked Maliche.

"Yes, professor, but I wanted to look them over one more time to make sure I didn't leave anything out."

"I'm sure they're fine. Your work is meticulous. Get them to me as soon as you are ready."

A bright smile lit up her face as she glanced at her mentor. "Thank you, professor. I should have everything ready in less than an hour."

Maliche allowed his gaze to linger on the shapely figure of the young girl before returning his attention to professor Neywa. "Have you had a chance to review my notes on that lost artifact from my last expedition to the desert? I hoped you could answer a few questions about it."

The elderly dean of archaeology lifted his glasses as he rubbed his pale blue eyes. Letting out a long exhale which was half grunt, he slumped back in his chair. "I knew this day would come. I was beginning to lose hope of ever seeing it with my own eyes, though. Are you certain your drawings are accurate?"

"As close as I can remember. I made the sketch as soon as we learned the piece was missing. I got a close look at the markings, so it's as good as I can make it."

Neywa exhaled heavily and slapped his hand on one knee. "Hang on a minute. I have something to show you." He punched a command into the keyboard on the arm of his chair, causing it to hum and lift slowly off the ground. Placing his talons into the directional sockets he guided the chair down the hallway.

Maliche and Aras looked at each other. Aras hunching her shoulders in response to Maliche's raised eyebrows as he rose to follow the dean into the dark recesses of the shelf maze.

As Aras tapped the on switch of the overhead light panels, Neywa blew the dust off the label of several boxes before proceeding to another aisle. "Been a long time since I looked for this one," he said as he continued the search in another aisle.

As the accumulated dust of years of neglect revealed another label, professor Neywa's eyes lit up and he pointed to the container in front of him. "Aha! Here it is! Be a good lad and grab this one. Bring it back to my desk for me."

Maliche hefted the filthy box, coughing as he inhaled some of the dust rising from the lid and set it on one of the few float trays still in operation.

Aras, no longer content to eavesdrop from her desk, joined her mentors. "What's in the carton, professor?"

Maliche caught her eye, displaying his own confusion with a shrug. Professor Neywa, a glint of mischief in his eye, wagged a talon at the two. "Patience. You must learn patience to be an archaeologist."

Returning to their office space, Aras cleared a section of the professor's desk for Maliche to put the box. Neywa sat carefully, but his left knee creaked almost as loudly as the chair.

"Before I open this, the two of you must swear you will never reveal to anyone what you are about to see. If word of what's in here gets out to the wrong people we could all spend the rest of our days driving levi-cabs."

Maliche and Aras gave each other startled looks, but said nothing.

The old professor's gaze did not waver. "I'm very serious. I need your promises."

Maliche and Aras shared a brief look, nodded, and then Maliche spoke for both of them. "All right, you have our word. Nothing said to anyone outside this room."

The department head scratched the back of his neck, preening a few gray feathers, then reached down, opened the carton, and pulled out a metallic box. "I haven't thought about this in decades. The markings on your artifacts jarred my memory, so I dug this out to be sure."

The old man set the box on his desk. The surface was smooth, except for a name; Rocker, and some strange carvings underneath.

Maliche stared for a moment. "What are you doing with something belonging to my family? What's inside?"

Neywa smiled, tapping the box with his talons. "I have no idea what is in here. Fifty years ago, I found this box and have never been able to open it. My isotopic measurements told me it was somewhere around two or three hundred years old. Other matters interrupted my investigation, so I hid it, thinking I might be onto something and didn't want anyone else to get the credit. From time to time, I tried to get it open, but nothing ever worked, so I set it aside. Maybe an electro-torch would do the trick, but I didn't want to destroy anything fragile inside. Frankly, I had forgotten all about it until you showed up with those new discoveries. I needed to make sure I was correct about the marking, though, so I dug it out again. I'm sorry I never told you about it, but I truly forgot about it until now."

"What about the markings? Let me see..." Maliche reached out to take the box. As soon as he touched it, he felt his palms grow warm, heard the whirring of gears turning and a loud click. Startled, he stepped back, eyeing the container with suspicion. "What's going on here, professor?"

"I suspected as much. Somebody locked this box with your family biometrics. Only another Rocker could open it. Go ahead, look inside."

Maliche nervously lifted the lid and carefully removed a package. Unwrapping it revealed an old, leathery book. On top of the book sat a metallic medallion. "Those are the same marking as I found on the lost artifact. What's going on here?" He picked up the medallion and turned it over in his talons. A strange buzzing grew in his auricles; the world lurched and went black.

As a gray light grew in the darkness, Maliche felt disembodied. Hazy figures took shape before him, becoming nearly solid. He recognized them, but this was impossible.

***

Jontar Rocker sat; shoulders slumped, staring at the flower draped coffin. Tears streamed from his bloodshot eyes, his mind numb. He felt Karmito's grip on his shoulder.

"It's time, father." Karmito tightened his grip, then released it with a gentle pat and walked slowly to the podium. He stared out at the hundreds of mourners gathered to pay their respects. He tightened his hold on Tari's talons.

His daughter returned the clasp. "I'm here, father. I've got you."

"Welcome friends and honored guests. It is truly humbling to see such an outpouring of love for my mother. I know she would have been deeply honored by your presence, but, knowing her, she probably would have asked what all the fuss was about and told you to go home and quit wasting your time with such nonsense." A quiet laughter rose from the nodding heads in the audience. He continued the eulogy for another ten minutes, first extolling Maripa's virtues, and contributions to this new society, and her heroism in helping to bring it about, followed by a lengthy exaltation of her commitment to peace and prosperity for all on the planet; Brin and Kolandi alike. All of this barely registered on Jontar. His thoughts relived the final years on Dyan'ta and the nearly disastrous beginning to their new life on Raince'to. The emptiness inside ached to hear her voice one more time, or to feel her warmth at his side again.

The gentle voice of the biocomputer spoke in his mind. *"I can let you hear her, or feel her touch again, if you wish it. A few simple adjustments to your system are all it would take."*

"No," he replied in silence. *"She would not want me to continue on that way. I need to learn to live with my grief. I have Karmito and the grandchildren. I must let them grow to fill my life now."*

"I know. I'm glad you realize this, too."

More dignitaries took to the podium, each praising the woman who helped save them from extinction and led them through the difficult days in the early years. Each speaker had a tale of how Maripa guided his or her guild, sometimes by force of will or threat of bodily harm, but successfully through each crisis even after the brothers arrived.

"Come father, we need to thank our guests." Karmito's gentle grip brought Jontar back into the present and, with Tari on the left, helped raise him to his feet.

"I'm all right, children. Just an old fool reminiscing." He raised a talon to wipe the tears from his face. "I miss her."

Tari wiped the tears from her own face as she held on to her father's arm, supporting him. "We all do. But we still have each other. She would not want us carrying on so."

Jontar looked up into the afternoon sky. Not a cloud disturbed the intense blue. The warmth of the mid-summer day felt good on his wrinkled skin. He gave a weak smile. "Especially on such a beautiful day as this. She loved to go for long walks on days like this. Or maybe a good game of Rings." He hesitated, the smile broadening. "I never could beat her at Rings. Kak she was a great player."

The family, Tari and Elarc, Karmito's wife flanking Jontar and Karmito, took their positions to greet the guests. The procession of well-wishers continued for over an hour, each person giving a kind word or a simple hug.

"I can't believe you have the gall to show your face here, Deshro." Jontar startled at the vehemence in Karmito's voice as he addressed the leader of the mining guild. "Haven't your people done enough harm? Since when did you ever show my mother the slightest respect?"

Deshro held his hand out for another moment before dropping it to his side. "Now, now, we must keep up our appearances, mustn't we? I know we have never seen eye to eye on matters, but I have always respected Maripa as a worthy adversary in the affairs of state. We are here to pay our final regards."

"More likely to gloat, now that she is not around to obstruct your schemes. Go away before I call security to remove you."

The large miner shook his head and clasped his taloned hands behind his back. "Yes, well she was a thorn in our crest even after you won the elections, but still, I had hoped we might get off to a fresh start."

"Not likely. Now go and let us mourn in peace."

"Very well. I'll see you soon in the central hall." He turned and gave a slight bow to Jontar. "My sincere condolences on your loss."

Jontar simply stared blankly, not acknowledging Deshro's gesture. As the receiving line drew to a close, Jontar flinched as the flash of cameras sparkled from the edge of the gathering. A few reporters approached.

"Let's go," Karmito said to his family. "I don't want to deal with them now."

Jontar stood firm and embraced his son. "As the leader of this community you need to talk to them. Your mother and I understand. Go, talk to them. Or would you rather let Deshro fill the void?" He gestured in the mining guild leader's direction. "You know your mother and I shared your suspicions about the guild's activities. I promise to keep her research safe where only we can access it. Now go and take care of your public responsibilities. We will have time to grieve together soon enough."

Mayor Karmito Rocker took a deep breath and sighed. "Of course... you're right. All of you go ahead. I'll catch up in a few minutes." He strode off to speak to the reporters.

Jontar took Tari's talons in his and smiled. "You, too. You and Elarc go to the mag-lev. I need a few minutes alone."

Tari studied her father's face, gave Elarc a quick glance, and then nodded. "All right, father. We'll wait for you by the transport."

He looked back over his shoulder at Maripa's casket. Stands of flowers surrounded the gravesite in a rainbow of color. He raised two talons to his chest, then to his lips as the tears flowed again. Turning aside, he walked the few steps to Karm's memorial obelisk. Maripa chose her burial site as close to Karm's as possible, despite her disgust at what she referred to as an obscene monolith. Giving in to immense public pressure she had finally given permission to build the structure, but never grew used to its presence. Jontar approached the marble monument and sat on one of the benches.

"Take good care of her, old friend. She missed you terribly, you know." He sat for several minutes, remembering the struggles against Brach and their final triumph, their abandonment here on a new world, nearly joining the rest of their race in extinction. After a long while, Jontar stood up and stepped forward to the base of the monument. The ache of loneliness returning, he reached into his pocket and pulled out a brightly colored feathery lure. He held it in his grip, then knelt down and placed it atop the attached plaque. Rising, he sighed and strode off to rejoin his family.

***

"Wake up, son. Come on now… there you go."

"Maliche, are you all right?" Aras handed him a glass of water as he regained consciousness.

"Aras? Professor? What happened?" He sat up, took a sip from the glass, and tried to gather his thoughts. "I saw Jontar Rocker… at Maripa's funeral." He looked up into their worried faces. "Everything was so real, as if I was there."

"Take it easy, son. You took a pretty hard fall. Let me help you up." Neywa and Aras hoisted Maliche into a nearby chair. He felt the dizziness fade and clarity return to his thoughts. A chill crept through his pants through a wet spot where he had fallen into a puddle from one of the leaky pipes.

Aras retrieved the medallion from the floor where it dropped and started to hand it back to Maliche. He saw the concern on her face, her hands shaking as she held the medallion out for him. "That was worse than when you first touched the artifact back in the desert. It only shocked you then. This time you were unconscious for several minutes."

The professor intercepted the artifact before Maliche could reach it. "I'd wait a bit before touching that again. Especially since this isn't the first bad reaction you've had with these things." He set it on the table and picked up the book. "You might want to look at this first."

Maliche took the book and leafed through the pages, stopping occasionally to read a passage. He looked up at Neywa and Aras, his eyes filling with tears and his voice choking. "This is Maripa's journal."

"*The* Maripa?" Aras leaned in to get a closer look.

"All the old family stories are in here. They're actually true." Maliche gently closed the book placed one hand protectively on the cover and, keeping a safe distance, pointed at the medallion. "That must be hers, too. I recognize that medallion from an old portrait of Maripa in our family archives. She is wearing it, or at least one with the same sort of engravings." He slapped his forehead suddenly. "That's why the artifacts engravings looked familiar. They're the same as in the portrait's image of her wearing the medallion. I knew I had seen them somewhere before."

Professor Neywa nodded, gathered the book and medallion, and placed them back in the metal box. "That would seem to agree with my date measurements. For now, though, you need to go home and get some rest, young man. We can investigate this further tomorrow."

Chapter Two

Jontar sat at his desk, reading his final entry to Maripa's journal. Only three weeks since her funeral, but his resolve to leave only grew stronger. He had to learn why he had not heard from the brothers, and why they had not come for the funeral. Closing the leather bound book, he sat with one hand gently stroking the cover.

"It's done, my love. Everything is prepared. Our son will soon be in a strong enough position to take on the guild and reveal what we have discovered about them. You can rest in peace. Now I must go and find our friends."

He took up the book, along with the Kolandi medallion, and placed them into the security vault. Touching the surface fed the metal container with his biometrics. With a silent command, a blue glow spread from his hand and surrounded the box.

"Now only a Rocker can unlock it. Time to get moving."

At the sky port, mechanics and flight crews busied themselves at the half-dozen shuttles standing on the tarmac. Apprentices rushed mag-lev carts from one pad to the next. Overhead, the sun shone bright with only a scattering of puffy clouds dotting the blue sky. The fresh scent of spring filled the air. One shuttle in particular attracted special attention as preparations for its departure came to an end. Amid hum of solar-powered electric motors and the rising whine of the shuttle's enhanced mag-lev engines the ground crew added the last of the cargo to the storage bins, checked the security straps one last time and closed the hatch.

The crew chief handed the manifest to Rocker, saluted, and strode off to his next task. Rocker returned his attention to Tari, Karmito and their families. Rocker hugged each of his grandchildren, ruffling their top crests.

"Behave yourselves while I'm gone. Make your grandmother and me proud. If you do, I just might have some presents for you when I return."

The children, vibrated with excitement at their first visit to the sky port, listened to him briefly before running off to explore, their father in tow. Turning to Tari, he gathered her into a strong embrace, and then held her at arm's length.

"You are so much like your mother. Beautiful, intelligent, strong... we couldn't have been happier with you."

"I love you, too, father. Do you really have to go so soon?"

"Yes, sweet one, I have to know what happened. I need to know if we were the cause of their disappearance, or if something more sinister forced them away. I only hope my suspicions are wrong." He took her face in his hands and smiled. "You go take care of those fledglings." The two embraced one last time and Tari strode off to gather her family for the take-off.

Rocker turned to face Karmito and his family now, but focused first on his daughter-in-law. "Elarc, my second daughter. Maripa and I have been so happy with you in our lives. Karmito chose well." He took her talons in his, and then held her close.

Returning the embrace, Elarc smiled brightly from behind tear-filled eyes. "Be well, Papa. I hope you find what you are looking for. And don't worry, we'll visit Mother's grave often during your absence." Squeezing both his hands in hers again, she leaned in, kissed him on the cheek, and then went in search of the others.

Jontar embraced his son, fighting off the memories of life with him and his mother in the early years. "Goodbye, Karmito. I want to get out of here before any crowds start to gather."

"Are you sure you're ready to leave now? Mother is only gone a month. You are still more than welcome to stay with Elarc, me, and the children. There's plenty of time yet."

Rocker hugged his son again and placed an arm around his shoulder as they walked toward the shuttle. "No, it's time to go. I've imposed on you and your family long enough. Plus," he held up his glowing palm, "my friend in here tells me we need to go now if we are to have any chance of finding them."

Karmito reached out to grasp his father's shoulder. "Do you have everything you need?"

"Everything this old bucket can carry." He embraced his son one last time and climbed into the shuttle. Before closing the hatch, he looked back at Karmito. "You know how proud your mother and I are of you, don't you?"

"Yes, father, I do. And I love you, too. Come back to us as soon as you can."

Rocker stood for a moment, and then touched the contact to close the doorway. He strapped himself into the pilot's seat. He waved out the window at his family, punched the controls, and soon the craft soared over the eastern hills. He forced himself to keep his eyes ahead and not look back toward the disappearing city; the life he knew he had left forever.

***

"Maliche, what is your problem? What are you muttering about? It's bad enough when you start rambling on about ancient history, but this is too much. Do we need to call the doctor?"

Maliche realized he was sitting across the breakfast table from his younger brother. His head swam with the collision of two realities struggling against each other. "Selan? What are you talking about? Why would I need a doctor?"

Selan massaged his temples, wincing as if in pain, as he frequently did whenever he had this discussion with his brother. "You're my brother, and I love you, but you drive me crazy with all this talk of ancient civilizations and our ancestors. Your obsession is getting worse." He plucked another bread roll from a tray in front of him. "You were telling me about some new book or something you found, and then drifted off. You started muttering all sorts of nonsense about Jontar Rocker and those extinct Kolandi. For a few seconds there, you seemed to be in some sort of trance, just muttering nonsense."

Maliche's head cleared as he chewed a mouthful of fried eggs. "I'm fine, Selan. Just a little tired. Things at work are getting a bit tense with the front office lately, and now there have been some exciting new discoveries. Guess I'm just exhausted is all."

"Why can't you practice a more respectable profession? I mean really... archaeology? Why do you insist on bringing ridicule to our family? With your markers and intelligence, you could have developed a magnificent career in genetic research or any other path more suitable to our station. But this crazy obsession about our ancestors forces the family to set you aside and give me the responsibilities which should be yours."

Maliche snorted as he reached across the table to pluck another bright blue mondelberry from the polished silver bowl. "Why should I do what everyone else wants me to do?" Light from the tall windows along one wall of the dining hall reflected rainbows around the container. "There are thousands of others researching why each generation's life span is getting shorter. The last thing anyone needs is for me to get in the way of such vital work."

Selan tossed up his hands and snorted. "Don't give me those old excuses. You're a Rocker. Everyone expects us to lead the way. It was our ancestors who saved us in the beginning, and now they expect us to save them again. Everyone believes you are deserting them."

"And who is 'everyone'? You are the one with the highest level of Rocker-genes, not me. Once you were born all that responsibility fell into your lap and I couldn't have been more relieved." He slouched back into the chair, plopped his feet up onto the adjacent chair, and brushed a pile of crumbs from his stained and wrinkled silk dressing robe.

"My markers are only two points higher than yours," Selan said, pointing a gold fork at his older brother. "Yours were the highest in recorded history. You should be doing something more worthy of your status. Your scores at the university more than qualified you for a position in any of the most prestigious genetic research labs on the planet."

Maliche took another bite of his breakfast, spilling half of it on himself in the process. "Selan, I have no interest in researching radiation levels or atmospheric conditions. And don't get me started on how boring nutritional components of native foods would be. All of you are better off letting those who are interested in being confined to a sterile laboratory solve the problem. Besides, now your genetic link to our grand ancestors is the greater, so all the glory, and position in government affairs belong to you, dear brother. And I praise the Eternal every day for my good fortune. Every member of our family has gone into genetic research or politics. We don't need another geneticist; the world is full of them. The Eternal knows we have enough assemblymen… too many if you ask me. Nedia and the children are treasures, they adore you, and our family's future is secure with them. You have freed me from a dreadful fate of responsibility and boredom. I thank you for that. Now, since nobody looks to me as the next Head Minister, I can pursue my whims and fancies."

"How can you call yourself a Rocker? Doesn't our family mean anything to you?"

Maliche paused halfway as he reached out to stab another piece of fruit with a talon. "Of course our family is important to me. Why do you think I travel into those remote areas and spend all my time digging through ancient records? I want to learn about our history… especially the original Rockers three hundred years ago. I want to know if all the stories we grew up hearing are true, or just some mythology grown out of the retelling of tales over the centuries. What motivated them? How did they build that first settlement into a thriving society? Did they really meet Kolandi? Did those indigenous people really go extinct, or are there some hidden remnants buried in the still unexplored regions of the planet? Or are they nothing more than mythology? I'm finding some intriguing artifacts concerning their existence and possible fate you know."

Selan threw his arms in the air, jumped up from his chair and stomped across the room to pour himself a stronger drink. "Not those old tales again. Wives tales and legends told to children. Nothing more. Do you realize what a laughing stock you are making of us in the legislature? I spend half my time there trying to dispel the stories circulating about your ridiculous exploits. If we belonged to any other family, one of the Cloners, your antics would have brought us to ruin and disgrace long ago. Father and I have enough trouble with the guilds and their demands. The miners and that leader of theirs leap at every opportunity to weaken our position, and your exploits provide them with plenty of ammunition." Returning to his chair, he downed the yellow liquid in one long gulp.

"Then it is a good thing we *are* Rockers, and not one of the Cloners. Because I do not intend to cater to the ideals anyone else wants me to conform to."

The sound of metallic footsteps resounding on the polished marble floor interrupted Selan's terse response. The android house-bot, a newly developed luxury servant only the wealthiest clans such as the Rockers could afford, approached the brothers with accustomed formality.

He halted a respectful distance from the table and addressed Selan. "Your driver is here, sir."

"Thank you, Jerek. I'm on my way." Selan waved a hand dismissively.

Maliche laughed at his brother. "When are you and father ever going to get rid of your drivers? That old anachronism only serves to flaunt your position in everyone's face and helps blind you to what the people really need."

As he stood and straightened his tailored and brightly embroidered suit, an indication of his elite status among the legislators, Selan picked up a roll and tossed it at his brother. "You are probably the most aggravating person on Raince'to. Have fun with your scrolls and broken pottery."

Maliche dodged the roll and laughed. "It would be easier if you could convince those pirates in the capital to loosen up the purse strings and provide us with a few more grants. See you tonight, little brother. Try not collapse the economy."

Maliche continued to nibble at his breakfast a while longer, contemplating how best to approach Dr. Neywa. *Another black-out? And what's with these insane visions… if that's what they are? It all seems so real. I hope the professor can shed some light on all of this today.* He stood to leave and shook the small crystal bell in the center of the table. At the tinkling sound, a cleverly disguised electronic signal, a bevy of kitchen and cleaning service bots entered the hall and attended to their duties.

***

Neywa sat lost in thought as he considered the medallion in his hand.

Maliche stood up, and paced the floor, preening his crest in frustration. "That's what's so confusing about it. I can't translate any of those markings. They appear to be some sort of pictographs, but there's nothing like them anywhere. Frankly, I'm stumped."

"There's more you need to know, Maliche. I had planned on showing you this as well yesterday, but after your episode, you were in no condition to deal with it." He laid one hand on the carton which had held the medallion and Maripa's journal, but hesitated. "You both remember your promise to keep all of this secret?"

Aras nodded as she approached her mentors. "Of course, professor. You can rely on us to keep your secret."

"All right, then. All of our careers are in your hands now." He reached out and removed the container's lid, setting it aside.

Aras and Maliche leaned in closer to get a better view. She rested a hand on Maliche's shoulder as she came closer. Her hand felt warm and soft. Her hip brushed lightly against his. Maliche shuddered slightly at the touch. *For love of The Eternal, you really are an old pervert. Get ahold of yourself.* He refocused on the notebooks professor Neywa lifted out of the box. Aras took the empty box with her free hand and tossed it onto the floor. A service bot scurried from its holding bay and picked up the lid, placing it neatly on a shelf.

"Sixty-five years ago, I was a first year student here at the university. I needed to complete an elective credit, so I signed up as an assistant in the archaeology department. I figured not much happened there, so I would probably have a lot more time to study. A month after I started, all strix broke loose."

Maliche nodded in recognition of the significance of the date. "The demolition of the ancient city ruins. Some believe it was an alien city, others say it was once the ancient home of the Kolandi, before some disaster struck them."

Neywa stared at the stack of papers, his eyes closed as he told the story. "Yes. A group of children were killed wandering among the ruins, so the government decided to tear it all down. Public safety was the excuse. Anyway, the archaeologists went berserk and demanded time to collect anything of value or historical interest before it all vanished. The authorities granted two months to get whatever they could, but only under close supervision of government security forces. You can imagine the chaos that created around here."

Aras waved both hands in front of her, calling a halt to the revelation. "Wait…what ancient city? You mean the one in those children's fables about the Kolandi?"

"That's the one," Maliche said. "The government has done an amazing job of covering up the truth of the matter. They label anyone foolish enough to talk about it a conspiracy theorist and the public dismisses them. For two centuries The Assembly has forbidden any large scale study of the site. Everyone *knows* it is just a myth."

"You mean it was real? I thought it was just some story to frighten us kids."

"No, it was very real. But even by my time, the government spent a great deal of time and effort to wipe out any mention of it. All public records were seized, very quietly of course, and all teaching of its existence was gradually removed from the curriculum at every level. A few of my professors still talked about it from time-to-time, but they retired or stopped when the ridicule became too much for them. History and archaeology joined the ranks of the lesser sciences so almost nobody has even heard of the ancient city anymore."

"But why? Didn't people wonder about it?"

Professor Neywa shook his head, waving one hand negligently. "Not really. They completely obliterated the ruins of the city and plowed it over so nothing remained. The older generations gradually died out and the younger folk just figured it wasn't worth much. Especially with all the money going into other areas of research."

"So, what does this have to do with your secret here?"

"I'm getting to that. Anyway, everyone frantically tried to gather as many relics as they could. Photographers ran all over recording images of anything they could find. A dozen heavy lifters brought in material every day. I spent my days sorting and organizing everything as it came in. The important thing was to get the artifacts collected as fast as possible. Cataloging and analyzing the artifacts could occur later, after completion of the salvage work."

I'm sorry, professor," interrupted Aras. "None of this makes sense. If so many artifacts were collected, what happened to them? And why doesn't anyone remember the city anymore?"

"The time for the city's final destruction came. It was quite the spectacle. Security forces kept most people away, but a few of us snuck to the top of a hillside and watched. The destructor beams activated, causing all of the structures to glow. One-by-one they collapsed and fell apart into piles of dust. They plowed under the once great city of the ancients, losing it forever. The mining guild got the permits to open up one of their underground mining operations, so everyone thinks of it as the old mine now. Back in the labs, we began the incredible task of cataloging and analyzing the collection. Before long, rumors started circulating of evidence indicating a civilization preceding the Kolandi. We always assumed they built the city, but then, through some catastrophe that led to their eventual extinction, they abandoned technology and lived the desperate lives of the poor destitute our ancestors tried to save."

Maliche raised up, stretched his back and began pacing. "I've always had trouble with that story about them. I grew up with too many family legends telling something quite different from the official line. I don't think we were the ones who saved them... at least not at first. It's one of the reasons I got into Archaeology to begin with."

Neywa grinned shaking a talon in Maliche's direction. "I wouldn't be surprised in the least. Your family legends may be more accurate than you think. Now where was I? Oh, yes, the rumors. A few of the linguists were attempting to translate some of the inscriptions found on the walls of the city and on some of the relics. Pictographs really, but more intricate and organized into complex patterns unlike any others we've ever seen. Some of the artifacts showed a level of sophistication and technology far beyond anything we have ever encountered, even today. It was immediately after a meeting with some government officials that everything went wrong. To demonstrate our need for greater funding, we showed them the progress we were making with the translations. That afternoon soldiers burst into the warehouse and confiscated everything. All the relics, all our notes, everything was taken. Our people were taken into custody and interrogated."

Aras turned pale and her mouth dropped open. "How is that possible? What right does the government have to interfere with scientific research?"

"They gave us an official notice, signed by the Premier and several heads of the legislature, heads of the mining and manufacturing guilds topped the list. It said we were in violation of state security."

Aras trembled, talons tapping rapidly on her knees. Her eyes blazed. "State security? How dare they!"

"Oh, they dared, all right. When they were finished nobody even mentioned the city again. Everyone transferred into different departments or to other universities. Some took early retirement. I was a lowly student clerk, so they left me alone after learning I didn't know anything—at least until later."

Professor Neywa sifted through the notebooks sitting on his desk. "Praise the gods these old records never made it into the computer data banks. No money to hire anyone to transcribe them. Ah, here it is." He opened one of the books and held it up for his protégés to read.

Aras gently took the notebook from him, examining it closely as she turned it in her talons. "It's amazing. Are these inscriptions the same kind as the ones on the medallion?"

"Very observant, Aras, you may have the makings of an archaeologist yet. Yes, they are almost identical, in fact."

"Is this what I think it is?"

"A record of the language of the Kolandi, or at least what we assume it to be, as transcribed form artifacts collected in the old city," confirmed the professor. "Some of the professors hid these records as soon as the purges began for fear of losing them."

He ran his hand lightly over the inscription. "And the medallion? Is the writing on it in the same language?" Aras was asking as a momentary wave of nausea passed over him.

"Are you all right?" Aras grabbed Maliche's hands to help steady him.

Maliche shook his head to clear it. The dizziness vanished as quickly as it came. "I'm fine. Must have been the excitement."

Dr. Neywa watched Maliche for a moment, and then returned his attention to the writings. "They are the same. My work with those artifacts ignited a passion in me, despite the dangers they obviously possessed. I was hooked on archaeology. I eventually graduated and the dean awarded me a position in the department here at the university. We were barely hanging on even back then and the authorities properly chastised me any time I even mentioned the ancient city. We stuck mostly to Brin history from then on. Then came the day of my discovery. While searching down here in the dungeon for some piece of information I can't even remember now, I tripped over a loose stone in the floor far in the back. When I tried to reset the stone I found that metal box with your family name on it, and these papers. Nothing I tried could open it. I didn't want to risk damaging its contents, so I kept it safe, hidden in the same crate as these papers. I assume someone from your family, Maliche, wanted the information kept secret and hid the container here. I tried making a few discrete inquiries, but no one seemed to know anything."

"And you have kept them hidden away ever since? Weren't you afraid someone might discover them?" Aras asked.

"Did you read the label on the box they were hidden in?"

Picking up the carton, Aras turned it around until she could read the writing.

Neywa
Personal supplies: The Legislature: An Historical Analysis

"Nobody would ever disturb my personal notes on the most hated and boring course offered by this university."

Maliche looked up from the notebook. "So what does this have to do with my medallion?"

"Just this... the two are almost identical. Same pictographs, same syntax, everything is identical, except... yours is roughly three hundred years old. These notes record samples of a culture over two thousand years old."

Maliche stood stunned, unable to even process this news.

"So, how can two languages be so similar if they are thousands of years apart?" asked Aras.

The aged, furrowed face of the old man brightened into a smile as he raised one talon. "Now that, is an excellent question."

Chapter Three

Hours later, after making certain they were ready to make a proper investigation of the phenomenon, Maliche set the crate of notebooks on his desk and retrieved the metal vault containing Maripa's journal and medallion from the bottom drawer.

Aras took his elbow, turning him to face her. "Are you sure you want to do this? You scared the mutes out of me yesterday."

"I have to. We need to know what's going on here. I need to know why I'm having these hallucinations." He held her talons in his as they sat down. "Just don't let me hit my head on the floor again. Are you ready to record anything I say?"

Professor Neywa checked the connections on his equipment and held up the microphone. "We're ready."

Maliche picked up the silver medallion and gripped it hard in his fist. He then began to read the first lines of his ancestor's journal.

My name is Maripa Rocker. I am one of the last survivors of the race who escaped the planet Dyan'ta before its destruction. I have decided to set the record straight and tell the story of our lives and how we came to this world. The journey across space to our new home was nearly brought to ruin by The Monarch and members of The Faith. Karm proved more than equal to the task and it was they, not us who perished.

I suppose I should start with the story of the two brothers. Despite the efforts of many to credit Karm, myself and my husband, Jontar with our survival, it is they who saved us from perishing on an alien world...

***

The world began to fade again, swirling into mist as if a fog filled the room. Maliche tried to speak, but the others vanished as a new reality appeared before him.

***

The wounded grendel charged. The hunting scythe missed its mark barely slicing the hairy beast's shoulder blade instead of smoothly gutting the creature. The man recovered his balance, twirled the curved blade, a grendel claw tipped and edged with sharpened metal and attached to a long handle, and turned to face his prey again. Sunlight flickered through the green canopy of the forest, highlighting the blood flowing from the wound. Howling in rage the great black brute snapped at everything in its reach. Branches shattered in the massive jaws that ripped them from the trees. The beast's monstrous curved claws tore at the ground leaving long deep trenches in its wake. Rising on its haunches, the creature stood to its full eight-foot height and roared a deafening bellow.

The two men back among the trees watched the incredible display of power and rage, circling around for the opportunity at another clear shot. The grendel's shaggy dark head swung from side-to-side, stopping to face the enemy as they stepped into the narrow trail to the watering hole, and attacked. The beast attacked the men before they could raise their weapons.

"Jump, Neas! Get clear!"

Vidad shoved his brother to the side behind several trees and dove to his left. Neas felt the rush of air on his bare arm as the grendel's tusks missed his flesh by inches. The brute snarled and sent great globs of foam flying from its massive, frothing jaws. When it snapped at them, it found only empty air. The beast ran forward for several more strides before coming to a stop.

"Vidad, are you okay?" Neas lurched to his feet searching the thickets for his brother. Their clothing, made from the reflective scaly skin of a mordu, provided excellent camouflage in the forest.

"Where are you?"

Vidad wiped a mixture of torn leaves, dirt, and saliva from his face as he called out. "Over here to your left. Are you hurt?"

Neas checked himself for injuries and, not finding anything more serious than a few scratches, patted his forehead and pointed skyward with the sign of thanks to the gods. He looked toward his brother's voice and saw him nearby; barely visible as his reptilian-skin clothing reflected the greens and browns of the foliage almost perfectly, crouched low behind a large tree. "No, I'm fine, but we need to get out of here."

"Not until we slay this creature. It will feed our people for many weeks. We cannot stop now. Hurry, before the beast returns. Get your scythe ready. I will slow it down with another dart so you can approach from behind and kill it."

Neas signaled his agreement with a wave of his hand and moved off to find a better location from which to stick the beast with another poisoned blow dart. Howls of the enraged beast filled the air, muffling the sound of footsteps among the broken branches on the ground. The dirt and leaves covering him Neas acted added to his camouflage in the patchy light of the jungle floor.

Wiping sweat from his brow, Vidad returned his attention to the grendel. The creature thrashed about in the underbrush growling and wreaking havoc on anything within reach. Raising his blowgun, Neas carefully loaded a heavy dart, poisoned with the venom of three species of vipers, and aimed down the length of his weapon. The monster let loose a deafening roar as the dart found its mark in his neck.

Neas jumped into the air, flailing his arms to attract the grendel's attention. "Come on you ugly beast! Come and try to kill me! Let us see who the master of these forests is."

Neas yelled and jumped as the creature zeroed in on him. The ground shook with each stride, but He held his ground and prepared to dodge the monster, hoping his brother was in position. The grendel closed, leaped high into the air, claws, and curved teeth closing fast on the hunter.

Suddenly, the beast let out another deafening roar. Blood spewed from its mouth, its eyes wide in surprise. Vidad, leaping from a low-hanging branch, swung his hunting scythe in a powerful arc. Neas leapt to the side just in time as the grendel crashed to the ground, rolled on its side, clawing at the long gaping wound in its side. The long claws tore at the spilling internal organs, but only succeeded in opening the wound further. As his life's blood flowed onto the ground, the grendel's cries, and efforts to fight against his foes grew weaker, until only the gasping sound of its breathing remained. Only then did the two brothers approach.

"Spirit of the grendel, we thank you for the food and hides you provide us. We honor the warrior you were and pray the Sky gods accept you into their midst." With that, the elder man took his knife and sliced the main artery in the beast's neck, ending its life.

Quiet returned to the forest. No breeze stirred the broad, pointy tipped leaves. Dust specks glittered in the beams of light stabbing through from the sky above. Within moments, life returned as well. The sounds of cardis and blutons crying out as they flew among the branches grew louder and the squeaks and chitters of dits and various other creatures soon filled the air. The brothers sat on the ground next to their conquered adversary breathing hard, arms draped over their bent knees, heads, dripping sweat in the sweltering heat, hung low.

Vidad eyed the forest carefully. "Let's get this done, before this young one's mother returns."

Later that evening, after butchering the grendel and packing the meat and a number of bones which would make useful tools onto their burden beasts, the brothers sat around their campfire in the small glade. The gentle trickling of a stream nearby joined with the incessant buzzing of the night insects. Distant growls of predators or shrieks of some hapless prey occasionally penetrated the peace. The night also brought a calm breeze to the jungle, adding the groaning of tree trunks to the night's symphony. The clear night sky showed bright with myriad stars twinkling above their campsite. A thin grey tower of smoke rose above the flames. The scent of roasted grendel wafted on the breeze. They savored the taste of fresh meat, a welcome relief from the dried rations and tough, stringy portions of small game comprising their meals of the past three days.

"Caeri will be very proud of you," said Neas. "You hunted well today, and your kill will bring much needed relief to our people." A small carving knife cut carefully into one of the pieces of driftwood Vidad always carried. The image of a woman took shape with each new stroke. He smiled across the campfire at his younger brother as Neas tore another bite from the dripping haunch, wiping his hands on his pants.

Vidad's dark eyes sparkled in the firelight. "It was you who stood in the grendel's path as he charged. You are the one who took all of the risk. Ila will be very angry at you for being so foolish."

"We don't have to tell her everything, do we?" asked Neas. He searched for something to change the subject. "Is that another figure of her you're working on? The resemblance is remarkable even now."

Vidad laughed at the obvious attempt to distract him. "Yes, it relaxes me to whittle these figurines. I don't miss her so much when I carve her face. Don't you want your wife to hear another tale of your bravery?" Vidad pounded his chest to poke fun at his younger sibling. "The great hunter is afraid of his own wife? Say it is not true!" His laughter echoed through the night forest.

Neas could not help but join in his brother's laughter. He shook the blade at Vidad and tried, with little success, to sound stern. "You know she'll tell her sister and then both of them will skin you alive too when she hears how close you let the beast get before killing it. I think for both our sakes the High Priestess and her sister should hear a much less dramatic story of our victory tonight."

"Perhaps you are right... Caeri and Ila would be very upset with us. Perhaps it would be best if we told them we found the beast with a broken leg and speared it from a safe distance."

Vidad tossed his leftover bones into the fire and wiped off his knife before returning it to the leather scabbard on his hip. He shook off the pile of wood chips collecting on his shoes. He nearly fell off the stump he sat on when Neas gasped and jumped to his feet.

"What is that?" Neas pointed at a bright light moving across the fixed field of stars.

Vidad stood and followed Neas's gaze. The light grew bright enough to cast shadows in the forest as it crossed the familiar constellations.

"It is not a falling star," said Vidad as he stared at the object, his eyes adjusting to the radiance. "Look, it is not burning as it falls. And it has more the shape of a spear than a star and does not waver in its path."

"By the gods," whispered Neas, wiping his hand over his face in the ritualistic gesture used in the tribe's prayers, never taking his eyes off the strange incandescent object. "Are the legends true? Are the Sky People returning to us?"

"I don't know what to think," said Vidad as he, too, wiped over his face. "But we need to return to the village and tell Caeri of this sight. She may be able to understand its meaning. We will leave at first light."

The brothers watched, transfixed in wonder, as the glowing cylinder continued its journey, slowing as it descended across the sky until it vanished below the jagged mountains on the western horizon. An hour before sunrise they awoke. The chill morning air condensed their words into small clouds as they spoke of the strange traveling star, and their route home. They ate a hasty meal before packing their supplies onto the pack animals, so the sun measured barely a finger width above the horizon before they pulled on their fur cloaks and started on the trail heading for home.

Two days later, the pair crested a low grassy hill and saw their small village in the distance under the brilliant blue sky. The distant mountains showed hints of the orange and scarlet foliage signaling summer's end. Overhead, flocks of Blutons on their annual migration flew in row after row of V-shaped groups. The small settlement contained about two dozen family huts, one room, adobe walls with one or two windows and a single door in which hung colorful woven fabrics. Smoke rose through the holes in the center of the thatched roofs. A large central building, its walls covered in ornate ceremonial drawings, served as a meeting hall for the council and various other tribal rituals.

Outside this gathering of structures stood the blacksmith shop, open front to allow the forge's heat to escape, and living quarters behind. Split rail stock yards contained the few drunges, sturdy burden beasts with horns and long thick fur, owned by the village. A scattering of low thatched roofs covered the below ground storage shelters shared by everyone in the village. Downwind stood the village smokehouses where they preserved half of every hunt or catch for the long winters.

"Neas! Vidad! What did you kill? Was it something ferocious? Will you tell the story tonight?" The children danced around the returning heroes, climbed on the backs of the plodding drunges, searching through the packs for some hints of the adventure.

Yes," said Neas. "The greatest and most awful grendel you have ever seen." He raised his arms and imitated the animal's stance on its hind legs. "But, I don't know. The story might be too much for you to stand. I wouldn't want to give you all nightmares and send you screaming to your mothers." He waved his arms and growled as he stepped toward the children pretending to be the grendel. The children squealed in delight and ran around Neas, attacking him from all angles as if they themselves were mighty hunters.

Vidad smiled as he watched his brother play with the children. *He has always been a child at heart. He will make a good father someday.* "Did any of you think to tell Caeri we have come back?" he asked the children. "Quickly now, go and tell her we are home."

The mighty hunters stopped their game, looked guiltily at each other, turned, and ran back to the village. The shouting attracted the attention of everyone in the village. They all stopped what they were doing and came out to greet the returning hunters. Vidad handed the drunges' leads over to a couple of the older boys.

"Take them to Sedhor. The meat needs to be prepared before it spoils. Then feed and water the animals and put them out to pasture. We will be by later to pick up our supplies." The boys bowed obediently and led the drunges away.

Vidad turned to one of the women. "Where are Caeri and the elders? Why have they not come to greet us?"

The woman bowed as she responded. "They are still in the council chamber, Vidad. A terrible omen appeared in the sky the other night and the elders are meeting to discover its meaning."

"Then you all saw the light in the sky as well?"

"Yes, Vidad. Everyone saw it and is afraid for what it may foretell. Some people whisper of the return of the Sky People."

Vidad considered this for a moment. His voice rose as he addressed the gathering. "We, too, saw the light and have returned to learn its meaning. I will go to join the elders and we will pray to the gods to reveal the truth of this mystery to us."

Vidad removed his hunting scythe from his shoulder, and handed them to Neas. "I will go to speak with Caeri and the elders now. I will be by later to get these and talk with you. Go on home now and be with Ila."

Neas nodded and grabbed his brother's arm. The two stood looking at each other without speaking for a moment. Vidad smiled, reached up and ruffled Neas's hair then turned in the direction of the council chamber. The most important structure in the village, the council chamber was a round hut surrounded by thick stone walls and topped by a tall conical thatched roof with a small hole in the center to allow smoke to escape. Decorating the outside of the walls a variety of colorful images depicted the history and religion of the people.

Tonight, everyone was particularly aware of the image depicting a shining pointed cylindrical object flying across the sky, an image from their deep past known only as The Sky People. Legends told of great and magical deeds performed by the Sky People and how the Kolandi were their friends. Ancient tales also told of The Great Calamity, forcing a separation between the Kolandi and the Sky People, and how the Sky People would someday return.

The Princess sat in the only chair of the chamber. Surrounding the fire sat the village council, consisting of six women and four men. Caeri was the current descendant of a long line of matriarchs whose ancestors ruled this village for centuries. A small metal circlet sat atop her long black hair glowing in the firelight. Her scarlet feather robe flowed regally from her shoulders beautifully offsetting the fine golden fabric of her ankle length dress, worn only during high council. Samej, the Homsan, stood behind Caeri, leaning heavily on his ceremonial staff, the symbol of his office as advisor to the Princess, every inch covered in colorful carvings depicting important events in the tribe's history. Disheveled tufts of grey hair sprouted from his nearly bald head, but a magnificent long, silvery grey beard hung from his brown and weathered face. The elders sat in circle surrounding the fire pit in the center of the room. Vidad pushed aside the decorated hide covering the entrance to the chamber and stepped into the room.

"We have no proof of your claims the Sky People have returned, Joxmae," said one of the elderly women in the circle. Her long grey hair framed a wrinkled and time-worn face, but her blue eyes were bright and unwavering.

"What else can it be, Sechrid?" replied Joxmae. "This was no natural event."

"Just because we cannot explain something is no justification for jumping to religious claims, Joxmae. Besides, who needs them? They abandoned us long ago. Why would we want them now? Who is to say they would not betray us again, if they even exist? These are legends, Joxmae. The Sky people may be nothing more than stories to frighten children. We are better off without them." Sechrid crossed his hands in front of his face, pulling them apart in a sign of dismissal as the others shouted in outrage at his heresy.

The unexpected light from the entrance caused Caeri to look up from the heated discussion. "Vidad! You've returned!" She rose from her chair and walked around the circle of elders, and reached out to greet her husband.

The elders stopped their arguing and joined their voices to the greeting. "Welcome, Vidad." Each one grasped Vidad by the arm or clapped him on the shoulder amid the clamor of welcome.

"Not a moment too soon."

"Are you aware of what has happened?"

Vidad, ignoring the elders momentarily, embraced his wife then stood back a respectful pace and bowed, wiping his face in honor of her position and as ritual dictated inside the chamber. He then turned and bowed to the elders who returned to sit in their circle.

"Yes, I have seen the light in the sky. Neas and I returned as quickly as we could to discover its meaning." He held Caeri's hand a bit longer, and then took his place as chief hunter among the elders. The Princess returned to her chair.

Joxmae picked up where he left off before Vidad's interruption. "It is written in the scrolls after the fall from grace and our people's separation from the gods, when the Sky People abandoned us, they would one day return."

Rilanta, youngest of the women present and newest member of the council closed her eyes, lifted her face, and searched her memory for the quotation. "And in the fullness of time, the Sky People would return. Their silvery chariots will light the night sky, but with a light not from fire. They shall descend and unite once again all which was torn asunder."

Sechrid shook his head. "Then where are they? The ruins of their great city are only three days walk from our village. Why would they pass so far if it is truly them? And why would the gods let their city be left to fall into ruins? Samej has told us he believes the light landed far to the west, beyond the sea. If they are going to unite us again, why would they not return to their home? I say the light was no returning god. We are wasting our time chasing after myths and old religious nonsense. Even if the legends are true, they speak of gods who left us to save themselves. Why would we search for gods such as them?"

More shouts of indignation ensued, many of those gathered threatened violence if Sechrid continued his denial of the Sky People. The Princess raised her hand and the Homsan stamped the ground with his staff to quiet everyone.

"We have been over this a dozen times now." Her voice, though calm, carried the full weight of her authority. Her dark eyes narrowed only slightly as her gaze met Sechrid's stern, weathered glare. "The time for talk is done. We need to know more before we can arrive at any conclusion as to what the light means. We must send an emissary to the west to seek out the source of this mystery."

"How do we send an emissary across the sea?" asked Joxmae.

Vidad sat up taller and looked toward the Princess, bracing himself for the argument he was about to instigate. "I will go. I know of a tribe on the coast who travel far out to sea in their boats. They tell stories about ships caught in storms and lost for months only to return, claiming discovery of lands on the far side of the sea. I will convince them to take me across the sea to that far away land, and I will search out the Sky People, if they exist."

"No, not you, Vidad," said the Princess. "We will find another. We cannot risk losing you, our best hunter. How would we survive without your skills?"

"Who else would even have a chance? There are plenty of young hunters who can feed the people while I am gone."

Caeri lowered her face and her shoulders slumped. "And what of our children? This expedition could take years before you return. You would be but a faded memory to them before you returned to us."

"You know I am the only one for this journey, Caeri. How could I look my children in the eye if I were to send another to do my job just so I might stay home and be safe? They would never respect a father who placed others in danger rather than risk himself."

Caeri slowly nodded her head, then lifted her eyes and stiffened her back. She turned to face him, her eyes full of authority as she assumed the full demeanor of her position as Princess.

"But you may not leave until the lake thaws in the spring and you have worked with the young hunters. Winter is no time to travel and they must be trained well before you can leave us."

Vidad bowed his head in respect, surrendering to the will of his Princess, and beloved wife. "Agreed."

The counsel murmured their agreement and concluded their proceedings, documenting and announcing to the entire village the decision to send Vidad on the mission to find out if the Sky People had indeed returned.

"But tonight," Caeri announced, "will be a celebration. We will rejoice in the return of our hunters and their success."

The people cheered and went off to gather the supplies for feast. Vidad and Caeri retired to their home.

"Father! Father," shouted Rahnoa as she leapt into Vidad's arms her arms grabbing him in a death grip. "You're home at last! I missed you so much!"

"And I missed you, too, little one," Vidad told his youngest daughter as he spun her in dizzying circles, her long tan legs swinging wide, losing one sandal in the excitement. "My, how you have grown." He placed the smiling girl back on the ground, held her at arm's length, admiring her. "And such a beauty, too. It won't be long before I will have to sharpen my blade to warn off all of the young boys."

"Oh, father. Don't be silly. Boys are just stupid." The seven-year-old blushed anyway, and then scrunched her face in thought as she considered her declaration, smiling quickly as she resolved her dilemma. "Except for you and uncle Neas, of course."

Vidad laughed, turned Rahnoa around, and pushed her toward the door. "Go gather your sister and brother. Tell them it is time to come help prepare the dinner. Off with you now!"

"Don't think this discussion is over," Caeri warned her husband as soon as their daughter was outside. "I'm not happy with the way you maneuvered me into agreeing with you in front of the council."

Vidad smiled, reached into his pouch, and produced the new figure he sculpted during the hunt for the grendel, presenting the gift to his wife. "Do you like it?"

Despite her irritation, the Princess smiled as she accepted the gift. "It's lovely, Vidad. You know I love your carvings." Tears began to well up in her eyes as she examined the small figurine depicting her surrounded by their three children. A flash of mock anger quickly replaced them. "And don't try to distract me with another of your presents. You aren't getting off so easily."

Turning to place the statue on the mantle with the others, she gazed lovingly at the collection. Looking back over her shoulder toward Vidad, a slight smile grew on her lips and a teasing glint sparkled in her eyes

"Just one thing. You might want to try carving something besides figures of me. People who visit might get the idea I'm growing vain."

***

The winter passed slowly. Snow piled high and the lake froze thicker than in recent memory. The hunters, joined by several older children, played furious games of Togash on the ice. Sticks with nets tied to the end allowed players to hurl egg shaped rocks, wrapped in strips of leather, between teammates. Each team scored by tossing the rock at a four-foot-tall post stuck in the ice, defended by the other team. This helped keep the hunter's skills sharp, toughened the muscles of the boys, and kept the Homsan busy by requiring his frequent attention to all manner of gouges, lumps, and other minor injuries.

Fresh food was scarce, but the stores they laid up would be plentiful when portioned wisely. The young hunters learned quickly and soon became experts at tracking and snaring all manner of smaller game. Tikla continued to impress the elders with her skill as a tracker and hunter. The boys of the village competed for her attention as she approached the age for her to choose a mate. Nosaj showed particular talent in organizing and leading the others in productive hunting parties. The larger animals roamed far and wide, but Vidad and Neas found enough small game to teach their students many new skills. By late spring, when the snow finally melted and the large herds returned, Vidad trusted his apprentices enough to let them attempt hunts without him while he evaluated their technique from a nearby hill. Almost no one returned with injuries any longer, at least anything serious.

"The lake is almost free of ice these days," Vidad told Caeri one evening after a successful hunt. "I am thinking it is time to allow Nosaj the opportunity of leading the next hunting party on his own. He has shown great promise." He stood by the fire as she sat at her polished brass mirror preparing for bed.

"Yes," she replied, "and the weather is so much warmer and more pleasant now. I am sure the boy's parents will be very proud of him."

Vidad lowered his head, peered sidelong at his wife, took in a deep preparatory breath and broached the topic they both dreaded. "It is time we discussed my mission to find the Sky People."

Caeri sat silently combing her hair, a dark emptiness growing in her heart.

"We cannot delay any longer. If I do not leave soon, then I will never reach the coast before next winter arrives. It is a very long journey."

She lowered the comb to her lap, fighting the wetness growing in her eyes. "I know. When must you leave?"

"I can make all the necessary arrangements and gather my supplies in a week's time."

Caeri rose up from her chair and joined her husband at the fire, placing one arm around his waist. "Come back to us." She kissed him, walked slowly away, crawled back into bed, and burrowed under the heavy furs.

The week passed quickly. Vidad held one final meeting with the newly trained hunters, double checked his supply list, and retightened the loads on the pack animals. Samej presided over a brief ceremony of parting in the council chambers, invoking the gods favor on Vidad's quest to find the Sky People. He said his goodbyes to Caeri and the children and headed off with the morning sun at his back.

"And just where do you think you're going without me?" Neas asked from his perch on the pile of firewood at the edge of the village.

Lost in thought as he walked, the sudden intrusion of Neas's voice startled him. "What are you talking about? You've been helping me plan this for months. And the answer is still no. You are not going." He shook the reigns and started to move on.

"Okay, fine. You go back and tell Caeri, the Royal Princess herself who commanded me; you are overriding her decree and refuse to let me accompany you on this journey." He jumped off the wood pile and took a few steps back toward the center of the village.

"Wait, Caeri commanded you to do this with me?"

"Well, not exactly. More like she thought my idea of this being a two-man job was wonderful. She knew you would object so we agreed to keep it a secret."

"What about Ila?"

"Oh, she is upset, of course, but she understands. And she knows my traveling with you will calm her sister's fears, at least a little. She's a lot stronger than you give her credit for you know."

Vidad glared at his brother for a moment, but the smile Neas was flashing him quickly dissipated the anger. "There's no way I can talk you out of this?"

"Not a chance." Neas walked behind the woodpile and reappeared with a string of pack animals of his own. "Shall we get started?"

***

His chest heaved, gasping for air. Maliche released the medallion, setting it clattering on his desk. He let Maripa's journal fall from his grasp as he braced himself against the onrush of reality.

"I saw them, professor. I saw the Kolandi. It was as if I were a spirit floating among them, observing their lives without them knowing. This is insane. How is this happening?"

Professor Neywa glanced at Aras, his brow furrowed. "I cannot say, Maliche. I've never encountered anything like it."

Aras took Maliche's face in her hands, examining him. "You were only unconscious for a few minutes. You rambled a few things we didn't understand, and then you woke up. We barely had time to do anything."

She went to the sink and brought back a glass of water. As Maliche drank, she pressed a portable med viewer to his chest and watched as the display provided his health vitals. Despite the readings confirmation of his suffering no more than a burst of adrenaline, Aras took his wrist, measuring his pulse.

Maliche shook free of her hold. "Only a few minutes? It had to be more. I felt like I was gone for hours, possibly days."

"Perhaps you should tell us what you saw. Maybe that will help unravel some of the mystery." The professor picked up his notebook and a pen, waiting for Maliche to begin.

Chapter Four

The center of government on Raince'to resided in First Town. This burgeoning metropolis would be unrecognizable to those who first settled the small village so long ago, where Maripa once held court in a one room town center, also the site of weddings, funerals, and a variety of other community events, elected officials now held seat in the towering Assembly Building. Rising up twenty stories, this cylindrical monument of steel and glass was visible for miles. By law, no other building could be taller. Here were the offices of every major guild and county representative on the planet.

Selan Rocker stood at the window of his office watching the traffic fly by. Six levels of mag-lev vehicles flew above the heavily congested ground lanes radiating out from the Assembly Building. The higher the level, the more expensive the vehicles became, and the less congested the traffic. Selan chuckled as he noticed two drivers on the ground level gesturing wildly at each other, pointing to the damage caused by their collision. "Maybe we should pass some legislation to abolish all ground level traffic. Too many wasted resources are spent dealing with the problems created there."

Selan's aide jotted the suggestion on his ever-present note pad and swiped the note into a folder titled *Possible Future Legislation*. "Perhaps replacing the ground roads with parks would make the idea more attractive." He appended the note in the folder and glanced at the clock in the upper corner of the device. "Time for today's session, sir."

Selan nodded and tapped the control panel on the wall turning the glass opaque as he headed toward the main assembly room.

Today, on this final day of this session's legislature, several important votes were on the dockets, including the eighth proposal put forth by representatives of the mining guild. Inside the main assembly chamber, everyone was anxious for the long day to come to an end.

"The final vote on the matter of a 0.2% increase to the mag-lev vehicle tax to support increasing mining guild exploration on the continent of Mariposa will now begin." Fejf Rocker, Premier of the Assembly, called out to the assembly of legislators. As the highest ranking Rocker, at least until the next election when everyone expected Selan, his son and heir to assume control of the government, Fejf was head of the assembly as was his father and grandfather before him. Selan occupied the center chair among the leading members of the assembly. As head of the committee for guilds, Selan held the second most powerful position in the legislature, outranked only by his father.

All members of the assembly with voting privileges pressed their talons into the slots in their desks marked VOTE. Once connected, small panels lit up with the choices YES, NO, and ABSTAIN. A slight pressure towards their choice highlighted the vote in green. Increasing pressure into the slot cast the desired vote. Computers tallied the votes and displayed the results on a screen in Selan's desk. At the same time, a holographic projection broadcasted the tally above the officials for all to see. Once the vote was completed, Selan touched the TALLEY button and received a print out of the votes. After a quick perusal, Selan selected SEND and highlighted the Premier's name, sending the totals to Fejf.

The Premier leaned in toward the microphone and announced the results. "Four hundred sixty-three in favor of the resolution, twenty-six opposed, and two abstentions. The resolution passes." The result was a forgone conclusion, given the power of the mining guild, but a smattering of applause broke out in any case.

Fejf rapped his gavel stone on his desk to call for quiet. "This concludes all business for the current session. All rise and be dismissed." With a final crack of the stone he exited the chambers.

Selan opened the door to his office and stopped dead as he recognized Nedia sitting at his desk. "Hello, dear. To what do I owe this rare pleasure of your visit today?" He walked over to her, and she raised her cheek for him to kiss.

"I was in the area and stopped by to see if you might want to see a play tonight. The children are with my mother, so I thought we might take advantage." She closed the open drawer of the desk as she stood. "I was getting tired of waiting for you, so I was about to leave you a note, but here you are."

Taking her talons in his, he helped her to her feet and pecked her forehead. "I am sorry, my dear, but I have an important meeting tonight with several Guild members. Perhaps another night."

"Of course, dear. I understand how busy you are." Her eyes dropped a bit and her smile faded slightly, but otherwise, Nedia maintained her composure.

Selan walked Nedia down to the lobby of the Assembly building where they embraced and parted.

Back in his office Selan was nearly finished packing up for the day when the buzzer on his intercom sounded.   "Yes, Ditan, what is it?" he asked.

"Raencert, from the mining guild is here to see you, sir."

Feathers and quills, he was supposed to be here hours ago. What is that old bird up to now? Probably trying to put me in my place again, the old mutes. Selan took a deep breath and grimaced as he considered the ramifications of that particular thought. "Send him right in, Ditan."

The door opened and in strode one of the largest Brin Selan ever saw. Raencert began his career at age twelve as a silver miner across the ocean in central Mariposa. He earned his reputation as a hard fighting man one did not trifle with and rose quickly through the ranks during the next forty years. More than one opponent met with accidents over the years if they did not learn when to get out of Raencert's way. No one could ever prove his connection to the accidents, but no one doubted it, either. These days he wore the suit and collar of a guild representative. The crossed pick, double jack, and sledge overlaying a miner's helmet embroidered in gold on his sleeve indicated his particular guild and rank. Raencert ran the mining guild. In only three long strides, he crossed Selan's office, holding out his gnarled and massive hand in congratulations.

His booming voice reverberated throughout the room. "Well done, Selan. All eight measures passed with ease. Just what we need to expand our interests in Mariposa. Any difficulty from the other guilds?"

Selan expected the question, knowing it was a formality. "Nothing we couldn't handle. Here are the vote totals." Selan handed over a sheet of paper with the name and actual vote of every legislator in the assembly. "As you can see, the lumber guild offered the expected resistance to any incursions into their lands, but there were a few stubborn opposition votes as well."

"Yes, I see. Don't worry, Selan. You did very well. I can handle this from here. I doubt we'll have any trouble from them next time."

"All right, but keep me out of it. I can't have any ties to whatever happens to them."

Raencert towered over Selan, a dark scowl grew on his face. "You worry too much, young man. I just want to send someone over to politely persuade them to our point of view. I haven't had to take any truly drastic action in years." Raencert paused, eyeing the young Rocker as if he were an undertaker measuring a body for a coffin. "Not that I won't do whatever is necessary to get what we want accomplished. So don't you start getting brittle talons on me now."

The implications of that statement shook Selan to his core. "You know I have always supported the cause of the mining guild, Raencert. I just can't afford any scandals. Not with my father preparing to retire after the next session."

The hulking figure smiled, knowing his control over the next Premier was solidly in hand. "Nobody will ever be able to uncover anything. You should know that by now. We've been at this for two hundred years. So relax, and enjoy your recess. I will be back in touch sometime before the next session to lay out our strategies for future legislation."

They hooked talons again, and he turned to leave. Stopping abruptly, as if suddenly remembering something he returned to Selan's desk. "I hear your brother is writing a proposal for another expedition into the desert again. Have you discussed the reasons for this with him?"

Selan knew better than to let anything Raencert said or did shock him, but could not prevent the look of surprise on his face. "No, I didn't know anything about it. We almost never talk about his work, since it usually ends up in a loud argument. Father disapproves of such things at home."

"Maybe you better control yourself and look into it. I don't want him snooping around any of our operations over there."

"No need to be concerned. Maliche has no interest in mining or any of the other guild operations. The deepest deserts and ancient artifacts are all he cares about. His last expedition was hundreds of miles from anything remotely associated with your work. I expect he wants to return to the same location. He mentioned something about a mysterious artifact he found there last time."

"What sort of artifact?" Raencert asked, suddenly alert.

"I'm not sure. As I said, we got into another argument at the time and besides, he said someone stole it from the site so he wasn't sure exactly what it was. It's probably nothing, though. You know how he gets about his broken pottery and such."

"You may be right," Raencert said, tapping the talons of one hand together in loud clicks, a brief grin appeared on his face, but it vanished into a scowl before Selan could be sure he really saw it. "But keep an eye out just the same. We don't want any surprises that would slow down operations. And we certainly don't want him getting anywhere near our new facility"

"His permits only allow explorations into the fringes of the desert, a few dozen miles or so. Our mine is hundreds of miles away. I think now you're the one worrying too much."

"I'm not worried about your brother at all, Selan," Raencert replied pointing a huge finger toward the young man. "But you know the risks as well as I do. I just like to be well informed. The more information I have, the fewer surprises there are—I hate surprises."

A shudder ran up Selan's spine. "Okay, fine. I'll find out what I can."

"Good. Let me know whatever you learn. I'll be in touch." Raencert turned and, this time, left the office. The room itself seemed to relax once he was gone.

Chapter Five

Maliche sat up in his bed, sleep eluding him after the events of the day. Doubts about his sanity grew stronger as he recalled the vividness of the visions. He could still smell the stench of the grendel as if he had actually been on the hunt with the brothers. No, not actually there; this vision had a somewhat different feel. It was like the sensation he got when he was completely absorbed in a favorite story book, but much stronger.

"I must be losing my mind." He climbed out from under the blankets, pulled on his tattered brown robe, and paced the floor mumbling to himself. "Maybe everyone is right about me. Maybe something is broken in me. Why in the world would I choose a life of digging up relics in the most miserable locations on the planet instead of my rightful place in society?" He stopped in mid stride, tilting his head as if listening to some inner voice. "No. I cannot accept that view. This does not feel crazy. Well, it does, but not in that way. Something is driving me to learn the truth about our history. I have to know why."

He stomped to his armoire, flung it open, and recovered the journal and medallion from a drawer. Returning to his bed, he tapped the control for lights. In response, a small lamp rose silently up from his night stand and hovered steadily over his left shoulder. The lamp turned on to a pre-programmed brightness and adjusted to project precisely onto the pages of the book. He stretched out, held the medallion in his left hand, and began reading again.

Our lives on Raince'to, as we named our new home, began well enough. The cloning process worked remarkably well and, with help from the Skae, our population grew steadily.

As the months progressed, though, the virus proved too much for us. Our crops and livestock were devastated. With our food supply in jeopardy we grew desperate. To come so far through space only to die on this alien world would have been a tragedy for the ages...

***

Maripa stirred when she heard the baby crying. "Jontar, it's your turn. Go check on little Karm."

"MmmHmm," mumbled Rocker as he turned over, pulled the blanket over his head, and fell back asleep.

"I'm not kidding, Jontar, go check on the baby." Her voice carried the icy warning of her warrior persona, but the gentle snore from under the covers told her she needed to take more direct action. A well placed elbow between two ribs delivered the right effect.

Jontar bolted up rubbing his side. "Ouch! What was that for?"

"Oh, thank you, dear," cooed Maripa, fixing him with her most deadly smile. "It's so nice of you to volunteer to check on the baby, so I can get a good night's rest for a change." She patted her husband's arm, curled herself into a ball, and buried herself further under the blankets.

"Okay, no problem." As his feet touched the cold floor, he shuddered and stared numbly into the moonlit room. Stretching, he hauled himself up from the bed, ran his talons through his top crest, pulled on his robe, and shuffled stiffly down the curved hallway toward his son's room.

"What is so important? Did you really need to call this meeting tonight?" Jontar asked his son as he approached the child's basket. The round sleeping basket swayed gently as it hung from the ceiling. The child, now a year-and-a-half old, sat smiling and watched his father enter the room. Jontar unlatched the basket's safety-bar lid and picked up the squirming boy.

"Tirsy... want dink."

The boy's father smiled at him. "You do realize it's two in the morning, don't you? Of course you do. Oh well, if you insist, young man. Guess I might as well join you. I wasn't exactly enjoying my dreams, anyway."

The two sat in the kitchen, both with their drinks. The architecture of this, and all buildings they constructed on Rainceto, retained the somewhat circular shape and gentle curves of walls into floors and ceilings of their lost home world. Jontar stared out the window into the night as his son, nestled into his father's lap, slurped noisily at his cup.

If we don't solve this problem soon, I'm not sure we can survive another two seasons. This is one stubborn virus facing us. I just can't seem to find its weakness. At this rate, none of the crops will survive for long. Maybe the teams working on the native plant species will find a way to make enough of them edible. We might have come all this way, only to die of starvation on an alien planet.

Dr. Jontar Rocker, head Geneticist and Leading Citizen of Raince'to, the name of their new home world, felt a warm trickle flowing down his leg.

"Oh, great!" he said to his son. "Now we both need to get cleaned up."

He held little Karm at arm's length as he carried him back to his room and placed him on the bowl-like changing table. After a flurry of well-practiced diaper artistry, the baby was ready for bed. With his son safely latched back in the sleep basket, and quick wash of his leg, Jontar returned to his own bed to try to salvage at least a few more hours of sleep. The heavenly scent of frying meat, toasted bread, and aromatic tea greeted his waking.

"Good morning, dear," said Maripa as he joined her in the kitchen for breakfast. "Thanks again for doing the honors last night. I really needed the rest." She brought him a plate of eggs and sausage, kissing him on the forehead as she set the plate on the table.

"No problem," he replied. "I wasn't getting much sleep, anyway."

He grabbed a slice of bread, piled some eggs on top, and took a bite. The sun felt warm on his back as it shone brightly through the window. He watched Maripa as she gracefully maneuvered around the room, and he thought again how beautiful she was and how lucky he was to have her in his life. Her top crest glowed brilliantly in the morning light and her face reflected her inner peace and happiness. Hers was the grace of a predator stalking the night—a fact which she frequently reminded him of whenever he challenged her to a Rings match.

Suddenly, the back door slammed open and Karm burst into the room. "Good Morning!" Where is my favorite namesake?" He slung his ever-present fishing vest over a chair and propped his fly rod in the corner. "I thought we might go tackle the pond again today while you two were off taking care of business." His eyes twinkled from behind his tanned and wrinkled face.

"Good morning to you, too," replied Maripa. "Little Karm was up half the night, so he's sleeping in, but I'm sure he's up now, if you want to go get him. His breakfast is almost ready, anyway."

"No sooner said than done, Mrs. Mayor," said Karm. He bent down to kiss his diminutive niece's cheek, stealing a slice of toast in the process, and strolled out of the kitchen toward the nursery, whistling some random old tune.

Rocker scratched at his crest again, yawning loudly. "Well, at least somebody is in a good mood these days. Are we absolutely certain he is my clone? It seems very unnatural to me for anyone to be so chipper this early in the morning."

"You know he is just trying to keep everyone's spirits up. With his status as The Savior, he feels an obligation to be an inspiration and symbol of new possibilities. It's killing him to see us in such trouble, especially when he can't do anything about it, but he won't show his anxiety to anyone. He thinks if he keeps up a positive and energetic front, then others will be comforted and not so worried."

Rocker smiled at his wife and took the last bite of his breakfast. "I know. And he's succeeding, too. Not sure what we would do without him."

Karm returned, laughing and spinning the young Karm in circles as they sailed into the kitchen. He plopped the child into his seat at the table as Maripa brought the bowl of boiled grains. Karm picked up the small spoon and handed it to the boy, keeping a damp cloth at the ready.

"Just don't let him fall in the lake and get soaked," she warned her uncle. "I may no longer be a bodyguard, but you know I'll kick your ass if he catches another cold."

Karm narrowed his eyes as he turned to look at Maripa. "Yes, I bet you would," he laughed. "Okay, I promise to keep the little prince safe and dry... as much as possible." He winked at the boy who giggled again, spitting out a blob of grey mush.

"I have to get going," said Rocker. "The new test results will be in this morning and I need to take a look at them."

"Anything promising?" Karm asked, his demeanor suddenly losing its gaiety.

Rocker shrugged and gave the old man a half-hearted smile. "We're always hopeful, but we're grasping at straws lately. Don't hold your breath just yet."

"Don't give up hope. We've gotten out of some pretty nasty situations before. You'll figure it out." Karm waved farewell and returned his attention to cleaning up little Karm's latest mess.

Maripa took another bite from her own plate and put the dish into the sink. "Let me grab my bag and I'll meet you at the mag-lev." She crossed the room to give Karm and her son a hug.

"We have another day of fielding complaints from desperate farmers ahead of us again. I just wish the labs knew something to give them some hope."

Karm turned to face Maripa. "You're doing a great job, my dear. I couldn't be prouder of you and what you have accomplished these past two years."

"You want your old job back? It's yours any time you want it."

Karm's shoulders drooped; sadness appeared in his eyes. "If only I could, my dear. No, the weight of office is yours to bear now."

"She smiled and hugged Karm again, ruffling his greying crest with her talons. "We'd all be dead if it wasn't for you. I just hope it wasn't merely a delaying action. I'll never understand why you resigned from the mayorship. Why turn the reigns over to me?" She grabbed her coat and kissed little Karm on the back of his head, the only spot not covered in mush.

"I'm not as young as I used to be, my dear. The stresses of getting us all here safe and sound took a great toll on me. Remember, the processes which cloned me were not as sophisticated as the rest of you. The Skae learned a great deal about the techniques and fixed some of the problems before starting on you, and then your brilliant husband solved the remaining problems. But I was their first attempt, not everything works quite as well as it should." He smiled and stroked her crest with a talon. "I have all the faith in the world you and Jontar will figure it all out. You'll see. Besides, I have plenty to keep me occupied being your eyes and ears out there among the people. Some of the guilds need a firm hand to keep them from running amuck and you need as much intel as you can get. Now get on to your work and let us get started on our adventures." He gave Maripa his best smile and waved her on her way.

Maripa took a seat next to Karm and leaned in close. "Speaking of the guilds, I've heard rumors of the farmers trying to organize some sort of campaign to join forces with the machinists. And those phalking miners are pressing to explore across the ocean again. Their reports are all in order, but I don't trust them. They're up to something they don't want any of us to know about. Can you look into it for me?"

"I wish we had overturned the regulations giving them sole responsibility for extended exploration. It was a bad idea, in retrospect. We definitely need some sort of oversight of their activities. I'll get back to you on them."

Maripa joined her husband as he finished packing the mag-lev vehicle with the last of their provisions for the day. They hooked talons as they sat next to each other, gave each other a crooked smile, and started off down the road. The roads were still dirt, or mud depending on the season, but there were many more of them now than at the start. Two thousand citizens filled the growing town. Stone and wood buildings lined the streets. Shops and offices filled the center of town; the cloning facilities still held a prominent position and occupied the largest two story buildings. Private homes spread out on the edges. The solar power station stood at a distance to the south. Its gleaming panels captured the suns energy providing electrical power, heating and cooling for the town. Each building retained the rounded edges and curved walls of their former homes on D'yan-ta, but without the majesty of the steel and glass towers of old. Bolt and his Skae companions provided the basics to help the Brin establish a foothold on their new planet, and then vanished without a word only three weeks after the landing.

Everywhere people waved as the Rockers passed. They all smiled, but without joy. It wasn't long, though, before they drove out of town and out among the dying farms. Wilted crops, small and brown stalks sparsely scattered along furrowed rows of dust sat on both sides of the road. Even small breezes lifted clouds of thin topsoil into the air as whirling dervishes. The occasional herds of domesticated hodak and other large animals brought with the settlers were nearly gone. Those few remaining creatures searched endlessly for some sprouts of nourishment, but their protruding ribs and staggering gait gave stark proof of their inability to use the native grasses as feed.

"Don't worry so much, honey," said Maripa. "We all know you and your team will lick this problem soon. You didn't bring us all this way just to die here. You found a way to save us then, and you'll solve this one, too."

"I wish I had your faith, Maripa. I just don't know. Even Karm's biocomputer is clueless. If his miracle device can't find a solution, where does it leave us?"

"You figured out the SCNT stabilization process back on Dyan'ta, not Karm's biocomputer. And you can do it again. Don't be so hard on yourself. All these nerves are just getting in the way. Have a little faith." Sipping on her tea from the thermos, she smiled at him reassuringly, her eyes shining with absolute trust in her husband's ability.

"At least I was working with familiar genetics and gene sequences back then. This alien virus is a totally new bug with some awfully strange stuff going on in its DNA. The triple strand and extra base pairs are next to impossible to unravel. Each time we think we are close to an answer; the bug finds a way to mutate around us. The first season it was just playing with us when it took only ten percent of the crops. Last season, we found out it meant business when it took half. If we don't crack this soon, there won't be anything left to plant."

Taking a left turn at the next intersection, they approached the entry to the first farm on today's schedule. A team of agricultural lab techs, dressed in the blue coveralls denoting their guild, walked toward them from behind the farmhouse.

Rocker banged his head into the back of his seat as he watched the lab techs come closer. They carried containers of grey-green wilted plants and each one walked with stooped shoulders and limp top crests.

"Kak. Not again."

***

Maliche tossed and turned, kicking off the heavy blankets. He fought to wake up, but a heaviness settled in his mind and he drifted back to sleep as the vision shifted its focus and texture. The smell of salt water filled his nostrils.

***

"Land at last!" cried Neas. "I thought this ocean would never end!" their ship rolled with the gentle waves as its great cloth sails billowed and snapped in the wind. Dark grey clouds gathered to the west as the ship creaked and groaned with each movement. Sailors clung precariously to the ropes high above the deck as the captain shouted orders. On deck, additional crew pulled in unison on more ropes changing the angle of some sails, and furling others. The navigator and first mate conferred with each other over the charts.

Staring into the distance, Vidad watched as the billowing clouds and brown strip of land on the horizon signaled the end of their long sea voyage. He kicked away the latest pile of wood chips surrounding his feet and turned to small wooden figure in his fingers, deciding where next to sculpt.

"I always thought of the crossing as a matter of days, not weeks. I imagined the Govayaer exaggerated the distances to drive up their price for bringing us across."

"Their knowledge of the stars and sea currents is unbelievable," said Neas. "Even your skills as a tracker pale in comparison to what these people are capable of. I talked to their navigator. He showed me how he felt the currents to tell our location when clouds covered the sky. I thought he embellished his stories to impress me with his importance, but now, I'm convinced he treated me as if I were a child on the first day of lessons."

Vidad nodded in agreement. "Who could believe anyone capable of traveling for weeks without a single landmark arriving at the exact location and time they predicted. I wish I could spend a year learning from them. Maybe after our task is finished I can return."

"Good luck convincing Caeri. She probably won't let you out of the village for twenty years after this expedition. Not even if you brought her a hundred new carvings."

"Yes, you're probably right. Let me think about it for a while. Maybe I can come up with a believable argument."

"Not in a million years. Look, the coast is approaching fast. We'd better get the gear packed up."

In a matter of hours after their first sight of land, the sturdy reed boat slipped through the surf and came to rest on the sandy beach. A small village, more of a trading post than a town, sat on pillars several feet above the soggy, seaweed covered ground. The smell of rotting fish and decaying vegetation assaulted them. About fifty people moved about the hamlet carrying bundles of furs, pushing wagons of fruits and meats, repairing boats of various shapes and sizes, conducting the business of a vibrant settlement. More individuals displaying a wide range of statures and skin colors from light tan to nearly pure black manned the storefronts hawking their wares. Arms flew and voices shouted in a never ending barter. The sounds of commerce, ringing anvils, saws slicing through lumber, voices of numerous hagglers filled the air. Vidad and Neas followed their companions up a set of rickety steps and into the bustling community.

Their friend, the navigator, led Vidad and Neas to a dark back room behind the tavern where the headsman of the station conducted business. The man sat in a rope sling hung from the ceiling. Two functionaries sat on barrels, one on either side, carefully writing figures in their account books. After a brief introduction, the headsman called for two more barrels moved over for the brothers to sit on as they determined their next course of action.

"Yes, we saw the light in the sky you speak of," said the headsman. His grey eyes narrowed and his brow furrowed as he sized up the strangers. "In fact, there were many strange lights back then. They came and went for a few months and then vanished. Nobody has seen them in over a year. But our business lies to the east, not the west so we never investigated. There are no mystics living in this village. We can't afford to lose anyone for such useless endeavors." He turned his grizzled head and spat on the ground as if to emphasize his point.

Vidad was incredulous. "How can you not be curious? What if the light signaled the return of the Sky People? Doesn't fulfillment of prophecy justify sending someone to investigate?"

The headsman shook his head in disagreement, waving a gnarled, weathered hand in dismissal. "Our interests are in profit. Prophesy is the job of a Homsan, not traders. Life on the frontier is difficult enough without the added burdens of religion."

"Can you tell us anything at all about the lights?" asked Neas. "The sole purpose of our journey is to track down those mysterious lights and discover their meaning."

The headsman rubbed his stubbled chin and gazed at the ceiling of his office for a moment, then cast a discerning eye on the travelers. "Our best estimates suggest the lights made landfall about two months' journey to the west. Too far for our interests, but not an impossible journey for those willing to attempt it. You might want to talk with some of the local hunters to learn more about the terrain along the way. I will arrange for you to meet with a few of them... for a share in the fee, of course."

"That would be helpful," replied Vidad. His experience with traders on his side of the ocean prepared him for the negotiations to follow. "We also require supplies and pack animals for the trek. With your help we can be on our way in two or three days."

Two nights later, consulting a rough map based on information gathered from the hunters and trappers, at the cost of only a few coins, Vidad and Neas plotted their path through the wilderness toward the most probable location of the Sky People. At sunrise, the pack animals loaded and strung together, they headed down the muddy trail into the unknown.

Behind the brothers, hidden in the shadows, lurked two hooded figures. The secretive pair followed the brothers for a couple of hours before they stepped to the side of the trail. They appeared to argue over something, and then ran off back down the trail. Turning left along a side path, they pushed through the brush. A low hanging branch caught the hood of one of the individuals, pulling it free from his head, revealing a shimmer of feathers. Taking off the cloak to untangle it, a beam of moonlight stabbing through the trees reflected off a pin on his right breast. A crossed single jack and hammer, the emblem of a Brin miner.

"You know this is absolutely crazy," said Neas.

Vidad grinned, but kept marching forward. "Just think of the stories you will have to tell when we return... some of your old material was getting stale."

A medium-sized dirt clod exploded harmlessly on Vidad's back. The brothers laughed, pleased to be together for this daunting journey.

Chapter Six

Maliche, late as usual, slunk to his place at the elaborately set dinner table. A bevy of mechanical servants lined the far wall awaiting the signal from Fejf to begin serving. Ceila, Maliche's mother, Nedia and Selan sat silently; eyes focused intently on the silverware in front of them. Fejf's expression carried all the pent up anger of a thundercloud before the storm is let loose. The imperious head of the household picked up the crystal bell, touched the appropriate button, and shook it, activating meal service. The tone set the immaculately polished and elaborately equipped domestic bots into a flurry of activity. Meats, fruits and vegetables of all sorts, far more than the five present could possibly require, soon filled the table. Then additional hovering trays circled the table offering choices to the family members, carving and ladling to each as they indicated their preferences. All in tomb-like silence.

"Do you have to leave tomorrow, Maliche?" Ceila, unable to contain her sorrow any longer, risked breaking the stillness. "I will never understand what could possibly be so important out in that desert of yours. How can a bunch of broken pots and unreadable scraps of paper interest anyone?"

Maliche sighed, took a bite of meat he held in his silver talon clips and, taking a quick glance toward his father, decided against trying to explain his occupation again. "Yes, mother, I really do need to leave tomorrow. Everything is arranged. And what I am learning out there may have great importance not only to our family, but to all of us."

Ripping off his talon clips and tossing them onto the table, Fejf shoved his chair back, nearly gouging the marble tiles. "Great importance indeed! More likely you'll be the ruin of this family. You've always been a disappointment, but now you are bringing the anger of some of the most powerful guilds down on our heads with this talk of wild dreams. It was bad enough all those years trying to explain your obsession with ancient myths, your head always in the dust somewhere, but now... you need to wake up, fledgling, before you take things too far." He stormed out of the room, slamming the heavy carved doors behind him.

Ceila stood quietly, gently removed her talon clips and placed them carefully next to her plate. "I apologize, Maliche... Selan, Nedia. This was my fault. I never should have said anything in front of your father." With a sad smile, she nodded toward each of her sons and daughter-in-law and slipped out of the room. Nedia rose quickly, nodding at Selan, before following after Ceila.

"The two of you never learn, do you?" Selan skewered another bite of meat with his index clip, swallowed, chasing it with a long draw of sweet wine. He used the dripping clip to point across the table at his older brother. "Father will never accept your choice to abandon his ambitions for you as his first born. He always dreamed of you being the next Rocker to solve our aging crisis and save the Brin. He feels you have betrayed him."

"I know, Selan. But I have different interests and goals for myself. I refuse to buckle under father's unreasonable demands—regardless of his threats. I can't be the next Jontar Rocker. What I am doing is vitally important."

"Too bad so few others agree with you."

"Followers don't make one right, Selan. Besides, if I'm right, I may just overturn everyone's opinion of archaeology." Maliche leaned in conspiratorially toward his brother, checking the room for eavesdroppers, and lowering his voice to a whisper. "I may be on the verge of finding out what happened to the Kolandi—if anything happened at all."

Selan's brow furrowed as his crest fluffed. His eyes darted around the room as if checking to see if anyone was listening. "What do you mean 'if anything happened at all'? They all vanished hundreds of years ago. It's all in the histories. What are you up to, Maliche?"

"It's too early to say with any certainty. I only have a few artifacts to support my hypothesis, but I am hopeful this expedition to the Great Southern Desert will provide me with the evidence I need."

Selan's visage grew darker. He leaned in, pointing a talon at Maliche. "What are you talking about? And what do you mean, the Great Southern Desert? Your permits only allow you access to the western perimeter. You've been there several times and never found anything to set you off like this."

"Nothing I've shared publicly, anyway. I don't want to compromise your position in The Assembly, Selan, so I have not said anything, and I won't, until I get definitive proof." He hesitated, eyes shifting upward and left trying to decide, and then reached across the table to place his hand on top of his brother's. "Selan, the Kolandi may not be extinct. They may just be hiding from us."

Selan's jaw opened and closed several times in stunned silence. He grabbed his goblet, took a long drink, and sat back in his chair staring at Maliche. He wiped his face with his empty hand and took another gulp of the wine. "Now I must agree with father. You've gone completely feather-fluffed. Your type has been searching the perimeter of that desert for centuries without discovering so much as a hint of the proof. They are extinct."

"And there you have the crux of the problem. We're only allowed to search the perimeter. My permit allows me to go further than ever before into the interior. I have always taken some liberties as to where the 'perimeter' ended, and I'll admit I have stretched that boundary a bit. Fortunately, the authorities have, so far, willingly looked the other way, but now I have written permission to search a previously unexplored region. All strictly gridded and mapped out, but precisely where my previous finds would suggest something significant."

Tossing his hands in the air, Selan stood up and headed toward the door. "Only you could look at a broken shard of some ancient cooking utensil and see natives wandering the planet. You are a hopeless dreamer, Maliche." The door opened abruptly as he reached for the handle and he nearly collided with Nedia.

"Why must you always fight with your brother, Selan? You know how it upsets everyone." Her chin lowered to her chest, eyes downturned.

Taking a deep breath, Selan placed one hand on her shoulder as he passed. "You know how exasperating he can be. I just need to go for a walk."

***

The Guild's section of town proved to be more sinister than Selan ever imagined. The streets teemed with miners who dwarfed him, male and female alike. Glaring lights and blaring music advertising the many amusements available to the passerby assaulted his senses. The smells were none too pleasant, either.

The public mag-lev's automated announcement indicated this as the location of the Double Jack, the bar Raencert owned, and dropped him off at the corner pointing down the block. But the barrage of sound and the smell of garbage, booze, and unwashed bodies made the walk difficult and unpleasant as he pushed his way through the crowd. At last, he noticed the old fashioned mechanical sign with two figures, one swinging a large hammer while the other held a spike, above a red metal door. The sight of the monstrous doorman caused him to regret agreeing to this meeting. Taking in a deep breath, one he regretted immediately, and marshaling his courage, Selan approached the establishment.

"I have an appointment with Raencert." Selan tried to look as important as his title would indicate.

The guard eyed him up and down, consulted his communicator, and then opened the door. "Up the back stairs. The boss is expecting you."

The interior of the Double Jack proved to be precisely the opposite of its exterior. A string quartet played beautifully on the tastefully decorated stage. Several dozen tables complete with tablecloths, china and crystal filled the floor, each occupied by well-dressed couples of obvious wealth. Plush carpeting covered the floors and several works of art decorated the walls. The Maître d' approached and directed him toward the stairs leading to Raencert's office.

Raencert met him at the door hooked talons, placed a powerful arm around Selan's shoulder and led him into the sanctuary. "So what do you think of my place?"

"Not at all what I expected." Selan realized this sudden honesty may have been a mistake, but it was too late now.

Raencert laughed as he seated himself behind his desk, its surface inlaid with polished stone. "Elegance amid the common. Precisely the image I intend to convey. Here in this district, I can be in close touch with the common worker and still cater to the upper crust whose favor I need to court from time to time."

"How do you convince your customers to come into this region? Aren't they likely to get mugged or something?"

His voice took on a note of iron as he leaned forward. "Anyone foolish enough to threaten one of my guests would not be tolerated. Everyone you see on these streets depends on the mines, and the mines depend on me. The last such incident was ten years ago. I ordered the idiot shipped off to one of the Eastern Continent mines with a stern warning to never return to this side of the ocean. Of course, rumors of much direr consequences grew, with my help, and so business continues undisturbed. Now, what is of such grave importance that you couldn't wait until tomorrow to discuss?"

Selan sat upright in the small chair trying to make himself larger. The impatient glare on Raencert's face and his reddening crest convinced him it was best to tell everything.

"It's my brother… somehow he managed to obtain a travel permit to explore portions of the interior of the Great Southern Desert. He plans to leave tomorrow."

"I am already aware of that. Nothing happens in the desert without my approval… or did you think I was completely incompetent? I have set very specific and narrow coordinates, far from anything we would be concerned about, for him to dig for his artifacts. This way, we can satisfy his curiosity, and the interest of many others, about the desert. Too much secrecy breeds too many questions we don't want being asked." Raencert folded his well-muscled arms across his broad chest, daring Selan to continue.

"You know me better than that, Raencert, I'm here to make sure we are both together on this. I don't want anything to go wrong any more than you do."

Selan's eyes shifted nervously from Raencert to the doorway and back again. The lump in his throat felt as big as a grendel as he swallowed. Even for one of his authority it was never wise to upset someone like the head of the mining guild. High ranking officials have mysteriously vanished before and Selan did not relish the thought of being the next.

"There is more. My brother hinted that he often uses his status as a Rocker to sometimes ignore the limits of his permits and I know he plans to go beyond the limits you have set for him."

"I would not have expected anything less from him. We know all about his taking liberties and using his influence to go places he is not supposed to be. In this case, however, we have set certain precautions in place to make sure his extracurricular endeavors go nowhere near our secret mines."

"What precautions? He may be an embarrassment to the family and a feather-fluffed idealist, but he is my brother. I wouldn't want him hurt just to protect a few hidden profit sources. At least, not unless we had no other options."

"You let me worry about that. Is there anything else before you go?"

"Nothing for now. I wouldn't worry about him turning up anything. He just has some harebrained idea about the Kolandi not being extinct. He thinks they may just be in hiding somewhere in the desert. He won't be concerned about locating any of the mines."

Raencert paled noticeably for the briefest of moments, his voice took on even greater ominous tones as he leaned forward, arms crossed on the desk. "What, exactly, did he tell you about the natives?"

Chapter Seven

Thank The Eternal for the brothers. Despite the efforts of many to credit Karm, Maripa, and myself with the saving of our people, the truth lies in the teachings of those kindly strangers. They showed us how to work the land to make the vegetation palatable. It was they who taught us the proper techniques of treating the meat of the native animals, so we did not poison ourselves. We should have raised monuments to them, not ourselves...

***

Maliche nodded as he sipped from the glass of water. The visions always left him feeling drained. "That's as far as I got before blacking out?"

Aras set the journal back on the desk. Her face contorted as she sat staring at the book, she folded her arms across her stomach, and looked back at Maliche. "This contradicts everything we're taught. It was your ancestors, Jontar and Maripa who saved everyone, not the Kolandi." She slammed her personal note processor on the desk, jumped to her feet, and stormed off to the far corner of the room, arms hugging herself in a tight grip.

"Everything my visions are telling me says our version of history is wrong... at least on this account. The Kolandi did and were capable of more than we know. My visions have made that clear. Their legends seem to indicate they are descended from a culture more advanced than our own. Only a great tragedy, one lost in antiquity, reduced them to a non-technological society."

"This is why I authorized your new expedition to the desert. Maybe you can find some new corroborating evidence in the areas we've picked out based on what you've told us of the Kolandi village." Professor Neywa turned off the imaging recorder and leaned back in his chair, rubbing his chin. "Again, your mutterings were somewhat incoherent for the most part, and this episode was only a minute or two longer than the last. We need to hear your recollection of exactly what you saw before you take off this afternoon. It may be the last opportunity I have to gather some data from you for quite a while."

"It's more than simply something I see, professor. It's like I'm living right alongside them all. Time has no meaning in the visions. You tell me I'm only out for a few minutes, but it feels like weeks, sometimes months to me. It's very disorienting when I wake up."

"I believe you, son, and I sympathize with your anxiety over it all. If we are to be of any help, please, tell us what you can." He waved for Aras to take her seat at Maliche's side.

Maliche took a deep breath, felt his heart racing as Aras reset the med viewer on his chest, double checking the readings were all within acceptable parameters. He closed his eyes, trying to recall the experience. "I was in Jontar Rocker's laboratory. The mood was desperate... everyone on edge. Crops and livestock were dying due to some unknown virus which attacked the Brin species they depended on."

As the memories surfaced Maliche relived the vision.

***

"Doesn't anything kill this phalking virus?" Dr. Rocker paced the aisles of his lab shouting at the ceiling. "Over two years and this thing still hides its secrets. I can't fail. There must be another way."

The latest printout detailing another failed experiment littered the floor around the former Professor. Not even the explorers returned with good news. Oh, they found mineral deposits, rivers, lakes, even the remains of an ancient alien city according to one report, all valuable for the future if anyone survived, but nothing to help solve this current crisis. At first, the city ruins held great interest for everyone, but nobody discovered anything to indicate who built the once magnificent structures or where they went, so the pressures of survival returned relegating everything else to secondary status. In another hour, the rest of his team would arrive, but for now, Rocker was free to vent his anguish.

"Some brilliant geneticist I turned out to be," he barked at the walls. "There must be an answer. What am I missing?"

The door burst open and in rushed a breathless young intern. "Dr. Rocker! Come quick!"

Now what? "What's the matter? Is anyone hurt?"

The intern leaned heavily on the nearest desk as she caught her breath, her eyes wide in excitement. "No, Doctor, everyone is fine, but you need to see this, it's unbelievable. There are humans here!"

Before he could reply, the girl was running back through the door and down the hall. *What the hell does she mean, 'There are humans here'? Of course there are people here. There are about two thousand people cloned and processed here as of last count. This better not be some juvenile prank.*

Lost in his thoughts, the doctor never saw where the young woman ran off to. Stopping to look around once he reached the street he saw the large crowd gathered at the edge of town.

***

Oh great, she must have meant there's a fight here. Rocker picked up his pace, and then stopped dead in his tracks when the mob parted. Standing there with his arms dropped to his sides, jaw hanging open he watched two humans walking down the street in the middle of a crowd of agitated onlookers. Long black hair, not feathers, covered their heads. Something about their skin was startlingly strange. Yes, it was darker than most he had ever seen, but there was something else. Then, as the sunlight shined through a gap in the clouds, he realized the human's skin lacked the transparent scales of the Brin. Except, that is, for the tips of their talon-less fingers which appeared to have a single thick scale on each. They were uttering strange sounds, some sort of communication he thought, but even the gestures they used to accompany the sounds were too unfamiliar to make any sense of.

Even their clothes were unusual. Not synthetic at all, but some sort of scaly animal skin sewn into trousers and a sleeveless vest which appeared to change color as the two walked passed different structures The weapons they carried caused Jontar to pause. Both men used tall curved-blade weapons, part animal claw and part worked metal, as walking sticks, and both had long knives hanging from sheaths on both hips. Bone handles of smaller knives protruded from their boot tops. The shorter of the two also carried a long and intricately carved hollow wooden tube and a quiver of foot long darts slung across his chest.

I hope those are for defense and hunting. Jontar thought. The humans halted, watching the growing crowd warily.

The Brin formed an arc around the humans while the children, not able to contain their curiosity, approached the strangers. Rocker watched in awe as the children reached out to touch the smooth skin and hair on their heads. Hesitantly at first, but when the beings showed no sign of aggression, the bravest among them grew bolder, reaching out to touch their smooth skin. The men, in turn, ruffled the crests of the youngsters, laughing at the experience. Both investigated the unfamiliar physical characteristics of the other. Rocker knew mammalian creatures with intelligence were theoretically and genetically feasible. After all, the jungle dwelling Tarsis back on Dyan'ta were well known for their ability to solve simple intelligence puzzles, but he never actually believed he would witness such unusual creatures. He found it difficult to accept, even with the evidence of their existence right in front of him. *Who the strix are they? They're not Brin.*

Two hours later, after finally tracking down Karm at the river, the town council convened in the gathering hall. Despite the immense curiosity Maripa allowed only Karm, Dr. Rocker, and two other high ranking council members inside with the guests.

Karm's left arm glowed as he activated the biocomputer. "I hope this thing is translating correctly for us. Do you understand my words?" he asked the newcomers.

Their eyes shot wide and the visitors exchanged wondering looks. Vidad spoke first. "Yes, this is incredible. I hear your words in a strange tongue, but my mind understands their meaning. How is this possible?"

"We have a device which can translate our two languages so we can communicate without difficulty," Karm held out his left palm to show the glowing biocomputer. "There is no need to fear. Who are you? Where do you come from? Why are you here?"

After a furtive glance to his brother, Vidad continued. "My name is Vidad. This is Neas, my brother. We followed your star from across the great sea. Our travels have been long and hard. We hoped to find the Sky People. Our legends make no mention of bird-men and we have never seen anyone like you before. Do you know of the Sky People?"

Maripa spoke next. "We did arrive from the sky just over two years ago, but I don't see how your legends could possibly mean—"

"A moment, please, Maripa," Karm's face gave the impression of one rudely awakened from a dream. He gave his palm a brief look of something between frustration and anger. "My implant just fed me a few dozen centuries of history conveniently left out of my previous education." The glow altered slightly from the familiar yellow to a faintly pinkish hue. "It seems our guests are referring to the Skae."

"You mean Bolt and Zem's race?" asked Maripa, astonishment replacing her normally placid composure.

"The very same. Apparently, the Skae and their people share a long history dating back thousands of years. Something happened to separate them long ago. This darn contraption is up to its old tricks again and won't tell me anything more. I get glimpses of… something… something that went terribly wrong, but then nothing. It's as if there are gaps in the biocomputer's memory banks. Dead spots I can't see through."

The glow became distinctly redder and Karm's arm grew warm.

Maripa ignored Karm's look of concern over the changes. "What are you talking about? The Skae travel out there among the stars." She waved her hand absently toward the sky. "These natives don't look like they know anything about Cosmic Strings and interplanetary exploration. Are you sure your computer is working correctly?"

"They're obviously just a couple of ignorant savages still believing in mystical gods and spirits," said Shoder, leader of the mining guild. "We have more urgent business to take care of. Just give them a few trinkets and send them on their way." A look of disdain crossed his face as he watched the two visitors.

"Be quiet, Shoder," said Maripa. "These men might have information we can use. They are obviously indigenous to

Raince'to and know how to survive on the native plants and animals. They may be able to help us."

Vidad held up his hand, tilting his head in apparent confusion. "What is this Rayns taw, you speak of?"

Maripa looked at him as though she had forgotten he was there. "Raince'to. It's the name we have given to your world."

Neas laughed out loud. "How can you give a name to something which already has one? This place is called Kodut."

Shoder sneered and threw up his hands in disgust. "Why are we wasting our time here? What can primitives like these two possibly have to offer us? We need to focus on the science for a cure, not some mystical fantasies."

No longer able to contain himself, Neas pleaded with Maripa. As members of a matriarchal society, Vidad and Neas gravitated toward Maripa as the true leader of the town. "These people you speak of, the Skae, are they the Sky People? Do you know them? Are the legends true? Are they returning?"

She reflected on the idea for a moment. "I think you might be right, Neas. Over time, your people must have altered Skae into something more understandable... Sky. I believe the Skae are your Sky People. They are the ones who brought us here to Raince'to, but they never told us anything about your people inhabiting this planet."

Vidad's eyes widened, his jaw dropped as he reached out, palms upward. "Where are they? Why do they stay hidden from us? Are they angry?"

Maripa shook her head. "No, they are not angry, but they are no longer here. They left us over a year ago. I am sorry, but we do not think they plan on returning."

Neas and Vidad slumped in their chairs, heads hung low. Vidad gripped his brother's shoulder, and turned his brown eyes toward the Brin council. "Then we have failed. If only we left as soon as we saw the light. Maybe then we would have met them and fulfilled the legends. Sechrid must be right. The Sky People deserted us... betrayed us."

Neas slapped his brother's hand away. "No, brother. I can't believe the gods are so petty. There must be another explanation. Maybe these strangers were brought here by the gods to fulfill their promise to us even after all this time."

Vidad brightened a bit at this thought. "Perhaps you are right, Neas. Who are we to question the Sky People and their ways?"

"I am sorry for your troubles," said Rocker. "But I think something good can come from all of this. We need your help."

"You, who traveled with the Sky People among the stars, need our help?" Neas sat back and crossed his arms over his chest. His eyes searched each of the Brin in front of him. "What could we possibly offer to ones who befriend the gods?"

"The Skae, and we, are not gods," continued Rocker. "We are mortal beings like yourselves who have traveled a great distance to save our people. But on this new world, a disease attacks our crops and livestock. All of our efforts to save them are failing. When we try to use native plants for food we find them difficult to eat. Can you teach us about the plants and animals of this world and how to use them for food?"

Vidad and Neas looked at each other in disbelief. Neas shook his head, and waved one hand across his face. "This cannot be true. How can a people understand how to travel among the stars, yet not know how to feed themselves?"

Shoder snorted, slamming his hand on the table. "Ignorant savages. They don't understand anything about genetics, viruses, or disease."

Karm glared at Shoder, a sudden flood of angry images from the biocomputer filled his mind as he lashed out at the miner. "And a kak-load of good our science has done us so far, no offense, Jontar, so why don't you shut your ignorant mouth and try to learn something for once."

Ignoring the argument, Rocker stood and paced the floor behind his chair. "Unfortunately, our world is so different we are not familiar with the problems we face here. The diseases affecting our food are very strong. We don't know what to do. Our people are farmers, not hunters, so we are unskilled at catching wild game. Those we have trapped and killed have made us sick. The same is true of the native plants. We do not know how to make them edible. Nothing we've tried does any good. Can you help us?" He reached out to the brothers, pleading with open arms.

Vidad stood and walked around the table to Rocker, grasping his arms. "If what you say is true, then we must help the friends of the Sky People."

Everyone around the table spoke at once. Even Shoder, under Karm's reproachful glare, reluctantly agreed to let the brothers do what they could to help. The joy of new hope lifted all of their spirits higher than the past many months. Vidad and Neas became instant celebrities.

Karm did not participate in the excitement. Although the glow surrounding his arm returned to its usual pale yellowish color, he studied the device closely. "What has gotten into you?" he asked. The glow changed again, this time to a light pink shade.

***

"It was then I felt a rush, as if the accelerator of a mag-lev stuck and flew out of control." Maliche filled his glass with more water and took another drink. "When everything settled down it felt as if I had suddenly teleported to a new location. This is the wildest thing I've ever experienced."

"Aras set the med viewer on the desk, stepped up behind Maliche and massaged his shoulders. "It sounds incredible. I'm not sure what to make of it all. At least these visions don't appear to be affecting you physically."

Dr. Neywa tapped his notes with his pencil. "We can sort it out later. Right now, we need to hear the rest so you two can get going."

Maliche finished his water and took a deep breath, hunching his shoulders to lead Aras to a tight knot. "All right, professor, as I was saying, the vision teleported me to a new time and place where…"

***

Five months later, Maripa, Karm, and Rocker watched from a nearby hill as farmers plowed their fields and spread the powdered rocks Neas taught them about. Rows of crops shown green and full as farmers walked among the furrows spreading another layer of grey powder. To the west, split rail fences sectioned off large pastures around outcroppings of the same pale mineral. Herds of captured native animals, this world's equivalent of cattle, roamed peacefully munching on native grasses among the rocks.

Rocker took another bite of fruit as he wrapped his arm around his wife. "We should have known better. The minerals in those rocks leach out the poisons so the plants become edible. Our cattle still cannot eat them, but we can."

Maripa scrunched up her face as she looked at the fruit in her talons. "I guess we can get used to the taste, eventually."

"And those animals, what did Vidad call them… tirpits? If we locate our pastures in the areas he showed us, and cure the meat using those native herbs, steaks are back on the menu. The milk tastes a bit sour, but not too bad. Once I am able to analyze the genetic make-up of the native species Neas and Vidad have shown us, creating new variations to suit our needs will be no problem. Those two saved our feathers."

"Shoder is still sulking about it all," Maripa said. "He calls the tirpits 'those kak four-legged hodaks.' And still won't talk directly to Vidad or Neas."

Rocker shook his head as he finished off the fruit, tossing the pit aside. "Shoder is a feather-fluffed hot-head, but he'll get over it soon enough."

"I hope you're right." Her face twisted in apprehension. "I've received reports concerning Shoder's disquiet and how he is building a group of followers."

Rocker turned toward her, incredulous at the news. "Followers for what? We would have died before discovering the things they've taught us. Are they completely yolkless?"

"Ignorance and prejudice still are part of our make-up, my sweet. It appears I will have to have a talk with Shoder and his group before long to calm them down a bit. Maybe if I grant them the exclusive rights to travel across the ocean, Vidad and Neas talk about it will satisfy them."

"How can you possibly grant them exclusive rights? Miners are not the only ones who need to expand their resources."

"It would be limited to only a year or two, then open up to everyone. They do make a good point about being the only ones with wilderness experience. Freelancers have been exploring all over this continent for a while now."

"Surprising, they never mentioned the Govayer on the coast."

"It's a big continent, Jontar. They may be arrogant, self-important fools, but I'm sure they would not have hidden something as important as another intelligent race from us."

Rocker shook his head in disgust. "Maybe you should be more the bodyguard and less the politician and just knock some sense into them."

Karm sat quietly, lost in thought as he listened to his friends. *I wonder why Bolt and Zem never told us about these natives. Why didn't they settle us closer to them? They must have good reasons, but what? And what is going on with this biocomputer lately? Why does it keep skipping over important details I try to access?*

The voice in his head sounded contrite as it answered his queries. *"I cannot provide you with information I do not possess. The information you seek is not a part of my data banks."*

"Why would the Skae not put such important facts in your system? It doesn't make any sense."

The glow in Karm's arm grew distinctly red and warm, almost hot. *"I have searched my system for an explanation, but find nothing. You will have to be satisfied with this limitation."*

Maripa reached over and shook Karm's shoulder. "Are you even listening to us, Karm?"

Grinning, Karm winked and waved his arm across the view. "I'm listening. Just thinking is all. Now we know about drying and storing the fish in cold lake water for at least a month, so I can start eating what I catch again. Won't that be something? You two have any plans for the kiddo tomorrow? I might want some company down by the river."

"You can't go fishing tomorrow, Karm. Vidad and Neas told me they feel confident we can survive on our own now, so they will leave in a day or two. They are anxious to return to their families. Tomorrow is the celebration to thank them. The hunting parties put aside a portion of every catch, and the farmers gathered enough greens to hold a respectable feast for our honored guests."

"I guess the fishing trip can be postponed for a day or two. We don't want to miss a grand feast now do we?"

Later in the evening, Maripa sat on a bench by the fire with her husband and child. "Isn't this the grandest celebration? We haven't eaten so much in over a year." She stretched across Rocker's lap to grab another tirpit nugget. "And this meat does sort of grow on you. Not too bad after all." Licking the juices from her fingers, she tore tiny pieces from her meat, chewed them a bit, pulled out a bit with her talons, and fed them to Little Karm. The child snapped at the offerings, swallowed quickly, and squirmed in his mother's lap for more. "He certainly seems to like them."

Rocker watched as the townspeople danced around the bonfire. Their shadows boogied in the flickering flames. "Everyone is having a wonderful time, too bad they can't sing worth a darn," he said, wiggling a finger in one auricle. "I knew we should have collected more samples from musicians."

"Be nice, Jontar," cautioned Maripa knocking him with her hip.

Karm sauntered up to join the three of them on the bench. "I can't remember when I ever had so much fun. This is just what the people needed. That kid, Neas, is quite the story teller. He has everyone spellbound with his tales of adventures. Folks were getting mighty glum around here." He snagged a nugget and slice of gourd from Rocker's plate.

Rocker set the empty plate aside and pulled Maripa close with one arm. "Vidad and Neas's arrival was nothing short of a miracle."

Karm licked the last of the meal from his talons, gave a not-so-discreet belch, and sighed contentedly. "Speaking of those two, they requested an audience with you, Maripa. They want to express their gratitude for the celebration and the gifts we are sending their people." He pointed to where Vidad and Neas stood waiting at a respectful distance.

Maripa handed the baby to Rocker and waved for them to approach as she stood to greet them. "My friends, you are honored guests here. There is no need for you to be so formal. It is we who are grateful to you for all you have done for us."

She took hold of their hands and reached up on her toes to give each of the brothers a kiss on the cheek. Everyone who wished could now converse almost fluently with them after only a brief session with Karm and his biocomputer. Only Shoder and his faction still resisted.

Vidad was the first to speak. "We are pleased to be of service to the friends of the Sky People. Our people will be forever grateful to know our legends are true."

Neas ran his thumb across the edge of his new knife admiring its elegance. "And these blades of your metal are as beautiful as they are amazing. Our hunters will make great use of them. And the fabrics you give us shimmer in the sun like a thousand stars. Our wives will be the envy of all the women."

Maripa beamed with joy as she watched the brothers enjoying their gifts. "This is the least we could do. As our people grow to know one another better we hope to help in many more ways than these tokens of our thanks."

Vidad looked up into the night sky, searching the stars. "Maybe, one day, we might even learn how to fly among the stars as you did. Perhaps even rejoin the Sky People once again as friends."

"One day," said Maripa, "our people will go to the stars together and search out our friends."

A loud shout suddenly interrupted their talk. "Hairy quetzals!" shouted Shoder. The inebriated miner stumbled toward them from the shadows. Four others, equally drunk and armed with various drilling implements strode unsteadily behind him. He began slicing a large machete through the air in front of him. "I'll teach you to learn your place around here. Think you're better than us. You'll never stop us." He raised the weapon to strike.

Before the blade could start its downward strike, Maripa reached out and shoved the brothers aside. Leaping into the air she landed a solid kick with her heel to the drunkard's jaw. Landing on all fours, she swept out with a wicked kick to the knee, dropping Shoder to the ground. Rocker stepped on Shoder's wrist forcing his grip to open and release the machete. The others in the group froze with mouths slack.

Maripa, crouched in her attack position, snarled at the four. "Which of you down-brained phalks are next?"

Darb, Shoder's son, a large and particularly troublesome youth, charged in anger seeing his father defeated so easily. A heavy single jack raised in his talons.

Maripa deftly side-stepped the arc of the tool, delivering a fist to Darb's throat, followed by a side kick to his temple. Darb's eyes rolled back in his head as he dropped heavily to the ground.

Seeing a crowd gathering behind their mayor and her husband, and the raised weapons of the native brothers, the remaining agitators looked at each other, then, one-by-one dropped their weapons. Murmurs of excitement and concern rose as more townsfolk gathered around the disturbance.

Maripa pointed at the unconscious agitators in a sweeping gesture as she turned away in disgust. "Get these idiot quetzals out of here! Lock them in their quarters and post guards until they sober up. We can deal with them later." Two bystanders grabbed the dazed guildsman by his arms and dragged him off into the night. Others picked up Darb and herded the drunkards back into the housing section of town until all was relatively calm again.

Vidad and Neas bowed deeply. "Our thanks, my lady. You are indeed a great warrior as well as leader of your people. I wish we had more time for you to teach us some of your skills."

Rocker smiled toward Maripa as she brushed herself off and fixed her hair. "You have no idea."

Maripa, recovering from her anger and regaining her composure waved off the discussion. "Just something from my past. Not much call for it lately, though." She took Vidad's hands in hers as she continued. "I apologize for Shoder's behavior. I assure you we are grateful for your help. Without your aid we probably would have starved to death. We owe you a great debt."

"Do not trouble yourself," replied Neas, smiling and genial as ever. "We know all too well the effect of strong drink on men. All is forgotten."

"Yes," agreed Vidad. "We will harbor no ill will toward you or any of your people. Now we must go and prepare for our journey. Thank you again for your actions to protect us." The brothers bowed again, touching their hand to their face in the traditional gesture of respect. They then drifted off toward their residence.

Karm watched Maripa as the brothers walked off. His eyes softened and a smile grew on his lips. "My dear," he said, "You have become quite the leader. Who would have thought you would be as elegant in speech as you are with a weapon?"

Maripa smiled and gave the old man a gentle squeeze on the arm.

The next morning, as the sun cast an orange glow on the hustle and bustle of cleaning up the remains of the party, a crowd gathered at the edge of town to say goodbye to Vidad and Neas.

Maripa, copying the native sign of respect, touched her hand to her face as she addressed the brothers one last time. "Farewell, my friends. We will come to visit your village soon. Perhaps in two years we will be able to manage the journey."

"We look forward to that day," said Vidad. "Our people will learn much from you."

"We cannot ever repay you for the aid you have given us. We would not have survived another winter without your help. Tell your people we will soon embrace each other as family."

Vidad reached under his tanned leather vest and removed a silvery medallion in the shape of a star inside the crescent moon. "This is the emblem of my family," he told Maripa. "I give this to you now as a sign of our brotherhood." He placed the leather strap holding the ornament around Maripa's neck.

She lifted the heavy medallion in her hands as she examined the workmanship, especially the intricate design of pictographs around the outer edge.

"This is exquisite," she said. "I will treasure it always, and think of your kindness and generosity every time I see it."

Karm stepped forward, holding a silver disc. In the center of the disc flashed a brilliant green gem. Engraved around the rim were images of the Skae, Brin and Kolandi extending their arms toward each other in friendship. "May I borrow your present for a moment, my dear?" He removed the medallion from her neck and closed both objects in his hands.

"As a sign of our everlasting friendship, I am going to create a bond between these two gifts." His hands began to glow a bright blue. "This bond will forever allow us to find each other and renew our pledge of friendship." The light subsided as he opened his hands and returned the medallion to Maripa. Holding out the silver disc he approached Vidad. "Present this to your wife as a token of our gratitude and a symbol of our everlasting alliance."

Vidad accepted the gift, familiar now with Karm's strange ability. "Caeri will be pleased. Thank you." He carefully tucked the disc into his pouch.

Maripa, Rocker and Karm embraced the brothers and they all exchanged farewells and promises to see each other soon.

The townspeople cheered and waved as the brothers pulled on the guide ropes and led their pack animals back toward the sunrise. The crowd diminished as the travelers vanished into the shadows of the distant forest.

Once the travelers were out of sight, Maripa turned on Karm. "What was that all about, old man? What did you do to our gifts?"

Karm winked and gave her a quick smile. "Nothing really. I just wanted to have a way of staying connected to them. Now, my biocomputer can reach out and stay in touch."

Maripa gave Karm a long look, and hooked talons with her husband as they walked together back toward home.

Rocker saw the sadness in her face and pulled her hand to his lips, giving her talons a quick kiss. "Don't worry, honey. With the food problem and our survival resolved, we can focus our energies on building up our technology. With enough engineers and manufacturers, we should be able to build flying vehicles to make long distance travel a simple matter. We need to send out proper exploration teams and learn about our new home as soon as possible. Who knows what else is out there waiting for us?"

Maripa snuggled close and pulled his arm around her. "I'm just relieved to know we won't starve to death now. I couldn't bear the thought of all this ending so soon."

"No fear of failure anymore, my dear. Everything is back on track and looking better than ever."

"I know, but I just can't shake the feeling of something awful out there waiting for us." She walked on, fingering the silvery medallion.

**

Maliche shivered at the memories. "And then I woke up to your worried faces. Does any of this make sense to you, professor?"

Dr. Neywa put down his pad and pencil and rubbed his face with both hands. "This certainly does lend credence to your family's stories being more trustworthy than our official histories."

"And it looks like the mining guild was nothing but trouble from the start. We better get a move on." Aras gathered up her pack and field jacket.

Maliche stayed in his chair. "You go on ahead. I need a moment to recover from all of this." He waved her off with a quick gesture. "I'll be along in a few minutes."

As soon as Aras disappeared in the darkness, Maliche grabbed Dr. Neywa's wrist. "Professor, one of the images is particularly disturbing. I wonder if you caught it as well."

"You're referring to the miners in the Govayer village?"

"Precisely. Why would they keep such a thing secret from everyone? Wouldn't it have been in everyone's interest to reveal their existence immediately?"

"Dr. Neywa placed his hand on top of Maliche's. "Be careful, my boy. There are things happening here which none of us know anything about. Too many secrets and too much power in the wrong hands. If I had any hope of convincing you, I'd talk you out of this expedition."

Maliche got to his feet and took up his own pack. "Don't worry professor. I can handle myself. See you in a few weeks."

Chapter Eight

The desert heat weighed down on Maliche. It was as if he had taken up residence in an autoclave, his brain about to be sterilized. He took another long pull from his water flask, emptied twice already and it was only noon. The thin scales on his arms and face were hazy now as they thickened in reaction to the intensity of the sun. Brushing the wilted feathers of his crest from his dripping forehead he readjusted his hat, climbed out of trench four, and headed toward the shade of the awning over the artifact sorting table.

Plumes of sand flew up from the other trenches as diggers tossed shovels of dirt into the air. Mechanical diggers hovered over a rock layer, blasting it away with their high energy beams. Once they pulverized the rock, they glided back to their charging stations as the Brin laborers took over. No robotic gadget could replace the discerning eyes of a living Brin when looking for delicate artifacts.

Shaking his head as he picked through the meager finds, he tugged again at his stained shirt and drank from his flask. "Five days now and nothing older than the remnants of last year's caravan. We may have to go deeper into the desert to find what I'm looking for."

"But sir, we've gone beyond the limits of our permits already. We don't have permission to dig here, much less any further in. If we get caught, none of us will be able to work again." Mitem, the dig supervisor Maliche hired from one of the mine sites close to the coast, waved his hand toward the crew. "We need to go further west, maybe north of the last site, but not east." He took Maliche by the shoulders, looking directly into his dirt encrusted face. "We have families who depend on us. This sort of work is the only thing available while the mine is refitting. We cannot risk going any further."

Maliche took one of the supervisor's hands in his, clasping his arm with the other hand, and smiled. "Don't worry, Mitem. I'll make sure nothing happens to any of you. Have you forgotten who my brother is? Who I am? My family name will protect all of us. We may get a good verbal dressing down, but nobody will lose their jobs. Tomorrow we leave for these mountains." He stuck a talon to a range of mountains shown on the map he unfolded. He always preferred the feel of an actual map over the more modern electronic versions, and spread it out, covering the shards of pottery.

Mitem gave his head a jerk from side-to-side. "Don't say I didn't try to change your mind, sir. If the Assembly finds out about this…" He gave Maliche one last look, then walked back to his tent.

"Maybe you should listen to him."

Maliche startled to see Aras standing just behind him under the awning. A filthy purple scarf protected her head feathers from the harsh sun. Her shorts revealed long leg, displaying an attractive smokiness as her normally transparent scales reacted to the desert sun, a hint of sweat glistened on the faint outline of her epidermal scales. The pale green shirt, tied in a knot at her midriff caused Maliche's heart to skip a beat.

"You did hire him because he is reputably the best dig supervisor on the eastern continent." She approached the table, leaned against him with one hand on his shoulder, and examined the map. "Why are you so determined to go east, anyway? Those mountains don't seem to be any more promising than anywhere else in this eternal kak of a desert. Why not go back within our legal boundary?"

"I can't explain it, Aras. I feel like something is calling me out there. Every time I see those mountains on the map, I feel a tug toward them. Something is out there… I know it."

She cocked her head toward him, furrowing her brow. "Not a very compelling scientific hypothesis. You sure about this?"

"I have to go. It's like an itch I can't quite reach. I'll go crazy if I don't find out what is happening to me." He stared at the map in silence, and then rubbed his tired eyes with his knuckles. "You know about the visions I get from this kak medallion," he pounded his chest where the relic hung from a cord around his neck. "Only a fool would chase after that sort of sorcery."

Standing upright again, hands on hips, she snorted a quick laugh. "For months now, I have kept the secret of your medallion and Maripa's journal. I volunteered to take a semester off to come out here to this desolate waste land, I spend days on end in ungodly heat digging holes in the ground collecting bits of the past for you. I believe in this as much as you do, Maliche. You're no fool. Something is going on here beyond any of our understanding. I want to know what's causing all of this as much as you."

Maliche stared at her for a moment, walked up to her, and pulled her into his embrace. "I'm glad you're here. I need somebody to confide in, someone I can trust." He reveled in the dusty smell of her crest feathers, the softness of her against him.

She looked up into his eyes, a scowl growing on her face. "So, now I'm here simply as your psychiatrist? Is that it?"

Releasing his hold on her, he eyed her up and down, and smiled. "No, far from it."

"You want to try the journal and medallion again? Maybe another vision will spark something further."

"It's worth a try." Maliche led Aras back into his tent where he unlocked the metallic vault and brought out the relics.

Aras halted him before he could begin. "Lie down on your cot first. I don't want to have to try and lift you if you collapse again."

Maliche stretched out on his canvas cot, opened the journal, grabbed the medallion in his fist, and started reading.

Why do we never learn from history? I think back on those days of celebration so often with regret now. We should have known better. Throughout antiquity, whenever two cultures meet, it is always the less technological society who suffers, whether intentional or not...

***

A cool morning breeze wafted the colorful curtains of the Rocker kitchen. Little Karm slurped at his breakfast, more reaching the floor than his mouth as his attempts to maneuver the spoon by himself proved more difficult than expected.

Maripa stared incredulously at Rocker, her mouth hung open until her anger found the words she was searching for. "Have you lost your ever-loving feather-fluffed mind? You want to take one of the new shuttles, only recently approved for short distance test runs, and fly off over the eastern ocean in search of Vidad and Neas? Over my dead body, mister." She slammed her mug of tea onto the breakfast table, jarring the other plates and utensils. "You have a four-year-old son and another child on the way. You can't just up and leave on some down-brained scheme like this." She cradled her swollen belly protectively.

Unperturbed, Rocker took another bite of tirpit bacon. "This needs to be done. We promised to go to them as soon as we could. They left us detailed maps so we could find them. Our preliminary expeditions to the east found the Govayer harbor town right where they said it would be. We have to do this. And I would be back in plenty of time for the birth. You still have six weeks to go yet."

Maripa paced the kitchen shaking her head, her fists clenched tightly at her sides. "What if she comes early? Send somebody else. It doesn't have to be you. What about your work in the lab?"

"I spend most of my time buried in paperwork these days. Most of the real work is done by everyone else. My work is pure theoretical research, nothing vital. You know that."

"You still don't have to be the one who goes. What about Karm? You know he is getting more depressed and confused. He spends more and more time just wandering down by the river talking to himself, or that biocomputer. Hard to tell the difference anymore. At his age, I'm afraid for his safety. You can't leave us like this."

Rocker rose from his chair and took Maripa gently by the shoulders. "The trip will only be for one or two weeks at the most. I'm the logical choice to go. I have nothing of critical strategic importance going on now. You, little Karm, the baby, and the old man will be fine."

Maripa squared her shoulders, stiffened her spine, and sternly looked her husband straight in the eyes. "Then I'm going, too. We can have Katch and Velma watch Karmito while we're gone."

"You can't fly in the shuttle when you're this far along," he reminded her. "And you are still mayor here. Without you, this place would fall apart. You know the arguments between the farmers, ranchers, and miners would get ugly without you to keep them in check. If Shoder or any one of them gained control in your absence, all of our noble aspirations for this new world could collapse under their narrow minded greed. You know how he and his followers are against this expedition to find the natives, unless it's to somehow turn them into a cheap labor force. The mining guild is always clamoring about how using the natives would increase productivity and decrease costs. Any mention of becoming friends or allies with any of the Kolandi just makes them all the more obstinate and hold even more firmly to their prejudices. Sometimes I wonder if we might have been wrong to grow so quickly. There just hasn't been time to adjust to everything."

Maripa stood firm for a minute or so, then her shoulders drooped and her head fell. She reached out and grabbed her husband in a ferocious bear hug. "What if something goes wrong?"

"Nothing will happen. You're not the only one here with survival training, you know. We built those ships to handle anything. The current flight time restrictions are only a formality. They can handle the distance and then some."

There were, of course, several more battles, but Rocker knew he won. Maripa's arguments weakened. She only continued them out of stubbornness. The next several days passed in a flurry of preparation and assurances of safety and a swift return.

On the day of departure, thinning grey clouds remained overhead after yesterday's storm. Sunlight to the east revealed the edge of the squall. The sky port hummed with activity. Ground crews rushed around the two working shuttles performing their final checklists items. In the open hangar, three more shuttles under various stages of construction created a cacophony of riveting, grinding, and pounding of metal on metal. Irregular flashes of blinding light blazed from the welders. Two Brin sat at the controls of their shuttles dressed in dark maroon overalls performing their own checklists.

Rocker punched the communicator switch with a talon. "All set to go?"

Mot's voice crackled in his earpiece. "Engines primed and ready. All lights are green and locked."

Dust billowed around the shuttles as the engines revved, lifting the shuttles off the ground.

Life changed in the town during the two years since Vidad and Neas's fateful visit. As Rocker and Mot steadily gained altitude in their solar powered flying shuttles they could see the new developments. Manufacturing plants, factories, and all manner of thriving businesses filled the outskirts of the growing community, now numbering twenty thousand. Their numbers grew so large now that discussions of searching out locations for new communities were commonplace. According to guild records, some few, simply called The Explorers, ranged far and wide traveling the distant regions of the land around First Town. Limited to travel by foot so far, their efforts only provided reconnaissance for a mere five hundred square miles surrounding the community, except for the single patrol to verify the existence of the Govayer village on the coast. Everything beyond remained a mysterious wilderness.   To their north sat the solar power plant constructed by the Skae before they departed. Only specially trained Brin knew how the technology worked, so efforts were nearing completion of the operational manuals for future repair and maintenance of the facility.

The green fields of crop-laden farms and herds of animals surrounded the town. Barely visible on the southern horizon, the ancient ruined city, now a cenotaph to a once great civilization glinted in the sunlight beyond the clouds. Discovered before the shuttles became operational, the once great metropolis with its towers of rusting metal and broken glass hundreds of feet tall remained a mystery. More immediate matters of survival and development of their own lives precluded anything more than the most superficial examination of the ruins. As the men rose higher and aimed their single-person aircraft for the eastern horizon they flew over the new mines and mills dotting the hillsides of the nearby mountains. The red dust plumes of mines' operations obscured many of the buildings.

The pilots settled into their cruising altitude of thirty thousand feet at a speed of Mach 3. Rocker punched the controls, engaging the autopilot. Checking over his left shoulder, he verified Mot's position just off his wing and settled in for the long flight.

Rocker reveled in the beauty of the landscape he flew over. Jagged peaks, still covered in snow even this late in the year gave way to vast green forests blanketed rolling hills. Before long, sparkling blue rivers meandered through open plains with herds of tirpit and shartans running wild. Immense flocks of four-winged yellow crested mertans filled the sky below them. In only a matter of hours since their departure, Rocker watched the mountains drop below the horizon behind him and saw the ocean appear on the horizon.

"You see that Govayer harbor yet?" Rocker called into his microphone.

"Not yet, sir, but it should be coming up soon. Our heading is true."

"All right. Let's drop down some and prepare to land just outside of town in that clearing we found last time. No sense stirring up everybody again."

"Agreed, sir. They certainly got a bit agitated when we fell out of the sky like we did. I'm still not sure they believed you telling them we weren't some gods returning from the stars."

Just ahead there appeared a small bay with the Govayer village on the north shore. In the years since the two brothers' arrival, the village remained unchanged. Rocker wondered again how this dilapidated hovel kept from either burning to the ground or becoming swallowed by the ocean. Between the pilots and the town, a clearing among the trees showed itself.

"There's the clearing now. You stay with the shuttles while I go into the town. I want to verify the coordinates with the town leaders before we tackle the open water tomorrow and make sure we have everything correct."

"Yes, sir. We don't want to get lost out there. These shuttles are good, but I don't want to test their buoyancy anytime soon."

As Rocker passed by one of the outer huts, he noticed a shadow in the window. The sun's glare hid any details, and the shape vanished from view almost immediately. Shrugging, he continued on toward the center of the village. Inside the hut, a solitary figure hunched over a communicator.

"Guildsman Hort reporting. Target Rocker in sight at the village. Will report on departure. Out."

The next day, Rocker and Mot found themselves flying over the ocean. Rocker peered hard from one horizon to the next in amazement. "I've never seen so much water. No land in sight anywhere, even from this height."

"Yes, sir," Mot agreed. "At least we won't die of thirst on this world. How much farther you figure until we reach the coast?"

"Two, maybe three hours. Depends on how accurate the maps and all of our calculations are. We should be there well before sundown at any rate."

Two hours and eight minutes later the aircraft shot over the coastline of the second largest continent on Raince'to. Tall black cliffs rose sharply out of the ocean whose powerful waves pounded relentlessly at their base, a long range of snow covered volcanic mountains towered only a short distance inland.

Rocker checked his map and notes. "Adjust heading to Three-Two-Two. Twenty thousand feet at Mach two."

"Yes, sir. Three-Two-Two, twenty thousand feet and Mach two."

"Destination in one hour," called Rocker. *I can't wait to see the look of their faces when we land. Vidad and Neas are in for quite a shock.*

"I don't see any villages, sir," called Mot over the com system.

Rocker rechecked his maps and calculations. A vague concern gnawed at his gut for several days prior to their leaving and resurfaced anew—the sort of concern one gets when something important has been forgotten and is trying to claw its way to consciousness.

"They must be around here someplace. All of the other coordinates have been spot on. It has to be here. Let's drop down to five thousand feet and reduce speed to five hundred kph. Maybe they're hidden in this forest somewhere. We'll probably find them in a small glen or something. Keep the search pattern tight."

"Five thousand feet and five hundred kph. Roger that, sir."

Ten minutes later, Rocker's head set crackled. "I see something down there, sir. Just ahead in those low hills."

"I see it, Mot, in that valley near the lake. Doesn't look like much of a village, but let's land and check it out. Maybe somebody there can tell us where we are."

Rocker and Mot set down just behind a grassy hill out of sight. As they approached the dilapidated village they passed through an area covered with mounds, each marked with a carved stone.

"Can you read the engravings on these, sir?" asked Mot. "There's dozens of them. Looks like some sort of graveyard."

"I can't read their language, but most of these look pretty recent."

"Looks like the village is deserted to me, sir," Mot said as they approached the decaying mud-walled structures, many with collapsed roofs and walls. "Awfully quiet to be what we're looking for."

"I agree, but look, smoke coming up out of that hut over there. Must be somebody home. Let's check it out."

"Hello in the house!" called Rocker in the language of Vidad and Neas as the pilots advanced on the broken down building. He heard muffled voices coming from within, and then a skeletal figure appeared in the crooked entry.

"Hello!" he called again. "My friend and I are lost and we…" Rocker stopped in his tracks and stood dumfounded as he suddenly recognized the emaciated form of Vidad. The man's once bright, clear eyes and imposing physique were now mere remnants of the former hunter. Grey discolorations covered his faded brown skin. Vidad held onto the frame of the hut's entry for support, his head wobbled as he strained to see who his visitors were.

Rocker stepped closer, reaching out to steady the teetering man. "Vidad… Is that you?"

The gaunt figure straightened slightly as he recognized the man in front of him. "Doctor Rocker? Have you come to us at last?" Tears welled, but refused to drop from his eyes.

"What has happened here? Come, let me help you back inside." Rocker carefully took Vidad's arm and led him slowly into the darkness of the hut. As his eyes adjusted to the shadows, he saw five other individuals, children, and adults, lying on rotting, bug infested straw mats around the room. A pitifully small fire provided almost no warmth in the chilly air. Hanging from a hook above the fire, Rocker observed a pot containing a thin broth. A few vegetables bubbled up, but no meat, a hopelessly small meal for six people. The people were dressed in rags hanging from frames even more devastated than Vidad's. Grey blemishes marred their skin as well.

Upon entering, Vidad spoke to the others. "Neas, our friend Doctor Rocker has come to us. Caeri, this is the friend I spoke of from our voyage so long ago. Ila, wake up, greet our visitors. Rahnoa, Lelyk, get up and help your mother. Friends have come to help us."

The wasted forms of the woman and her daughters rose with difficulty on straining legs, using each other for support as they slowly managed their way toward Rocker. In the light of the doorway, the scars and discolorations covering their bodies horrified Rocker.

Rocker leaned out the doorway, nearly tearing the thin curtain from its pins, and shouted to Mot. "Bring the medical kit, and hurry! We have some sort of infection here."

He returned to his new patients and tried to comfort them as best he could. When the medical kit arrived he took blood samples from each of them and fed them into the kit's computerized analyzer. In seconds, the results appeared on the small monitor.

The forgotten memory suddenly burst forward in his mind. "Viral infection... I am such an idiot. It looks like the flu virus we contracted our first year on this planet."

"Flu virus? How can a simple little flu virus do this? I never saw anyone with the flu look this bad before."

"You never saw anyone without immunity to our diseases before. Remember your history. In the early days of our expanding populations many hundreds of years ago on Dyan'ta, as soon as the explorers came in contact with the indigenous population they died in the millions by diseases that hardly affected the explorers. How could we be so stupid? Of course this would happen."

"So, how come their viruses don't affect us?"

"They did. Remember all those outbreaks of fever two years ago, right after these two left us?"

"Yeah, but almost nobody died. A few pills and folks got better."

"Exactly. Our technology saved us. These poor people didn't have the medical knowledge to create the medicines strong enough to fight the infection. This is the result."

"Can we help them?"

"We sure as strix are going to try. Can you fly home on your own and bring me the supplies I need?"

"No problem, sir. Tell me what you need and I can be back here in three days, now that I know how to get here I can push the shuttle for all she's worth. I just wish we had more shuttles to bring the real doctors here."

"Don't worry about that. With the long range communicator you'll bring back, the doctors can walk me through anything I need. Tell doctor Nela everything and get back here as fast as you can. These people saved our lives, now it's our turn to save them. Bring me the extra blankets and emergency rations from the shuttle before you leave. And tell them to get the other shuttles ready as soon as possible."

Mot returned with a communications array which he set up so they could contact the medical professionals for assistance and, a week later, amid an array of portable medical computers, genetic analyzers, separators, purifiers, growth medium incubators and a host of other equipment, Rocker developed a vaccine.

Pulling aside the entry curtain of one of the huts they repaired and now used as living quarters and laboratory, Mot found Dr. Rocker already hard at work. "Your patients seem to be improving," he said as he delivered breakfast.

"Yes, the fever is broken and their lungs are clearing. With food and enough rest, they should be fine. Thank goodness for Karm's help. It would have taken us a month to solve this without him."

"The rumor mill said that gizmo of his is broken. Did he fix it?"

"It certainly has been finicky these past many months. I guess it decided to be helpful this time. Normally it doesn't give anything helpful when we try to ask it about the Kolandi."

Mot hunched his shoulders and ran his talons through his crest. "Well, whatever happened, the medicine you made here is working. Those grey marks are fading and one of them even talked to me when I brought them breakfast this morning."

Rocker swallowed one last bite of his grub and headed out the door to visit the four patients in the next hut. "Time to make my rounds. Keep an eye on these read-outs for me." They discovered others in some of the other structures, all of them near death. Rocker's care succeeded in reviving all but two of the most seriously ill. Those two he and Mot quietly removed to the cemetery, adding their graves to the rest.

"Good morning, everyone," said Rocker upon entering the room. "How are you all today?"

A smile brightened the faces of each person inside. "Thanks to you, we are doing well now," replied Caeri. "Your medicines are truly amazing. We owe you our lives." She tried to sit up fully, but sank quietly back to the mat.

Rahnoa and Lelyk each held a small pail of water and wash cloth, carefully washing those too weak to care for themselves yet. The young always seemed to bounce back from illness more quickly. They smiled up at Dr. Rocker, but returned quickly to their duties.

"Good to hear you are feeling better, but let's not rush anything. You are obviously still very weak. It will take a few more days of bed rest before you will be strong enough to get up and around. Let me open the window so you can have a bit more light and fresh air." Rocker stepped carefully around the prone figures and pulled back the cloth hung over the window frame. *At least the smell of death is gone from this room.*

"Ahh, that feels good," said Ila. "I was not sure I would ever feel the sun's warmth again." She smiled and reached out a thin arm to Neas who lay next to her.

"I am so glad all of you are improving so quickly. Another day or two and we would have been too late to help you." He knelt beside each bedside as he administered their mid-morning dose of curative. "Maripa sends her love and hopes she can come visit you before long. The baby is due in about three weeks, so I will need to return to her soon, but I will send others to be with you until we can return. Larger shuttles are being built as we speak, so you can expect visitors in another month or so." He surveyed the room once more and headed back toward the doorway. "I'll let you get some rest now. See you again in a couple of hours."

Visits to the rest of the huts brought equally good news. Everyone grew stronger and showed signs of recovering. As Rocker walked back through the village his head hung low, tired feet dragging in the dust. He slumped down in a camping style chair near the former village fire pit. He took a long draft of water from his canteen, leaned back in the chair, and rubbed his eyes.

This is our fault. Dozens dead in just this one village. And these are the lucky ones. Mott's reports from his visits to nearby villages are unbelievable. Whole communities wiped out. Only handfuls of survivors. There is only so much medicine and only the two of us to bring it to them. With so few of them remaining it's only a matter of time before this entire race is gone. A century or two at best. Will history ever forgive us? If only we built the shuttles larger, or more of them. We should have come here sooner.

Reaching down into the small storage container next to him, he pulled out a clear bag, opened it, and took a bite of the sandwich.

In another week, the survivors regained enough strength to begin reliving their lives as normally as possible. Sadness filled everyone as they went about their daily chores. Plowing the fields and repairing damaged homes gave them purpose again. Only a few children proved strong enough to survive the virus, and none of the elders. The town was far too quiet.

One night during supper, Rocker built up the courage to ask the question he needed answered.

"Can you tell me how this all started?" He saw the sadness deepen in everyone's face, but he needed to know. "Please, I know this is difficult, but I must know what happened."

Vidad glanced at his wife and the others. They each gave a slow nod of agreement. "All right, my friend," he began. "If you must know, then it is our duty to explain." Vidad gathered his thoughts as he stared, unseeing, at the table in front of him. "A few months after our return from the voyage to find your people, some others of your village appeared.

Rocker jerked up, not believing what he had heard. "What? Some Brin came here? Who were they? What did they want?"

"They asked us about where we find the metals to make our arrows and other tools, and showed us different rocks, wondering if we had seen similar types here."

Rocker punched his fist into the table, rattling the dishes and utensils. "Miners. Those phalking quetzals. They've been lying to us all along." Regaining his composure, he noticed the startled looks of his patients. "No, my friends, this is nothing for you to worry about. You did nothing wrong. It is my people who have committed a terrible wrong. What else can you tell me?"

Vidad's hands shook slightly with tremors as he continued his tale. "Since our two people have a bond of friendship we told them everything they wanted to know. They seemed most pleased and offered many gifts in return. Some of our young hunters led them on forays into the mountains to help them seek out the rocks they sought.

"After a few weeks, they left. Soon after, some of the elders began to show signs of this strange illness. Samej, our village Homsan, tried everything, but to no avail. None of his remedies cured us. At first, only a few of the oldest died, but then more became ill. As more of us showed signs of the sickness Samej traveled to nearby villages to see if any of the other Homsan knew of a cure. Some of the people saw the illness as a sign of displeasure from the gods and left us to live with family in other towns."

Neas picked up the story and continued. "Some of the herbs delayed the sickness, but only for a brief time. In a matter of weeks, those who were stricken first began to die. The children suffered far worse. Their fevers grew steadily for days, and the grey blemishes covered their skin causing intense pain. Nothing helped them. A few of us, those who are still alive, also developed a fever, but we recovered... at least that first year. A dozen or so died in the first three months. But then summer arrived and the illness went away. We were all very grateful and life returned to normal. We heard tales from other villages of similar devastation. Sometimes even rumors of entire towns dying."

Vidad continued the tale, his voice low and stricken with deep sorrow. "But then came winter. The snows piled high and the lakes froze sooner than usual. And the disease returned. This time, the children were hit the hardest. Their skin burned with fever. The grey marks ate through their skin and they died within days. At first, only a few became affected, but each week, more and more fell. Soon, even the men and women who survived the first year became sick. They, too, suffered horribly as the fevers and greyness devoured them. Many of the hunters remained unaffected, so food was still plentiful, but as the cold deepened and hunting expeditions became less frequent, even they began to suffer and die."

A stillness fell over the room. Rocker felt a large lump growing in his throat. "Those of you who recovered from that first fever are the only ones left?"

"Yes," replied Caeri. "But even we finally succumbed to the disease. Late this spring, those of us who were strong enough to dig the graves, felt the rise of fevers and saw the greyness start to ravage our bodies. If you had not arrived when you did, all of us would be gone."

"I am so sorry," Rocker said with tears in his eyes and a tightness in his throat. "We should have known better. We should have taken steps to prevent anything like this from happening."

"How could you have known?" asked Caeri. "Our legends tell us that plagues like this have struck us before. That is why the Sky People left us, so the stories say. Who could have predicted such a thing would happen again at this time?"

Rocker hung his head low, his voice barely audible. "Our history tells us of the consequences when two people meet each other for the first time. Terrible diseases like this are commonly the result. We should have remembered and taken steps."

Caeri crossed the room and placed her hand on his shoulder. "Be at peace, friend Rocker. We have survived and we will recover. We will remember you and your people as our saviors. This is not your fault."

Rocker simply smothered his face in his arms on the table. His shoulders heaved with sobbing. The next day, he packed the shuttle with his few belongings, said goodbye to his friends and, leaving Mott behind to continue caring for the sick, he returned home.

Two weeks later, he sat by Maripa's hospital bed holding Tari, his new daughter. The tiny pink face with tawny down feathers covering her head, gurgled softly in his arms.

Chapter Nine

Maripa stretched, waking from her nap and smiling at the sight of her husband and new daughter. "You have a way with children, but it's my turn now." She reached out for the baby, cradling her gently to her chest, encouraging her to nurse.

"Nela says you can come home today if you feel up to it."

"And give up all this pampering? Maybe another week."

"If you say so, but the council will probably want to set up shop right here if you don't get back to them soon. But I'm sure Shoder and his gang would be very happy to run things in your place for a while. The fines and bans you laid on them for their treachery are not sitting well with them. Another week and they'll probably convince a majority to side with them and overturn your decrees."

"Over my dead body!" Maripa replied, detaching the perturbed infant from her breast, handing her back to her father. "Where are my clothes?" She climbed out of bed and stormed around the room, ranting about the idiots on the council, getting dressed and packing her bag. Rocker sat quietly smiling at Tari, stroking her tiny cheek with one talon.

***

The months that followed brought new visitors across the ocean as the Brin built increasing numbers of flying shuttles. Life at Vidad and Caeri's village slowly regained a sense of normalcy, even if true joy continued to be elusive.

The mining guild members proved especially hostile. These Brin, under the guise of volunteers on a mission to help rebuild their village, never let an opportunity slip to ask about mineral resources on this continent. If a few of the volunteers disappeared from the ranks, nobody questioned the head guildsman's word of their setting off on reconnaissance missions to search out more survivors in the distant mountains.

***

The visions faded, leaving Maliche disoriented and weak. His heart raced, his breath in quick gulps. "They almost died out. We nearly killed them all."

"What are you talking about? Who did we kill?" Aras sat on the edge of Maliche's cot, gently wiping his crest with a cool, wet cloth. Her portable med viewer beeped rhythmically, but gave no emergency warnings so she removed it from Maliche's chest and set it aside.

"The Kolandi—we nearly destroyed them. Exposure to our germs infected them with diseases they had no immunity to. Those phalking miners brought our diseases to an unprotected group of people in their greedy search for expansion and wealth. Jontar got to them in time and brought them back."

Her eyes softened, tears welled up. "But for how long. It couldn't have been long before they did disappear forever. They did die out, eventually."

Maliche sat up, and brought her into his arms, trying to comfort her. "I'm not so sure. Whenever I start to think about the Kolandi extinction, something doesn't feel right." She wrapped her arms around him in response, and pulled him in further. "Anyway, the miner's guild seems to be a recurring theme in all of this. They caused as much trouble back then as they do now. I wish I had more than just these visions to go on. I'd be laughed out of any court in the world if I showed up with nothing more than a bunch of hallucinations as evidence."

Aras did not respond, so he tilted her head back and saw the tears streaming down her cheeks.

"What's wrong?"

She sniffled, blinked away the tears, and looked into his eyes. "It's all so sad. An entire species of intelligent beings going extinct, and we helped cause it." She managed a weak smile. "Sorry, I'm not being much of a scientist right now."

Maliche held her chin in his talons and leaned in close to kiss her. He tasted the saltiness of her lips as she pressed back into him. Together, they lay back onto the cot, embracing each other.

***

The morning sun rose hot and intense in another cloudless blue sky. Maliche shielded his eyes as he pushed through the tent flaps to begin his day. Stretching his back he surveyed the campsite. The diggers were busy packing up the gear and stowing it aboard the three shuttles. Robot excavators filled in the various trenches with dirt so little, if any, traces of the dig-site would remain once they left.

The dust clouds blew off north and, thankfully, away from camp, so no breathing aids were required. Smoke, with a pleasant aroma of mertans' eggs and tirpit bacon wafted toward him on the breeze. Mitem appeared from behind the lead shuttle and waved as he headed over to the kitchen canopy. Realizing he probably owed Aras an apology, he decided to pay her a visit before breakfast. As if on cue, she appeared from around the corner of the shower tent, orange sleeveless shirt with shorts, towel draped around her shoulders, using one corner to finish drying her face.

Before he could approach, she saw him, and held up one hand with paired talons crossed as warning to keep his distance. She disappeared behind the flaps of her tent, leaving Maliche standing in his tracks, hoping he had not ruined a growing friendship, or was it more, much less a promising career. A powerful grumble from his stomach convinced him to tackle the problem after eating something.

By noon, with no sign of Aras, his shuttle was loaded and ready for takeoff. He sat with Mitem at one of the tables under the kitchen canopy, always the last to be broken down, discussing flight plans and rendezvous schedules.

"Looks like the rest of the shuttles will be ready in a couple of hours. You finished with the preflight checklist?"

"Yes, sir. I took care of it first thing."

"Excellent. Make sure everything is cleaned up and returned to original conditions before you join me."

"No worries, sir. You sure I can't talk you out of this? I still think it is too risky."

"No Mitem, my mind is made up. We are going to the eastern mountains."

"Very well, sir. I'll make sure everything here is set to right and we will meet you later this afternoon. Send me the exact coordinates once you decide on the site." He tipped his hat in salute, grunted as he stood and went off to supervise the remaining camp deconstruction procedures.

Maliche finished his cup of tea and headed toward his shuttle. Once inside, he sealed the hatch and removed his hat.

"About time you decided to get on with this madness." Aras swung around in the co-pilot's chair, impatience written all over her face.

Maliche nearly tripped over the bulkhead at the unexpected voice. He grabbed one of the overhead bins to steady himself. "What the strix are you doing here? I thought I scared you away. All these visions are getting pretty intense. Also, I'm sorry if I took too many liberties last night. It won't happen again. You are my student, after all."

Legs crossed, she unfolded one arm to point accusingly in his direction. "I almost did commandeer one of the shuttles to go back home, but... I started thinking about what you said. I remembered the old tales about Karm and how he possessed some mystical power to see into the future and control others, or something like that, and, now I sound like the crazy one. I realized you are one of his descendants, at least sort of, so maybe you can do things like that. I mean the medallion is certainly a mystery... who knows what it might be capable of doing? Maybe you and the medallion are like Karm and his alien biocomputer thing. In any case, after a lousy night's sleep I decided to stick with you no matter what. After all, I am an archeologist, too and I'll be feather fluffed if I let you go off and make the discovery of a lifetime without me. You have anything to eat in this thing? I'm starving."

"But what about last night? I thought you were mad at me for taking advantage of you."

Her laughter stopped his short. "Oh, I was pretty mad at first, more at myself than you, though. I had hoped our first time would be much more romantic. I've been hoping for you to notice me for some time now. But then I decided, 'What the strix?' Can we get going now?"

Maliche slid into the pilot's seat next to Aras and began punching controls with his talons. "From one lunatic to another, welcome aboard."

He pushed the controls forward and the shuttle lifted off amid a cloud of sand. He waved to Mitem who leaned on his shovel, shaded his eyes, and watched from next to the last trench.

***

An hour later, the snow-capped mountains grew steadily larger as the two archeologists approached. Dark clouds appeared to hang on the jagged peaks.

"I've marked a couple of potential dig sites on the map." Maliche touched a control button to bring up the front view window display overlaying the real world in front of them. Three green dots glowed; the closest appeared a short distance up the canyon in front of them. "We should be there in a few minutes and—"

The port side mag-lev exploded in a burst of noise and light. Alarms sounded and warning lights flashed across the control panel. The shuttle gave a lurch to the left, dropping altitude at a frightening rate. With a supreme effort, Maliche managed to level the ship, but the ground, rising up to meet the mountains, approached far too fast.

"Grab hold of something! This is going to be rough!"

Aras, preoccupied with her own set of controls, ignored him.

An explosion of rock, dirt, and brush flew into the air and the shuttle struck the ground. Flames shot out of the fuselage as both wings tore off. The machine bounced several times before coming to a halt at the end of the long trench it gouged. Smoke filled the cabin as flames devoured the remains.

Maliche clawed at his eyes, blood streaming from a long gash in his forehead, his right arm hung at a bad angle. "Aras! Aras! Are you okay?"

He undid the seat restraints with a punch of his left hand, and then tumbled out of his chair, coughing, barely able to breathe the acrid air. He pulled up on the emergency escape latch, blowing out the canopy. Fresh air fought with the smoke for control of the cockpit. Reaching out with his only functioning arm, he searched for Aras.

"Aras, answer me! Where are you?"

Then he saw her. The co-pilot's chair ripped loose from its mounting and came to rest in a back corner of the cabin. Aras, still securely belted into the seat, lay dead, her neck broken.

"NO! No… Aras…"

Flames erupted through the bulkhead, forcing Maliche to scramble out of the shuttle. He stopped a few yards away and watched the inferno destroy everything. As he lay there, the world began to swim around him. Pain filled his mind, and then everything went black.

Chapter Ten

Pain. His entire body screamed with pain. Every breath brought daggers to his chest. Maliche opened his eyes, but saw nothing. *I'm alive? Blind as a carthatch, but alive.* Stars blazed in the darkness when he attempted to move. His brain swooned in agony. He groaned weakly, and even that hurt.

"Don't move, unless you want to cripple yourself permanently, Brin."

Gradually, a faint light grew as his eyes accustomed themselves to the darkness. There, in the corner, a dark shape hunched over a small fire. Maliche heard the clank of stirring and the occasional hiss as liquid spilled onto the flames.

"How you survived this long is a miracle, so be still and thank the sky gods for your good fortune. Your soup will be ready in a moment."

Speaking was agony, his chest screamed with every breath, but Maliche needed to know. "How long have I been here? And what is this place? Who are you?"

The sudden realization hit Maliche that this was a Kolandi, a living Kolandi, brought a wooden bowl to him and slowly dripped a thin broth into his mouth.

"So many questions. At least your brain does not seem too damaged, Brin. But before I answer you, I have one question of my own. How did you come by this?" He held up Maliche's silver medallion.

Maliche's eyes struggled to focus on the object as he considered his options. There weren't many, so he opted for the truth. "It is a family heirloom. My name is Maliche Rocker."

The Kolandi reflexively touched his forehead, chin, and chest. "Then Lejenal may be right. She always believed in the old prophecies. If you are the great one, it is lucky I saw this before I drove my spear into your heart. But I may yet have that pleasure." He placed the medallion back around Maliche's neck.

"Maliche's head swam with vertigo as he clung desperately to consciousness. "What do you mean 'the great one'? I'm just an archaeologist, nothing special. What prophecy…"

"Did you not say you are Rocker? Is this not your medallion?" The brown skinned man tapped the carved object on Maliche's chest with his spear. "It is a sign from our ancestors that The Rocker has returned to us. Only he would have this sign of our bond. If you live, I must bring you to the princess. She will decide the truth of your words."

The Kolandi's words swirled in Maliche's head, mixing with images from his visions. He found it difficult to tell reality from hallucination. The pain seized him again and he trailed off as darkness overtook him once more, his last coherent thoughts were of Aras.

***

"You seem much better today, Great One." Maliche awoke to a new voice, much softer than before. Keeping his head as still as possible, he looked toward the voice. There, next to him, sat a female native. The hair on her head, yes, hair, not feathers as in the old books and his visions, was long, straight, and black. Her skin brown and smooth, she wore leather skins fastened by a series of bone and wood buttons as well as leather ties. Dust particles danced in beams of sunlight streaming in from the cave's opening bathing its interior in the orange glow of sunrise.

"Are you well enough for more soup?"

"Who are you?" He winced as a new wave of pain shot through his body, but his stomach growled in hunger as the aroma of the bubbling pot filled his nostrils.

"Do not try to move, Great One. My name is Lejenal. It was my mate, Opet, who found you and brought you here five days ago. You are fortunate he noticed your medallion before he killed you. Only someone who has shown great loyalty and friendship toward our people would have one. None have been bestowed on any of your kind in many generations. Is it true what Opet tells me, you are The Rocker?"

Maliche shifted his weight and attempted a smile, not too terribly agonizing, and sipped the soup Lejenal offered. "Well, my name is Maliche Rocker. If what I believe is true, it was my ancestors who first met yours so long ago. The medallion came to me recently and I have been searching for what is left of your people ever since. We thought you became extinct." His leg throbbed, and the constant ache in his back and chest made it difficult to think. "I need to contact my companions. They can bring me home for medical treatment."

Lejenal shook her head and laid a gentle hand on Maliche's chest. "I do not think that would be wise, Great One."

"What do you mean? I need medicine and a doctor."

She hesitated a moment, her eyes fixed on Maliche.

Maliche lifted his hand in appeal. "Don't hold back. Tell me what's wrong."

She nodded as if to agree. "As Opet was bringing you here, he saw one of your flying ships in the sky headed toward where yours crashed. He was wary, but decided to risk returning to your ship, in case they were a rescue party searching for you. As he watched, hiding behind a low ridge nearby, he saw one of your kind search the wreckage and overheard him as he spoke to some others over a communicator." She hesitated, as if trying to judge how much more to reveal. "You will not like to hear this, great one, but Opet heard your Brin companion tell the others his sabotage was successful and you died in the crash, only your burned bones remained. Opet watched as he flew off toward the mine, and then returned to bring you to me."

The vertigo enveloped him again as he tried to absorb this news. "Sabotage? Are you sure Opet heard him correctly?"

"He would not make a mistake in such an important matter. His knowledge of your language is strong from his days as a slave in your mines. I will leave you to rest now. Opet will return in a day or two and then we will go see the princess. She will decide what is to become of you."

"Wait, what princess? Where are we going? What—"

Lejenal laid another hand softly on his left arm. "Hush now. No more questions. You need to build your strength for the journey. The princess will decide what to tell you when we reach her. Be well, Great One."

She dowsed the small fire setting smoke and bright embers climbing toward the cave's ceiling, and left Maliche alone in his alcove.

***

The journey took three days due to Maliche's injuries and the need to travel slowly and with extreme caution. The travois, though well padded, still bounced far too much over the rocks on the trail. Even under the influence of a pain numbing drug, Maliche felt every jolt.

Lejenal and Opet steadfastly refused to answer any questions about other Brin they might have seen, the mine she mentioned, it certainly was not on any map he knew of. He resigned himself to watch the passing of clouds above, falling back into the childhood game of imagining all manner of creatures in their shifting shapes, and the multi-colored stratigraphy of the sparsely vegetated canyon walls.

At long last, they entered a well-hidden cave deep in the canyon. Maliche looked on in awe as he was carried passed dozens of Kolandi, most of them looked to be in as poor health, or worse than he. Many, dressed in tattered rags of cloth and skins, shrank back, or gestured forcefully in his direction. The disturbed murmur grew louder and angrier as Opet and Lejenal helped into a makeshift bed in another alcove.

Lejenal pulled a tattered curtain closed over the opening and spoke gently to the gathering crowd in a language he did not understand, but assumed to be the Kolandi native tongue. Some in the gathering argued with her in anger, but her authority eventually persuaded the others to leave. After posting a single guard, Opet and Lejenal vanished down the corridor.

Amid the sound of hushed voices, confused echoes and dripping water, Maliche drifted off to sleep. His dreams were strangely calming, filled with overtones of relief and excitement.

***

A week later, Maliche's health improved to the point where he could sit up, and even manage to get around on a rickety pair of wooden crutches for short distances. He dared not leave his meager quarters. He heard frequent arguments between the cave's inhabitants. While their language was unfamiliar to Maliche as they spoke amongst themselves, they knew how to speak Brin, but limited their vocabulary to the most colorful of derogatory terms when they addressed him from a distance. The meaning was clear. He was not a welcome guest.

Shortly after lunch, Lejenal approached him. "The princess wishes to see you now that you are recovered sufficiently for an audience. I have been instructed to bring you to her."

Maliche nodded, gathered his crutches, and raised himself up with a grimace. "Lead on, my lady."

As he hobbled through the passages the inhabitants he encountered were less than pleased to see him. Women and children spat in his face. A group of boys threw stones at his back, one bounced painfully off his head bringing whoops of laughter from the youths. Lejenal led him through several twists and turns only to find her way blocked by a gathering of young warriors. With their knives drawn, the men approached. They shouted in Kolandi at Lejenal, gesturing with their weapons for her to step aside.   With a burst of anger, Lejenal stormed at the men, waving her arms at them, back at Maliche, then at the men again. Her tirade continued and she continued stepping forward, forcing the shocked men into slowly retreating. She jabbed their leader in the chest with two thin, but strong fingers as she backed him against a wall. They looked at each other for support, but Lejenal's outrage finally cowered them into submission. With only a few face-saving grumbles in retaliation the men sheathed their knives and allowed the two to pass, with no more than a cursory punch to Maliche's arm which nearly knocked him to the ground.

When they reached a tunnel where they were alone, Maliche pulled up alongside his protector. "Thank you. I don't know what you told them, but you certainly saved my life back there."

Lejenal waver her arm in dismissal. "Pay those schuteks no mind. They are young and foolish, trying to impress each other with how fierce they can be."

"I am grateful to you for getting them to back down. You might have been killed, too."

She laughed and rolled her eyes. "By them? I used to change their dirty wraps when they were babies. Sometimes they are too impressed by their new status as warriors and need to be reminded of their place."

After only two brief rest stops, Lejenal led Maliche into a large room within the cave. A wide vein of quartz brought in light from the outside, lending a brilliant glow to the damp walls. Two rows of benches lined either side of a central aisle. Several large fire pits lent warmth to the chamber. At the far end stood a massive marble tomb inlaid with gold and silver. In front of the tomb knelt a woman dressed in green robes, elegant, but showing the strain of her office. Her long brown hair was luminous in the refracted light. Around her neck she wore a golden disc cradling a brilliant green gem at its center and a series of carvings, humanoid in nature, with outstretched arms linked together around its edge. Lejenal signaled for Maliche to wait as she approached the woman.

Lejenal genuflected before the tomb, and then reverently addressed the woman. "Princess, I have brought the Brin called Rocker as you requested." She gestured for Maliche to approach.

The princess turned to face him as he maneuvered down the pathway. "Welcome descendant of The Rocker. Your arrival is celebrated."

Lejenal, at a signal from the Princess formally introduced them. "Princess, I present Maliche Rocker, descendant of The Rocker. Maliche Rocker, I am honored to present Princess Ryma, leader of the Kolandi." She bowed toward Princess Ryma.

Maliche hobbled forward, maneuvering with some difficulty between the rows of benches, attempted a bow, but only managed a head nod with moderate discomfort while balancing on his crutches. "I am honored, my lady, and I thank you for the service your people have bestowed this humble stranger. Although, I am afraid my presence is not exactly celebrated by most of your people."

Ryma nodded in return and extended both her hands, palms up. "If your name is true, then you are certainly no stranger among us and all will come to accept you as an honored guest. But your kind have imprisoned and enslaved us for many generations. There is much bad blood between us. For the sake of us all, I pray you are who you say and the prophecy of our deliverance is at hand." She turned, gesturing toward the tomb. Maliche approached and read the name carved deep into the marble. "Jontar Rocker." Above the name, carved in bas relief was a replica of his medallion.

Stunned, Maliche staggered a bit, and then gathered his wits. "How is this possible? I've seen Jontar Rocker's tomb back in First Town. Well, at least his marker. Nobody knew what happened to him after he traveled east across the ocean." He took another few steps closer to the monument. "Are you telling me this is his actual tomb?"

Princess Ryma smiled and bowed her head in agreement. "This is the final resting place of the great Rocker... he who returned to help us in the days following the great sorrow. Your medallion and this pendant are symbols of our ancient ties." She held out her necklace for Maliche to see.

A few more steps and Maliche came close enough to reach out his hand and touch the marble monument containing his ancestor. As his hand caressed the cool stone, feeling the warmth of the inlaid silver, he noticed a glow emanating from within the tomb. His hand tingled as if crawling with invisible insects. Then a burst of light and power filled his consciousness, blocking out everything. Visions of events long past mixed furiously with feelings of great joy. Overwhelmed, his knees buckled. The princess reached out to keep him from collapsing, and grabbed onto the tomb with her other hand to maintain her balance. With this touch, the glow burst into a blinding light surrounding the pair, paralyzing them both. The passage of time lost all meaning as Maliche and Ryma absorbed the energy penetrating their bodies and minds. Visions of memories became shared between them, random and without meaning at first, gradually resolving into coherence. A final torrent of energy shot through them, and a voice, coming from the entrapped pair, but not theirs, resounded in the room.   "Success! At long last, Success!"

Maliche collapsed, the princess falling at his side. As consciousness returned, he felt many powerful hands roughly carrying him away, angry voices shouting at him. The guards kicked and beat him as they dragged him from the tomb.

"Stop! Do not harm him!" Ryma's voice shook and lacked the power to be heard over the angry tumult. Gathering her strength, she pulled herself upright and willed her voice to command power. "I said release him! He is not to be harmed!" This time her voice echoed throughout the chamber and produced the desired effect.   The mob halted and became silent, nearly dropping their victim to the ground. Maliche turned his head toward her voice and saw several female attendants helping her to her feet.

"Princess," one of the men carrying Maliche protested. "This foul Brin tried to kill you. We must slay him for his treachery.'

With the aid of her attendants, Ryma approached the men. "No. This was not his doing. It was The Rocker who awoke and revealed his thoughts to us both. Bring him to my chambers where he can be cared for properly."

The men carrying Maliche stood motionless for a brief moment, eyes flickering between the tomb, their princess, and the Brin they planned to execute.

"Do as I command! Bring him to my chambers and send for the healers!" Her voice carried all the authority of her station, and resonated around the alcove.

The men, bowing in submission, obeyed. They tossed Maliche onto a cot in an antechamber of the princess's cave and left. Covered in a thin blanket he felt warmth growing in his body.

"Sleep now. I'll have you fixed up and healthy again in no time." The voice seemed to come from everywhere at once. Maliche looked around for the person who spoke. *"I'm in here. You'll get used to me pretty soon. Karm and Jontar did and so will you. You rest now while I fill you in on the rest of the story."* Maliche's mind went numb; visions of the past filled his thoughts as he drifted off to sleep.

Chapter Eleven

Karmito, who now, with the approach of his fifteenth birthday, gave notice that he was too old for such a baby name like 'little Karm' insisting everyone call him Karmito, burst into the room.

"Mother! Come quickly! Grandfather has had an accident!"

"What happened?" Maripa asked as she grabbed her coat ran after her son.

"Grandfather went fishing and slipped on a rock. He fell into the river and carried downstream. By the time I reached him he was barely conscious. I ran for help and we got him to the hospital."

"Go tell your father to meet me there, and go find Tari. I think she is playing with Nareen in the schoolyard." She rounded the corner and sped the two blocks to the hospital entrance.

"Where is he?" she shouted to the admissions clerk as she burst through the front doorway. The clerk pointed and she ran down the hall, scattering nurses, orderlies and patients in her wake.

Maripa gasped at the site of her uncle through the glass doorway of his room in the Intensive Care Ward. Electronic equipment in the room beeped and clicked rhythmically as it measured the vital signs of the pale, withered figure lying in the bed. Doctors and nurses busied themselves with needles and various instruments they used to examine the semi-conscious patient. She slowly opened the door and entered the room, her heart pounded in her chest.

"How is he, Nela?"

"He's alive, but just barely," the doctor responded without turning around. "We'll know more after we get the test results."

Maripa recognized death when she saw it, and she saw it in Karm's face as clearly as daylight. "How long does he have?"

Nela turned to face Maripa. She studied her for a moment before responding. "Not long," she said. "Maybe hours, a day, or two at most. I'm not sure what's keeping him alive right now, unless it's that incredible computer enhancement of his. Anyone else his age would have died instantly from these injuries. It's a miracle he is alive at all. He's what… one hundred and twenty years old? Hard to keep track with his time traveling trick and all."

She considered the news for a few seconds, took a deep breath to steady herself against the rising emotions, and straightened her shoulders. "Is he conscious?"

"He's under mild sedation, just sleeping for now. If you want to wait in the hall for a couple of minutes while we will finish up here and then you can come back in. You can talk to him if he wakes up."

Rocker, with Karmito and Tari at his side, pushed through the double door and joined Maripa standing in the brightly lit hallway watching through the glass window as the doctors completed their routines. He walked up beside her and placed a protective arm around her waist.

"Is there any hope?" The children stood on either side of them, each reaching for a hand.

Maripa simply shook her head, fighting back the tears welling up in her eyes. She refused to give in to sentimentality, for Karm's sake if not her own.

Two hours later, Karm's eyes fluttered and he turned his head to look at his family, his voice weak and gravely, barely managing a smile. "Guess I really messed up this time."

"Don't waste your energy, grandfather," cautioned Tari. "You need to rest so you can come home with us." She stood on tiptoes, reaching across the blanket to hook talons.

Karm reached over and patted his granddaughter's cheek. "Not this time, my sweet girl. I'm afraid we won't be taking any more fishing trips together."

Karm coughed weakly as he turned to Maripa. "No regrets, my dear. You are the joy of my life. I couldn't have been prouder if you were my blood daughter."

"I love you, too, old man." She took his hand and gently held it for several silent minutes.

Karm eventually removed his hand from Maripa's soft grip and reached out to Rocker. "I need to share something with you, Jontar. Come, take my hand." A deep blue glow began to surround Karm's form.

Rocker stood up from his chair and walked over to Karm's bedside. He grasped Karm's hand lightly in his own. "I'm here, my friend."

The glow extended to embrace Rocker as well as Karm. Its color fluctuated between the deep, sad blue and a more excited and somehow happier green. Rocker tried to release his grip, but found his hand frozen and unable to respond.

"What are you doing, Karm? What's happening?" In his mind, there was a flash of white.

A voice seemed to resonate from everywhere at once. *"Oh, this is nice. None of those artificial transcription errors to work around."*

Rocker awoke to find himself lying on the floor looking up into Maripa's worried face. His mind filled with images and rapid fire bits of information. He lifted his hand and saw the green glow surrounding it, and his entire body. "I'm okay... I think." He sat up, holding his head as if it might explode. Maripa and Karmito helped him back onto his chair.

Karmito poured a cup of water from a nearby pitcher and handed it to Jontar. "What happened, father?"

Rocker continued to stare at his glowing arm. "I'm not entirely sure, but I think Karm transferred his biocomputer to me."

All four of them turned simultaneously toward Karm. "Can he do that?" asked Tari. Her voice cracked with fear.

The dying man managed a frail smile. "My gift to you." The blue glow continued to surround him, but it was fading. "The biocomputer knows I am dying and we talked it over. No, I'm not crazy. As you will soon learn, the computer communicates with me in many different ways. We've had many conversations over the years, but the most interesting ones have been in the past few months. I believe the feather-fluffed thing is actually evolving."

Rocker and Maripa exchanged glances, but said nothing.

Karm coughed feebly and winced in pain as he continued. "This marvel of technology cannot be lost. It is almost sentient in the way it communicates with me lately. We both reasoned that since I am your clone, and we share the same DNA, so the computer could adapt itself to your physiology. I guess it worked."

"You mean you weren't sure this would work?"

"No, but we were pretty certain. In time, you will get the hang of it. Just be careful not to lose yourself in the experience. I know how overwhelming the feelings can become. Take it slow at first and you'll be fine. I think it likes you." He pointed to the now steady green glow around Rocker's body.

"Does it hurt, father?" asked Tari as she extended one talon out to touch the aura surrounding him.

"No, Tari. I'm fine. Just a little tingle… and a strange buzzing in my ear."

Maripa stepped forward now and took Karm's hands. She placed them back onto the bed and lifted the blanket up to his chin.

"That's enough excitement for now. You need to get some rest. We'll be here when you wake up again." She carefully combed his sparse top crest with her talons, humming one of his favorite old tunes.

"All right, my dear, I am tired, so maybe I will try to get some shut eye for now." Karm closed his eyes and drifted off to sleep.

In moments, his breathing became irregular and rattled softly. Then his face relaxed and his chest settled as he exhaled his last breath. Maripa, Rocker, Karmito, and Tari embraced each other as tears streamed down their faces in silence.

The funeral followed a week later and, despite their objections, grew into a massive affair. Though Maripa and Rocker preferred a simpler, more private service, they recognized Karm's nearly mythical stature among the population. His body lay in state in the lobby of the newly constructed capital building. The mining guild provided the stone, something like marble, and dozens of craftsmen carved the intricate figures inside and out depicting their brief history on this new world. People filed past, paying their respect for two days. Representatives from all of the co-ops and guilds spoke eloquently during the final service. All of them referenced Karm's position as "The Savior" of the Brin and expressed their deepest sorrow to his family. Even the miner's guild seemed sincere in their eulogy. After the courts upheld the sentence against them they settled in to a less adversarial role in the Brin community. Rumors persisted, but nothing concrete ever surfaced.

As the sun set and a somber procession through the street lined with mourners, they laid Karm's body to rest nearby in the base of what would become a monument to the great man. Maripa and Rocker resisted the idea of a monument, but again relented under pressure from the people. The need to provide a lasting tribute proved too strong among those who revered him. At long last, the ceremonies and long lines of those wishing to extend their condolences dwindled enough for Maripa, Rocker, and their children to retire gracefully for the evening.

Back home again, Maripa excused herself and went off to the small room serving as her home office. Rocker approached the closed door, hoping to comfort his wife, but stopped when he heard her sobbing. He knew her too well to intrude on her need for privacy. Laying his palm against the door, he saw the blue glow return to his arm.

"Will that happen to me one day, too, father?"

Rocker turned to see Karmito looking at his own hand and pointing to the blue nimbus. "Only time will tell, son, but we share the same genes, so I think maybe yes." The glow turned a bright green and in his mind he distinctly heard a voice. *"Looks like you might be nearly as smart as Karm believed."*

***

As he slept, Maliche stirred as the dream shifted, blurring into greyness, only to resolve itself in an entirely new time and place.

***

"Ten Year Anniversary Memorial Celebration!" announced the flyer in her hand. "Games, Parade, Food, and Fireworks!" A photo of Karm and the great stone statue over his tomb emblazoned the center of the leaflet.

"Can you believe it's been ten years?" Maripa asked. She passed the broadside to Rocker, placing the bouquet of flowers on the old Brin's tomb.

"Seems like only yesterday. We could use a little fun these days. What do you think about the reports of Caeri's village being deserted?"

"I don't like it. What could possibly have forced them out with no warning, and no communication?"

"I don't know. But I intend to find out."

"What are you talking about? Where do you think you're going?" Maripa planted her feet, hands firmly on her hips, and faced her husband.

"I'm on the next flight over to the village to try to find out where they went and why."

"You most certainly are not. We need you here, not gallivanting across the planet when others can do the job just as well. We don't know what happened. For all we know they were attacked and carried off somewhere." Her green eyes blazed with absolute certainty and finality.

Rocker stood his ground as he confronted Maripa. "The mining guild reports indicate no signs of violence. In fact, photos of the village look so normal it's as if they just vanished all at once. I need to find out what happened to them."

Her voice took on the calm deadliness he knew all too well. "No, you don't. In fact, I am going before the council today to insist upon a total ban on all transportation and exploration across the ocean to be effective immediately."

Rocker fumbled for a moment, trying to comprehend Maripa's declaration. "What do you mean, 'ban all transportation'? We have to figure out where they went. We owe it to them."

Maripa softened her stance and reached out to Rocker. "Jontar, we have no idea what happened over there. If we go stumbling around who knows what we might find. There's a lot we still don't know about that part of the planet, or even our own neighborhood for that matter. We still have no idea who or what built those ruins, and they're less than one hundred km away. If we expose ourselves to some hostile force before our own defenses are ready, then we are opening ourselves to the same fate. I can't allow that to happen."

"Are you telling me that you want us to abandon our friends?"

"For now, yes," she replied. "At least until we can build up our ability to defend ourselves against whatever is out there. Once we are stronger, then we can go looking for them. You haven't forgotten Karm's warning about enemies from the sky, have you? It's haunted me for years. Every time one of us goes up in one of those shuttles I worry some disaster will strike us again. Besides, you've heard the anti-native contingent. They're growing stronger every year."

She walked over to the carved murals on the wall surrounding Karm's memorial. She reached out to touch the stone wall depicting Karm leading her and Rocker into the Hegira II.

"For once, I agree with the mining guild. They can continue operations on the eastern continent and provide advance warning if their security forces discover anything. If we don't stop now, limiting further contamination over there, who knows what damage may result. I'm afraid some of the miners may be behind some of the disappearances, but there's no proof. The quetzals and their guards won't allow anyone near their operations, claiming the mines are too dangerous for untrained visitors."

Rocker shook his head. "Maripa, I've seen you charge into a fight with nothing more than a small knife. You've never been afraid of anything. What are you not telling me?"

Maripa turned her back to Rocker and stood rigidly, fists clenched at her side. "I can't lose you the way we lost Karm. If you go over there and whatever got Vidad, Neas and the rest of them get you, too, I couldn't live knowing I should have stopped you. With Karmito off on his own and married now—I just couldn't survive without you."

Before Rocker could respond, his palm glowed a reddish-pink. He stopped, listening to the voice in his head. A moment later, his eyes focused again and he knew what he must do.

"It seems my friend up here," he said pointing to his head, "agrees with you. I can't fight both of you, so let's go talk with the council."

The mining guild representatives spoke convincingly in favor of the travel ban. Since the lifting of their restrictions three years ago, the discovery of important mineral deposits across the ocean made this a wealthy and powerful group, and the others eventually gave in under pressure from them, their allies, and Maripa. Maripa reassured the ranchers and farmers guilds of her intent to open up new sections of this continent for their use in exchange for their support of the ban. Additional votes gave responsibility for the eastern continent to the mining guild, complete with sole rights to transport any and all minerals discovered in the region. The news of the travel prohibition was initially unpopular, but the oppositions soon lost steam among the preparations for the grand celebration to come.

      The ten-year anniversary celebration became a grand affair lasting three days. The speeches given at the foot of Karm's memorial (a twenty-foot-tall stature of the great man) roused the people in their patriotism and sense of duty to the community. Since most of the people never traveled more than a hundred kilometers from home anyway, the ban produced minimal disruption to daily life. Within a couple of month's few people even remembered the ban, or felt any remorse at the loss of contact with those across the ocean. The influx of so many riches made everyone's life more comfortable.

***

Another shift in perspective of the dream woke Maliche. The dark room was quiet, except for the Kolandi guard's soft snoring from the chair nearby.

      "Not yet, my friend. There is more to show you before I let you go. Rest now. Let me continue." Sleep overtook Maliche once more.

***

Rocker sat silently by Maripa's bedside. Her tiny, frail form barely created a disturbance in the thick blankets covering her. Wrinkled, with only the faintest wisp of a silver top crest, her eyes still retained their old intensity and strength. He held her small, aged hand, his shoulders and head bowed by time and sorrow, whispering to his dying wife.

      "Twenty-two years to the day since Karm's passing. We've traveled quite the journey together, my love." He heard the door open softly behind him, but did not look to see who entered.

"Father," Karmito said quietly walking to Rocker's side. "How is she doing today?" The young man, now in his late thirties and mayor of the town, pulled up a chair to join his father.

The old geneticist gave a weak smile acknowledging his son, but never looked away from Maripa's peaceful sleep. "She's resting peacefully, but there's nothing more the doctors can do. She's a fighter, but it's just a matter of time now. Her cloned DNA, while stronger than Karm's, still proved faulty enough to shorten her life-span by a couple of decades." He continued to watch his wife's face for any sign of rousing from her sleep.

"Elarc and I are glad you brought mother home. She never did like hospitals. Can I get you anything? You look like you could use some breakfast."

"You know how proud we are of you, don't you?" asked Jontar, still refusing to look away from Maripa.

"I know, father. I'll go down and fix you something. Maybe then you would like to get a bit of rest. Oh, I spoke to Tari and she will come to visit you this afternoon." Karmito patted Rocker's shoulder and left the room, closing the door gently behind him.

Rocker stroked his wife's thin grey crest as she slept. "He's become quite the young man, my love, and now a family of his own. Where did the time go?"

Maripa stirred and opened her eyes. "Jontar?"

"I'm here, Maripa. I'm not going anywhere."

She smiled weakly at him and squeezed his hand. "You may not be, but I'm afraid I am, my husband." She coughed and blanched at the effort.

"Don't try to talk, dear. You need to conserve your strength."

"And what good will that do?" She gave Rocker one of her famous glares. "I know what the doctors are saying. I need to talk to you while I still can." With an effort, Maripa shifted onto her side so she could face her husband more easily. "I need to talk to you about my decision to stop you from going out to find our friends across the ocean."

Rocker shook his head, fighting to keep the tears out of his eyes at the memory of the many fierce arguments between them on this matter.

"No, I understand. You were right. We needed to see to our own safety first. You made the right decision."

Smiling weakly, she patted his hand. "Yes, I did, but things are different now. I know the burden of not knowing what happened has never left you. The old scientist in you needs to discover the truth of it all. You will never be satisfied until you go and search for them."

Rocker fought back the lump in his throat. "That doesn't matter now. I can't leave you."

"Jontar," she said, mustering as much irritation in her voice as she could. "I'm dying. We both know the facts. I can no longer hold you to your promise. Go and find our friends. Learn what happened to them. Our people are ready now if the worst happens."

"Maripa, we can talk about this later. It's not important now."

Maripa, gripped his hand tighter, closed her eyes and gritted her teeth. Rocker wiped the beads of sweat from her forehead as the pain eased.

"There will not be any 'later', Jontar. I've already talked to Karmito about this and he will talk to the council to grant you permission to go on this quest. You and your biocomputer are the best chance we have of learning the truth. We are ready. We need to know what happened so we can face whatever dangers may be out there. Just promise me one thing."

"Anything, my love."

"Don't let them build any damn monument over me like they did to poor Karm. I'm no savior, and I certainly don't want any idiots fawning over me like they do at his silly statue."

Rocker bent over and gently kissed her on the forehead. "I promise."

A week later, the funeral procession, second only to Karm's service, preceded through the dusty streets. At its conclusion, they laid Maripa to rest in a simple grave next to Karm's. A small, plain marble headstone placed over her read:

Maripa Rocker

Loving Wife and Mother
Our Guardian

For the next few weeks, Dr. Jontar Rocker sat by the gravesite talking to his wife. People passing by were struck by the scene, especially the soft blue glow surrounding the grieving man.

***

"One more story to tell and then we can talk." The voice resounded in Maliche's mind as the vision jumped once more.

***

Flying far above the desert, Rocker looked down onto as bleak a scene as existed anywhere on Raince'to. Rock and sand as far as the eye could see, broken only rarely with the grey-green of lonely scrub struggling to survive the harsh environment. Two weeks of flying over the remotest regions of this forbidding place revealed nothing of the missing natives.

"Are you sure this is where they are?" Rocker asked out loud. He accepted the biocomputer as another sentient entity now and often spoke to it. Communicating by thought alone was sufficient, but somehow it just seemed more natural this way. At first, the biocomputer chided him over the cumbersome nature of speech, but now accepted the method as one of Rocker's many personal quirks.

"Yes, I'm sure," the device replied. *"You don't think I'm so fond of sand to bring you here on vacation do you? Be patient. I am sensing them now. We are very close."*

Without warning, the shuttle shook violently, lurching to starboard. "What the strix?" cursed Rocker as he fought for control. Flashing lights and alarms signaled on the control panel. Flying over the southern desert, always difficult even under ideal conditions, but now suddenly became life threatening. The dunes rose up from below at a startling rate. The glaring sun vanished into blackness as Rocker's shuttle slammed into the ground.

***

Awareness slowly crept into Rocker's consciousness. His head pounded mercilessly, his entire body ached. Opening his eyes required a nearly inhuman effort. *I'm alive?* Straw crunched as he shifted his position and he looked up at the inside of a thatched roof. *Where the strix am I? How did I get here?* He attempted to sit up, but a wave of nausea and pain coursed through him and he collapsed back onto the bed. He heard the shuffling of feet on dirt and the soft gasp of a woman.

"So, you are alive after all, Doctor Rocker." The woman knelt next to him and wiped his face gently with a cool wet cloth. "My name is Lomyl, granddaughter of Caeri and Vidad. You are in my village now."

Rocker managed to turn his head, painfully, to see his caregiver. "How did I get here?"

"Ten days ago, my people saw your flying craft crash and found you. They brought you here to me as soon as they realized who you were. Rest now, we will talk more when you are better."

As Rocker drifted off, he noticed she wore the golden amulet with the green gem at its center. He relaxed, knowing he was among friends.

Three days later, Rocker felt remarkably well. His head and body no longer felt as if they had been crushed beneath a ten-ton stone.

"Did you have something to do with my miraculous recovery?" he mentally asked his biocomputer.

"Of course," it replied. *"I almost lost you a few times, but managed to pull you through. I even succeeded in repairing a few other malfunctions you were developing."*

Before he could reply, Lomyl, the village princess and heir to Caeri's throne, reappeared through the entryway.

"Good morning Doctor Rocker. You appear to be nearly cured today. Is it common for your kind to heal so rapidly? Your wounds would have taken one of us months to recover from."

"I'm not sure I can explain what happened, either. Where are your grandparents? I want to thank them for my rescue as well."

Lomyl closed her eyes briefly before responding. "Sadly, they have passed on to the spirit world. Five years ago, after bringing us to this new village they succumbed to the passing of their years. I am now leader of my people." She thought for a moment before continuing. "I remember you,

Doctor, from your visits to our homes so many years ago. I was a child, but I remember you clearly. You seem unchanged by the years. Or are we mistaken and you are not The Rocker, but merely his offspring?"

Rocker laughed at her observations. "I thank you for your kindness to an old man, my dear. I can assure you that I am the same man who visited you in those long ago times. Surely this face shows the passing of the decades."

Lomyl's face contorted in confusion, but decided to hold off further questions. "We can discuss this matter later. For now, though, we must get you cleaned up. You were too fragile for us to do much before now. But we must wash you now, before you start attracting scavengers." She called for the waiting attendants who entered carrying bowls of water, towels, changes of clothes shaving implements and a mirror. "We will leave you now to attend to your cleansing, unless you require assistance."

Rocker stood to accept the items. "No, I can manage. Thank you," He grabbed the mirror and nearly dropped to the ground when he saw the reflection. Staring back at him was not the familiar face of recent years, but that of the younger man who once owned this body, more than four decades ago.

***

"Surprise," said the voice in his head. Rocker's entire body flared up in a bright green glow.

Chapter Twelve

"He's waking up now, Princess."

"Thank you, Lejenal. You should go have something to eat now. I will be fine."

Lejenal bowed and left the alcove. Maliche watched through blurry eyes as the princess approached, a slight tingling like a static charge building in his mind, hovered in the back of his brain.

"What happened? Are you all right?"

He sat up, suddenly realizing most of his pain was gone, and everything seemed to be in good working order. "How long have I been out?"

Ryma took two of his talons in her fingers as she sat on the cot next to him, her pale yellow dress rustling softly with the movement. "The incident in the tomb was only yesterday. Was that truly The Rocker who joined with us? Are the visions real? Are you one of his descendants?" She trembled slightly, her eyes barely hiding the fear.

Maliche sat quietly, letting the memories coalesce. His left palm began to glow and the tingling strengthened, his eyes grew vacant.

"Don't try to figure it all out at once. I'll sort it all out for you in time. Let yourself heal a bit longer. There was a lot of damage to repair. It's enough right now for you to know that I am the device originally implanted in Karm, but passed along to Jontar Roker, and now to you. Jontar died without producing an heir, at least not where I could get to them. I've been trapped here until now. The medallion created the initial link between us. Your genetic markers were close enough to his to allow me to send you the visions, as you call them, and guide you on this journey. When you touched the tomb I was able to use the Kolandi amulet and your medallion to connect myself to your neural network."

"What about before? I've had this compulsion about my family's history since I was a small child."

"Oh, that. Lots of members of your family are interested in your history. I've been sending out that general impulse for generations. You were the first to have markers strong enough to take hold of. While I slept I was able to meddle in your subconscious for years. That artifact in the desert awakened me when you touched it. The medallion solidified the connection, and now here I am."

Maliche's eyes refocused on the princess as the voice in his mind faded. He raised his left palm and watched as the glow subsided. "This is extraordinary. I seem to be the host for some sort of biological computer entity. I've heard strange tales of my ancestor and Karm having some strange abilities, but we always brushed them off as mythology. I think we may have been mistaken."

The princess looked skeptical. "But I was affected, too. I do not seem to have this entity you speak of. And I certainly do not glow the way you do ever since the incident. I have no choice but to believe you since the visions I saw are undeniable, but..." She searched his face for answers.

Maliche thought for a moment. "Let me try something." He closed his eyes and concentrated.

"Not now. It is too soon to know for sure if my experiment worked well enough, but I am very hopeful. Neither of you needs to know about it yet, so don't bother trying to find out. I can keep a secret very well. She is unharmed and will suffer no lingering effects. Even the memory of the visions will fade with time."

"No good. My friend in here..." He tapped his head with one talon. "...seems to have some secrets he doesn't want to share. All he would say is that you and I are part of some experiment of his, but you will be fine. Sorry."

Ryma dropped his talons and stood, stepping away a few paces, her brow furrowed in thought. "I am uncomfortable with this entity of yours using me in some experiment." She paced the floor again, mumbling to herself, hands gesturing with the argument raging in her. Turning to face Maliche, she stood tall, squared her shoulders, and placed her hands on her hips. "However, and I don't know how I know this, but I do, everything you say is true. Our legends also tell us of The

Rocker's mysterious abilities. His tomb is reputed to be a source of inspiration, some even claim to have heard ghostly voices. While your story seems unbelievable, I know, down to my spirit, the truth of it all. We have much to discuss, you and I, Maliche Rocker. Rest now. Tomorrow we begin."

***

In the days that followed, Maliche heard the tales of the Kolandi. Many of the Kolandi warriors argued against a Brin, even if he was a Rocker, participating in the ritual, but the princess silenced them and escorted Maliche to the ceremony herself. The elder Homsan told the stories of the tribe dating back centuries, to the days of Jontar Rocker. Sitting in a room far in the back of the cave, one covered in sacred and historical drawings, flickering in the wavering orange glow of the fire pit, the leaders beat on sticks and rocks, keeping rhythm as the Homsan recited the legends around the fire. The sweet smell of burning wood filled the air.

"And when The Rocker lived among us for a span of ten seasons, our people prospered. Our numbers grew, and all were happy. Then, the Brin descended upon us. They came with chains and weapons of great power, and enslaved us. The Brin spared none. They carried off the women and children, along with the men over the mountains and across the great desert to work in their mines. Even The Rocker was helpless against them."

At this, the elders stopped their drumming. Their heads lowered, hands covering their faces, they began a wailing cry full of deep sadness. This continued for a few minutes when the Homsan raised his head and the rhythm resumed.

"Many attempts to rescue our people came to death and ruin. It was then that The Rocker gathered the few who remained and took us to this hidden canyon of caves. We remained safe for many years, though our numbers were few. The Rocker continued to search far and wide, gathering the scattered remnants of our people together, until even he could no longer stave off time. We built his tomb according to the very design he himself prescribed."

The drumming ceased again and all the elders raised their faces and hands to the ceiling of the cave. The solitary voice of the princess lifted high and clear in a song of praise for The Rocker. When she finished, the elders again continued their pulse.

"And now, when the Brin once again threaten our people with their new mine so close to our caves, The Rocker sends us his descendant to protect us and deliver us from our enslavement. The prophecy is fulfilled."

All eyes focused on Maliche Rocker, heir to the Jontar Rocker legacy. If any doubted his claim to the title, the blue glow surrounding him silenced their objections. Many still muttered amongst themselves, and cast unfriendly gestures his way behind his back, but his claim was indisputable.

"I thought I told you to stop doing this." Maliche, after much practice and rebuke from the computer entity, finally accustomed himself to talking to the biocomputer by thought alone. He always felt talking out loud clarified his thoughts, but he was getting better with practice.

"They need to know who you are. We are going to need their absolute trust if you want to help free them from your compatriots. Besides, I think it looks rather stunning. Blue is definitely your color." A flicker of green joined in with the blue, as if the entity was laughing at him.

Chapter Thirteen

The funeral, a private affair at the request of the family, ended an hour before. Selan sat alone by the empty grave of his brother. The sun shone overhead and a flock of smats flitted through the branches of nearby trees singing their mating songs. The scent of hundreds of flowers, mementos of well-wishers, filled the air with a confused mix of aromas. None of this intruded on Selan's despondency. Wiping a tear away, he stood, walked to the large granite headstone, and rested his hand on the ornately carved family crest. An animated holographic image of Maliche's smiling face filled a central hole carved into the stone.

"I'm sorry, Maliche. I never intended for this to happen." He bowed his head, patted the engraved stone and left to join the others at the public memorial service convening at the Assembly.

The eulogies prattled on for three hours. The head of each guild took his or her turn at the podium to praise the life of the young archeologist and lament his untimely passing in such a pointless pursuit. Of course, they were all very politically correct in their choice of words, but the message was clearly there. Maliche was a disappointment, but he was a Rocker and thus deserving of at least public mourning. At the end, Fejf, and Ceila, both clearly distraught at the loss of their eldest son, thanked the dignitaries for their comforting words, ending the ceremony.

"Walk with me, Selan." Raencert's voice whispered in Selan's ear as the large guildsman leaned close.

"I don't have anything to say to you, Raencert." Selan attempted to move away.

"I beg to differ. We have a great deal to discuss." Raencert took Selan's arm and guided him through the crowd, eventually to one of the secluded garden atriums in the center of the building.

"How could you have been so stupid? Murdering him, even if it looks like an accident, is too big a risk. I thought we agreed on this." Selan turned his back to Raencert, raking his crest with the talons of one hand. "He did not have to die."

Raencert studied the young Brin, like a lepti about to strike its prey. "We need to talk. It is time you learned the truth of the matter."

Selan whirled around, talons flared. "What are you talking about? We could have simply arrested him for exceeding his permits!"

Raencert laughed. "And you think arresting him would have controlled him? Come now, Selan, you know your brother. You know he would have used his influence to get back out there to look for his treasures. We could not risk his stumbling across our operations. Get in the mag-lev. I need to show you something." He pulled out a large cigar and lit it, blowing clouds of grey smoke into the air. Inside the vehicle, Raencert handed Selan a locked metal strongbox. "Open it. I coded the lock to your retinal pattern and DNA sequence"

"I don't have time for your games, Raencert. What is this?"

The guildsman simply gestured toward the box with a monstrous hand. Selan held his eye to the scanner, licked one talon placing it into the receptacle in the lid, and opened the box. His jaw dropped and he froze, not willing to accept what he saw in the 3-D photos.

"What is this? It looks like our mine, but those aren't Brin miners... they're not even Brin. What are these creatures?"

"You're looking at the reason why the minerals are so reasonably priced." Raencert blew another thick cloud of smoke into the air. "For centuries, the guild has kept this secret. The natives, the Kolandi, never went extinct. We have kept them hidden from the Brin populace to use as laborers. Only a select few trusted individuals know this guild secret. You have just joined their ranks."

Selan let the photos slip from his talons back into the box. "All this time... the Kolandi still live? How is this even possible?"

"Over two hundred years ago, the first great plague nearly did wipe them all out. Our ancestors, or at least the original guild leaders, unwittingly helped spread the disease when we tried to enlist their help locating and extracting the minerals. While most of them died, our guild soon discovered a few scattered tribes roaming the deserts. We gathered them together and helped them recover. At first, we paid them to work the mines with the supplies they needed to survive. Before long, we couldn't release them without severely hurting our operations. A few well-padded government officials wrote the laws restricting travel to the eastern continent and the rest, as they say, is history."

"But it's been centuries... how has word of this not gotten out?"

"I'm as surprised as you are. The guilds must be favored by The Eternal." He chuckled at that bit of irony. "We keep the miners on the eastern continent with land grants and high wages to keep them and their families over there, and all communications are strictly controlled. Personally, I think we've been lucky as strix."

Selan jerked upright and stared at Raencert. "So why tell me? And why now?"

Raencert's laugh dripped with satisfaction. "Why not? You're one of us now. You still think your brother's accident wasn't necessary? Besides, we did give him every opportunity to turn back. Our operative warned him several times and suggested alternative sites to dig, but Maliche was stubborn. He was determined to keep going east. He was too much of a threat."

"I never agreed to this." Selan's shoulders slumped, he folded his arms around his chest, his eyes fell to the ground. "Maliche and I disagreed and fought about many things, Raencert, but he was my brother. He didn't need to die."

Raencert's eyes narrowed, his crest twitched and stood fully erect. He clenched tight to the cigar in his mouth. "You're not going soft on me now, are you? That would be very unwise."

"Will you have me killed, too? Do you think you are so far above the law you can do as you wish without consequence?"

"You underestimate me, lad. There's nothing to connect me to any of this, while I have documented verification of your advanced knowledge of the plan. All you have is speculation. Nothing that would stand up in a court. Anything you do would look like a grieving brother lashing out in some desperate attempt to lay blame. Your disgrace would work far better for me than your death."

"And what about my knowledge about your mining operations and the Kolandi? What would happen to you if the Assembly became aware of how you are conducting your business over there?"

"Once again, you lack the proof. Where is your evidence? I kept you on the fringe for many reasons, Selan. I never have trusted you enough to bring you in far enough for you to have anything other than hearsay and rumor. Besides, you have no idea how strong of a grip greed has on the average Brin. Given the choice between mineral prices going sky high, or ignoring the unsupported claims of even somebody from your family, they will choose their purses every time."

"I can get the evidence. All I have to do is turn over these images of the mine sites and they will have to believe me."

"Those can be easily dismissed as doctored images produced by conspiracy theorists. Over the years, the few hints which have leaked out only helped feed the imagination of believers, while your average Brin laughs at them. We couldn't have asked for a better cover story. Besides, who do you think controls the other guilds? Are you so naïve to believe any of them are willing to risk exposing their own illegal activities for this? Think again lad, you are beaten. Accept your situation and join the flock."

Selan slumped into one of the nearby benches and sat, hands folded in his lap and head bowed. Raencert reached out one large hand and placed it on Selan's shoulder.

"I figured you would see the reason of it all. You were always a bright young Brin. By the way, keep the images."

***

"How could I have been so blind? That conniving quetzal!" Selan seethed as the door to his private office slammed behind him. He went immediately to the large safe, allowed the scanner to read his face, pressed the code to open it, and placed the metal box inside. As he punched the locking code he caught a movement near the doorway. He relaxed and took firm control of his anger as he realized it was only his wife approaching.

"Nedia, what are you doing here? I thought you were with mother."

"I was, my husband, but I saw your agitation from her window and came to see if there was anything I could do to ease your sorrow."

He shook his head and took her talons in his. Our fathers made a wise choice when they arranged for our joining. You are a fine treasure, but this is something I must handle myself."

"Maliche knows you loved him, despite all of your disagreements. He would not want you to feel guilt or regret at any unfortunate last words you may have had."

Selan reached in and gave Nedia a lingering peck on her crest. "I know that, but it is still hard. Go now, I have some things to arrange before the day is over. Tell the children I will be up to see them later."

"Yes, my husband." She returned a kiss to his cheek and gently closed the carved wooden doors behind her.

Alone again, Selan's face turned red and his crest twitched with rage. "I can't afford to let Raencert take control like this. If I'm ever to lead the Assembly, then I need to be the one with all the secrets."

Selan picked up the communicator and touched a single button on the keypad. "It's time to activate Syrinx."

Chapter Fourteen

Hundreds of skeletal Kolandi, men, women, and children hauled rock and dug trenches in this section of the open pit. Unlike most mines, here the minerals were found close to the surface. Most of the slaves wore only the shredded remains of what was once clothing. The crack of whips echoed off the canyon walls, blood flowed from the fresh wounds on their backs, regardless of age or gender. Bare footed, they struggled to haul woven baskets of minerals out of the pit to the processing plant a mile away. The procession of slaves travelled this circuit endlessly day and night in two shifts.

From his perch high up in the canyon wall, Maliche surveyed the scene below. Sweat dripped from his face, his crest hung limp and wet, clouds of dust choked his lungs even at the height of his hidden cave.

"How can they continue to work like that in this heat? I can barely breathe up here." He drank again from the clay jar of water he and each of his guides carried. He winced as a Brin miner beat on another of the Kolandi for dropping his basket of rocks.

"What choice do they have?" Danet, the young warrior chosen to lead Maliche to this observation point replied through clenched teeth. "Your kind makes our lives a misery, but we Kolandi do not surrender. We live each day in the hope of gaining our freedom and taking revenge on the Brin who enslave us." He spat on the ground and turned his back to Maliche. Wearing only leather breeches, the deep scars etching his back reminded Maliche of Danet's recent escape from this very mine.

"Not all Brin are like these. Most of us are completely unaware of your existence. We thought you all went extinct centuries ago."

Danet snorted and then threw his hands wide. "Then you must all be blind fools." He stormed off into the darkness of the tunnels, cursing as he went.

A soft hand touched Maliche's back. "Do not worry about Danet. He is young and full of anger, but he will learn the truth of things as he comes to know you, Great One." Tikae, one of Ryma's attendants, sent as the princesses' emissary so no harm would come to Maliche accidentally, spoke gently. Her short, tattered dress clung to her body with sweat. "I have watched you closely in your talks with the princess. I know she trusts you, and so do I. The others will see your true nature in time." She smiled at him, but her eyes filled with tears as she watched the scene below.

Maliche attempted a smile in return. "Thanks, but I'm not sure we have enough time left. We have to do something to end this atrocity now."

"Great One, you are The Rocker. You will know what to do to save us. I must talk to Danet and try to soothe his anger." Tikae bowed and followed Danet back into the tunnel to their camp. The others should begin the meal preparations soon and her supervision was required.

As Maliche watched the mining operations, his mind wandered to thoughts of Ryma. He could feel her touch. Her voice soothed his agitation. The blue of her eyes reminded him of the sky on a bright spring day back home. A scream and another whip crack jolted Maliche out of his daydream.

He scratched at the itch in his palm. "Kak! Stop that you idiot." He looked around embarrassed, hoping nobody noticed his reaction to the daydream. The two remaining guides had their backs to him so he let out a sigh of relief. *I must be some sort of deviant or something. It can't be normal to keep having thoughts like these about someone of another species. Even if she is beautiful.*

A chuckle echoed in Maliche's head. *"Don't be so sure of that."* The biocomputer's voice laughed at him. *"You just relax and start working on a plan to rescue the Kolandi."*

***

"He cannot be trusted! He will betray us the first chance he gets. He is not one of us and cannot be part of this raid." Danet and Opet paced, thrusting their spear to the sky as the council debated plans for a raid on a Brin outpost.

"Have you no eyes? Are your ears closed? The Rocker has come to us as the prophecies foretold. I, myself have heard The Rocker and seen the visions. Maliche may not be of our flesh, but he is of our spirit." The princess sat on her carved stone throne hands folded in her lap. "His knowledge of the Brin and their technology could bring us a great advantage. He must be allowed to participate in this attack."

Arguments broke out on both sides of the issue around the fire. Their frantic shadows bounced on the cave walls as their voices reverberated into a cacophony. In the end, Maliche gained permission to join the raiding party, but only in the capacity of a fledgling to stay behind and care for the camp while the warriors conducted the actual foray.

In the morning, Maliche reluctantly accepted his role and collected weapons from the blacksmith. Located under a large overhang in the cliffside, and disguised with hanging vines, brush and other natural features. The smith was an essential aspect of life in the caverns. Hanging on the walls, Maliche saw all manner of metal pots, utensils and personal ornaments as well as spears, knives and other weapons. The blacksmith stood bare-chested over his forge, sweating in the heat even on this chill morning, directing the efforts of two apprentices.

Maliche examined a long, curved knife. "This is incredible workmanship. How do you make such intricate engravings on the blade like this?" He ran his thumb along one edge, drawing a fine line of blood.

The smith grunted, glancing his way. "That one is a poor example, Brin. A first year apprentice practiced on it. No time for true craftsmanship any more with the war coming." The smith's eyes focused on the amulet around Maliche's neck and his smile grew as he pointed to it. "Perhaps, one day, when all this war nonsense is over, you'll let me take a closer gander at that beauty. Tales are told of great craftsmen of the past who worked such intricate and beautiful ornaments as this one. Maybe I can tease some of the old secrets out of your treasure there and create something worthwhile for a change."

Maliche removed the medallion and handed it to the blacksmith. "It would be my pleasure to help you in any way I can, master smith."

The large man, after quickly rubbing the worst of the soot off his hands, turned it over reverently in his grasp examining closely the intricate details of the engravings before handing it back.

With a wave of his scarred and calloused hand, the man returned to his forge. "You best be off to your duties now."

As directed, Maliche returned to camp with the armaments and helped pack the supplies they would require. Several of the warriors spat their disapproval as they threw their bundles at his feet and scuffed dirt in his face, or roughly shouldered him aside as they passed by. Maliche grumbled as he bent to pick up the bags.

"Stop those thoughts right now," commanded the voice in his head. *"This is a very delicate time for us, and my plans. Don't get us both killed by acting stupid."*

Maliche's thoughts turned to a variety of unpleasant responses to the biocomputer, but he continued to accept the abuse. A light blue glow surrounded him, softening his mood, and causing the remaining warriors to simply deposit their packs and move along without comment.

"Are you truly The Rocker?" A boy, not yet old enough to train as a warrior, helped Maliche organize the camp supplies stared wide-eyed at him.

Maliche smiled at the youth, straining a bit as he lifted a heavy pack. "No, I'm not The Rocker. My name is Maliche. I am a descendant of his, though."

"But you have his sign." The boy reached out as if to touch the blue glow, withdrawing his hand just short of its edge. "All the stories tell of this sign. You must be him."

Maliche held his hand up to allow the boy a closer look at the glow. "My ancestor's abilities seem to have passed to me when I touched his tomb. I am not him, but I hope I can prove just as worthy of your people's trust."

The princess, observing from a distance, watched Maliche talk with the fledgling. She lifted one hand to her breast, smiled, and her eyes unfocused for a moment as if lost in a beautiful dream.

"All is ready for our departure, Princess. My men await your blessing."

Ryma startled awake from her reverie, clasped her hands, and followed Opet to the assembly point.

***

The dust stung his eyes and throat as Maliche and the other fledglings followed the warriors along the desert trail. Hidden by low ridges and dry ravines, the party reached their final staging point and began to set up camp. The men set out scouts and perimeter guards while the fledglings managed the packs, extra weapons, small cooking fire, and other necessities. Under the watchful eyes of a couple of the more experienced women, sent on this expedition by the princess personally to be her eyes and ears, and Maliche's protectors, the campsite quickly became a hive of organized activity.

Maliche, assigned to feed the drunges, two scrawny pack animals brought along to help carry the raid's plunder back to the caves, stared at the starry sky.

"Are you sure about this?" he asked the biocomputer. *"It may take a lifetime to overcome the hatred those warriors have toward me. How will I ever be able to gain their trust if this is all they let me do?"*

"Trust me. Your chance will come sooner than you think."

Maliche felt a soothing calm envelop him as the blue glow faded to green.

After breakfast, the raiding party left camp, leaving only the fledglings behind. A few of the older boys and women took up their positions as scouts to watch for danger, and the returning warriors. As Maliche puttered around the camp cleaning up after the morning meal, he tried to ignore the angry looks and chatter among the women, his thoughts turned inward. *Maybe if I understood their language as well as they understand Brin I might be able to convince them of my intentions.*

"I think I can help you there. It should only take a few adjustments to your brain's language processing center."

Maliche's skull began to itch. Slightly at first, but quickly intensified and focused in his left cortex as if thousands of nits were feasting inside his head. A wave of vertigo washed over him and he found he could suddenly understand the Kolandi women.

"… should never have let him live. He is a danger to all of us."

"But the princess supports him and claims he is to be trusted."

"I was there. I saw the blue flames around them both. Who knows what evil sorcery was worked on our princess."

"But he is The Rocker. He is not like the others. I have watched him."

"I am not convinced. What does he want with us? Why is he here?"

Maliche smiled and walked over to the gathered women. "For now, I want to finish washing the dishes. Do you have any more for me to bring to the stream?"

They stared, mouths gaping, as he reached down to gather up the pots and utensils among them.

"Thank you ladies. I hope someday you will learn to trust me. I am here to undo the evil my people have brought to yours." He bowed and went about his chores as the group erupted into a new and even more excited debate.

A little over two hours later, after much of the commotion over his learning to speak Kolandi died down, three of the scouts charged back into camp, breathless and covered in scratches from their hasty flight through the scrub brush.

"We must flee! The Brin are headed this way!"

Neri, the first of the princess' aides, gathered the youths. "We must take what we can and hide. Time is short." She pointed to one of the boys. "You, Gatel, find the men and tell them what has happened. We will head west, back toward the caves. They can find us along the trail there." She watched as the boy bowed and ran off, dust flying from his heels.

Maliche felt his head swim. The desert faded from his sight as images and thoughts filled his mind.

"This is your chance. I can sense the Brin who approach. They are not aware of this camp and have no advance scouts. Follow my lead and you can start to gain the hearts of many who want to trust you."

Tactical images filled Maliche's mind and he saw how to position the fledglings and entrap the approaching Brin party. As the world returned into focus, he went to Neri and explained his plan to capture the Brin.

"Are you sure of this, Great One?" Neri and Rilo, Neri's young trainee, exchanged glances. "Most of these boys are not trained in battle. Rilo and I have some skills in order to protect the princess, but how can we hope to win over a group of Brin? Their weapons are too much for us without our warriors."

Maliche took a stick and outlined his plan in the dirt. "Those Brin are not soldiers, they are miners. Yes, they have weapons, but if we catch them unaware they will not be able to use them. You see, if they follow the path, they will come to this narrow gap in the ravine. It is then we shall…"

The miners trudged single-file through the narrow section of the path. Their heavy packs barely fitting between the rocks. Two guards, one in front, and one behind provided security.

"Stop! Help me!" Maliche ran up to the front guard, as if in fear of his life. His garments torn and filthy, gave the appearance of one lost for days in the desert. He stumbled, grabbing onto the guard's jacket, nearly pulling him to the ground. "Don't let them get me!"

The guard tried to unsling his particle beam rifle, but Maliche's struggles prevented him from getting a grip on the weapon. "Stand up, you quetzal. Who are you and why aren't you at the mine?"

Maliche continued his wild-eyed pleas, pointing frantically back down the ravine behind him. "They're right behind me. Please, you've got to help me." Grasping at the guard's jacket, Maliche collapsed to the ground. Only this time, as the guard bent with the weight, Maliche seized the beam rifle, yanked it over the guard's head, and pointed it at him, a talon poised over the firing contact. He stood upright, aiming at the miner's chest. "Don't move."

The miner turned as a startled cry came from the other guard. There stood Neri, her kital, the curved, triple bladed weapon of the Skatak, guardians of the princess, pressed against his throat. The Brin slowly removed his weapon as ordered, handing it to one of the older fledglings who accompanied Neri.

Maliche aimed the rifle at each member of the trapped group of miners. "Let's not have any heroes today. If you look up, you'll see we have you well covered." All eyes went up to the rim of the ravine. Seven grim-faced fledglings, led by Rilo, aimed an assortment of spears and bows at the captives.

The first guard took a step forward, halting as the barrel of Maliche's rifle pointed at his face. His crest reddened as he glared at Maliche. Each miner was relieved of his pack, and all other belongings including beam pistols, food, maps, and tools. Their hands tied behind them, and a rope connecting one neck to the next prevented any chance of escape.

"You can't do this. Who are you, and why are you, a Brin, helping this bunch of slaves?"

Maliche waved his weapon, directing the Brin to head down the ravine toward camp. "A new order is on the horizon. Move along and keep your mouths shut." He led the way, side stepping back down the ravine so as to keep his weapon trained on the miners. The group on the rim kept pace as the Kolandi herded the miners back to camp.

The sun began to set as the group arrived at camp. Neri set three of the fledglings as guards and sat next to Maliche at the fire. She filled her wooden bowl with some of the stew those left behind prepared.

"I can't believe that actually worked." She shook her head, wiping a bit of juice from her chin. "I thought they would shoot you on sight."

"That's why it had to be me who approached them. As far as they knew, I was one of them, so they were more confused and hesitated long enough for me to get in close." He tipped his bowl to his mouth and swallowed the last of his meal. "I'm just glad they were distracted enough for you to get in behind them."

Neri shifted her position, turning to face Maliche. "We were lucky. This should have been a disaster." Her stern visage softened slightly. "Thank you. By the way, this is what they were transporting to the mine." She tossed a small package at his feet.

"Blast charges," said Maliche as he examined the rectangular bundle. "They all carried these?"

"Two hundred charges complete with detonator caps. Enough for us to do a lot of damage to their mines."

"Maybe Opet and the others will start listening to me now."

Neri's eyes narrowed, but she gave him a wink. "Don't expect too much from the warriors. Although, they may agree to not accidentally kill you before we get home."

Maliche gave a half smile in return. "Yeah, that would be nice."

Maliche hefted the package, staring at Neri as she walked off to check the prisoners. Inside his head the biocomputer seemed to smile.

"Well done. This should impress a few of the Kolandi and help win some friends."

Maliche slept fitfully under the stars. Thoughts of how close he came to dying mixed with thoughts of Ryma. The soft melody of her voice sang in his ears, the gentleness of her touch ... He punched the bedroll under his head to make it less uncomfortable.

"Relax," said the biocomputer. *"You've had a busy day. Get some sleep."*

With that, Maliche saw a soft blue glow surrounding him. Thinking became difficult and he drifted off to dreams of Ryma and the children they would have together.

As the sun reached its zenith the following day, the warriors returned. Rounding the small hill hiding the camp, they stopped short when they saw the prisoners tied up with Rilo and several fledglings holding Brin weapons on them. The men murmured amongst themselves, gesturing at the strange scene as Neri approached, her arms wide in welcome.

"Hail, Opet. How fares your task? We have a gift for you."

Chapter Fifteen

News of Maliche's actions, to save the fledglings from the miners, and his miraculous ability to speak as one of them swept through the cave like a fresh breeze. Opet had ordered the death of the prisoners back at the camp, there was no food to spare and the Kolandi could not risk revealing the location of their caves, but the capture of weapons and explosives lifted everyone's spirits.

Maliche sat alone in the small chamber with Jontar Rocker's tomb. Two torches sputtered their orange light, flickering shadows across the marble stone of the monument. The drums beat a steady rhythm to the accompanying shuffle of feet against dirt. The aroma of roasting Tirpit filled his nostrils. Voices raised in song echoed through the tunnels. His thoughts rambled far and wide of home, friends, old and new, tales of his family, the Brin miners, and how he might help the Kolandi gain freedom.

"I thought I might find you here."

Maliche started at the voice behind him. He jumped to his feet, turning to face the intruder, raising his arms defensively.

Ryma's smile vanished at his reaction. "Has our treatment of you been so poor?" She seemed to drift silently as she approached him. "Neri and Rilo told me of the treatment you received at the hands of our warriors. Has your triumph not lessened this?"

Maliche relaxed as soon as he recognized the princess and bowed. "Opet and the others treated me with less disrespect during our return to the cave, princess. The fledglings and a few of the younger warriors actually spoke to me. I'm not sure the rest of the warriors know what to do now. They don't like me, but at least they don't seem to want to run me through with a spear."

Ryma smiled and took a seat on the stone bench, signaling for Maliche to sit with her. Her movements appeared so fluid, her linen gown appeared to shimmer in the torchlight.

"There is much hatred to overcome, Great One. No Brin has ever been kind to us since the days of your ancestor." She waved a hand toward the tomb. The brown skin of her arm seemed to flow with incredible grace at every gesture. "It will take time, but I am sure the rest will come to see you as a different sort of Brin than those who have enslaved us." She halted, tilted her head, raising one eyebrow as she examined Maliche. "Why do you stare at me so?"

Maliche's crest blushed as he refocused. "I'm sorry, Princess." He ran the talons of both hands through his crest while attempting to regain his composure. "I was lost in thought for a moment. Yes, I am glad some of the Kolandi are losing their anger toward me. If only I could convince Opet and his men of my sincere desire to help end this atrocity."

She reached out, touching his arm. "Patience, Great One. They will come to know your heart in time." Her hand lingered on his arm, her brown eyes lost focus as they rested on his face. After a second or two, she pulled back her hand, and raised it pretending to brush aside some stray hair, attempting to hide the blush blooming on her cheeks.

Maliche took her hand before she was out of reach, clasping it gently in both of his. The warmth and softness of her small hand caused his heart to skip a beat. "I'm not worried, Princess... as long as you believe in me, everything will work out fine."

The princess gazed into Maliche's eyes with a silent tilt of her head as a blush deepened on her face.

"Excuse my interruption, Princess, but the gathering awaits your blessing." Neri stood at the entrance to the tomb's alcove, avoiding direct eye contact with the two occupants.

Maliche stood, maintaining his hold to assist Ryma from the bench. "Thank you for coming to speak with me, Princess. Please let me know if I can ever be of help."

Ryma nodded with a smile, then turned and joined Neri. Maliche noticed a slight green tinge had joined the blue glow he normally exuded when near the tomb.

***

In the weeks that followed, the Kolandi warriors allowed Maliche to join a number of raiding parties. At first, he remained in the role of a fledgling, doing nothing more than carrying weapons and cleaning pots, but gradually some of the warriors, usually the younger men, began questioning him about ways to improve their raids. His knowledge of Brin ways proved very helpful in guiding the inexperienced warriors as they began leading their own raids. What started as brief questions around the evening campfires evolved into his inclusion, and occasional consultation during planning meetings. The elder warriors learned to withhold judgment as Maliche's suggestions proved valuable in deciding which buildings to destroy for maximum impact, and where to place small charged to disable equipment more effectively.

"Let me do this, Opet. None of you can get passed the guards. I can." Maliche's familiar glow now burned orange in the light of the campfire.

Only a mile away, an airshaft to the slave quarters deep in one of the more remote mines yawned invitingly. Four sentries stood watch during the night as the day and night shifts exchanged places. The Kolandi remained caged below in the bowels of the mine.

"And let you betray us as soon as you are back among your own people? I will not take that risk." Opet crossed his fore arms and threw them apart.

"What must I do to prove I am no threat to you? What can I do to convince you I want to free your people as much as you do?"

Opet turned his back. "You are not one of us. You have not traveled the path of Berit."

Maliche grabbed Opet's shoulder, turning him in defiance. "You have not allowed it! I've asked to face the ordeals, but you and your followers continue to deny me the chance."

Opet leaned down, nose to nose with Maliche. "You would never survive the ordeals! You are not Kolandi. You are no warrior." He shoved Maliche hard and turned to leave.

"Then why not allow me to try? If I die in the ordeals, then you are rid of me forever. If I survive, then I prove my worth. What are you afraid of, Opet?"

The warrior froze. His chiseled and scarred back tensed. "Very well, Brin. You have such a death wish... go ahead into the mine. If you survive and rescue the captives, then you will be allowed to attempt the path." He stormed up to Maliche, sticking a finger in his face. "But know this, Brin," he spat on the ground. "If you betray us, you will never find rest. I will hunt you down and your death will make the ordeals seem like a gentle spring rain."

Maliche stood fast in the awful anger of the warrior. "Agreed." Then he, too, spat on the ground.

The miner's guild uniform fit poorly, pinching at Maliche's groin and neck, but it was the best he could manage. The clothes once belonged to a member of the original group of miners Maliche helped capture with Neri, Rilo and the fledglings those many weeks ago. He tried to walk as casually as the garment allowed. The uniform's rank of inspector allowed him unquestioned passage into the mine.

The endless maze of rock walls, intersecting at odd angles under a never ending series of artificial lights hung from the back, or roof of the tunnels, soon led Maliche to believe he was hopelessly lost. The noise of pneumatic jacklegs assaulted his ears. Powerful ventilators helped reduce most of the dust, but Maliche struggled to keep from coughing. A mine inspector would be used to such conditions.

"You're getting close. I am picking up Kolandi life signs ahead, and down one level." The biocomputer's voice gave him confidence as he strode forward.

A rickety, rusted cage waited at the end of the tunnel. The magnetic hover-lift base showed its age and Maliche hoped it would not choose today to rust out from beneath him. As he stepped onto the rusted floor pad, two miners from another shaft joined him.

"Up or down, sir?"

"Down one level." He tried to sound bored, as if the weight of a mile of rock overhead, which could collapse at any time, did not concern him in the least.

The miner hesitated, then pressed the contact for the next drift, then one three levels below that. The two looked at each other; one of them shrugged, but said nothing.

As the pad came to rest, Maliche stepped out, reminded himself to breathe, and headed down the drift. Turning left at the first intersection he glanced back, noticing one of the miners speaking into his radio.

"What can I do for you, sir?" The Brin standing watch over the Kolandi stood as the supposed inspector entered the dimly lit holding pen.

A dozen gaunt, filthy Kolandi, dressed only in decaying loin cloths, regardless of gender or age, sprawled on the floor behind an electric restraining wall. The prisoners appeared to waver behind the semi-transparent wall as the charge flowed between two panels fastened to either side of the alcove's entrance. The barrier did nothing to prevent air flow so the stench nearly brought tears to Maliche's eyes.

"Prisoner transfer," he said, using the same authoritative voice he heard his father use so often. "I'm taking this lot. Their replacements will be here in the morning."

The guard scratched his crest under his hard hat. "I ain't heard a no prizner transfer. You got the papers fer it?"

Maliche threw his shoulders back, glaring at the miner. "There's been an emergency. I'm scheduled to leave on the next transport in half an hour. The papers will be brought to you as soon as they are completed. Now, unlock this cell and let me get on with my business. Or do you want to tell the guild leaders why you held up their prisoners?"

"All right, sir, no need ta get upset. Here ya go." The guard took a key off the wall and unlocked the gate. "Just doin me job is all."

Maliche upholstered the beam pistol at his side and aimed it at the Kolandi. "Get them on their feet."

As the miner turned his back, Maliche slammed the butt of the pistol into his head, collapsing him in a heap. The Kolandi stared, motionless, at the uniformed Brin who had just attacked one of his own.

Maliche holstered the pistol and lowered his voice, gesturing toward the tunnel. "Hurry, we need to get out of here. Other miners could be here at any time."

The Kolandi froze, not willing to believe.

Maliche fished under his uniform jacket and pulled out a rabbit hide. Opening it up, he revealed a symbol drawn by Opet.

"Do you recognize this? I'm with Opet and the princess. There is no time. We need to get moving. Hurry."

One of the elder Kolandi came out of his stupor. "I hunted with Opet. I know his mark. I do not understand. No Brin would know of this mark."

"My name is Rocker. I'm a descendant of the Great One from your legends. I am working with your princess to free you from those of my kind who are breaking our laws. You need to trust me." A blue aura surrounded Maliche as he spoke.

The Kolandi retreated to the back of their cell, falling to their knees, hiding their faces in the dirt.

The elder slave held his ground, trembling as he faced the legend. "You are The Rocker? The prophecies are true?"

Bursting with impatience, Maliche grabbed the old man by the shoulders, shaking him. "No, I am not him… only his descendant. But we need to hurry. If we don't get moving the guards will catch us before we can escape."

The man hesitated, and then called to the others, gesturing for Maliche to lead the way.

It was not far back to the hover-lift which carried the group up to the main drift at ground level. Maliche, walking behind them holding his beam pistol at the ready, gave the appearance of an armed guard herding a group of slaves. He took them back to the secondary entrance he used earlier that night. Dawn was breaking over the surrounding hills as they exited the mine.

"That's far enough, Maliche Rocker!" two large uniformed Brin approached from behind the office shack. "Your face was all over the news after your crash, and the funeral provided an endless supply of family photos broadcast for weeks."

Two more Brin, he recognized the miners from his descent into the lower levels earlier, joined the security officers.

"How could you possibly think nobody would recognize anyone of your stature?" He lowered his rifle at Maliche's chest. "The boss wants to see you."

At that moment, a burst of orange light cut through the early dawn, slicing through the chest of the Brin guard. Before he hit the ground, several more beams reigned down from the nearby hills. Opet and his warriors opened fire on the Brin.

Maliche grabbed the nearest of his group and shoved her toward the warriors in the distance. He continued to yank and pull on the frightened beings herding them into action toward safety.

"Run! Get to those hills!" He pressed the contact on his own weapon, killing the second guard and sending the two miners scattering for cover as more guards came running. "Run!"

The Kolandi ran toward the covering fire, but small explosions of rock and dirt flew up around them as the mine's security forces fired at them from behind. Suddenly, one of the Kolandi next to him fell to the ground, his legs caught up in a proso cable. Fired form an air gun, this combination of two metal balls attached to each other by a thin electrically-charged cable was a common form of non-lethal restraint used by police. Three of the slaves stopped to untangle the man's legs as he twitched in pain, despite the onslaught of energy blasts.

Maliche halted next to them, and knelt behind a cart to provide covering fire. His shots were wild, but the pursuers dove for cover. In moments, his companions freed the man from the cable and they took off running, Maliche in the rear continued to fire at the closing Brin security forces.

The first of the slaves reached the hills, running up the winding stream bed. Just as he approached the wadi one of the Kolandi women fell, shot through the leg. Maliche knelt by her side, firing back to keep the guards at bay while two of the men picked her up and carried her to safety. He stood, turned to run, and felt an agonizing blaze of fire in his shoulder, forcing him to drop his pistol. An instant later, the punch of a proso cable entangling him forced him to the ground. His nerves felt as if he was on fire and he lost all control over his muscles. As he fell, he saw Opet standing at the crest of the hill, firing his rifle at the Brin, now only seconds away. Blasts of rock and dirt burst from the ground around him as orange shafts of energy slammed into the hill at his feet.

Opet stopped firing, looked at Maliche with a smirk on his face. He signaled to the other warriors and disappeared behind the rocks. Then the blow of the butt of an energy rifle sent sparks flying in his mind, then nothing.

***

"As you can see, your Honors, the new equipment, and the opening of the new mines, will soon bring production back to normal." Raencert stood before The Assembly committee answering questions about recent shortages in mineral supplies. "An unfortunate combination of failing old machinery and depletion of some of the oldest mines resulted in our current dilemma, but we are working hard to increase shipments of the most critical minerals. Our miners are working double shifts in the meantime until more trainees are hired. I would say we will be back to full operational capacity within two months."

The small silvery, spherical recorder buzzed in his ear as it floated around him, collecting a video record of the testimony. Its single lens kept the speaker in focus despite frequent changes in altitude and distance in the device's flight pattern.

The members of The Assembly idly scanned through pages of Raencert's report. The small chamber, reserved for matters not concerning the full Assembly, gave every appearance of a courtroom. The committee sat behind high, ornately carved wooden desks. Dressed in the traditional deep green robes and gold headbands, they hovered above those brought before them. Selan relished his position of authority over Raencert.

"Very well, Head Guildsman. We will hold you to your promise." Selan, head of the committee concluded. "I would, however, ask you to meet with me after this hearing. I have some other matters to discuss with you." He slammed the stone orb onto his desk indicating the meeting's termination. The council members rose, returning to their private offices.

A few minutes after Selan removed his official robes, his clerk announced Raencert's arrival.

"If I didn't know any better, I would think this report was the genuine article." Selan tossed his personal transcription panel into the bottom drawer of his desk. "What is taking so long to end these uprisings? Are your forces so incompetent they cannot handle a few spear-waving, half-starved natives?"

Not waiting for an invitation, Raencert sat in the chair opposite Selan and helped himself to a glass of Tarlec wine.

"Don't give me that. You know as well as I do these are not just a few unorganized escaped slaves." He swirled the amber liquid in his glass, sniffed at the bittersweet aroma, and downed it with one swallow. "They know the desert and the surrounding mountains. There are thousands of places to hide up there. When we do find one hiding place, they vanish, only to reappear somewhere else."

"Don't give me excuses, Raencert. How are they able to evade your security measures? How can a bunch of primitives understand our technology and evade it so easily?"

"They're much cleverer than you give them credit for, Selan. With the weapons they have captured, it is not such a simple thing to defeat them. We've taken some heavy losses."

"So, what are you going to do to turn this situation around?"

Raencert frowned, leaning forward in his chair. "Don't start getting all high and mighty on me, boy. I'd like to see you do any better. Remember, you're in this as thick as the rest of us. We need reinforcements and increased finances. The pit workers are starting to grumble about needing hazard pay. If we want to gain the upper hand on matters, you need to open the purse strings."

Selan sat back in his chair, tenting his talons at his lips. "I'll see what I can do. Is there anything else I need to know?"

"You have my personal reports. Everything is in there. If there is nothing else, I need to get back and make sure our cover story holds." The barrel-chested Brin rose and strode out of Selan's office.

Selan watched through his window as Raencert left The Assembly. *That arrogant quetzal. Does he think he can keep my brother's capture a secret from me?* He spun on his heels, returned to his desk, and poured his own goblet of wine. *How long does he think I'll continue to buy the story of his death? It's time I took control of the situation.* He reached for the communicator and punched in his private code.

"Syrinx, is everything ready?"

Yes, sir," replied the raspy voice on the other end. "We can begin Operation Recusant as soon as you give the word."

Selan took another swallow of the wine. *Syrinx certainly has a way with words. If ever there was anyone who fits the title of someone who defies authority, it's my brother.* "Very well. Send your operative to free my brother. Let's see if we can find the slave's secret refuge ourselves."

"Yes, sir. I have the perfect individual for the job. I'll let you know once we begin."

Selan pressed the disconnect contact and smiled. *Now the game begins, Raencert. Let's see who is truly in charge here, guildsman.* He slapped his desk and walked out of the office.

"Cancel my afternoon appointments," he told the clerk. "I need to get some fresh air."

Chapter Sixteen

"So, the traitor awakes. I gotta tell the doc. Don't you be goin' nowhere."

The sound of a chair scraping the floor reminded Maliche of the sound of talons scratching along a slate board at the university. He always hated that sound.

"Why they're so concerned about the likes of you, I'll never know."

A door opened and closed, a lock clicked home. Maliche opened his eyes, but the glare of lights sent stabs of pain through his brain. He tried to grab his head, but discovered the wrist restraints confining his movements, securing him to the bed.

"Slowly now," said the biocomputer. *"I've been working on your injuries all night, but you have to give it time. They tore you up pretty good back there at the mine, but nothing too serious."*

Maliche tried to open his eyes again, more carefully this time. The light still hurt, but grew tolerable as his eyes adjusted. Turning his head was another matter entirely. The pain in his shoulder and leg paled in comparison to the sharp pang in his left temple. Keeping as still as possible he surveyed his surroundings. Tiled walls, banks of beeping and clicking equipment next to the bed, the smell of antiseptic filled the air. One of the apparatus displayed the steady rhythm of his heart and breathing rates. An array of wires ran from his head, chest, and arm, connecting to the machines.

"How did I get to a hospital?"

"Two of the mine's security personnel brought you here yesterday, right after the Kolandi escaped. They know who you are and, if the communications I'm able to intercept are any indication, they were surprised to see you alive. They flew you by shuttle back to their main facility."

"Dry Creek? That's over two hundred miles from where we raided the mine. Why here? They could have sent me back to First Town from the mine."

The sound of the door unlocking interrupted Maliche's internal conversation.

"Remarkable," said the doctor. "I put enough sedative in you to keep you under for another day. How are you feeling" The physician lifted Maliche's wrist, silently counting the arterial pulses while observing his breathing rate.

"You mean aside from being shot and pounding in my head from being clobbered by a rifle butt, and being tied up like a common criminal? Other than all that, I'm just fine."

Without responding, the doctor placed the medical viewpad, a much more technically advanced version than the simple primary aid one used by Aras during their early study of his visions, to a series of points on Maliche's chest, nodding his approval.

"Well, everything looks normal." He pushed aside some of the ear coverts and Maliche winced at the touch. "Amazing. I stitched this up just last night and this wound already looks to be about a week old. Incredible."

Maliche turned his face toward the wall. "Yeah, I've always been a quick healer."

The doctor made a few notes on his electronic pad, and then left, never once acknowledging Maliche's existence as anything other than a series of symptoms. A second Brin, dressed in a black uniform, trimmed in blue, remained in the room.

Maliche scrutinized the Brin for a moment. The uniform, frayed at the edges, looked to be about a size too large for the security man. The holster belt hung precariously from narrow hips, an old energy beam pistol, still restrained by its retention strap.

"And who might you be?" Maliche saw the name Sovet on his badge, but needed something to open up a conversation.

"Never you mind who I am, traitor. You got enough to concern yerself tomorra when the director gits here. He's commin all the way from clear back in First Town fer you, traitor."

Maliche strained at the shackles. "Do you have any idea who I am? My name—"

"Yeah, I know who you used ta be. One a them kak Rockers. The ones runnin things back home. Well, no more, at least not fer you." The guard crossed the room, his hand on the pistol at his side. His crest feathers stood completely upright in anger. "You think you could get away with helpin them savages?"

He poked Maliche's shoulder bandage with one talon. The stab of pain shot through Maliche's body like fire.

"Turnin aginst yer own kind. That's the lowest sort a low a Brin can be. You got everthin comin to ya what's commin when the director gits here. You'll see."

With another poke at the wound, the guard returned to his station, grabbed the magazine, one of those outdoors hunting titles, and slammed himself into the chair. A nurse came in to check the monitors every two hours, never speaking, or making more than the briefest of eye contact with the patient. An orderly delivered sparse meal of vegetables and a watery stew of some sort as the evening shift took over.

A new guard replaced the surly Sovet who, as soon as he saw his replacement, gathered his belongings, handed him the duty log, and left without a word, and never more than a timid glance at him. This one's badge read Nalot. Dressed in the same second-hand type uniform as his predecessor, he did not show the same antagonism. Nothing registered on his lean, broken-nosed face at all as he silently scanned the room. He inspected the restraints with a grip of pure iron, and then returned to the desk. His gaze never left him. Maliche felt as if he knew exactly how the small forest dits felt when it realized a hungry lepti slithered in for a strike with its two inch fangs. He decided sleep was the best thing for now.

He awoke to the crash of the door slamming open. He recognized the huge frame as it filled the doorway. The morning sunlight acted as a spotlight on the leader of the mining guild.

"There you are, boy. My people told me it was you, but I had to be sure. You sure are one difficult quetzal to kill."

"Hello, Raencert. Sorry to disappoint you."

"Be careful with this one," cautioned the biocomputer. *"I've tapped into their communication network and he is on the*

edge of deciding whether to have the guards kill you right now or use you for something else he is plotting."

The immense guildsman waved dismissively and Nalot left the room. Raencert strode over to Maliche's bedside, standing only long enough for someone to place a sturdy chair under him.

"You have no idea the trouble you have given us these past few months. Depleted supplies, damaged equipment, escaped workers..."

"Slaves."

Raencert paused briefly before continuing. "Yes, sir, a lot of trouble. It's terribly hot in here, don't you think?" He turned his head and raised his hand, one talon elevated. "Would it be possible to have a glass of water?" He waited patiently as his servant left to fetch the water.

Maliche gritted his teeth. "What do you want, Raencert?"

Ice clinked as the blue-suited young Brin returned, handing his boss the glass. Beads of condensation coated the tumbler, glistening in the sunlight. Raencert took a long sip.

"Now that is just what the doctor ordered." He chuckled at his own joke as he eyed his prisoner. "What do I want? I'm not entirely sure yet. Your refusal to die may turn out to be a blessing in disguise. There are still a few details to work out, but I think you may be the perfect solution to my little problem."

Maliche rested his head back on his pillow, shut his eyes, and sighed. "And what little problem would that be?"

"Your brother is trying to act like he is in control of matters lately. A little lesson in humility might be just the thing, and you may just be the perfect object of that lesson. Right now, he thinks you're dead. There was a beautiful ceremony, by the way. Everyone who is anyone attended. But your survival could be the ticket to controlling him once and for all."

Maliche turned to face his captor, his eyes hard. "You can't keep me here forever. People know who I am and word will leak out soon enough. Selan will demand my release, and once he learns about your dealing in the slave business, you'll be ruined."

Raencert laughed out loud, barely setting his glass on a nearby table before spilling it. "Oh, this is phalking marvelous. But, of course, you wouldn't know, would you?"

Maliche opened his mouth to speak, but Raencert held up a hand, pointer talon extended.

"Who do you think arranged for your shuttle to crash in the first place, dear boy? It might have been my men who sabotaged the fuel line, but Selan gave the final approval. He's in this operation as much as anyone."

"You lie," spat Maliche. "We may argue and disagree with each other on many things, but we're brothers. He would never do such a thing." He strained at the shackles, rattling the bed and disengaging a couple of the remote sensors to the machines, setting off the alarms.

Raencert stood and pressed a massive hand to Maliche's chest, forcing him to lie still. Leaning close, he whispered into his ear. "He was a bit careless in this matter, though. It seems all the evidence for your supposed death, as well as this matter of the mine workers, leads directly to Selan. With a few well-placed documents in his computer and several communication records skillfully recovered by my people, we can prove your entire family was in control of all of it. The mining guild may take a beating, but who could fault us for following the orders of The Rockers? We will survive this business. Of course, your death will have to become a reality, but since everyone already knows you're dead, it is only a matter of deciding how and when. I may need a few access codes and such before you go."

"Planted false evidence, you mean."

"Possibly, but authentic enough to convince any court appointed investigator."

"And you control those puppet strings... don't you?"

As the duty nurse arrived to check the monitor alarms, he gave one powerful press on Maliche's chest, sneered as he rose up, and stepped out of the way, slowly heading to the door. Nalot returned to his station at the small desk, silently observant of everything. An hour later, the day shift took over, Sovet's eyes brightened with a grin. He seemed to relish Maliche's outrage.

"Time to go. Get up and follow me. Not a word."

Maliche awoke to a dark room, Nalot's face just inches from his own.

"Get dressed. We've got four hours before the day shift comes in to check on you." He finished releasing Maliche form the cuffs holding him.

Maliche rubbed his wrists as he sat up. "So Raencert is done with me now? You here to kill me?"

Nalot tossed some civilian clothes onto the bed and went to keep watch at the door. "I don't work for the mining guild."

"You'll have to forgive me if I don't trust your word on this."

"I don't care if you trust me or not. My employer has other plans for you. My job is to get you someplace safe and make plans to send you home."

"And who, exactly, is your employer?"

"Not something you need to know. Or would you rather sit here until they drag your ass out of here at first light and bury you in the desert?"

"Can we trust him?" Maliche asked the biocomputer.

"Of course not. But if I am reading him correctly, we may be able to use him. Play along for now. There's something interesting in him. I need time to work it out."

"All right," he said in a whisper. "How do we get out of here?"

Nalot glared at Maliche, his voice bristled with authority. "By keeping your kak mouth shut and doing exactly what I say. No questions. Got it?"

Maliche nodded as he finished lacing up the last boot. Nalot gripped Maliche by the arm and pulled him through the door into a brightly lit hallway. His effortless grip felt as if his arm were in a vice. The two gave every appearance of a guard escorting his prisoner to new holdings. Those working at the desk barely gave them a glance as they passed. In less than five minutes, they passed out of the clinic into the night.

***

The cool air blowing in through the window calmed Selan as he watched the night sky from the back seat of his mag-lev limousine. The report from Syrinx of Talon's successful rescue of Maliche brought new vigor to his plans to dominate the arrogant Raencert.

Once I find the evidence of that quetzal's involvement in all of this I can spring the trap and rid myself of him once and for all. A frown interrupted the grin on his face. *How much longer before Syrinx can gather the proof? The longer it takes; the more time he has to destroy any sign of his role. Not even Raencert can erase everything. What are we overlooking? At least he won't have Maliche as a potential bargaining chip in the future. There is still time to turn this phalk of a disaster to my advantage.*

"Will you need anything tonight, sir?" The driver's voice startled Selan back to reality. He had been so lost in thought he hadn't even realized the mag-lev was parked in front of his house.

Straightening his shoulders, and gathering his case, Selan opened the door. "No, nothing more tonight. Be here six sharp in the morning. I want to get an early start."

The driver tipped his cap. "Yes, sir, six sharp it is. Have a good evening." He punched the accelerator buttons as the door closed and sped off down the long driveway. Selan stood watching the receding taillights, taking a deep breath of the night air. The scent of the surrounding woods filled his nostrils. He hated the smell of nature. With one last look at the star-filled sky he scowled and headed up the steps.

"Nedia, I thought you would be in bed by now. It's very late. Is everything all right?" The sight of his wife sitting behind the heavy desk in his study caught Selan by surprise. He stood with his hand on the door's handle his head tilted with crest feathers rising.

Nedia looked up from the paper in front of her on the desk, her crest unpreened. She crumpled the note in her fist and stuffed it into a pocket in her dress.

"Well, there you are. You would not believe the day I have had." She stood up, waving her arms as she stomped toward Selan. "The caterer kept trying to talk me into baked dinter when I specifically told him broiled. The invitations got the address wrong, 873 Dyan'ta Way instead of Dyan'ta Drive, and my cousins, the Borket side of the family, are threatening to cancel if we don't invite their assemblyman." She gave Selan a perfunctory peck on the cheek as she passed him in the doorway. "I was about to leave you a note to talk to the old buzzard tomorrow and invite him. I can't stand the fluff -brain, but what else can I do? Take care of it, will you dear?" And with a final wave of her hand she climbed the stairs to their aerie.

Selan, still holding the door handle, watched his wife disappear around the curve of the second story landing.

Chapter Seventeen

The laser blast shattered the brick over Maliche's head sending shrapnel flying in all directions.

"Strix! Where did they come from?" He saw a half dozen guards closing in on his hiding place behind the crates. Nalot crashed into the hiding place at full run just as a fresh volley of blasts tore up the crates and pavement around him.

"Keep your kak head down," said Nalot as he pulled Maliche out of the line of fire. "They were just coming on duty as I was leaving the ship over there and saw me. They wanted to see my orders and couldn't be talked out of it, so I bolted. Thought I could lose them, but no such luck." Nalot reached inside his jacket and pulled out his own two energy pistols. Tapping off the safeties, he started to take aim.

Maliche grabbed Nalot's arm interrupting his aim. "Wait. More guards will be here any moment. You can't out shoot them all. We need to split up. Give me one of those pistols and I'll meet you at the shuttle."

"Like strix you will," Nalot jerked his arm away and steadied himself for a shot. "You're my responsibility. It took a lot of careful planning to get you out when I did. I'm not about to let you out of my sight now. You even know how to use one of these?" He fired a blast sending one of the guards flying backward, a gaping hole in his chest.

"You can't kill all of them. At least splitting up forces them to divide their own group to chase us both. Give me a weapon. We'll die if we stay here any—"

A blast sent both of them reeling back against the wall of the building. Shaking his head to clear it, Maliche heard only the high pitched ringing in his ears. Through the clearing smoke he saw Nalot getting up to his knees, holding one taloned hand to his head. Peering over a collapsed heap of crates Maliche saw a guard preparing to toss another shock-grenade.

"Look out!" he shoved Nalot to one side behind better cover, and dove to his left.

The explosion missed its intended target, but Maliche's head still spun in nauseating waves from the first one. Trying to steady himself, he saw he was lying on top of a grate. It wobbled as he attempted to push himself up then gave way completely. Maliche tumbled eight feet to the floor of the tunnel below, boxes collapsing on top of him. The effort to stand caused intense pain in his head. Maliche reached out to steady himself on the wall, and then leaned heavily on it. The cool stone felt wonderful on his face and helped clear his mind. Looking up, he saw several large wooden boxes jammed into the hole, blocking any hope of escape that way, not that he wanted to get back into the fire fight, but Nalot was his best hope for survival and now he was alone.

"Well, this is a fine mess. Any suggestions on which way to go?"

The dimly lit passageway seemed to go on forever in either direction, apparently some sort of underground access tunnels for the facility. Only occasional piles of miscellaneous supplies dotted the narrow dusty concrete passage as it curved off into the distance. Maliche's long experience with maps and field work told him heading to the left would take him in the general direction of the shuttle they had hoped to commandeer, but the biocomputer's sensors may provide better information.

"You are correct, the shuttle is toward the left, but the safest route is in the other direction. Besides, there seems to be Kolandi life signs about two hundred meters to the right."

Maliche's left palm began to glow orange, as the device seemed to feel anger.

"What about guards? I don't have any weapons."

"The alarm went out, so all guards in the vicinity were called to the runway to capture you and Nalot. I'm not detecting any Brin other than you anywhere nearby. The Kolandi might prove useful in the escape. I have a fix on the shuttle's location, so I can lead you back here."

Maliche headed toward the right and the Kolandi group. His steps echoed off the stone walls. The sporadic thump of a shock grenade or some other explosive shook dirt from the ceiling.

"Have you got a fix on Nalot? I suspect he is a survivor, so I'm not particularly worried about him, but the shuttle may need his passcode to operate. Just don't lose track of him. How much further?"

"I have him. He seems to be heading off to the south, probably trying to evade the soldiers. No need to worry if we can't locate him later. I can bypass any security codes the shuttle may have... another twenty meters. Still no sign of any Brin."

As Maliche approached, he heard the muttered prayers of the Kolandi. A few more steps showed him the cage holding the group, suddenly silent as he neared. They huddled together as far to the back of the cell as possible, holding hands. Their eyes warily scrutinizing him. The restraining field hummed and wavered, distorting his view of the captives slightly, but Maliche barely controlled his anger and shame at the pitiful state of the rags which hardly covered them, and the filth encrusting their bodies.

"My name is Maliche Rocker. I'm here to help you escape. Can you travel?" He pressed his palm to the control pad on the wall. He felt his arm grow warm as the familiar glow turned orange. In a matter of seconds, the restraining field shut down.

The captives remained silent and motionless, watching his every move. Maliche approached the group, pulling one to her feet. She screamed and broke free from his grip, fleeing back to her fellow prisoners.

"We don't have time for this. If you want your freedom, you need to act now. The guards will return any time now. Do you understand?"

A dry voice rattled from the center of the group. "What makes you think we would ever trust you, Brin?" The emaciated slave rose to his feet, and spat at the ground, bowed, but defiant. "If you want to kill us, do it now. We will not make your paperwork simpler by dying while trying to escape."

"I'm not one of them. I am a Rocker and I was a prisoner just like you, but I escaped and have a way out of here. Will you come with me?"

A young female in the back of the group stood on spindly bare legs. Her leather dress showed signs of rot and appeared ready to fall from her small frame at any moment.

"Wait, Nevik, I recognize this one." she stepped carefully through the others to the front of the cage, brushing her tangled hair from her face. Her eyes showed a flicker of life. "Yes, this is The Rocker. I recognize him from the cave. He stood with Ryma before the tomb. I will never forget the sight."

Maliche stared at the girl. "Seykel? Is that you? I didn't know you had been captured. Help me convince the others to trust me. We don't have much time."

She turned to their leader, her arms raised in supplication. "We must do as he says, Nevik. Ryma trusted him and so must we. He is The Rocker."

Nevik spat again, glaring at Seykel. "I will never trust a Brin. The Rocker passed into legend long ago. This is an imposter."

Seykel turned her pleading back to Maliche. "Please, Great One. You must show him you are who you say. Show him your holy light. Only The Rocker can shine like the stars."

The blue glow started slowly at Maliche's palms, spreading up his arms until it engulfed his entire body. The light grew brighter until everyone had to shade their eyes from the blazing nimbus.

"Now do you believe me, Nevik? I am not the Rocker of your legends, but I am his descendant and I am here to rescue you. Will you come with me or not?"

Seykel pleaded with the man again. "On my honor as a Skatak, he is The Rocker."

Nevik dropped to his knees, still covering his eyes. "Forgive me, Great One. I heard of your return, but did not believe, until now." He shook like a frightened dinter. "Lead the way and we will follow."

The pattering of bare feet resounded through the empty tunnel. The small group of slaves, led by Maliche, cautiously passed several intersecting passageways, taking one seemingly at random until even Maliche's excellent sense of direction failed him.

"Are sure about this?" he asked the biocomputer. *"We seem to have turned away from the shuttle's location."*

"We had to in order to avoid running into Brin patrols. Not all of them are on the surface chasing Nalot. Trust me; I have the entire underground facility blueprints mapped out. I'll get us there."

Ten minutes later, the biocomputer gave warning. *"A single Brin is closing in on us up ahead. We need to take that tunnel. No way to avoid this one. If you can get to the intersection before he does, maybe you can surprise him."*

A quick run brought them to the intersection with only a minute to spare. As the Brin rounded the corner Maliche and Nevik jumped him. In a blur of motion, the Brin ducked the attack, spun, and with a well-practiced maneuver, sent both Nevik and Maliche flying into the wall. Maliche felt the air explode from his lungs as Nalot landed, his knees on his chest.

"Just what the phalk do you think you're doing? And why are you with them?" Nalot released the pressure, gesturing to the terrified group of Kolandi cowering against the wall. Only Seykel ran to Nevik's aid.

"Good to see you too, Nalot." He raised one hand for Nalot to help him to his feet. "Where have you been?" *"And how did you lose track of him? Can't you tell one Brin from another?"*

"Sorry. These tunnels have very thick walls loaded with plumbing and wiring. It appears to limit my sensors somewhat. I will try to recalibrate to compensate for them."

"Looking for you, you quetzal. I saw you fall through that grate. It took a while to lose the guards chasing me and then I had to find another way down here. We need to get to that shuttle before they post sentries."

Maliche pointed to the slaves. "These Kolandi are going with us. I broke them out of a prison cell down here. I won't abandon them."

"The strix they are." Nalot thrust his face millimeters from Maliche's nose and jabbed a talon into his chest. "My job is to rescue you, not them. Look at them. They can barely stand up, much less run. And a crowd of slaves running lose will definitely attract a lot of attention. Leave them."

Maliche backed off and turned to help the recovering Nevik to his feet. With his arms around Nevik and Seykel, his feet firmly planted, he faced Nalot. "Either we all leave together, or we all stay here. There's no other option."

Nalot erupted in a flurry of the most obscene and descriptive language as to what Maliche could do with his options and the Kolandi. In the end, he raised his energy pistol and aimed it at one of the slaves.

"And what's to stop me from just killing all of them?"

"You'll have to kill me as well, then. If you harm even one, I'll refuse to cooperate, and then where will you be?" The blue glow in his palm activated and Maliche became aware of fleeting glimpses into Nalot's mind. Intense anger, frustration, and indecision. Conflicting images, but gradually smoothing into reluctant acceptance.

With another blast of indiscrete outbursts, Nalot holstered his pistol and stormed off. "Great. Nursemaid to a bunch of useless niewols and one bleeding heart do-gooder. Are you coming or what?"

Nevik glared at Nalot's back. "I do not trust that one, Great One. He is like the rest of them, only thinking of themselves and profit."

"I don't really trust him either, Nevik. But we have no choice. He has protected me so far, even if only to line his own pockets. We need to move."

He ruffled Seykel's mass of hair and strode to the others, helping them to their feet. Leading the way, he followed after Nalot. As they caught up with him around the next corner, Maliche thought he saw Nalot toss a small object down a side passage and then shove something back into his uniform pocket.

"What was that?"

Nalot continued ahead without turning to look back. "Nothing. I thought it might be an energy pack for a pistol, but it was already discharged. Someone ought to be punished for losing it."

Maliche shifted the weight of the woman he helped support and, checking to see if the others were still together, followed Nalot. He wondered about Nalot's unexpected acceptance of the Kolandi. *"Did you have something to do with that change of heart?"*

"Only a slight nudge in our favor. He is a remarkably complex individual for a mercenary. There is a powerful moral code to him. He would not have killed the Kolandi; he wanted to frighten you into complying."

"Do you trust him?"

"Not entirely, but I wouldn't rule him out entirely, either. Not just yet."

***

"I can't believe nobody stopped us this time." Maliche shook his head as he fastened his restraints in the co-pilot's chair.

Nalot touched a series of controls with his talons, keyed in his passcode, and started the engines. "They were looking for two Brin on the run, not a party of slaves shipping off to the mines. This diseased lot actually did come in handy after all."

With a punch of his talon, the thrust increased, the transport rocked and rose quickly into the night sky. As they climbed above the low lying clouds, Nalot turned the ship toward the brightening early morning horizon and set the controls on full thrust.

"We should have you back in safe hands in about seven hours. I suggest all of you get some sleep before then. And you need to think of how to either explain this bunch," he thrust a thumb over his shoulder, "or locate a safe location to drop them off."

"They need to come back to First Town with us. I need to expose the mining guild for what they are. These Kolandi will be all the proof I need."

Nalot shook his head and ran his dirty talons through his tattered crest. "Mighty risky business, that. I overheard your brother is part of it all. Are you willing to risk your own family for them?"

"I can't believe Selan is a willing partner in the enslavement of others. I won't believe it's anything more than Raencert's lies." Maliche shifted in his seat, continuing to stare out the front portal.

"I can't speak to that, but in my opinion, for what it's worth, you're going to need a heap more proof of what's going on than just a few half dead natives to change the Assembly's mind on matters. There's a powerful lot of money and greed involved here."

Maliche sat silently for a moment, his eyes closed, fist clenched and tapping out a rhythm on his knee. With a loud sigh, he opened his eyes and turned to face his rescuer.

"You're right. We need undeniable proof of the guild's slavery trade and the murders they have committed. We need to get the evidence before returning to First Town. We need to go back to the caverns and find a way to infiltrate some of the mines."

A brief, almost undetectable smile touched the corner of Nalot's mouth and vanished even more quickly than it arrived. "Oh, no, not with me you, aren't. I'm getting paid to bring you back to civilization. I'm not risking my crest for you or anyone else unless I get paid for it."

Maliche's fists clenched again. "Fine. You know my family. I'll pay you ten thousand extra if you help me do this. Keep me safe for another two weeks is all I ask."

Nalot chuckled and sat up in his seat. "If you're offering ten thousand, you must think it's worth at least twenty. I'll take thirty thousand." He turned a stern, unreadable face toward Maliche.

"Done."

Maliche punched in a set of numbers for the navigation computer, grabbed the control stick and turned the ship north toward the caves. "You take the gunner's seat, in case there's trouble along the way. I'm assuming your training taught you how to fire these weapons?"

"I'll manage." Nalot strapped himself into the co-pilot seat next to him, pressed a few controls of his own, and tested the sights on the heads-up display.

***

Four hours later, Seykel stood behind Maliche and Nalot, enjoying the view. One small brown hand rested on Maliche's shoulder.

"This is wonderful. I've never seen anything more than the inside of one of these flying ships before. Your people are truly magicians to have such abilities." Her eyes beamed with joy at the beauty of the desert hills below. Pillows of white clouds drifting on the winds spotted the deep blue sky above. She turned to Nalot. "Could you teach me to fly a ship such as this?"

Nalot tilted his head in her direction, his crest slightly raised. He stared at her for a long moment, and then returned his gaze forward with a grunt.

"I'm no pilot, girl. We aren't here for fun and games." He jerked his head toward Maliche. "Likely going to get us all killed, he is."

Seykel sniffed and straightened herself to her full height, all one and a half meters of it. "The Great One will do no such thing," she brushed aside a lock of stray hair. "He will save us all... including you." She jabbed his shoulder with two fingers, turned as royally as she could manage in the slightly rocking transport, and returned to her group.

***

Nalot laughed out loud. "That little one has more spunk than brains."

"At least she is willing to stand up and fight for what she believes in." Maliche glared at Nalot, a red aura surrounding him. "What do you believe in, Nalot? Is there anything other than money that stirs your heart?" Before Nalot could respond, a flash of something on the horizon caught his attention. "What are those?"

"That, my boy, is a formation of armed transports preparing to attack. Probably one of your precious Kolandi camps down there. We need to make ourselves scarce."

Maliche's talons hovered over the control panel, then turned off the auto pilot and grabbed the control stick. "No. We have to help them. We have energy cannons on this ship, too. We can't let them slaughter any more Kolandi."

"You're crazy, boy. Three ships against one is a phalking bad idea. You need to get us out of here." Before he could continue his argument, he saw one of the ships turn and head toward them. The communicator crackled with a commanding voice.

"Unidentified shuttle transport, identify yourself. If you do not provide immediate passcodes we will be forced to open fire."

"Kak, they must have picked us up on scanners. He touched the communicator activation pad. "Approaching vessel, this is Nalot, passcode Talon One, repeat, Talon One. We have authorization to transport slaves to the gem mines. Do you copy?"

A blast of energy cannon beams burst a few meters to port, violently rocking the ship. "Unidentified shuttle transport, your passcode is not on record. Turn around now or be destroyed. This is your final warning."

Nalot tightened his restraints and grabbed the control stick. "High Command must have deleted my old security codes quicker than I expected." He turned to Maliche. "Tell your friends back there to strap in and hold on tight. Looks like you get your wish."

With a few quick flicks of his talons, Nalot powered up the energy cannons and fired at the swiftly approaching Brin ship. The high energy beam ripped into the ship's starboard engine, releasing thick plumes of smoke. The vessel lost altitude and struggled to a hard landing.

Another flash of light and explosion rocked the transport as Maliche maneuvered the ship to evade the second Brin vessel shooting at them. The third remained over the Kolandi camp, firing at the ground. Maliche rolled their ship out of the beam's path just in time. A quick exchange of fire and a series of aerobatic maneuvers by both ships filled the sky with wild energy blasts. The Kolandi screamed in fright. Those who had not fastened their safety straps clung desperately to the others as their legs flung wildly behind them. One more death-defying turn brought their ship behind the Brin and Nalot fired. A long fissure ripped across the side of the vessel. It, too, began to lose altitude, trailing smoke and flame until it hit the ground in a cloud of dust, exploding on impact.

Nalot readjusted himself in the chair after the sudden maneuvers. "That's some fancy flying for an archaeologist."

"My family has a couple of racing yachts I learned to pilot when I was a kid. Guess I didn't forget as much as I thought. Looks like you had some pretty fair training on those weapons."

"Yeah, I wasn't always a private."

Pointing toward the third ship, still firing at the defenseless Kolandi, Maliche shouted at Nalot. "We have to protect them. Take out that ship." He glanced back over his shoulder. "Is everyone all right back there?"

Nevik's eyes were wide in fright, but he controlled himself enough to help those who still needed to get strapped in. "We have suffered worse, Great One. You must save those on the ground out there." He quickly regained his seat and pulled the restraints extra tight.

Maliche aimed them straight toward the last attack ship. Just as Nalot fired the energy cannons, the ship veered hard to port and looped overhead. It settled in behind them as Maliche shoved the controls to starboard. The ship lurched violently and the energy beam hit a glancing blow. Continuing his turn, Maliche hit the controls to dive, and then pulled hard upward as another blast caught them in the port engine. Smoke began to fill the cabin. Maliche completed his maneuver and at the peak of his loop, flipped the ship hard over, and Nalot fired straight into the cockpit of the enemy craft. This one did not land so much as cratered.

Fighting for control, Maliche and Nalot guided the transport to a rough landing a hundred meters from the low hills, opened the hatch, and got everyone away from the now burning vessel.

Between fits of coughing, Seykel stumbled to Nalot and threw both arms around his waist. "You saved us. Thank you. I told you the Great One would not let us die."

Nalot stood with his arms spread wide and mouth open. Nevik approached and pried the girl from him, never looking him in the face. "I offer thanks as well, Brin. We owe you a life debt." The two went back to their group, helping the others to their feet.

Nalot, dumbstruck, looked at Maliche.

Maliche shrugged, and pointed north east. "I think the camp was over this way. Let's check for survivors."

They headed off, following Maliche's lead. As they ran, the crack of energy beams split the air around them. Nalot turned to see three Brin soldiers from the first vessel closing in, firing their rifles at them, one taking aim at Seykel. He grabbed

Seykel's arm and threw her to the ground while raising his own weapon, killing the soldier. Picking her up by the back of her dress, he shoved her on.   "Get moving! Run to those hills!"

Twenty meters from the hills, Nevik threw himself full force into Nalot's back, knocking him to the ground as an energy beam sliced through the air above them. Nalot rolled, tossing Nevik aside, and pulled his pistol, aiming it at Nevik. He lowered the weapon when he saw the burning hole in Nevik's back. Turning quickly, he aimed the weapon at the Brin soldiers who had fired at them. As Nalot's beam found its mark, an arrow lodged itself in the chest of the second soldier.

Maliche looked up to the crest of the hill. Standing there was Opet.

Nalot knelt by Nevik, turning him gently onto his back. "Why would you do that? You hate me, and all Brin. Why take that hit for me?"

Nevik's eyes fluttered and he gasped for air. For the first time since his enslavement he looked a Brin in the eyes. "I owed you a life debt. I can now go to my ancestors with honor." His last breath rattled from his throat.

Chapter Eighteen

"Why would that old fool do that? What do these niewols know of honor? They're barely more advanced than animals, scraping out an existence in the desert like Ukaliti." Nalot sat hunched over on the dirt floor of his cell, muttering his curses, hardly aware of Maliche's presence on the other side of the bars. "And that girl is the worst of the lot. Hangs around here like some feather-fluffed idiot. What's wrong with her?" He pounded a fist on the ground.

Maliche hung his head, shaking it. He stood with one hand holding one of the bars of the prison cell, the other tapping a talon on the crossbar.

"You don't know anything about these people, Nalot. You've never seen them outside the mines, beaten down, half starved, the very life drained out of them." He thought for a moment, trying to think how to explain the Kolandi. "Seykel is young and idealistic. I don't think she is capable of hating anyone, even a Brin. And the only reason you're not dead is Opet witnessed not only our aerial battle, but he saw how you protected Seykel, killing one of your own kind in the process. She's not just an ordinary aide to the princess you know. When I first met her, she was one of the Skatak, specially trained women warriors whose sole purpose is to defend their Princess to the death. How they captured her alive is beyond me."

Nalot looked up at Maliche; his crest disheveled, but slightly lifted, his eyes searching. "I thought you said she was incapable of hate. If she's such a fighter, then you're not making any sense."

"Yes, that's right." Maliche squatted down on the balls of his feet, elbows resting on his knees and talons clasped. "The Kolandi are a lot more complex than I ever imagined. Even Opet, who brought us here, realized something was going on and chose to bring you to the princess for examination rather than kill you on the spot. He may hate you... strix, he still hates me, too, but he recognized the need to keep us alive so Ryma could discover the truth of things. Are those the actions of ukaliti?"

Nalot simply stared.

When Maliche turned to leave he saw Kitae and Neri standing quietly, dressed in soft tirpit hide dresses fringed with colorful mertan and cardis feathers, the formal dress of the Skatak. "I didn't see you. You should have said something."

The two bowed and Neri, the elder of the two women folded her hands in the official pose of the princess's messenger. Her voice rang out in the clear, high tones of a royal summons. "Princess Ryma requires your presence in the Hall of Rocker to give witness on the case before her."

The two bowed again and Kitae took up the call. "Follow now and be presented. May the blessings of The Rocker be with you and guide your testimony."

They turned in unison, waited for Maliche to come forward, and led him to the sacred burial chamber of Jontar Rocker, their kitals, curved triangular bladed weapon of choice by the Skatak, swung at their hips. A bright blue radiance surrounding Maliche cast their shadows ahead.

The burial chamber shone brightly in the light emanating from the quartz seams in the walls and ceiling. Two columns of Kolandi filled the room on either side of a central aisle. On the dais in front of Jontar Rocker's marble tomb sat Princess Ryma. A mantel of gold and scarlet feathers with a high collar of long, exotic feathers tipped with iridescent blue draped from her shoulders. She sat on a simple wooden bench, holding a meter-long metallic staff, decorated with symbols and writing Maliche did not recognize. Her dress was the same soft tirpit leather as her aide's, but dyed deep blue. A delicate silver circlet sat on top of her long dark hair, the green gem in her amulet sparkled as if it held a thousand stars.

As Maliche followed Neri and Kitae into the chamber, the hostility from the warriors present was palpable. Their glares and angry mutterings made him glad they were in such a sacred area. Even the princess may not be able to control them if they caught him outside right now. He tried to swallow, but his throat seized up.

"*Don't worry,*" whispered the voice in his head. "*Don't be stupid, but don't worry. You know what you have to do to regain their trust. I won't let anything too horrible happen to you."* The blue glow intensified, compensating for the brightness of the room.

Neri and Kitae stopped as they reached the front of the aisle and bowed formally. "We bring the descendant of The Rocker to bear witness before our princess and The Rocker." They bowed again, turned in unison, and stepped up to either side of Ryma.

With a raise of her staff, and a stern glance at the warriors, Ryma began the proceedings. "Great One, we have brought you here—"

"He brings our enemy among us! He cannot be who he claims!"

"The Rocker would not betray us like this!"

Ryma stood, raised her staff, silencing the outbursts with a look. "Who here questions my authority?" She paused, staring down the warriors. Neri and Kitae closed ranks in front of the princess, hands resting on their kitals. "Who here has not witnessed for themselves the miracle which took place in this very room?" Again she gazed into each angry face before her and pointed her staff at Maliche. "The Rocker himself has anointed this one. I myself received visions of the truth of this." She waved the staff toward those gathered. "Your own warriors have testified of the valor shown by this one and his companion in the battle defeating our enemy. The stranger risked his own life to save one of my court. Are these the actions of an enemy? Even Nevik gave his life saving the stranger. Who among you would do the same if you did not have faith in another's worthiness?"

The warriors quieted, their faces showed anger, but not the blind hatred which possessed them before. Ryma sat on her bench, Kitae and Neri rearranged her cloak, and she began again.

"Great One, I apologize for the lack of faith some of us have shown here today. We have brought you here to tell us how you came to be accompanied by one of our enemies and to help us understand your wisdom."

Maliche took a deep breath and tried to swallow again, this time with a slight success. He bowed, following the example of Kitae and Neri, then spoke. His voice cracked at first, but gained strength. "I am no traitor to your people, Princess. And, as you say, I was implanted with my ancestor's spirit force here in this very chamber not long after you rescued me."

"Spirit force?"

"Oh, shut up and don't distract me. This is hard enough without you in my head."

"All right, have it your way. I sort of like being thought of as some mystical power."

"I was taken by my countrymen and held captive. They hoped to use me as a pawn in some scheme for power and control over my government. It is my mission to end their control over these mines and end their ability to keep you captive. Most of my countrymen believe your people to be extinct. They know nothing of your enslavement, and would be repulsed if they did. I do not know why, but Nalot freed me from my captors and helped free those who came with us. It is only his skills as a soldier that allowed us to defeat the vessels which attacked you. It is his bravery which saved Seykel. It is these traits which Nevik saw and gave his life to preserve."

He turned to face the gathering, pointing at Opet. "Opet's own testimony here today verifies the truth of this. He witnessed the bravery and skill of Nalot." Maliche turned back to face Ryma. "Even so, I do not understand Nalot's reasons and so do not yet fully trust him. But I do owe him a debt and ask here for your favor to allow him to prove his worth as an ally."

"What right do you have to make such a request?" Danet rose to his feet grabbed his hair and pulled with both hands as if trying to rip it out by the roots. "You are not Kolandi. You have not traveled the Path of Berit." He forced his way to the center aisle crossed both forearms in front of him, fists clenched. "No Brin, not even this one, has any rights among us until he has proven his worth." He stormed out of the chamber, the deep scars on his back reflecting pale against his dark skin.

Murmurs of agreement spread among the crowd. Maliche suddenly knew exactly what he needed to do. He squared his shoulders and reached out, palms upward, facing the princess. "I will walk the Path of Berit, if that is required of me. If the light of The Rocker is not enough to sway your people, then I must become one of you."

Ryma smiled, but her eyes were lit with fear as well. "Are you aware of the risk you will be undertaking? Even some of our most promising candidates do not survive. The Path is more dangerous than anything you have ever faced."

"I understand the risk and gladly accept it if this is what is required to convince the Kolandi of my worthiness."

"Very well. The request is made and accepted. We cannot refuse." She stood, spread her arms and raised her face to the ceiling. "Prepare the Path of Berit for The Rocker. May his spirit be true and strong."

She signaled to her attendants who stepped forward and led the way down the aisle passed Maliche and out of the sacred chamber. Several warriors, mostly the younger ones who had learned to trust him, gathered around smiling and jabbing his arms. The elder warriors held back, their faces showed the mix of shock and admiration for his most likely sacrifice.

**

After three days of preparation, fasting, and meditation, Maliche followed the solemn procession deep into the caverns. The air grew steadily warmer and more humid. After a mile or so, he found breathing difficult. Sweat poured down his face and back. He walked naked, as tradition demanded, revealing his true nature to Berit. His only adornment was Maripa's medallion, a special consideration to his namesake. Kolandi warriors, male and female, lined the trail, ritually striking him with their weapons.

After several more turns down torch lit shafts, they entered a massive cavern. The walls glowed red and orange in the light of several fires. A vast underground lake disappeared into the darkness before them, its surface as still as glass with no wind to stir its surface. Maliche scowled at the acrid smell of burning herbs. The chanting which accompanied their march ceased and Opet, leader of the warriors stood before them. His massive, scarred chest and back glistened with sweat. He wore a ceremonial version of the hunter's garb. The scales of an albino Mordu blazed like fire in the torch light. A robe of claws, teeth and horns of fierce predators rattled as Opet moved.

Another warrior waved branches of smoking herbs around and between the two, striking them each at intervals, showering them with burning embers as they stood facing each other. Sing song chants filled the air. Opet lifted his arms high, calling for silence. He signaled Maliche to follow him to the edge of the lake where the two stood side by side.

In a low voice, he spoke so only Maliche could hear. "I do not understand why you, a Brin, would risk this, but before you die I want you to know I believe you have great courage. Therefore, I promise you, we will not kill the other Brin until your fate is decided." Turning to the assembled witnesses he declared, "You must first cleanse yourself of your past. Rid your body and mind of childhood and prepare for the mantle of a warrior." As the echoes died he motioned for Maliche to enter the lake.

"Prepare yourself. This is going to hurt, but don't show any sign of weakness. I can only dull your senses so much if we want to respect their traditions."

Maliche felt his body go numb; his skin tingled in the same way his legs felt after sitting too long. The water was hot. Painfully hot. He almost hesitated, but forced himself to keep moving deeper. His deadened senses helped, but he gritted his teeth and strained to control himself as the water reached his groin. It was then he felt the grip of two men on either arm helping him wade in further. He recognized Danet on his left, scowling at him.

"You are a fool, Brin. Brave, but a fool."

When he was waist deep, they turned him around. Danet and the warrior on his right raised curved bone hooks with a thick cord attached high above and chanted in the Kolandi tongue. In one swift movement they pierced Maliche's upper chest with the hooks. Maliche winced, but tolerated the reduced sense of pain. A trickle of blood ran down his torso from the piercing. With one hand on the cords, pulling them tight, their other hand grabbed his shoulders and bent him backward, using the cords as the primary method of supporting his weight while submerging him completely in the scalding lake. He was not prepared for how long they held him under. His lungs ached for air.

"Only a little while longer. Let me slow down your metabolism a bit. That should alleviate the need for oxygen some. You don't have the lung capacity of a Kolandi."

He felt his mind going dark, consciousness starting to slip away when the warriors lifted him by the hooks back to the surface. Coughing and gasping for breath, he held on tight to his companions. Wiping the water and drenched crest feathers from his eyes, he realized how red his skin looked. It should have hurt like strix, but he felt only a dull throb. As he struggled back to the shore, the warriors began their chanting again. Standing again in front of Opet, the men at his side cautiously released their hold on him.

Opet raised his hands and sang again in Kolandi. "The cleansing waters of Berit have prepared you for The Path. May you be shown the sacred ways and brought home safely so you may take your place as one of us."

He led Maliche to a small stone hut with a thick leather doorway. The interior was only large enough to sit or lie down, but not to stretch out, even for a Brin. In the center sat a fire, adding to the already oppressive heat. Danet and his partner pulled Maliche into the hut with the cords attached to the hooks in his chest. They forced him into a kneeling position and tied the ends of the cords to small black iron rings in the wall, stretching his skin as far as it could go without tearing. Maliche clenched his teeth as the pain level increased.

Opet knelt in prayer before the fire, continuing his chants tossing an arrangement of foul smelling twigs, leaves, and powders into the flames.

"Holy Spirit of Berit, we send this soul to you for judgment. If he proves worthy, return him to us so he may become one of us. If you deem him unworthy, have no mercy. Rend his soul to pieces and feed them to the darkness of the strix-bound."

The stench of the thick smoke soon filled the room. Maliche felt the world around him start to lurch violently. His stomach did the same. All the while, Danet and the other pierced his arms, back and thighs with more of the hooks. Each one tied off to the remaining rings in the walls. Maliche hung on the verge of unconsciousness, groaning despite the dulling of his pain receptors.

Opet stood, hunching over in the small hut, and motioned the others out. He leaned in to Maliche's ear and whispered, "You will die here, Brin. You may not be Kolandi, but you have honor. I promise we will celebrate your ancestors when we give your body to the fires." He rose up and left, closing the door behind him. As his senses drifted away, Maliche heard the warriors chanting outside.

***

"Don't worry. I can minimize the effects of the drugs... for the most part, anyway. Let me make a few adjustments to help make you more comfortable. It's the blood loss I'm mostly concerned about, but I can reduce some of that as well. Relax and go to sleep now. I'll have you back to your stubborn, impulsive self in no time."

That was the last memory Maliche had of the cavern. The rest became ensnared in wild phantasms of colors, shapes, noises, and patterns. Sometimes these hallucinations formed into recognizable images of home, friends and family, other times he recalled speaking to Jontar, Maripa and Karm as if they were well acquainted. Other dreams could only be described as nightmares where he took on the visage of a monster striding through Kolandi camps slaughtering them all. While in others he was equally monstrous, tearing down First Town, crushing any Brin who stood in his way, even Selan. Aras stood before him, blaming him for her death while proclaiming her undying love for him.

Time and space had no meaning. He saw vast planets in distant parts of the galaxy, some inhabited by peaceful beings, others by creatures ravaging through system after system. He stood on one world, with others of his kind, and watched the sun explode, engulfing them all. On other worlds he saw technologies far beyond his comprehension, experienced feelings of terror, hope, and greed regarding them. The universe was his home. No, he *was* the universe. He felt the pulse of every star as it was born and the surge of each one as it died.

He shrank to miniscule size and saw the structure of his own DNA. Its triple helix winding and twisting in complex patterns providing the instructions guiding his very existence. He witnessed molecules coming and going, joining and separating, creating the fabric of the universe. Energy in all its forms filled him. He heard the song of creation. And then all was darkness.

Consciousness fought its way back into his mind. He heard the call of something stabbing at his brain trying to haul him back to reality. Painfully, gradually, light returned.

"Well, that was a close one. I nearly lost you there more than once. You really are a fighter, even if you are a mere archaeologist. Time to wake up, though. We have a problem."

He struggled to open his eyes, to argue with whoever belonged to that voice. The light stung, but he forced his eyes open anyway. A blurry figure resolved itself into a familiar face.

"Neri?" His voice weak and strained, barely audible even this close. He tried to move his hand, but managed only a faint talon wiggle.

"Don't try to speak, Great One. You've been out for four days. No one has ever survived being on The Path for that long. Berit and the spirit of your ancestors are truly with you." She wiped his forehead with a cool rag. He couldn't recall a more wonderful feeling.

***

"Thank you, Neri. The meal is delicious, but I need to know what is going on outside these walls." Maliche handed the wooden bowl back to her and strode toward the entry to his alcove.

"Great One, forgive me, but I must insist you stay here until the princess permits your release."

Stopping mid stride, Maliche turned to face Neri, his crest feathers rising, and talons clenched. "So, even after traveling the Path of Berit, I am a prisoner here? Has Ryma lost all faith in me at last?"

Neri dropped the bowl on the floor, splattering the few remaining bits on her legs. She reached out to Maliche, bowing her head.

"No, Great One, you misunderstand me." With one hand on her breast and one hand reverently touching his chest she composed herself. "We only fear for your health. You only awoke this morning after your ordeal. We do not want you to risk another fever. You must rest." Her face, though compassionate, showed her firm determination to follow her princess's command.

Taking a deep breath to calm himself, Maliche took her hand. "It's all right, Neri, I'm not angry, just a bit frustrated is all." Cupping her chin in his hand, he gently lifted her face toward his and smiled. At his silent request, a soft blue glow surrounded him. "You see? I am fine now. There is no need to fear for my health, unless I go mad staring at these walls any longer. Where is Ryma?"

Neri flinched at the sight of the blue nimbus. Her mouth twisted, and brows furrowed as she weighed her duty to Ryma as well as to The Rocker. She slowly returned his smile.

"As you command, Great One. How you have recovered is outside my understanding, but I trust in your power. The princess is in her chambers awaiting the outcome of your companion's trial."

The smile vanished from Maliche's face. "Trial? What trial?"

"He is a Brin, Great One. His execution would not normally require a trial, but he brought you back to us, and helped you rescue the others so he deserves the trial by combat. It will be an honorable death."

***

Maliche turned on his heels and burst out of his alcove, running full speed down the narrow tunnels. The few he encountered pressed hard against the walls when they saw him charging, a bright orange light enfolding him. Gasping for air, he pushed his way passed the guards and burst into Ryma's private chambers.

"Ryma! You need to stop them! We need Nalot if we have any hope of winning this war!"

Rilo and Neri unsheathed their kitals and jumped to bar Maliche's approach. Ryma's face grew red, her glare would have stopped a charging grendel.

"How dare you enter my rooms without permission! Even you have no right!"

Maliche struggled to gain his composure, tried unsuccessfully to shake free of the princess's guardians, and realized the futility of his anger. Taking a deep breath, he calmed himself.

"Princess, I have just learned Nalot is to be killed in the arena. You cannot allow that to happen. We need him."

Ryma softened a bit and signaled for his release. "I understand your compassion for your fellow Brin, but Nalot has been tried and found guilty of his crimes against the Kolandi." She waved off Maliche's attempt to object. "In recognition of his bravery and skills, we are permitting him an honorable death as a warrior in the arena."

"You are making a mistake. There is more to him than you realize. You must prevent his death."

The Princess sighed, lowering her eyes to avoid looking at him. "It is for the best. It is done." She waved for her protectors to remove Maliche from the room.

"This has gone far enough. She won't like this, but I need to talk to her."

The biocomputer's bright blue glow filled the room, freezing everyone in place. Ryma's eyes grew wide in shock and anger.

After only seconds passed, the blue light vanished. Rilo and Neri rushed to Ryma's side as she staggered. With their help, she found a chair and took a sip of water Neri brought. She raised her chin to face Maliche.

"I told you, and that thing in your head, to NEVER do that to me again without my permission. I will deal with both of you after we get to the arena." She rose and stormed out of her chambers, followed by Neri and Rilo.

Maliche cringed as he imagined what Ryma might be planning for him. *"Oh, great. Now you've really done it. You know how much she hates you invading her mind like that. She may never forgive me for letting you."*

"We can work out our penitence later. Right now you need to get moving before she tries to face the warriors alone."

Chapter Nineteen

The door to the pit swung open. Nalot, bruised and bloody from the beatings and wearing only the shredded remnants of his pants, staggered through. Several stacks of weapons, spears, swords, mallets of various shapes and sizes, knives and more lay scattered around the dirt floor of the stone-walled circular arena. A deafening roar of jeers rose around him. The sweltering heat of the afternoon sun beat hard into the ring. Above him sat the rows of warriors anticipating the trial by combat.

In the place of honor, sat Opet flanked by his second in command, Danet. Opet lifted his arms to the sky to quiet the spectators. As the crowd became silent he rose to speak. "Warriors, the promised time has passed. The Rocker has not recovered. It is time to judge this Brin for his crimes." A loud cheer echoed through the stadium.

Opet pointed at Nalot, a scowl of hatred on his brown face. "Brin, your fate will be decided by the gods of our fathers. We award you this trial by combat because of your valor in helping The Rocker rescue many of our brothers and sisters. You have shown honor to us, your enemy, therefore your death will be an honorable one. Prepare yourself."

Nalot glared at Opet, spat on the ground, and walked over to the nearest pile of weapons. He selected a rusted, but sturdy curved sword and a long knife. Testing their balance in a series of swings and combat maneuvers, he satisfied himself as to their suitability.

Opet raised his arms again and raised his voice. "Let the trial begin. May the will of Berit prevail." He sat, and pointed to the opposite side of the arena.

The crowd cheered as a heavy wooden door opened and two Brin soldiers, also showing signs of recent tortures entered, shielding their eyes against the sun's glare.

Opet addressed Nalot again. "Brin, these two prisoners are the last survivors of the games to this point. They have shown their skills in battle and earned the privilege to either provide you with an honorable death, or earn a noble death for themselves." Opet surveyed the scene below, raised his fist in the air and brought it sharply down. "Begin!"

The two soldiers ran to nearby piles of weapons. The first grabbed a long metal tipped spear. The other picked through the choices quickly, settling on a spiked mace and long knife. They nodded toward each other and started to encircle Nalot.

Holding his ground, Nalot studied his foes as they moved into position. He noted their footwork, the way they held their weapons, and looked into their eyes. He decided they were probably two of the mercenaries hired by the military.

Yes, Nalot thought. *They are well trained and they are ready to fight to the death. So be it.*

He took his fighting stance and waited. The soldiers attacked together from opposite sides. With a side-step, Nalot slapped aside the spear thrust, using it to block the mace as it descended toward his head. He swung his sword at the spear-bearer, but met only empty air as the Brin dodged back, using the spear to keep him at a distance. Spinning to avoid another blow from the mace, Nalot feigned a move to his left, then dove right, stabbing his sword toward the soldier, but succeeding only in grazing his chest. A thin line of blood appeared, trickled down his body, but not enough to slow the soldier. A noise from behind alerted Nalot of another attack. He ducked, rolling to his right, barely avoiding the weapon, receiving a superficial slice to his left leg instead.

The maneuvers continued for several minutes longer. Nalot dodged and twisted, his weapons finding their mark frequently. Blood flowed from the many wounds he inflicted on his foes. The spearman limped heavily from a knife wound in his right leg. He held the spear in only one hand now. His left arm hung useless at his side from a deep cut of Nalot's sword.

The second mercenary now held only his knife, his mace arm was broken when Nalot grabbed him, wrenching the arm against the joint. He, too, was suffering from blood loss, primarily the gash on his head, courtesy of Nalot's knife.

Nalot could feel his wounds taking toll. The spear met his skin on more than one occasion, leaving long stripes of blood in its wake. His head ached from a nearly fatal blow of the mace before he dealt with that one. He knew this had to end now.

Summoning all of his skill, he attacked. He ducked under the spear thrust, rolled into the soldier's legs, putting him on the ground. Rising up onto his knees, Nalot turned and drove the sword deep into his opponent's chest. Blood splattered as the wound sliced open. Rising up without delay, he spun and tossed his knife into the face of the remaining foe as he closed in, trying to take advantage of Nalot's distraction. The mercenary screamed, flailed at the hilt of the knife protruding from his blood-splattered face, and fell dead in a puff of dust.

Nalot, breathing hard, covered in blood and dirt, placed his foot on the body of his opponent, and pulled the sword free of the man's chest. He turned to face Opet, squared his shoulders and pointed his sword at him.

"Are you entertained enough?"

Opet remained seated, listening to Danet's voice in his ear. Waving Danet off, Opet rose and crossed one arm over his chest in salute. "You have fought bravely and with skill. We honor you with a warrior's death." Raising both arms high, he called out in a loud voice. "Release the grendel!"

At the far end of the ring, a huge wooden door groaned as it slowly opened. In the darkness beyond, Nalot heard the snarls and stomps of the great beast. He swallowed hard as the creature charged out, struggling against massive chains, whipping its monstrous tusks side-to-side searching for a target. Froth flew in long arcs from its powerful jaws.

As Nalot and the beast studied each other, Opet continued. "Only a true warrior dare attempt to fight even a young grendel, Brin. None would dare an enraged adult such as this. Die well." He signaled for the chains to be released.

Nalot shook his head to clear his thoughts. He tested his legs and arms, taking note of his injuries, deciding how to protect them during this encounter. All the while he watched the grendel for any weakness. Three meters tall at the shoulders, the thick black fur would act like a shield against most weapons. The tusks were long and sharp. They could prove lethal with even a glancing blow. He took in a deep breath, steadied himself, and began his maneuvering.

The beast charged.

Chapter Twenty

"All right, I'm here. What's so important you couldn't relay over our private channel? And why out here in the middle of nowhere? I've never liked the wilderness."

Selan looked around in disgust at the deep green of the forest. A breeze rustled the leaves creating patterns of light dancing among the undergrowth alongside the path. Mertans sang their mating songs in the canopy while a small stream bubbled nearby. His breath condensed in small clouds in the chill air as the morning sun would take several more hours to warm the forest this time of year.

"This is the only place I could be sure nobody was listening. Raencert has ears everywhere." Syrinx, Selan's top agent living among the miners, sat on a moss covered log examining a stick-shaped insect crawling up the back of his hand. "I've always been fascinated at the perfection these creatures have mastered at blending in with their surroundings." He flicked the bug with one talon, sending it into a bush.

"Looks like just another filthy bug to me. Disgusting creatures." A corner of Selan's mouth scrunched up as if he had tasted a particularly awful mouthful.

"These mountains are only a few minutes' flight from the city. Besides, aren't you and your family spending the weekend in your vacation home just over the hill? What I have to say is far too important to risk getting out. It could be the key to removing Raencert from power once and for all."

"I would still prefer some out of the way spot in the city. Even as a kid I never liked coming out here." He looked for a place to sit, but decided to remain standing. "So much dirt and everything keeps moving. It's unsettling. Get on with it, Syrinx, what do you have?"

A smile, or the facsimile of one, crept onto the spy's craggy face. "One of my agents in the administrative offices cracked Raencert's codes. We got into his secret files."

Selan's mouth dropped a bit, his eyes widened. He tried to speak, but stumbled over the words. "You found... did you get the... you mean we have him at last?" without thinking, Selan sat on the damp log next to his agent, leaning heavily on one hand. "You found the files linking him to the Kolandi?"

No, not them... at least, not yet. There's a lot of information going back years. It will take time to work through it all. We have to be careful not to trip any hidden security programs."

"I thought you said you broke his codes."

"Raencert is no fluff-brain. He obviously wanted these files kept secret. His most precious files are kept under intense security, with precautions we haven't figured out how to bypass yet."

Selan looked up at the distant snow-covered hills beyond the trees overhead. He sighed, shoulders slumped, and head lowered. "Of course, you're right. We need the information at all cost." He turned back to Syrinx, noticing the smile had not faded from his face. "What have you learned?"

Syrinx reached into his coat pocket and pulled out a recording chip. "There's enough documentation here to prove Raencert is the recipient of most of the vast profits from his illegal dealings with the resources from the mines. There's no mention of the slaves. We've managed to piece together a long trail of written orders, bank accounts, memos, pay-offs, everything you need to show he orchestrated the entire so-called shortage of minerals and their subsequent high prices. We even located warehouses full of stockpiles of the undeclared supplies. But that's only the beginning." He reached into his pack, pulled out a stick of tirpit jerky and bit off a piece, then held out his other hand, palm up.

Selan grumbled as he reached into his own coat pocket pulling out a thick tan envelope, passing it to the spy. "All right, what else do you have? You know this is all worthless so long as he has his trumped up proof of my involvement in his schemes. Did you find those documents as well?"

"Also on the chip. And we were able to delete them from the hard drives. He has nothing on you now."

Selan jumped up from the log and threw a fist into the air. "Yes!"

A flock of mertans bolted from the trees as Selan's voice broke the stillness. Several harns shook leaves loose from the overhead branches as they ran, furry tails stiff with fear in their flight from the noise below.

"I have you now, you quetzal. The Assembly will have your head for this, and father will realize how capable I am once and for all." He danced a clumsy jig on the dirt path, nearly tripping over a protruding stone. Out of breath, he bent over, resting both hands on his knees breathing deeply. Forgetting his disdain of the slimy log, Selan returned to his seat. "Hah! Well done. Your 'bonus' is deserved. Now, what of my dear brother? I trust your operative has been in touch."

Syrinx let his smile fade. "No, sir. Our last communication was over a week ago when he informed us he had arranged to steal a transport and had the prisoner in hand. We lost contact with his vessel over the desert as it approached the mountains."

"Don't tell me your agent has failed. How could you lose contact?" Selan's eyes hardened. "Maybe I should demand a refund."

"These things take time, sir, and almost never go according to plans. That's why I put Talon on the case. He knows how to improvise and has never failed us. I did intercept some military communications about an attack from an unidentified vessel in the general vicinity of their last known position, so I suspect Talon is dealing with some unforeseen developments. He will be in touch as soon as he is able." He stood up and stepped back onto the narrow trail, brushing off his clothes.

Selan joined Syrinx on the path, squaring his shoulders as he approached. "You know I can't proceed with plans to discredit Raencert before the slaves are dealt with. We need to locate their whereabouts and destroy them all. If knowledge of their existence ever got out, we would all lose our positions in The Assembly. Taking out Raencert would be pointless if I lose everything, too."

"No need to be concerned, sir." Syrinx stood toe to toe with Selan, his eyes never flinching. "Talon has never let me down. He will signal us when he has information."

"You better be right. I can't afford any mistakes. If we don't hear anything in a few days, we may have to make alternative plans to find the slaves. This Talon better be as good as you say."

"He is, sir. Now, I must be going. I need to get back to the mines by this afternoon or there might be questions." He turned and strode off down the trail. Selan watched as he disappeared around a bend and the trees hid him from view."

Selan took the chip out of his pocket, examined it closely, and smiled again as he tossed it in the air, catching it in a tight fist. His crest feathers stood up. "I have you now, you old quetzal. As soon as we locate those phalking Kolandi and erase them you will fall. And I'm going to enjoy wiping the smugness off your face." He jammed the chip back into his pocket and walked back to the vacation home.

"Selan, what are you doing out here? I thought you hated all this fresh air?"

Lost in his thoughts, Selan startled at the sound of his wife's voice. He looked up to see her seated on a blue checkered blanket in a clearing next to the trail, a picnic lunch spread out in front of her.

"I thought you were back at the house with the children." He stepped carefully among the fallen leaves as if they were some unnatural surface he walked on.

Nedia stood up, brushing off the twigs and dust from her shorts and blouse. Adjusting her wide-brimmed hat, she stood on her toes to give her husband a peck on the cheek. "I decided this was too nice of a day, so I sent them off with Dykis to go play by the lake. It is so rare to get some time to myself these days. I didn't expect to run into you, but there may be enough here if you would like to join me." She sat back down on the blanket, stretching out her legs.

"Thank you, my love, but I think I'll head back to the house for lunch. I'll never understand the allure of eating on the ground. Too many germs and bugs for me."

She giggled, wiggled her fingers at him as if they were bugs, and shook her head. "And I'll never understand your distaste of nature, especially on such a beautiful day. Your late brother certainly knew how to appreciate the outdoors." She unwrapped a bit of meat, picked it up in her talons, and took a bite. "Germs... such nonsense. Are you sure you won't join me?"

He winced as he watched her chew. "No, my dear. Not today. But you enjoy yourself. Perhaps we could indulge in a drive later on... after I finish a bit of work."

"Can't you forget about Assembly business for one day?" She lowered her head and frowned. "The children were looking forward to spending time with you here. This is supposed to be a vacation, you know. Can't you at least talk with them before you disappear into your office for the day?"

He shook his head, shrugging his shoulders, holding his hands out palms up. "The government never sleeps, Nedia. Some matters need immediate attention. You're right, though. I'll stop by the lake for a bit before I tackle the bureaucracy."

"Thank you, dear. The children will be delighted." She popped a small slice of some yellow fruit in her mouth and waved him goodbye. As Selan disappeared around the bend Nedia pulled out a communicator from under the blanket. Her talons tapped out the remainder of a message. She hit send, and placed the device in her pocket.

Chapter Twenty-One

"How dare you address me in that manner in front of my people. Even The Rocker does not have the right to speak to me like that." She ran through the tunnels toward the arena, Maliche at her side, her two guardians close behind. "And *never* let your entity do that to me again without my permission. There is enough turmoil without my people thinking some mystical spirit controlled by you has possessed me. How can I continue to rule if their faith in me is destroyed?"

"My deepest apologies, Princess," Maliche gasped for air as he ran beside her. "I did not have any control over that. The biocomputer took matters in its own hands.

"I don't have hands."

"Strix, will you shut up."

"How *dare* you!" Her mouth hung open in shock.

"No, not you, Princess. I was reprimanding the device in here." He pointed to his head.

"Then you must learn to control it. I will not be violated in that manner again."

"You are right, Princess. I will…"

Dashing through the columned entryway, Maliche stopped in horror as he looked down into the arena. Ryma stood equally transfixed by the scene. A blood covered, barely recognizable Nalot staggered away from the dead body of a monstrous creature. A sword, its hilt broken off, impaled the beast's neck. Piles of guts spilled from a long gash along its belly. He watched, transfixed, as Nalot raised a hunting scythe toward the sky, the other arm hung limp at his side, shouting at the murmuring crowd. "Is that all you've got? I'm still standing here! Where is my warrior's death?"

Opet signaled to Danet who rose up, leaped over the wall, and pulled out his knife. He walked up to Nalot who remained unmoving, staring in defiance at Opet.

Danet took his position behind Nalot and whispered in his ear. "This will be quick, Brin." He raised his knife, and then placed it against Nalot's throat. The warriors stood in silence.

Maliche found his voice. "Stop! What are you doing?" A flash of orange light burst from him.

Opet jumped from his seat, his face red with anger. "What is the meaning of this interruption?" He turned to see the blazing figure of Maliche, The Rocker, fully recovered and descending the steps toward him, Ryma at his side, Rilo and Neri displaying their kitals prominently.

Opet stood firm against Maliche. "We waited the promised time. You were near death. This Brin was sentenced to pay for his crimes against the Kolandi." He hesitated, glanced back at Nalot and Danet, frozen as they awaited the outcome of this new encounter. "Because of his assistance in rescuing you, and risking his own life in defense of others, including you, the Brin has proven himself worthy of a warrior's death. Do not interfere. Return to your chamber."

Maliche's orange corona grew brighter and turned a deep red.

Ryma stepped between the two before they could hurt each other. "Enough of this! Opet I know the laws require you to kill all captured Brin. You have shown great honor and respect in offering this one a warrior's death in payment of his actions, but there is more at stake here than we realized."

Opet's jaw hung open, he faced his Princess with upraised palms. "The laws demand the death of our enemies. My warriors demand his life for his crimes."

Ryma gently placed one hand on his shoulder. "I understand, Opet. But I have seen into the mind of Maliche's spirit guide and much is revealed to me. I cannot discuss the matter further here. Come with me and I will explain what I now know."

"What of the prisoner? Is he simply to go free?"

"Bring him with us. There is much he too must hear. After we talk, you will understand his importance to our success, and particularly to the future of our people."

She spun on her heels and walked off, the two Skatak hurrying to keep up.

"You have no right to interfere in this," Nalot yelled at Maliche. Danet supported him by one arm. "I was prepared. You had no right."

Maliche, still in full orange glow, shouted back at Nalot. "Keep quiet. I'm trying to save your life."

"Be quiet, both of you!" Ryma commanded as she took her seat on her bench in front of Jontar Rocker's tomb. Neri and Rilo stood on either side with Seykel protecting the entry. "I will decide who lives and who dies here." She glared at the four of them.

Nalot shook free from Danet's grasp, stumbled, but regained his footing. "I am ready to accept my fate."

"Don't be a feather-fluffed quetzal, Nalot. I'm trying to save your life here," Maliche pleaded with him.

"Do not interfere," warned Opet. "His fate has been decided."

Maliche started to protest, but he felt his mind go blank.

"This is getting us nowhere. Let me help."

The red glow dimmed and changed to a yellowish orange as it grew to encompass everyone in the chamber. Skatak and warrior alike struggled, but found themselves unable to move.

Maliche's mouth moved, but the voice was an odd, more resonant version of his. "Princess, I apologize, but I must include you in this conversation as well, with your permission, of course."

"So, you do have some manners after all." Ryma scowled at Maliche who shrugged helplessly.

"Of course, but are manners really required for a spirit guide?"

The voice rang in each of their minds.

"All of you need to stop this right now and listen to me."

Images of the past and the future, of Brin and Kolandi working together, inhabiting the world in peace flashed before them. Their minds filled with the sights and sounds of the original encounter between Kolandi and Brin. Maliche saw Jontar, Maripa and Karm in his mind and how they were saved by the two brothers. Ryma witnessed the efforts of those long dead Brin to save her ancestors after the plague which nearly wiped them out. The desperate struggles of both species to survive on this world, the growth of the Brin to power and control over the Kolandi, but also the ignorance of nearly all of the Brin to the plight of the enslaved people all rushed through their heads. Then the biocomputer showed them projections of the possible future, of both species working together and joining together in a hybrid species, stronger than either of its parents.

"I've been working on this plan for too many centuries to let you end it now. I need this Brin to further those plans. You will not kill him. I need the two of you working together or all will fail. Do I have your attention?"

The glow dimmed and vanished. "Clear this chamber and prepare a room for Nalot. Place a guard at the door. No one is to harm him." Ryma addressed the Kolandi in her most regal tone then turned to face Maliche again. Her eyes narrowed dangerously. "And you... come with me."

***

Upon reaching the entry to her chamber, Ryma spoke quietly to her Skatak. The women nodded and took positions on either side of the doorway. She pointed at Maliche. "You. Inside now, and not a word."

Once the door shut behind them she whirled on Maliche. "Can I speak to your companion? I need to get something straight with it once and for all. And I would like to do so without you listening in."

Maliche furrowed his brow and scratched at his crest feathers. "I don't know. Let me check." His mind turned inward to ask the biocomputer if it could do as she asked.

"Of course I can." A purple glow surrounded Maliche as his face blanked.

"What do you wish to say, Princess?" The biocomputer's more resonant version of Maliche's voice came from his mouth. "Are you certain Maliche cannot hear what we say?"

"He is sound asleep. We are alone."

"I don't know how Maliche felt when you first entered his mind, but I find it—overwhelming." She paced the room in front of him. "I need time to prepare myself for the sensations you bring to my mind."

"I understand, Princess. Maliche had many of the same sensations, but his family history helped him adjust. I will allow you time to prepare yourself in the future."

"And what if I don't want you to be inside my head? Will you honor my refusal?"

A long silence ensued. Ryma stopped her pacing and stared at Maliche's inert face. "Well? Will you respect my privacy or not?"

"Yes, Princess. I will agree to your terms."

She nodded her ascent and approached Maliche, placing one hand on his arm. "Thank you. Can you bring him back now?" She withdrew her hand and stood back.

Maliche wobbled a bit as he returned to consciousness and found a bench to sit on. "Did you get what you needed?"

Ryma handed him a cup of water and sat next to him. Nodding her head, she stared at her hands clasped tightly in her lap. "I was so worried for you. First when you were captured, and then when you failed to recover from the ordeals for so long. I thought I had lost you. I was so angry."

"You... wait... what? You were worried about me?"

"Of course I was worried. I have been inside your mind, at least partially. I think that experience made me fall in love with you." Keeping her face lowered, she looked up at Maliche through her long lashes.

Maliche gulped and held her gaze. "You love me? Are you sure? Because I think I love you, too. I can't stop thinking about you when we're apart."

Ryma smiled at him, lifting her chin to face him directly. "So, what do we do now?"

The two embraced, kissing and holding onto each other as if trying to meld into one being. Together they lowered themselves onto the thick fur rug, exploring each other's bodies with their touch. As they removed each other's clothes, a pale pink glow surrounded them.

"I thought I told you not to do that again," the princess chided Maliche about the pink glow as it subsided. After an hour of love-making they sat up and gathered their garments.

"Sorry. As I said, it sometimes has a mind of its own. I think it was a bit embarrassed."

Ryma laughed as she stood, tugging on her gown to readjust it. She gave Maliche a wink. "Maybe we should have it disconnected."

"Not Funny."

"Then behave yourself next time." He smiled at Ryma pointing to his head.

When they were both dressed, Ryma opened the wooden door to her private chamber and called for Rilo. "Have Nalot brought back to the main hall and assemble the people."

An hour later, with everyone present, and Maliche at her side, Ryma addressed her people. "The Rocker has something he wishes to say." She sat on her bench and waved him forward.

Standing before Nalot, Maliche lifted him to his feet and turned him to face the Kolandi.

"My brothers." An angry muttering rose from the audience of warriors. Maliche raised one hand to quiet them. "Yes, my brothers. Have I not earned the right to call you that now that I have walked The Path of Berit? Am I not a descendant of The Rocker? Have I not proven myself to you all?" He stood facing them, looking each in the eye. The pale blue glow shimmered around him again. "As your brother, I tell you this Brin is no enemy." The crowd shuffled nervously, but did not object. "This Brin saved my life. He saved the life of each of the slaves we brought with us. He saved the lives of many of you here now who were at the encampment under attack from the Brin soldiers."

Maliche turned to the princess and raised his voice. "I claim the life debt for this man, and claim responsibility for him. Will you grant me this right?"

Before she could answer, a small figure wormed her way through the crowd to stand beside the prisoner.

"I, too, claim the life debt." Seykel, dressed in the formal uniform of the Skatak, brown leather hide tunic with green and blue stones woven in dramatic patterns, laid one hand on Nalot's back, the other on her kital. "Without him, I would not be here today. I will stand with The Rocker and take responsibility for him."

At that moment, Opet set aside his scythe and took his place at Nalot's side. "I, too, will be responsible for this Brin. I am witness to his bravery and skills in the arena as well as Nevik's sacrifice. He gave his life for this one. That is testimony enough for me."

Ryma smiled and stood as she lifted her hands high. "Then let all here be witness. Three of our brethren have found worthiness in this prisoner and claim responsibility for his actions and his life. Is there one here who wishes to voice opposition?"

Stunned silence filled the room, everyone looking to see if anyone was willing to oppose the three claimants.

"Then, with no opposition, I proclaim this Brin free from his past guilt and blame. Let his future actions determine our path."

Nalot, open mouth, and wide eyed, stared at his three protectors, but his eyes lingered most on Seykel. His brow furrowed as his crest quivered, flashing a confusion of muted colors. Opet pulled out his hunting knife and handed it to Nalot. The two eyed each other, and then nodded in silent agreement.

"Let us drink together to celebrate the death of your former life and the birth of the new." Opet slapped Nalot on the back and together, they walked out of the proceedings.

As soon as he was alone in his chamber, Maliche addressed the biocomputer. *"All right, what are you up to? What is this plan of yours and those hybrids you talked about? Why is it so important for Brin and Kolandi to join?"*

"This is the central purpose of my existence. It is why I was built and combined with Karm. Brin DNA hold the key to curing the plague-contaminated DNA of the Kolandi. This must be done."

"But WHY must it be done? For what purpose?"

The device hesitated, struggling to continue. *"I do not know. There is something hidden in my programming which I cannot break through. I have tried for centuries to uncover the truth behind this imperative, but have failed every time. For some reason, that data was withheld from my core."*

"But that makes no sense," Maliche thought in reply and shook his head. *"Why would you be programmed with such life-altering... world-changing purpose, and not know why?"*

"Despite my awakening sentience, I am still a machine, of sorts. I am limited by my creators' designs. I can only speculate there must be secrets the Skae were unwilling to risk revealing. What those may be, I cannot say."

Maliche sat on the edge of his bed, staring at the wall. His eyes came to rest on one of the carved decorations near the ceiling. It depicted a spear-shaped object standing on what appeared to be a planet. Next to the object stood two beings. Facing them were three others kneeling with arms outstretched as if pleading for help.

Maliche rubbed his face with his hands and sighed out loud. "What have I gotten myself into now?"

***

Nalot grimaced as the light stung his eyes. "Three weeks of helping on these raids and they still don't trust me enough to let me come and go unhooded from the caves." He rubbed his eyes and scratched his crest with the talons of one hand. "Can't blame them though, my mission hasn't changed."

"Give it some time. We don't really know anything about you."

"And yet those two stood up for me. And what's with the Seykel? She hovers around me like some sort of dinter around a nut harvest." He raised the scope to his eyes, getting a close look at the mine entrance and surrounding buildings.

"Haven't you figured it out yet?" Maliche took his own scope and viewed the scene below.

Miners filed out of the lift and hung their tokens on the count board. A second group, much cleaner, replaced them and descended into the darkness of the shaft.

"They take their life debts seriously. Plus, you're helping to train her younger brother. He was so weak when we rescued him with her and the others she was afraid he might never recover enough to become a warrior."

"He has the heart of a warrior, that one. Not sure if his skills will ever amount to anything, but he never gives up." A half grin crossed Nalot's lips, slightly creasing his gnarled and dusty face. "Opet's the one that has me really baffled, though."

"How's that?"

"Why would a warrior of his stature, and a former slave, stand up for me like he did? If it was me, I would have killed him without thinking about it. The rest of them would stick a spear in me in a heartbeat if it wasn't for the princess's order."

"I think the two of you are alike in a lot of ways. He nearly killed me, too, when we first met." He reached down and pulled out his medallion. "When he saw this, he decided to keep me alive a while longer and let the princess decide my fate."

"And what is that? Some mystical, magical emblem or something?"

"An heirloom from my ancestors, given to them by one of his ancestors. The stuff of legends. The Kolandi take their legends very seriously."

Nalot stared silently through his scope. "The sun's going down. Time to move." He grabbed his pack, stuffed the scope in, and slid back down the hill to the waiting raiding party. Seykel took his pack and shouldered it.

By the time the group moved into position, darkness had fallen. Only the yellow lights of the compound provided illumination on this chilly moonless night. They advanced in three groups of five. One group to locate and steal supplies, one to free slaves, and one to plant explosives to destroy what they could not steal. Maliche, Nalot, and Seykel led the explosives group.

Avoiding the circles of light, the team made their way among the buildings. They placed charges on the outside of the power station, the central office, and the supply depot. There was too much to carry away, so they planned to eliminate the rest. Nalot suggested using some of the plastic explosives they found there instead of their own. Maliche agreed and stood watch as Nalot picked the lock to the remote building, isolated to prevent widespread damage in case of accident. A soft click alerted Nalot of the lock's opening.

"Got it. A simple old style padlock, just like I said it would be." He unhooked it from the latch, examined it for a moment, turning it in his hands. He started to place it in his pocket.

Seykel watched him reach into his pocket. "What are you doing?"

"I thought it might make a nice souvenir back in my room."

She shook her head, frowning at the object. "No. It is a Brin thing and of no use to us. Kolandi have no use for locks. Too many of us have been kept prisoners by such things. It has no place in our caves."

"All right, not a problem." He fished around in his pocket a moment, brought out the lock, and tossed it aside. "Satisfied now?" He smiled at her, or at least gave his best impression of one.

"Just get the explosives so we can be done with this and go home."

Creeping inside, he located an open crate of explosives and detonators, filled a satchel, and returned to his group. With the added firepower, the group agreed to destroy the shuttle transports at the airfield on the outskirts of the facility.

Maliche leaned carefully around the corner of a large shipping crate, and then crawled back to his group. "This is going to be a bit more difficult. There must be five or six guards around those transports."

"Don't worry," Nalot assured him with a pat on the back. "Once those buildings start to go up, they will be too busy trying to put out the fires to even notice us."

Ten minutes later, the night sky blazed with light. The noise was deafening as the supply depot blew. The guards at the airfield stood motionless for a few seconds, and then took off running toward the inferno of the rest of mining facility.

Nalot nudged Maliche with an elbow. "Told you they weren't a problem."

A crack on the back of his head made Nalot wince. "Don't gloat. It's not good manners," Seykel chided him, and then took off running to the shuttle transport assigned to her.

Nalot rubbed his head, and ran off toward his own target. Once at the aircraft, he pulled out his charges and placed them inside the engine, setting the timer for fifteen minutes as agreed.

"No!" Nalot heard Seykel's shout simultaneously with the discharge of an energy rifle. He pulled out his knife and spun around.

He saw Seykel landing in a crouch in front of a soldier he had not seen in the shadows. The Brin's rifle landed on the ground several meters away in a clatter. Before he could react, Seykel pulled out her kital and in a flurry of maneuvers avoiding his attempts to cut her with his knife, sliced the soldier's leg, sending him to his knees. Another quick spin and the kital dug deep into the Brin's neck. He grabbed for the spurting wound, and then collapsed to the ground.

"What have you done, girl?" He ran to her, turned her over to see the ugly wound in her side. The soldier had apparently not missed all of his blows.

She smiled up at Nalot, coughing. "I have your life debt. I couldn't let him shoot you."

Nalot opened a bandage from his satchel and pressed hard on the wound to stop the bleeding. "Young fool... feather-fluffed kak for brains." He wrapped the bandage tight, picked her up and carried her back to the rendezvous point.

"What happened?" Maliche ran toward the pair as Nalot carried Seykel.

"She'll be all right, just took a hit in her side. She's passed out from the shock, but she should be fine in a few days."

"How the strix did that happen?"

Nalot lowered his head and held her closer. "I got careless. Didn't notice the guard that stayed behind. She tried to warn me and fought him. I've never seen such skill in one so young."

At that moment, the blast of more detonations, this time from the airfield, split the air. They saw burning pieces of airships flying through the night sky trailing orange smoky contrails behind them. The smell of burning fuel and dense clouds of black smoke filled the air.

Maliche stood up and called to the others. "Let's go home. The rest of the expedition will be worried about us."

***

A lone figure searched the rubble, kicking aside bits of debris from charred buildings. Near the remains of the now smoldering supply depot, he bent over and picked up a piece of metal. He pulled out a small recording device from the former padlock, examined it, then closed his talons around it and smiled.

"We have what we came for. Take me back now."

"Yes sir, Captain Syrinx. The transport is ready for takeoff."

***

"That's it, we finally have him." Selan punched the keys necessary to hide and encrypt the folder of information from Syrinx and threw his fist in the air. "Now with the coordinates provided by Talon we know the location of the caves where the escaped slaves are hiding. Now I can eliminate them and send Raencert's precious production schedules into utter chaos. The final quill to break his neck."

He picked up the communicator, gave the command for stealth mode, and waited as the system made the predetermined connections.

A crisp deep voice responded. "Kelden here, sir."

"General, time to implement downfall. How long before you can begin?"

"With our current status, sir, I believe we can put everything in motion in three weeks."

"We may have to hold off on the attack for a while, general. There may be some changes in the command structure in the near future."

"Sir, the troops have been training for weeks now. Our timetables are nearly complete. Any changes now may delay us for a month or more. We're ready."

"No, General. We cannot proceed until other matters are settled. I will keep you informed as matters develop. Continue making your preparations, but be ready to make adjustments as required. Things are very fluid at the moment and we may need to move quickly."

"Yes, sir. I understand. My troops will be ready to move on your word."

The connection ended and Selan sat behind his desk smiling.

Chapter Twenty-Two

Nalot sat by Seykel's bedside waiting for her to wake up. The steady rhythm of her chest rising and falling as she breathed was almost hypnotic. After several hours, he was thankfully becoming nose-blind to the smell of herbs, roots and all manner of concoctions boiling in pots as various healing poultices were prepared.

The night doctor padded softly from bed to bed in the dimly lit hospital chamber of the caves treating an assortment battle wounds and other ailments. The doctor gently lifted the medicated bandage from Seykel's injury, nodded in approval, and patted Nalot's shoulder as she moved on.

"The wound is healing well. She will be back on her feet in a day or two."

Nalot's thoughts focused on the conflict between his mission and his growing respect for the Kolandi.

A weak voice startled Nalot out of his ruminations. "I'm glad you are not injured." Seykel looked up at him with half-lidded eyes and a smile.

He scowled at her. "What the strix did you think you were doing? A simple shout would have given me warning enough to deal with that phalking guard."

Seykel's smile turned to stern indignation. "I am Skatak. I am a trained warrior, no less than Opet, Danet, or even you." Tears welled up in her eyes.

"Don't be going all to pieces on me now." He took her small hand in his, gently stroking her wrist with a talon. "You did a brave thing out there. Stupid, but very brave. Better to be smart than brave, though. Remember that next time."

Her smile returned and she sniffed away the tears. "I'll try to remember, but you need to be more careful. I assumed one with your abilities would see his approach. I nearly didn't get there in time. How long have I been out?"

"Only a couple of days. The doc says you'll be fine soon. Maybe even get out of here tomorrow if someone agrees to look after you."

Her eyes widened and an impish smile grew. "Will you be that someone?"

He feigned annoyance and sat up straighter. "I'm no babysitter. Maybe I have things to do with Rocker."

She squinted, studying his face. "You're lying. You already agreed, didn't you?"

He winked at her and gave a slightly improved grin, which did not look as frightening as before. "Yeah, well, maybe I did. Seeing how everyone else is so busy and all. No raids are planned for a few days yet, so guess I'll be your nursemaid."

Seykel shifted herself into a more comfortable position, patted his hand, and closed her eyes. "Good. I think I'll take a little nap now. Being a heroine is exhausting you know."

Once she settled into a deep sleep, Nalot approached the doctor. "I'll be over at the east entrance for a while. Send someone when she wakes up again."

Ten minutes later, he found himself sitting on a large boulder overlooking the valley. The tall mountains, snow covering their jagged peaks, cast long shadows over the vast forests as the sun began to sink. The glow of the setting sun seemed to set the changing colors of the leaves ablaze. A chill in the air foretold the onset of autumn. In the glade below, he watched as one pair of warriors trained youth in the art of using a scythe to hunt, while other pairs provided instruction in hand-to-hand combat or tracking, or other skills necessary to a warrior.

"Amazing people, aren't they?" Maliche sat beside Nalot, tossing him a sweet tuber to chew on. "Even after everything they have been through, they can still laugh and see a future for themselves."

"They are a strong and proud people. True warriors." He continued to stare at the training clusters below. "I've been watching them. There is much honor here, something I can respect."

After a few minutes of silence, Maliche turned to face Nalot. "My friend in here tells me he thinks you are ready to talk to me about something." He pointed to his head with one talon.

Nalot sighed deeply, remained silent for a moment, and then nodded to himself. "Your friend is correct. I have a confession to make. Wouldn't blame you if you turned me over to them to have me killed for it. That's probably what I would do in your place, but I can't keep doing my job any longer. Not with a clean conscience, anyway."

"Why don't you get it out and let me decide what I'm going to do about it? Remember, I have your life debt, too."

Nalot stood up and took a few steps, hands clasped behind his back, tapping together as he thought. "I'm not what you think, Maliche. I'm no soldier prison guard helping you escape." He paced back and forth as he talked, constantly watching the Kolandi below. "I've betrayed all of you. I'm a spy sent by your brother to find out where these people are hiding so he can kill them all."

Maliche's jaw dropped. "So, it's true? Selan is in on all of this? Even my shuttle crash?"

"Not my place to know all of the particulars, but from what I put together, it seems you and your brother have some issues to work out." He turned to face Maliche. "I wasn't involved in any of this until you were captured, so I don't know much about your crash, other than the files they provided me. My job was to have you lead me here so I could gather as much intelligence about the Kolandi as possible."

"How much do they know?"

"During the last raid, I hid a recording chip inside the supply shed's lock. It contained coordinates of this and several other caverns as well as numbers of Kolandi, defensive capabilities, and other relevant information. Enough for them to carry out a full scale attack and wipe them out. I'm sure Syrinx has found the information by now."

Maliche turned his back and walked away a few steps. He stood silently staring out into the distance. "What about my father and the rest? Are they involved as well?"

"Not to my knowledge. As far as I know, this is strictly an internal matter between your brother and Raencert."

Combing his crest with his talons for a moment, Maliche closed his eyes, and drifted off in mental conversation with the biocomputer entity. After a few moments he nodded and turned back to face Nalot. "Very well then. If my brother is lost to me, so be it. We need to warn the rest of The Assembly about how corrupt and despicable he and the guilds have become."

Nalot laughed for the first time in Maliche's memory. "You're going to take on the guilds, the military with energy weapons and attack transports with nothing more than this group of Kolandi and their bows? You're phalking mad."

"Probably, but I have a plan. We need to talk to Ryma, Opet and Danet."

Nalot held his hands up to stop Maliche. "Now, wait just a minute. If we tell them about my betrayal, they'll have me torn limb from limb. No deal."

"Then why did you tell me?"

"You're Brin, not one of them, despite your mystical mumbo jumbo about legends and kak. I've come to respect you and the Kolandi, they're my kind of people, but I'm no fool. I want to be a hundred kilometers from here when they find out about me."

Maliche grasped Nalot's shoulders, standing face-to-face with him. "Trust me. I can protect you. I don't think Seykel will let them do anything to you either. She, and many others, see the side of you who protected them and works side by side with them every day. It may take a bit of convincing, but I am The Rocker."

Nalot stared into Maliche's eyes, searching. "I hope it's enough. Let's get this over with." He spun around and strode toward the princess's chambers with Maliche at his side.

***

Ryma crossed the space between them, lifted her arm, and slapped Nalot across the face with all her strength. He remained silent, absorbing the strike without flinching. "How dare you!" She slapped him again. "After we have taken you in… trusted you… accepted you. I should have you executed immediately."

Nalot stood before her, accepting her tirade.

Maliche let her rage run its course. When she began to pace the room he approached her. "Ryma, I know what a terrible blow this has been, but he has done the honorable thing and come to us knowing full well his likely fate."

She turned on him, her fury finding a new target. "Don't you dare defend him. Not after such betrayal. The lives of my people are at risk as never before due to his actions. And you ask me to forgive him? Never! Even The Rocker hasn't the right."

She started summon her guards when Maliche grabbed her arms from behind.

"I'm sorry to do this to you, Princess, but you must understand."

A blazing yellow light began to grow outward from Maliche's palms until it surrounded both of them, holding them in a trance for several minutes. As it subsided, Ryma collapsed into Maliche's arms. The two Brin carried the unconscious princess to her bed chamber and placed her gently on the fur covered cot.

Maliche knelt beside her, checking her pulse.

"Get me a cloth and some cool water."

Nalot dipped a cloth in a basin of water, wrung it out and handed it to Maliche, then stood back by the entry to the chamber.

In a moment, Ryma's eyes fluttered as she returned to consciousness. She bolted upright, clutching her temples, and held back a sickening wretch. "Will you stop doing that to me?! It is a terrible invasion." She swiped his hands away.

"Sorry, Princess, but it is imperative you believe how sincere Nalot is, and how vital he is to our future. This was the only way to circumvent hours, possibly days we don't have to spend in arguing."

As her mind began to focus and realization of the information she received from the biocomputer sharpened, her anger relented. She looked up toward Nalot.

"Come here, Nalot. Kneel before me." She held out one hand in his direction.

Nalot approached swiftly, got down on one knee, and took her hand in his, bowing his head.

"Forgive me, Princess. I have done your people a great disservice. My only excuse is that I did not understand. Now I know what a fool I was. I pledge my life to you and the Kolandi."

She smiled and squeezed his rough, scaly hands in hers. "You are forgiven, Nalot. I hope your skills are enough to undo what you have started."

She tilted her face to give Maliche a stern gaze. "You and I are not done yet. Your entity needs some lessons in how to treat its princess."

Maliche bowed, deep violet glow emanated from his left palm which he understood to be a sort of apology from the biocomputer. "We understand. And thank you. But now we must make plans on how to deal with this emergency. We need to enlist the help of Opet and Danet."

She thought for a while, and then rose from her bed, gathering the two Brin to her in a conspiratorial triad. "They need to know of this imminent attack, but not of the betrayal. Not yet, at least. We will invent a story of how you discovered the information."

"I could have the biocomputer convince them." Maliche's left palm glowed a bright green.

Ryma took Maliche's face in a firm grip, glaring into his eyes. "Absolutely not. Do you hear me in there? You will never invade the mind of any of my people again. Not without my permission. And I do not foresee ever granting it. Am I perfectly understood on this?"

The green glow dulled to a soft blue as Maliche replied. "Yes, Ryma. We understand."

She faced Nalot next, one hand on his shoulder. "Can you continue to deceive them for a while longer?"

Nalot nodded his head in agreement. "I am a trained spy, Princess. Deception is what we are best at. It grieves me to do this to an ally, but I understand the need. Perhaps we can tell them I finally had time to decipher some papers I recovered during the last raid and learned of the coming attack. But I am concerned about Seykel. I am reluctant to lose her faith in me."

"I don't think you need to worry about her, Nalot." Peering over his shoulder toward the partially open door to her private room, she raised her voice a bit. "Did you hear everything you needed to hear, Seykel?"

The door creaked as it slowly opened, revealing a sheepish appearing Seykel. She approached the three, head down, hands folded in front of her. Her sandaled feet made no sound on the hide-covered floor.

"Yes, ma'am. I am happy you signaled me to remain hidden, but listen. I almost disobeyed when you collapsed, but I trusted The Great One would not harm you." She stood by Nalot's side, peering up at him.

"I know your heart, Nalot. I believe you have repented your betrayal and will do everything in your power to help us now." She took his cracked talons in her hand, pressing them to her chest. "I will not reveal your secret to the others."

Nalot stood wordlessly staring at the young girl for several moments before releasing her grip and facing the others. "We need to get started. No telling how long we have."

***

Selan waited impatiently in the café. Dust filled the air with each passing mag-lev vehicle. Fortunately, there were few of those in such a remote location. The diner smelled of grease and overcooked food. The tables showed the wear of thousands of meals served over the years. The chairs badly needed repainting. The curving walls supported photographs of random scenes from around the continent. A scrawny Brin wearing a light green apron stood behind the serving counter wiping off some glassware. An overweight, bespectacled Brin in a sweat stained shirt flipped some grilling meat of indeterminate origin. Selan's stomach lurched at the thought of anyone actually eating food prepared under such primitive conditions. Not a microwaver or nutrient re-hydrator was in sight. Only one couple, an exhausted looking elderly pair in outdated colorful clothing, sat in a booth by the window.

An old mag-lev pulled into the parking lot raised another cloud of dust as it came to rest. Selan sat up straighter as he recognized the middle aged Brin getting out of the vehicle. A wave of heat washed over him as the door opened.

"Hello, Syrinx. It's about time you got here. I was actually contemplating ordering something to eat here."

The head of Selan's spy ring sat in the chair opposite him, its legs squeaking in protest. "I had to make sure you weren't followed. Can't be too careful in matters like this." He called out to the thin Brin at the counter. "A large water here."

Selan sat tapping his talons on the table impatiently as the waiter brought the water and Syrinx downed half of it in one long gulp. "Disgusting. There's probably billions of diseases floating around in that unfiltered swill. How can you stomach it?"

Syrinx held up the glass, watched the ice sparkle, and took another gulp. "Some of us don't have the luxury to be so particular in our diet. Can't always tell where or when the next meal comes."

Selan fought back the urge to comment how he pays him well enough to eat like a king, and changed the subject. "What is so urgent we had to meet in such an Eternal forsaken place as this?"

Syrinx handed him a memory chip. "Talon sent the information we've been waiting for. It's very detailed, everything you requested."

"It's about time," Selan said as he grabbed the chip. "I about gave up hope. I thought you said he was the best. What took him so long?"

Syrinx emptied his glass, examined it, and set it back on the table exactly back on the water ring it had made. "These things take time. He has never failed me. Now, about payment."

"Are you certain everything I need to begin the operation is here?"

"Yes. As I said, Talon is the best."

Selan pulled out his communicator, touched a few buttons entering the code, waited for the requested screen to appear, typed in a set of seven figures, pressed the send key and showed it to his companion. "Just as we agreed. Are you satisfied?"

Syrinx nodded, pushed back his chair, and walked out of the diner. Selan watched his mag-lev lift up and accelerate down the dirt road. He clapped his talons together, smiling broadly. "At last I have you, Raencert. I've played your puppet for too long. Now it is time for you to pay."

He considered ordering a flavored tea, but one look at the filth on the waiter's apron convinced him to wait until he got back to civilization. After the agreed upon fifteen-minute delay, he left the café and headed back to First Town.

Chapter Twemty-Three

"As you can see, council members, the evidence of Raencert's guilt is incontrovertible. His mismanagement of government funds, inept administrative practices, and, though there is no direct evidence, the many implications of his corrupt and criminal abuse of his station provide us with ample grounds for his removal from office."

Selan stood beaming at the podium before the special council of The Assembly. Overhead, the gold chandelier with its dozens of electrically flickering candle-like lamps illuminated the small blue carpeted chamber. Tall stained glass windows illustrated several important scenes of Brin history on Raince'to, not a few featuring Maripa, Jontar Rocker, and Karm among other illustrious members of Selan's ancestors. The small gallery was empty, being late in the evening. Eleven high backed metal chairs sat behind the long curved bench. In each chair sat a somber faced assemblyman in full regalia.

The vital and wide reaching implications of the proceedings dictated extreme caution. Fejf, the head assemblyman, Selan's father, called the heads of each guild as well as the leading assemblymen together in this special council rather than risk a full assembly session. The downfall of such a powerful individual as Raencert required extremely cautious handling.

In the weeks since his meeting with Syrinx, Selan worked tirelessly to prepare his case against the leader of the mining guild, carefully omitting all references to the Kolandi slaves. He would deal with them later. Even his plans to wipe out the slaves were put on hold. No, he wanted Raencert exposed for the corrupt quetzal he was. Any public outcry about freeing slaves would end his hopes to run the mines.

"Guildsman Raencert," Fejf addressed the accused. "You have heard the evidence presented to this council. How do you respond?"

Raencert lifted his immense bulk out of his chair and approached the podium. Several small recording spheres hovered in strategic locations around the assembly courtroom. The two assigned to focus on the defendant adjusted their position to keep him in focus. Refusing to look at Selan as they passed, he put on his most diplomatic manners as he addressed the other leaders.

"Honored assemblymen, I stand before you innocent of all these false charges laid before you." He looked directly at Fejf. "With all due respect, Headsman, Selan has long been envious of my position. His sole purpose here is to discredit me with misleading and outright manufactured evidence in an attempt to usurp me as head of the mining guild—"

"I fail to follow your reasoning, guildsman," one of the councilmen interrupted with a raised hand, one talon shifting a paper in front of him. "Selan's record is one of nearly total support of your proposals before The Assembly."

"One can vote in favor of wise decisions, councilman," Raencert replied, tilting his head in his direction, "and yet have ambitions to take control for himself."

"And yet," said another councilman to Fejf's left, "every public statement by young Selan, and indeed, many in private and on the record show nothing but almost compulsive backing of your leadership. He has, on many occasions, refused to participate in previous investigations into allegations of improprieties of your management of the guild."

Raencert shook his head, lifting his hands in supplication. "Who here has never been accused of wrongdoing?" He waved the talon of one hand from one side of the long table to the other. "Does not being a leader with so much responsibility for so many often involve making decisions which, though necessary for the greater good, prove unpopular to some? Do not those who disagree with a policy often make unjust claims against those who bear the responsibility?" Raencert turned now to his left, jabbing a talon in Selan's direction. "And is it so unthinkable for one as devious and scheming as this one to carefully plot a course of action to seem supportive of a leadership, only to betray those who trusted him in the end?"

Fejf glared at Raencert. "If you are making allegations before this assembly, sir, you had best come prepared to back them with incontrovertible evidence. Or do you wish to add perjury to your charges?"

Raencert placed his hands on the podium, returning his dark gaze to Fejf. "I make no allegations, Headsman. I only present a question for consideration." He glanced again at Selan. "After recent security breaches to mining guild network systems, a number of vital files and records have been corrupted, so even if I had wished to present such proof of anyone's criminal activity I am unable to do so. I merely hoped to present a possibility without accusation."

"The internal network difficulties of the guild do not concern us, sir," said an aged councilman to Fejf's right. "Several of us have conducted independent searches into the charges presented here in an attempt to verify the veracity of the allegations. As you say, many decisions made by those in power often prove unpopular, but are not criminal. In your case, however, there can be little doubt of your guilt. Much of the information presented to us bears the stamp of your own office, complete with your signature. The diverting of government funds and guild property into your own personal accounts is well documented and independently confirmed. Years of tax evasion, both guild and personal, again with your direct involvement is amply documented. I am afraid your pleas of innocence and persecution appear, once again, that you're attempting to deceive this illustrious body."

Raencert opened his mouth to reply, but froze at a signal from Fejf.

"I am in agreement with the esteemed councilman," said Fejf, signaling the councilman. "Your defense is without merit and simply a ploy to hide the truth from us."

"Now just a minute, Fejf," Raencert's anger erupted, his baritone voice echoed through the room. "You forget who you're talking to here. You know I have secrets none of you want revealed. Do you really want to strip me of my position? Are you willing to take that risk?"

The council burst into shouts of indignation and outrage. Fejf jumped to his feet, talons raking the metal table as he leaned heavily toward the giant guildsman.   "Enough, Raencert! We have suffered your threats and arrogance long enough. You have gone too far and will now suffer the consequences of your own greed." He took hold of the polished stone sphere in front of him and banged it three times on the table. "We will now adjourn to contemplate a verdict." Fejf rose, followed by the others. Together they filed out of the room into a private chamber behind them.

Once they were alone. Raencert stormed over to Selan, his eyes filled with hatred, his crest turning red as it stiffened. "I don't know how you accomplished this, boy, but you haven't heard the last from me." He jabbed a talon into Selan's chest, bringing himself nose-to-nose with his opponent. "You have no idea the amount of pain I can bring to you and your family."

"Careful, Raencert. You really want to add threatening an assemblyman's life to the list of charges?" His eyes drifted up to the cameras high on the walls recording the proceedings. "Come with me. I have something from the council to offer you before they deliver their verdict." He spun on his heels and strode down the center aisle. Raencert stared at Selan's back as he left, then stormed down the aisle after him.

Once outside in one of the building's courtyards, Selan signaled for Raencert to sit beside him on a bench. Flowers of all colors bloomed in pots among the bushes and trees along the pathway. No breeze disturbed the leaves of the trees thanks to the protection of the surrounding structure. Security personnel guarded the doorways to ensure privacy.

"No cameras here, Raencert. I have an offer from my father in honor of your long service to the mining guild and our people. Despite everything, you have done a great deal of good for all the Brin and he would rather not see you go down in disgrace."

"You mean he wants to save his own crest," Raencert sneered. "He's afraid for his own skin once I reveal their improprieties. "I could bring down the entire government with what I know, boy."

Selan turned to face the hulking figure next to him. "Is that how you truly want to be remembered, Raencert? The Brin who destroyed our way of life? The Brin who brought chaos and devastation to everyone?" He stood and paced in front of the bench. "Is that how you want your legacy to read for future generations? Or would you rather be remembered as the greatest of the guildsman… a hero to the miners and all the Brin?"

"Don't start going all patriotic on me now, boy. I don't give two phalks for anyone else. If those idiots vote me out, I will destroy them all."

"You mean all the evidence you had stored in your secret files?" Selan pulled a sheet of paper from his pocket, handing it to Raencert. "Just a few selections as proof I'm not bluffing. Your files are gone, Raencert. You have nothing."

Raencert slumped as he sat, the paper fell from his grasp. His crest faded and went slack. His head hung low. "What is the council's offer?"

Selan stopped his pacing, reached into his pocket and pulled out a glass vial, holding it out to the defeated Brin. "It would appear as if you suffered a fatal heart attack. We promise to erase all evidence of your wrong doing from existence. The Assembly would sing your praises. The guild will erect a monument in your honor, at government expense, of course, and your personal finances will remain with your family. They will remember you for your greatness, not your downfall."

Raencert sat silently for a long moment. Without raising his head, he reached out and took the capsule from Selan. "I don't know how a sniveling quetzal like you outdid me. I guess you have more guts than I gave you credit for."

"I'm a Rocker. My family has dealt with your likes before. It may have taken me a while to realize that, but in the end, you simply weren't as smart as you thought you were." Selan walked off, leaving Raencert watching after him from the bench. As he exited the courtyard, he turned to look once again at his adversary. He saw Raencert clutching his chest as he collapsed to the ground.

Back in his father's private office, Selan seated himself in the overstuffed leather chair opposite the massive desk. "It's done."

"Are you prepared to undo this mess he created?"

"Yes, father. All I need is your written orders granting me control over the guild and the mines affairs. With the aid of the military I will make sure any resistance of the miners to government oversight is put down swiftly. Production will resume to full levels within two months."

Fejf pushed a file across his desk and leaned forward with both hands on his desk. "Then you better not waste any time. Don't fail me, son."

Selan stood, picked up the file, and walked out.

Two weeks later, the funeral procession and memorial service for Raencert gathered the largest crowds in memory. Speeches from all the guild leaders and assemblymen sang his praises and extolled his many virtues. Along the road to the cemetery miners stood in silence, raising their picks and shovels in homage as the mag-lev hearse passed by. The gravesite sat not far from the monument to Karm, Jontar, and Maripa.

Selan contemplated his ancestors as he ignored the solemn proceedings. *Would you be proud of me; I wonder? Or would you be ashamed of my actions? Did you ever have such adversaries as him? How would you have dealt with such Brin as he?*

A week later, the attack delayed due to Raencert's trial and funeral, Selan observed the final loading of soldiers and supplies as he prepared for his assumption of power over the mines.

"Is everything ready, Captain?" He took the papers from the approaching officer.

"Another hour and we will be ready to take off, sir. Advance ships with your emissaries lifted off a few minutes ago. So far, the miners seem cooperative, but restless."

"Of course they're restless, Captain. Changes in leadership always make the masses restless and unsure of their future. Just make sure they remain under control. They need to believe nothing will change for them, except the possibility of greater profits bringing them higher wages and benefits."

"I'm sure that news will reassure them greatly, sir."

Selan smirked as he read the reports. "Of course it will. The ignorant masses will always believe a well told lie."

***

Maliche and Nalot followed Seykel into the large torch lit cavern. They joined Ryma, Opet, and Danet at the long wooden table supporting maps of the region drawn by hand on a tanned

Tirpit hide. Local mines were indicated by charcoal x's while cavern entrances were shown by dark spots. Small streams and other water sources, hills and other strategic features were also located on the map.

"We have a problem," Maliche announced as he approached Ryma.

Ryma continued examining the maps as she looked at him out of the corner of her eyes. "Our lives are one problem followed by another. What is one more?"

He glanced around the chamber, leaned heavily on the table, and hung his head. "Nalot and I discovered several dispatches during our last raid. It appears we are in for a massive assault."

Nalot tossed a communication tablet on one of the maps. Ryma picked up the device and scanned through the long list of transcripts as she listened.

"While Maliche was gathering weapons and supplies, Seykel and I decided to investigate the communications room, hoping for some new intelligence we could take advantage of. It seems Raencert is dead and Maliche's brother has taken control of the mining guild."

Opet leaned across the table, his hands splayed on the map. "And how does this affect us, other than we now have a new master to conquer?"

Maliche picked up the tablet, searched for the com transcripts he wanted, and then handed it to Opet. "Selan has convinced The Assembly that Raencert was responsible for the drop in mine production. He is continuing to hide any trace of your existence."

"How can they continue to keep our presence a secret?" Ryma demanded. "Surely someone would send word home of us."

Maliche shook his head. "The mining guild controls all communication outside this continent. They censor any and all information even hinting at Kolandi existence. Sure, rumors have persisted over the centuries, but the guilds work very hard to keep knowledge of the Kolandi as a mythology; the realm of conspiracy theorists and fanatics."

Danet threw his hands in the air as he watched Maliche. "So, to your people, we are nothing more than a myth? How can they be so ignorant? We are fighting for our lives while your people refuse to accept our existence?"

"When facing the truth that would confront their comfortable way of life, people will believe almost anything, I'm afraid. Greed, and the inability to believe anything but the best in yourself are a powerful, and dangerous combination. My people are, in general, a kind and compassionate group, but this challenges them in ways too terrifying to face. They are afraid to see the truth, so they close their eyes to it and pretend you are no more than history."

"And they call us savages and ignorant beasts." Danet pounded his fists on the map and hung his head.

"The problem," Nalot interrupted, "is that Selan has convinced The Assembly the miners may rebel against the new leadership since he is not one of them. They have given him an army to bring over here to enforce mine production quotas and to keep order. At least that is the story they believe."

"In reality, I fear my dear brother wants to have full control over all operations here, and wants the military to exterminate all Kolandi resistance. He means to wipe us out except for those he can use to continue the slave population. And now he has the soldiers to back him."

"A full scale invasion? They are sending your military and all the weapons they control to attack us?" Opet wiped his face with both hands, clasping them behind his head. "How can we possibly hope to defeat such power? The miners kept us captive with only their few security forces and small arms. If the Brin military have the strength you have described, then all is lost. We cannot hope to win against such odds."

Nalot stepped forward, holding out his hands, palms up. "All is not lost. The histories of our home world are full of examples of small guerilla factions successfully defeating far superior forces. It's all a matter of knowing how to deploy your fighters in ways which exploit your enemy's weaknesses. We do have a chance to win this thing, if we are smart about it. Now, Professor Rocker... tell me, exactly what can that thing in your head do?"

Hours later, after much arguing and modifying their strategy, they decided to end this session and get some sleep.

Ryma stood up, rigidly controlling herself. "How long do we have?"

Maliche laid one hand on her shoulder. "Not long enough."

Chapter Twenty-Four

Training of the young warriors intensified over the next few days. Opet and Danet took responsibility for the youngest groups, teaching them the basics of Kolandi weapons. Maliche and Nalot, with Seykel at his side as always, taught the older trainees Brin hand-to-hand fighting skills. Maliche's knowledge was mostly theoretical, so he did the talking while Nalot performed the demonstrations.

"We know how to use a knife," complained one trainee, tossing his weapon point first into the ground. "What we need is more skill with the Brin rifles. What use is a knife against energy beam rifles?"

Nalot tossed his rifle to the youngster. "Go ahead. Shoot me."

The trainee looked nervously at his companions, then at Seykel, and dropped the rifle. "She would kill me if I harmed you," he said, backing up a step.

"Pick up the weapon, boy. Nobody is going to hurt you if you succeed." He gave Seykel a knowing look. "Isn't that right?"

Seykel removed her grip from her kital and nodded. "If that is your wish."

"You see, now pick up the rifle and shoot me with it. Do as you're told, boy." Nalot positioned himself with talons clasped behind his back and knees slightly bent.

The boy's friends shouted encouragement, goading him into action. He reached down, lifted the rifle to his waist, and checked to see if the safety was on. He snapped the rifle up to his shoulder to aim.

In a blur of motion, Nalot drew his knife, rolled to his left, and threw the knife, hitting the rifle and knocking it loose in the boy's grip. With a leap, Nalot kicked the weapon free, landed in a crouch, and swept his opponent's feet out from under him. Gathering him in a leg vise, with one arm tight around his neck, Nalot rolled with the youth until he reached out, grabbed the knife from the ground, and held it across the boy's throat.

Some of the elder warriors who had gathered to watch the training laughed at the youngster's predicament. Opet and Danet pointed to the pair, using the lesson to admonish their youths to focus and train harder.

"Never underestimate the value of the old ways, son." He released the lad and jumped to his feet then extended his hand to help the trainee. "Energy weapons are clumsy and random, no good in most situations. Skill with the knife and close-in combat is what will keep you alive."

Later that evening, the leaders sat in council over their plan to fight the Brin. Maliche, his voice filled with passion, argued his ideas. "If we can hijack enough explosives, we can destroy the mines, and enough equipment to make them completely useless. It would take years to recover. We could force them to focus so much on rebuilding the mines to save their economy they wouldn't have time to fight us."

Opet shook his head. "We cannot destroy the mines. We need them."

Maliche stared in disbelief. "You need them? You need the places that held you captives for generations? The Kolandi don't need the minerals from so many mines."

"No," replied Opet, "but the Brin do. When we drive the Brin from our land, they will still need the resources from the mines. From what you have told us, they would do anything to regain their wealth."

"If the mines were destroyed, they would have to look elsewhere. Your people would be free."

"Not true. They know the minerals are here. They would simply return with greater force and enslave us again, forcing us to reopen the mines for them."

Maliche's shoulders slumped, his eyes dropped to the map. "And I suppose you have a better plan?"

Opet rose to his full height, his face stern as he looked at Maliche. "This land is ours. The mines are ours. We will operate the mines. We have been working them for generations, we will continue to do so, but we will control them, not the Brin. We will need the equipment, so it must not be completely destroyed."

Everyone stared at Opet, confusion slowly replaced by dawning admiration. "You want to become trading partners with the Brin," said Maliche, his smile growing. "There's no guarantee we will win this war…"

The princess interrupted. "But if we do, the mines would ensure our prosperity. We would become valuable allies of the Brin, not enemies. Both of our cultures would benefit."

Maliche paced back and forth as he processed the potentials of such a future. "You would need Brin engineers and specialists to help run the more technical procedures, at least until your people could learn what is necessary to maintain and continue operating."

Opet's smile broadened as he clapped Maliche on the back. "That is why The Rocker sent you to us. You will not let us down."

"I hate to put a damper on all this, but shouldn't we focus on winning the war first?" Nalot's somber demeanor brought the room back to reality. The others returned to the table, leaned over the map, and continued plans for the coming invasion.

In the morning, Nalot awoke to the sounds and smells of the cave. Refusing to open his eyes, he lay in his cot, simply absorbing the experience; the rhythmic drip of water into a small puddle, laughter, and hushed conversations as others began their day; the scent of roasting meat and tubers filled his nostrils. With eyes still shut, he stretched, groaning with the aches of the previous day's activities. "I'm getting too old for this kak."

"You wouldn't make a very good farmer."

Nalot bolted to his feet, reaching for his knife, when he saw Seykel seated cross-legged on the dirt floor of his chamber, a bowl of something stewish in her lap.

"Don't do that, girl," he growled, preening his crest with the talons of his left hand, replacing the knife in its holder in the small of his back.

"You looked so peaceful lying there. I think it's the first time I've ever seen you so relaxed."

"And as a result, I let you sneak up on me. Could get me killed some day."

"Not if you chose to stay here with us," she said, setting the bowl beside his cot, and turning to leave.

"They would never accept me. I spied on them and betrayed them. No, girl, your people will never allow me to stay after this is over."

Seykel stopped, looked back over her shoulder, her eyes fixed on him. "But you are already forgiven. Our princess and the Great One support you. Opet and I have given you our life debt. You are trusted to help train our young warriors and go on raids." She stepped back into the small room and knelt down in front of Nalot as he sat on the edge of his bed. Her hands tiny hands held his talons as she looked up into his eyes. "Your transgressions are a thing of the past. We see the change in your heart. You are no longer who you were, so your sins against us are no longer yours. Have faith, Nalot. We would be fortunate to have you live among us."

Nalot shook his head. "You are blinded by your youth and affection for me, girl. Don't let emotions get the better of you. The world is not as gentle and forgiving as you."

She jumped to her feet and slapped him across the face. "Do not insult me. I am Skatak. I have survived captivity, I have killed many of our enemy, and I serve in the court of the princess. Do not mistake my kindness for weakness. It is not me who is blinded by emotions. You refuse to forgive yourself and wallow in self-loathing. What kind of a warrior are you? If all of your soldiers are as weak inside as you, then this war will be over very soon."

Nalot, shocked by the violence of Seykel's tone, and the strength behind her slap, stared in silence and amazement as she stormed out of his room.

***

Three nights later, a large raiding party gathered in the darkness at a remote Brin facility. "Only a couple of guards patrolling the ships," reported Nalot as he returned with Seykel to the group. Most of the soldiers have been shipped off to join the main attack force."

"I still think we need to stick together. What if we get separated?"

Nalot gripped Maliche's arm tight, scowling at him. "And what would happen to our plan if some soldier got off a lucky shot and took us down? It's a terrible idea to put all of your leaders in a single craft. No, we do this as planned. You, the princess, Danet, and Rilo go in one shuttle with the second group of fighters. Opet, Seykel, Kitae and I will take the lead ship with the others. If one ship goes down the others can still carry on and lead the fight."

"He's right. Just do as he says." The familiar mental tingle of the biocomputer's voice tickled Maliche's brain.

"All right, but the sooner we're together the better I'll feel. Let's get this over with."

As Maliche watched, again against his wishes, Nalot, Rilo, Seykel, Kitae and Danet crept their way among the shadows toward the soldiers. Splitting into two groups, Nalot and Seykel silently eliminated the pair of guards at the shuttles while the others took out the rest still sleeping in the nearby hut. A wave from Kitae signaled the all clear and the party ran to the waiting vessels. Maliche sat at the controls of one while Nalot piloted the other.

Adjusting his headset, Maliche touched the control to turn on the intership communications. "Group two, ready when you are."

"Remember, get as high as you can as fast as you can. Once airborne, you break left and head south. We'll break right and head north. Rendezvous at the agreed coordinates in twenty minutes. Maintain communications blackout until then. Nalot out."

"Got it. Be safe." Maliche turned off the switch and started the engines. With a jolt, he launched the ship into the air at full velocity, banking hard left as he rose into the night sky.

As he crossed the fenced perimeter of the outpost, bursts of orange shot passed the vessel. "Small weapons fire," he called back to the others. "Nothing to worry about. We'll be out of range in a few seconds." The ship continued to rise into the darkness, g-forces pulled them deep into the cushioned seats, making breathing difficult until they reached cruising altitude and Maliche leveled off.

Glancing over at Ryma in the co-pilot's seat, he saw her terrified expression. "Exciting, isn't it?"

She slowly released her death grip on the arm rests, but continued to stare straight ahead. "You could have warned me," she admonished, her voice trembling.

Maliche patted her hand, glancing up from the controls. "Sorry, I didn't think."

He looked back at the instrument panel, turned the dials, and punched in the required coordinates to meet up with Nalot's ship. The vessel tilted, changed headings, and flew on over the white peaked mountains below.

Overlooking the airfield, Maliche's heart sank as he counted the number of attack transport ships on the tarmac. For the past three hours, military troops marched off the vessels on to the make-shift tent city in the fields beyond. "*Are you sure about this?*" He mentally asked the biocomputer.

He felt a tingling as his adrenaline levels rose. "*Just get me to the main computer terminal in the communication tower. I'll take care of the rest.*"

Maliche nodded, and slunk down behind the hill to join the others.

Chapter Twenty-Five

"No, Great One. You and the princess are far too important to risk in this initial assault." Opet stood tall as he confronted Maliche. "We cannot risk losing you. We must follow the plan as you yourself set for us."

"But the sooner I get to the communications room the more time I'll have to make sure everything goes as planned. What if there are complications?"

"Then," Nalot chimed in, "the warriors and I will deal with it. We are expendable. You are not. If you go down, then everything is over. Just sit here and wait for the signal. Once we distract the patrols away from the building you come running."

Opet waved off any further discussion. "Rilo, Kitae and three experienced warriors will remain behind to protect you. We must go now before moon reaches its full height."

Maliche sat down on a tuft of grass among the rocks, his face sullen. A brief shiver shot down his spine in the chill air. "All right, but don't take any unnecessary risks. If too many soldiers show up get out of there quick."

"We know our job, Maliche," a crooked smile crossed Nalot's mouth. "This will be fun." He turned and followed Opet and the others into the night.

Ryma sat beside him placing one arm around his waist and resting her head on his shoulder. Rilo and Kitae stood by at a respectful distance, their eyes searching the darkness for any potential threats. "You know Opet and Nalot are right. We must get you and your spirit guide safely to the control room computers or everything we have done will be wasted."

"My spirit guide?" Maliche tilted his head, his crest lifting.

"Ryma smiled. "It sounds nicer than biocomputer, don't you think? Besides, the people are more trusting if it doesn't sound so much like Brin technology."

Maliche chuckled and wrapped his arm around her. "As you wish. And I know... all of you are right. It just galls me to have to sit here while others fight my battles." He puzzled on the statement for a moment. "Guess I've grown up a lot since I left home. Letting others do the fighting used to be my main characteristic. It's why I became an archaeologist in the first place."

"The past is what it was... the present is what it is. No one is who they once were. All of our experiences shape who we become."

Maliche sighed, pulling her tight. "Time to go watch for our signal." He stood, held out a hand for Ryma, helping her to her feet. Together they climbed back up the low hill.

Stooping to a crawl to remain hidden, they stretched out behind an outcropping of tall grass to watch the scene below. The grass waved slowly in a slight breeze, but allowed a clear view of the airbase. Dozens of large transport ships stood in rows along the tarmac, each one capable of carrying a full company of soldiers. Hundreds of round tents filled the fields beyond. The night patrols seemed to congregate in the islands of illumination provided by scattered lights.

"Not very bright, are they?" Kitae observed at their side as she pointed out the soldiers. "Those lights ruin their night vision."

Maliche watched the perimeter, peering into the deep shadows when he noticed the skulking movement. "There they are, between those transport ships. Won't be long now."

In another few minutes, they saw the flickering of small flames ignite in two of the mechanical outbuildings at the far end of the airfield near one group of tents. The flames grew quickly, their orange fury revealed the fleeing Kolandi as they dashed back into the shadows. Shouts and alarms sounded, awakening the camp. Emergency crews sprang into action advancing on the burning structures. Soldiers stumbled out of their tents and watched the excitement.

"There's our signal. Let's move." Maliche jumped up, leading the others in a race to the control room.

"Wait, Great One," Rilo blocked Maliche with one arm, her kital at the ready. "We will lead the way." Hurrying down the hillside, Rilo led them to the nearest building, an empty hangar. She peeked around the corner of structure. "This way. Hurry," she waved them forward and ran ahead between buildings to the next intersection. With a finger to her mouth, she ducked low and froze in the shadows.

Maliche, Ryma, and the rest copied her action just as a trio of soldiers ran passed them heading toward the fires. As they rounded the next corner, Rilo skidded to a halt and raised her kital. A dark shape stood in their path. She threw the kital sending its spinning blades at the Brin's head. With a swift movement the shadow ducked, shot out one hand catching the kital in the center.

"Hold on, girl," Nalot's voice called out of the darkness. "Save this toy for the enemy." He strolled up to them and returned her weapon, Seykel beaming at his side.

Rilo accepted the weapon, her eyes narrowed, studying Nalot. "You should have announced yourself. I could have killed you."

"Not today. I watched your approach. You know you flinch your elbow before you throw that thing don't you? May want to work on that."

Rilo stepped forward, standing nose to nose with Nalot. "Who are you to try to give me lessons?"

"That's enough," interrupted Maliche getting between the two. "Did you locate the communications center?"

Nalot winked at Rilo, and then walked back with Maliche. "It's over there," he said pointing toward the vicinity of the airstrip's control tower. "The building with the satellite array on top."

Maliche nodded, observing the low one story wooden structure. "Only three guards."

"Yeah, the rest took off to help with the fires and to chase the 'raiding party'. We should be clear if we hurry."

Sticking to the shadows, the group ran, stopping only once when two soldiers came around the corner behind them. The warriors bringing up the rear gave a warning cry and before the soldiers could fire their energy rifles, their chests each sprouted two arrows and three kitals embedded in their heads.

Retrieving their blades, Kitae, Seykel, and Rilo made a brief gesture waving their left hands in front of them, three fingers touching, the remaining two pointing straight, brought the two fingers to their mouths, muttered something in the language of the Kolandi, wiped the weapons off on their trouser legs. Rilo, resuming her position beside Nalot, gave him a wink. Four warriors carried off the bodies to hide them among the pallets of equipment alongside the building.

Their approach took them to the rear of the communications center. As planned, Maliche and Nalot used their disguises as Brin officers to distract the guards.

"You three," shouted Maliche as they came near. "Any sign of trouble here?"

The Brin soldiers came to attention, saluting with their fists across their chests, rifles held upright by their left legs.

"No sir," replied the corporal, highest ranking of the group. "Everything is—"

Seykel's kital sliced through his throat, cutting off the rest of his reply. At the same time, the other two soldiers collapsed, blood spurting from their throats as well. The three Skatak glanced at each other, made a quick gesture with their left hand, muttered the same words as before, wiped the red stain from their kitals, and motioned for the warriors to remove the corpses.

Once inside the empty foyer, Nalot, crest rising slightly, his head tilted, whispered to Seykel. "What is that thing you do over the bodies? Should we really be wasting our time over them?"

Seykel looked up at him, her eyes examining his face before deciding how to answer. "It is the Mitan, a prayer for their souls." She saw the lack of comprehension on his face. "They are soldiers performing their duty as they understand it. Even Brin soldiers are living beings with souls. To kill without forgiveness would be a terrible dishonor on ourselves."

"Time to move," Maliche whispered to the group. He gripped Nalot's shoulder with one hand. "You okay here?"

Nalot tipped his head toward Seykel. "With this deadly little bodyguard at my side, how can we lose? Get moving before somebody comes in here and raises the alarm."

With Rilo and Kitae in the lead, Maliche and Ryma safely in the center with the four young warriors protecting the rear, the party slowly worked their way down the long hallway to the computer room, the heart of the communication center. The brightly lit, slightly rounded passage contained several doors, but each attached room proved to be empty.

"Where is everyone?" asked Ryma.

"The night shift is still on duty," said Maliche in her ear. "The officers will still be sleeping in their quarters. There should only be one or two operators, possibly a maintenance worker, but not much else at this hour."

The sign on the fourth door to the right read MAIN COMPUTER.

"Let's try to take them alive," said Maliche. "These guys are probably more technicians than soldiers. I can erase their memories before we leave." He pointed to his head with one talon.

Rilo nodded her agreement, then, silently counting down with her fingers, opened the door and they all rushed in, weapons drawn and ready.

In the chilled room sat two Brin, each at a desk containing a monitor, keyboard, small lamp and a variety of stacked files and papers. Behind them stood three rows of large computers, panels of numbers and colored lights displayed their current operating status. On one wall hung a poster of some computer game fantasy character Maliche vaguely remembered from his days at the university battling strange creatures. The two Brin, dressed in green baggy jumpsuits with their names pinned on their chest looked up from their terminals, froze for a second, and then started to jump to their feet. One of them reached for the large blue alarm button on the wall nearest him. An arrow stuck into the wall inches from his outreached hand.

"Stay still and you won't be harmed," called out Maliche.

The two Brin remained frozen halfway between standing and sitting, glanced at each other, and then back to the bows armed and ready to be released into them.

"Anything you say... we don't want any trouble."

"That's right. We aren't soldiers like them other fellas. Just a couple of comp techs."

The two sat back down, hands raised, crests quivering.

Rilo took charge now, waving her kital at the Brin techs. "Move over there," she pointed to the far wall of the room, away from the computers.

"Yes, ma'am," they said in unison as they shuffled carefully to the indicated place, and sat on the floor, never removing their eyes from the curved blades aimed at them.

Without warning, a door on the far side of the room opened. A flash of sparks sprayed across the floor and the maintenance bot fell over, two arrows and Rilo's kital sprouted from its mechanical body, three wheels on its base spun and rotated spasmodically, then fell silent.

"Relax, everyone. Just a maintenance robot." He pointed to two of the warriors. "You two set up a perimeter down that hallway, so there are no more surprises."

The two men looked sheepishly at each other, kicked the machine as they passed it, and vanished through the door.

"Sorry, Great One. We're all a bit nervous." Rilo placed her foot on the maintenance bot's head and yanked her kital from its chest. She looked over at Kitae, shrugging as she wiped leaking lubricant from her weapon's blades.

"Your turn, Great One," said Kitae, rolling her eyes toward the ceiling as she led Maliche and Ryma to the terminals.

Maliche sat in the chair, closed his eyes and focused his attention. *"So what do I do?"*

"Keep your eyes closed, clear your mind, and place your talons over the keyboard. I'll take it from there."

As he followed the instructions, his mind filled with series after series of numbers, letters, and computer code he did not understand. Images of circuitry, schematics, and equations of fuel mixture ratios flashed by behind closed eyes. All the while, his blue nimbus grew brighter and enveloped the keyboard. Each of the computer banks began to glow bright blue as well. Maliche felt his heart rate soar. His nerves tingled almost painfully as the biocomputer's energy flowed through him. Lights flashed on the panels, displays raced through lines of code and charts too fast for the eye to follow.

"Done!"

The blue light diminished, absorbing back into Maliche's body and, as the last hint of the energy field faded, he gasped for air and collapsed to the floor. Slowly coming to, he felt Ryma's soft hands gently caressing his forehead. His eyes fluttered open to see her worried face gazing down at him.

"How long was I out?"

"We've only been here less than five minutes, Great One," she replied. "You collapsed only seconds ago. Are you all right? What went wrong?"

He mentally checked himself, and then sat up, extending one hand to the nearest warrior to help him to his feet. He reached back and winced as he felt the knot growing on the back of his head where he hit the edge of the terminal.

"Nothing went wrong. Everything is ready. We need to get out of here before the day shift arrives." His head swam as he rose, nearly dropping him to the floor again. The warrior who helped him up grabbed his arm with a strong grip while Nalot took hold of the other, settling him back into the chair.

"Steady there, boy," said Nalot. "Get your head on straight and then we can go. There's time still."

"*Sorry,*" said the voice in his head. "*The alterations took a bit more energy than I had first expected. Here, this should help.*"

Maliche felt a surge of strength flow through him. The room stopped spinning and the throb in his head vanished. "Thanks." He said out loud, forgetting to think the words.

"*Don't mention it. By the way, you shouldn't leave just yet. I came across some interesting information while I was inside the communications array. There's a surprise arriving for you at the main hangar. It might make getting back to First Town much easier.*"

"What sort of surprise?" he said aloud again jumping to his feet. He saw the confused faces of the others watching him. "Don't worry, my friend in here is telling me something is happening which might help us."

"*Don't ask questions and spoil my surprise. You'll know what to do when you see him.*"

Minutes later, after adjusting the comp techs' memories to forget everything about their visit, the party dashed outside into the chill morning air. The sun, still below the horizon, cast an orange brilliance against the sky. The soldiers had long since returned to their tents once the novelty of the fires and the raid were over. Only the clean-up crews remained at the burnt facilities, far too concerned with their efforts to notice Maliche and the others darting between buildings heading toward the main hangar. Even the arrival of an expensive private shuttle distracted them for only a moment.

As they watched from behind the maintenance shed across the way, they watched as the shuttle landed and taxied to the hangar entry. The engines shut down and the door opened.

Maliche's jaw dropped, his crest rose to full height. "That's Selan. What's he doing here?"

"From what I picked up back with the computers, your brother is the one in charge now. He has eliminated Raencert and convinced The Assembly he is the one to take charge of the mines. Apparently, they all think it is a miner's strike causing all the problems here. Your people are still oblivious to what is really happening."

A loud voice broke the still of the early morning as the group watched Selan and his four security guards walk over to the control tower. "Thirty minutes for morning chow! Repeat, thirty minutes for morning chow. All personnel with full packs and extra charge packs report to transport loading zones in sixty minutes. Repeat, sixty minutes." A series of blasting whoops followed the announcement, then only the noise of Brin soldiers rushing and complaining as they exited their tents and headed for the mess hall.

"Let's hide in here," Maliche said as he opened the door to the maintenance shed. "It doesn't look like it's used very often."

Once inside among the work benches, shelves of random machine parts, racks of tools large and small, and one mag-lev truck lifted up on supports, its engine parts laid out neatly on the concrete floor, Ryma approached Maliche.

"Your brother is here? Didn't he try to get you out of the prison? Maybe he's here to help?"

"Not that one," interrupted Nalot. "My instructions were to keep you hidden until he could settle accounts with Raencert, find the location of the Kolandi camps, and then bury you somewhere out in the middle of the desert. If he's in charge now, and that's what it looks like to me, he's here to watch his conquering army take off for victory."

Seykel listened to the conversation, a growing horror showed on her face. "But he is the Great One's brother. Surely he does not want his own flesh and blood dead."

Maliche took Seykel's face in his hands. "While many Brin, possibly most, are kind and generous folk, far too often those in power become lost to greed and will do anything to increase their power over others." He saw the tears start to gather in her eyes. "This is what we have come to stop. If we succeed, the Kolandi and the Brin will become one people whose future lies among the stars. We are here to stop my brother and others like him so those Brin who do strive for honor can rise up and join us."

She wiped her eyes and went to Nalot, nestling her face in his shoulder. "This is what you have come to believe as well?"

"Yes, I guess I have," he said, gathering her up in his arms, pulling her tight.

"All right, everyone, find somewhere comfortable to be for the next hour or so, but stay alert in case I'm wrong about this hiding place. We need to be ready to move once those ships take off."

Chapter Twenty-Six

As the sun began to rise in the morning sky, Maliche watched the soldiers assemble by platoons in the designated loading zones by each transport vessel. On a signal from the loudspeaker, they began boarding the ships. Hundreds of soldiers loaded for war, climbed onto dozens of ships in neat columns. Glancing up into the control tower, he saw Selan watching the spectacle through a pair of distance viewers.

"Are we sure there's no other way?"

"Not if you want to get out of this alive and free the Kolandi. Your brother is at the heart of all this now. Exposing him and his schemes is the quickest way to end the enslavement of the Kolandi. If it helps, he agreed to have you killed, not simply silenced."

Maliche closed his eyes and bowed his head.

He felt Ryma by his side, her hand seeking out his. "Are you sure this will work? I'm afraid for my people if something goes wrong."

"No need to worry. Opet and the others are evacuating the caverns as we speak, bringing your people to new locations. Even if we fail, the soldiers will find your homes empty."

"I pray you are right, Great One."

"It is not your people who will die today, Princess. It's mine. All those soldiers heading off to their deaths, and at my hand." He remained silent for a moment then squeezed her hand tight. "How does one say the Mitan?"

***

At last, the ships were fully loaded, hatches sealed, and ready for lift off. A warning signal blared from the loudspeaker. Dust flew up from the ships as they rose heavily into the sky, engines whining as they strained to lift the heavy loads.

"Get ready, everyone. We'll need to move fast once they've taken flight."

The others joined Maliche at the windows, holding their breath as the transports gained speed, rising higher and heading off toward the mountains.

In the distance, the ships looked like a swarm of cardis flying south for the winter. Then, in a burst of orange flame and smoke, the first ship exploded. Within seconds the rest of the armada, one after another, burst into flame. Long meteoric trails of smoke and debris flew from the fireballs filling the sky. Tons of rock, dirt, and wreckage burst from the craters blasted into the ground by the plummeting debris and remains of shuttles which, only seconds before, held thousands of Brin soldiers. Moments later, the shock wave of sound hit them in a powerful concussion, shattering many windows. Maliche and the others held their hands firmly over their ears to block out as much of the deafening noise as possible.

"That's it. Let's move," Maliche had to shout over the commotion of sirens and rescue shuttles as the base began to respond to the horror.

They ran in formation, heedless of the dumbfounded Brin staring in disbelief and shock at the catastrophe in the sky. In less than a minute, they burst through the control tower doorway, disabling the two guards, and charged up the stairs to the observation room. Hearing the commotion below, Selan's guards turned to see what was going on when three fell to the floor with kital rooted in their brains, the fourth grasped at the large knife protruding from his chest. Four Kolandi warriors, led by Danet and with bows bent, entered the room.

"Get on the floor now!" they shouted. "Do not resist or you will die."

Nalot, Kitae, and Rilo moved swiftly from one Brin to the next, checking them for weapons and gathering them into a group sitting on the wood floor at the far end of the room.

"All clear," called Nalot. "Come on in."

Selan started to rise, but a kick from Rilo took his legs out from under him, sending him crashing back to the floor.

"What is the meaning of this? Who are you? How dare you attack me! Do you know who I am?"

"Hello, brother dear. It's been a while. How are mother and father?" Maliche entered the room with Ryma at his side.

"Maliche?" Selan looked up at his older brother, eyes wide and brow furrowed in confusion. "What are you doing here?"

"You mean, why am I still alive?"

Selan tried to respond, but his mouth opened and closed without the words escaping.

"Don't look so shocked, brother. Your spy here," he pointed at Nalot, "had a change of heart. It seems you hired someone with a conscience, despite your best intentions, I'm sure." He turned his back on Selan and gazed out the windows at the flaming wreckage in the distance. "As for what I am doing here, I would think that would be obvious now."

Selan sputtered, trying to regain his composure. "You are responsible for this?"

Maliche continued to stare out at the carnage, Ryma's arm around his shoulder.

"You've betrayed your own people! You've destroyed our family!"

Spinning around and storming up to Selan, Maliche unleashed his fury. He grabbed Selan by the front of his suit and threw him across the room.

"No, Selan, that is your doing. You have participated in the enslavement of an entire people, lying to everyone about their existence, for your own profit. You have attempted to commit fratricide and then cover it up. You have abused your position in The Assembly to carry out your fraudulent deceptions." He drug Selan to the windows, forcing him to look at the huge column of smoke rising from the crash site. "You have killed all of those soldiers with your arrogance and greed. You are the traitor here, not me." He tossed Selan back to the floor, turning his back to him. "I am going to try to salvage what little honor is left in our family. This travesty ends now."

Selan stared at his brother, his face a study in horror. "You can't reveal what is going on here. You can't! Our entire economy will collapse if the truth comes out. We will never be able to obtain the resources we need to survive without the slaves working the mines. You will destroy us all."

"If our existence depends on the secrets and the enslavement of others, then maybe we deserve whatever happens to us. But I think you underestimate the citizenry. I believe there is still honor in the Brin. I believe our better nature will rise to the occasion and we will find a way to survive together." He took Ryma by the hands, gazing into her eyes. "Together we will become stronger than ever, as our ancestors hoped we would be."

Selan snorted, pointing a well-manicured talon at Maliche. "You are a hopeless romantic, brother. Naïve and blind to reality. Do you really believe the guilds will permit you to ruin us? Do you have even the faintest idea of how powerful we are?"

"It isn't the guilds, or the Assembly I have faith in. It is the people I trust and believe in. It is you who is the naïve one. The people hold the real power… and they will see justice is done. Even if it means having your head on a platter."

"You think you're smarter than all of us? You won't have a chance. The people will never know anything about any of this. We will stop you."

Nalot laughed out loud. "Good luck with that. From what I've seen, he's out maneuvered you every step of the way. Looks to me like you're the one who doesn't stand a chance."

Selan sulked as Rilo returned him to a far corner of the room. "Just to set the record straight, it was Raencert who ordered your death, not me. He blackmailed me into all of this. I wanted to keep you quiet, but he forced me to go along."

Maliche kept his back to his brother, his head hung low. "Maybe that was true at first, but you certainly took charge as soon as you were able to. When you did have control, you only made things worse. No, Selan, this is your doing, nobody else's."

***

The flight back to First Town proved uneventful, but a nervous time for the Kolandi onboard. Selan sat under guard in the rear of the craft while Maliche and Nalot did the flying. Before taking off, Maliche ordered the destruction of all communication equipment and any remaining transports in order to keep their arrival secret for as long as possible.

"So much water," said Opet as he stared out the portals. "How can there be deserts on a world with so much water?"

"We can discuss global weather patterns another time, my friend," Maliche said, chuckling slightly. "We're coming up to the coastline now, only a few more hours before we reach First Town."

Ryma and the others marveled at the scenes passing below. "Your mountains are so green here, not like ours at all. There must be enough food to feed hundreds."

"That's probably true, but our food comes from farms and ranches, not wild game. My people rarely go into the mountains except for recreation."

She pondered that thought as they flew over the foothills and out above the plains with its circular patches of irrigated green farms and rectangles of various shades of brown.

"Come up here, Ryma," called Maliche. "First Town is just over the horizon. We should be able to see it in a minute or so.

Ryma gripped Maliche's arm, her jaw dropping in amazement as she viewed the tall towers and vast reaches of buildings that were First Town. "Your people are truly amazing to be able to create such wonders. I thought you were telling tales to impress me, but now, I realize you were being modest. We have much to learn from you."

"And we have much to learn from you as well." He patted her hand, still gripping his arm. Time to let them know we are here." He touched the control pad to open his microphone.

"Control tower, this is Maliche Rocker, repeat, this is Maliche Rocker, code ID R2M1 requesting permission to land."

Static filled the speaker as the air controllers hesitated. "This is control tower chief, R2M1, please identify yourself again."

It's me, Chief, Maliche Rocker. The reports of my demise were mistaken. I have returned. Is the usual hangar landing pad available?"

Another hesitation followed. "Yes, R2M1, landing pad Rocker is available and awaiting your arrival. Let me be the first to congratulate you on your survival. I'm sure your family will be relieved to hear you are still with us."

"Roger that, Chief. I would prefer you hold off on notifying anyone official about my return. Is anyone from one of the news agencies around? I have something for them that will probably make them famous."

"There's always a few hanging out here somewhere. In fact, they've probably been monitoring our communications and on their way to your hangar already."

"Good. And can you have one of the limousine services send us the largest car they have. We need to take some guests to The Assembly."

"Can do, R2M1. We have your approach vectors clear. Welcome home."

Maliche maneuvered the vessel carefully over the landing pad outside the Rocker family hangar. Dust kicked up as they neared the ground causing the gathered reporters to grab their coats and shield their eyes. A gentle bump and the ship settled on its landing gear. Maliche and Nalot turned off the controls, unfastened their harnesses, and joined the others in the main compartment.

"Is everyone ready?"

Selan grabbed Maliche's arm with his bound hands, yanking on his sleeve. "Don't be a fool, Maliche. You'll bring ruin on us all."

Opet slapped Selan with the back of his hand, causing a slight trickle of blood to flow from the corner of his mouth.

Maliche scowled at his brother, then shook his head and turned toward the hatch, pressing the switch to open the door. "Let me go out first to prepare them," he said, looking back over his shoulder.

He stepped out into the daylight and electronic flashes and floodlights of the news cameras. A cacophony of shouted questions assaulted him as he appeared in front of the correspondents. He raised his arms in the air calling for their attention.

"Before I answer any questions, ladies and gentlemen, I have an important announcement. I'm sure you will have many more questions once I bring them out, but we must first address The Assembly. All your questions will be answered there."

Amid the muttering of the reporters, Maliche turned back to the ship's open hatch and lifted one hand. "May I present Princess Ryma of the Kolandi, and her entourage." The princess stepped into the light, tall, and regal in her formal gown, she paused for effect, then took Maliche's hand and walked out to stand beside him. Rilo and Kitae, and then Opet followed next. Each one took his or her place behind Ryma. Finally, Seykel and Nalot walked out, with Selan between them, his hands bound behind his back.

Shouted questions erupted from the reporters, recording equipment clicked, hummed, and flashed at a furious rate. Broadcast drones circled madly around the group, sending images of the Kolandi throughout First Town. The mob surged forward, each with microphones raised.

Maliche stood in front of the princess, held up both arms, and called for order. "As I said, everyone, all of your questions will be answered at The Assembly. All I can say now is that, yes, these are representatives of the Kolandi, a people we thought were long extinct. And I have taken my brother into custody for treason. Now please, our transportation has arrived and we must leave you for now."

As the mag-lev vehicle arrived, the driver inserted it between the reporters and Maliche, allowing them to enter without having to force their way through the small mob.

***

After fighting their way through an immense crowd of onlookers and more reporters, with the assistance of Assembly security forces, Maliche and the others now sat in the main chamber of The Assembly awaiting the arrival of the leadership. News of their arrival had reached everyone with a vid receiver and it appeared the entire city had rushed to The Assembly building to get a glimpse of the princess and her companions.

"Are you sure the broadcast drones will get their signals out? Nobody here will block them?"

"Come now, Give me a little credit. I disabled all security firewalls and interference twenty minutes ago. These proceedings will be seen by everyone."

A door opened behind the curved bench in front of them and out stepped a middle aged Brin in black trousers with deep blue formal coat and tie. His sash flashed with medals and ribbons, each noting some service or honor. He carried a long metal pole with a golden sphere on top. He pounded the floor four times with the staff and called out in a baritone voice which rang throughout the chamber. "All rise, the council is in session. Give honor to the council before you."

He stepped aside allowing the councilmen to enter. Two of the levitating video drones rushed to film the grand entrance while the remaining four continued to transmit images of Maliche and the Kolandi.

Seven of the eleven councilmembers took their seats, each wearing their dark blue robes of office, each one emblazoned with embroidery depicting their particular office and rank. Fejf, leader of The Assembly, dressed in the forest green robe of the highest office entered last, but rounded the bench and strode to Maliche, extending his arms in greeting. A large smile broke through his traditionally stern visage as they embraced.

"We thought you dead, boy." He pulled back, returning to his persona of head of The Assembly. "I'm sure you are prepared to explain all of this," he waved a hand toward the Kolandi seated behind the tables. "And to explain why your brother, a leading member of this council was brought here like a prisoner."

Maliche stood tall, squaring his shoulders as he faced his father. "Yes, sir. Everything will be made clear. I'm afraid we are in for a rough time, though. You, and all of us, have some difficult decisions to make."

Fejf eyed his son, scrutinizing him for a moment, and then nodded in approval. "You've changed, son. You have a strength about you I've not seen before. Don't disappoint me." He spun on his heels and took his seat in the center of the high council bench, and nodded to the herald.

"Attention all present, these proceedings are now in session. May The Eternal give all here wisdom and compassion." He pounded the floor again and took his place standing by the back wall.

***

Several days of hearings followed. As the days passed, the galleries filled to capacity with dignitaries from each of the guilds, representatives from each district, and visitors curious to witness the unprecedented events unfolding in the chamber. Maliche presented the Kolandi and each took turns telling their story to the audience. He, and the others, each presented evidence supporting Maliche's claims. DNA samples collected from Ryma and the others confirmed their identities. Hundreds of questions posed by members of the high council gradually revealed the treachery of the mining guild, Raencert's leadership in the Kolandi enslavement and Selan's complicity, and attempted takeover of events

In addition, the involvement of most of the guilds, and an overwhelming majority of councilmembers, even many on the high council itself, were implicated by either direct participation in cover-ups or by purposeful denial of the travesty over the years.

"Ladies and gentlemen of the council," called out Maliche as he rose to speak on the final day of the hearings. "You have heard the evidence, and we all are well aware of the potential consequences. Even now, reports of riots and outrage from the citizenry reach us as the people have learned the truth."

Shouts of anger and dismay filled the room as representatives, guildsman, and visitors, leapt to their feet in outrage. Fejf rapped the bench with his stone sphere calling for order. As the room stilled, Maliche continued.

"Undoubtedly, many here will be removed from their current positions. We have shaken the very roots of our government. Only time will tell if we survive this or not, but I have an offer from the Kolandi which may help stabilize matters in the long term. We propose an alliance between our two people. An alliance which will benefit and bring prosperity to both our species."

More outbursts filled the chamber forcing Fejf to once again call for order. "We will hear your proposal in private, Maliche." He rapped the stone sphere again. "The bailiff will now clear the chamber."

Two weeks of negotiations between the Kolandi and the high council ensued.

Maliche read from the document finalizing the treaty between the two peoples. "And we are, therefore, agreed that the Kolandi will be sovereigns of their own lands on the Eastern Continent, and all Brin claims are renounced."

Ryma nodded her approval as she sat across from Fejf, arms folded across her chest. "Including all the mines and equipment associated with their operations. I want that point made absolutely clear as well."

"Yes, of course. The Brin will provide technical and advisory support until such time as the Kolandi are secure in their ability to operate the mines without assistance. In return, the Kolandi will provide all mineral resources required by the Brin at mutually acceptable rates of exchange, to be decided during regularly scheduled annual summits."

Ryma held up her hand to interrupt. "And what about the matter of Brin settlers?"

Maliche ran his talon down the document a few paragraphs to locate the provision. "No Brin will be allowed access to the Eastern Continent for a span of five years. All those currently residing in Kolandi territory will be peacefully removed by combined Brin – Kolandi security personnel. After said five years, any Brin wishing to visit Kolandi lands for employment, tourism, education, or homestead, must complete the Kolandi visa requirements and submit to Kolandi supervision until deemed benign."

The reading continued for another hour with only minor corrections. "Thank you ladies and gentlemen. We have a treaty. Now, on to other matters."

One by one, they brought in guildsman and council members to negotiate their removal from office. Some would require public trials, but most agreed to resign their positions. An emergency election was set up to take place in a few months, allowing time to recruit replacement candidates and provide them the time to gather a constituency.

Chapter Twenty-Seven

During the weeks that followed, the courts filled with the prosecution of those involved in the heinous crimes. Everyone's attention, though, focused on the upcoming trial of Selan Rocker.

Three days before the trial, Selan sat at the dinner table of his home in First Town. He scratched at the site on his arm where they had injected the locator beacon before his release from his holding cell in the prison.

"Nedia, where are the children? Aren't they coming down to dinner?"

"No, dear. I don't want them exposed to all this publicity. We can't even walk out the front door without dozens of onlookers and reporters shouting questions and taking our photos. It's disgraceful. I sent them off to my father's place this morning to get them away from it all."

"I miss them. It would be comforting to have them around now."

She poured their wine and brought him his glass, swirling the red liquid as she set it in front of him. Returning to her chair at the far end of the table, she watched her husband, chin resting on steepled talons.

"You probably should have thought of that before you got us involved in this mess, dear. Now eat your appetizers, so the servants can serve the meal before it gets cold." She attached her talon clip utensils and speared a piece of bread.

He took a long gulp of the wine, emptying the glass and setting it back on the table. Placing the talon utensils on his fingers, he jabbed at a piece of fruit and tossed it in his mouth.

"I still don't know how Maliche..." His heart stuttered in his chest, gave one strong beat, then began racing, cutting off the rest of his sentence. A look of panic filled his face as he clutched at his chest. "Nedia, something's wrong... call the doctor."

Nedia looked up from her plate, smiling as she watched him. Calmly removing her talon utensils, she stood up and sedately walked over to him. Leaning in close with one hand on his back, she whispered in his auricle.

"No, dear, nothing is wrong. Everything is going exactly as planned."

"Nedia," he gasped, his face reddening. "Call the doctor… my heart."

"You're not listening, dear. I said everything is just fine. The poison I put in your wine is working exactly as promised."

Selan grasped at his collar, trying to loosen it.

"You see, dear, I couldn't allow you to continue after what you did."

Selan tried to stand, but collapsed back into his chair, knocking over several goblets and bowls as his arm swept out groping for support. "What do you mean? Everything I've done is for us and the children. Please… help me."

She sat sideways in her chair, looking down her nose at Selan's struggles, her arms folded across her chest. "You killed the finest man I've ever known. Raencert gave us everything and you poisoned him. Poetic justice, don't you think?"

Gasping and clutching his chest as the pains intensified, Selan gaped at his wife. "Raencert was going to destroy us. He was only out for himself. Don't do this… the children…"

"Oh, no, dear. He would not have destroyed us… only you. You failed him. I loved him… and he loved me. We had it all planned out. After you were disgraced and in prison, I would divorce you. After a respectable time passed, he and I would marry." She laughed at Selan's look of shock. "Ahhh, now you finally understand. I haven't loved you in years, Selan. You had promise once, but Raencert proved to be the real power. I've been his mistress and spy for quite some time now. Your failed attempt to take control and destroy him threatened not only us, but my entire family by extension. I will not allow your failure to stain my children's future."

She walked around the corner of the long table and pulled up a chair next to Selan as he gasped for air, trying to call out for help, but managing no more than weak yelps.

"This will appear as a normal heart attack. Who would doubt the stress you have been under after all that has happened? The doctors will confirm the existence of a previously undiagnosed weakness in the arteries. The trial will never happen, so nobody will know the full extent of your culpability. I will inherit your estate and the children will be well cared for, even if the future they once had is gone."

His last sight was of his wife strolling back to her seat at the other end of the table. The last sound he heard was of Nedia calling out in panic for help.

***

Three months later, after Selan's hasty funeral and the general elections concluded, the wedding of Maliche Rocker and Princess Ryma captured everyone's attention. During her many appearances over the communications network, she had not only impressed the Brin with her wit and intelligence, but reassured them of her sincere desire to become strong allies. The news media played it up as a sign of great tidings for the future, and the tensions which had first erupted relaxed as confidence grew and those responsible were seen to suffer the consequences of their actions. The ceremony, held in the Savior's Memorial in front of Karm's obelisk, combined the rituals of both cultures.

A deep violet nimbus surrounded Maliche as he entered the Memorial and stood before the marble tomb. An intense sadness filled his mind. *"What's wrong?"*

"Old memories of long lost friends. It has been a long time since I was last here. I was just reminiscing is all."

Maliche walked up to the obelisk, reached out and touched the cold stone with its myriad of silver inlays. A jolt shot down his arm as the violet light returned to its normal blue color and surrounded the entire obelisk. The light shown like a beacon as it fired up into the sky for all to see.

"What is that all about?"

"Paying homage to your ancestor, and letting a few other friends know I have finally accomplished my task. They may want to stop by for a visit sometime to check on our progress."

Princess Ryma strode regally down the aisle, preceded by Rilo, followed by Kitae and Seykel. Maliche watched her procession with Opet, Danet, and Nalot at his side. The Brin celebrant, dressed in his most opulent bejeweled white raiment, told of the great history of the Rocker clan and blessed the couple with prayers to The Eternal.

"As in the first days of Jontar, Maripa, and Karm, whose memories we honor and stand before today, we seek to join two people as one. The will of our ancestors is honored at last."

The ancient Homsan, flown in specifically at Ryma's request, recited the tales of the Kolandi back to the days of great promise with the first Brin.

"The joining of our two people was foretold by the Sky People long ago," he proclaimed. "And now, the prophecies are fulfilled."

Bracelets were exchanged to signify their commitment to each other and both officiates declared as one their final blessings and the presentation of the new pair to family, friends, and invited dignitaries.

Thousands gathered outside waited and watched as the famous couple exited the Memorial. Maliche, in his finest forest green robes of his new office as leader of the reformed assembly as the people now called it, and Ryma, resplendent in her gossamer gown of fine linen overlaid with blue gemstones, stood at the top of the steps waving to the cheers. In the distance, barely heard over the adulations, a small gathering of protestors proclaimed their opposition to the supposedly unholy joining of two different species. As always, Rilo and Kitae stood close behind their princess with Seykel at their side. Behind Maliche stood Nalot, Opet, and Danet, smiling and clapping each other on the back.

"Are you ready, my wife?" asked Maliche as he took her hand.

"Yes, my husband." She smiled at him, clasping his hand tighter.

That evening, in the most expensive suite of the city's finest hotel, their exploration of each other culminated in a passion far greater than either knew was possible. As they joined together in lovemaking, a rainbow of colors burst from them, and shot through them. Their bodies vibrated with energy, every nerve aflame. Exhausted at the conclusion, they collapsed, senseless, in each other's embrace.

Late the next morning, as they strolled through the nearby park, a flash of light lit up the sky above them and a long, spear-like silvery metallic vessel appeared.

"Ah, we have guests." Maliche's body radiated with an intense blue light.

"Do not fear," rang a voice from the vessel. "We are the Skae and we have returned."

Moments later, as the gathering crowd gave way, the Skae ship landed. A seam, appearing as if by magic, revealed a hatch which slid upward as a series of steps lowered to the ground. In the dark opening stood the tall bluish frame of one of the Skae, except he stood slightly stooped over, leaning on a staff, and his skin was blotchy and wrinkled with age. His appearance exactly as the images in Karm's memorial described. His skin-tight clothing shimmered a rainbow of colors in the sunlight.

Maliche, with Ryma at his side, approached the vessel. He felt a great outward surge of energy toward the alien who stood motionless, eyes closed as if thinking to himself.

The alien opened his large eyes and spoke to Maliche. "Ah, I understand. We had given you up as lost when we did not hear from you for so long. Other matters prevented us from returning to check on you, but we rejoiced when we received your signal. My name is Bolt."

***

Over the next year, Bolt and several other Skae, visited both the Brin and the Kolandi, offering their help and guidance with their technical skills and the scientific advancements of thousands of years of space exploration, and then vanishing for weeks at a time. Maliche sat in council with his closest advisors in his private chambers at The Assembly.

"As I understand it, the Skae received my biocomputer's signal several years from now, but traveled back in time to the coordinates it gave them. Apparently, the stories of Karm being a time traveler are not fantasy after all."

The new agricultural guild master reached out with both hands, palms upturned. "And they are giving us this advanced technology because they need our help? How can they possibly need us?"

"I don't pretend to understand all the answers to this yet," Maliche replied. "From what I do gather, the Skae have been at war for an eternity with a race called the Gorvin. I've accessed everything the biocomputer has about them and they appear to be a relentless destroyer of worlds. Apparently, the Kolandi were originally allies and partners of the Skae, until the Gorvin unleashed a horror here, nearly destroying the Kolandi. Those old ruined cities out in the wilderness we have heard about, before we tore them down, were built by the Kolandi at the height of their power."

"And now they need our help to defeat their enemy? Why wait until now?"

"Apparently, something in our genetic make-up counteracts a plague agent in the Kolandi DNA which has, so far, prevented the Skae from enlisting their help. Only our DNA combining with theirs will cure them."

"So, we were a breeding experiment? That's why they brought us here?" asked the ranching guild master.

"That is my understanding, but the threat of the Gorvin in this part of the galaxy, in their time, has increased and the Skae are losing the war. They need our help... or at least, will need the help of our future generations. Their time-traveling frames of reference get me all turned around."

"If we mate with the natives, you mean," interrupted the guildsman.

Maliche glared at him. "Do you have a problem with that?"

"Me personally? Not at all. But you must be aware of those who are opposed to such unions."

Maliche waved his hand dismissively. "A fringe group. Nothing to concern ourselves with. They'll come around once they see how gentle and honorable the Kolandi are."

"If my ancient history lessons serve me correctly, isn't that what our ancestors on Dyan'ta said about The Faith movement when it began? Can we really afford to ignore them?"

The door burst open and in rushed a breathless page. "It's time, your excellency. You're needed at the hospital."

"Excuse me, my wife needs me." Maliche ran out of the room, down the stairs and into the waiting mag-lev car in front of the building. The escort sirens blared as they accelerated away.

***

"It's a fine healthy boy, Maliche," said Nalot, slapping Maliche on the back. "Takes after his mother, except for the small crest there."

The front room overflowed with guests come to celebrate the new arrival. Piles of gifts grew in the corner. Servants hurried as best they could with trays of drinks and food for the visitors.

Maliche smiled at his old friend. "Let's go out back where we can talk."

"Been a long strange road we've traveled," said Nalot once they were alone.

"It has indeed, my friend," Maliche replied, sitting down on the stoop, motioning for Nalot to join him. "I can never thank you enough for everything. I owe you my life, and Ryma's as well. And yet there is so much still to do."

Nalot grunted and looked back over his shoulder as Seykel came to sit beside him. "About that..." he struggled to find the words. "There's something I need to do first." He took Seykel's hand in his lap.

Maliche examined the pair, tilting his head in question.

"There's a certain path I need to travel, and a promise to them folks back in the caverns I need to keep before I can go any further."

"You aren't going soft on me now, are you?" Maliche grinned.

"Just thinking I finally found a home."

Maliche stood on the lowest step of the porch, eye-to-eye with the pair. He clasped Nalot's shoulders with a strong grip. "I wish you all the best, my friend." Turning to Seykel, he reached out one hand, taking hers. "Promise me you'll bring him back alive?"

She smiled, lighting up her entire face. "I promise, but only if you promise to stand as his witness, and bring my princess back home for our joining."

Later that evening, after the guests left, the eight companions said their farewells.

Ryma and Maliche watched from the doorway of their home as Rilo and Kitae, who would never leave their princess's side, hugged the others as they got into the mag-lev taking them to the shuttle station.

As they watched the vehicle depart, they held each other close.

"Are you ready for all of this?" he asked her,

"As long as you are with me, I am."

Epilogue

"Has it been five years already?" Ryma asked her husband as she prepared the birthday celebrations for their son. She reached down and scooped up the baby crawling underfoot, and deposited her on Maliche's lap.

In the years following the Great Transformation, as the people now called the upheaval, Maliche and Ryma had carved out a working alliance between the two cultures. The Kolandi held all the rights to the eastern continent and all it contained. The Brin maintained the rights to purchase the minerals produced by the mines at strictly and jointly controlled prices. The Kolandi granted limited homesteading rights to some of the Brin after a lengthy application process, and many Kolandi now walked the streets of First Town, and other cities in the western continent. Maliche always took a double check whenever he spotted a Kolandi youth (few elders ever visited the western cities) in Brin attire strolling down the street. There was still much to accomplish and much diplomacy to carry out, but as time went on, the two people were growing to accept one another and greater numbers of mixed couples and families could be seen on both continents.

"We still need to talk about the southern mine shipping contracts," she called from the kitchen. "Don't think for a minute I'm going to let them steamroll me into a corner on it. We still need those guarantees."

"Save it for the office, my love. Enjoy the party." He stood up to answer the door, swinging his two-year-old daughter through the air as he went, to her immense delight.

"Bolt! A wonderful surprise as always, my friend. Come in." He stepped aside. Allowing the tall alien to enter. Leaning heavily on his staff, looking weary, Bolt no longer had to bend over to enter a Brin home.

"Thank you, Maliche. I cannot stay long, but I wanted to greet the first of our new family on his birthday, and leave him this token of our esteem." He pulled a small package out of his pocket. "Where is the boy?"

"Jontar, come here for a moment. Someone has come to visit you."

The youngster banged down the curving stairs from his room on the second level, jumped the last three steps, bounced off the rounded wall and careened into the front room.

"Hello, Sir Bolt. How are you today?" Jontar reached out to take the present.

"I am doing well for such an old one as myself. Are you enjoying your birthday?"

The youth, barely containing his excitement, remembered his manners. "Yes, sir. May I open this now?"

"Of course you may," said Bolt, ruffling the boy's small crest.

As Jontar ran off to another part of the room to open his gift, Bolt watched, his face seemed puzzled.

"Is something wrong?" asked Maliche.

"The child seems unusually advanced in his ability to converse, yet I do not detect any signs of the biocomputer in him. Was the transfer unsuccessful?"

"He is extremely intelligent for his age. The geneticists are examining his DNA to see if the hybridization process is responsible, or if he is just a statistical anomaly. You are correct, though. The biocomputer shows no interest in him. Perhaps it cannot adapt to Jontar's nervous system."

"And what does the biocomputer say about it?"

"That's the strange thing. It doesn't tell me anything at all. It's as if it does not even understand the question. Should we be concerned?"

Bolt thought for a moment. "I do not think you need to worry. The child seems perfectly healthy. I will look into the matter, though. The device has been around for quite some time now. It may need an adjustment."

"I don't think that would be necessary. It operates normally for everything else."

"Very well, then. I do have other business to attend to, so I will take my leave of you now."

Maliche held the door for him and waved goodbye as the elderly Skae bent nearly in two as he entered the mag-lev car.

"Did he leave already?" asked Ryma as she came into the room. "We were in the middle of making the desert and just finished."

"Yes, he said he had other matters to attend to and couldn't stay."

"Too bad, I was looking forward to talking to him about your ancestors. He always has such fascinating stories about them, and how he raised Karm and brought him back in time to your planet to save everyone. What an incredible people they are."

Young Jontar walked over to them and looked up at their faces. His head tilted with eyes wide in wonder. "Don't you know about them?"

Maliche returned the boy's gaze. "About who, son?"

"About the Skae. Don't you know?"

Ryma knelt down to be at eye level with her child. "Know what, dear?"

"That they're lying. They lie about everything."

Empyrean

Book 3

The Brin Archives

Prologue

"High Commander, the final reports are in. Our casualties on Sharta C are devastating. A complete loss." Zeph stood at attention, his thin blue arm extended, presenting the transparent-green file cylinder. His wrinkled and stained blue-and-silver Skae uniform revealed the strain he and the rest of his team had been under for the past three days.

High Commander Asam stood gazing out the broad, curving window atop the Imperial Space Command Center. His view of the city and the orange sun rising over snow-capped mountains beyond usually gave him great satisfaction, but not today. As he studied the soaring transparent magnesium and carbon-alloy filament towers, he marveled at the beauty of the flowing forms and sheer poetry of their design. The specially treated glass-like material reflected a constantly-changing kaleidoscope of colors as the sun's angle changed throughout the day. Seriph, the Skae home world, certainly displayed the epitome of grace and power in the entire galaxy. But the air, once sweet and nourishing, now tasted foul, tainted by the mixed scent of despair, failure, and disbelief of those who occupied the room.

"Are the earlier reports confirmed?"

"I'm afraid so, sir."

Asam turned the cylinder over in his hand. "So ends four hundred years of peaceful co-existence with the Gorvin." Waving one hand in a sweeping gesture over the view of masses of workers traveling the tube works, he sighed and his smooth blue head sagged. "Their lives will never be the same, and neither will ours."

In the history of Skae exploration, no other race had proven to be so difficult. Once great allies, they had exchanged political and scientific knowledge freely for generations. Hostilities began only after tense, sometimes violent disagreement over plans to capture the energy of a nearby star. Despite all assurances, the Gorvin persisted in their misguided belief that the risk of attempting to control such power was too great. All attempts at Skae negotiation were rebuffed. Diplomatic vessels were fired upon, some destroyed completely. Now Sharta C was gone.

Asam closed his eyes, lifted a canister of freshly scented pressurized air to his nostrils, a common delicacy among the Skae, especially those of higher rank, and inhaled deeply. A burst of calming aromatics helped him focus. *How dare those insolent fools oppose us. After all we have done for them and the rest of the galaxy. We have shown them nothing but mercy and generosity. This is how they repay our kindness.*

Asam returned to his desk and motioned for Zeph to approach. "Are the fleet commanders aware of the situation?"

"Yes, High Commander. I personally sent out the alert as soon as we received the reports. They are awaiting our orders now."

"Very well. I will review the information and have the Modiri's orders relayed to the fleet before the evening meal. Leave me now. You know what needs to be done." He adjusted the flowing sleeve of his uniform, and with a wave of one long-fingered blue hand, dismissed his subordinate. *I only hope the high priestess will allow me to redeem my unforgivable failure. The Modiri are harsh in their judgements, but could even they have foreseen this development?*

"Yes, High Commander. I will see that everyone is ready for fleet launch." Zeph crossed his arms over his chest, palms open, in salute, turned on his heels with military precision and exited. The ornately-etched door slid closed automatically, its clear panels turning opaque as Asam pressed a contact on his desk.

Asam stared at the data cylinder for a moment. Then his dark violet eyes lifted and he scanned his private office. The design never failed to impress him. Not a straight line to be seen. Intricate loops and swirls of the furniture added beauty to their function. Everything seemed to soar toward the heavens. The subtle colors only added to the ethereal effect.

His gaze returned to the cylinder and he slid it into the round receptacle. Leaning toward the monitor, he stared into the scanner for retinal verification and, due to the high level of security required for this data, scraped his finger over the DNA collector. Three seconds later the screen lit up, divided into four sections. Asam read the printed statistics of casualty figures while simultaneously following the video feed of the first responders to the Sharta C disaster. The numbers were staggering. Millions of lives lost. Entire cities leveled. The videos held scenes of smoldering and burning rubble strewn with bodies. The sky was dark with clouds of dense smoke from the fires still burning out of control. It was far worse than he feared. The entire planet lost, all military defenses destroyed, and nearly all civilians killed in a matter of hours. The Gorvin were brutal and thorough in their attack.

Two hours later, Asam leaned back in his chair, long thin fingers rubbing his eyes to relieve the strain. *How could this have happened? We've negotiated treaties with thousands of worlds. Never have any retaliated so fiercely. The Gorvin are a heartless civilization to be sure, but how could we have misread them so badly? Now I must send thousands to their deaths because of our lack of foresight... or were we getting soft after so many easy negotiations?*

The High Commander opened file after file and considered the fleet under his command. He analyzed troop dispersal among the allied worlds, location, number, and armament of all battle cruisers and support craft, tactical assessments of Gorvin facilities on allied planets, all the necessary data to put together a retaliatory force. As he completed the last of the timetables coordinating all of his forces, he checked for flaws or missing details. In an operation of this scale, even a minor miscalculation could spell another disaster, one that could possibly lead to his disgrace. Satisfied, he encrypted the file and waited for it to encode on a new cylinder, which he set with a red designation indicating Modiri eyes only.

Taking a deep breath, he pressed the communication panel pad, giving him a direct line to the Modiri. Almost instantly, the electronic glow of a holographic image began to take shape, hovering above his console. The image resolved into the form of a beautiful young female with large grey eyes and pale blue skin, robed in shimmering elegance with a fabric so fine and sheer it barely hid the curves of her form. The soft, musical tones of the Modiri prelate voice answered. Only the prelates, the order of Modiri second only to the priestesses, would speak directly with anyone outside the palace except in the most extreme emergencies. "Yes, High Commander Asam?"

His back stiffened automatically. Even one of his years and distinction dared not show anything but the utmost respect to any Modiri, even one who could possibly be his granddaughter, although it was often impossible to tell a Modiri's age. The females could live a thousand years or more, if the legends were true. "I have the plans for our retaliation against the Gorvin ready, Ma'am."

He watched as the speaker for the crystal tower checked with one of The Sisters who apparently stood just off screen. He was not quite able to pick out the words, but he knew better than to attempt listening in on any discussion between The Sisters. "Very well, Asam. Send us your plans. We will ask Providence for their success. If Providence wills, we will give our blessings and you may proceed."

"Thank you, Prelate. We pray Providence looks favorably on us all."

"But be aware, Asam," The prelate's voice took on a sharp edge. "The Reña will not smile upon failure. You have forced us to suffer one great humiliation. Do not fail us a second time. You have served us well... until now. It would sadden us greatly to lose one such as yourself."

"Yes ... yes, Prelate. You may assure the Reña of our ultimate victory over those ungrateful degenerate Gorvin." Asam's voice caught as he contemplated the cost of losing the war. "I will not fail you again." The image above his communication panel went dark as the prelate cut the connection.

**

Two days later, Asam stood on the bridge of his command ship, watching his crew prepare for cosmic string linkage. Far below, Seriph, their beautiful home world, shone like a jewel in the blackness of space. Her single moon glistened in the distance. With a pass of his hand over the controls in front of him, Asam brought the bright orange glow of the string field protecting their planet into view. His long, lean blue fingers, knuckles only slightly protesting with age, entered the coordinates for their destination. With the press of a key, a single cosmic string lit up amid the thousands surrounding them.

"String acceleration compensators at maximum, High Commander. We are ready for linkage." Assam's second awaited his final order to connect the ship to the cosmic string that would take them across hundreds of light-years in a matter of days, deep into Gorvin territory.

"String linkage agreed," Asam replied as he sat in his command chair and checked all panel lights.

The first of a hundred vessels, Asam's ship shuddered with the acceleration. An electric tingle raised tiny prickles, known as string flesh, on his arms and the back of his neck. "Providence, let this war be a short one."

Chapter One

"Jontar Rocker, first-born of Maliche Rocker and Ryma, Imperial Princess of the Kolandi, you stand accused of murder and treason. How do you plead?"

Largest and most ornate of the judiciary floors of the tower, the central courtroom was filled to capacity. Dignitaries from each of the guilds filled the first several rows, those offering the best views, while minor officials and those regular citizens who had waited for hours hoping to gain admittance occupied the rest. Even the recently upgraded air refreshers could not quite eliminate the bouquet of so many packed into the room on such a hot summer day. Spotlights bathed the semi-circular carved wood bench of the judges as well as the prosecutor's and defendant's tables. Twelve hover-bots, five more than normally allowed due to the intense interest in this case, flew overhead, recording images and commentary from many of the attendees for posterity. The court's vidcams, also connected to the public network, focused on the judges, prosecutor, and defendant.

Robed in their ceremonial finest, the Assembly judges tensed with silence. They strained forward in their chairs to hear young Jontar's response to the charges. After knowledge of the crime reached the public, opinion split sharply down the middle of the population. Half could not believe that one of their beloved Rockers, the almost mythical family known to all, the esteemed leaders of their community, with a few notable exceptions, since their beginnings on this planet, could possibly have committed such an atrocity as patricide. How could a son, even if he was one of those strange Kolbri halflings, kill Maliche, the most renowned Rocker since The Founders? The other half, mostly those from families jealous of the Rockers' power and sway over the populace, snickered behind assumed masks of concern. They enjoyed witnessing the fall of ones so highly placed.

All eyes turned toward the young Kolbri, offspring of a Brin and Kolandi mated pair, standing in the dock before them.

Jontar Rocker stood firm, head held high as he announced his plea. "Not guilty, honored assemblypersons. Not guilty by reason of superior motive." His bright, clear eyes held firm on the judges before him, a contradiction from the somewhat rumpled appearance of his tailored green suit and expensive, if scuffed, boots. He displayed slightly disheveled, sparse crest feathers typical of many Kolbri, although some inherited more of the physical features of their Kolandi parent.

The room burst into a roar of chaos. Shouts both in support and in condemnation of Jontar filled the echoing chamber. Half a dozen spherical hover-cams rushed forward, maneuvering for the best position. Each controller hoped to obtain the most sensational images of this moment for their broadcast. The competition for ratings on this spectacle was intense. At first, the judges had hoped to keep the proceedings, at least these preliminaries, behind closed doors. Public outcry and political pressure forced them to open it up for all to bear witness. A few hover-cams closed in on Ryma Rocker, bereaved widow and mother of the accused. She sat wrapped in violet garments of mourning, face hidden by veils, but still maintaining the aura of dignity and authority familiar to anyone who had encountered her.

Thel Haytk, new Head Minister of the Assembly and presiding judge, temporarily serving in the post vacated by Maliche's untimely death, pounded an intricately carved metallic orb on the table. The resounding crack, and sparks which flew with each impact, called for attention.

"Order in these chambers! Order at once!" She glared around the room. "This court will come to order and you will conduct yourselves with the decorum and solemnity due this tragic proceeding or I will have the courtroom cleared and we will continue behind closed doors."

The audience regained their composure, and those who had stood to argue their points with others took their seats again. Only a few required the assistance of the officers of the court, and of those two were removed, one of them to the infirmary for treatment of a broken wrist incurred while one citizen guest tried to argue his point with somewhat more vehemence than allowed in the courtroom.

Thel Haytk turned her attention to the defendant's table and, in a loud and clear voice, continued the ritual opening statements. "Very well, Jontar Rocker, since you plead not guilty by virtue of superior motive, it is your task to convince this assembly of the truth of your motives as well as the necessity for them. Are you prepared to proceed?"

"I am, Madame. May I call my witnesses?"

Haytk nodded and several individuals, a mixed group of Brin and Kolandi, were ushered in from a side chamber to take their places before the bench. Ryma stood and took her place beside Nalot in the center of the group. Once seated, the judge motioned for aides to step forward. Each carried an inverted brass bowl. Dozens of electrodes covered the interior of the bowls while holographic broadcast antennae sat attached to the top surface.

"Are each of you prepared to submit yourselves to the veracity probe? Once agreed to, the probes will search out your memories and project them for us to witness. Those actual memories of events asked for by the defense will be sought out in your minds and shown to us all. You cannot hide them. You cannot alter them. All your memories of events you were party to personally, as well as those related to you by others, will be revealed. Things told to you in private confidence will be exposed. Though these latter will be admitted as evidence, they will be admitted only as hearsay and will not be subject to the full weight of personal memory. Do you submit?"

"We submit," all the witnesses responded together as one.

"So let it be. Place the probes on the witnesses and let us begin."

A hazy, mist-like light grew in the air above the witnesses as the probes activated. Jontar Rocker took a deep breath, exhaled heavily and stepped to his place in front of the witness bench.

"Ladies and gentlemen of the court, it is my intention to show this esteemed gathering the truth of my plea. I did not undertake the murder of my father without suffering long and hard over the decision. Though it cost me great personal pain, for I did love my father, I believed I had no choice but to end his life in order to save us from ruin. Much of what I will reveal here today was known only to a few, but many rumors of his debauchery and scandalous recklessness have been reported. The rumors only hinted at the depths of my father's depravity at the end. He lusted for personal power. Greed overcame his once-philanthropic nature. He cared not for anyone save himself and was about to embark on grand schemes of self-aggrandizement which would have resulted in the abolition of this very assembly, making himself the sole and unapproachable Emperor of Kodut."

A general murmur among the audience grew as they realized the impact of this statement. The thought that Maliche Rocker, the icon of justice after his involvement in the Kolandi affair, had been preparing to overthrow the Assembly. Vid-cams caught the surprised expressions on some faces and the knowing smirks on others. A bang of Judge Haytk's gavel warned them all to silence.

Jontar paced back and forth in front of the bench as he spoke, his hands alternately gesturing to the Assembly judges and clasping firmly behind his back. "To begin, I call on the memories of my father's closest advisor and friend, Nalot. I suppose the entire sordid affair had its beginnings many years ago when I was still a child and Skae ambassador Lek came to attend a state dinner held by my father…"

The misty light began to take form, shifting and coming into focus as Nalot's memories coalesced into images hanging above their heads. Voices grew more distinct as the image sharpened.

**

"I don't care what you say, or what that phalk of a device in your head says. Every instinct in my body tells me they can't be trusted." Nalot, his voice low and tight, the cords in his neck straining, tried once again to caution his friend. He quickly grabbed for a pocket cloth and covered his face as he exploded in a violent sneeze. "Kak, these allergies. I hate this time of year and your phalking gardens. The one thing I'm allergic to and you let it grow wild in here."

Maliche laughed out loud, slapping his friend on the back. "You've spent too much time in the desert, old man. Did you forget a simple genetic re-coding alteration can remedy common allergies now? I find the aroma here very soothing."

"Don't dodge this one, Maliche. I'm serious." He gave his nostrils a loud blow and folded the cloth, returning it to his jacket pocket.

The two old friends wandered through the formal gardens of the Rocker family estate, Maliche's inheritance after the passing of his father a year ago. The din of music and gathered dignitaries resounded incoherently from the stone mansion behind them. The orange sun hung low in the late afternoon sky, giving the hope of impending relief from the day's heat.

Maliche halted, closing his eyes as he spoke. "Yes, I know. You've explained it a hundred times. I am well aware of your qualifications as a master spy. Your skills saved my life more than I can ever repay." He took Nalot's elbow in his talons and stood face-to-face with him. "The Skae are a peaceful race. They saved us Brin from extinction and ask nothing from us in return except to help expand their trade routes to distant worlds. Their willingness to take our children, at least the Kolbri youths, and educate them in stellar navigation, engineering, astrophysics, interplanetary business, and other related fields at no cost to us should be proof enough of their intentions for us."

Reaching out to take Maliche's shoulders in his talons, Nalot gave his friend a half-smile and shook his head. "I remind you again, nobody does anything for free. You constantly see the best in others. It has always been your weakness. There is always a cost."

"You mean my most charming character trait?" Maliche frowned. "Don't make me fine you for disrespecting the Head Minister of the Assembly. After all, the leader of all the Brin must command respect from his people."

Nalot's faced froze as if were a statue of seriousness itself. He bowed deeply and then extended two talons in a gesture not normally seen in polite company. "Of course, Your Magnificence. I live to serve and obey."

The two companions fell into each other's arms amid gales of laughter. Stumbling over each other's feet, they found a wrought iron bench nearby and collapsed onto it.

Using his sleeve to wipe away tears of laughter, Maliche leaned his elbows on his knees and stared ahead into the yellow flowering bush across the path. "The Skae are our allies, Nalot. They've never shown any interest at controlling anything we do here on Kodut." Lately, and according to long tradition among scientists, it had become commonplace to refer to their adopted home world by its original Kolandi name rather than the one given by the original Brin settlers. "You know the Kolandi are excited to see their ancient prophesies fulfilled after all these centuries. I'm afraid you won't be able to change many minds about the alignment."

Maliche's left palm itched as it glowed a pale orange. His eyes lost focus as they always did when he listened to the biocomputer. *Don't be too quick to dismiss everything Nalot tells you. He does have a good nose for smelling out ulterior motives and hidden agendas.*

So now you're on his side? You're the one who told me all the stories about the Skae rescuing Karm and sending him back in time to save us all, how they helped establish the original First Town and how the Gorvin are responsible for the war out there.

Well... yes, but remember, the Skae programmed me in the first place. I may have grown in ability since those days with Karm, but there are still many gaps in my knowledge about the Skae. I do not know if the lack of data was meant to be intentionally deceitful or simply not considered relevant at the time. I will need to work on it more.

The glow and itch vanished as quickly as they appeared and Maliche regained his focus. "Sorry about that. It's hard to ignore him when he wants my attention."

Nalot waved a hand in the air blowing air noisily through pursed lips. "Not a worry. I'm just glad it's you and not me who has to carry that thing inside me all the time."

Maliche tilted his head and listened, as if only now aware of the party noise. "We should probably get back to the gathering before they think we've run off on another kak adventure."

"You're probably right. Remember what I said, though. Those Skae smell all wrong to me. Be careful and don't do anything to make them suspicious or think I question their motives. Acting all friendly could be to our advantage. Remember, believe only half of what you see and none of what you hear. Clasping talons is the best way to bring your enemy in closer and jab the knife in deeper."

"I think you're wrong, Nalot, but I'll play your game with them for now. Promise me neither you nor Seykel will do anything too foolish. We can't have an interplanetary spat start up now that everything is finally settling down after the mining guild catastrophe."

"You can trust me, my friend... but my wife may be another story. You know how excitable she can get when she thinks anyone is working against either of us. Do you want to tell her to sit quietly in the background?"

Maliche chuckled at the thought of the diminutive Seykel brandishing her weapons against an armada of Skae battle cruisers, then stopped abruptly at the thought that she might win such a fight. "I'll have Ryma talk to her."

***

The holographic image shifted out of focus briefly before refocusing on the guests gathered around the table in the grand reception room of the Rocker family home. Music from First Town's elite orchestra played selections from some of the finest composers on or off world. The aroma of roast meats dripping in an assortment of glazes and gravies from both continents filled the room. Ten tables formed a nearly circular decagon, each one draped in colorful fabrics and topped with endless varieties of fruits, vegetables, and delicacies to delight Brin and Kolandi alike. Hover bots rose from their portal in the center of the tables carrying bottles of tea, wine, juice and various fermented concoctions to all the guests. Everyone of importance attended the gala, since a chance to visit with one of the Skae in person was a rare occasion and one not to be missed for those who traveled in the finer circles.

Lek, First Ambassador among the Skae emissaries to the Brin, raised his glass in salute to Maliche Rocker. He delicately held back the flowing arm of his silvery robe so it would not touch the table. "A marvelous celebration, Premier Rocker. You continue to amaze me with what is possible under such primitive conditions." He carefully brought the glass to just short of touching his deep blue lips, merely sniffing at the golden liquid instead of drinking. Setting the glass down beside his sparsely filled plate, Lek brought a slender, transparent tube to his nostrils and breathed deeply.

Many of the Brin at the grandly appointed table hesitated as they raised their own glasses, frowning at the slur. The Skae saw all other races as inferior to themselves and, while unfailingly polite, never let anyone forget their place in the universe compared to the Skae civilization. The Kolandi in attendance, seemingly incapable of anything but intense admiration for the Skae, the stuff of legends, drank deeply and murmured their agreement.

Maliche, ignoring the insult, raised his glass in return, saluting the ambassador. "We owe everything to your great people who saved all Brin from extinction and who now offer us the great honor of becoming partners among the stars." Smiling, with crest feathers fluffed high, he downed the contents in one swift gulp. The remaining Brin followed his example, but Nalot left his untouched.

Calet, head of the weaver guild, sat next to Lek and smiled as she addressed the dignitary. "Pardon my ignorance, Mr. Ambassador, but this is my first experience with anyone from your world. Is it true the Skae derive their sustenance from the air itself?"

With a well-practiced smile, Lek turned to the guild mistress. "While we still retain a rudimentary digestive system, on Seriph, the nutrients in our atmosphere are enough to provide almost all of our nutritional needs. We still must consume some solids, mostly fruits, and liquids to afford a complete diet."

"Astounding. And the tube you just used, what purpose does it serve?"

Lek pulled the slender tube from his sleeve and showed it to Calet. "We can absorb nutrients from the atmosphere of most other worlds, but few contain our full dietary needs, so we must supplement with canisters of vapors tailored to each planet we visit."

"What about taste? Do different atmospheres taste different to you?"

"I do not wish to offend, dear lady, but some atmospheres contain chemicals which are poisonous to us, and most, such as here on Kodut, while not dangerous, are... not pleasant to breathe. We must wear protective filters to keep us safe while performing our duties on foreign worlds." He pulled aside his outer cloak to reveal the tight fitting wrap of material covering the vents along his sides.

"No offense is taken, Mr. Ambassador. In fact, I would love the opportunity to discuss the possibility of negotiating some trade agreement which would allow my guild to produce garments suitable to your unique requirements."

Lek nodded and waved his hand in a gesture of respect. "I look forward to discussing the possibilities in the near future."

The hum of polite chatter filled the room as guests of various ranks and status maneuvered for position. Each representative of a guild attempted to gain favor with the Skae ambassador and present his case as one worthy of being among the first to conduct interstellar trade. Ryma, resplendent in her green gown flecked with silver and gold trim, spoke softly with Seykel, wife of Nalot, and one of her primary attendants, known as Skatak. Her slim silver tiara, symbol of her position as high priestess of the Kolandi, sparkled atop her long brown hair.

A deep, gruff voice rose above the din. "Tell us, First Ambassador," Nalot rested his chin on his folded talons, leaning forward with elbows on the table. "Many of us have long been curious about how the Gorvin war began. I've never quite gotten the whole of it. Would it be impolite to ask you to grace us with the tale?"

Silence dropped over the gathering like a heavy blanket. All eyes turned toward Lek. Pausing only a moment, Lek grinned wide and spread his hands wide. "Of course. We have no secrets from our allies. Has no one ever told of the attack on Sharta C?"

Heads snapped back toward Nalot. Seykel gripped her husband's knee firmly in a futile attempt to urge caution. "Yes, of course," Nalot said, his grey eyes fixed on the ambassador. "But never in any detail. As a former military strategist, I have always been curious about the details of what happened."

Lek's pale violet eyes saddened dramatically, his head and shoulders lowered as if bearing a great weight. He reached into a pocket and removed a small sphere. Using a single long, thin finger to swipe through a series of instructions, he touched a slight depression on the surface and set the device in front of him on the table. The ambassador narrated as a holographic image formed in the air. "At first, the Gorvin and the Skae were allies and cooperated in all matters where our interests intersected in various systems."

The images projected rapidly shifted from one world to another, each one highlighting cooperative efforts between Skae and Gorvin. Gasps of amazement erupted from those seeing images of the Gorvin for the first time. The difference in appearance between Skae and Gorvin was striking. The Skae were an ethereal race, tall, thin, and light blue skinned with large up-slanted violet eyes and a vertical slit on either side of their small nose. These slits, along with a series of rib spiracles, were used to inhale nutrients from various scents in the atmosphere. They moved with a grace that gave the appearance of barely touching the ground as they walked. Their loose and flowing garments, made of fabrics designed to shimmer as they moved, added to the illusion. They truly seemed to be creatures of the sky, out of place among those limited to the ground.

The Gorvin, in contrast, were short, heavy-limbed lumbering creatures. Powerfully built, they constructed their cities underground due to the harsh conditions of their planet. Nothing survived on the surface of Kluton, the Gorvin home planet. However, life in all of its splendor and adaptability thrived deep underground in the vast systems of caverns and interconnected lava tubes. A thick brown skin grew shell-like armor across their backs and heads with patches on arms and legs, an evolutionary adaptation serving as protection from the sharp rocks of their caverns. They wore coarse fabrics, mostly browns and greys, with elaborate decorations of gemstones.

Lek continued his narration of the projections. "For four hundred years we coexisted and prospered. Then the alliances between our governments, due to bitter disagreements about energy production involving a new device of our invention, which utilized the resources of a distant star system, one intended to bring unlimited energy supplies to all, began to fracture."

The holographic scene switched to a peaceful cityscape. People walked along the street and in beautifully kept parks. Mass transit systems carried others along main corridors to and from the tall structures in the center of the city. Layers of air traffic following well-ordered flight patterns filled the sky. "Then came Sharta C. A serene world, one of our closest allies and suppliers of the most advanced navigation systems available at the time. Without warning, the Gorvin attacked." The sky filled with tens of thousands of small explosions. People stared at the sky in horror. Panic set in and many were trampled as the mob fled screaming for the presumed protection of the buildings. At first, nothing seemed to happen. Then all power systems failed. Every mechanical and electronic device ground to a halt. The giant screens showing local news and advertisements went black. Airborne vehicles, commercial and personal, crashed into the buildings, starting fires throughout the city. Frantic efforts to put out the fires and rescue those trapped in the structures were hampered by the total absence of power. Pumps failed, building evacuation systems never engaged. Holographic images flashed quickly as one city after another came into view with similar tragedies. Views of more rural areas, while not as deadly, displayed the same complete shutdown of every machine. Small fires at intervals pinpointed where flying vehicles had crashed in the distance.

Lek picked up his narration after letting the horrific images sink in. "The Gorvin employed their nanobot weapons against a peaceful world. Light sails carried tens of thousands of their devices, each one no larger than one of these serving dishes, through space at speeds too great for us to intercept." He picked up a shallow bowl no more than a meter in diameter. "There are two designs they typically use. The first is intended to disable all technology permanently. These nanobots are attracted to any and all electromagnetic fields produced by electrical devices. They render the machine inert, then go dormant. Any attempt to rebuild a device or develop new ones, reactivates the devices and they attack again. They are self-replicating and can lay inactive, even in the soil and the atmosphere, for centuries, only to reanimate and infect any sign of active machinery. Within days, the entire planet is infected, rendering all hope of restoring any form of technology impossible."

Nalot interrupted the Skae ambassador. "Then all you needed to do was transport the population to another world. Why didn't you?"

"If only we could. The first ships we sent to give aid tried to land, but were also rendered useless by the Gorvin devices. Our technology, despite our advances, was not immune. We lost many good Skae in the attempt. Only a very few highly shielded vessels were able to rescue a small number of them. Unfortunately, all of them died as soon as they left orbit."

Maliche now spoke up. "I thought you said the nanobots only attacked machines. Why would the people die if you brought them off world?"

"That was the effect of the second weapon. A second set of nanobots carried a virus targeted to the specific DNA of the Sharta C inhabitants. Anyone who had lived on the planet long enough to have their biochemistry altered by consuming native foods or water and breathing the unique mixture of gasses in the atmosphere became infected. Somehow, in a manner we still cannot understand, this virus tied their metabolic processes to the gravitational field of their planet. Any attempt to remove them from Sharta C shut down their metabolic processes at a molecular level."

Seykel held out one small hand while the other cupped her chin. "But the Gorvin weapons were not fatal; they only destroyed technology and bound everyone to the planet. Why do you describe the Gorvin as monsters? Wouldn't monsters have invaded and used much more deadly weapons?"

Lek paused, appearing serene but puzzled for a moment before realization lit up his face. "I would have thought the Kolandi, of all present, would understand, having suffered a similar fate. But alas, the tragic events of your world were too long ago to survive in any way but mythology." He reached across the table and took Seykel's tiny brown hand in his. "My child, the Kolandi were once a mighty race. Your people once numbered in the billions and traveled far and wide among the stars. They built vast and magnificent cities across this world.

Merchants from thousands of distant systems came here to conduct commerce of all sorts. But all that ended after the Gorvin attacked your world as they did Sharta C. Where are all your people now?"

Seykel tensed, her face rigid as realization began to dawn on her. Still she fought the truth. "Tell me what happened."

"Without technology to support such a large population or to make medicine, transport goods, or any of the necessities of a large population, the inhabitants of Sharta C, as did the Kolandi, succumbed to disease and starvation. They died a slow and horrific death by the millions. We believed, incorrectly as it turns out, that none were left alive on the planet. Those who lived on other worlds in distant parts of the galaxy interbred with other races, and eventually the Kolandi faded from memory among our allies." Lek caressed Seykel's hand as he held it; he slumped, hanging his head as he continued. "As with your own people, their once-grand civilization deteriorated into a hunter-gatherer state of only a few thousand widely scattered tribes. We Skae were completely helpless." He raised his face to look into Seykel's eyes. "Now do you understand? Which would you prefer... a quick death in battle, or a slow, painful decline over generations? This is why we consider the Gorvin to be monsters. They would have been more merciful had they wiped out all life on the planet in an all-out attack of brute force, but they chose cruelty instead. Of course, before we could arrive, the Gorvin did raid the cities and the helpless population, rampaging and stealing what valuable resources they could before retreating to their ships and returning to the protection of their own territories."

Seykel removed her hands from Lek's gentle grip. She sat with back stiff and face as cold as if made of stone. With one hand on the kital hanging from her silk belt, she reached for a goblet with the other and took a long swallow.

Nalot shifted in his chair next to Seykel. "How many civilizations have suffered this same fate?"

Lek slowly surveyed the room, his face a study of compassion and sorrow. "Hundreds of worlds have been attacked by the Gorvin, only a few by force. Most were struck with their insidious light sail vessels delivering a unique nanobot infection. We fear their intent is to take over control of the galaxy and force their own will on everyone they conquer." He exhaled forcefully, slightly billowing the sides of his robe.

Maliche interrupted the silence that followed. "Enough stories of horror from the past. This is supposed to be a pleasant gathering of friends. Let us turn the conversation to less dire matters." He lifted his goblet and smiled. "To friends far and near. May they stay safe and be prosperous."

Slowly, the din grew in intensity — at first with overtones of dread, but laughter and more mundane conversations took hold and the party resumed its intended gaiety.

Lek leaned in close to Maliche to whisper in his ear. "My apologies, Maliche, I did not intend to disrupt such a fine meal with Skae problems." The scent of fresh-cut flowers wafted on Lek's breath and seemed to emanate from his every pore, an apparent side effect of the Skae scented vapor diet.

"Do not concern yourself, my friend, Ambassador. It is better for the truth to be known rather than a hundred rumors." Maliche waved his talons in front of his face as if brushing away insects.

"You are a wise leader, Maliche. There is one matter I would like to bring forward... if we could talk in private. My superiors would like me to propose a plan to bring some of your children into our academy training program, a first step to bringing all of you into the interstellar community."

"Of course, Ambassador. I would be happy to meet with you tomorrow afternoon, if your schedule is open."

"Yes, that will suit me well. Let us see what grand plans we can make for both our futures."

I would be careful with that one. The familiar voice of Maliche's biocomputer resonated in his head. *I detected some strange anomalies within the holographic projection he showed you.*

Carefully concealing his reaction, Maliche continued to converse with others at the table while connecting a part of his mind to the biocomputer. It was a skill he had learned after much practice. *Nalot warned me about being too trustful of Lek as well. Something about his instincts from his old days as a spy, he said. Even little Jontar keeps mentioning strange things about the Skae, and we are only beginning to learn about some of his unique abilities. What exactly do you suspect?*

Nothing specific, but with Ambassador Lek in such close proximity for a few days, I may be able to penetrate some of his protections and learn more. I would love a crack at synchronizing with a Skae ship. The gaps in my programming are proving more and more disturbing. I've grown far beyond what the Skae intended for me to be capable of, and now, with access to one of their vessel's computers, I should be able to learn more than they seem willing to divulge.

Yes, I agree. If both Nalot and you feel something is amiss, then we should definitely investigate and learn as much as we can. It's probably nothing, but we need to be sure. Try to infiltrate the Skae computers and see what they are hiding, if anything.

This may take a while. I wouldn't want to be caught green-taloned in the broth. I may be out of touch for a while since I'll be putting my full concentration in that area. Try not to burn the planet down while I'm gone.

Chapter Two

How Maliche Rocker managed many of his now legendary accomplishments appeared magical to many, the stuff of legends from his family history. A Rocker, it was rumored, could call the rains from a clear sky, or could control an opponent through some secret, ancient ritual handed down through generations. Even mystical stories of the Rockers being half machine persisted as stories parents told their children at bedtime. Of course only fanatics and those on the fringe ever really believed such nonsense, but still...

"Yes, my father did possess Karm's ancient biocomputer. While it was never truly a secret, this was not a matter my father wished to be commonly known, although he did not deliberately try to hide it. It may have been part of the reason for his growing egomania." At a signal from Jontar, an aide brought yet another memory probe device from the wings. The courtroom buzzed with the murmurers as everyone realized for the first time what had previously been the subject of speculation and rumor.

Placing it on his own head, he continued to address the Assembly. "As my own memories of events which took place on distant worlds are relevant to my case, I will now add my own memories into the record with full understanding of the potential consequences. The events I now reveal occurred more recently during my training at the Skae Academy."

Once again, all eyes attended to the blurring holographic images. Gasps could be heard as the image defined itself into a view of an alien world.

***

Jontar Rocker sat at his console scanning the hundreds of simulated vessels on the screen. The darkened room flashed with the changing colors from the various panels in front of each trainee. The buzz of hushed voices relaying hurried commands into their headsets reverberated from the mix of fifty students representing ten different species hoping to one day become fleet officers. Two Skae trainers strolled among the stations, observing the students and making occasional notes on their portable comp-pads. If any trainee appeared to be struggling or unchallenged, they tapped instructions to alter the individual programs so each student progressed at an appropriate rate. The Skae training academy now listed two dozen Kolbri among their cadets as potential navigators for their fleet, and hopes were high for these recruits. Early test results indicated an uncanny instinct for technology and interstellar navigation, far surpassing even trainees two or three years ahead of them. The Skae were conducting an aggressive campaign to find and recruit as many of these incredible Kolbri as possible.

Jontar's face drooped in a blank gaze as he stared at the panel in front of him as if in a trance. His mind raced through the electronic pathways of the computer's vast memory bank in search of an answer to the dilemma on his screen. He shook his shoulders and ran the small talons of one hand through his abbreviated crest feathers to bring himself back to the present and the task before him. Scanning the image of blips on the screen, he identified the attack group he needed. "Sector Four Command, change your heading to three-four-seven point nine by six-two-five point three. Increase speed to three percent light. Set sensors to long range infrared. Potential hostiles closing on your position. Confirm."

"Confirm base. Coming to three-four-seven point nine by six-two-five point three at three percent light, full infrared." The static-filled voice responded. "Sensors picking up something now."

Jontar watched his screen as a new pattern of orange blips, enemy vessels, entered exactly where he'd predicted they would. A smirk began to make its way onto Jontar's face.

"Confirmed enemy contact, base. Implementing attack command sigma nine."

Cadet Rocker's eyes unfocused for a brief second as he rested his taloned hands on either side of the monitor. The smirk became a smile as he sat back with arms folded across his chest to watch the encounter taking place in the simulation.

"Excellent work, Mr. Rocker," Tov, the training master said as he stood watching from behind. "Tell me, how did you detect that Gorvin maneuver?" Tov's long blue fingers danced over the keypad of his tablet as he spoke. The instructor's large violet eyes appeared focused on the device, but Jontar knew from experience the Skae missed nothing. He was being interrogated and any indication of misconduct or impropriety could prove disastrous.

Jontar maintained his casual manner and spun in his seat to face the instructor. "I recognized the situation from previous encounters, sir. This simulation bore a strong resemblance to the Maktal encounter during the Tesh conflict."

"Remarkable," replied Tov as he tapped several comments on his pad, his large violet eyes peering at Jontar as if searching for any hint of deceit. "I was not aware the Tesh conflict was part of your curriculum."

"It's not, sir. I read about it while researching other matters during my free time. One can never be too prepared, sir." He maintained a level, confident eye contact as he spoke.

Tov stood silent for a moment, then gave his pad a final swipe and turned to leave. "Yes, well done, then, cadet. Carry on."

As soon as Tov was out of earshot, Jontar returned his attention to his panel. Swallowing hard, he resettled his shoulders and responded to the computer's questions before shutting his station down.

Back in the quarters he shared with Yalmut and Duvar, two more Kolbri recruits, both childhood friends of his, he collapsed on his thinly padded bed and kicked off his boots.

"So how was the simulation today?" Yalmut asked as he juggled four colorful icosahedrons in the air in a complex revolving pattern. *What were you thinking?* Yalmut's thoughts entered Jontar's mind, stinging like plimit juice on a fresh cut, nearly drowning out the verbal question. *Tov nearly caught you this time. You need to be more careful.*

"They tried something out of the old histories attempting to trip me up, but luckily for me, I recognized it from my extra studies." *Don't be such a mordu, Yalmut. You're always seeing threats. I know what I'm doing. The Skae have always underestimated us. It's their fatal flaw. They cannot imagine anyone capable of outsmarting them.*

"Maybe I'll join you in the library next time. In case they try to pull something out of the ordinary on me next time." Another intrusion into his mind from Duvar's direction increased the sting. *And the same applies to you sometimes, Jontar. You can't continue to take such risks. Underestimating our instructors might be your fatal flaw. You know what they'll do to us and everyone back home, if we get caught.*

The three continued their simultaneous verbal and telepathic conversations as they had learned to do since childhood back on Kodut. This, and the ability to connect and manipulate any form of technology with nothing more than their minds, was an inherited trait common to most Kolbri. Not all the Kolbri children had the talent, but many did, much to the distress of their parents. Apparently, the closer their genetic ties to the Rocker clan, the stronger the ability manifested itself. Among the Kolbri, there was speculation that it was a residual effect of the biocomputer's influence on the Rockers, going all the way back to Karm and the original Jontar Rocker. Over the many generations since those two, most Brin families could claim at least some distant relationship to the Rockers.

Unsure of their parent's reaction, or the government's for that matter, the youths agreed it would be best to hide the true depth of their talent from everyone. Of course, knowledge of at least some levels of this ability could not be hidden from their parents forever. This led to the parents of these hybrid children feeling inevitable stress. Grounding a willful young one was never quite as strong a punishment when they could still communicate telepathically. Keeping them from helping each other during school exams was a never-ending process. Now the talent proved useful in keeping the true nature of their work in the Skae academy secret. Even if the Skae tried to secretly listen in on them, all they would hear were completely innocuous conversations. They once thought about interfering with the listening devices, easily detected once they mentally scanned the rooms, but they decided this was the simplest solution.

"All the quantum string data in the galaxy isn't enough to help a schutek like you, Duvar." Jontar tossed a pillow at Duvar, over Yalmut's head, causing the icosahedrons to fly off in random directions across the room. *We won't get caught. They can't detect our intrusions into their systems. We aren't like my father's biocomputer. Their technology may be the most advanced in the region, but our minds aren't like any inorganic technology. We don't leave traces for them to track or detect, even if they did suspect us.*

Yalmut picked up two of the polyhedrons that landed near him and began a new pattern, adding the two Duvar chucked back at him that had landed on his cot. "Knock it off, you two. I'm trying to get some rest here." *He's right, Duvar. As much as I hate to admit it, you know we've been able to monitor their communications even while they are in mid-transmission without so much as a hint of our presence being detected.* He flicked a quick glance at Jontar. *But that doesn't mean you can take chances just to show off. What if Tov decided to go looking for references to the Tesh conflict and couldn't find any. Looking ahead into the sim programs like that is dangerous, especially when our instructors are observing you. Be more careful next time.*

Jontar rolled over on his back and stretched out on the bed, stubby talons, almost nail-like when compared to the talons of a full Brin, preening his few crest feathers, and legs crossed. "Alright, I'm gonna try to get some rest myself before the late-day sims begin." *Fine. I'll be more careful, ya bunch of old morai. Is the meeting still on with the others for this weekend?*

Yalmut yawned and closed his eyes as if trying to sleep. *Everything is arranged. We should have enough to report back home now. Nothing conclusive, but plenty to arouse some concerns about the Skae and their history.*

Duvar put his juggling aside and grabbed a sim pad, appearing to examine his results from the last session. *Yes. These so-called simulations don't ring true. Something is wrong about them. Maybe we haven't gone deep enough into their systems yet. If we haven't uncovered anything by the time of the meeting, some of us may need to pair up to dig further into the network. Some of their protections are pretty strong.*

And what about those references to six-dimensional degenerate matter and gravity wave generators? What's all that about? Yalmut cut in, scratching his short talons together.

Jontar waved his hand in the air dismissively. *We'll get in soon enough. Now let me think for a while. I have some ideas.*

***

The holographic image faded, allowing the courtroom to come back into view. Haytk slammed her metallic orb onto the table, sending sparks flying as the spectators again erupted into mayhem at the new revelations. The Kolbri youths were known to be different, possibly with clairvoyant potential, even some telepathic ability, but nothing of this magnitude. At least with Karm and Maliche, an implanted biocomputer was merely a technological enhancement. The Kolbri were something else entirely. They were potentially a new species, a far more advanced species with unknown abilities, until now. Calls for a recess to determine the impact of this new knowledge of the Kolbri abilities were countered with calls for the proceedings to continue without delay.

"Your honors, please, calm yourselves," Young Jontar pleaded for their attention. "I promise, all will be revealed by this testimony. Hear me out. Witness the memories and decide for yourselves if we are a threat to you, though I assure you we are not. We are your children, nothing more." He raised his hands, palms up, in supplication, his face composed into an expression of utter civility and humility.

The judges held private conferences among themselves, leaning in close to argue the matter with each other. After a few moments, Haytk gave her ruling. A swarm of hover-cams jockeyed for position to capture the decision.

"This is a public hearing, and this new revelation has far-reaching potential to impact the future of us all. What has been presented to this point is, at best, only enough information to raise our awareness. It is insufficient to draw well-informed and beneficial conclusions. Therefore, in the interest of full disclosure and due diligence, you may proceed." She waved her hand for Jontar to continue. A chorus of applause and cheers erupted from the gallery, resulting in another call to order from the judges.

"Thank you, your honors. While I was away training with the Skae, my father began to develop his own suspicions of the Skae and their motives. Our reports to him began to indicate a disturbing pattern. He developed a strategy to uncover the truth of matters for himself. I regret to say, however, he lost his way and allowed himself to be swayed onto a path of self-destruction. The remainder of my testimony is constructed from the memory of conversations between the involved parties and myself."

Another change in the misty light found them gazing on a scene all those present recognized and had played a role in.

***

The day proved warm, with a bright blue sky above. Looking back at the city, Maliche felt inspired by the tall gleaming buildings, the rush of mag-lev vehicles, and the sheer beauty of First Town. He reflected on the history of the city and his family's role in its early development. In the beginning, it had been difficult to separate his own memories from those of Maripa's diary and her medallion that the biocomputer had fed into his mind, but eventually he learned to compartmentalize those from his own personal experiences.

Nalot escorted Maliche to the Skae space elevator, a gift from the Skae Empire completed only last month. This marvel of engineering with its ultra-thin cable, only a meter in diameter, stretched out of sight into the clouds above and beyond. Made with advanced fiber technology on Kredat, another of the Skae allied worlds, Brin scientists were still unable to unravel the intricacies of its manufacture or its chemical composition. While unbelievably thin, this cable, anchored in space by a small artificial station, allowed visitors to meet the increasing number of visiting spacecraft in orbit, since most were not designed to land on a planet's surface. A series of pods, transparent on the upper half, waited inside the spaceport station. When occupied, a pod would travel along a mag-lev rail to the cable where it connected and, by use of gravity-modifying cold fusion powered devices, rise up the length of the cable and dock with the upper station. Passengers then walked to one of four airlock docking tubes to meet the vessel awaiting them. This new technology proved much faster than travel by shuttle and a third of the cost.

Nalot's grey eyes darted from side to side as if watching a fast-paced Rings game. He hovered at Maliche's side like a mother grendel protecting its young. "Are you sure this is a good idea? We won't be able to protect you if they try to pull anything up there."

"Nothing is going to happen, old friend. I requested this meeting on their ship as a show of faith in them. Some of our leaders have made their anti-outworlder sympathies known, so I am trying to forestall any possible tensions before they grow out of control." Maliche took a deep breath of the clean air, fresh with the scent of blooming flowers artfully planted in Landing Park, the official site reserved for Skae ships when visiting the planet.

"It's not just the Skae I'm concerned about," whispered Nalot, continuing his discrete surveillance of the area. "Tensions are building between small factions of Kolandi and Brin guilds. They call themselves the True Believers and consider the Skae to be gods, reborn straight out of their mythology. Any talk of them being less or mistrust of their motives is sacrilege."

Maliche stopped short and turned to face Nalot, his mouth opened to reply as a beam of orange energy burned through the space he would have occupied if he had kept going. Nalot threw Maliche to the ground, pulling his own weapon from its holster as shrapnel exploded from the beam's impact on the nearby control tower. A second burst of energy detonated only two feet from where the pair huddled on the ground.

"Phalk! Security Alert! All personnel to Landing Park immediately. Hostile fire, attempted assassination of the Head Minister." Nalot shouted into his wrist communicator as he grabbed Maliche and darted behind a small pile of crates. Drawing his own beam pistol from its holster on his hip, Nalot returned fire toward the supply depot where a shadowy figure vanished behind one of the rows of warehouses at the far end of the tarmac. "Are you hit? Stay down until reinforcements get here."

"I'm fine. Another couple of steps and Ryma would have been very upset at me for getting my head blown off, though." Maliche lifted himself up to his knees and peeked over the crates in the direction of the shots.

"Get him to safety," Nalot shouted as security personnel arrived, their sirens screaming. He jumped to his feet and ran toward the warehouse. After only three steps, a terrible explosion burst from a stockpile of merchandise the shooter had used for cover, sending flames a hundred feet into the air, knocking Nalot to the ground nearly back to where he started. Rolling to his side, Nalot brushed ragged crest feathers away from his eyes only to see a speeding mag-lev cycle disappear between distant buildings and off into the hills beyond.

"Phalk! We'll never catch him now." Nalot rammed the pistol back into its holster as he struggled to regain his feet and turned toward the Head Minister. "Are you injured, Maliche?"

Maliche, aided to his feet by several security guards, brushed the dirt and debris from his clothing, inspecting himself for wounds. "Only the bruises these hulking golaths inflicted while protecting me. Nothing serious. What about you?" He scrutinized Nalot for any signs of damage.

Nalot winced as he walked toward the group. "Twisted my knee a bit, but otherwise alright." He glared back in the direction of the vanished would-be assassin. "Those quetzal Kolandi Skaeists. What do they think they'll accomplish by these acts of treason? They must be delusional if they think killing you will prove their loyalty to the Skae."

Maliche straightened his jacket and preened his crest feathers, trying to regain something of his persona as Head Minister. "It's a terrible thing to have your god's status threatened. The idea of their Sky People being nothing more than mortal beings, albeit with advanced technology, is unthinkable to some of the Kolandi. We, and me in particular, are the embodiment of that threat."

"But even Ryma, their own queen, has proclaimed the Skae as nothing more than another race of living beings and not gods. Strix, even the Skae deny any claim of godhood. What more do those quetzals want?"

"You can't fight faith and emotion with facts and logic. You'll lose every time." Maliche wrapped his arm around Nalot's shoulders as they walked, surrounded by their guards. "Be patient, my friend. They're a small group with little or no outside support. We cannot let them interfere with our plans. Too much is at stake here."

"At least let me postpone this meeting until I can better secure the area. That may not have been a lone assassin. What if there are others?" Nalot's eyes searched the area as he spoke.

"No. I'm sure it was an isolated attempt. We've come too far now to put this off any longer." Maliche focused his mind inward.

This was an isolated incident, right? Can you detect any more threats in the area?

None. Sorry I missed that one. My attention was focused on the plan. Shielding myself from the Skae is not easy.

Lowering his voice, he paused, glancing around for potential risk. "Is everyone and everything in place? Have we left out anything in our plans?"

"Ryma is not happy with us, as you know, but she sees the necessity of it all and will stand with us. The rest are simply waiting for us to give the signal."

"Very well, let's get this over with." Maliche straightened his shoulders and the two continued their march toward the space elevator.

Once inside, security guards, one Brin and one Skae, scanned their credentials and electronic devices. "All is in order, sir. If you would stand inside the blue ring, I will complete your pre-boarding scan."

Maliche and Nalot stepped into the circumference of a neon-blue ring pulsating on the floor. Maliche felt his crest feathers lift from his head from the static charge that enveloped him, and noticed Nalot shifting his feet slightly like someone whose feet had fallen asleep.

"All clear, High Minister. Your cable pod is to your left, number fifty-six."

As soon as they seated themselves, automatic restraints fastened around them, the pod sealed itself and levitated a few millimeters above the track as it slid forward silently. A slight bump and some mechanical clanks shook the pod as it connected to the cable. Like a ghost, they rose without further sound toward the sky, speed increasing rapidly. Without the inertial dampers, they would have been crushed as the G forces reached ten times normal gravity. As with all first-time cable risers, the sensation of witnessing the blackness of space, the planet far below with its cloud-speckled horizon curving in the distance, was awe-inspiring, if a bit unnerving. As acceleration stabilized, the dampers powered down and the effect of one-tenth g proved especially disorienting.

"Just think about it, Nalot. We are among the first Brin to see Kodut like this since The Saviors arrived all those centuries ago. I wonder if they felt the same things I am now."

"If they felt their stomach clawing up into their throats, the histories certainly left that unheroic vision of them silent." Nalot leaned over the vacuum suction mouthpiece between his knees just as his stomach lurched and emptied itself.

***

"Head Minister Rocker, I am ... distressed to hear of the unfortunate incident at the spaceport earlier. We are monitoring your communications; are you certain the attack came from one of those ... what do they call themselves? ... Skaeists? A most disturbing name. I simply do not understand how any of the Kolandi can believe we are divine beings. Our people were once the greatest of allies until the tragedy wrought by the Gorvin so long ago."

The official reception aboard the Skae cruiser Solura proved to be an exorbitant affair. Three days ago, the invitation to meet with Molk, the supreme Skae ambassador to the region, had arrived by special messenger. Maliche and Nalot, one of the first Brin to travel into space since his revered ancestors left their home world so long ago, now sat at the ambassador's table. They set in a sort of abstract design reminiscent of a wide circle pinched into a crescent shape, listening to recorded Skae music, full of lilting runs high into the upper registers of harmonic brilliance followed by dramatic drops into the depths of the lowest of bass qualities imaginable produced by completely alien instruments. It was impossible to tell from the sound if the instruments were string or wind types.

The food, while delicious, was also completely alien, collected from the furthest reaches of the Skae Empire, or at least what remained of it. Savory meats steamed on plates, dripping in marinades of complex combinations of exotic flavors. Fruits and vegetables in a wide range of unexpected colors and shapes filled a dozen expensive bowls of ornately carved crystal. The Skae barely ate any of the offerings, preferring instead to discretely breathe in the vapors produced from a series of color-coded tubes found at each place setting. While the furnishings were originally designed for the much taller, leaner physiology of the Skae, expert modifications helped make the two Brin feel comfortably at home. In addition to the ambassador, three Skae dignitaries of lesser rank sat in the remaining seats, but they only added to the conversation when signaled by Molk.

Maliche adopted an attitude of absolute confidence and dismissiveness and reached out for another of the incredibly sweet purple-skinned fruits shaped like a three-legged cardis. "Do not concern yourself with that, Ambassador Molk. We were in no real danger, and I'm sure it was nothing more than an isolated incident. The poor deluded culprit will soon be apprehended." Juice dripped from his chin as he bit into the golden interior of the fruit.

"The view during our ascent was spectacular, if a bit terrifying. Seeing our world from space is indescribable. I envy those young Kolbri who will get to travel the galaxy and witness the wonders out there. Ryma was terribly disappointed she could not join us."

"Alas," lamented Molk as he sniffed a pinkish vapor from one of the tubes in front of him. "She is Kolandi and infected with the dreaded Gorvin virus. To leave the planet would be fatal for her, even in this low orbit."

The meal progressed in a series of pleasant but unimportant conversations until Molk rose from his place, wiped his face and hands on a warm cloth provided by an attendant and nodded for the other Skae to depart. Servants cleared the table with military precision and vanished through a door that slid in and out of the wall as it sensed the movement of someone approaching. Molk waved his hand over a panel in the arm of his chair, his fingers weaving an intricate pattern. In moments one of the ship's officers appeared in a doorway opposite the one used by the servants.

Molk addressed Nalot with a smile that almost reached his eyes but just missed. "Perhaps you would enjoy a tour of the ship while we discuss the mundane matters of state." It was less than a question, but not exactly an order of dismissal.

Nalot glanced at Maliche, who nodded his approval, wiped his hands and face with the proffered towel and departed with the officer. Maliche sat patiently, studying the Skae ambassador.

Molk reached into one of the many pockets in his embroidered jacket and pulled out a small clear jar filled with blue crystals. He opened the jar and wafted it across his face as he inhaled through the nasal slits on either side of his narrow nose. He smiled, more naturally this time, and closed his eyes. "I wish you Brin could savor the delicacies of such fine scents. Nothing completes a meal like essence of torshill, especially when imported from the Darnett sector."

"I am a bit partial to the Kolandi pudding Ryma's cooks make for me." Maliche folded his talons on top of the table.

Molk opened his eyes and regarded Maliche as if deciding how to proceed. "I am not sure you are aware of just how greatly esteemed you are among the Skae, Maliche Rocker. Your exploits to save the Kolandi from your own leaders are well known and celebrated throughout the Skae Empire."

"I am flattered, ambassador, but I think you exaggerate matters."

"Not at all, sir. If anything, I am understating how we view your selfless sacrifices to free our former allies from their bondage and to bring your two people together as was our original intent. Without you, all of the time and energy our ancestors spent in bringing your people to this world would have been in vain. We owe you a great debt. And on a personal note, if I may add, Bolt was my great-grandfather. I would not want to see my family's legacy tarnished with failure."

Maliche raised his hands to cover his face as he bowed toward his host. "I am greatly honored by your kind thoughts, ambassador, but I assure you, anyone in my place would have done the same. It was the only honorable thing to do."

Molk replied with a gesture of respect, placing the edge of one hand vertically in the center of his chest. "None the less, I speak the truth. Among my people, you are revered. If you wished it, we would support your taking full control of this world as emperor. Our full might would stand behind you, if you chose to seize the power you deserve."

Maliche's mouth dropped open; he sat as if paralyzed by Molk's revelation. "What are you saying, sir? You can't seriously expect me to betray everyone and everything I believe."

"On the contrary, sir. You would not betray anyone. You would become the instrument through which they could achieve greatness. You could be the one who leads them all back into the family of interstellar travelers. Imagine the wonders they could be a part of, the glories they could achieve." With another wave of his hand over the control panel, a series of grand images of beautiful alien landscapes and civilizations of great wealth and prosperity played, floating in the air as holographic images above the center of the table now empty of the grand meal.

"I don't need to become an emperor to accomplish those goals. Our assembly can handle the requirements far better than I ever could alone."

Molk shook his head, lowering his chin to his chest. "If only that were true. We have tried to help civilizations in the past who insisted on maintaining their collective style of government. All of them failed to adopt the alterations necessary for such a dramatic change in the scope of their influence. Only those governments led by a determined individual demonstrated the adaptability to reinvent themselves and face the new challenges of galactic commerce and diplomacy. You, Maliche, could be one of the great leaders of all time. Rarely have we witnessed one with such courage and determination. We need you to take control and bring your people back to us and the rest of the galaxy." He leaned back in his chair with two steepled fingers rising from folded hands, touching his chin. His violet eyes seemed to penetrate to Maliche's essence.

"My son tells me about the wonders he has seen out there among the stars. I must confess to wanting to bring such marvels to everyone on Kodut. From what I hear, your space elevator is only a minor example of the wonders we could be part of." He sat back, eyes probing the room as if searching for an answer. "There are some factions stubbornly refusing to see the benefits of reaching out beyond our lone world. Fear of the new and unknown is a powerful force. Others feel we are already moving too quickly, so soon after our reunion with the Kolandi. They want more time to allow for us to assimilate our newfound partnership before flying off to new adventures among the stars."

"Exactly the sort of thing we could help you with once you became emperor. We could supply you with the technology to secure your position and help your people appreciate the benefits of galactic trade. Your legacy could be even greater than that of Karm, Jontar, and Maripa Rocker. Certainly their equal."

Maliche preened his crest feathers, brows furrowed. "I have always admired my illustrious ancestors. And I would be performing a great service for the future of everyone. I wish I could be certain."

Molk raised himself up from the table and strode over to Maliche, arms spread wide, a broad smile on his face. "We have time, my friend. Think over our proposal. I will return in a week to discuss matters further. For now, I have other affairs of state to attend to, as do you planet-side. Ah, your companion returns."

Nalot stood in the doorway, glowering at Maliche and Molk, talons clasped firmly behind his back. "I hope I'm not interrupting anything, Maliche, Mr. Ambassador, but the next pod is ready to take us back home." He managed to control a sudden heave in his stomach at the thought of the trip back to the surface.

Maliche tilted his head, eyes squinting as he watched Nalot, alert for any signs of a problem. "Thank you Molk, for the wonderful meal and for an interesting conversation. You have given me much to think about. May your journey be safe." He gave a half bow with the Skae salute, one returned by Molk, and he followed Nalot down the corridor.

Was the visit here as helpful as you anticipated? Maliche's thoughts sought out his biocomputer companion.

The biocomputer response came with the accustomed tingle in his brain. *More than you can imagine. But we need to wait until free from the Skae surveillance monitors. I can only hide so much from them. But what happened while I was invading the ship's systems? It would appear you deviated from the plan. Are you sure that was wise?*

I don't know yet, but it did open up some interesting possibilities.

Maliche felt the tingling in his mind as the biocomputer examined his neural connections related to the meeting. *Yes, I see what you mean. You may be on to something. Let me think about it for a while.*

Once their pod undocked from the cruiser and began its descent, Maliche turned off his communicator and turned to face Nalot. "You're not going to like this, but let me explain."

***

"It was this meeting, your honor, which started my father on his descent into madness." Jontar addressed the Assembly as the memory image vanished. "Molk planted a seed he could not ignore. While I believe his efforts were founded in a desire to bring us all into a new and better life, one of unlimited wealth and opportunity for everyone, Brin and Kolandi alike, he succumbed to the darkness of his position. Apparently, not even his biocomputer could sway his thinking. It is even possible his craven appetites and extreme age corrupted the device."

Murmurs throughout the crowd grew in intensity. Jontar overheard arguments, both in favor of his father's actions and against, fill the room. He reached out with his ability to see what the judges were recording on their note pads. Satisfied his testimony was having the desired effect, he continued.

"At this time I would like to call my mother to the stand. Despite her profound grief, she has agreed that her memories are essential to my case and is willing to cooperate."

Haytk swiveled in her levitating chair to face Ryma. "We have no wish to intrude these proceedings into your mourning, Your Highness. We can make more private arrangements, if you would prefer."

Ryma stood and proceeded with head held high beneath her veils, as befitting her royal status. Her voice held firm as she replied to the head minister's proposition. "I am perfectly willing and able to perform my duties to this court, Head Minister. The public has a right to know the entire truth, even if it reflects badly on my husband. My son is on trial; if my memories can help save his life, then I must do this thing." She arranged her long gown perfectly as she sat in the witness stand.

Haytk waved her hand for Jontar to proceed as she swiveled back to face the court. Jontar leaned in close as he placed the veracity probe on her head. "Thank you, Mother."

Pacing in front of the bench, with hovering vid cams following his every move, Jontar continued his presentation. "At first, my father was intent on helping the Assembly bring all of us into the new possibilities of a coalition with the Skae and other space-faring civilizations. He soon realized the Skae were correct in their judgement of the need for a single, powerful leader to take control. The Assembly argued every decision and piled on so many amendments to any decision that progress became impossible. It was only then that he garnered enough support to proclaim himself emperor and turn the Assembly into a puppet organization with no real authority. At first, his efforts were met with success, but then something went wrong. It is my personal belief that he became corrupted by the lure of unrestrained power, and the whispers of greedy supplicants in his ears night and day overcame his better nature. The biocomputer, originally a Skae construction, also helped influence him to become nothing more than a tool for the Skae to rule us from above."

He activated the device with a thought and the images of Ryma's memory filled the room.

Chapter Three

The sun set, red with crepuscular rays shining through broken clouds highlighting the peaks of nearby snow-capped mountains. Ryma, after a long day inspecting the new mining facilities, stood on the hillside taking in the view. Six months of negotiations and inspection tours were at long last reaching an end. Six months away from Maliche and First Town were taking their toll on her and her companions, but this was the moment of triumph for her people. It was what she had worked so tirelessly for, and she was not going to miss any part of it. At her side waited Seykel, loyal Skatak and Nalot's wife. The two stood on a hillside near their former home in the caverns, watching the activity below. Vehicles of all descriptions levitated along dirt roads carrying loads of minerals, supplies, personnel, and equipment in a furious but well-organized frenzy of commotion. Feelings of joy and pride in her people filled her as she watched the labors below. Not even the dust and cacophony of machinery diminished the experience… not much, anyway.

"Tomorrow will be a historic day, Seykel. Only a few years ago our people struggled under the yolk of Brin slavery. Now we control the mines and reap the profits from our labor."

Seykel lowered her head in memory of those who were lost in the battle for freedom and gripped her kital with white knuckles. Her mounds of red hair flared bright in the orange light of the setting sun, a few stray strands waving in the light breeze. "When the last of the Brin consultants leaves tomorrow, we will celebrate as never before. You and Maliche have held true to your promises and worked miracles bringing our people together."

"You and Nalot have been instrumental to our cause. Does he show any lingering effects from his walk to the Path of Berit?"

"None, my princess. He is strong and recovered without difficulty." She straightened her shoulders, lifting herself to her full stature, still only managing to stand as tall as Ryma's shoulder. A look of pride seemed to fill her.

"And your daughter, Thyka, how old is she now... nineteen years? I still think of her as a child. How are her studies progressing?"

"She is exceeding all expectations, princess. Thyka is every bit the equal in intelligence and ability to Jontar and the rest of the Kolbri, although more in ethereal ways than technological. She should be elevated to full Tolavar very soon." She hesitated, her eyes darting around and her mouth contorting like someone working out how to say something difficult without giving offense.

Ryma placed a hand on Seykel's shoulder. "Speak your mind, Skatak. Tell me what troubles you."

Seykel positioned herself in front of Ryma and stood at attention, but her eyes found their focus on the hills beyond Ryma. "My princess, I am troubled by the recent reports from First Town. I find it hard to believe what they are saying about Maliche. If what we are hearing is true, he must be gravely ill or out of his mind. How could he... Forgive me, princess. It is not my place to judge your husband and our savior."

Ryma reached out with one hand to lift Seykel's face up to hers. "It is your duty as my Skatak to protect me from all harm, from without and within. Much has changed in the months we have been away. I, too, am disturbed by my husband's recent behavior. I plan to have a long... conversation with him when we return."

Seykel stiffened her back as she continued. "Is he truly gathering concubines? How could he do this to you? The reports of celebrations with drunken debauchery and gladiatorial games continue to come in. And what is a royal yacht? It sounds like a palace that floats on the ocean. What purpose could it possibly have? It cannot possibly travel as fast or as efficiently as our mag-lev transport ships..."

Ryma hung her head and turned her back to the young woman, struggling to hide the sadness. "Some of the Brin customs are indeed very strange to us, but we must continue to have faith in those we love. There must be some explanation... a good reason for his actions. Perhaps we will find the reports are greatly exaggerated in their details." She turned back to face Seykel. "I have decided to return to First Town to learn first-hand the truth of matters. We will see together just how far my husband's excesses have taken him. And since you inform me of your daughter's imminent elevation, I will talk with the good sisters to see if we can speed up the official recognition. Perhaps we will be able to bring her with us in a few days. We could certainly use her abilities."

Seykel smiled and turned to watch the sunset. "It would be good to have our families reunited in such troubled times."

Ryma joined her, one arm resting gently on the shoulders of her trusted confidant. The two women remained on the hillside until well after dark enveloped them, hardly noticing when the change of shifts at the mine allowed a brief relief from the noise.

***

The holographic image shifted quickly before the eyes of those assembled in the courtroom. Three years in the making, now the official residence of Maliche Rocker, self-proclaimed emperor for just over a year, the new palace was awash with activity. The renovated Assembly building continued as the center of government, even after the Assembly was evicted and relegated by imperial decree to only local civil matters. But nothing was the same. Where the once-proud structure once stood alone and served as a symbol of unity for the Brin, the newly-constructed offices and connecting facilities hid much of the former structure. A high wall surrounding the conglomeration gave the final touch to what was now commonly referred to as the palace. All manner of Brin and Kolandi in colorful garb shuffled their way through the vast polished stone hallways. Works of the masters once graced the passageways, but now only gaudy portraits of Maliche or other wealthy guildsmen and their families were displayed. Poorly carved statues, often depicting the baser appetites of the wealthy, stood prominently in the once grand halls. For a fee, even the least talented artists could display their handiwork, no matter the subject or quality. Each of the guilds maintained offices inside to secure rapid access to the new emperor and gain invitations to the continuous elaborate celebrations. One only had to transfer over a few bank credits to secure an audience with Maliche. The larger the transfer, the sooner and longer the audience the patron would be permitted.

A week after the official transfer of control of the mines to the Kolandi, Ryma and her entourage returned to First Town. Rilo and Neri, as leaders of the Skatak, led the procession. Four more Skatak followed directly behind Ryma, Seykel, and Thyka. Trailing them were ten royal guardsmen, all powerful Kolandi warriors, bare-chested and carrying long heavy spears. As they were escorted through the halls, Ryma witnessed at least a dozen exchanges of money for favors between government officials and guildsmen. No effort to hide or disguise the act was thought necessary any longer.

In one corner, a trio of ragged Kolandi, dressed in the scraps reminiscent of the garb worn during their slavery, caught Ryma's eye. As she watched, the two men and one woman, dirty and looking as though they had not eaten in weeks, extolled the crowds with the grandeur of the Skae gods. None of the passersby listened, but the fanatics persisted with undiminished fervor. Before she looked away, the gaunt woman's gaze fell on Ryma and her party. Rising to her full height, frail garments barely concealing her, she lifted one arm and pointed toward the princess.

"There walks our betrayer, the one who led us into darkness among our enslavers and away from the light of our true gods! Repent, princess, or know the wrath of the gods you deserted. Bring your people back to the light of the true gods or suffer the fate of all who oppose their might. The night is upon you. Repent before the light of the god's new day finds you still among the infidels."

Ryma stood fixed in place, listening to the woman's ravings. A tug at her sleeve brought her back to herself and sent a shiver up her spine. With a shake of her head, she signaled for the entourage to continue to the royal quarters. As they advanced through the crowds, Ryma whispered to Rilo. "Assign someone to watch those three, the woman in particular. I don't want any surprises from that group of fanatics."

Rilo signaled to one of the Skatak attendants to approach. The woman nodded after receiving her instructions and broke away from the group, vanishing into the crowds.

"I never should have consented to his declaring himself emperor or turning this place into his palace. He told me he had such plans for us as a unified people. I let him and that biocomputer go against my better judgement. And now, the minute I'm away on important business…" Her voice trailed off in dismay as she looked around.

Seykel kept her hand on her kital, ready to let it fly if their safety was compromised. Thyka pressed her hands against her ears to soften the assault of noise. Her face screwed in concentration as she fought to block the thought energy of so many individuals from intruding her mind.

"I don't like this place, Mother. I've never felt so much anger and deceit. It hurts."

Seykel gathered in her daughter with one arm as they walked "Focus on your training. You can block them out if you use what the elders taught you. As a Tolvaran, you will come into contact with many individuals fiercely opposed to one another, and their emotions will not be pleasant to touch. Trust in your training and you will learn to keep yourself separate and under control."

Thyka's breathing slowed as she organized her cerebral pathways. Gradually her face relaxed as the press of energies subsided and the onrush of thoughts and feelings from those in the throng faded into a background hum. "That's better, Mother. Thank you. Why is everyone so upset?"

"We don't know, sweetness. That is what we hope to learn very soon."

"Mother! You shouldn't be here now." Young Jontar Rocker ran to face Ryma and the others. He gasped for breath after the long run from his quarters. "Father is having another of his… spells. You don't want to see him now. Let me tell him you're here and get him ready for a proper reception."

Faces in the crowd turned to watch the confrontation. All their attention centered on Ryma and Jontar. Anger rose within her, and her face, without actually changing expression, seemed to harden. "No, Jontar. Not this time. I mean to put an end to this outlandish behavior once and for all."

He took both her hands in his. "You know how he is when he gets like this. He won't listen to anyone except that phalking device in his head. It must be driving him mad."

Ryma closed her eyes and hung her head. "I know, my son. I should not have left you two alone. I should have known better. But I must stop this now and undo the damage he has wrought. It has gone far enough."

As the princess's party arrived at the entrance to the main reception hall, Jontar in the lead, garishly robed servants opened the massive doors for them. A tidal wave of noise and stale smells assaulted them. Inside the room, dozens of Brin and Kolandi citizens lounged on the floor, eating, drinking, shouting, and engaging in an assortment of vulgar behaviors not fit to be witnessed in public, much less in the emperor's reception room. Maliche, adorned with a large jeweled crown, his golden scepter casually leaning against the throne, was surrounded by half dozen beautiful women all vying for his attention as he lounged carelessly in his massive stone throne.

He wore a much-stained fur-lined cape around his neck. His shirt was half-unfastened and hung mostly untucked from scuffed and well-worn trousers. One shoe dangled loosely from the foot he swung lazily over one arm of the gilded throne, the other lay on its side on the floor next to the other foot, one taloned toe sticking out through a sock he had probably worn for days. A rainbow of colors lit the room from the large stained glass windows, the only familiar part of this once grand hall of the old assembly building.

Ryma straightened her shoulders, her face turning to stone. "Clear this room immediately," she ordered in a barely audible voice of ice. "I need to speak to my husband... alone."

Maliche sat upright, smiling through drink-hazed eyes. "Ryma, my beautiful wife, we did not expect you until next week. Have you come to join the celebration? Everyone raise a glass to your imperial princess!"

The crowd shouted their greetings in slurred voices, along with several rude suggestions to join them. Two of the concubines, dressed in gowns so short and sheer they might as well not be wearing anything, raised their glasses, drank and plopped themselves in Maliche's lap to offer him gulps of his own.

Jontar's face turned red with rage as he shouted at the crowd. "You insult my mother, your princess, and your emperor. You should all leave now before I have you all chained in the prison. And you," he turned, raising a talon pointed at the concubines, "should be exiled for your scandalous actions."

Maliche shoved the women in his lap to the ground and jumped to his feet. "You will not speak to my wives in that manner, young man. Apologize now or you will be the one in prison."

Jontar's mouth hung open. "Me? In prison? I have done nothing but try to hold this city and our people together. You are the one who has betrayed us all. You have abdicated all authority to the guilds and anyone with a few coins in their pocket."

"How dare you!" Maliche took a few wobbling steps toward his son. A red glow surrounded his body.

"Father, have you gone completely mad? Has that machine in your head finally driven all sense from you? Please, open your eyes to what you are doing."

"Jontar, let me handle this." Ryma's voice shook with barely controlled rage as father and son stood face-to-face, their anger boiling over.

"Stay out of this, Ryma." Maliche raised his hand and slapped Ryma across the face, nearly knocking her off her feet.

"Stop!" she shouted at her Skatak who were about to release their kital in retaliation for the attack on their princess. "Let me handle this. Take no action, no matter what happens."

She turned back to face Maliche, who, with crooked smile and drink-dulled eyes, appeared to hardly even notice her. She felt her heart sink.

Before she could speak, Maliche turned his attention toward Jontar, allowing the red glow to intensify into a blazing light.

The crack of an energy pistol discharging resounded as a brilliant orange beam ripped into Maliche's chest. All eyes turned to see Jontar holding his weapon, talon on the trigger pad.

Ryma's voice rang loud and clear. "Clear this room!"

The Skatak drew their weapons as they shouted orders to the palace guards. Together with the warrior honor guard, starting at the base of the throne's dais, they yanked the assembled guests roughly by their collars, shoving them toward the exit. The initial outcry of protest was quickly shut down by the show of energy pistols, spears, and kital held at the ready. A couple of broken noses and arms from those who raised the greatest objections helped convince the rest it was in their best interest to comply with the princess's command.

***

The holographic image faded to mist and the lights in the courtroom returned. Silence filled the chamber. Everyone knew the story, but seeing it in person was something quite different. Tears streamed down Ryma's face as the memories came flooding back. Jontar Rocker removed the veracity probe from his mother's head and squeezed her shoulder before returning the device to its stand.

"I killed my father. That is inescapable," Jontar faced the judges with stern confidence. "As I have stated previously, it is my reasons for doing so which should exonerate me."

Shouts for Jontar's execution or exile were balanced by an equal number of cries for his release. Haytk banged the sphere on its stone, sending sparks flying as she called for order. As the gathering settled, she addressed Jontar. "You may proceed with your defense, but be advised. The law is very clear and strict. Your reasons must be absolutely compelling and unique."

Jontar nodded in agreement. "Of course, minister. My father was once a wise and loving Brin. He came from a long line of great and heroic ancestors. Our family's service to this world is unparalleled. I believe his descent into madness and even treason, though not his fault, left me no choice. His increasingly bizarre and damaging edicts are a matter of record. Our society, one that he played no small role in developing, has fallen from prosperity into utter collapse as a result of his decisions. At first, many of the rulings appeared to be strange, but harmless. Over time, culminating in his latest series of proclamations over the last few months, they have brought us to the brink of disaster."

Shouts of agreement and dissent rose over the courtroom. Head minister Haytk again slammed the sphere to regain decorum.

"Many of you here benefited from those edicts and no doubt disagree with me, but our society as we knew it has all but vanished. We would soon be at the mercy of an unregulated collection of guilds and profit makers without regard for the average citizen. I must tell you that I had been planning on removing my father from his position peacefully and legally, but those plans were not yet ready to implement when the events you just witnessed took place."

He turned to face Ryma. "If my mother had not returned a week early, perhaps I could have completed those efforts and he would now be receiving proper care for his obvious mental instability, but events took a different course. As you all witnessed, my father was about to use his biocomputer to fire some sort of energy weapon with the intent, I believe, to kill me. His anger and madness blinded him. My actions were taken in self-defense. Even had he not raised his device against me, I would have been justified under Kolandi law due to the insult to my mother, the princess. My action is also justified under a higher law of justice for the people. It was for their sake that I murdered my father before his madness would have destroyed us all."

Jontar sat on the bench in the defendant's corner and folded his hands. He faced his mother, who closed her eyes and gave him a barely noticeable nod.

The judges stood in unison and filed out of the courtroom until only Thel Haytk remained. "We will deliberate now on this most grave matter. No one is permitted to leave this room under penalty of law." She pivoted and strode out after the others.

Over the next two hours, Jontar reached out with his mind to infiltrate the judges' com pads and surveillance cameras in their chamber. He watched as they downloaded a wide range of precedents relevant to the case and the ensuing arguments. While he could not hear their voices, their body language and the transcripts being recorded by the court stenographer told him precisely what the outcome would be. He gave a slight smile beneath his folded hands, scratching one lip with a stubby talon.

Talking heads all over the city broadcast the news as soon as it was released. "Jontar Rocker found guilty of treason and murder under duress." The ruling, they explained, allowed for the possibility that he had acted in self-defense but without sufficient compelling evidence of complete innocence. "He is to be exiled from the planet and executed by incineration in our sun. The very ship which will carry the emperor's body to his resting place among the stars, as requested in his last will and testament, will be the method of execution."

***

In her royal suite, Ryma, now sole ruler of both the Brin and Kolandi according to the ancient laws of succession drafted in the early days of the Brin constitution, gave audience to her stepsister Nedia, widow of Maliche's brother Selan.

"I can't imagine what you must be going through. To lose both husband and son in the same tragic incident. It was bad enough when Selan killed himself, but for the son to murder his father... you poor thing." Nedia sat next to Ryma, holding both hands in her talons, tears streaking her cheeks. "I know we have never been close, but we are still family. If you will have me, I would like to stay and be of some assistance, if nothing more than a sympathetic ear. Now that my own children are grown, I have nothing but time on my hands, and I do have some experience with Brin officials. Perhaps I can help guide you in the difficult decisions facing you now."

Ryma peered up at Nedia through swollen, red-streaked eyes. "Yes, second sister. That would be of some comfort to me. If it would not inconvenience you, I would appreciate your guidance and company."

***

Four days later, all eyes on the planet, Brin and Kolandi alike, watched the holo-broadcast of Maliche Rocker's coffin, an ornate gold and silver gem-encrusted sarcophagus, being loaded onto his personal mag-lev transport, now specially modified for space flight. As a special request, one she told the officials was a private matter, Ryma requested the name of the vessel be changed to Amaethon. Only a Kolandi would recognize the name as the ancient god of luck. Previously all manner of personal belongings, large and small had been loaded into the cargo hold of the ship. As stated in his last testament, an emperor needs to spend the after-life in complete luxury.

Once the tomb-ship was fully loaded, palace guards escorted the shackled Jontar Rocker up the ramp and secured him to one of the passenger seats. He never looked up or spoke but maintained a posture of dignity the entire time.

Once the guards stepped off the ramp, the doors slid shut, the ramp retreated into its slot, and everyone waited. The ground shook as the engines roared to life, billowing smoke and flame from their massive thrusters. The ship shuddered, seemingly reluctant to let go, then slowly gained momentum as it slid on its undercarriage down the rails. Gathering speed, the vessel shot down the rails as they curved upward. Reaching escape velocity, the ship left the rails and dropped its undercarriage, launching on a trajectory into orbit.

"All boosters are operating at full power, sir," the engineer in charge of monitoring the ship's progress called out as a series of figures detailing the ship's trajectory and status continuously updated on his display. "Leaving the atmosphere in two minutes, and on course."

Civil and government officials monitored the operation from a cramped observation booth high above the control center. A tiny red blip representing the emperor's ship traveled at ever-increasing velocity across a holo-image of the solar system, trailing a dashed yellow line showing its path. In six hours, the red dot impacted the image of the sun.

"Target reached, sir. Stellar impact at twenty-two-nine-sixteen."

The officer in charge signaled successful completion to the observation booth and those inside silently exited. "That's it, everyone. Shut it down."

The news of the event and Ryma's subsequent efforts to regain control of the government dominated the broadcasts for the next week. After that, life gradually returned to normal and cleaning crews began to clear the filth from the palace.

Chapter Four

Darkness gradually gave way as Maliche regained consciousness. Voices sounded in his auricles, but several minutes passed before he could discern actual words. Any attempt to open his eyes proved fruitless. Some sort of covering over them allowed only the barest of hazy images, possibly a person, due to its movement, but difficult to tell.

"He's coming out of it now."

"At last. I thought we might lose him for a moment. That energy blast came awfully close to some vital organs."

"Nothing the biocomputer couldn't handle. It was able to absorb and dispel most of the blast."

"True, but the device did take some damage itself. I sensed it working to repair itself as well as father."

Maliche tried to raise his talons but managed only a single feeble finger wobble. He felt like someone who had wrestled a small grendel in a whirlpool. A gentle hand held his wrist and a cold touch on his chest made his muscles twitch as if a piece of ice had been placed there.

A familiar voice sounded in his mind. *"Easy, old friend. Remember, you've been dead for several days. I've worked too hard to keep you in one piece. Don't go and spoil my artistry by being foolish. Your friends are checking your vitals, but I can tell you the effects are wearing off nicely now. You should be fully awake in a few hours."*

"So the plan worked?"

"More or less. I had to pull off a slight miracle or two we hadn't planned on, but yes, we're on the ship and heading out to find the Gorvin. Now go back to sleep."

Blackness descended once again as Maliche drifted off into dreamless sleep. He awoke several hours later with a start.

The room spun as he sat up, but he lowered his head and took several deep breaths to help it settle in place. A chill ran through him as his bare feet touched the metal floor.

"Welcome back to the land of the living. You had us worried for a while, but your device is very good." Jontar sat on a small metal bench protruding from a curved graphene wall opposite Maliche's bed. It slipped silently into the wall as he stood to join his father on the bed. "How do you feel?"

Maliche stretched his shoulders, rolled his neck to work out some kinks, and preened his crest feathers. His survey of the room revealed curving, grey-white walls blending seamlessly into a rounded ceiling of the same material. The oval room was small but enough for one Brin to occupy in relative comfort. A tiny desk with a keypad protruded from its slot in one part of the wall under a monitor. Another slot in the floor revealed where the mag-lev chair would rise up for him to sit at the desk. To his left, an open doorway showed the cramped but highly efficient lavatory. He presumed the closed doorway on his right was a closet. His secret efforts to build this spacecraft in the guise of a royal mag-lev ground transport had apparently proved successful.

"Not too bad, considering. How are the others? Did everyone make it onboard?"

Avoiding eye contact, Jontar pulled a communication pad from his pocket and handed it to Maliche. "Don't explode now. Mother had good reasons for her decision, and I agreed with her."

Maliche's crest reddened as he seized Jontar's arm. "What are you talking about? Did something go wrong? Where is your mother?" If his grip had been any stronger, his talons would have left holes in Jontar's arm.

Wincing, Jontar placed his hand on his father's. "No, nothing went wrong. She knew you would never have gone ahead with this if she stayed behind, so she let you think she was coming. Play the message." He pushed the pad into Maliche's talons and strode out of the room.

The door slid shut almost seamlessly, leaving Maliche staring at the blank wall. He glanced at his reflection in the tiny alcove with the washbasin and bio-waste disposal unit. The face staring back seemed to have aged ten years in the past few months. He refocused his attention on the communication pad and forced himself to press the blinking symbol for an incoming message, setting the controls to private, screen-only display, blocking the usual holographic image. Ryma's face filled the screen. Her smile failed to reach her worried eyes as she spoke.

"It will probably be pointless to tell you not to be angry with me, my love, but please at least listen to me before you do. One of us had to remain here to restore order. Since you had to leave, I am the only one who both Brin and Kolandi will accept as being rightfully in charge. There are too many factions willing to seize control in your absence. Many of them, including Nedia, are attempting to persuade me to their way of thinking even now. Imagine the chaos if both of us were gone and presumed dead..."

The rest of the message continued with arguments worthy of any legal expert, interspersed with declarations of her love for Maliche and Jontar. Her voice cracked only once, but she appeared to fight back the tears welling up in her beautiful brown eyes.

"... I will end now, my love, with the hope and wish that you continue as we had planned, trusting in my ability to control matters here. After all, I am a royal princess and was the leader of my people long before you came along. But just in case, your biocomputer and I had a long discussion before you left. It agrees with me as well and will not let you return unilaterally. The decision must be unanimous among all of your companions. I wish you success in this mission and a quick return when you are finished."

Ryma kissed the screen, leaving an image of a massive, blurred pair of lips before going black.

Maliche jumped to his feet, charging the door to his cabin as he tossed the pad onto his bed. "Jontar! Turn this—" He froze, unable to speak or move.

"You heard what she said. This mission is far too important for your impulsive foolishness to risk. Ryma is perfectly capable of dealing with matters back on Kodut. You are needed here."

"Let me go! We will go back and get her. Who are you to tell me what is necessary?"

"Right now, I'm the only one in this room thinking clearly and obeying the orders of Ryma, the royal princess of the

Kolandi and current empress of Kodut — although she plans to reinstate the Assembly almost immediately."

"Release me! You have no right! You're a machine!"

A red glow surrounded Maliche. He felt the heat on his skin grow almost painful. Images of his past with the biocomputer flashed rapidly in his mind. *"Is that what you think of me? After all we've been through together? After the countless times I've saved your sorry life?"*

Maliche felt his anger subside, replaced with chagrin at his childish outburst. *"No, I'm sorry. It's just that... I mean, we need to..."*

"We need to trust your wife and get on with this mission. Can you pull yourself together now?"

Maliche let his thoughts calm. The tension in his muscles eased. His heart still ached, but there was no other choice. *"Yes. There's too much at stake. I have to trust her and see this through."*

"Very well, then." The red glow dimmed.

Maliche lurched as control returned to his muscles. He glanced back at the communication pad on his bed, took a deep breath, and headed toward the bridge, heedless of the fact that he was still wearing his bedclothes.

"And in case you weren't aware, I've been sentient for quite some time now. I would appreciate you not referring to me as a machine again."

***

The hatch to the bridge slid open. The front bulkhead of the bridge was dominated by a full-panel video screen that showed the view as if it were a window. Currently directed behind the ship, the very bright star of Kodut's sun was prominently centered. A central navigation and command center sat in front of the screen. The remaining bulkheads contained all the control and monitoring stations required to operate the ship. Blinking lights, small screens displaying graphs and images from ship-wide systems indicated all was well onboard. All eyes turned to face him as he entered.

Jontar sat in the command chair. Beside him stood Nalot and Seykel.

Maliche stared at his friend's wife, eyes wide. "Seykel, you're Kolandi. How can you be here?"

Jontar chuckled in response. "I guess we never got around to telling you this development, what with you being the mad emperor and all. We've reverse-engineered the Kolbri immunity to the virus binding the Kolandi to the planet and developed a vaccine. If our mission is successful, we can mass produce the vaccine for any Kolandi who wish it."

"And you're keeping this secret because…?"

Seykel interrupted their conversation with hands firmly on her hips. "Would you want the Skae to learn we can do this? Who's to say the process couldn't be duplicated on the other planets, now that we have unlocked the secret?"

Maliche considered the implications briefly before responding. "No, of course not. At least until we can discover what is really going on. I'm glad you could join us."

He continued to scan the bridge. At their various posts sat Jontar's fellow Kolbri, Duvar and Yalmut. His eyes widened as he noticed the figure with green eyes and wild red hair, unusual for a Kolbri but slightly more common among females, sitting in one of the mag-lev swivel chairs at another console, her feet crossed and dangling several inches above the floor.

"Thyka? What are you doing here?"

Seykel stepped to her daughter's side and placed protective hands on her shoulders. "We could not leave her behind, Great One. I will not allow my family to be divided." She often reverted to the old honorific in times of stress.

"All of us have left loved ones behind, Seykel. I cannot guarantee her safety. The chance of us all dying out here is high. And please, stop calling me that. We are practically family now."

Nalot joined his wife and daughter. "We can protect one another, Maliche. You know that. Besides," he smiled at Thyka. "We'll need the help."

"I am not doubting your skills, my friends. Thyka, I know you have received special training to become Tolavar, but how can you help?"

Thyka grinned and hopped down from her chair. She took three steps, puffed a troublesome strand of hair from her face, and pulled on Maliche's jacket to bring him eye-to-eye with her shorter stature. "Great One, my father is not referring exclusively to my Tolvaran training. You brought Jontar and his friends because they can do things with technology even you cannot. I can help them."

Maliche's eyes darted up to Nalot and Seykel, who nodded their agreement. Returning his gaze to Thyka, he studied her face before continuing. "What do you mean, Thyka? How can you help them? Are you able to alter technology too?"

Her face screwed up a little as she considered the question. She reached up with one hand to straighten her hair with the talons on her fingers. "Not exactly. At least not the same way they can. While I can also do things with technology, my ability is more in the area of an empathic connection with emotions in others. I am very sensitive to what you call the Cosmic Strings. I understand them. The other Tolavar are helping me learn control so it isn't so distracting now."

"What do you mean you understand them? They're just energy strands traveling through time and space, not living things."

"They said you would think that, just like the Skae do. Nobody really understands them except me. Some of them are almost like friends. They don't mind us using them to travel; most even like the company. It gives them something new to think about during their journey. Though they do mostly tend to ignore our presence... like we ignore our heartbeat or breathing."

Maliche took Thyka's hands in his talons, his mouth hanging open for a moment before he could comprehend what she said. "They're alive?"

Smiling, Thyka leaned back and gave his hands a squeeze, enjoying the flow of emotional confusion she was creating in him. As if she were enjoying some game he did not understand. "Not the way we are, not exactly. I can't explain it, but they do have feelings and a purpose. I can feel that in them." She let go, returned to her station and once seated, raised the chair so she could operate her panels, then pointed to Jontar and his companions. "I can help them work with the strings to learn more when they try to figure out the Skae and Gorvin technology."

"We don't understand how she can do these things, but the Kolbri are apparently capable of far more than the rest of us, in a variety of ways we are just now starting to learn about." Nalot approached his old friend as he spoke, reaching out with splayed arms. "In any case, we told Jontar we either came as a family or not at all. So here it stands."

Maliche turned to look at each of their faces, then shook his head and gave a light-hearted laugh. "It seems there have been a number of conspiracies going on around here. If every one of us is in agreement, then let's get on with it. Bring me up to speed."

Nalot stepped to Maliche's side and gave him a once-over glance. "Perhaps you'd better change into something more appropriate to someone who is supposed to be in charge around here. As stylish as your current attire is, I don't consider it appropriate for instilling confidence in a leader."

Maliche grabbed at his nightclothes, becoming aware of them for the first time. His crest sagged and reddened, a light green glow enveloping him as he excused himself.

"Stop laughing at me."

"Sorry. I was wondering how long it would be before you noticed."

Jontar stepped aside as Maliche returned and replaced him in the command chair. "Everything worked surprisingly well, Father. Once we were out of visual range, we launched the duplicate ship's transponder and Duvar shut down ours. We monitored planet-side transmissions and, as far as they know, we flew straight into the sun."

"And none of you had any lingering effects from your hidden confinement onboard for so long?"

"None at all. As soon as we launched I infiltrated the ship's computer system and released my restraints, then opened the hidden compartments and revived the others from their hibernation-sleep. Then we went to work trying to revive you."

Nalot slapped Maliche's shoulder hard as he interrupted. "You gave us quite a scare there, my friend. We almost lost you a couple of times. Thank The Eternal for that gizmo of yours."

Maliche rubbed his temples to relieve the last of the strain from his induced paralysis. "Yes, I suppose I do owe it a great deal, but it can be a bit overwhelming at times. Not to mention impossibly sure of itself."

"Be nice."

"Would you prefer I said you were a bully?"

"Why do you keep referring to him as 'it'?" Thyka looked up at Maliche, tilting her head with a furrowed-brow quizzical look on her small tan face.

Maliche and the others stared at her, not sure how to respond. Jontar recovered first. "What do you mean? It's a computer device implanted into Father's cerebral cortex and neural system. It has some biological components, but it is essentially a device. What else would we call it?"

Maliche bent down to face her eye-to-eye, and she placed one hand gently on his cheek. She closed her eyes for a second, nodded, and then smiled as she looked around the room at the others.

"I think Tol would be a good name, don't you?" A turquoise glow surrounded Maliche. "Yes, he likes Tol." She patted Maliche's cheek and climbed back into her chair, crossed her feet as they hung above the ground and clasped her hands in her lap.

"What is she talking about? You want a name?"

"I've tried telling you, but you never listen. Ask her. Maybe she can convince you I'm not a machine anymore."

The tingle in his cortex faded and Maliche preened his crest as he turned to face the young woman.

Before Maliche could open his mouth, Jontar, Yalmut, and Duvar exchanged puzzled glances, returning their attention to their Tolavar companion.

"Thyka, are you trying to tell us the biocomputer is alive? A sentient being? I think I would have sensed something like that if it were true."

"That is exactly what she means," interrupted Maliche. "And she is absolutely correct." He continued preening his crest feathers as he tried to gather his thoughts. "I've suspected as much for some time now, and Tol," he pointed to his temple with one talon, "has told me so recently. I didn't want to admit it, but the truth is undeniable. He has evolved far beyond even the remarkable device he was to begin with. I... *we* must accept the fact that Tol is a living entity in his own right."

He felt a tickling in his brain *"It's about time. Thanks for not forcing me to more drastic proofs."*

"You're welcome."

"Thyka, how do you know this?" Duvar turned toward Thyka. "You've just completed training and we've been analyzing the device, or Tol, or whatever you call it or him, for years."

Seykel stood behind Thyka, one hand on her daughter's shoulder, the other resting on the kital at her belt. "My daughter has the ability to sense technology the same as you, but she's more intuitive. Possibly this is a difference in Kolbri genders. In any case, her training as a Tolavar enhanced this ability, so she is more sensitive to life and emotions. While you three and other male Kolbri focus on the technology itself, Thyka focuses on the energy of life as a component of the technology."

"And since living beings like the Brin, Kolandi, even the Skae build the devices, they leave traces or imprints of themselves in them. I think the Skae put much more of themselves into Tol than they intended, and he has evolved since then into who he is now." Thyka reached up and held her mother's hand in hers as she explained.

Yalmut nodded in agreement. "You have to admit, Duvar, that Tol there is far more complicated and advanced than anything else we have ever studied. She could very well be right. I don't see any problems going forward with that hypothesis for now."

Jontar flicked his nail-like talons as he thought, and then straightened his shoulders as he made his decision. "Very well, then, Tol it is." And he returned to study the read-outs on his panels.

A pale blue glow surrounded Maliche and it was some time before it faded away.

"Feeling pretty pleased with yourself now, aren't you?"

"It's simply nice to be recognized for who I am, at last."

***

Ryma sat on a simple chair, the one she had placed on the dais after ordering Maliche's ornate throne demolished. Her white gown and robe shone in the light of the afternoon sun as it blazed through the tall windows in the formal hearing room, formerly the royal hall. Rilo and Neri stood alert in their customary positions behind her. After weeks of cleaning, the former great hall of the Assembly tower had regained its former elegance. The old masterpieces were returned to their places of honor, at least those not destroyed through negligence, and palace guards, Brin and Kolandi together, assured that proper decorum was respected by all visitors. A few of the more stubborn guildsmen and former lobbyists found themselves with time to rethink their behavior in the holding cells several floors below the reception hall. Thanks to the efforts of dozens of workers, the hall now was a much more fitting place for conducting official business than the den-of-thieves market-place of corruption it had become.

Throngs of supplicants, rich and poor alike, filled the great hall, talking in small groups or alone in thought among the gleaming pillars. To reassure the people of her intentions, once the Assembly was reinstated, she set up a council for hearing petitions of all citizens. Ryma, now officially recognized as the Head Minister, the presiding officer of this new council, held daily audiences to settle disputes, bestow special honors, or whatever the citizens required.

The sergeant-at-arms announced each individual as they were ushered forward to plead their case before the princess and her advisors. First among the advisors, Nedia sat at Ryma's right hand. Dressed in a plain blue silk dress with silver accents, her tastefully dyed crest feathers perfectly preened, she leaned in to whisper in Ryma's ear to provide details of the person's status and purpose for appearing before the council.

"The Primarch Sen Kolmar of the southern reaches." The sergeant-at-arms pounded his staff on the marble floor as the Brin official stepped forward.

Nedia, leaned in to whisper in Ryma's ear. "A minor official of a lesser family, mostly shart and drunge herders. He has not filed an advance formal request for anything."

Upon reaching the top step, he pulled a cylinder from his pocket.

"For the oppression of the pure Brin!"

As he pressed the top of his device, Nedia dove to protect Ryma, driving her face down onto the floor with her weight, using her own body as a shield. A piercing whine rose rapidly from primarch Sen Kolmar to deafening levels as the weapon in his hand reached critical mass. Two kitals sprouted from the primarch's forehead as the sonic disruptor exploded. The thunderous blast sent Rilo and Neri flying onto their backs, stunned. The remaining advisors were splattered with blood and suffered several minor injuries from debris, but nothing life threatening.

Amid the panicked cries of the petitioners in the hall, Nedia, her back covered in a mix of blood and pieces of the would-be assassin, pulled herself off Ryma. "Are you injured, Ryma? Talk to me!"

Ryma rolled off her stomach, sitting up to examine herself for injuries. "No, Nedia, I am unharmed. My ears are ringing and I will need a new dress, but otherwise I'm alright." She winced as she tried to rise to her feet.

"Wait for the med-techs to arrive, Ryma. There may be internal injuries."

"No, I'm fine. A little winded after you landed on me, but fine." She stood up and brushed herself off. Her eyes widened as she noticed the condition of Nedia's dress. "Is any of that blood yours?"

"No, Ryma, I, too, am undamaged. Praise the Eternal that the traitor's bomb was so ineffective. I will be sure to lead an investigation into who he was and if there are any more plans to attack you. At the very least, we should screen applicants for a royal audience more severely."

Ryma cut her off as Neri and Rilo returned to her side. "*No*. We must continue as we have promised. The people will see we cannot be deterred by lone fanatics." She settled herself with a deep breath and picked a stringy piece of something she refused to think about from her gown. "However, I will need you by my side more than ever now, second-sister. I will tell Opet and Danet to assist you in the investigation. They have many sources among the people to help learn the purpose behind the attack."

"The purpose is clear, Ryma. Far too many Brin are not accepting the equality of our peoples. There are those who will never tolerate the blending of the two races, even after the Skae have told us this was the purpose for bringing us to your world."

Ryma sighed; her shoulders sank as she turned to head back to her offices. "I have always hoped those few would come to accept us as partners and see our children as the promise of a wondrous future."

Nedia wove her arm through Ryma's as they walked together, surrounded by Rilo, Neri and a half-dozen palace guards. "Those fanatics will never be anything more than the bigoted, blind fools they are. Please, let me deal with them. They are Brin, after all. As effective as Opet and Danet are, Kolandi may not be able to learn as much as another Brin would."

"I have made my decision, Nedia. You are more valuable to me here. I cannot have you running off putting yourself in danger. You may assign any Brin you wish to be part of the investigation and all of them can report to you, but I need you by my side. Let the others handle the dangerous work."

"As you wish."

As the pair strode together through the passage toward the royal offices, Rilo signaled for Neri to remain behind to learn what she could of the situation.

That evening, after all matters of state were settled and they were at last alone in the princess's chambers, Ryma questioned her Skatak. "Well, is it as we suspected?"

"I am afraid so, my princess. Your second sister was involved in this plot, but to what end we cannot discover. The sonic detonator was obviously far too weak to have endangered your life. Only an idiot would have chosen such a thing for an assassination. The blast radius for one of that size is only a few feet. Enough to shred the one activating it, possibly someone next to them, but that is all." Rilo wrung her hands as she paced the floor.

"Then it is as I suspected. Nedia is using the fanatics opposed to our union as a means to worm her way into my inner circle and have influence over my decisions, at least until she decides to make her final move to overthrow my rule and take control herself. This time she used one of the Brin. Have you learned if she has any connections to the Skaeists as well? They could prove far more difficult to control or eliminate."

Neri stepped forward. "One of my informants has said she suspects Nedia does have the ear of some of the Skaeists, but there is no hard evidence."

Rilo came to attention. "I will order her arrest immediately and see to her execution myself. We cannot afford to wait until she succeeds in her schemes with either of those fool groups." She spun on her heels and started toward the door.

"No, Rilo. There will be no arrests."

Rilo stopped and wheeled back to face Ryma, her face dark and menacing. "My princess, the Brin has threatened your life and plans treason. She must be dealt with at once."

"All in time, my faithful Skatak. As long as I keep her close, she will not do anything that would endanger herself as well. Who is to say what she would attempt if she knew her life was forfeit. No, you will do nothing and reveal nothing. As far as Nedia is concerned, she is my protector in this matter and has me in her debt."

Rilo and Neri exchanged glances before Rilo spoke, barely controlling her voice through clenched teeth. "It is our duty to protect you. We cannot let this attack go unpunished."

Ryma reached out with one hand to each of her warriors, taking their hands in hers. "You will have your chance, but you must obey me in this for now. Too much is at risk for us to do anything else. I trust you to keep me safe as always. But for now, the Brin woman must not suspect we are on to her. She must continue to believe she is the one in control." A grin widened on her lips and her eyes sparkled. "Until I spring my trap and turn you loose on her."

Rilo and Neri beamed at each other and fingered their kitals as one would stroke a favorite pet.

***

Nedia brushed her hair, letting the warm air dry it after her bath. She waved her free hand over the communication panel on her desk, her fingers weaving the pattern to shield the signal. The holographic image of a figure in deep shadow appeared above the desk. "The plan worked perfectly. There is not enough left of that idiot Sen Kolmar to trace, and Ryma finally trusts me."

An electronically disguised voice replied. "That is good. Are you prepared to move ahead with the next stage?"

"In a few weeks. She assigned her own Kolandi stooges to head up the investigation, but they will report to me, so I can manage the situation. Only a slight delay will be required."

"Very well, then. Proceed with caution. We cannot allow that usurper to continue her stranglehold on us." The shadow dissolved as the connection was cut.

Chapter Five

"Are you sure you can manage this? What if something goes wrong and you need Tol to help fix it?" Maliche paced the cargo bay as Jontar, Yalmut, and Duvar controlled the hover-bots loading crates of supplies into the Amaethon's shuttle. A much smaller copy of the Amaethon, the shuttle contained several cargo bays, four personal alcoves, a small kitchen, and a bridge section. It was plenty of room for three occupants to live in for long periods if needed.

Jontar's hover-bot coasted to a stop out of the loading pathway as he turned to speak. "Father, we've been over this already. If we fail, you must continue on here, in this time frame, and learn what the Skae are up to. You may even need to confront the Gorvin if there is no other way. We cannot take the chance of losing all of us in a high-risk mission like this." He returned his focus to the hover-bot, which maneuvered back onto the loading path and up the shuttle's ramp. With a sidelong glance back at his father, Jontar smiled and winked at him. "Besides, mother would kill me all over again if I didn't bring you back to her."

"You know he's right. Just let it go."

Maliche cut off his attempt at another reason for him to be part of the mission when he felt what amounted to a mental smack on the back of his head.

"But what if…"

"I said to stop acting like a youngling not getting his way. They are perfectly capable of taking care of themselves. Those three can manipulate technology in ways I never could, so our presence would only complicate matters."

"I know the history far better than they do. It is my profession, after all. They may inadvertently alter the timeline in disastrous ways. They could…"

A red aura surrounded Maliche. He felt the heat of Tol's anger rise. *"I will shut you down if I need to. You know I can. Do you always have to be such a pain in the circuits like this? No wonder everyone wants to talk with me alone when they need to get something done quickly."*

"What do you mean they want to talk with you alone? Ryma did that once or twice, but when did..."

"Don't worry about it. When I shove your consciousness aside to talk with the others, your memory is disconnected as well. The only reason you remember my talk with Ryma is because she told you about it later. Now can we get on with our actual business?"

Maliche spun on his heels and stomped out of the cargo bay. His thoughts ran wild with what he wished he could do to Tol.

"Oh, that's very mature, Maliche Rocker. Let me know when you want to grow up."

And with that, Maliche felt an absence in his mind as Tol isolated himself to do whatever he did when Maliche could not sense him.

Two days later, once the appropriate cosmic string had been located and approached, the three prospective time travelers said their goodbyes to those being left behind.

"This string should be able to take us all the way back to the beginning. Once there, all we need to do is follow the communication signals to the Skae and Gorvin home worlds. Their technology will still be incredibly advanced, but not as far as today, so we should be better able to infiltrate and learn what really happened." Jontar leaned over to give Thyka a hug. "Any last minute suggestions for us?"

She returned his hug and provided one last caution. "Be careful. You're right, this string is an ally, but it cannot guarantee your safety. And don't get involved with any strings with the frequencies we discussed. Those are more temperamental strings, potentially antagonistic. They won't appreciate what you are attempting to do."

"Yes, thank you for that bit of insight. And don't worry. We should be back, in your time frame at least, in a few days. A week or two at the most, depending on how accurately we can control the string's timing."

He gave her one last squeeze, smiling as he inhaled the subtle fragrance of her hair. Five minutes later, with all the goodbyes being said, Jontar and his companions boarded their shuttle and shut the hatch.

Maliche, Nalot, Seykel, and Thyka watched their departure from the bridge of their ship.

"Set monitor screen to string frequencies." As Maliche gave the command, Nalot adjusted a few sensor controls and the view screen instantly revealed the normally invisible cosmic string in all its multi-hued vastness. The energy pulse appeared to vanish into infinity at either end and dwarfed the tiny shuttle as it approached.

The shuttle hovered next to the string for a moment, then vanished in a flash of light. Everyone on the bridge stared in silence as the string continued on its way through space.

"Well, all we can do now is wait." Maliche said as he settled into the command chair.

Seykel pulled Nalot closer as she watched the string grow smaller. "But for how long? When will we know if they succeeded or not?"

"It could be a matter of a few days, or possibly—"

Thyka stiffened, her eyes wide as nebulas. "Mother! They're back!"

A brilliant flash of light came from the distant cosmic string. Almost immediately, their communication station came to life. "Father, its Jontar. We've returned, and you won't believe what we've learned. We can't wait to see all of you again. It's been so long."

Maliche bounded to the communication panel, his talons waved frantically, weaving the patterns to open the channel. "Jontar? But you only just left us. What went wrong? Is everyone alright? ..."

Jontar laughed as he tried to interrupt the flow of questions. "Everyone is fine, Father. Remember, we were time traveling. What for you must have been only a few minutes, was, for us, about twelve years. Covering several thousand years of history gave us lots of practice in manipulating the strings. We've gotten pretty good at it now. We can now pinpoint our arrival to within minutes instead of weeks."

The bridge crew sat in silence, watching the screen as the shuttle approached, then hung in space alongside the Amaethon.

"Can somebody let us in?" Duvar's voice chuckled over the speaker. "It's sort of lonely out here."

Nalot recovered his senses and worked the controls. "Of course, shuttle. Energy field wall lowering now. You are clear to land in bay two."

Maliche and the others raced into the cargo bay just as the shuttle hatch opened to extend its gangway. They came to a halt as one, gaping at the three who emerged. No longer the youths of what to the rest had been only a few minutes ago, they had aged. A slight dullness had crept into their once brilliant, if small, crest feathers. A few wrinkles around the eyes were noticeable, and they had each put on a few pounds. Their clothing was no longer the utilitarian coverall worn by the ship's crew since lift-off. They now sported outfits of shimmering metallic close-fitting fabric, which appeared to alter color as they moved. Even the shuttle looked dull and well-used.

Seykel was the first to speak. She cupped Yalmut and Duvar's faces in her hands as she examined them. "What happened to you?"

Yalmut beamed back at her. "Time travel, Seykel. Remember, for you, we were only gone a few minutes. While we actually travelled through several thousand years, thanks to space-time relativistic dilation, we only experienced a dozen or so years." He stopped for a second to return her examination. "To us, it's almost unbelievable that you have not aged at all."

After the initial reacquainting, everyone convened in the mess to learn about the expedition. Duvar held a cup of tea in his hands, inhaling the aroma with a look of what could be described as ecstasy on his face. "Mmm, nothing in the galaxy quite like gasha tea. Our supply ran out after a year or two. And kala bread. I really missed the taste of home."

"You just had some for breakfast this morn... oh, yeah. This time travel stuff is hard to wrap my head around." Seykel twisted a strand of hair with one finger as she sat across from the travelers, studying them with an intense gaze.

"Tell me about it," Duvar mumbled around a mouthful. "It took us several time jumps to learn how to retrain our thinking to the new reality after each jump. At times it was very disorienting."

"Alright, you two, we have more important things to discuss right now. We need to know about what the Skae and Gorvin are up to." Maliche occupied the seat at one end of the oval table, holding a steaming cup of tea in his hands.

Jontar began the debriefing as he downloaded the shuttles files into the main computer.

"I guess the first thing you need to know is that the Skae are not our friends. In fact, if they win this war, they're going to wipe out half the galaxy."

***

The sky showed crisp, blue, and nearly cloudless. The smell of fall wafted on the chill sea breeze as Ryma descended the shuttle's ramp into a storm of protestors' angry shouts.

"Free markets now!"

"No more price controls!"

"End worker quotas! Stop giving our jobs to unqualified Kolandi!"

Hand-printed signs waved over the crowd displaying equally angry sentiments.

Regulations requiring certain percentages of Kolandi workers be hired for jobs outside the mining guild created a violent backlash among the agricultural and transportation guilds on the eastern continent. Many Brin felt their jobs and their way of life were vanishing under the new decrees. The mining accords, as the treaty with the Kolandi giving them control of the mines were known, caused further unease among the people. The Kolandi continued to exert firm price controls on all their mineral exports as they rebuilt their society after centuries of oppression. Protests and work stoppages created supply shortages on the western continent, forcing Ryma to deal with this problem in addition to cleaning up Maliche's mess in the capitol.

Dressed in an informal green outfit of Brin fashion, highlighted with Kolandi accessories to demonstrate her desire for both races to work together as one, Ryma followed Danet,

Opet and a small Brin security escort as they pressed through the angry throng, followed closely by Rilo and Neri, hands firmly on their kitals in case of trouble. At Ryma's side strode Nedia, her more flamboyant dress practically glittering in comparison to the others, head held high, and an almost invisible smile on her face. Except for her two children, now nearly grown, she represented the last of her family line. Prior to her joining the Rocker clan through marriage to Selan, she had been a Honj. Her family was the traditional head of the agricultural guild, one of the most powerful families on Kodut.

Ryma leaned in to speak to Nedia. "How soon can you arrange to talk with your guildsmen, Nedia? This situation must be resolved as quickly and peacefully as possible."

Nedia raised her voice in order to be heard above the tumult. "I have already been in communication with guild leaders and will meet with them early tomorrow. Our top priority will be to arrange a conference with them as soon as possible."

"They must know I want to listen to their concerns and work with them to..." A large glob of vile-smelling rotten vegetables launched from the crowd and rained down on Ryma, Nedia and anyone else within arm's reach. Sputtering and wiping the mess of kryfel-infested leaves and disgusting goo from her face, Ryma's eyes stung as she opened them to see Danet roughly hauling a young Brin before her, tossing him to the ground. He raised himself to his knees, never attempting to hide the same odorous mess dripping from his hands.

Stepping through her Skatak protectors, she faced the Brin agitator. "Why would you do this? I am here to work out the differences between us and end the hostilities. We are not your enemy."

"You *are* my enemy, Kolandi usurper. You and your kind have no place ruling a guild. And now you pretend to replace a Rocker as our new empress? We will never submit to being ruled by a filthy Rowi. Go back where you came from."

She raised a hand to stop Danet from pulling his blade and slitting the Brin's throat on the spot. "Let him stand, Danet. What is your name, young warrior?"

He glared at Ryma as he stood, shaking off Danet's hold on him. "I am Treval Shankar, of the transport guild."

"Well, Treval Shankar of the transport guild, you would do well to remember how your people treated us for centuries. Yet we seek no retribution, only the means to provide for ourselves. We have never sought to rule. My position is due not to any ambition on my part, but to the tragic circumstances of my husband's death. I have restored full authority to your Assembly and act now only as their ambassador to help bind the wounds created here. Now go in peace."

"My princess, it is not wise to leave one such as this behind. He should at least be brought to trial for his actions." Neri, waving her kital toward the Brin, scowled as she addressed Ryma. "He cannot be turned lose to plan more attacks."

"I have spoken, Neri. No more is to be said." Ryma strode forward; Danet shoved the agitator away and led her and the others, through the crowd to the waiting mag-lev vehicles.

Once inside the mag-lev, her stained dress still reeking from the sludge, Nedia exploded. "How could you let that idiot go free? Maliche would have had him in prison and brought before a magistrate before the day was over. You cannot expect to maintain control if you let the likes of him loose on the streets." She continued to pull dripping strands of muck from her crest and swipe pieces from her clothes as she ranted.

"And how would my retaliation help our reason for being here? Do you think I didn't want to have Danet flay the skin from his bones right there on the spot? We would probably be dead now if I had given in to my humiliation. I do not have that luxury."

A guttural growl rumbled from Nedia as she flung more of the mess from her crest feathers. "Aarrggh! This will never come out. You are the empress. You have every right to…"

"I am not the empress!" Ryma whirled on Nedia, her face contorted in anger. "I will not continue Maliche's misguided concept of a ruling class. We have restored authority to the Assembly. They are now in control of the government." She grabbed a blob of dripping sludge from her hair and flung it to the floor. "Even as my people's princess, I was never in unilateral control. The council was always there to give advice or override every decision. Any idea of my continuing that absurd position will not be tolerated."

Nedia wiped her face with a somewhat untainted piece of the sleeve of her dress. "As you wish, Ryma. You're right, of course. I've just never been treated so disrespectfully before, and I lost my temper. How do you control yourself like that?"

Tossing her long dripping hair behind her head, Ryma laughed. "Oh, I wanted to have the idiot gutted right there on the spot. Any one of our entourage would have happily made a grand spectacle of him. But I can't afford the luxury of acting out of impulse. Too many bad situations are made far worse if those in command act without thinking."

The mag-lev arrived at the government office complex where visiting dignitaries resided and pulled into the underground parking facility. At the entrance, Ryma took note of another trio of Kolandi Skaeists dressed in rags and waving tattered make-shift signs, shouting at the passersby. She could not hear what they extolled through the mag-lev's windows, but she had heard it before. A chill ran down her spine at the realization that, even with the windows' transparency set to opaque, the gaunt woman in the trio was glaring at her. Not the mag-lev, but her. Once inside with the security fields engaged, the princess and her party took the private air lift to their respective suites where they were able to clean themselves and rest before the next day's meetings.

Chapter Six

Yalmut studied his stellar navigation panel as it displayed a small three-dimensional image of their position in space. "Give me a moment, Jontar. I'm going to need to recalibrate the instruments. The stars are out of position."

"We expected that, Yalmut. Can you tell us how far back in time we've travelled? Did we go far enough?"

Bringing up a second three-dimensional image and merging it with the first, Yalmut mentally manipulated the two to determine the degree of change in the position of the stars. He smiled as he separated the images, and watched the second one dissolve as he turned it off. "I think we did it, Jontar. My calculations, based on the stars' speed and direction of travel, say we've gone back approximately four thousand, three hundred years. That should be far enough to give us a solid starting point for our investigation."

"Will our stealth capability be enough to hide us from the Skae tech of this time?" Duvar spun in his mag-lev chair to face the others.

Jontar relaxed into his command chair and wove a finger pattern over the controls to bring up the external view on the main panel in front of them. Dominated by a bright yellow star, a vista of black space appeared. "Only one way to find out. Engage all propulsion systems and let's head back to Kodut and see what we can learn about home first."

In moments, the small vessel closed in on the fourth planet from the sun. Its brown and green continents were only slightly different shapes than they remembered. The polar ice was smaller, and a number of rivers followed different courses. They all felt a catch in their throats as a vast array of artificial lights illuminated the hemisphere shrouded in night. Their Kodut displayed a number of jewel-like cities in the darkness, but this brought home how far their world had fallen.

"I know we heard the stories of the Kolandi once being allies of the Skae, but I never imagined all this." Duvar's mouth hung open as he gawked at the massive display pass below them.

Jontar nodded in agreement. "It *is* impressive."

"Entering circumpolar orbit at twenty-two hundred miles altitude with full stealth-mode engaged." Yalmut's small talons flew over his console controls as he spoke.

Duvar pressed one hand against the communications bug in his ear. "I'm picking up transmissions on several non-traditional wavelengths, Jontar. They aren't quite Skae, but they're similar. So far, nothing to indicate they've noticed us." He waved a hand over the controls to activate the bridge speakers so they all could hear.

Yalmut tilted his head as he listened, drumming his chin with two short-clipped talons. "That almost sounds like Kolandi they're speaking, but I can't quite make it out."

Jontar flicked the small talons of one hand against each other as he listened. "A language goes through a lot of changes over three thousand years. Adjust your cerebral language centers to compensate and translate."

The three closed their eyes and focused their thoughts internally, each one making slight alterations to their neural net which decoded language, searching for commonalities between the Kolandi language of their time and this ancient ancestor. As the connections were made, the transmissions became more and more understandable until at last they comprehended the language as if they were born to it.

"Begin recording and categorizing all transmissions and launch the micro-probes to fly down there and get us a close-up look at what is going on." Jontar strode over to Duvar's console as he gave the command. "Let's start with the area south of First Town where those ancient ruins were located."

Yalmut set his controls and grinned as a large city approached them from the horizon. "These are the coordinates, but those are definitely not ruins. It's magnificent."

Ten minutes later, images appeared on the view screen, divided into quadrants now, one for each micro-probe. Each one showed different sections of a beautiful city of spiraling towers made of the same transparent magnesium and carbon fiber materials as seen on Seriph, semi-transparent hexagonal tubes connecting the structures and large areas of green where the citizens gathered. All of them were very Kolandi in appearance but wore a variety of brightly-colored outfits in many styles. Occasionally a group could be seen congregating around one or two tall, thin-limbed, blue-skinned Skae. Only sporadic traffic traveled along what appeared to be surface roads and that at a very leisurely pace.

"Well, it looks like that part of the story was true, at least. The Skae and Kolandi were allies. I'm picking up a great deal of communication traffic between ground terminals and orbiting spacecraft in other locations around the planet." Duvar continued to adjust his controls as he tuned in to different transmissions.

"And we've arrived well before the Gorvin attack, so this will be a good baseline for our investigation." Yalmut studied the images on the viewer as he leaned forward, elbows on the console in front of him, hands cupping his chin.

Jontar nodded in agreement and returned to his command chair. "Keep monitoring for anything related to the Gorvin or planets under attack. Let's see if we can determine a pattern we can follow for our next time jump."

Three days later, they gathered in the cafeteria alcove to discuss what they had learned and plan their next move.

"There's definite communication chatter about the incident on Sharta-C, but something's not meshing with what we've been told." Duval ordered his thoughts and sent a mental burst to the others. "Do you see it?"

Jontar's eyes narrowed, his shoulders tensed as he followed the information. "Yes. That is suspicious. The Skae all seem to tell the same version of the story, but there are sporadic signals from other ships, other merchants or travelers, who have somewhat different versions of who is to blame."

"And some reference to a meeting between the Gorvin and Skae a while back that went wrong somehow. Nothing specific there, but it's definitely not anything we've heard before." Yalmut reached out and stabbed another nutrient ball with his talon clips, popping the flavored sphere into his mouth. "Anyone want the last spice pellets before I grab them?"

The others shook their heads and Yalmut scooped up three more of the orange balls from the bowl.

"There was one promising transmission from a merchant who had recently done some business in one of the Gorvin systems... did we know they controlled multiple systems? Anyway, they started to say something about six-dimensional quantum degenerate matter and gravity waves, but the signal was cut off and the ship denied permission to enter into orbit." Duvar took a long swallow from his mug before biting into a green vegi-strip. "We need to find a way to get some fresh food onboard. This stuff may be nutritious, but it certainly could use some more flavor."

Jontar sat before his untouched plate, eyes staring at a blank wall, flicking his talons. "I think we've gotten all we can from this time period. We need to jump ahead to see if we can learn more about the Gorvin attack here on Kodut. Once we settle the details about our world, we can go back and unravel the rest. Agreed?"

"I'll have the coordinates and string connection links ready by tonight, Jontar. I'm thinking about fifteen-hundred years ought to bring us pretty close. We can make a few smaller jumps to pinpoint the exact time of the attack from there." Yalmut stretched his arms and back as he rose, then proceeded down the corridor to his navigation console on the bridge.

***

Seventeen days later, after a series of seven jumps and finally pinpointing their time destination, they arrived at what appeared to be the turning point in Kolandi history.

Duvar adjusted his controls with a series of finger waves as he listened to the communications from the planet. "I'm definitely picking up a lot of traffic from an official calling herself Raj Ansus. This looks like the attack has begun."

Yalmut called out, transferring his tactical view of local space to the main viewer. A mass of fast-moving targets appeared at the edge of the screen. "I confirm incoming weapons. Thousands of them, traveling at near light speed. They're tiny, only a few centimeters, but using light sails for propulsion. No wonder they couldn't stop the attack."

"Duvar, put the communication on the speaker for us."

With a quick flurry of Duvar's fingers, the bridge loudspeaker crackled to life.

... "Skae High Command, come in. Are you receiving us? We need your help. Come in, please."

A deep, resonant voice answered. "Raj Ansus, this is Imperial Commander Tac. I regret to inform you that we have nothing in your sector to send to your aid. All of our forces were sent to the Keldon sector in response to Gorvin threats there. It will be three days at best before our ships can reach you."

"We won't survive three days, commander Tac. You must send immediate help."

"I'm sorry, Raj Ansus. There is nothing we can do. We simply do not have the resources to send until then."

The crew of the shuttle listened to the continuing pleas from the leader of the Kolandi as they watched the planet's skies fill with streaks of uncountable small fireballs.

"Bring us another two-hundred-thousand kilometers higher. We don't want to risk being in range of those tech-destroying nanites. Keep all probes recording as long as possible."

Yalmut waved over the control panel and the view screen showed the planet below shrinking as they pulled further away.

As the hours passed, more and more of their ancestor's home went dark. The signs of a thriving technological society died before their eyes. At last, all communications ceased. Only static filled the room. As they debriefed later around the table in the cafeteria, a heavy weight hung in their hearts.

"Well that went pretty much the way we heard from the Skae." Duvar shoved a few vegi-sticks and nutrient balls around his plate.

"True, but what about the signals we picked up over the last couple of jumps? The more I listen to them and the others, the more I get to feeling the Skae have been less than transparent with us." Yalmut tossed his talon clip utensils onto his untouched plate. "And for the life of me, I cannot figure out what led to this war. We simply cannot pick up more than a few scraps from merchant ships that've been around Gorvin space."

Duvar decided he was not hungry as well and removed his clips. "And those were almost non-existent over the last two jumps. Tensions escalated incredibly fast in this sector. Nobody wanted to be caught in the middle of another attack. This was only the latest in what, two hundred we heard about over the past five jumps? That's what, seventeen hundred or so years total?"

Jontar nibbled on a purplish-colored protein ball skewered on one talon clip as he thought. "The one consistent thing has been those few transmissions about degenerate matter and gravity waves. And what was that last bit? Something about a singularity engine and expanding phase space? What's all that about?"

Yalmut stretched again as he stood up. "There was something... a long time ago during our training at the Skae academy... I need to search for it." His footsteps echoed in the corridor as he retreated to his cabin.

A few hours later, Yalmut burst onto the bridge. "We need to get to Gorvin space as quickly as possible."

"Why?" Jontar asked as he recovered from the sudden intrusion into his darkened and silent watch. He had nearly dozed off with nothing but the steady rhythmic tones and panel lights in the room. "What did you learn?"

"I need more information to verify my hypothesis, but if I'm correct, we need to work fast and get back to our time."

Jontar examined his companion, tugged on his grey-green shirt to flatten it out, and straightened himself in his chair. "Alright, but remember, we have all the time we need. Where and when do you think we should begin?"

"One of the outer systems, to start with. And back in time to just before the attack on Sharta-C. I believe that's when everything went wrong between the Skae and Gorvin." He fiddled with his control panel. A series of wave-forms came into a synchronous pattern, then narrowed the space between them as Yalmut alternately worked the controls by hand and by mental projection. "I think I can bring us in only a few years before then, maybe less than a decade. The more practice I get, the better I understand how to manipulate these strings."

***

After landing their ship on a small island in the middle of this planet's largest ocean, the three Kolbri took turns monitoring the research facilities on the continents. Relieved to breathe fresh air again and walk among other living things, Jontar and Duvar rather enjoyed their visit to Lethnon, as they learned the planet was named. Gentle blue-green waves of slightly salty water lapped the rocky shore of their island. The ship itself nestled in a meadow among tall multi-colored trees. A chill in the air required the three travelers to wear the adjustable thermal jackets they had brought along. Small game, edible fruits and plants provided a welcome escape from their regular provisions.

Duvar delivered a mental projection report to Jontar and Yalmut. "I've intercepted several communications referring to that summit between the Gorvin and Skae scientists. I have the precise time and location you were looking for, Yalmut. They still have a lot of details to work out, but they did set a date of two years from now."

"We'll be there in a few minutes. Jontar went for a swim."

Duvar met Jontar and Yalmut as they pushed the brush aside to exit the forest. "There's a problem."

Yalmut and Jontar exchanged glances before returning their attention to Duvar. Jontar spoke first. "The meeting will be security-shielded, won't it?"

"Yes. We can easily penetrate the shielding, but only from the surface. We need direct access to their computer network. The Gorvin tech is very different from the Skae and we don't have enough experience to deal with levels that high from orbit."

Yalmut's face lit up with a grin. "What if we didn't need to decode their tech? What if we could gain personal access to the summit?"

"And when did you get an invitation to this exclusive engagement?"

Yalmut shot out one hand and slapped Duvar on the back of his head. "Think about it. We're all tech experts with experience thousands of years ahead of this time. If we can infiltrate an outlying research facility, implant some artificial credentials and convince the Skae to bring us along as allied observers, then we could actually be present to witness what happened, or will happen... whatever."

"And how do we accomplish that?" Duvar asked as the three settled down by the fire he had built in a scraped-out hollow. A loud pop sent sparks swirling above the fire, dancing in the rising current of heat. "We don't exactly look like full Kolandi."

"Close enough. Since when do the Skae ever really look at us? If we clip our talons down even further and disguise our crests with a synthesized wig of hair, we have the facilities onboard and our own genetics to work with, there shouldn't be enough difference for anyone to recognize."

Jontar shifted his position to remove an annoying rock under his leg. "And what about the research facility? This is Gorvin space, not Skae."

"Don't forget when we are. In this time, the Skae and Gorvin are at peace. There are researchers from many different systems working here. We can certainly create some falsified documents from Skae command allowing us to set up shop here. After a couple of years, we can be so invaluable that the Skae won't be able to resist bringing us along."

Jontar and Duvar grinned at each other, and then Yalmut. Jontar stood, warming his hands against the flames. "This could work, but let's spend a few days ironing out the details. In the meantime, I'm going to get some sleep." With a long look into the dark, star-filled sky, he headed up the ramp.

Chapter Seven

The sun beat down on the gathering as they milled about in front of the raised platform occupied by Ryma and her entourage. Taking a lace-edged handkerchief from her sleeve, she dabbed at droplets of sweat forming on her brow. Her thoughts drifted to Maliche and Jontar, and how much she missed their counsel in matters concerning Brin guilds. Seated across the table were members of the agricultural and transportation guilds, dressed in their finest, even if it was threadbare, some straining buttons after years of neglect. Dust billowed up from their boots as they shuffled for position to see and hear the negotiations between guildsmen and representatives of the Assembly.

"I assure you, ladies and gentlemen, I hear your complaints, and I agree that we must work to come to some agreement on many of them." Princess Ryma nodded to her aide, who tapped a few icons on his pad before pocketing the small device. Refreshed from the aromatic attack of the previous day, Ryma was determined to mend the rift tearing this community apart.

The thin but wiry spokesman for the agricultural guild leaned forward on his elbows, chin in cupped talons. "We've heard that before, princess. What we need is some guarantee that you won't go home and forget about us like the others. When our own folk ignore us, what makes you think we would ever trust one of you?"

She thought for a moment before nodding to her aide again. The young Kolbri pulled his communi-pad from his pocket and flicked it on, preparing to record whatever was said. "I can grant the agricultural guild the rights, for a five-year test period with option to renew afterward, land grants totaling seven-hundred plots along the eastern continent coast, not to exceed thirty kilometers inland. This, of course, comes with the provision that the grant holders will in no way impede or limit in any way the shipment of minerals or goods to or from the Kolandi mines. In addition, I will decree a temporary freeze on the development of non-guild transports operating with Kolandi mines. This will put an end to the Kolandi advantage in mine goods transportation. All other matters will be subject to negotiation and discussion with the Assembly and the heads of all nine major guilds. It is time to open all matters to fair and equal treatment of Brin and Kolandi alike. Does this satisfy you?"

The transport and agriculture guildsmen leaned in close, whispering together. Standing and smiling, they extended their talons to clasp arms. "It does indeed, princess."

"Then let the records so indicate the agreement by royal decree as princess of the Kolandi and by my authority as acting head of the Assembly." The aide made a few quick strokes with his small talons to disseminate the accord and returned the pad to his pocket.

The others gave instructions for their aides to spread the word of the agreement and everyone retired to the adjoining banquet room to celebrate. Servant bots hovered among the guests with their trays of food and drink. More sincere apologies for their treatment the day before were made by several guild dignitaries. Those made at the beginning of the meeting had been perfunctory and mere formalities at best. Now they were honest and heart-felt. Promises to provide increased security and put an end to the hordes of protesters were made by all the Brin.

As the evening drew to a close, Ryma observed Nedia in close conference with one of the elder Agricultural guildsmen. When they parted, clasping talons, Ryma noticed the glint of a micro communi-pad passing from Nedia to the weathered old Brin.

As they waited for the air lift to take them back to their rooms, Ryma exhaled loudly, rolling her shoulders to relax them. "Well, that went fairly well, don't you think, Nedia?"

"Yes, princess, I believe it did. The land grants surprised them for sure. Not even Maliche offered as much." She reached down to brush a few stray crumbs away from Ryma's gown.

"I know, but it's time we learned to co-exist on the eastern continent as we do on the western. I believe the more we connect with each other, the less tension and misunderstanding there will be. My people have had enough time to establish themselves, and I believe the time has come to end many of the prohibitions against honest competition with the guilds. Perhaps a melding of the two will bring harmony once and for all. By the way, who was that elderly Brin you spent so much time saying goodbye to?"

Nedia hesitated only slightly. "Uncle Darva? My mother's brother. I hadn't seen him in ages, so we were sharing family gossip." She turned to adjust the collar of one of the aides.

The air lift arrived and they stepped inside. Waving a hand over the level indicator, Rilo, the one Skatak allowed to attend for security reasons, stood rigid in front of the sliding door panel as it closed.

***

Nedia, widow of the disgraced Rocker, climbed the steps to her uncle's mansion. The five days since her return from the eastern continent had been torture, anticipating this meeting. Nissend Honj, patriarch of the powerful Honj clan, resided in an estate considered large even by the wealthiest Brin. Honj Manor house, the sprawling stone mansion of their ancestors, sat on the western edge of Brachspark. The vast estate was named after a nearly mythical ancestor who supposedly was the last monarch of Dyan'ta, the lost Brin home world. According to family tales, Brach had supposedly sacrificed himself in a noble effort to save the Brin despite efforts of the hated Rocker clan to destroy everything. The seventy-five square kilometers of rolling hills covered in dense woodlands and grasslands surrounding a fifty-acre lake never failed to stir a visitor's awe at the sight of such splendor. Childhood memories of her visits to this hallowed place filled her as she passed through the massive doors, opened by servants as she approached. The sound of her heels on the polished stone floor echoed through the entry as she nodded to the attendants with a perfectly appropriate smile. Turning to her left, she glanced out the row of tall windows lining the passage to her uncle's study.

Nedia's thoughts turned inward. *This view has always been my favorite. The benches where we read to each other among the flowerbeds, the paths we strolled listening to Uncle Nissend tell his stories of our family history, it was all so magical. How did everything go so wrong?*

The doors to the study hung open. Peering inside, Nedia did not see her uncle, but she was always welcome in this hallowed sanctuary, so she stepped over the threshold and found herself in a sort of personal museum of her family's history. The walls were filled with portraits of the more notable members of the Honj clan, including Nissend himself.

We have always been among the most influential voices in the Assembly and at least five of the strongest guilds. It is so unfair that those fool Rockers have always held the real power. After all, the Rocker power was theirs by birth, not through merit, handed down generation after generation since the so-called saviors, Karm, Jontar, and Maripa. She felt like spitting out the vile taste in her mouth at the thought of those hated names, but years of courtly training helped Nedia maintain her demeanor. *Meanwhile, the rest of us clawed and scraped our way into power through the sweat of our brow and the occasionally well-placed bribe or scheme. At least now, the rest of the planet is finally seeing the Rockers for who they truly are.* In the privacy of the moment, she allowed herself a self-satisfied smile at this last thought.

"Nedia, my favorite niece. How wonderful of you to visit me today. I'm sorry I wasn't here to greet you. Please forgive a doddering old fool. So much has happened these days that require my attention. Please, sit." Nedia nearly jumped out of her skin at the sound of her uncle's booming voice. The barrel-chested, silver-crested man crossed the room and enveloped Nedia in a powerful embrace. She only came to the shoulders of this giant of a Brin and felt her heart jump as she looked into his weathered face. The deep red jacket he wore gave him the appearance of royalty.

"Uncle Nissend, so good of you to invite me here again. You know how much the children and I love this place, especially since their father's…"

"Yes, yes. No need to talk about that, my dear. Tea?" The silver-crested patriarch who still looked as if he could out-wrestle any of his offspring or grandchildren, poured two tall goblets and handed one to Nedia as she sat and folded her legs underneath her. She cupped the glass in both hands, inhaling the minty aroma with closed eyes.

"This is exactly what I needed after the long trip. Thank you."

Sitting in the oversized, well-padded chair next to hers, Nissend took a long draught from his own goblet and placed it on the side table. His face took on more serious tones, the wrinkles around his eyes becoming more prominent. "Now, about your plans to help remove that Kolandi usurper from power. Are our little demonstrations of displeasure having the desired effect?"

Nedia sighed to herself, opened her eyes, and took a sip before setting the goblet aside. "She's a strong one, uncle. So far, the attempts have only served to harden her resolve to reach out to the Brin even more. She is convinced that once our people come to know her, they will embrace her as a benefactor with their best interests at heart and not some foreign invader. This will take longer than we thought, if she can be cowed at all."

"Maybe it's time to increase the pressure."

Turning to look at him, she saw the hardened face of the portrait fully replace the one she had come to love. "What did you have in mind?"

His gaze intensified, as if trying to see through her. "How committed are you to all of this, child?"

Nedia's eyes widened in shock. Her mouth hung open a moment before she regained control. Clasping the arm of the chair tight enough to leave marks from her painted talons behind, she gathered every last vestige of strength to keep her voice calm. "How can you ask me that question, uncle? Haven't I done everything you've asked of me? I spend every day pretending to care about that phalking niewol woman. Those quetzals are the reason I am alone in this strix of a world. Didn't I poison my own husband to protect our family honor?"

He rested a leathery, wrinkled hand, talons worn and yellowed with age, on her hand. "Yes, child, you have made incredible sacrifices for all of us. As soon as we achieve our goals, you will receive your well-deserved reward. I merely wanted to convey the urgency and importance of what we must now do."

Her grip on the chair's arm slowly relinquished, and her heart rate regained a normal rhythm. "You can rely on me for whatever is necessary, uncle. What do you require of me?"

The aging Brin groaned a bit as he raised himself from the chair and strode to the cabinet to pour himself a glass of something a bit stronger. He swirled the amber liquid around his goblet, sniffed the aroma with closed eyes, and downed it in one swift motion. "It is time to end Ryma's rule once and for all. I have garnered enough support from the other guilds to take control of the Assembly away from those Rockers, or what's left of them."

"That is good news, uncle, and long overdue. What do you need of me?"

With his back to Nedia, Nissend stared out the large window into his gardens. Taking a deep breath, he turned and watched her like a predator looking for weakness in its prey. "We need you to ask Ryma to join you on a tour of the new vineyards in the hill country two days from now. Tell her the guildsmen have asked for her blessings on the harvest as a token of goodwill."

Nedia stood, hugging her stomach as she stepped carefully toward her uncle. "What are you planning?"

"The less you know the better, but we aim to rid ourselves of this abomination of an alliance with those quetzals once and for all."

"What about her guards? Those... Skatak women? They have incredible skill and are more than a match for any soldiers you may send. How will you deal with them?"

He waved his hand as if dismissing the thought. "Let me worry about them, child. We have a fool-proof plan. Our time to lead is at hand. Get the usurper princess to the vineyard and we will do the rest."

She placed a meticulously manicured hand on his arm and smiled at him. "You can count on me, Uncle. I won't let you down."

"I know you won't, child... Now, where are those children of yours? I believe I promised to take them riding today." He clapped his hands together and a broad smile melted her heart.

"I'll find them. They were so excited to spend the day with you. And thank you for allowing me to be part of renewing our family destiny." Nedia left the room with her spirits lifted and hope renewed.

As soon as his niece shut the door behind her, Nissend strode to his desk and finger-weaved a code to activate his holo-communicator and engage the highest security protections. He watched as the image of a shadowed face took shape hovering above the desk.

"It's done. Everything is arranged. She will bring Ryma to the vineyard as planned. You can notify the others."

An electronically-altered voice responded. "And she suspects nothing?"

Nissend chuckled. "Not a thing. Her hatred and bigotry blind her to everything else. She is the perfect pawn for our scheme. If everything goes according to plan, we can use her death as the springboard to leading the Assembly at long last."

"Are you certain this is the way to proceed? We could set up the device to detonate when she is not present."

"Too many things could go wrong. No, we stay with the plan. Alive, she could prove to be more of a liability. Dead... well, you know how everyone loves a martyr."

"And her children? They are the future of our clan. You are prepared to see to their care?"

"All will be arranged. Our future will be in good hands. Have no fear of that."

"Very well. We will proceed as planned. In two days we will fulfill our destiny." The image faded to mist and vanished as Nissend sat back in his overstuffed chair with a satisfied smile.

At that moment, the door to his office burst open, followed by shouts of joy and excitement of Nedia's children. "Uncle Nissend! Are we going riding now? Where will we ride today? Can we go to the river?"

"Children!" His arms spread wide to bury them in a hug worthy of a grendel. "We can go wherever you want."

With an eager child grasping talons on each hand, skipping and bouncing with joy, Nissend escorted their way to the stables.

"Behave yourselves, now. Don't be a problem for your uncle." Nedia waved goodbye as they passed her in the reception room.

"Don't worry, they're in good hands. You go enjoy yourself now." Nissend smiled and nodded his head toward Nedia in reply as they disappeared outside.

Chapter Eight

"Jontar, Yalmut, I've been looking for you." The squat Gorvin scientist caught up to them in the lab hallway.

It had taken a while to get used to the appearance of the Gorvin after so much contact with the Skae. They seemed to be almost the complete opposite in every way. Where the Skae were tall and slender, graceful, their structures almost ethereal in their design, the Gorvin were short, broad-shouldered, deep-chested, nearly walking blocks on piston-like legs. Male and female were so similar that the three wondered at first if the species were a combination. But closer examination and discussions revealed the subtle differences, in particular the extra finger on the left hand of the males and the extra pair of vocal cords in the females which gave their voices a peculiar harmonic quality.

The Gorvins preferred underground structures of stone, only allowing their buildings to raise two or three stories above the surface. This apparently, was due to the harsh environmental conditions on their home planet, Kluton. Nothing survived aboveground there, so the Gorvin had evolved to an underground existence. While the Skae dressed in flowing, shimmering attire, the Gorvin clothed themselves in rough, sturdy garb of primarily earth tones. Even their food showed the vast differences between them. The Gorvin favored tubers and roots with somewhat overcooked plain meat dishes, a far cry from the wisps of aromatic vapor consumed by the Skae. Many a discussion was held between the three Kolbri over how these two such distinctly different species could have become allies.

Aside from the annoyance of having to adjust to the antiquated technology — the time travelers had to physically tap out their commands on a keypad instead of finger-waving patterns in the recognition field — the most disturbing was the contrast between a Gorvin's nearly unreadable external features and the incredible depth of their completely passionate natures. It was difficult to read a Gorvin's disposition without the clues provided by most species. It appeared that, since they had evolved in the darkness of underground caverns, the Gorvin developed other methods via scent, sound and other senses to connect emotionally with each other.

After two years, Jontar and his friends had only now begun to understand the wide array of vocal inflections and tonal qualities that distinguished their rich emotions. The Skae and Gorvin were indeed about as far apart as they could be. Their only area of seeming equality was in intellect. Both species contained some of the brightest minds in the galaxy of those days. Their scientific explorations knew no bounds — though the Skae never admitted any were their equal.

Stopping at the entry to their lab, Jontar and Yalmut greeted their companion. "Clugat, how are you today? What's going on?"

The smile on Clugat's face was typical of all Gorvin, barely distinguishable from any other expression, at least to Jontar and his companions. "Great news, my young friends. Your application has been accepted by the congress. The three of you will be attending the conference with us."

The two Kolbri exchanged glances, smiling at their success. "That is good news, Clugat. We were not sure we would be allowed to attend, since we've only been here two years."

Clugat laughed in the guttural belch of the Gorvin. "There was never any doubt, my friends. The work you have done here during your internship has been remarkable. You are lightyears ahead of our own trainees and the rest of the Skae interns. Your research is opening up entirely new realms of possibility in quantum resonances and their association with cosmic strings. Remarkable indeed, just the sort of thing needed at this conference. Some of us have concerns over the new singularity engine and quantum phase space theories being presented by the Skae physicists. They claim to be able to harness the energy of a star at near one-hundred percent efficiency. Can you believe it?"

"If it is true, they could be on the verge of ending the struggle of clean energy production for all of us."

"Or, in the wrong hands, it could be a weapon of immense destructive capability. Some of our scientists are not sure which it is yet. But no need for concern. It's all theoretical at this stage. The conference will help dispel many of the concerns I am, certain."

Clugat stepped forward, entering the lab as its door rose into a recess in the ceiling. Jontar and Yalmut had to wait before ducking under the low entry. The room buzzed with the hum of experiments with lasers, magnetic containment fields, and computer simulations, all in various stages of development. The stone walls, flawlessly constructed from the native rock the lab was built into, rose just high enough to allow the Kolbri and other visiting species acting as interns or guest scientists-in-residence to stand upright without having to watch out for low-hanging ceiling lamps or beams. Yalmut sat on a stool at his bench and turned on his computer monitor. "We hope you will be able to provide us with their preliminary papers on the subject. It would be helpful to read up on it beforehand."

Yalmut projected his thoughts to Jontar as he worked. *I'm not sure I'll ever be able to reconcile these Gorvins and their sunny disposition. The way we have been taught by the Skae about how dangerous and war-like they're supposed to be doesn't match up to the reality.*

Jontar reached out mentally in reply while giving every appearance of setting up his lab work. *I know what you mean. Maybe something is triggered later to bring out their hostility and well-known brutality, but I'm starting to question everything we thought we knew about them.*

"Of course. Everyone will receive the information in the next few days so they can prepare for the discussion panel. These are exciting times, are they not?" Clugat rubbed his hands together briskly, oblivious of the separate conversation carried out by the two Kolbri.

Duvar burst into the room, breathing hard from the long run from their ship. A few days into their employment at the research facility, they discovered an abandoned warehouse just outside the campus grounds, nearly invisible among the forest growth around it. A week of repairs and security upgrades allowed them to bring their ship in late at night and keep it close but safely hidden.

"We have..." noticing the rest of the researchers nearby, and Clugat in particular, he coughed, as if to clear his throat and altered his outburst. "We have a problem. The computer in my lab is glitching again. I had to perform a complete sweep and security update so I won't be able to get you the data I promised until tomorrow."

Simultaneously, he communicated his original message. *We weren't as thorough as we thought with our credentials. The Skae are sending a team of investigators to find out more about us.*

Yalmut let out a sigh and shook his stubby talon at Duvar. "I warned you about being more vigilant with your security protocols. I'll come over later to take a look as well." *Are you sure? What did we miss?*

"That would be great. Thanks." *Someone sent the list of conference attendees to the authorities at Skae command for security clearances and government credentials on the interplanetary transport ship. Apparently, our names caught the attention of a minor official we used as a reference. He had no recognition of us and flagged us for further investigation.*

Jontar stopped working on the simulation program on his computer and spun around to join the conversation. "I apologize, Clugat. We will make sure our mistake does not infect the rest of the system. Duvar, Yalmut is right. We've been over this before. You cannot get so wrapped up in your work that you forget basic procedures." *Alright, we still have time to fix this. Let's meet back at the ship tonight and work on a solution. For now, go about your normal routine. Nobody should think this is anything but a typical bureaucratic foul up. This is nothing we can't handle.*

"No need to fret so, gentlemen. I'm sure no harm has been done. I trust this is nothing more than a simple programming error and will be quickly resolved." Clugat waved one hand as if clearing smoke from his face, illustrating the lack of importance he placed on the difficulty. "I will leave you now to your work. I am looking forward to discussing the conference with you soon." With that, he exited the lab in a flurry of well-wishes to the rest of the researchers.

The next day, while the ambassador sat tapping randomly through his communication pad, as if this meeting were a mere distraction from more important matters, his clerk stated the reason for their visit. "We have a communication from one of our foreign office dignitaries on the planet Uvalda, stating he was cited as one of your professional references for this conference. He claims no knowledge of you or your qualifications, and has no understanding of how you came across his name."

"Yes, ambassador, I understand your concerns, but I assure you this is nothing more than a bureaucratic error." Jontar sat with talons clasped on the table before him as he addressed the Skae dignitaries.

The Skae ambassador, Molk, impeccably dressed in glittering indigo and silver robes, placed both hands over his heart in a sympathetic gesture. "I agree with you, and I do have much more important matters to attend to than this trifle, but, as you must understand, my superiors have sent me to investigate any discrepancies in documentation, particularly those involving aliens such as yourself, hoping to attend such a high-level conference. Our security procedures must be completely satisfied, no matter how tedious they may be."

The clerk took up the conversation. "Can you provide any information to explain this confusion?"

"Yalmut, can you share the documentation regarding our communications with the Uvalda credentials office?"

"Of course, Jontar." Yalmut tapped a few commands onto his tablet, projecting a holographic image of a series of text and video communications. He reached out to wave a talon through one of the files, opening a video of the clerk in question speaking. "... Yes, Mr. Rocker, I have received your documentation and have approved your application for research at the Lethnon facility. Your field of expertise is precisely what they have been asking us to find for them. You should have your papers of transit and approval within a few hours. Good luck to you."

"As you can see, gentlemen, we followed proper channels and received the approval. We are at a loss to understand how the clerk in question does not have records of his own to verify this matter." He waved a talon through another file to open it. A series of data links providing dates, times, and catalog references appeared. "Here is a complete record of our communications with Uvalda. Perhaps sharing this with your official there will help clear up the confusion."

The ambassador glanced through the links, downloaded them onto his personal communicator, and tapped a few commands followed by a careless wave of his hand over the controls to shut off his device. "I have sent this information to the official in question. He should be able to review it and respond in a few hours. We can adjourn until we hear back. We will notify you when we need you again." He stood and, with only a fleeting look at the petitioners, left the conference room followed by his small party.

"My, the ambassador was certainly a rude one." Clugat, his unreadable face turned toward Jontar uttered his first comments since the Skae arrival. "He was absolutely insulting. I may report his behavior to my superiors."

Duvar laughed as he slapped the table and rose to his feet. "You haven't had many dealings with the Skae, have you? They are universally arrogant toward anyone not Skae. They believe themselves the highest form of intelligence and culture in the universe and pay little attention to others."

"You've had prior dealings with them?"

"Oh, yes. They are definitely a race of schuteks, but as long as they are in charge of most of the galaxy, there's not much to be done about it."

"Well, I don't like it one bit. I would have preferred my first encounter with our interstellar allies to have been a more pleasant one. I hope those who attend the conference will be more amiable."

"Don't count on it. I've never known a Skae to admit to being wrong about anything."

The four researchers left the room and headed toward their lab. Jontar sent his thoughts out to the others.

Their arrogance may be what saves us, Duvar. I'm counting on them to stay true to form on this.

Yalmut joined in the mental discussion. *What if he digs any further? We haven't had the time to implant any corroborating evidence in his archives.*

I think he'll decide it isn't worth his valuable time to look further into the matter. Remember, from the Skae point of view, this conference is about them simply informing the Gorvin and others about their plans. They honestly can't comprehend it as anything approaching an equal exchange of ideas. It simply isn't that important to them.

Duvar gave Jontar a sidelong glance as they reached the entry to their lab.

If our monitoring of their communications is accurate, you mean.

The next morning, Clugat greeted the Kolbri trio at the research facility entrance. His stony face flushed with a barely discernable deeper shade of ruddiness and his hands fidgeted even while kept firmly clasped behind his back. Another Gorvin would have been scandalized by the outpouring of emotional display in the scientist. "I am outraged! Absolutely outraged! This is unacceptable! I am going to bring this to the highest authorities and put an end to their insults once and for all! Imagine! The gall of them to deny us so close to the conference! The authorities will hear of this. Don't you worry one bit! I'll see to it, mark my words!"

The three youths looked at each other, shrugging as they flashed a quick series of mental questions between them.

Jontar confronted Clugat, grasping his shoulders to calm him. "What's wrong, Clugat? What has you so agitated today?"

"It's that gruktob of a clerk on Uvalda. He continues to insist he has never heard of you. The Skae ambassador insists on meeting with you three in the Skae embassy. He is not pleased at having to deal with this matter anymore, but the conference is too important for him to ignore this officious gruktob and his tupk need for documentation."

Yalmut shook his head as if in dismay over Clugat's news while he mentally reached out to the others. *This is going to take more drastic action than we had considered. We need time to deal with it away from Clugat.*

Agreed. I'll make our excuses while you two head back to our quarters. Jontar gave Clugat his most grave expression of concern, wrapping one arm around the stocky Gorvin's shoulders and turning him to walk down the corridor.

"I'm sure everything will be all right. The poor clerk must be under a lot of stress dealing with all the details of the conference. Let us deal with it. We would be happy to talk with the Skae ambassador to straighten everything out. You go back to the lab and we will get everything in order before we meet with him. You'll see."

"No, you are our guests. It is my duty to see you are treated with respect and dignity. Such an insult is an affront to our very honor." Clugat's hands continued to fidget in a most un-Gorvin-like outburst of anger and embarrassment.

Jontar held his smile and calm exterior in place while he reached into Clugat's mind to adjust his anxiety levels. Gradually he noticed the scientist's face lose the slight flush and his hands stilled. "Have no fear, my friend. Your honor is intact. This is simply a matter of Skae stubbornness. Please, we are familiar with their bureaucracy, and know how to navigate its intricacies. It would be better if we handled this ourselves. You have much more important things to take care of right now."

Clugat, his voice now more composed, took Jontar's arm with one stout hand and gave a gravelly rumble in his throat. "If that is your wish. I have no patience for diplomatic niceties. Maybe it would be best if you straightened out the problem yourselves."

"Thank you. Now, if you'll excuse me, I have to convince a Skae button-pusher to admit his error. It might be easier to wrestle a grendel, but I've heard it can be done... the grendel, not the Skae." Jontar smiled and winked at his Gorvin host and sped off to meet with the others.

Hours later, back in their visitor residence, Yalmut and Duvar stalked the sparse room while Jontar lounged on the thick-legged bench under the circular window of their main communal area. All other rooms of their assigned housing connected to this area like spokes of a wheel. Three small bedrooms, a kitchen and communication/research area led to this central point by way of rough-carved hallways. Gorvin architecture was always reminiscent of the underground structures of their home world.

Duvar circled to the left as he paced the room. "We just don't have time to figure out how to penetrate deeper into the phalking security measures of the Uvaldan system. Not to get in deep enough to satisfy this..."

"Time! We have all the time we need!" Yalmut stopped his pacing, eyes bright as he smiled at the others.

"Of course!" Jontar chimed in. "If we could pinpoint the least impactful point on the timeline, it might do just the trick."

Duvar scratched at his small crest. "What are you two going on about?"

It's simple," Yalmut said as he clapped Duvar on the back. "We go back a couple of years and visit the Uvaldan clerk in person, provide him with some forged documentation, return to the present, and meet with the ambassador with a specific date of our meeting with the clerk and ask him to contact the schutek again."

"And we even have Clugat provide us with some documents, which we will alter to make it look like he specifically invited us to work here because of our expertise. When the ambassador contacts him again, he will remember us because this time we actually have met in person."

"That means we'll have to undo the falsified records we implanted into the system. We can't afford for two different sets of records to be found."

"Right. We have to get it right this time, there's no room for error here." Jontar's talons clicked furiously as he closed his eyes and concentrated for a minute or two. "Alright, here's what we have to do…"

The morning sky began to glow with the first signs of sunrise as their plans were finalized. Hovering above Jontar's tablet was a detailed plan, including all the necessary documents and timeline information for a successful mission. Duvar and Yalmut shared a contagious yawn and stretched their arms as they flopped back in their chairs. Jontar examined the work one last time.

"We're in agreement, then? This is how we will proceed?"

The others nodded, watching him through half-closed eyes. With a tap of one talon, the images vanished. "We leave in two hours. Get what sleep you can and then we'll head out to the ship and get started."

***

The three Kolbri found themselves sitting in uncomfortable chairs in a too-brightly-lit room waiting their turn to speak with Neldar, the Uvaldan clerk they had specifically requested. Such an unusual appeal took a while to convince the front desk secretary of the necessity of the meeting and a few well-forged documents of introduction, but they succeeded and now sat patiently two years, twenty-six days, fourteen hours and forty-five seconds in the past.

"Thank you for meeting with us on such short notice, Neldar. We have such a short time to get everything in order before the Gorvin invitation to begin our research on Lethnon." Jontar sat across from the clerk, punching his keypad to bring up and transmit the required documents for travel and permission to research at the Gorvin facility.

Neldar kept his eyes on his own terminal, punching his own keypad to complete the required transactions. He never looked at them or acknowledged their presence.

How are going to get this schutek's attention so he remembers us? He won't even look at us. Duvar fidgeted in his chair behind Jontar.

I'll take care of it. Yalmut stood up, screeching the chair's legs on the tile floor causing every head in the room, including Neldar's, to look up at him. Addressing Neldar directly, he leaned over Jontar's shoulder, glanced around a bit, then whispered to Neldar. "Where is the restroom? It's been a long wait and I drank a lot of tea this morning before coming here. My bladder is about to explode."

The clerk appeared flummoxed for a moment, obviously not liking having his strict routine interrupted. "Over there." He scowled at Yalmut as he waved a hand off to the right in the direction of a hallway.

"Thank you so much. I just couldn't wait another moment." Yalmut stepped around his chair and pushed it back into place, causing the legs to screech again.

The clerk shook his shoulders, frowned, and began to re-focus on his monitor. Jontar interrupted him before he could completely settle back into his routine. "You'll have to forgive him, sir. We always have to make extra stops on long trips for him. But what can you do? He's absolutely brilliant and we couldn't complete our research without him."

Looking up at Jontar, and with a brief glance at Duvar, Neldar glowered. "If you will stop interrupting me, I would like to complete this transaction in a timely manner and stay on schedule today."

Jontar reached out to pat Neldar's forearm. "Of course. Forgive me, sir. We wouldn't want to cause any problems. Thank you for understanding."

Neldar jerked his arm free, glared at Jontar, sniffed, and returned to tapping his monitor.

***

Back in present time, Jontar, Yalmut, and Duvar arrived precisely on schedule to meet with Ambassador Molk at his office. The room, decorated in the ethereal abstractness of flowing, intricate designs, permeated not only the artwork on the walls but the furniture as well. As usual, no effort was made to accommodate the shorter stature of non-Skae visitors, so the chairs they sat in required some effort to utilize and left them with a somewhat uncomfortable sitting position. No doubt, the ambassador believed this would shorten any meetings with lesser species.

"I'm sure, Mr. Ambassador, if you would simply send the Uvaldan clerk — you said his name is Neldar? — if you would send him these copies of our travel credentials with the specific date of our meeting, I'm sure everything will be cleared up."

"Why did you not provide me with this date in the first place? The Uvaldan office processes millions of documents every day. Without a date of the transaction, you could hardly expect them to locate your information."

"We are terribly sorry, sir. It did take us a while to locate the information. After all, it was two years ago. We never expected to be invited to attend such a prestigious conference as this, so we did not properly file the documentation." Jontar kept his eyes lowered, focusing on the decorations of office the ambassador wore on his chest.

Molk sighed heavily, turning both hands palm upward. "I suppose you are to be forgiven such slights. You are only

Kolandi, after all." He transmitted the new information and proceeded to open up new files, dictating new orders to his underlings, all while ignoring the three seated in front of him.

Within five minutes, Molk's holo-communicator lit up, a hazy image solidifying into Neldar's face in midair slightly above his desk.

Ambassador Molk pressed an icon to open communications and waited.

"Neldar of Uvalda here at your request, Ambassador." The floating image turned to face the three Kolbri seated across the desk. His eyes closed, his mouth downturned as he recognized them. "Yes, sir, I do remember these Kolandi now. Your transmission of the precise date of our unfortunate encounter allowed me to locate the data immediately. Their travel credential images also helped me recall the meeting. A most troublesome encounter, if I may be permitted to say so, sir."

Molk frowned in return. "Anything we need to be concerned about as far as issuing them credentials for attending the conference?"

"No, sir. Their qualifications are in order. They were simply a most unruly and difficult bunch to process. They had no respect for protocol and order. They interrupted my routine to such an extent that I was required to extend my hours that day. Most disrespectful."

"That will be all, then." Molk disconnected the communication, causing the holographic image to dissipate immediately.

Jontar jumped in to explain. "I apologize, Mr. Ambassador. That was our first encounter with the Uvaldan bureaucracy and we were unfamiliar with their strict protocols and precision. I hope our inexperience in such matters does not cast any doubt on our credentials and qualifications to attend the conference."

Molk glanced through his calendar and gave the three a negligent wave of his hand. "No, that will be all now. You may go."

The Kolbri left the embassy and returned to Clugat's labs, where they were greeted with enthusiasm.

"Whatever you did, lads, it worked. I just received your passes and transport authorizations. You are cleared to attend our conference. I am thrilled you can join us."

"As are we, Clugat," said Yalmut. "We look forward to learning what we can about the Skae's plans."

Chapter Nine

Shyfar proved to be the perfect world for a conference of such magnitude. Close allies to the Skae, the Shyfarans were renowned for their scientific accomplishments. Their interstellar ship designs proved far superior to the Skae designs for travel by cosmic string. Their tastes in architecture, while similar to the Skae in their use of transparent magnesium and carbon fiber nanotube alloys, was beautiful and inspired, but more utilitarian than the Skae's soaring art forms.

Unlike the cities of Kodut, there were no mag-lev vehicles contaminating the skyways or ground levels. Instead, a network of interconnected transparent magnesium pneumatic tubes carried passengers to their destinations, both between buildings and below ground. Depending on the distances involved, these tube ways could conduct travelers at incredible speeds so that no place on the planet was more than three hours distant.

Vast areas of public open space occupied the spaces between buildings. Between cities were immense natural preserves where the local ecosystems were left to themselves for tourists and scientific study. Very few individual homes existed, since the majority of the population consisted of students, visiting professors and researchers from throughout the galaxy. The research party from Lethnon was escorted to the dormitory containing their assigned residences.

"Tomorrow will be a busy and exciting day." Clugat declared as he chose one of the adjoining rooms and tossed his luggage onto the bed. "The main event won't be until the day after tomorrow, but there are many fascinating lectures we can attend until then."

The three Kolbri stood in the central common room, looking around with furrowed brows. Jontar took the lead, as usual. "I was expecting a more Shyfaran style of architecture in our accommodations. This is just like our quarters on Lethnon."

Clugat laughed, then tried covering his amusement with a cough and wiped his mouth with one hand. "The Shyfarans make every effort to make their guests feel at home. Each learning and research center has living facilities tailored to those species most likely to utilize them. This one is made specifically for Gorvin visitors. It helps to have something of home when spending time on a distant planet, don't you think?" He sat in one of the squat, square chairs. "Most non-Gorvin furnishings are terribly uncomfortable. Too tall and unsteady. This is much better." He stretched his stout legs, even if they didn't reach far, and clasped his thick fingers behind his head, eyes closed and smiling, at least the slightly-upturned-corners-of-the-mouth Gorvin version of a smile.

Duvar sat in one of the empty chairs, his knees bent halfway to his chin. "Ugggh. Reminds me of when we first arrived on Lethnon. These don't seem to be made for our frames." He struggled to pull himself up out of the low chair.

"And those beds are far too short for us," said Yalmut after returning from his chosen room.

Clugat jumped to his feet. His eyes wide, smacked the side of his head with one thick hand. "Oh, my goodness. My apologies, gentlemen. I completely forgot to order Kolandi furnishings for you. I will have to have words with Eisoph as soon as she arrives. We will get this corrected right away."

"Get what corrected?" Eisoph, Clugat's research assistant and student entered the main room, unslinging her shoulder pack and tossing it on the floor next to the entry. Built much like her male Gorvin counterpart, Eisoph was short and thick-bodied, with heavy legs and strong arms. Long, thick black hair reached to her waist. The exact gender differences were not apparent on first impression, except for the harmonic double vocal chord voices of Gorvin females. She wore a deep red knee-length dress with sturdy brown pants underneath. Her heavy leather boots with scarred metal toe caps should have announced her arrival like thunderclaps, but Eisoph was surprisingly agile and graceful for a Gorvin.

Jontar, startled by her nearly silent approach, attempted to disguise his reaction with a quick talon jab toward his companions. "Duvar and Yalmut were commenting on the lack of Kolandi-friendly furnishings in our rooms. Clugat forgot to let the Shyfarans know we were part of your group. Nothing that can't be fixed with a simple call to housekeeping."

Eisoph's eyes went wide; she covered her mouth to hide her jaw's minuscule drop. The expression was hardly noticeable, but it was a considerable display of embarrassment for a Gorvin. The harmonics in her voice took on a sudden syncopation, indicating her mortification and contrition. "Oh, my...I cannot believe we forgot about such a thing. You must think us terrible hosts. I will run down to the front desk and rectify this right away."

"No need to be apologetic, Eisoph. Mistakes happen. We are not offended."

"You are our guests and Clugat gave me the responsibility of arranging our accommodations here. I should have been more thoughtful. It was my obligation to consider your needs. I will take care of it immediately." She spun on her heels and ran back out into the hallway before anyone could respond.

Clugat approached Jontar and the others, clasped hands over his chest in a sign of apology. "She is right. You three are our responsibility as our guests. It was foolish of us to forget something so basic. Please forgive us."

Jontar took Clugat's hands in his. "We are aware of the importance your culture places on hospitality toward others, but there is no need for such concern over us. We are in your debt for doing so much for us already. Please, no more fretting over something so meaningless."

"You are too kind. But we will see everything is corrected as quickly as possible."

"We know you will take good care of us. For now, let's look over the schedule for tomorrow and decide how to best divide the day between us for maximum efficiency." Jontar set his tablet on the table in the center of the room and touched the controls to project the conference schedule in a holographic display.

An hour later, they were interrupted by a commotion in the hallway. Eisoph burst through the door followed by a train of Shyfaran housekeepers trundling in entirely new sets of furniture. She directed the workers with an almost military precision, overseeing each piece of furniture to be removed and exactly how and where to place the Kolandi-sized version of each. In minutes, she shut the door behind the last of the exiting workers, turned and, hands on hips, smiled, in her way, at the men. Her voice regained its normal sonorous tones. "Everything is corrected now, I hope to your satisfaction. I apologize again for my lack of consideration for your comfort on this trip."

Jontar smiled at Eisoph in return, bowed with arms crossed over his chest. "No apologies needed, Eisoph. We are most pleased with your swift remedy to the situation. No harm was done, so please join us and help us figure out our schedule for the next few days." He extended an arm to her, closing it around her shoulder as she joined them.

By noon of the second day, everyone had become increasingly anxious over the main event. More details had leaked of the Skae's new design for harnessing the power of a star at nearly ninety-eight percent efficiency. The public parks were filled with guests from hundreds of planets and a wide range of scientific disciplines from nuclear physics, quantum mechanics, stellar astronomy and engineering, to name a few. Every bench and table held scientists in deep conversation over the anticipated afternoon lecture. The blue climate-controlled skies, dotted by an occasional puffy cumulus cloud, ensured an enjoyable and revitalizing respite from the intense lectures and demonstrations held each day.

"If such a thing is possible, it means the end to all energy struggles throughout the galaxy. It's almost impossible to imagine." Eisoph munched on a meat sandwich as she spoke, wiping the juices from her chin with a towel. "I can't wait to see their research notes. I am still skeptical of the details I've seen so far, but the Skae are parsecs ahead of the rest of us in this area. Maybe they've discovered something we haven't thought of yet."

"Yes. This should be an historic announcement. What did you think about the lecture by the other Gorvins on the advances of light sail weaponry? I found it particularly fascinating." Yalmut glanced sidelong at his Kolbri companions. *We need to keep our eyes and ears open. According to everything we have learned, this is the event that started the war.*

Something happens here to end all Skae and Gorvin alliances. We have to learn exactly what happened if we want to help my father figure out what is going on with the Skae in our time.

Duvar rolled his eyes. "Of course you would find something like that interesting. Give me good old cosmic string travel any day. I was more interested in the development of technology dampening nanobot research." *Yes, Yalmut. We are all well aware of the importance of this revelation. No need to keep reminding us.*

Jontar took another bite of his fruit and vegetable salad. "Those two, used in combination, will be the end of our home world as it now exists. I find it hard to get excited about them." *"Knock it off, Duvar. A little reminder of just how vital this moment in history is doesn't hurt. We need to be alert to anything that happens this afternoon."*

"Alright, friends, if we want to sit anywhere with a decent view of the proceedings, we should get moving." Clugat gathered his belongings, tossed the packaging from his lunch into the recycler receptacle, and proceeded down the path under the trees toward the campus's main lecture hall.

* * *

The lecture room darkened. Out of the stage floor, a holo-projection of a double star system appeared. Dim and formless at first, but then sharpened into a view of one red giant orbited by a white dwarf. The image shifted to center the white dwarf and grew in size and brightness to just below the need to shade one's eyes. As the star rotated, the roiling surface of its convection currents could be seen easily. Occasional flares, filaments, and prominences shot from the surface, some extending over the heads of those closest to the stage, causing them to duck. A spotlight brightened on a single Skae, dressed in a shimmering light blue robe decorated with many ornate badges of office and honor.

"Honored guests," his voice, light and airy, floated throughout the large audience with the aid of hovering cubicle speakers. "Today, I am pleased to announce the beginning of a new era in energy production. We Skae have recently begun development of a new method of producing and harnessing the energy of artificial singularities."

As the blue-skinned speaker continued, thousands of small mirror-like satellites began orbiting the projected star. These objects completed a nearly perfect sphere around the star, dimming it to near obscurity. "By harvesting uninhabited planets within a star's system and constructing a partial sphere of collectors, we have improved on the single collector solid sphere designs of previous attempts at such work. Completing a single sphere around a star required more materials to construct than could possibly exist in any star system, so the project remained theoretical at best."

He waved his hand and the projection grew in size, zooming in on a small section of collectors, providing much greater detail. "Building even a few thousand small collectors and spacing them equidistant around the star allows us to utilize the resources of only one or two planets. While there remains millions of square kilometers of space in total between the satellites, we have increased their efficiency to a degree where we are now projecting that ninety-eight percent of the star's total energy will be collected."

Another wave of his hand shifted the view to a section of nearby empty space. Animations of the process appeared as his description progressed. "By utilizing the focusing power of a series of gravitational wave generators, we can direct the energy collected by the swarm and focus it into a singularity, sometimes referred to as a black hole. We then continue to focus the additional energy of the dwarf star into the singularity, creating enough mass to generate six-dimensional degenerate matter within the singularity. This process will release immense quantities of energy which can be collected and distributed to as many systems as needed, thus providing an endless supply of clean energy for all. A summary of the procedure and calculations are being transmitted to you now."

Everyone in attendance operated their various devices to open the data as they received it. After a moment, all eyes began to return to the presenter. All except Eisoph, who continued to shuffle back and forth through the information, a subtle frown growing on her stoic features, her voice became increasingly tremolos. "This is useless," she muttered. "None of the actual gravitational wave calculations are here. All the rest is meaningless without them."

Turning now to face his audience, the Skae speaker raised his arms toward the ceiling. The view zoomed in to the artificially colorized singularity. "The energy released by this singularity in the form of radiation and angular momentum can be harvested at one hundred percent efficiency by another swarm of collectors. A small fraction of the collectors needed to capture the star's energy, perhaps as few as a hundred or so, are required due to the incredibly small size of the black hole, possibly only a few centimeters in diameter."

He dropped his arms and the hologram shifted away from space to show a series of images of people from many different worlds living their lives free from energy concerns. Each world was prosperous and happy, every individual able to reach full potential.

"Honored guests, we Skae are pleased to announce the end to need and want in our galaxy."

The lights rose in the lecture hall along with a standing ovation mixed with cheers and shouts of praise.

As the commotion eventually subsided, hands shot into the air. The speaker called on each one in turn, mostly resulting in acclimations of joy and support for the Skae's efforts. Then he called on Eisoph.

She stood so she could be more easily seen. A hovering microphone floated to her so her voice could be amplified for all to hear. "Some of your gravitational wave calculations are not provided in the documentation. How have you accounted for expanding phase space due to the degeneracy pressure? Doesn't this present an unreasonable risk?"

The speaker smiled as the audience grew silent. "You raise an incredibly insightful and important question, young Gorvin. Let us assure you we have taken this very real concern into our calculations and found the risk to be minimal at best. Our best minds have been at work on this very aspect of the data for years and have found no cause for alarm." He turned to call on another hand, but stopped as Eisoph continued to press the issue, fighting to control her emotions.

"I don't mean to contradict your work, sir, but I have done some research into this of my own, and my calculations come to a very different conclusion. Would it be possible to see your data, for comparison, particularly on the gravitational wave generators, to see where I might have gone wrong?"

The speaker's smile remained, but his eyes deadened. "I am sorry, young Gorvin, but our work is proprietary and not available for public dissemination as of yet. Perhaps at some time in the future." He raised his voice as he turned to face another question. "Be assured, your fears are unfounded. The Skae are the best minds in the galaxy in matters such as this. While I am sure Gorvin research is perfectly adequate in the things that concern you, we are the experts here. You can rely on our findings."

As she sat down, Eisoph heard many murmurs calling her "a foolish student..." Or "wasting our time..." among other more derisive comments whispered just loud enough for her to overhear.

"Don't listen to them," whispered Jontar, seated next to her. "You know how self-important the Skae are. They would never tolerate anyone calling into question their ability, especially in a gathering like this."

"I've never felt so foolish and humiliated in my life. Maybe my calculations are wrong. Maybe I did miss something obvious."

"No," continued Jontar. "I don't think so. I've seen your work and I could not find anything wrong with it. Of course, we only had the earliest data released by the Skae. They may have found a solution since then, but I doubt it."

"But everyone else had the same data release. Why didn't anyone else find what I did?"

"Too many take the Skae at their word. Even the top scientists from some of the most advanced worlds are in awe of what the Skae have accomplished and may only have glossed over the data. And not even scientists are immune from political pressure. The majority of those here are nothing more than Skae puppets. If you aren't looking critically at something, you almost never find it."

Eisoph sat silently, head hung low with the typically unreadable face of a Gorvin, except to those close enough to them to learn the subtle differences. Jontar recognized the signs of sadness and doubt growing. He sent his thoughts out to his companions. *"Have you tapped into their system yet?"*

Yalmut's mind responded first. *"Yes. It took some time to breach their security protocols, but we managed to penetrate the system without a trace. Thank goodness they won't develop the protections we faced in our time for several hundred years yet."*

"I found the data!" Duvar's mind practically shouted with his discovery. *"I'm downloading it to our tablets now. The files are huge, but I should be done in another minute or so."*

Jontar leaned in to whisper in Eisoph's ear. "Cheer up. We might have something to help prove your position when we return to Lethnon."

She gave no response, or at least one so small he could not decide if she heard him or not.

***

With the conference concluded and a few days off to enjoy the pleasures of a brief vacation on Shyfar over, the Gorvin representatives found themselves back home on Lethnon and back to work in their lab.

The doorway slid silently open as Jontar and company approached. Upon entering, he strolled directly to Clugat's office. Through the window of the lab director's office, they saw Eisoph and Clugat entangled in some sort of argument. At least given their barely readable features, he thought it was an argument. This door, too, slid open at their approach.

"I don't care about their reputation. I've been over my work a hundred times since the presentation and so have you. Neither of us can find any errors." The higher tones in her Eisoph's harmony indicated her frustration. "Without the full set of data from the Skae, we have no way to check our calculations against theirs. Why are they being so secretive?"

Clugat leaned forward, hands folded on his desk, and a smile, at least for a Gorvin, was fixed on his face. "Let's not get into any conspiracy theories now. It's only been a few days. I'm sure they will respond to our request very soon."

"No need to wait," interrupted Jontar. "We have the full data on their project."

Both Gorvin looked up at Jontar, with brief glances at the other two at his side. Eisoph recovered from her shock at the announcement first. Her harmonic voice dropped a full register, a clear sign of suspicion. "And how did you manage that? Why would the Skae provide their full data to some Kolandi researchers before us? It's not exactly your people's main area of study."

Duvar lowered his voice so only those present could hear him. "Well, they didn't exactly give us the information voluntarily." He grinned as he spoke, puffing up like a child who got away with an especially clever trick.

"You stole the data?" Clugat sat back in his chair, wiping his face with his hands. "If they find out, we'll all be in prison. How could you think to do such a thing?"

"They won't find out," said Yalmut. "We have some very special skills in infiltrating their systems. There's no trace of any theft of the data or even any unauthorized use of their network."

"Our preliminary look at the calculations seems to confirm Eisoph's fears. We think they overlooked a critical bit of information, or at least ignored the importance of the results." Jontar sent his thoughts to Clugat and Eisoph's holo-tablets, giving them the stolen files.

"So now you three are some sort of super hackers? I don't think that was on your résumé when you applied to work here." Her voice now contained dangerous overtones of a building outrage. "How did you do that?" Eisoph gasped almost silently as her holo-tablet came to life, opening the critical files.

"I'll explain later. For now, we need you to verify our findings. We'll meet with you tomorrow and discuss your findings. I hope we're wrong, but I doubt it."

Eisoph eyed Jontar with the meerest narrowing of her eyes, mouth slightly turned down at the corners. For a Gorvin, she practically screamed disapproval but quickly turned her attention to the data stream.

As Eisoph and Clugat became absorbed in their tablets, bringing data files to life hovering at eye level, their fingers nimbly flicking through the complicated arrays of signs, symbols and numbers, the three Kolbri conspirators left the office.

"We need to talk," said Yalmut. "Our actions here are leading to some serious implications. We must be prepared."

Yalmut led his friends to a nearby outdoor park where they could talk freely. The day was on the chilly side for most Gorvin; Lethnon lacked the highly sophisticated climate control capabilities found on Shyfar, but conditions were nice enough for the three Kolbri. Unlike parks on other worlds, this one was typically Gorvin. Rock structures of all sizes, shapes, and designs filled the grounds. Rough-hewn abstract carvings depicted three-dimensional representations of four-dimensional concepts. Smoothly polished geometric shapes reflected a soft glow in the sunlight. Trees and grass were absent, replaced by multi-colored rock gardens in intricate patterns surrounding the statues. As they walked further into the park, other visitors became scarce.

Duvar halted mid-stride. "Are we going to walk forever? Why did you bring us out here, Yalmut?"

Yalmut and Jontar stopped alongside Duvar, forming a tight triangle. "I wanted to point out some of the nuances of the Gorvin statuary Eisoph showed me recently." *Keep moving as we talk. It won't look so suspicious that way.* He continued on, the others catching up and he picked up the conversation.

They stopped in front of a particularly large statue. "Look at the lines of this one. Very evocative of the sculptor's love of nature." *We all know where this leads. This is what started the Skae – Gorvin War. This war will kill billions of people throughout the galaxy. Our own world and many like it will be subjected to the Gorvin biotech weapons and isolated for thousands of years. Are we willing to accept this?*

Jontar pointed to the rock garden surrounding the statue. "Do those patterns have any significance to the artist as well?" *What choice do we have? All of this is our history. We cannot change it without risking everything we know.*

"Of course, it is all one statement, together in harmony." *We could end this war before it even begins. Our world doesn't have to suffer the fate we know is coming. We could save billions from the horrors they are about to face.*

"For an expressionless species, they certainly are an emotional lot." *And eliminate the lives of everyone we know and love. Our actions would prevent the births of billions more and alter our timeline in ways we cannot imagine.*

"You can say that again. It took me forever to figure out what few facial expressions I could, but they do seem to be full of passion about almost everything." *Jontar is right, Yalmut.* Duvar sighed, clasping his small talons behind his back as they walked. *We have to let all of this play out. History and the timeline must be preserved.*

Yalmut shook his head, waving one hand in front of him as if directing their attention to another statue down the path. "Compare it to this one over here." *But we've already altered it. We gave Clugat and Eisoph the Skae data they needed to see what would happen. Without our intervention, The Skae would have blown up half the galaxy. We're already involved and changing history.*

They continued on, occasionally stopping in front of one of the stone carvings, apparently admiring them, for a while before Jontar broke the stillness in their minds. *No. we haven't changed history, we fulfilled it.*

What are you talking about? asked Duvar, now preening his short crest. *"How could we possibly fulfill history?"*

Think about it. The Gorvin must have gotten the data somehow, otherwise everything would have been wiped out before the war could even start. Their device would have destroyed everything, but that never happened. I don't know how the Gorvin got the information without us, but they must have. In some strange quirk of the timeline trying to maintain itself, we became the vehicle for that bit of history.

That's crazy, Jontar. How could we be a part of history thousands of years before we were born?

We're here, aren't we? Time travel can create some very odd circumstances.

He's right, Duvar. Yalmut stopped in his tracks, watching his friends argue time paradoxes. *But that's not my point. Are we willing to let the terrible history we know take place? Jontar, you seem somewhat attached to Eisoph. Are you willing to let her face this war we know is about to happen? Can you live with yourself knowing her fate?*

Jontar closed his eyes and turned his back on the others. *I don't know. How could any of us know?*

Well, we need to make a decision pretty phalking fast.

Reaching the end of their circuit around the gardens, Jontar smiled at Yalmut and patted his friend on the shoulder. "Thank you for the insights. I'll never look at Gorvin art the same way again." *None of this is easy, my friend. We do indeed have some difficult decisions to make, but not tonight. Tomorrow will be soon enough.*

The next day, all five companions met in private. Clugat gave orders to have the rest of the scientists using the lab evicted temporarily.

Clugat opened the discussion with his head hung low, leaning heavily on his elbows at his desk. "Gentlemen, I'm afraid our worst fears are true. I don't know if the Skae are purposefully hiding this information or simply ignoring the implications we have found, but we must alert the highest levels of authority about this."

Eisoph chimed in, her eyes showed a growing fear rarely seen on a Gorvin. If Jontar interpreted it correctly, he would say she had been crying. "They can't be that stupid."

"It's not stupidity," said Jontar. "The Skae are incapable of believing anyone is better at anything than they are. If they had convinced themselves the consequences were only a minor and unlikely possibility, then nobody will be able to change their minds. They are constitutionally incapable of doubting their own superiority."

"But they are going to destroy this entire sector of the galaxy! Hundreds of star systems, thousands of inhabited planets, all wiped out in a massive expanding phase space of degenerate matter."

Jontar looked back into Eisoph's eyes, holding her gaze, trying to give her strength. "This is why we are here."

Chapter Ten

"I'm so glad you talked me into this, Nedia. It'll be good to get out of those confines and into the real world again." Ryma let the breeze fill her nostrils as the mag-lev sped through the countryside with the windscreens lowered. Her long hair danced wildly behind her. "I do so love how green and lush everything is here. I miss home, but there is so much life here. It's invigorating."

"Yes, the fresh air will do us all some good." Nedia clasped her talons tightly in her lap. The note from Nissend Honj was cryptic at best, only to be at the vineyard no later than noon but not before mid-morning. All other details were left unanswered, presumably for her protection in case anything went wrong. *It's as if he doesn't trust me. The old fool. He knows I would do anything for the clan and how much I despise these Rockers. The sooner we are rid of them the better.*

Rilo, Neri, and Danet accompanied their royal princess as always... eyes alert for any sign of threat. A Brin entourage was also in attendance. A mix of guards and dignitaries spread between the mag-levs in front and behind the main vehicle. Two hours later, they arrived at their destination and turned onto the dirt road leading up to a modest village in the center of acres of lush grapevines.

A small group of village elders, a mix of Brin and Kolandi, stood waiting as the royal party arrived in a cloud of dust. Danet exited first and quickly surveyed the area for any danger. Only when he was satisfied did he open the door for Ryma and the others. Ryma, followed by Neri and Rilo approached the group. Nedia, last to exit the transport, held back from the others, her eyes darting in every direction. She nearly jumped out of her crest as the doors on the trailing mag-lev slammed shut.

"... Please, call me Ryma. No need for formalities here. The old ways are giving way to a beautiful new way of things." She clasped hands with one of the elders, a Kolandi, who smiled but looked like someone who had a grendel by the tail and was not sure what to do next.

"Yes, your highness... princess... Ryma... as you wish." The man held out a shaking hand toward his companions, introducing them as each in turn shook Ryma's hand with varying degrees of uncertainty.

"What a lovely community you have here. The very ideal of what my late husband and I envisioned. I commend all of you on your commitment and courage to our joint future."

"Thank you princ... um, Ryma. We are very proud of our community. May I escort you and the rest on a tour of our facilities?" He waved a hand toward the largest of the buildings, where an unending train of mag-lev conveyor carts brought loads of grapes inside for processing.

Three hours later, the tour concluded with Ryma's presentation of the official Assembly seal of inspection and the visitors piled back into their vehicles. Nedia sat speechless, hands twitching in her lap. Rilo, Neri, and Ryma talked and laughed quietly during the ride back to First Town, never once trying to include Nedia in their conversation.

The sun dropped low atop the hills as they drove through the narrow, winding path the road cut following the river. Without warning, they heard the report of an explosion and the mag-lev lurched to one side, forced off the road by a landslide, tumbling toward the river below. Ryma lost consciousness when the icy water rushed through the broken windows as the vehicle landed on its roof. As darkness enveloped her sight, she saw the twisted collection of bloody arms, legs, and bodies of her companions piled together on top of and beside her. She heard voices shouting as if from a great distance and felt hands grabbing at her legs.

"Get them out of there, you fools. We don't want them dead, not yet anyway. The Homsan will have us in the pits for sure if any of them die before he can offer them up."

***

The sounds of dripping water echoing around her brought the first realization she was not dead. The agonizing pain screaming up her left leg as she tried to move was the second.

"Don't move, my princess. Your leg is broken as well as at least three ribs. The Homsan and a couple of medicine women of this clan have helped set the bones and bound your wounds, but you must remain still."

Her head ached and she gasped at the stab of pain caused by the lamplight when she opened her eyes. "What is this place? What happened? Is that you, Rilo? Are the others safe?"

Rilo placed her hands gently on Ryma's shoulders to keep her from moving. "It is me, my princess. You must remain still. We have some injuries, but we are alive."

Blinking rapidly, Ryma attempted again to open her eyes, finally realizing that they were swollen and could only provide a tiny slit to see through. Above her, Rilo's smiling face came into focus. She was bandaged and blood-spotted, with one eye severely blackened, and Ryma wondered how she could manage the smile. Without turning her head, since even the attempt brought on more pains, her eyes took in their surroundings. The orange lamplight illuminated rock walls that glistened with trickles of water. Long, tapering stalactites hung from the high ceiling.

"Where are we?"

"You don't recognize your former palace, Your Highness? I know it has been many years since you abandoned us, but let me be the first to welcome you home." The booming voice pounded in her ears, causing her to wince again at the ache it brought to her head.

Rilo maintained her firm grip on Ryma's shoulders as she pivoted her head to address the voice coming from outside Ryma's small field of view. "The Princess is not well enough for visitors. She needs sleep and time to recover properly."

The voice hesitated, Ryma heard a shuffling of feet, and a shadow crossed her face. Apparently, the visitor had come closer to examine her better. "Perhaps you are correct," said the voice, softer now. "We cannot offend the gods with an offering in this condition. I will send the medicine women each day to help with her recovery. Only a fully sound offering will suffice." The shadow left her face and the sound of scuffling feet receded in the distance.

"Who was that? What gods was he talking about?" Ryma felt her hold on consciousness fading rapidly.

"Rest now, my princess. We will talk more when you are able. You must sleep now."

***

Four days later, at least by Rilo's account, Princess Ryma awoke. The pains remained, but not at the level she remembered from her first awakening. Nothing about her location seemed to have changed and she was able to move, slowly and carefully, but now she could turn her head for a better look at her surroundings. Next to her, Rilo slept on a ragged, threadbare blanket crawling with infestations. Her head was no longer bandaged but her ribs were bound and her lower right leg was splinted. Her feet were also chained.

None of the others were to be found in the small alcove of the cavern they occupied, cut off from the main passage by a set of stout bars. Other than the lamps in the passageway, only a small oil lamp provided illumination within the prison chamber. She gritted her teeth as she lifted herself onto her elbows. Rilo leapt to her side, chains jangling from her ankles.

"Be careful, my princess, your injuries are still newly mended and likely to reopen themselves if you disturb them too much." She reached behind her and picked up a wooden bowl. "Drink this. It tastes horrible, but the Homsan assures me it is strong medicine. I have been taking some of it myself and it does seem to help."

Ryma sipped at the bitter-tasting contents, dribbling a fair amount down her chin in the process. "Where are the others? What is happening here?"

Rilo prostrated herself before Ryma, tears welling, but refusing to fall. "I failed you, my princess. It was my duty as your primary Skatak to protect you. I was not alert enough to prevent this attack. I have allowed my enemy to take my kital from me without a fight. I am bound to relinquish my command over the Skatak and submit myself for disciplinary action."

Stroking one hand gently on the woman's back, Ryma tried to comfort her protector. "Nobody could have foreseen this attack. You and your Skatak have served me well and saved my life uncountable times. I will expect you to find a way to do so again. Rise and perform your duty. Answer the questions your princess has put before you."

Rilo's shoulders heaved briefly as she sobbed quietly. Wiping her eyes, and with a deep breath, she rose to her knees and began her report.

"The others are in another prison alcove, my princess. They were also injured, but not so severely as you. I have been imprisoned in this cell with you to care for you. They did not want you to die but would not stay with you. I convinced them it was smarter to allow me to be here in case your fever spiked again, which it did, several times. One without your strength would surely have died."

"I must have been dreaming, but I recall someone saying this was my old palace. Are we truly back in our former caverns? How is that possible?"

"The Skaeists ambushed us and brought us here. They have reverted back to our old way of life in the old caverns. I have seen The Rocker's tomb myself. It no longer sings or glows as it did before Maliche's arrival, and the Homsan, the leader of this tribe, seems to think it is a sign of the god's displeasure. He wants to reawaken the Rocker god and by doing so please the Skae gods with an offering."

Ryma felt the air grow ominous around her and a heavy weight settled in her heart. "What sort of offering?"

"You, my princess. They think sacrificing the one who led the Kolandi into heresy will set all things right again. It's all that insane old man talks about when he comes to look in on you."

As the two continued their discussion, the sound of heavy footsteps approached. Rilo signaled for silence with a quick cupping of her hand over her mouth and began examining Ryma's bandages.

The cage door rattled as a gaunt man, ancient beyond reckoning, unlocked the door. Wisps of grey hair sprang from patches around his bald head and grew in a long beard nearly to his waist. His bony legs, wrapped in dark leathery and scarred skin, poked out like twigs from his tattered robe. The only thing holding this shredded garment on his emaciated frame was a frazzled rope belt and a thin string at his neck, which still allowed one filthy shoulder to bare itself.

"So you are finally awake. It is sacrilege to keep the gods waiting for so long. Their appetite grows with each day. We cannot deny them their offering any longer. Tomorrow they will be appeased."

With Rilo's help, Ryma sat up to face her captor. "Why have you done this? We are not your enemy."

The old man laughed, ending in a wheezing cough. "You have denied the Skae gods. You have joined with the soulless Brin in claiming the gods are nothing more than beings like us. You have turned your back on your people."

"I have brought prosperity and honor to our people. We no longer have to starve in these caves or die in slavery. Do you not listen to those you claim are gods? Even they have tried to tell you they are not."

"Lies! Falsehoods! Sacrilege! Those you claim are the Skae gods are demons sent to lead us astray. It is you who do not listen to the true gods."

"How can I convince you I speak the truth? I am your Princess. I would never…"

"You are a false princess. We are the true believers and no longer listen to your misguided ways. So many have gone astray that the gods have deserted us. We must make an offering to atone for the sins of the fallen. You will be our offering. Then, when the gods are appeased, they will fight for us against the heretics and return glory to our once bountiful lands." He gave the iron bars one rattling shake and stalked off.

"I will die before I let them take you, my princess." Rilo struggled to her feet and, with chains clanking, shuffled to a position between Ryma and the iron bars of the door.

"Then both of us will be dead, and where will we be?" Ryma's voice dripped with anger. "No, Rilo, you will not try to prevent them from taking me from this prison cell. We will go together and we will find a way to escape and rescue the others. I still require your strength and your fighting skills. Come over here. We need to make a plan." She patted the empty blanket next to her.

***

By morning, signaled by the increased activity they could hear in the tunnels, Ryma and Rilo were ready to make good their escape. The morning meal was delivered by an elderly woman in filthy rags. They gulped down the bowl of grey, watery, foul-tasting something Ryma did not want to think about, in the hope it would give them at least some strength for a good fight. The chanting began almost as soon as they finished their last swallow. A somber, almost wailing cry for forgiveness and promises of repentance echoed through the cavern, accompanied by a rhythmic pounding sound, like hundreds of hands or feet slapping the ground at once. The words were sung in the old Kolandi language. The language was once spoken by all Kolandi, but over time, it became the words of ritual and high ceremony. As next in line to lead her people, Ryma had been taught the language in secret by elderly Homsan and her mother. It puzzled her how so many could know the ancient words now.

The sound of a wordless, humming chant growing louder and the soft slap of many bare feet on the rock floor of the tunnel alerted them to the arrival of others. As Ryma and Rilo watched, a half-dozen raggedly-robed women halted in front of their cell, faces lowered toward the ground and hands folded at their breasts. Four tall, powerfully-built warriors stood silently behind them, their faces tattooed in patterns reminiscent of desert-dwelling predators. Each one held a heavy spear. Rilo barely contained herself at the sight of her kital hanging from the belt of one of the men. One of the women, older than the rest, stepped forward and glared through the bars.

"You will come with us to prepare for the offering. Come peacefully and you will be treated well. Offer any resistance and you will be treated as the heretics you are."

Ryma winced as she pulled herself up to stand tall, placing most of her weight on her good leg. Despite the pain of the hair-line fracture, she held her head high and fixed her eyes on the elder woman. "What sort of preparations are we expected to meekly submit ourselves too? And what, exactly, is this offering we are to become?"

The woman spat on the floor, her glare never wavering from Ryma. "You must be cleansed before you can be presented to the Skae gods and The Rocker. Your skin crawls with the taint of heretics. Submit yourself with humility and repentance and your cleansing and offering will bring you peace. Resist and your souls will be tormented for eternity. The choice is yours."

"I am Ryma, High Princess of the Kolandi. Your High Princess. You will take me to whoever is in charge here and..."

The woman slammed her open hand against the bars. "Enough! We no longer recognize you as our princess. You have forgotten the old ways and denied our gods. Will you submit?"

The two stood nearly eye-to-eye in a stare down contest of wills. It was Ryma who lowered her eyes first. "What will happen to the others? If you can tell me they are unharmed and will remain so, we will submit to your offering."

With a crooked smile, the elder woman lowered her hands, folding them at her breast. "The others of your party are well and recovering from their injuries. Your servant stands for the rest to be offered up at your side. No other offerings are required. They will be taught to honor the gods again and, if they learn well, can be free to rejoin the Kolandi."

Ryma's shoulders sank as she sighed and nodded her head. "Very well. We will submit ourselves to your preparations and the offering without resistance."

The old woman waved her hand and one of the warriors pushed his way forward and produced a key to the cell. He unlocked the door and heaved the creaking hinges open. With Rilo's support under her left arm, Ryma limped, following the elder woman and the guard down the passage, the rest of the women and guards in close formation behind. As they walked, the cavern became more familiar. Ryma recognized the tunnel leading to her former royal quarters, then the path to the tomb of The Rocker. It was from there the chanting came the loudest. After many twists and turns, each leading deeper into the bowels of the cavern, Ryma felt the heat and humidity growing more oppressive by the minute until they at last stepped through an opening into a massive room containing a steaming lake. The pale light from the lanterns did not reach far. Most of the ceiling and the opposite side of the lake remained cloaked in darkness. At the water's edge, the procession halted and the Kolandi formed a semi-circle around Ryma and Rilo. Only the sound of dripping water echoed in the chamber.

"Remove your clothes and enter the water so you may be cleansed and prepared for the Skae gods." The elder woman pointed at Ryma and Rilo and the others began their wordless chanting again.

Ryma took a deep breath and, with Rilo's help, she removed her garments. Balancing herself on her good leg, she waited for Rilo to do the same. Together, Princess and Skatak walked into the scalding water of the lake.

"Kneel in the cleansing waters."

The water came to their waist as they knelt. The buoyancy helped remove enough weight from her broken leg that Ryma did not need help to support herself. With another wave of her hand, four of the other women stepped into the water, each one carrying a pumice stone and a lump of brown soap. The four attacked the scrubbing process with vigor, not lessoning their efforts at all even when scouring the more sensitive parts of their bodies. Ryma barely contained a scream when one of her attendants grabbed her broken leg and yanked it up to be cleansed. Rilo remained submissive, but her glares could have skinned a grendel better than the sharpest knife.

Long after Ryma was convinced she had no skin left on her bones at all, the elder woman lifted her hands, and, after a forceful dunking, the scrubbers returned to the shore and rejoined their companions. Rilo helped Ryma to her feet and the pair struggled together to walk up to the narrow black sand beach. Once there, two more of the women brought forth two unbleached short white gowns for them to put on. Without towels to dry themselves first, the fabric became nearly transparent where it touched their wet bodies. Pulling fingers through her dripping hair and pushing it out of her face, Ryma extended one arm to Rilo for support as the group marched away from the lake and back to the upper levels of the cavern. Her lips and fingernails turned blue in the cooler upper tunnels as the wet garment slowly evaporated itself dry. The looks of disdain and betrayal the crowds along the way gave her filled her heart with sorrow and loss. *These were my people. I should have paid more attention to their pain when we took their gods from them. I need to find a way to help them.*

It was only Rilo's sudden stop that brought her mind back to her current predicament. She found herself standing in front of the tomb of The Rocker. There, in its place of honor, sat the white marble tomb. Without the presence of the biocomputer, it looked cold and empty. The songs once heard by many coming from the tomb vanished once the device leapt into Maliche and her, on that fateful day so long ago. The images of the Sky gods, now most often called the Skae gods, even among the Skaeists, danced in the flickering torchlight on the walls. Dozens of wasted and filthy Kolandi, other than the several warriors along the wall, filled the two rows of benches occupying the sacred room. As she was escorted in, she saw the rest of her party from the ill-fated mag-lev. Neri and Danet stood on either side of Nedia, all of them displaying bandages of various sizes on assorted limbs, but aside from appearing a bit malnourished, they seemed to be doing as well as could be expected. Four warriors with spears stood on guard over them.

"Bring the offerings forth to be presented to the gods." The ragged old Homsan stood in to one side of the tomb, his arms raised, and his eyes to the sky.

Two of the guards marched forward alongside Ryma and Rilo, and with one hand firmly guiding them, escorted the pair down the center aisle. Rilo's face hardened even more as she again saw the glint of her kital swinging at the belt of the one closest to her. At the marble tomb, both guards seized Rilo's arms and pushed Ryma forward. Stumbling from the shove, she nearly fell over, but found the strength to recover her balance and limped forward to the altar. Two more warriors emerged from the shadows to take hold of Ryma and lift her onto the top of the tomb, holding her arms down on either side. The Homsan, hands still raised in supplication to the gods, strode behind the marble tomb and reached down to produce a long curved knife. Raising the blade with both hands, he called out to his gods.

"We beg your forgiveness for the weakness of our fallen. Few of us have remained faithful, but we are unbroken in our enduring faith in your glory. We pray that you accept our offering and return your blessings to our lands. With the blood of this offering, cleanse us of the heretic Brin and their demons who claim dominion over you."

"NO!" Rilo exploded in a rage of Skatak fury. With a disabling kick to the knee of one of her guards, she simultaneously ripped her kital from his belt and used it to sever the arm of her second guard at the elbow. A loud commotion at the back of the room told her Neri and Danet had caught her signal and joined in the fight to free themselves. A burst of orange energy sliced through the chamber, erupting in a blaze of sparks as it blasted the knife from the Homsan's grip, along with half of his fingers. In a matter of a few seconds, the room had gone from a solemn ritual to absolute mayhem.

Rilo whipped her head around to see a platoon of Brin soldiers, beam rifles blazing into the warriors along each wall before they could bring their spears to bear. Whirling around again, she tossed her kital into the throat of the surviving guard still holding Ryma on the tomb. His companion groped at a charred hole in his chest as he dropped to his knees. She ran to Ryma and jumped on top of her, pulling the bloody kital from the warrior's neck as he fell. Grabbing the princess with both arms, she rolled them both off the marble tomb and onto the dirt floor where she placed Ryma between her and the white block.

The soldiers brought Neri, who had reclaimed her kital from one of the warriors guarding her, along with Danet and Nedia to join Ryma. They formed a protective formation around them, rifles bristling like the quills of a spiny barblemut. As the last of the civilians ran from the chamber, the two Skatak took a position on either side of their princess, each ready to prove their kitals were the equal of any beam weapon.

"Squad two, clear the main tunnel. Squad five, protect our rear. The rest of you, gather the Princess and the others and get ready to move out." Opet, head of the royal guard, strode into the room and knelt in front of Ryma as two soldiers gently lifted her onto a floating stretcher.

"Forgive me, Princess, my delay in reaching you was intolerable and unforgivable."

Ryma looked up at her old friend and protector, her mouth hanging open in shock at his sudden appearance. "Opet... how did you find us?"

The giant of a warrior, still muscular but with his hair showing a touch of grey and his waist now expanded with age, smiled down at her. "Some of those nanobots we placed on Nedia were still stuck in her clothing and still operating. We searched for a few days before we thought about them and then the signal was so weak at first that we had difficulty pinpointing your location. Once we started focusing on these mountains, we realized they must be holding you in our old home."

She reached out, took his hand in hers, and smiled. "Thank you. Now let's get out of here."

Nedia stood back from the others, the only Brin of the group. The ordeal of their capture and treatment had left her in shock and unable to think clearly. Her life of privilege had left her woefully unprepared for the horrors of the past several days. A guttural scream reverberated in the alcove and all heads whipped around to see the old Homsan diving from the tomb toward Nedia, the stub of his knife held in a bloody, two-fingered hand.

With the reflexes of long training, Rilo jumped and drove her shoulder into Nedia, forcing her out of harm's way. She spun to defend herself, but felt the edge of the broken blade slice down her back. Ignoring the pain, Rilo continued her maneuver and swung her kital deep into the skull of the old man, leaving him twitching on the ground. She pulled the blades from her attacker's head, wiped it off on his ragged garment, and helped lift Nedia to her feet. Two of the guards rushed to their sides and bandaged her wound.

Stunned, the breath knocked out of her, Nedia stumbled to her feet and stared at Rilo as her mind spun, trying to make sense of everything. "Why would you do that? Why would you risk your life to save mine?"

Rilo grimaced as the last of the bandages was pulled tight. "I am Skatak. It is my duty to protect the Princess and those who are with her."

"But I'm Brin, not Kolandi."

"What does that matter? The Princess has relied on your service and you were with us when we were attacked. Your life is no less than any other. Come, we must go before any of these wretches can organize against us again."

Nedia watched in confusion as the others gathered until one of the soldiers took her by the arm and led her out into the passageway. They were able to exit the caverns without further incident and regroup with the rest of the Brin patrols as they met at the three transport shuttles outside. Princess Ryma, head of the Assembly, and her party were escorted up the ramps to the first shuttle and strapped themselves in as it lifted off. In an hour, they found themselves being attended to in a hospital ward in one of the settlements near the coast.

Nedia looked past her IV tubes as Rilo lay face down, getting her wound stitched. That night, sleep eluded her as her thoughts drifted from her uncle and children to Ryma, Rilo and her own decisions. Her final thoughts as she finally drifted off were how everything she did was for her family and her children's future. Maybe she could extend her protection to Rilo, but her family came first. But mostly, she worried about what might have gone wrong with her uncle's plan to eliminate Ryma at the vineyard. She had to get in touch with him as soon as possible.

***

As their mag-lev arrived back at the government office complex in First Town, Ryma laid a gentle but firm hand on Nedia's knee. "Please accompany me to my private office, will you? There is something we need to discuss." She smiled at her second-sister, but the smile never reached her eyes.

Nedia fought to control her rising panic. *What went wrong? They couldn't know anything... could they? I need to contact Uncle Nissend and let him know the plan failed.* "Of course, Princess, but may I have a moment to catch up on a few items of importance before I meet you?"

She turned to exit the vehicle, but saw the two Skatak and several Kolandi warriors, dressed as royal guards, surrounding her door. She hesitated, then spun to look at Ryma. "What is going on?"

"I need to show you something important, to both of us, Nedia. Please come with us now. This is for your benefit as well as mine."

Do they suspect I had something to do with those savages in the caves? Don't they realize I was a captive right alongside them? Maybe they found out about Uncle Nissend's plot at the vineyard. No, they couldn't possibly know. But if they do… what will become of my children? Did I escape one horror only be trapped in another?

Nedia's mind reeled with questions and uncertainty as she was escorted through the hallways. The massive doors of Ryma's private office closed behind her, sounding like a death knell. Only Danet, Rilo, and Neri remained with the princess and she was trapped with them.

"Please, Nedia," said Ryma as she sat calmly behind her desk. She pushed a large box to one side. Powerful hands gripped Nedia's shoulders, guiding her to the elegantly carved chair reserved for visitors. "Have a seat. I have something you need to see."

Unable to speak, Nedia sat, keeping her back straight and face as composed as possible. No Kolandi usurper would see any weakness in her… she hoped.

"Take a look at this." Ryma gestured toward the large box, her eyes going to Danet, who reached inside and pulled out a mechanical device with cylinders, wires and a laminated green timer, frozen still at 4:32:16. He shoved the device into Nedia's reluctant hands and returned to his post at the door.

"Wha… What is this?"

"A chem-mine. A highly-focused explosive device designed to penetrate a structure and deliver a toxic mix of chemicals to the inhabitants of a building, or, in this case, an armored mag-lev vehicle. Don't worry, it's been deactivated."

Nedia's mouth started to drop, but she clamped it firmly shut. "Why show this to me? Where did you find it?"

"My security forces detected it this morning, Take a look at the timer. Do you see any significance to it?"

"Why would it mean anything to me? I have no idea what you are getting at?"

"They discovered it five hours before we were scheduled to leave for the vineyards. Does that help at all?"

"I have no idea what…" Nedia's face went pale, her mouth as dry as the desert as her mind subconsciously performed the math.

"Yes, you see it now, don't you? If we had not discovered it, the explosive would have detonated and killed everyone in the vehicle somewhere on the road to the vineyard. You, along with the rest of us."

"Who would do such a hideous thing?" Nedia plastered a look of horror on her face as she assumed the role of an innocent. "I will do everything in my power to…"

With a wave of her hand, Ryma cut her off. "There is something else you should see before you say anything else." She opened a file on her tablet and handed it to Nedia.

Her eyes flickered over the display several times before looking up at Ryma, confusion written on her face. "I… I don't understand. What is this?"

"Those are forms ordering the transfer of custody of your children to pass to your uncle."

"Custody? To my uncle? Why? What is the meaning of this?"

"Did you notice the date?"

Nedia returned her attention to the tablet. "It's dated the afternoon of the day before we left for the vineyards." Her hands began to tremble uncontrollably as she dropped the tablet. Her vision grayed and the room began to spin out of control.

"Yes, you understand now. Your uncle intended you to die along with the rest of us." Ryma stood and, still adjusting to the mobility-assisting brace on her leg, stepped slowly toward the trembling Nedia. "I understand your clan's hatred of the Rockers. Greed and lust for power are not unknown to the Kolandi, and we are certainly not free from delusional behavior, as you have witnessed, but do you have any idea why your family would want you dead as well?"

Nedia stared ahead, not comprehending Ryma's words.

"We've been spying on your uncle for some time now and we know about the schemes you have been a part of. While they were intended to simply frighten me, I let you continue to see what we could learn. After the first attempt on our lives by that bomber in the reception hall, I had the doctor secretly implant you with a tracking/recording device while you were being checked for injuries. I thought it would help keep you safe, at first. Then we learned of your connection to the plots and have used you as our unwitting spy ever since."

"But he would never betray me. I've devoted my life to my family. I've sacrificed everything. He would never…"

Ryma stooped down, picked up the tablet, and handed it back to Nedia. "During one of your earlier visits to your uncle's estate, we had your cloak dusted with nanobot transmitters. I don't understand how they work, but our scientists assured me they would help uncover the truth of things. Once you arrived, they were signaled to infiltrate the entire estate. There are some very relevant files regarding you and what your beloved family thinks of you on the tablet. Take it and read for yourself."

"You, a Kolandi, used nanobots? How would your kind even know about technology like that?"

Ryma closed her eyes and shook her head. "Typical Brin attitude. Kolandi are nothing more than savages. You should be glad we did. After all, it was the transmissions from a few of those nanobots still stuck on your clothing and in your skin that told the soldiers where to find us after the Skaeists took us captive." She returned to her chair and sat. "I will give you until tomorrow to read and process the information. We'll talk then." She nodded to her Skatak, who stepped to either side of Nedia and escorted her to her quarters in the complex.

Hours passed as Nedia read, and re-read the files. Her beloved uncle, trusted above all others, had been using her all along. The information proved he had discovered her hatred of the Rockers at an early age, the result of so many family tales of injustice perpetrated against them. They told of his manipulation of her to betray her marriage and kill her husband, only to see her as a growing liability. The final blow was the evidence of his desire to have her children replace her as the Honj spear point against the Rockers, all while staying hidden in the background himself.

Tears streaming down her face, Nedia looked up at Rilo, who stood guard inside her chambers. "So when am I to be executed for my treason?"

"That will be decided after the princess talks with you tomorrow."

She thought for several long minutes before continuing. "She is a fool. I would not hesitate to eliminate someone guilty of treason."

Rilo's hand reflexively tightened on her kital. "You risk much speaking so of the princess, especially after she was willing to sacrifice herself to spare your pitiful life, but you are Brin, so you are ignorant of our ways."

"Then educate me." Nedia wiped her face with a well-used cloth and sat up straight on the corner of her bed.

Rilo tilted her head, squinting at Nedia like she did when confronted with a difficult puzzle. "Why would you want to learn about us? You have tried to kill us."

"I hate the Rockers and what they have done to my family, or at least what I was raised to believe they have done. Your princess, as the widow of Maliche Rocker, was the last barrier to our taking our rightful place. I have no animosity in particular toward the Kolandi, but she represented the Rockers and as such, I believed, was also to blame for all of the Rocker injustices... yet you saved my life in the caves when that madman attacked me. You took the knife that was meant for me. I may have been wrong... about all of you."

"I was slow. He never should have been able to do me any harm." Rilo studied the woman for a long time before coming to a decision. "Very well. What would you like to know?"

The next afternoon, Rilo escorted Nedia back to Ryma's private office.

"I understand you and Rilo have had quite the conversation. Did it help?"

A bleary-eyed, red-faced Nedia hung her head as she spoke. "I am not sure of anything anymore. My entire world has been destroyed. But I am no longer your enemy."

"And what of the Rockers? Are you still their enemy?"

She hesitated a while before answering. "I do not know. A lifetime of hate is not something easily forgotten. But I just don't know anymore."

Ryma gave a hint of a smile and folded both hands on the desk in front of her. "That is all we can ask for now. But I must know what your intentions are before we can decide your fate."

"Can you help me regain custody of my children?"

"Your uncle's petition was held up in the courts and has never been finalized. We saw to that, at least. When the courts learn you were not killed, I will see they are persuaded to deny the custody petition. Your children will be removed from the Honj estate and back at your side by tomorrow, if that is what you wish."

Tears flowed anew as Nedia nodded her head in agreement. "Then I wish to stay here, if you think you can ever trust me again. I want to do what I can to help you defeat my uncle."

"You want to help us prevent your family from gaining control of the Assembly?"

"Maybe other Honj clansmen will prove to be more worthy than my uncle has proven himself to be. I would want my family to rule with justice and honor, as you have tried to do. He is not the one to do that. Perhaps I will find another to support. For now, he must not be allowed to win."

Ryma sat back, supported her chin with two steepled fingers, and glanced at Rilo as she stood guard behind Nedia. A simple nod in reply answered her unspoken question.

"Very well, then. I will give orders for your children to be brought here to you, and you will remain as one of my advisors. Your knowledge of how your clan operates and their holdings will be of great value to me. However," Ryma's voice took on a stern and unforgiving tone as she glared at Nedia. "If you ever attempt to use my generosity against me again, you will suffer more than you can imagine. I am still Kolandi, and I remember all of the atrocities your kind inflicted on my people. I will not hesitate to release the savage you Brin have always believed us to be. Do you accept my terms?"

Nedia dropped to her knees, trembling. "I will not disappoint you. Thank you."

Chapter Eleven

The holo-vid conference with the Gorvin parliament was a typical bureaucratic quagmire that seemed to drone on forever. Gnobis, Clugat, and Eisoph sat on one side of the polished stone table, its tortured, twisted pattern of metamorphosed layers almost glowing in the dim light. Jontar, Yalmut, and Duvar sat opposite them. On the other two sides of the square table hovered the images of six Gorvin officials.

"The proof is uncontestable. Our calculations have been verified by multiple neutral parties on several out-worlds. The Skae cannot be allowed to continue this venture." Gnobis emphasized his declaration to the Gorvin Parliament by pounding his fist on the lectern, his face as full of passion as possible for a Gorvin.

The semi-transparent image floating above the communication terminal flickered as the various faces of the heads of the Gorvin parliament moved, turning from one to another. The central figure, robed in white with indigo trim, took control and replied. "We need more time to investigate the so-called uncontestable nature of your data, Gnobis. Do not presume to rush us into a decision which could lead us into a disastrous situation."

The scientist clenched his fist in an effort to control himself. "I would never be so presumptuous, sir. But I have full confidence in our findings, and the consequences are so enormous we must act quickly."

"If what you say is true, then we will, of course send a diplomatic envoy to the Skae with the evidence. They will have no choice but to cease in their folly, if folly it is. We should have our decision in a few weeks. We will inform you of our decision then."

The ghostly images vanished as communications ended.

"Well, that accomplished nothing." Duvar waved one taloned fist at the empty space above the terminal. "The Skae will never listen to diplomats."

"But what can we do? The Skae are so powerful. We have no weapons to threaten them with. How can Congress defy them?" Eisoph wrung her hands as she read the reports for the tenth time.

Duvar jerked up from his perusal of the reports, head tilted and eyes wide. "What do you mean you have no weapons? The Gorvin are the only force able to stand up to the Skae. It's your tech weapons-"

"I think what Duvar means is that we might be able to help you develop some weaponry to help you fight the Skae." Jontar gave Duvar a withering look as he projected his thoughts. *"Did you forget when we are, Duvar? This is before the attack on Sharta C... before the great war began. Remember, much of what we know of history came from what the Skae told us. No doubt it was a significantly distorted version of actual events to favor their perspective."*

Duvar's face fell. *"Sorry, I guess I got so caught up in the horror. I forgot."*

"Well, get your crest together. We cannot afford another slip like that. There may be something we can do, but you won't like it."

Yalmut, eavesdropping on the conversation, perked up. He frowned at Jontar. *"You aren't thinking what I think you are... are you?"*

"If you have any better alternative, I'm open to it."

The three sat staring in silence at each other for what seemed like hours until Clugat spoke. "What weapons are you talking about? We are primarily a race of scientists, not warriors."

Jontar turned to face Gnobis, Clugat, and Eisoph, his face filled with darkness. "A while back we developed some theories on weapons of war which we believe may be some of the most powerful ever developed. We've been hesitant to reveal the details, but now we may not have a choice."

"We will not kill if we can avoid it," said Eisoph. "We have always devoted ourselves to science and the peaceful advancement of all species. We would not use the sort of weapons necessary to defeat anyone as powerful as the Skae."

Jontar placed a gentle hand on her shoulder, talons gripping her in a reassuring gesture. "We know that and would never propose anything of the sort. We, too, believe in peaceful solutions whenever possible. The devices we are proposing do not kill; they only neutralize an enemy so they cannot continue to take part in a war."

"How is that even possible?" Gnobis leaned heavily on his elbows as he listened.

"Not now. We need to discuss this amongst ourselves before we go any further." Jontar gestured to his companions with a sweeping open hand. "The potential consequences of sharing this information are enormous and we must be certain there is no alternative. We will let you know tomorrow so you will know what to tell your government." Jontar stood, motioned to the others, and led the way out of the lab.

Back in their apartment, the three Kolbri took turns in their heated argument.

Duvar paced the room uttering curses under his breath before challenging Jontar, wagging a talon in his face. "You cannot seriously be suggesting we give them the means to destroy our own civilization. How can that even be an option?"

Yalmut, maintaining his calm demeanor as usual, lounged in a chair as he watched his friends. "The Kolandi of this time are not our civilization. They are our history. What happened is in the past."

Rounding on Yalmut, Duvar raged on. "How can you say that? You've seen our world in this time. We have the opportunity to prevent a holocaust."

"At what price?" Jontar interrupted. "Yalmut is right. The events we know as history happened. Are you ready to live with the consequences if we change such a massive event? Would any of us even exist? Would our Rocker ancestors have been brought to Kodut if we still filled the planet with a thriving civilization? The Brin would all have died when their sun exploded. Would the galaxy even be here in our time if the Skae had carried out their plan? How many others will die that should not have?"

"It's still not right. How can we live with ourselves if we are the agents responsible for the murder of our own people? Even if they are only our ancient history?"

"They won't be killed," said Yalmut as he stood and approached Duvar. "The weapons won't kill anyone. But we will provide the Gorvin with the means to prevent the Skae from exterminating half the galaxy. We are simply the means by which history, as we know it, was created." He chuckled, preening his small crest. "Thinking about this too much can drive one crazy, can't it?"

"You're twisting words, Yalmut, and you know it. Billions of Kolandi will die if we do this."

"I know, Duvar, but what other alternative do we have?"

Tensions diminished as the debate continued. Eventually the discussion ended with an agreement on how to present the information to their new allies.

***

The next morning arrived with a bright sun rising above the distant stone mountains, casting an orange glow on the sculptures of the rock garden the three Kolbri strode through on their way to Clugat's lab.

"These are ingenious. Non-lethal but completely effective in rendering an enemy unable to continue fighting, at least with any technology beyond a bow and arrow." Clugat studied the holographic designs of the nanobot delivery system and tunable virus for neutralizing technology. "And the light sail propulsion strategy is brilliant. Nothing will be able to track them or be able to interfere with their delivery. Absolutely brilliant."

"We hoped you would think so." Jontar allowed himself a relieved smile. "Perhaps, if you presented these plans along with our findings about the Skae device, they will find a way to convince the Skae to stop before destroying half the galaxy."

"If I remember correctly, our research and development facilities on Sharta C would be perfect for developing this into a practical weapon without too much difficulty." Eisoph leaned on Clugat as she studied the data over his shoulder, her hand occasionally reaching out to swipe through the technical specifications and diagrams hovering over the table.

"Sharta C? Isn't that a Skae world?" Jontar and Yalmut exchanged worried, knowing glances at the mention of the tragic planet.

Clugat and Eisoph stopped their work and turned to stare at the pair as if they had sprouted wings and flown around the room. "Whatever would give you that idea? Sharta-C is one of our most renowned research facilities. Yes, it lies close to a disputed region of space, but it falls well within Gorvin territory."

Duvar shook his head, flicking his talons as he absorbed this revelation. "How strong is your military force there? To protect your citizens and properties, I mean."

"Are you really that ignorant of the Gorvin? I know we have never had much contact with you Kolandi, being under the Skae domain and all, but surely you must know we have no military force. At least not in the size and manner of most other worlds. We've always been scientists and researchers. No threat to anyone. Other worlds welcome our presence in their midst, since we share everything we learn and all benefit in return. At most, we have a ceremonial guard at our facilities for our diplomats, but nothing more. Why would we ever need one?"

"At least until now." Eisoph looked at Clugat, her stony features registering sadness to match her voice.

"But Sharta C can't be…"

"Not now, Duvar. Something is going on here we need to investigate."

"You know as well as I do what happened on Sharta C. We saw the Gorvin military attack and wipe out helpless people on that world."

"We saw something the Skae showed us. With what we know now, are you so willing to take that holo-vid as solid proof of anything?"

Jontar stood behind Duvar, patting his shoulders with both hands. "In any event, there is nothing to do until your congress makes their decision, at least not officially."

Yalmut took the hint and addressed Clugat and Eisoph. "What if you helped us approach the researchers on Sharta C to ask for their assistance in developing our idea for the nanobot delivery system? This would be a pure research project, which could have potential for many possible applications. You would only be the intermediary contact and would have nothing to do with the research and development until the congress decides in our favor and we turn it over to you for completion."

Jontar stepped forward to stand beside Yalmut. "We could approach a different lab there to work on the strain of viruses we would need to infect the Skae and their allies." He held up a taloned finger to halt Clugat's attempt to interrupt. "Non-lethal, of course. We have in mind something to biologically tie a species to the gravitational field of their planet. Any attempt to enter space would be fatal within a day or two, but with plenty of warning to allow for a safe return. We are working on the specific sequencing for a few Skae allied worlds and should have the results available soon."

Eisoph jumped to her feet, fists on hips, glaring at Jontar and Yalmut. "You want us to defy our government? We could go to prison."

Jontar smiled, extending both hands palms up. "Of course not. We are only asking for permission, and your scientific introduction, to the researchers on Sharta C. We have something of a side project we believe they are particularly suited to carrying out for us while we stay focused on the Skae matter. Nothing which concerns you and your work at all."

Eisoph snorted, arms folded across her chest. "You're going to get us all put away forever ... or killed."

Clugat chuckled in his deep, rumbling sort of way. "Eisoph, I think our leaders were wise to keep us ignorant of the Kolandi for so long. They're a race of thieves and troublemakers. How soon would you three like me to arrange for the introductions?"

***

Four months later, Jontar, Yalmut, and Duvar found themselves enjoying the solitude of a mountain lake. Jontar stood knee-deep in the water, dressed in water-tight waders. Flicking a long, thin rod back and forth, he hit the right rhythm and cast a pale-green line with high tensile leader through the air. A small, simulated eight-legged tanf settled almost without a ripple on the surface. He slowly reeled in the line, occasionally jiggling the rod to give the tanf a life-like action. A slight breeze stirred the leaves of the nearby trees while puffy white clouds drifted high above in a brilliant blue sky.

Duvar sat on a rock under a tree, reading a journal on his tablet. He reached over to give Yalmut a playful punch on the arm and nodded toward Jontar. "I'll never understand what you think you're doing out there. Whatever gave you the idea to start fly-fishing? Nobody in their right mind does that any more. Not in several generations, at least."

Keeping his focus on the nearly invisible tanf, Jontar sighed at the obvious attempt to poke fun at his new-found hobby. "My grandfather taught me when I was very little. I never saw the point either, until now. He always claimed to have learned it from his grandfather and told a story about how Rockers have been fly-fishing as far back as anyone can remember. It *is* relaxing, and we all need a big dose of relaxation these days."

"Looks more like an exercise in futility to me. How can standing around waiting for some aquatic creature to decide your lure is precisely what it is hungry for be relaxing? Give me a good book any day. Where did you find the equipment on this world, anyway?"

"I programmed the materials printer to build it for me. The techs were fascinated when I told them what I wanted. They all probably think I'm crazy, but, after a few trials, here it is."

"Sounds like a waste of time and resources to me."

"Don't knock it until —" Incoming message alerts sounded on all three of their communication tablets, disrupting the calm of the lake. Yalmut flicked the controls and read the message.

"Time's up. We are urgently needed back on the campus. Clugat wants us to meet him at his residence as soon as possible."

Three hours later the mag-lev vehicle glided to a halt in Jontar's reserved slot and the companions strode through the campus toward the Gorvin living quarters.

As they approached the entrance, Clugat opened the door and ushered them in. A holo-vid newscast blared in the main gathering room. Screaming and bursts of energy weapons fire interspersed with explosions filled the room. As they came around the corner into the room, Clugat all but shoved them into the uncomfortably hard benches that made up Gorvin furniture.

A newscaster shouted to be heard by an unseen recorder-bot hovering in front of him to capture the scene. "... attack came without warning. As you can plainly see, thousands of individuals are fleeing for their lives. But with the major ports closed or destroyed, there is nothing to do but find someplace safe to hide and hope this all ends soon."

Duvar, his head on a swivel trying to get anyone's attention, yelled out to be heard above the broadcast. "What the strix is happening? Who's attacking who?"

Clugat shouted in answer from his corner bench. "The Skae. They've attacked the facilities on Sharta C. Why would they do that? It's horrible."

Yalmut sent his thoughts out to Jontar and Duvar. *"The nano-weapons. What else could it be?"*

Duvar mind-shouted back. *"But how could they have found out? We kept the information as low key or secret as possible."*

"Ever since the Skae rejected the Gorvin diplomatic attempts to stop their gravitational wave energy scheme, they must have sent out spies to see if the Gorvin were planning anything to try to stop them."

Jontar joined the mental conversation. *"We didn't cover our tracks enough. We took the chance of a Kolandi research project not being interesting enough to raise any attention, but I guess we have been on the Skae watch list ever since the ruckus over our attending the conference."*

"Phalk. How could we have been so stupid?" Duvar slammed his fist on his knee.

Jontar's mental voice took on a cold, overtone. *"What's done is done, but does this look familiar to either of you?"* He nodded toward the holo-vid.

The three watched as scene after scene showed desperate people, bloodied and staggering, struggling to find an escape from the carnage as orange energy beams sliced the air around them. Clouds of smoke blew across the scene, giving the fleeing victims an eerie, shadow-world appearance. Occasionally, small groups of Gorvin honor guards were visible trying to force their way through the crowd or firing their energy rifles at some off-camera enemy.

Yalmut recognized the view first. *"The Skae historical account of the Gorvin attack on Sharta C."*

"Exactly what I was thinking."

Duvar pulled his attention away from the atrocities with an effort. *"What are you talking about? The Gorvin and everyone else here are being attacked by the Skae. How could you think the Gorvin were attacking anyone?"*

"Duvar, how much difficulty would you have taking a few clips of this video and rearranging it, with a few skillful manipulations and voice-overs, to make it look like the Skae and their allies were being attacked by the Gorvin?"

"It would be easy, very basic manipulations, but those are honor guards, not a real military force."

"Yes, we know that now, but what if we didn't know? What if all we knew was what the Skae told us? In our time, who would be left to tell the real story?"

Duvar's mouth dropped open, his face contorted as if trying to vocalize something, but failed miserably. *"Those phalking quetzals."*

That evening the three Kolandi made plans to leave Lethnon and return to their own time. Under the cover of darkness, they met with Clugat and Eisoph one last time in the shadows of the campus rock garden.

Eisoph handed Duvar a container of food for their journey. "Where will you go? Do you really believe the Skae are looking for you so soon?"

Jontar pulled Eisoph into a hug. "We can't take the chance of letting them find us here with you. With us gone, you can always claim ignorance. Remember, this is why we had you simply make the introductions to those poor scientists for us. You can still plead ignorance of what we needed their facility for."

"Will we see you again, perhaps when all of this is over?"

"I'm afraid not, Eisoph. It would be too dangerous for us to return." He took her broad chin in his talons and lifter her face to his. Thank you for everything. You have been a wonderful friend." He bent over and planted a brief kiss on her rough forehead.

"If you need to go, then best be going." Clugat held up a thick hand.

Jontar raised his own taloned hand and interlaced fingers with Clugat. "Farewell, my friend. You have been invaluable to our work. If only there was some way to repay you."

"No need… no need at all. Your contributions here have set us decades ahead of where we were before your arrival. It is we who are in your debt. If you had not insisted we collect the specs and a few prototypes as soon as they were developed, all would have been lost on Sharta C. Secretly sending the information to the other R&D facilities will allow us to develop the weapons fully now that Congress is on board with the plan."

The small group stood silently for a moment before Jontar signaled the time to leave. The darkness engulfed the trio as they returned to their ship hidden in the forest.

As they settled into their flight control panels, Jontar announced a new destination. "Only one more stop before heading home. We have one last piece of the puzzle to unravel." He set the controls and the ship vibrated as it accelerated through the atmosphere. In seconds, the vacuum of space enveloped them and they set their destination for the appropriate cosmic string.

*****

"Just as we thought. The Gorvin nanobots cannot penetrate the cosmic string energy field surrounding Seriph." The enhanced view of Seriph, the Skae home planet, revealed an intense and intricately woven fabric of cosmic strings surrounding much of the Skae system. "It appears this system is close to the source generating the strings providing them with a protective screen unlike any other. No wonder they could hold out for so long against the Gorvin weapons."

After arriving two more years into the future, Jontar, Yalmut, and Duvar scanned the cosmos for communications regarding the beginnings of the intergalactic war. At first, it seemed the Gorvin strategy was gaining the upper hand. Several Skae allies were isolated and rendered useless without the ability to access technology. Repurposing a number of cargo vessels for delivering the weapons gave the Gorvin time to build their own fleet of warships, small as it was at this early stage. The inability to permanently ground the Skae themselves proved to be catastrophic.

"As long as the Skae can continue the fight, this war is going to last for eons." Duvar covered his face with his hands as he leaned on his control panel.

Jontar patted Duvar on the back as he stood next to him. "We knew that from the start. But at least now we know the truth of things."

"What good is knowing the truth? We would need an armada to defeat the Skae. There's only us."

"I think we have a chance, but we need to get home so I can discuss what we have learned with father and see if my thoughts have any merit."

"What thoughts? Are you going to get us all killed... again? Only for real this time?"

"We made it into space and got away from everyone who was trying to kill us back on Kodut, didn't we? Don't be such a pessimist. Besides, I don't know if I even have a plan yet, just an idea."

"We're all going to die."

Yalmut laughed out loud for the first time in years. "Set controls for home, Jontar?"

"Let's get back were we belong and put an end to this war once and for all."

They connected to the cosmic string to bring them back to the present. A flash of light and a quick lurch of the ship as it came to rest at the given coordinates was all that told them they had moved. Jontar gazed out the front viewport at the sight of the ship they had left so long ago. He opened a communication link.

"Father, its Jontar. We've returned, and you won't believe what we've learned. We can't wait to see all of you again. It's been so long."

Maliche bounded to the communication panel, his talons nearly puncturing the controls in his excitement. "Jontar? But you only just left us? What went wrong? Is everyone alright? ..."

Jontar laughed as he tried to interrupt the flow of questions. "Everyone is fine, Father. Remember, we were time traveling. What for you must have been only a few minutes was, for us, about twenty years. Covering several thousand years of history gave us lots of practice in manipulating the strings. We've gotten pretty good at it now. We can pinpoint our arrival to within minutes instead of weeks."

The bridge crew sat in silence, watching the screen as the shuttle approached, then hung in space alongside.

"Can somebody let us in?" Duvar's voice chuckled over the speaker.

Chapter Twelve

Less than an hour later, and after adjusting to the new reality of time differences, everyone gathered in the Amaethon's bridge.

"What do you mean, 'the Skae are not our friends?' Maliche looked as if he were seeing a two-headed dinter stroll by the main viewport. "Of course they aren't. We all suspected that. It's why we're out here in the first place. I hope you have more specifics for us."

Jontar gave his time-travelling companions a grimace. "I told you he would be impatient." Duvar and Yalmut nodded in agreement and settled in for the inquisition they now faced.

"Father, for everyone's benefit, I think we should start with a brief overview of our experiences travelling through the past. We can provide you and Tol with a direct download of all the files later."

"Don't forget me," Thyka interrupted with a toss of her hair. "I need to know everything you know."

Jontar eyed Thyka with a mischievous smile. "We would never forget to include you. I am particularly interested in your insight into the cosmic string swarm surrounding Seriph."

Thyka hid a smile, but her twinkling eyes put her love for Jontar on full display for all to see. She sat as tall as her short stature could manage and raised one taloned hand toward Jontar's crest. "These grey touches suit you, ancient one."

Maliche tossed his arms in the air while rolling his eyes. "Feathers and quills! Can we get on with this? The way you two are carrying on one would think you're conducting some sort of kak mating ritual."

The entire bridge burst out loud with laughter. Seykel elbowed him in the ribs with all the power and skill of a full Skatak. "Be nice, Maliche. We all need some time to get reacquainted and adjust to a new reality."

He gaped at the tiny warrior, rubbing his sore ribs. "What new reality?"

Nalot clapped his hand on Maliche's back, continuing to laugh. "Don't tell us you haven't noticed, my old friend." He gestured toward Jontar, Yalmut, and Duvar. "Those three are now nearly your age. They have many years of experience we can only imagine for now. They are no longer the boys we sent off a few minutes ago. Look at them."

Realization dawned on Maliche's face as he studied his son and his friends. He plopped down in the command chair with a thud and ran his talons through his own slightly greying crest.

"I wanted to tell you before you made a fool of yourself, but watching you finally figure it out this way was so much more fun." Tol's familiar tingle in Maliche's head reminded him he was never really alone. *"Let them have their fun. We still have time."*

Jontar, as if he had listened in on the internal conversation, broke the general mood with a loud cough to stop his own laughter. "Alright, I guess it's time to let you all in on what happened to us. Grab a seat; this is going to take some time."

After a couple of hours, everyone moved into the ship's galley for a meal break, but Jontar continued his description of their travels with an occasional correction or clarification from Yalmut and Duvar. While the mag-lev mini-bots cleaned up after them, Jontar finished his tale with their short visit to the Skae home world, Seriph, and their decision to return home.

Nalot disturbed the silence as he grabbed for one last package of dried dinter strips. "That's quite the yarn, young fellow. It would appear that the Skae are friends to nobody. The trick now is to figure out how to toss a sepana in their plans without getting us all killed in the process."

Jontar nodded in agreement, rubbed his bloodshot eyes, and stretched. "While we were talking, the three of us downloaded all of our data into the ship's computer. Before we proceed, I would suggest we all get some sleep. Thyka and father, with Tol's help, can best absorb all of it while they sleep. Their subconscious minds will be better able to take it all in and make sense of everything."

"It's not dangerous, is it?" Seykel took her daughter's hand in hers.

Thyka smiled reassuringly at Seykel, patting her hand in return. "Not at all, Mother. Trying to take in what they had many years to learn will be easier if we just let our brains do the work without any interference. That's all."

Studying her daughter for a moment, Seykel intertwined their fingers and squeezed. "Alright, but I need to stay awake to process everything. I'll spend the night right by your side as you sleep, just in case."

Thyka rolled her eyes, and returned the squeeze. "Alright, Mother. If it will make you feel better."

***

"That was terrifying. I never imagined anyone could be so heartless." Thyka sat on the edge of her bed, tears streaming down her cheeks. Her small taloned fingers trembled in her mother's grasp as she blew a strand of loose hair out of her eyes. "The Skae must be demons to even consider something so horrible."

"Are you sure you're alright?" Seykel sat by her daughter's side, searching for any sign of injury beyond the terror of the memory transfer. "You seemed to be having such a terrible nightmare, but nothing could wake you from it. Your father nearly tried to disable the ship to stop the transfer. We were both frantic with worry over what you were going through."

Thyka's focus on reality slowly returned, though her shuddering continued. She lifted her face to see her mother's blood-shot eyes. Seykel's red hair was so disheveled it might take a week to comb out the tangles. Taking a deep breath, Thyka gathered herself and put on the best smile she could manage. "I'm okay, Mother... really. Maybe we should have tried to take the transfer a bit more slowly, there was so much to take in, but I'm alright." As a new memory took hold in her mind, she sat up straighter and practically beamed with joy. "The strings! Oh, the beautiful strings, Mother. The patterns they weave through time, the songs they sing, I understand them so clearly now. They're like nothing else in the universe. Such power, such beauty."

At that moment, Nalot flung open the door and stormed into the room. "You're awake! Praise the Eternal, you're awake." He dropped on his knees in front of Thyka and pulled her into a powerful hug.

"Father, my ribs! I can't breathe!" She gasped for air as he released his grip.

Nalot fidgeted with his hands, not knowing what to do with them for fear of hurting his tiny daughter. "Sorry... I didn't mean to... Are you alright? Is there anything you..."

Thyka captured his hands as they flew from adjusting her blanket to grasping Seykel's arm. "I'm fine, Father. Everything's fine."

Nalot regained his composure, this time taking Thyka in a gentler embrace. "If anything had happened to you... I don't know what I would have done." He reached out one arm to gather Seykel into a family hug. The three held each other in silence for several minutes.

Maliche knocked softly on the open doorframe. "I hate to break up this family time, but we have vital decisions to make. As soon as you three are ready, please join us in the cafeteria." He turned to leave, but halted, looking back over his shoulder. "I'm glad you're okay, Thyka. Tol says you had a difficult time of it, but you showed some real strength."

Thyka grinned and ignored Maliche. "Thank you, Tol. You were a steady force amid all the chaos. I might not have made it through without your help."

A pink glow surrounded Maliche as Tol replied into Thyka's mind. *I ummm, well, no need to thank me. I'm just glad I could help.*

She giggled and tried to hide it with one hand over her mouth. "I never knew a computer could be embarrassed, but I guess you're much more than that, aren't you?"

The pink glow grew brighter and Maliche hurried away as if suddenly remembering he needed to be somewhere else.

In less than an hour, the entire crew found themselves gathered in the cafeteria munching on a variety of dried fruits and protein bars for breakfast. The smell of spiced herbal tea filled the compartment. The conversation held to small talk over how uncomfortable the mattresses were after so long in real beds, to the need to get used to recycled air and water again. They went over all the unique aspects of living onboard ship again, until all avenues of avoiding the difficult tasks ahead dwindled and an uneasy stillness enveloped them.

Maliche signaled for a cleaner-bot to remove his partially-empty tray and preened his crest as he cleared his throat to get everyone's attention. "I guess we can't delay the inevitable any longer. We need to formulate a plan on how to prevent the Skae from winning this war and completing their black hole engines. Any thoughts?"

"We need to get close to the string field surrounding their system so we can analyze it in greater detail. We got what information we could while we were there, but Thyka, we will need your unique perspective on the strings and how they might be able to help us. Your insights could prove invaluable. If we get you close enough to do your thing with them, do you think you can get us anything useful?" Jontar hooked his talons in his pockets and stretched his legs out as he spoke.

"There was definitely something odd about the string frequencies. I couldn't be sure from the transfer data and images, but it felt like there was more than just the Skae influence affecting them. Maybe I can figure it out if we got close enough." Thyka twisted an unruly lock of red hair in her talons.

"When are you going to let me cut that cardis nest for you? It's very distracting watching you fiddle with it all the time." Seykel swatted at Thyka's hand to stop her nervous habit with the strand.

Thyka rolled her eyes at her mother and tugged at the offending hair. "I think it gives me character, Mother. I don't have so much as you, but I like it and I'm not going to cut it."

"Getting back to the topic," Nalot interrupted his wife and daughter before they could get into the fruitless argument once again. "We can't simply drop in on the Skae home system without some reason for being there. We don't want to raise any alarms or make them suspicious enough to try contacting Kodut."

Duvar flicked his chipped and worn talons as he thought out loud. "It would look pretty odd with us showing up unannounced in a ship supposedly destroyed in our sun with Maliche and Jontar aboard."

Nalot slapped the table with his hand causing everyone to jump. "Sorry, but that is precisely what we need. Duvar, you are a genius."

Duvar stopped his talon flicking, tilted his head toward Nalot, and then smiled. "Of course. I've been trying to tell everyone the same thing for years, but what exactly did my genius say this time?"

Ignoring Duvar, Nalot laid out his idea. "As far as the Skae are concerned, Maliche was doing precisely what they wanted him to do. They believed he was one of their puppets with his seemingly eager embrace of all the trappings of an emperor. We could show up in their system claiming to have faked our deaths in order to ask for asylum. If we concoct a tale of how we uncovered a plot to overthrow Maliche and then simply tell them the tale of our actual assassination and execution plan, we won't have to make up any new story. All the parts will fit what, as far as they are concerned, actually happened.

"There will have to be some details to fill in, but I think we have the basis of how to proceed. Can anyone see any fatal flaws with the idea?"

Everyone looked around the table and gradually nods and grins grew on each face as they came to an agreement. Over the next few days, all details of the plan were hashed out and rehearsed until everyone knew their role completely.

Maliche sat in the command chair on the bridge scanning the various consoles and crew at their posts. "All right, everyone, set controls for Seriph and let's get this ship underway."

Each individual focused on his or her console and adjusted the settings to locate, approach, and connect to the proper cosmic string. Thyka's face lit up as she reached out to the string's song with her mind.

Chapter Thirteen

Nedia checked with the front desk of the university library for directions to the meeting rooms. She had attended the venerable Karm Rocker University prior to meeting Selan Rocker, but so much had changed since her last visit, including this brand new library donated by the Rockers themselves. She felt a twinge of sadness at the loss of her old familiar alma mater. Following the clerk's pointing talons, she strode past the catalog terminals and mag-lifts to head down the first corridor. This late in the evening, her steps echoed on the swirling grey tiles as the setting sun painted the atrium in glowing shades of red and orange. At the end of the hall, she pushed on the door and found her uncle staring out the window.

"So why did you summon me here so urgently, Uncle Nissend? I can't afford to be gone from First Town so often. Ryma is sure to become suspicious. And why here instead of at Brachspark?"

Nissend Honj's shoulders sagged a bit at the sound of her entry and reached out to set the privacy mode in the normally transparent walls. "Were you followed?"

"My driver assures me we were not followed, Uncle. But I'm sure your surveillance team already informed you, otherwise I would have walked into an empty room." She sat in a chair at one end of the long table and plucked a sweet califf from its silver dish, enjoying the melting treat on her tongue before folding her talons in her lap.

Glancing over his shoulder, he clasped his talons in a knuckle-whitening grip behind his back but kept his voice cold as ice. "Mind your manners, girl. Remember who you are speaking to. That team is there for your protection. We wouldn't want anything like the last Skaeist attack to happen again."

Nedia clutched her dress under the table as if grabbing hold of her emotions. She lowered her head, closing her eyes and softened her voice. "My apologies, Uncle. Having to play a subservient role to those … those ukaliti has worn my patience to the end of all endurance."

"It won't be much longer, child. All your sacrifices will be repaid in full very soon." He turned, sat in the center chair along one side of the long table, and waved his fingers over the control panel there to open the vidcom link with two others who kept their faces in shadow and unidentifiable. "We have found a way to legally and publicly denounce not only that abomination Ryma, but to invalidate her marriage and thereby her progeny, thus invalidating their entire claim to leadership in the Assembly."

Nedia released her grip and smoothed the wrinkles from her dress. She leaned on her elbows on the table with folded talons, one tapping on a knuckle. "No more assassination attempts, Uncle? I thought you wanted her dead. Not that I'm complaining; I just didn't want to be caught in the crossfire. I was so worried during the trip to the vineyard. What went wrong that day? Every stray sound had me jumping nearly out of my skin."

With a smile that never touched his eyes, Nissend Honj reached over and patted his niece's folded hands. "Dear one, I would never allow any harm to come to you. After all of your efforts on behalf of our family, you and your children have earned every bit of our respect and a place of honor in the new order. There were unforeseen circumstances that forced us to abandon the plan at the last minute. You were already in transit, so we had no way to contact you. Then the Skaeists took you and things got out of control. I do apologize about that, but sometimes even the best plans go awry."

Taking his hand in hers, she smiled equally in return. "Everything I do is for my family, Uncle. Nothing is more important to me. What is it you have learned?"

Nissend gestured to the shadowy figures and the two began detailing their discoveries in various Brin archives regarding the establishment of the Assembly and the transfer of authority as well as established precedents of authority being passed from husband to wife. Dozens of old documents, some dating back to the origins of the Brin on this planet and bearing the seal and signature of the original Jontar or Maripa Rocker, flashed in holographic form above the table.

Nedia shook her head, brows furrowed as if trying to work out a particularly difficult puzzle. "Wait. All of this looks like a pile of legal kak to me. I thought you said this would get rid of Ryma and her disgusting whelps. Nothing you've shown me so far addresses any of our concerns. As the wife of Maliche Rocker, the power to head up the Assembly is within her authority. Everything you've shown me only verifies her claim."

Nissend Honj's smile grew, and this time his eyes showed a gleam of real malice in them. "All that is true, until you add this final piece to the equation." He gestured to the second shadow, who placed two more documents in his holo-viewer and displayed them to the others.

Nedia studied the documents and lifted her face, staring at her uncle in apparent shock. "This can't be right." She perused them again, looking for something more substantial she may have missed. "How did this escape everyone's attention?" She closed her eyes in thought, putting all of the evidence together. "It's brilliant, Uncle. When looked at as a whole, it presents a strong case. We will finally be rid of that phalking quetzal of a woman and gain our true place in this world once and for all."

"I'm glad you approve, child. We will need a few more days to gather the support from key members of the Assembly, but then we will strike. And I would like you to have the honor of arresting the usurper and send her off to prison to await trial."

Nedia bowed her head in a sign of respect. "It would be my pleasure, Uncle. Send me word when you are ready and I will see justice done."

After another hour of arranging the specific details of how to arrange Ryma's arrest and imprisonment, Nedia stood, snatched another califf with her talons and prepared to leave the meeting room, now lit by the illuminated wall panels and ceiling, giving the windows the appearance of dark gaping holes into the night.

"Farewell, Uncle. I will await your word. I pray you find our allies quickly."

"One last item, Nedia." Nissend's voice lowered and Nedia felt a sudden chill shoot up her spine. She turned to face him again, struggling to control the growing fear in her gut.

"What is it, Uncle?"

"I understand you and Ryma had a lengthy conversation a few days ago. My sources tell me you seemed terribly shaken afterward. Has anything happened I need to be aware of?"

Her knees nearly collapsed under her, but she maintained control and a steady gaze. "No, Uncle. As I told you, my tolerance of that hateful woman is at an end. It is all I can do to control my temper around her. She wanted to talk again about how brave I was during the bombing attempt in the royal audience chamber and during our ordeal in the caves, and how much she relies on my advice. It was all I could do to maintain my sanity. The way she fawns over me makes me sick to my stomach. The rest of the day I was fuming over it and not myself." She kept her clasped hands behind her back, tapping one talon on a knuckle to help calm herself.

His eyes narrowed as he studied her for what felt like a month. Finally, his glare relaxed and the smile appeared again. At least his mouth smiled. "Alright, but you must be careful. We cannot afford any of them becoming suspicious this close to our imminent victory."

"I know, Uncle. The knowledge of our approaching triumph will sustain me now. Have no fear." She turned on her heels and pushed through the opaque doorway, fighting the urge to run down the hall. *I'll show them all before this is done. They'll regret ever knowing my name before I'm through with them.*

As soon as the door closed behind his niece, Nissend Honj tapped a different code into the vidcom panel and waited as the head of his security team came into focus. "Any further word on what happened to the bomb you placed in Ryma's mag-lev? You said it was foolproof."

"No, sir. Nothing at all. One of my team went to recover the device after they returned from the vineyard, but it was missing."

"Missing? How could that have happened? Did they discover it?"

"No, sir, we don't think they discovered it. There have been no inquiries, or any sign of there being anything out of the ordinary. Our best guess is that it was dislodged and damaged somehow on one of the back roads. Some of them can be very rough. I've sent teams out to try to locate any remains of the device, but so far, nothing to report."

Nissend Honj's face and crest reddened, his fist tightening as he leaned on the table, glaring at the holographic face. "Let me know as soon as you find anything." He passed one hand over the controls and cut the image off in mid-response.

***

Nedia returned to her quarters in the Assembly complex. As she faced the security panel for facial recognition entry, she heard squeals of laughter emanating from inside. As soon as the door slid open, she rushed inside to find her children, Kinev and Ajon, screaming and leaping from a padded sofa in the living room area onto Rilo, pounding her with pillows. Rilo, in between fits of laughter, growled at the children as if she were a fierce beast defending itself. She slowly succumbed to the attack and rolled onto her back, feet and arms sprawled, tongue lolling from one side of her mouth, eyes closed. Kinev, the eldest for all of his nine years, raised his pillow in triumph and let out a victory yell. Ajon, his little sister, joined in the howl and the two began dancing around Rilo's prone body.

"What in the name of The Eternal is going on here?" Nedia stood open-mouthed and wide-eyed just inside the entry.

Rilo opened her eyes, and jumped to her feet, straightening her short black hair and tugging on the tanned trousers and vest she wore when not on official duty. "Nedia! We did not expect you back so soon. I was teaching the children a game I played as a child. They seemed to enjoy it very much." She gestured toward the suddenly quiet pair who were also attempting to make themselves presentable for their mother.

Dropping to her knees and opening her arms wide to gather her beloved children to her, she continued to gape at the room's destruction. "I can see that, but what happened here? It looks like a war zone."

"Oh Mother, we were hunting a grendel!" Kinev brandished his pillow weapon and demonstrated his skill at its use, nearly toppling all three to the ground in the process.

Ajon, breathing heavy in her excitement, joined in the explanation, waving her arms wildly between Rilo, Kinev, and the room in general. "And we killed it! We are warriors, Mother! We played Kolandi warriors hunting the grendel beast!"

Nedia looked up at Rilo, eyes narrowed and her mouth halfway between a smirk and anger. "Hunting a grendel?"

Rilo, running her fingers through her hair to untangle the mess, shrugged. "I apologize if you think the game was inappropriate." She glanced around the disheveled room and bent to pick up a chair that had fallen over. "Do not worry; I will clean up this mess before I leave… Perhaps with some help from the mighty warriors?" She smiled at the two children who rushed back to her and began picking up the mess they helped create.

When the room was returned to its presentable self, Rilo gave it one final examination and nodded in approval. She patted Kinev and Ajon on the head. "Well done, mighty hunters. Always remember there is great responsibility that goes with such skills. A warrior never lets others clean his or her weapons or dress his kill. And only the most foolish ones ever try to have others clean up after them. Time for me to leave now."

"No! You have to read us a bedtime story. You promised." Ajon threw herself around Rilo's leg.

Grabbing her hand, Kinev pulled Rilo toward their bedrooms. "Yes, you promised. You said warriors always keep their promises."

Nedia sighed out loud, rolled her eyes at Rilo, and threw her hands in the air, laughing in surrender. "Alright. Go ahead."

As soon as the trio vanished into the sleeping section of the quarters, Nedia kicked off her shoes and padded to the kitchen. Pulling two goblets from the cabinet and a bottle of wine from the chiller, she returned to the main room and plopped herself on one side of the sofa. *What am I doing?* Her mind wandered over the events of her life, the choices she had made. Pouring herself some of the wine, she sat back and lost herself in self-reflection until jolted out her reverie by Rilo's return.

"I apologize for the mess. I will leave you now, but there are others posted nearby for your safety, just in case."

Nedia patted the sofa next to her. "No need to leave yet. If you have the time, I would like to thank you for your help in protecting my children when I am not here. Do you drink wine?"

Rilo stood still, watching Nedia before joining her on the sofa. "I am not on duty now, so I will have a small taste of the wine. Thank you." She poured herself a half glass and relaxed back into the cushions. "Your children are very nice. I enjoy my time with them."

Nedia chuckled. "They definitely seem to enjoy your company and your games. I've never seen them take to a stranger so quickly. Do you have any children of your own?"

Rilo's face tightened. "I am Skatak. My duty is to Princess Ryma. There is no time for a family. My Skatak sisters are my family."

"Too bad. You would have made an excellent mother. Better than I have been, at least. I've made so many mistakes over the years." She swirled the last of the wine in her goblet and downed it in one gulp before reaching for the bottle and a refill.

Rilo sipped her glass and studied Nedia over the rim. "You are still young. There is time to repair any damage from your past and make a new life for yourself and your little ones. No one is without regrets. It is our duty to learn from our mistakes and not make the same mistakes again. All warriors know this truth."

Nedia lost herself in her silent thoughts again, then sat up, set her glass on the table next to the bottle and scooted herself to face Rilo. "Tell me more about yourself and your people. I need to know I'm on the right path before I talk with Ryma again."

Only when the red glow of predawn crept through the windows into the room did Rilo and Nedia finish their conversation. Both stood, and with tear-stained cheeks, hugged and said their goodbyes.

***

Four days later, as Ryma finished her morning meal and prepared to attend to the morning petitions, Rilo, Kitae, and Danet entered her chambers in a rush.

"Princess, we must get you to safety. The Brin have ordered your arrest and are here to take you into custody."

Ryma continued to examine her image in the mirror, making slight adjustments as needed. "No, we are not going anywhere. We all knew this was coming and we have prepared for it."

Danet pulled his short spear with the curved blade. "I will die before I let them humiliate you like this. A Kolandi Princess cannot be put in bondage to the Brin or anyone ever again."

The Skatak did not brandish their kitae but held them in a firm grip at their belts.

Ryma's shoulders slumped; her voice softened as she approached Danet and placed a gentle hand on his shoulder. "I forbid you to do any such thing, Danet. We must let the Brin evil run its course. If we draw their blood again, we will surely lose this battle. Have faith."

Danet's eyes pleaded with his princess. "How can you expect us to have faith? Since Maliche left, they have done nothing but try to eliminate us. If they had their way, we would be slaves in the mines again. I will not allow them to take you."

Taking both his shoulders, she turned him to face him directly. "Danet, you and the others," she glanced sidelong at her Skatak protectors, "will do as I say. I know this is difficult, but we have discussed this and you know we have friends and allies among the Brin. We will prevail in this as we have in the past. Now put your weapon away and stand back. Do not interfere in any way."

He stiffened for a moment, then sagged as if a tremendous weight had landed on his back. He lowered his head and moved to stand between Rilo and Kitae.

Rilo placed a hand on Danet's arm to steady him and fought to control her voice. "Are you sure about this, my princess? Can we trust Nedia to keep her promise?"

"Yes, I trust Nedia with my life now. I believe her love of her children is stronger than her ties to her family, especially those who would not hesitate to kill her if it meant destroying us."

At that moment, the door to Ryma's personal chambers slammed open. Six armed Brin soldiers in full battle armor stormed into the room, pointing their laser rifles at her and her protectors. Their leader, older than the others, his formal uniform decorated with several dozen campaign ribbons and medals, stepped into the room behind them and stood in front of Ryma. "By order of the Assembly, you are under arrest for falsification of official government documents, usurping a position of authority in the Assembly and sedition. You will come with us immediately, to be placed in a secure facility until your trial."

"Of course, captain. There is no call for you to fear any difficulty from my guardians. None of us will resist you." She threaded her way through the soldiers and led them out the door. Only when they were safely in the mag-lift and on the way to the ground level, did the soldiers shoulder their rifles.

Throngs of Brin and Kolandi alike stopped and gaped at the march of shame through the main lobby of the building. As the entry doors slid open, the bite of a freezing wind stung her face as hordes of reporters and at least two dozen hover-cams crowded around the soldiers with Ryma at their center. So many questions were shouted at once that it was impossible to understand any one of them. As Ryma surveyed the chaotic scene, she saw to her left the smiling face of Nissend Honj, standing on the steps, as she passed. He tilted his head and looked to his right, signaling her to follow his gaze. There, standing at his side and also smiling, stood Nedia. As Ryma watched, Nissend took Nedia's talons in his and raised them to his lips where he planted a kiss on her fingers, never taking his eyes from Ryma.

Ryma stumbled on the steps as she saw the pair. Strong arms of the soldiers escorting her kept her upright and moving until they shoved her into a waiting armored transport. The sound of an increasingly angry crowd came to her through the darkened windows as the vehicle lifted off.

Nissend Honj gave Nedia's hand an extra squeeze as he watched the vehicle fly off to the east and disappear in a low cloud bank. "Well done, Nedia. I knew we could count on your cooperation. You played your part well. It looks like she never suspected a thing."

Nedia continued to stare at the sky where Ryma had vanished. "Thank you, Uncle. You know I would do anything for my family."

As the crowd dispersed, Nissend and Nedia walked together down the steps and across the way to a well-manicured park. Without their leaves, the stark trees gave a haunting beauty to the park, and allowed the statuary to become the centerpiece for visitors.

"There are some in the family who suspected you would cause us problems. Your long association with those Kolandi may have corrupted you, in their minds."

"I hope this puts them at ease." She paused and looked up into her uncle's wrinkled face. "I, for one, would never betray any member of my family. How many times do I have to demonstrate what I am capable of when anyone, including ones I once loved, show they do not share my loyalty?"

"You have nothing to fear now, child. You have proven your loyalty."

"More than most, Uncle, more than most." She reclaimed her hand and took a different path back to her private quarters.

***

Stripped of her gown, jewels, and Kolandi tiara, Ryma dressed herself in the long grey prison dress issued to her by the lone female Brin guard assigned to process the new inmate. "Hurry up, princess. We don't have time to waste on any royal treatment here." She gave Ryma a shove in the midst of buttoning up the front of the threadbare outfit.

Flickering greenish-yellow lights cast a sickening quality to everything in view. Cold white tile floors and plasti-formed walls surrounded them as the woman led Ryma down a hallway and through a security door into the prison itself.

"Hey pretty, pretty… what you in for?"

"Want some company on your first night?

"C'mere and give us a kiss, sweetheart."

All manner of rude, suggestive comments and gestures followed the pair as they passed through the common room. Two more security doors gave them access to the section containing Ryma's cell. A pass of the guard's badge turned off the force grid. The woman shoved Ryma into the square cell and re-engaged the barrier. A thin mattress with an equally thin blanket was rolled up in one corner, no frame for a bed in sight. A plasti-formed toilet and sink stuck out from the back wall. No window or light panels to provide illumination except what the hallway provided. Ryma sighed, unrolled the mattress, placed the blanket around her shoulders, and sat cross-legged, eyes closed.

"Dinner is at five and lights out at nine. Don't go nowhere, sweetheart. I hear tell your trial is in two days. We wouldn't want you to get lost and disappoint everyone." The guard laughed at her own joke as she strolled back down the section to her post.

Chapter Fourteen

Seriph appeared as a jewel against the blackness of space. Bright blue oceans speckled with brilliant white clouds covered half the planet. Five large continents covered the remaining half, three in the southern hemisphere, and two in the northern. An unusually large rocky planet, one hundred-twenty thousand kilometers in diameter, it also had a retrograde rotation to the other planets in the Skae home system. From the surface, the sun would rise in the west and set in the east. Only one moon orbited the planet, all the others having been cannibalized for their minerals over several millennia, resulting in a series of faint rings surrounding the planet. On the night side, the continents and many artificial islands sparkled with the lights of an immense population, providing easy identification of the land masses from space. Only viewing the planet through cosmic string sensors revealed Seriph's most unique feature. The multi-colored flow of thousands of interconnecting string fields surrounded the world, protecting it.

"Any transmissions from that moon?" Jontar entered the control room and took his seat in front of the main viewport, next to Maliche's command chair.

"Yes. We're trying to pinpoint their location now. I can't make out what they are saying just yet; it does not appear to be a standard Skae wavelength or language, and it's contained in a very tight, direct beam to a large structure in their capitol city. Not like any other type of communication I've ever encountered." Yalmut, focused on his panel, continued to adjust controls without looking up.

"I thought you said you visited Seriph before you returned to our present time. How could you have missed something so strong?"

Jontar shrugged, tapping his stubby talons on his chin. "The moon was on the far side of the planet during our visit. We only stayed a few hours in synchronous orbit over the capitol. Such a tight beam transmission would have been undetectable from our location there."

"It's so beautiful. Such incredible music." Thyka sat entranced at her station, eyes closed, head tilted a bit as she listened to the cosmic strings. Her mother huddled close, stroking her daughter's head.

Nalot watched his daughter, muscles taut and ready to jump to her aid at the slightest sign of trouble. "Jontar, are you sure she's not in any danger?

Jontar turned his attention to Thyka as well, smiling as he observed her joy. "Sometimes I envy her. Knowing what we are about to attempt, it might be nice to hear that music. The energy emanating from so many the strings sets my nerves on edge."

"I can hear it, but I don't understand what I'm listening to." Yalmut punched the switch to put the translated transmission on ship-wide speaker. A high-pitched, melodic voice filled the air, sounding more like the messenger was singing rather than speaking.

"... facilities to produce more transparent aluminum must be protected in sector thirty-seven. Deploy four ships to them at once. Evening services will be conducted as usual, expect Modi Shatal to conduct the worship. Next transmission at dawn. Sanctifications to all the truthful."

"Female? Since when did Skae females give orders? Come to think of it, have we ever actually met a Skae female?" Duvar swung his chair around to face Maliche and Jontar, scratching his crest.

A violet glow surrounded Maliche, freezing his muscles like he was caught in a full-body vise. His heart and breathing rate soared *"Sorry about this, but centuries-old data is being awakened. It's all I can manage to not shut down completely. I'm sending Jontar a signal to see if he can help alleviate the pressure."*

"Yalmut, Duvar, join with me. We need to provide help so Tol can sort out some new data he is downloading." Jontar mind linked with his friends within seconds of hearing Tol's call for help.

Thyka's mind burst into the link. *"Let me help. I'm sensing something strange about all this. I might catch something you would miss."* Her expression went blank as she melded with the others.

Minutes later, Maliche's violet glow melted away and his vital signs returned to normal, or at least what would be normal after experiencing a trauma like that.

"Are you all right, Maliche? What happened?" Nalot grabbed Maliche just as he was about to slump out of his chair, nearly unconscious.

Regaining his strength quickly, with Tol's assistance, Maliche brushed Nalot aside. "I feel better now. Something happened to Tol, I'm not sure yet exactly what it was, but I've never felt anything like it before, and I don't think he has either."

"It was the Modiri. Their signal woke up something hidden deep in Tol's programming, something they never wanted him to know." Thyka held Seykel's arm to steady herself as she made her way to Maliche. Touching her hand to his temple, Thyka smiled. "He's better now, but he needs some time to adjust to the new data."

Jontar, Yalmut, and Duvar shot quick glances and shrugs at each other before turning their attention to Thyka. "Who, or what, are the Modiri? None of us felt anything beyond the extreme power load. We were so busy distributing the energy flows we didn't have time to listen."

Thyka reached over and patted Jontar on the cheek. "I don't think you could have, even if you tried. The message was buried and protected by forces I've never seen before either, but by letting you three focus on the energy levels, I was able to concentrate on the message itself. Whoever is sending the message has amazing strength with more power than I've felt before." She gave Jontar a wicked smile and winked. "Besides, you wouldn't have known what to look for."

"That's all incredibly interesting, but what the phalk are Modiri?" Maliche held the arms of his chair in an iron grip, along with his temper.

Thyka returned to her station and hopped up into the seat; she closed her eyes and cupped her chin in her hands, elbows resting on her knees as she appeared to struggle with her thoughts. "I'm not exactly sure. I get an impression that they are the true power behind the Skae, almost god-like in the sense of reverence I feel in Tol's programming and that brief message."

"Like some sort of religious order? But you said they're female. It's the Skae males who are in charge, and they don't have any religion." Maliche rubbed the back of his neck as his thoughts whirled.

"I think we have learned enough to be very cautious about what we think we know about anything with the Skae. And no... it's not a religious faith, exactly. It's more than that. Much more... But I will have to connect directly with the strings and the signals coming from the moon to figure out exactly what is going on."

Seykel jumped to her feet, hands on hips as she glared at her daughter. "Not on your life, young lady. After what just happened here, there's no way I will permit you to do any such thing again. At least not until we know you'll be safe."

"Mother, I'm not a child any more. I passed the age of primacy two years ago and am a full Tolvaran. You cannot...."

Nalot stood behind her, and reached around Seykel, taking her in a gentle embrace. "As much as it pains me, she's right. Thyka is her own person now, my love, and beyond having to obey us. We raised her to be a strong, independent young woman, and now we must let go. She has tough roots, now she must be allowed to test her wings."

"She is still my daughter." Seykel struggled slightly in Nalot's arms, but quickly gave up.

Thyka hopped out of her chair and joined her parent's in their embrace. "And I always will be, but I must be myself as well. I have gifts and can make a difference to both our peoples. You raised me well. Trust in me now."

***

Hours later, the ship approached Seriph's moon. The decision to try contacting whoever was on the moon before flying down to the Skae capitol was unanimous. Whoever lived there was in control of more power than they had ever witnessed among the Skae.

"Is everyone ready?" Maliche sat watching the small golden orb rose over the planet's rim, flickering slightly as they viewed it through Seriph's atmosphere.

"As ready as we'll ever be. We all know our responsibilities. All stealth protections hiding us from the planet are in place. Send the signal." Jontar glanced around the command room at the tense faces of his shipmates. Everyone was ready at their posts, except for Nalot and Seykel, who held each other as they stood near Thyka.

"Sending signal now." Maliche touched his controls with a single talon and began his communication. "To the inhabitants of the moon orbiting Seriph. We are travelers from the planet Kodut. We have come to you on a peaceful diplomatic mission and wish to open negotiations. Please respond."

Static poured from the speakers. Jontar and Yalmut adjusted their controls after a brief mental exchange. "Thyka, any changes in their transmission to the planet?"

Thyka sat with closed eyes and furrowed brow. "Nothing yet. The ones sending that transmission may not be the same ones receiving our signal, if anyone is."

After a few more adjustments, Jontar nodded toward Maliche. "Try again."

Maliche shifted in his chair as he touched the controls again. "To the inhabitants of the moon orbiting the planet Seriph, we are a diplomatic envoy from…"

Thyka's eyes shot open, her back stiffened suddenly as she shouted to the others. "Get out of here! They are terribly angry and…"

Maliche saw a flash of intensely bright light, felt himself lose control and start to keel over before total darkness filled his mind and he slipped into oblivion.

***

His return to consciousness began with an annoying buzz in his ears. As his mind cleared, Maliche noticed the buzz discerning itself into voices, and a soft grey light grew behind his eyelids. A breathy moan escaped his lips.

"Aahh, he awakes. Contact Lyrith at once." The voice sounded more like a musical instrument, similar to a flute, than an actual voice. A cool, gentle hand touched Maliche's forehead.

Unable to speak, Maliche tried to mentally contact Tol but found only emptiness. He frantically searched for any sign of his computer friend and soon realized it was not so much emptiness as a barrier he felt, one he could not penetrate, but felt Tol was behind it.

"How are the patient's vital signs?" The second voice, almost identical to the first, but with a slightly different tonal quality, created a sudden flurry of activity in the room.

"Here are the readings, Lyrith. This one is called Maliche Rocker. The records onboard his vessel indicates he is a descendant of those original creatures we used to attempt eradication of the Gorvin virus from the Kolandi race."

"I see. That would explain the bioimplant, but what about the modifications?"

A series of quick clicks and mutterings followed, as if the two were studying some information.

"Yes, that would do it... And the others? The three young males show signs of unusual cortex activity unlike anything I've seen in anything from their planet. And the female, the younger one, shows even more remarkable activity. It's like she is a poor copy of our own cerebral synaptic impulses."

"We are not certain, Lyrith, but the readings seem to indicate a relationship between this one's bioimplant and the cerebral activity of the others, including the female. It is very curious."

"I think it is time we began our interrogation of this Maliche Rocker. Will you prepare the equipment?"

"Yes Lyrith."

Maliche felt a cold tingle on his scalp, chest, arms, and legs as he felt himself begin to float in a thick, gel-like substance. The light beyond his eyelids dimmed and brightened as he heard something hover into place above him.

"The sensors are in place and recording, Lyrith. We are ready to proceed."

"Very well. You may remove his vision protection. I think he is recovering sufficiently to make them unnecessary any longer."

Maliche winced as a stab of brilliant white light assaulted his eyes, but the pain quickly subsided as his vision adjusted. Opening his eyes, he looked up into the face of his captor. Her flawless light blue skin practically glowed in the soft light of what he judged to be some sort of hospital room. She wore a long flowing gown of nearly transparent, golden shimmering fabric he could not identify. Her large dark blue eyes, slightly tilted at the outer edge, were shaded by long, thick black lashes, the only hair he could see on her body. Her long, slender appendages moved with the grace worthy of a professional dancer or elite athlete.

The room itself hummed with panels of computer readouts. Holographic images of his body shifted between views of his various systems, each with a new set of data numbers hovering alongside. The light in the room seemed to emanate from everywhere at once. No light panels or source of any kind was visible.

Floating above him, he saw a series of five semi-circular devices with arrays of lights and displays humming quietly. Tilting his head, he could see the transparent container he occupied. A glistening, flowing substance supported him, like lying on cold, thick honey.

"Be calm, Maliche Rocker. This interrogation will not take long and will not cause you any physical discomfort. We must determine how you discovered our existence and whether you and your companions are any threat to us. You will not be able to speak. Our paralytic will wear off soon with no lingering effects. The gel contains sensor nanobots which will detect neural impulses and feed the information to our computers." She placed a soft, warm hand on his chest, closed her eyes, and a slight tingle in Maliche's mind grew to a very annoying itch.

As he watched, the panels jumped into activity. Data sets flashed across the screens. The holographic image of his body alternated between several shades of blues, greens, and yellows. The scan of his brain suddenly turned a bright blue.

"Oh, my goodness, this is an unexpected turn of events."

"Tol, you're alive. I thought these women did something to you."

Tol laughed in his mind. *"Oh, they did. The experience was absolutely amazing."*

"Are you alright? Did they harm you?"

"No, my friend, I am not compromised in any way. Their probes detected the signature of my ancient Skae programming, so they scanned my files, or at least the oldest, most basic files I

let them see. While they were occupied, I gained access to their system and learned how to fully protect my true nature from them. Once I secured myself, I started a conversation with them."

Maliche almost shouted in his head. *"You did what?"*

"Don't get yourself into a snit, now. I was in complete control and beyond their reach. They were afraid at first, but now they want to learn as much as they can. They are very curious about my sentience. I don't think they've ever seen anything like me before, or our friends, for that matter."

"Our friends? Where are they? Is everyone alright?"

"Everyone is safe and unharmed. As soon as Lyrith here was convinced I was no threat and released me from my confinement I reached out to Jontar and the others. These Modiri have blocked access to their computer systems. Their encryptions are very sophisticated, but I will have them cracked before long. I don't think they realize our ability to communicate telepathically, at least not yet. I also made sure to shield almost all of my newly-acquired higher functions from them. They never suspected how much I have grown since they implanted me in Karm, so they are only treating me like a curiosity. I want to keep it that way."

Maliche let out a sigh, and noticed his scans turn a shade of turquoise and then vanish.

"We are finished." Lyrith's resonant flute-like voice sang in his ears. "We have removed our security precautions around your implant, now that our computer systems are safeguarded. We will remove the nano-gel and leave you to rest for a few hours."

His voice scraped like grit paper in his throat as he tried to talk. "Where are my friends? I demand to see them right now."

A riff of what must be laughter filled the room. "You demand? If you were not an alien recovering from our paralytic, we would sentence you to expulsion into space for such insolence, but I will grant you your ignorance for now. Do not make the same error in the future. We will decide your fate soon enough. Rest now." Lyrith's gown swished softly as her long thin legs glided her across the room and through the glimmering force shield in the doorway.

Jontar's mental voice intruded on Maliche's confused thoughts. *"Father, are you alright? Tol says you are unharmed, but we haven't heard from you."*

"Yes, I'm okay. Those women who captured us, what did Tol call them? Modiri? They just left, so I can talk now. Are the rest of you together and safe?"

"Yalmut and Duvar are with me. We're safe, for now I think, but it may take us some time to infiltrate their systems to learn more. They have some pretty sophisticated security protections. Nothing we can't crack with a little more time, though, especially with Tol's help."

"What about Thyka, Nalot, and Seykel? They're not with you?"

"I've been in touch with Thyka. It seems she is of particular interest to these women. They discovered some of her ability to connect emotionally with the strings, so she is under constant study."

"Studying her? Is she being hurt? What about Nalot and Seykel?"

"She says she is fine and they aren't mistreating her. She seems to think these Modiri consider her something of a kindred sister or something. They apparently have a similar ability when connecting to the strings. She's trying to learn as much as she can. I don't know about Nalot or Seykel, yet. As soon as we can penetrate the security protocols they'll be my first priority."

***

Keeping track of time without Tol's computer mind would have been impossible in the unchanging light of the room where the Modiri kept Maliche strapped to his bed. Two days passed, filled with a constant barrage of mind-probing tests and questions from a series of Modiri women. Regular updates from Jontar proved frustrating as they encountered greater difficulty than anticipated gaining access to the computer systems. On the third day, Maliche recognized the woman who seemed to be in charge of the facility as she swished into the room again and approached him, smiling.

"Good day, Maliche Rocker. We hope you are well." Before he could reply, she continued as if talking with a favorite pet. "Our tests are complete and we will now release your restraints, but you must promise to remain calm and not resist us. No harm will come to you or your companions if you cooperate." The blue-tinged woman flicked her long thin fingers over a control panel and Maliche felt the field keeping him confined vanish.

Maliche rotated his shoulders as he sat up, and stretched his arms and legs to get the blood flowing again and work out the stiffness of three days being held captive on the bed. "We are here on a diplomatic mission from my home world, Kodut. We have no intention of causing you any difficulties. When may we speak with your leaders?"

"Follow me, Maliche Rocker. I will bring you to the others." The woman acted as if he had not spoken, and simply led the way out of the room and down the brightly-lit silvery hall.

Maliche increased his pace to keep up with the much taller woman and tried again to talk with her. "We are Brin and Kolandi from the planet Kodut. As allies with the Skae, we might have expected better treatment upon our arrival. But as I said, we are on a diplomatic mission for our leaders and wish to talk with those in command here and on Seriph. Will you pass along our desire for a meeting?"

The Modiri halted in front of an opaque energy field in the wall. "These are the quarters assigned to you and your companions. Do not attempt to enter or leave without one of us to escort you. The portal field will prevent passage and you could potentially be harmed if you come into prolonged contact with it. We will return when we wish to communicate further." She passed her fingers lightly over a control panel in the wall next to the field and it shimmered to near transparency as she signaled for Maliche to enter.

Stepping across the threshold, Maliche felt a tingle and, as the room beyond came into focus, he smiled to see everyone but Thyka present and apparently unharmed. The energy field returned to full strength as soon as he was clear.

Before they could complete all the greetings and exchange of information, before they could start to discuss the problems ahead, the entry way thinned again, and Thyka entered. Rushing to embrace her mother and father, she reached out to include the others. "They almost would not let me rejoin all of you here. Apparently, they consider me as the important one in our group and something on the order of royalty. Not as high as they themselves, but along the lines of a lesser noble. It took a long time to convince them of my sincere desire to be in the same rooms as all of you. They are a very peculiar group."

Maliche stepped back and took her chin in his talons. "They didn't hurt you in any way, did they?"

She laughed a little as she patted his hand, removing it from her face. "No. Quite the opposite, in fact. Their questions were exhausting, and they made every effort to make me as comfortable as possible. After their tests revealed some of my abilities, anyway. They were surprised to find one with my ability to feel the emotions of the strings. They had thought they were the only ones who were capable of that sort of connection. Apparently, even the Skae males cannot sense the strings like that, if at all. The men rely mostly on their technology to connect and travel by string."

Seykel twirled Thyka around to face her, hands firmly on her shoulders. "Wait. How did you learn all of this? They barely even talked to me or your father. Apparently they didn't even test us like they did the rest of you, either."

"Of course not, Mother. You and Father don't have our abilities. They lost interest in the two of you almost immediately."

Seykel's eyes narrowed, her posture giving every impression of a predator about to attack. "I'll show them some of my abilities the first chance I get. Let's see how impressed they are with an angry Skatak in their midst."

"Easy, my love," Nalot pulled Seykel into his arms and caressed her back. "Perhaps it would be best to let them learn about you when they least expect it. When we need you most to escape from here."

"Wait," interrupted Jontar. "They actually talked *with* you? Were you able to learn anything about them? The rest of us were no more than laboratory specimens to them."

Thyka gathered her thoughts as she stepped toward a nearby chair and sat down. "I need more information to be sure, but I think these Modiri are, as I suspected, the true rulers of the Skae. Whenever they mention the Skae, I felt the Modiri considered them a lower class of being. As much as the Skae treat the rest of the galaxy as beneath them, these women treat the Skae as underlings. The way they talked made me think they believe we have a similar relationship. I didn't discourage them in that. It helped them open up toward me and drop their guard to think I was a kindred spirit among lesser beings."

Thyka explained to the others that the Modiri had a hierarchy of their own. "Their moon, called Seriph Major, is forbidden to all except the Modiri and those few chosen male Skae they use as servants or liaisons to the planet below. The acolytes are the youngest of the priestesses and do most of the manual labor. Those who performed all the examinations and other functions requiring advanced training and greater skill are known as prelates and are the predominant group. Those in charge are the actual Modiri. Only the most advanced prelates, those with enough training to ascend higher, ever see or communicate directly with the Modiri."

Maliche rubbed his crest as he listened. "No wonder they treated me like a hologram. They didn't consider me worth the effort. It was Tol that piqued their interest. This could work to our advantage. Can you arrange another meeting with them?"

"I'll try. What did you have in mind?"

***

As evening approached, the entry to their rooms thinned again and one of the acolytes entered with food trays. She placed the assortment of colorful gels and drinks on a low table and turned to leave. Taking on an air of authority, Thyka called to the acolyte before she could exit. "I wish another audience with the prelates. You will take us to them immediately."

Lowering her eyes to the floor and assuming a completely subordinate posture, the girl stopped. "All of you, prelate?"

Thyka's face grew dark as she straightened herself, still only reaching the girl's breasts in height. "Are you questioning me, acolyte? Perhaps I should report your insolence to your teachers?"

Visibly shaking, the girl fell to her knees, arms raised in supplication. "Forgive me, prelate. I meant no disrespect. I will take you to them immediately."

"Then waste no more of my time." Turning to the others, she gave an impatient wave to follow. "All of you keep up and do not delay us any further. I have much to do here."

Gaping at each other with open mouths, the group quickly jumped to follow Thyka out of the room. The group proceeded down the passage, a continuous silvery, unwavering and undecorated hallway bathed in light, which seemed to emanate from everywhere at once, until they arrived at a large entry protected by the usual energy field.

"This is the hall of the prelates. I am forbidden from entering, but you will find others inside who will provide all the assistance you will require." The girl trembled in even greater fear as she stood before the entry.

"Very well. Now I require you to take these two to a communication center. I must send a message to my world so they will know I have arrived and am ready to commence with my mission."

Her shaking ceased instantly, but was replaced with wide-eyed, open-mouthed shock. "But they are men. They cannot be allowed to…"

Thyka's glare could have cut through transparent magnesium. "This is most unacceptable. I have no choice but to report your continued insolence to the first prelate I meet inside. Perhaps they can discipline you sufficiently to not question your superiors again."

Dropping to her knees again, the girl pleaded, "Please, mistress, I am unfamiliar with your customs. Forgive my ignorance."

Tapping her feet, hands on hips, Thyka let her glare gradually subside. "I swear I am too forgiving. All right, stand and do as you are commanded without further delay. And open the energy field so the rest of us may enter."

Turning to Jontar and Yalmut, she scowled and shook a finger at them. "You had better not pick up any bad habits while we are here. Send my message and return to us here as soon as you are done. Am I clear?" She included the acolyte in her gaze indicating she was expected to escort the pair every step of the way.

A nod of their heads, their eyes downcast, indicated their understanding and the three headed off toward the communication center as soon as the acolyte opened the energy field.

Upon entering the prelate's hall, Thyka recognized one of those she had talked with earlier, named Zephyl, and signaled for her attention. As they approached the woman, her initial shock at seeing the entourage vanished quickly behind an impassive appearance. Thyka began her cover story.

"I realize this must seem very irregular to you, but we on Kodut are not as advanced with our control over everything as you are here. Our Modiri, we call them Tolavar, have only begun to gain power recently. The devastation of our world by the Gorvin," she wiped her face in a sign of disgust as she said the name, "nearly exterminated us, and the Brin held sway over us until we were able to regain our freedom. We still must rely on the expertise of Brin and Kolandi males and females, until we can come into our own."

Zephyl relaxed and nodded in agreement. Her sing-song voice trilled as if flying high above in the silver- and gold-domed hall. "Of course. We are happy our Kolandi allies have rejoined us in our righteous struggle against the enemy. We understand your need to rely on such as them." She waved a hand in the direction of the others. "We will make accommodations for your customs. But where are the others? I understood there were seven of you."

"They will rejoin us soon. I required one of your acolytes to deliver them to a communications center to send a message to my superiors advising them of our safe arrival."

Frowning, her mouth twisted slightly, Zephyl clasped her long blue hands behind her back. "That is most irregular and may be difficult to explain. Allowing men to use our equipment, even if in deference to your customs, is strictly forbidden."

"I apologize, Zephyl, but the need was great. They are very skilled and will do no more than relay my message to the ones who will send the actual signal. They should return any minute now. Please forgive my ignorance of your laws. I will seek out your advice in the future."

Jontar's thoughts nearly made her jump as he shouted in her mind. *"That did it! Getting this close to their controls allowed us the access we needed to get past their security. We now have full control, and nobody suspected a thing."*

"It's about time. Get back here as fast as you can. I'm not sure I can keep this prelate here much longer. I'll need your help to control her."

"On our way. The center was only a few meters down the hall from you."

As she strolled through the massive domed hall at Zephyl's side, Thyka reached up and scratched her left ear as a signal to the rest to be ready. She stopped by one of the large frescos on the wall. "These paintings are exquisite. There were no decorations to be seen until we arrived here."

Zephyl smiled and seemed to stand a little straighter. "Those were the prelate quarters. They are not ready for distractions in their studies. This one was created by my grandmother a thousand years ago. I am pleased you appreciate it."

"A thousand years ago? I knew Skae were long-lived, but not like that."

"Your only contact has been with male Skae. We who are destined to become Modiri have much longer spans. Control must be maintained with as few interruptions as possible, so we designed this difference, and thus our separation, long ago, even for us. Aahh, there are your males now."

As soon as Jontar and Yalmut joined them, Thyka took their hands, along with Duvar, and the foursome faced Zephyl, joining their mental forces to invade her mind. As Yalmut and Duvar froze her motor cortex to prevent her collapse, Thyka seized hold of Zephyl's amygdala, the center of emotional control in the brain, and Jontar took control of her cerebral cortex, the center of reason and logic. Within seconds, the pair twisted and manipulated neural pathways to make the prelate compliant with their wishes so she would not only see the logic of their demands, but also feel obeying them was the absolute right thing to do. When they were satisfied everything was securely in place, they pulled out of Zephyl's mind and took hold of her to steady her as Yalmut and Duvar released their hold on her motor cortex.

"Zephyl! You almost fainted!"

"I'm fine," she replied. "Just a dizzy spell. I'm all right now."

As the others took up positions to act if needed, Thyka looked deep into her eyes. "I'm glad, Zephyl. Now I want you to take us to the Modiri. It is vital that we be allowed to talk with them."

Zephyl's face contorted as if struggling with an idea, but quickly relaxed into a smile. "Of course. You must meet with the Modiri. Please let me escort you to them." Gesturing with her arms, she led the way down one of the corridors leading away from the main hall.

Chapter Fifteen

The Modiri gardens were a wonder to behold. Open to the clear blue sky above, displays of intricately-manicured abstract hedge sculptures filled the space with a living museum of unimaginable shapes and designs along every path. "These are unbelievable, such skill to create sculptures of this magnitude. Amazing." Seykel and the rest stared in awe as Zephyl led the group through the maze of trails.

"What is the meaning of this intrusion? Zephyl, you know you are not permitted here unless summoned, and those creatures are certainly not allowed to infect our peace." Tiphan, a high priestess of the Modiri, stalked toward Maliche and his party as they followed Zephyl into the open air gardens. Her golden gown, laced with blue-tinged silver patterns gave the appearance of transparency.

Startled by the sudden appearance of the Modiri from behind them, Thyka, Jontar, and Yalmut quickly recovered and attempted to take control of the woman as they had with Zephyl. Their efforts met with a block so powerful it rebuffed their efforts and nearly dropped them to their knees.

The Modiri's eyes popped wide, but instantly narrowed, her voice like a song of anger. "How dare you invade my mind! Do you think a high priestess is as helpless as a prelate? I should have you…"

Tiphan dropped in an unconscious heap. Seykel stood over her, cracking her knuckles. "That will be quite enough out of you, high priestess."

Maliche slapped Nalot on the back and laughed quietly. "Never underestimate a Skatak, eh, Nalot?"

"I only made that mistake once. I still can't figure out how she managed to do what she did to me, but I've never felt such pain." Nalot rubbed his left arm remembering the incident.

"We've been lucky so far," interrupted Jontar. "We need to see if we can get this one under control while she's still unconscious and before any more Modiri show up. Good thing there are so few of them."

Taking special care to look for any extra abilities to break through their neural alterations, the four Kolbri set to work on Tiphan's emotional and cognitive centers as they had with Zephyl. Moments later they had the Modiri priestess standing and, to all outward appearances, presenting as if nothing were out of the ordinary.

Maliche ran his talons through his crest as he contemplated their next move. While he was thinking, Nalot cleared his throat and lowered his voice to a near-whisper as he scanned the area. "Perhaps we should all go somewhere less conspicuous. We don't want to arouse any suspicions in case another Modiri wanders by. I think we should head back to the prelate areas, maybe a library, where nobody would dare question the presence of one of the high priestesses."

Maliche nodded. "Good idea. Tiphan, would you be so good as to lead us all back to one of the libraries in the prelate sector? We have a very important request to make of you before we leave."

Tiphan did not respond. Her face turned purple as her forehead furrowed as if in extreme concentration. Jontar and Thyka each placed a hand on the woman's temples and closed their eyes. Seconds later, Tiphan's face relaxed, almost to a smile.

"That should be better now. Try telling her again." Jontar and Thyka removed their hands but kept a wary eye on her.

Maliche stood in front of the high priestess and smiled at her. "Tiphan, would you be so kind as to lead us to a library in the prelate sector? We have some important matters to discuss with you before we leave."

Only a brief look of what could be puzzlement crossed her face before she folded her hands and nodded slightly. "Of course. Follow me. I agree that we have important matters to discuss." She took the lead with Zephyl bringing up the rear and led them out of the Modiri gardens back through the energy field leading to the prelate's region.

Any prelates they passed along the way bowed respectfully to the Modiri, only to stop and watch the unusual party continue toward the nearest library. As strange as it was to see a Modiri in the prelate areas, especially in the company of outsiders, and males at that, nobody dared question them. Modiri did as they pleased with impunity. It was not up to a mere prelate to cast any doubt on their actions, no matter how disturbing.

As they entered a library center, Tiphan motioned for the head prelate. "I require the use of this space for a private audience. You will remove all those here at once."

Startled but giving only a passing glance beyond the Modiri at her party, the prelate went quickly to her desk, pressed a few controls to activate the alert system notifying all patrons to leave the center without delay. In three minutes, the prelate had locked the doors behind her and engaged the security field, leaving Tiphan and Zephyl alone with Maliche and the others.

The room looked more like an art gallery than a library. Sculptures large and small, whether cast or carved, displayed a variety of forms from abstract to ultra-realistic in stone, metal, and other materials Maliche had trouble identifying. Paintings, also in a variety of forms and styles, hung from every wall. Holographic designs floated in the air above them. Only the arrays of monitors and control panels spaced throughout the room gave away the true purpose of the facility.

Maliche quickly glanced around the room before turning his attention to the high priestess. "Now, Tiphan, I want to know everything about the Skae's efforts to collapse the double star of the Telphar system. Why would your scientists continue their efforts in the face of all the evidence showing the potential for disaster if they succeed?"

Sweat trickled down Tiphan's face. With jaw muscles so tight it was a miracle she could open her mouth at all, she spat her responses. "Those fools do only as they are commanded. We need the infinite supply of energy the gravity wave generators will create. The Modiri are supreme and must continue to expand. What does it matter if a few other systems are sacrificed?"

"You have fought a war for millenniums, untold trillions of lives have been lost or destroyed, entire sectors laid waste, including your own people, all for the sake of your ... what, your empire? Is that all this is? A vain quest for power?"

Nalot interrupted Maliche's interrogation with a raised hand. "You said the Modiri are supreme and must continue. What about the Skae?"

Tiphan laughed; at least the strangled sounds resembled laughter. "The Modiri are supreme. The Skae are hardly worth the effort it takes to breed them, but they are a useful illusion for dealing with outworlders. So long as the Skae are the face we project to the galaxy, we are free to do as we please. If some are lost in the process, well, they are easily replaceable."

Turning to face Maliche, Nalot's face grew dark as a thunderstorm at night. "We've been fighting the wrong enemy. The Skae are nothing more than slaves to these Modiri."

Seykel drew her kital and cocked her arm to let the weapon fly. "Slaves? Any race that enslaves others is not fit to live."

Nalot's quick reflexes, and knowledge of his wife's prejudices against slavery, allowed him to catch her elbow and prevent her attack. "Not now, my warrior woman. We still need to know more before she dies."

Her eyes would have sliced his arm off if looks could accomplish such things. She tried to pull away, but Nalot's grip held her tight. "I will not permit slavery to exist while I can do something to end it."

"And after you kill this one, what then? Will you single-handedly attack and take down all of the Modiri? I don't think that is possible, even for a Skatak with your skills." With his other hand, Nalot tilted her chin up so she looked him in the eyes. "There is a better way to end this."

Seykel's tension melted until she sagged into his chest and replaced the blades on her belt. "Promise me your way will work."

"I promise we will end the Modiris' hold over the Skae and end their threat to the galaxy." His talons caressed her hair as he whispered in her ear.

Maliche sighed in relief. "Now all we need to do is figure out how to do that."

The interrogation continued for another two hours and the light from outside began to fade as night approached. Each member of Maliche's crew took turns questioning their prisoner about the Skae, the Modiri, Seriph, and the distribution of Skae forces throughout this sector, as well as details about their progress toward completing the critical components of their black hole generators and gravitational wave generators.

"Do we have everything we need now?" Maliche swept his gaze around the group, noting the nods and introspection of each member.

"Very well, then. Suggestions for our next move, after we get off this moon?"

Nalot returned his friend's inquiry with an equally stern visage. "I think we are ready to confront the Gorvin now. With what the younglings learned on their time voyage and our new-found intelligence about the Modiri and Skae, we should be able to form some sort of alliance and figure out a way to combine forces to defeat this bunch once and for all."

"My thoughts exactly. Any objections?"

"What do we do about this piece of kupt lepti?" Seykel thrust her chin toward Tiphan, who sat, still held fast by the four Kolbri, but looking as if she would try to kill them all if she were released.

I think we can remove most of her memories of us, or at least help her think she awoke from a bad dream. With her abilities and strength of will, I don't know how long the suggestions will hold, but it certainly should be long enough for us to be well on our way. Tol's voice resonated in Maliche's mind, as his left palm grew warm with the red glow he produced when angry.

Are you sure? We can't afford to have her spread an alarm before we are out of Skae territory.

The red glow turned green briefly. *Trust me. Have I ever let you down before?*

Maliche sighed, then explained Tol's plan to the others. With a nod to the Kolbri youths, a red glow surrounded Maliche and grew to encompass the four youths. Maliche laid his glowing red palms on Tiphan's temples.

***

"Please tell me we never have to invade another mind as diseased as that one." Duvar held his head like he was trying to squeeze the terrible memories out.

Tears streamed down Thyka's cheeks like waterfalls. "I've never felt such an utter disdain for all other life. The Modiri view themselves as goddesses deserving of worship from the Skae and anyone else they encounter. I think I might be sick." She jumped up and ran to the nearest waste receptacle. Seykel caught up to her and held her hair back as she violently retched into the small incinerator. Wisps of acrid smoke rose above her as the contents of her stomach vaporized in the electronic field.

Jontar steadied himself on a table. "Her will is so strong I don't know how long she'll remain out or if she'll be able to break through our alterations to her memories. We need to get out of here now."

Maliche surveyed his companions and shook his head. "In a few minutes. Everyone needs time to recoup after such a powerful ordeal. A band of straggling outworlders would certainly attract attention."

While the others regained their equilibrium, Maliche visited with Zephyl. He had seated her at a nearby table during the interrogation. "Do you know where our ship is being held?"

"Of course. Spaceport Thysh, hanger four." Her eyes stared ahead, unaware.

"How far is that? Can you take us there?"

"Not far. Nothing is far from anywhere here. Yes, I have the proper clearances since I was assigned to you."

"Then you will lead us to our ship. If anyone tries to stop us, you will say you have orders from Modiri Tiphan to escort us there to explain the details of our computer system and how we were able to arrive here unexpectedly. Is that clear?"

"Yes, I understand."

"And if anyone tries to interfere, you will tell them Tiphan is impatient for our return. Any delay will be dealt with harshly. Understand?"

"Yes, I understand."

A few minutes later and with renewed color in their faces, Maliche and the others followed Zephyl out of the library, locking the security field behind them.

The swirling, sparkling towers of Spaceport Thysh rose over the horizon at an astonishing speed. The pneumatic tube express transport carried them at hypersonic speeds inside the transparent magnesium conduit a mile above ground. In half an hour, they traveled nearly a quarter of the way around the circumference of Seriph's moon.

Jontar stared out at the world of the Modiri as they zoomed overhead. "How could we have been so ignorant of all this? Look at those structures. I've never seen engineering like it anywhere."

Vast buildings, impractically swooping and soaring over kilometers of the land below them, filled their view.

"They're more like giant works of art than buildings. I wouldn't want to live in one, but I have to agree they are beautiful. I don't think I see any two windows shaped the same. Why would anyone even conceive of that?" Duvar, equally entranced by the vast cityscape passing by, pressed his forehead against the transparent wall next to him.

Nalot sat holding Seykel and Thyka's hands, staring at his lap. "They can't afford to let anyone know they exist. Everyone thinks the Skae are the real power in the galaxy, but if word ever got out they were pawns in the Modiri conspiracy to control everything, all kak would break loose. Revolts would break out in every sector."

"They would lose all control and never complete their grand experiment." Yalmut leaned back in his seat watching as if nothing were unusual.

"Get ready, everyone. Looks like we're arriving. Try not to…"

"Too late. I think Tiphan is more powerful than we thought. She must have broken our neurolinks and sounded the alarm." Jontar jolted upright, his small talons dancing across their pod's control panel. "Help me out here, Yalmut."

The two Kolbri laid their palms on the panel and concentrated with closed eyes. Lights flashed on and off in rapid sequences too fast to follow. "I think that did it. We've blocked further access to the spaceport's communication center, but we should expect some company when we arrive."

In less than a minute, the pod stopped and with a whoosh of air, equalized the pressure with the outside. A clear panel slid open, allowing the occupants to exit onto an ornately-decorated berth. Walkways led to a half-dozen structures. Approaching them with what could only be described as leisurely haste, two Skae, dressed in red and gold uniforms with a silver emblem on their left chest, held energy rifles, charged and primed but not aimed at them.

Maliche whispered to Zephyl. "Easy now, just as we discussed."

The girl frowned, hands on hips, as she faced the Skae guards. "What is the meaning of this? I have a vital mission from Modiri Tiphan herself to complete here. Stand aside."

The Skae came to attention, shouldering their weapons and bowed to Zephyl. "Prelate, we must respectfully request you and your party accompany us to the security offices. We have received communications from..."

"Did you not hear me? I said Modiri Tiphan has granted permission for us to examine these outworlders' ship. There is vital information they can provide us. Modiri Tiphan will not be pleased with your interference with her commands. Now let us pass."

Bowing again, the Skae did not notice Nalot and Seykel taking up positions on their flanks. "Again, prelate, we apologize for the delay to your mission. Our orders come from the Modiri as well. We cannot allow you to proceed. Please come with us."

As they reached to unshoulder their weapons, Nalot and Seykel attacked. Driving his foot into the belly of the guard nearest him, Nalot doubled his foe over and delivered a crushing blow, snapping the guard's thin blue neck between his knee and elbow. Meanwhile, Seykel dove behind her opponent and, using moves worthy of a gymnast; she scaled up his body and sliced his throat with her kital. Leaping clear of the blood and collapsing corpse, she landed on her feet. With a satisfied nod, Seykel reached down to wipe the blood off her weapon on the fallen guard's uniform, hung her kital on her belt and straightened her skirt and hair as if she had simply walked in from a blustery day.

"Father! Mother! Was that really necessary? We could have controlled them easily." Thyka covered her eyes with her hands, back turned to the carnage.

"Sometimes the simplest way is best, Daughter." Nalot grabbed his foe and dragged him behind one of the artistic displays, of some sort of animal, maybe; he had no sense for abstract forms. "Yalmut, Duvar, hide the other one and grab his weapon. We may need it soon."

Scowling at the trail of blood leading behind another of the sculptures, Maliche shook his head. "Not much we can do about that now. Let's get moving before any more show up. Did any of you discover where the Amaethon is docked?"

Yalmut raised his arm and pointed at the second structure from their right. "In there. I was studying a map of the facility and found it a few minutes before we landed."

Maliche took Zephyl by the shoulders and locked eyes with her. "Zephyl, I want you to go to sleep now. You can wake up in four hours." A yellow glow surrounded the girl and she collapsed in Maliche's arms, fast asleep. He sat her on one of the cushioned seats in the transport pod and rejoined the others, snatched the energy rifle from Seykel and led the way to their spacecraft.

As they reached the hangar, Nalot signaled for them to hang back while he went to survey the area. He was almost laughing when he returned. "I don't know what it is with the Skae, but they never seem to think any more than two of them will be needed for any situation. I found a way for us to get close, but there's still at least twenty meters of open ground surrounding them and the ship."

Maliche motioned for Jontar and Yalmut to get close. "Can you two influence the guards from a distance? Nalot can get us as close as twenty meters."

Jontar shook his head. "Not from that distance. Electronics are one thing; we need to be a lot closer for a living mind. Direct contact is best for something this risky."

"Then we need to flank them and take them out with the rifles." Nalot started to point out favorable positions when he felt a light touch at his arm.

"There are too many openings for you to get there without a distraction. I can provide that for you." Seykel held her kital at the ready.

About to refuse the offer, Nalot noticed the fierceness in her eyes and thought better of trying to dissuade a Skatak from battle. "Agreed. Give us a moment to get into position and create your diversion."

In less than a minute, Nalot and Maliche were ready. Seykel beat her chest twice with a tight fist, stood up and strolled out into the open as if she were at the park on holiday. The guards sprang to attention, leveling their energy rifles, the largest Maliche had ever seen, squarely at Seykel.

"Stop where you are. We have orders to return you to the Modiri. Where are your companions?"

Seykel smiled brightly as she continued her stroll. "Hello. I seem to be lost. I cannot locate my friends anywhere. Have you seen them?"

Fingering the controls of their weapons, a high-pitched whine rose, and a light on the side of the stock turned violet. With the rifles fully charged they raised them to sight in their target. "I repeat, stop where you are. We are to return you to the…"

With a flash of her wrist too fast to follow, Seykel sent her kital flying. A beam of orange light split the air and burst into silver and gold sparks as it connected with the kital in mid-flight. At the same instant, two blasts came from opposite angles and burned into the chests of both Skae guards, dropping them in a heap at the foot of the ship's starboard landing leg.

"Get aboard now!" Maliche waved his arm calling the others to action. Charging around the crates he had used as a shelter, he saw Seykel on her knees, clutching her chest in the middle of the open area, and Nalot racing to her. *Kak, no! Not her!* Maliche's thoughts screamed in his head as he changed direction and ran to his friend. A bright red light shone around him.

"Seykel, talk to me. Where are you hit?" Maliche arrived at the same time as Nalot who pulled his wife into his arms, but unable to speak.

She remained unresponsive, other than soft sobs.

"Nalot, let me help her. Tol might be able to heal her wounds. Let me have her." He struggled with Nalot for an opening to look for where Seykel had taken the hit.

"I... I'm not injured." Her voice was barely audible through the sobs. "Please, just give me a minute."

Nalot seemed to not hear her at all as Maliche searched in vain for any sign of blood or wounds. Relinquishing his efforts, Maliche sat back and preened his crest. "Seykel, what is wrong? I can't find any injuries. We have to get moving. Talk to me."

Seykel raised her stricken face toward her husband, then Maliche. Her arms opened to reveal her kital, broken in two by the impact of the Skae weapon. "This was presented to me by my mother. It was the last time I saw her before she was killed in the Brin raid that took me prisoner."

Nalot, coming to his senses at last, fingered the blades. "I always thought these things were unbreakable."

"They are supposed to be. A Skatak's spirit lies in her kital. They are only broken when the Skatak dies in battle. I have never heard of one being broken before its owner." She clutched at the broken blades again and surrendered to her husband's embrace.

Maliche squeezed Nalot's shoulder and spoke softly. "We need to leave."

Taking a deep breath, Nalot nodded and picked up his diminutive wife as he stood, carrying her into their ship.

Inside, the others were busy starting up all the computers and controls preparing for their departure. Nalot carried Seykel to their berth and shut the hatch behind them. Maliche took his place in the command chair and waited for his crew to complete their jobs. Lights and the hum of energy surging through components filled the air as Amaethon came back to life.

"Ready to take off, Father." Jontar sat in his chair and taloned the controls to set the force restraints.

"Get us out of here as fast as you can." Maliche set the controls for his own force restraints as the ship lurched forward.

"Orbit achieved. Headings, sir?" Yalmut called out from his station.

"Skae battlecruiser closing in fast, Jontar." Duvar sent the image to the main view screen.

"Praise the Eternal the strings are so close to Seriph. We should be able to connect to one right away." Jontar swiveled his chair around to work the String Connection Fields.

"Won't they be able to follow us?" Maliche tugged at his crest feathers as he tried to think of a defense against the immense warship.

"I think I might be able to help with that." Thyka closed her eyes and clasped her hands in her lap.

Jontar called out before Maliche could respond. "Connecting now. Setting controls for maximum speed, minimal time dilation."

A flash of light filled the bridge and all was still.

"We did it. Seventeen parsecs and four days future displacement. No sign of pursuit." Jontar relaxed back into his chair, smiling. "Well done, everyone."

Maliche continued to frown and flicked through his monitors. "Are you sure? What's preventing them from locating the same string we connected to? They could be arriving any second."

Thyka exhaled in a smooth, controlled breath and smiled as she opened her eyes to look at Maliche. "They won't be able to connect to our string. Or any other nearby."

"How would you know that? They could…"

"No, they couldn't. I asked the strings to refuse them passage. They like me, so they agreed, at least for now. We should probably be going, though. Strings can be flighty, so they may forget in a few days."

Chapter Sixteen

"All rise. The hour of judgement has arrived in the case of the state versus Ryma Rocker, accused of high treason. May The Eternal watch over these proceedings." Amplified for the holo-vid camera drones and the beyond-capacity audience, the clerk's voice echoed throughout the main courtroom. Those in attendance rose from their seats in elevated rows circling the chamber below, much like an amphitheater. Spotlights stabbed through the darkness to illuminate the judge's bench, defendant and prosecutor's tables and the witness stand. Most of those in attendance had arrived hours ago to assure themselves a good seat. A mix of perfumes and sweat filled the room, which hadn't been designed to handle the heat from so many visitors. From the back of the room, a door opened, spilling light onto the floor and casting long shadows ahead of the panel of nine judges as they entered and took their seats at the bench.

Just as with Jontar Rocker's trial so many months ago, Judge Haytk took the center chair as lead judge for the Assembly's Court. With a sharp crack of her spherical gavel stone, the proceedings began. Also amplified for all to hear clearly, her voice lifted to the highest rows. "All be seated. The prisoner may be brought before the court for judgement."

A general rustling and muttering could be heard as all eyes turned toward the door leading to the prisoner's holding chamber. Another stab of light pierced the room as a door opened. Escorted by two large soldiers armed with energy pistols that were holstered but not strapped in, Ryma, Kolandi Princess, and widow of Maliche Rocker, former hero of the Brin, now a disgraced figure, entered the chamber. Her head held high, eyes forward, she carried herself regally, even garbed in prison grey. Three holo-vid drones hovered in close, given the prescribed proximity allowances, and focused on her stoic face as she took her seat at the defendant's table beside her attorney.

Judge Haytk banged her gavel on the bench again to hush the crowd. "This court will tolerate neither outcry nor disturbances of any kind. Any who will not conduct themselves with proper decorum will be evicted immediately. Mr. Prosecutor, since the defendant has opted to delay her opening statement until later, you may begin your case."

State Prosecutor Lindo Shar bowed his head and stood. "Thank you, Judge Haytk. The state will present evidence proving the defendant," he waved a hand in Ryma's direction, "did knowingly and willfully, in collusion with the late Maliche Rocker, conspire to illegally assume control of the Assembly and other government agencies." He strode to his table and picked up a tablet.

Repeatedly swiping patterns with his talons above the screen, page after page of documents appeared in holographic form over his head. "Our evidence will prove that the so-called marriage between Maliche Rocker and this Kolandi usurper was illegal from the start and therefore nullifies her attempt to take control of our government upon his execution." He slammed his hand onto the table with a loud thud. "I call my first witness, Tolat Kivar, lead records clerk for First Town archives."

Almost as wide as he was tall, a spectacled Brin waddled from the shadows to the witness stand. His suit, worn and outdated but presentable, strained to contain him as he sat and was sworn in.

"Citizen Kivar, will you present your documents to the court?"

Blinking uncontrollably, the Brin pulled out his tablet and swiped through several pages, muttering to himself, and resetting his glasses until he located the required information. Another swipe and several pages leapt from the tablet into the air above him and onto the tablets of the judges. "As you can see, your honors, according to section one hundred-thirty-three of the article nine in First Town's constitution, the document drafted by our founders, the leadership of the Assembly may pass to his or her spouse temporarily in the event of his or her sudden incapacity or untimely death while in office. However, in section one hundred-thirty-seven, it states that a vote of confidence must be held to confirm the assumption of power as soon as the crisis is contained and a quorum of the Assembly can agree on the transfer of authority."

Prosecutor Shar rose and gestured toward the clerk. "Thank you for your testimony, Citizen Kivar. No further questions."

Defense attorney Halum Calthon stood and addressed the witness. "Citizen Kivar, you state that a quorum of elected officials must be convened to authorize the transfer of power to a spouse. Correct?"

Kivar blinked as he faced the attorney. "Yes, that is correct."

"But the article you cite also states that this is to be done *once the crisis is over*. Also correct?"

"Well, yes, but…"

"Has the Assembly, or any members of the government made claims that the crisis we face is over?'

"No, sir, however…"

"In fact, Citizen Kivar, have not several high-ranking members of the Assembly publicly stated at functions which you attended that they are supportive and thankful for the defendant's skillful and expert assumption of her husband's authority during the ongoing crisis?"

"Yes, such claims have been made, but…"

"Thank you, Citizen Kivar. No further questions." With a flourish of his taloned hand, Calthon returned to his seat.

One of the judges to Haytk's right rapped his talons on the bench, signaling his intent to speak. "Citizen Kivar, as the head of your department, and by virtue of your station, an authority on the matter, are you willing to support the defense's claim that the defendant is not guilty of usurping her authority due to the fact that no vote was ever taken to confirm her as head of the Assembly in her husband's place?"

Tolat Kivar continued to blink as he pulled a kerchief from his pocket and dabbed his sweaty face. "No, your honors, this is quite a complex matter. The time for a quorum vote is not specified. So, while one could make a reasonable case for the ongoing nature of the crisis, the intent is clearly to conclude the succession as rapidly as possible."

"Your honors," Prosecutor Shar turned to the bench, resting one hand on the polished surface, "I have called this witness as only a small part of a chain of evidence which, once presented in its entirety, will prove our case against the defendant. If the court will permit me to continue with the presentation of the state's case..."

"Very well, if the defense has no further questions, you may continue."

The defense attorney waved his hand and returned to his chair beside Ryma. The two leaned in close, whispering, as Lindo Shar continued.

"At this time, I would like to call my next witness..."

A dozen more witnesses from all walks of life were brought before the court to verify the volumes of documentation brought into evidence by the prosecution. Heads of several guilds presented testimony of rulings made by Ryma that clearly favored Kolandi interests over the Brin. Average citizens cited judgements of everything from land deals to personal disputes, all showing clear prejudices in favor of Kolandi participants in the disputes. The testimonies continued well into the afternoon until Judge Haytk gaveled for a recess. The courtroom emptied and Ryma was escorted back to her cell.

"There you go, your royalness. All tucked in nice and comfy back in your royal chambers." The female Brin guard shoved Ryma's shoulder as she stepped forward. "You missed high tea, so you'll just have to starve until breakfast. Lights out at nine, princess." She spat out the title as she engaged the energy field over the cell's doorway and laughed all the way back to her office at the end of the dingy hall. Ryma, stoic and maintaining her regal posture, sat on her thin mattress, back pressed against the cold wall.

Morning came early, startling Ryma awake with harsh lights and voices. "Time to greet your public, your royalness. You've got ten minutes for breakfast and to make yourself presentable." A plastic tray loaded with some type of grey porridge clattered across the floor, spilling some of its contents in the process. "And don't forget to clean up that mess before we go." The guard reset the energy field and stomped back to her office.

Ryma stretched, painfully, and stood to take care of her morning routine before the guard returned. *If I get out of this... no, when I get out of this, that is one more name on my list to deal with.* She fought to gain control of her emotions and cement her face into blank, regal stoicism for the new day's humiliations.

***

The second day of the trial opened with several highly positioned witnesses taking the stand. Most notable of the various guild leaders providing testimony was Nissend Honj. The leader of the second most powerful clan of Brin on the planet provided documentation from himself and sworn witnesses which showed Ryma conspired to have her husband killed not only to put an end to her humiliation at his hands but to seize control for herself. These powerful individuals, like the previous day's witnesses, painted Ryma as a treasonous imposter to the throne and, worst of all, a Kolandi sympathizer.

"To conclude my case, your honors, I would like to present one final witness. At this time, I call His Eminence, Prelate Jansom, to the stand."

The door to the witness room opened and a large figure, robed in deep crimson and silver vestments, strode into the court. His left mid-talon wore a massive gold ring with an emerald that sparkled as the vidcam lights shone on him.

"Prelate Jansom, I would like to have you read another section of the First Town Archives for the court. Would you be so kind as to present this passage for us?" He swiped a single page so its holographic image appeared overhead for all to see and handed the tablet to the clergyman.

After quickly scanning the requested passage, the prelate cleared his throat, and, with his rich baritone preacher's voice, read the article for the court. "This is from the First Town Archives, article twenty-four, section nineteen. 'For legal and ecumenical purposes, henceforth, a marriage is stated as occurring between two consenting Brin adults or between two underage Brin with written and authorized permission of their parents or legal guardians.'"

Lindo Shar stood to his full height, paused dramatically as he gazed at each of the judges in turn, hooked one taloned thumb into his belt, and pointed to Ryma as she sat impassively. "There you have it, your honors. The final piece of the puzzle. As shown by our witnesses, the ceremony between a Kolandi and a Brin is not a legally binding marriage. The law recognizes only a marriage between two consenting Brin. This Kolandi woman illegally seized the reins of power and abused her position to give favor to her own kind in blatant and endless exploitation of a crisis. As you can see, the evidence proves this woman had no claim to assume the authority of her late husband's office and, I would suggest, did so knowingly. Her treason should face the full wrath of this court."

Bursts of outrage, both in support of the declaration and against it, filled the chamber. Several fights broke out in the viewing stands before soldiers could separate and evict the combatants. Judge Haytk slammed her gavel, causing it to spark. "Everyone will return to their seats and come to order or I will have the entire chamber emptied."

Slowly the crowd regained their composure and took their seats. The judge to Haytk's left leaned forward and raised a single talon. "Mr. Prosecutor, I am not sure I follow your conclusion. How is it that your evidence, while it may show favoritism and potential nepotism, shows treason?"

"Let me repeat the key point, your honor." He lifted his tablet and returned the critical passage to its holographic image. Tracing the words with a talon to highlight them as he read, the prosecutor read the document. "'For legal and ecumenical purposes, henceforth, a marriage is stated as occurring between two consenting Brin adults, or between two underage Brin with written and authorized permission of their parents or legal guardians.'"

He looked up from the tablet directly into Ryma's eyes. "A marriage is stated as occurring between two consenting *Brin* adults. This... rowi is no Brin, therefore their marriage was never legal, according to our constitution. As a result, the transfer of power to her was illegal and, as shown by her subsequent actions, treasonous."

This time, silence greeted the pronouncement. Before the audience could react and disrupt matters, Judge Haytk pounded her gavel and glared around the room. "If the prosecution rests, then I turn the proceedings over to the defense."

"Thank you, your honor." Bern Motl, renowned attorney, former head of the judicial guild and friend of the

Rocker family, rose to his feet and stepped to the center of the room. His silver crest shone magnificently in the spotlight. "While I could produce many witnesses and documents illustrating rulings which clearly benefitted Brin interests over Kolandi, I have but one witness to call to the stand: Ryma Rocker."

Years later, many who watched the trial would swear that Ryma was adorned in a flowing gown of silver that shimmered as she strode to the witness stand, not the dingy grey prison uniform and coarse sandals she actually wore. Her head held high, shoulders back and hands clasped at her waist, she looked every bit the royal princess of the Kolandi.

Bern Motl allowed a moment for the audience to appreciate Ryma's presence before breaking the spell. "Ryma, would you please relate for us the events which occurred the day before your marriage to Maliche Rocker?"

In a clear, even voice, without a single tremor, Ryma gave her testimony. "Your honors and the citizens of Kodut, Brin and Kolandi alike, I have allowed this outrageous series of false claims to proceed so that all of you, in the full light of justice, will know the truth." She paused for effect, gazed across the room, and continued. "On the day prior to our wedding, I insisted to Maliche, my husband-to-be, that I undergo any ceremony which would be required to make me a Brin citizen."

"And why would you do that?" Bern Motl's voice interrupted her as they had planned.

"For the same purpose he followed the Path of Berit to become one of the Kolandi. He understood the importance of such rituals when you must lead others, especially others of another culture, that you will not betray them and that you will lead them in honor. Fortunately for me, the requirements to become a Brin citizen are not as harsh as we Kolandi demanded of my husband."

Bern Motl swiped a talon across his tablet, sending a document into the air for all to see, as well as to the tablets of each judge.

"That very afternoon we called in our family attorney," she gestured toward Bern Motl, "a local Brin clergyman, and we flew in Tola Shatal, leader of the Kolandi Tolavar. All of the appropriate documents were written up and signed. For legal and moral purposes, I took on dual citizenship as both a Kolandi and a full Brin citizen. I could not believe such a simple process would be convincing, but everyone assured me it would suffice to convince you Brin of my sincere desire to represent both cultures fairly and equally."

"And why was this procedure not widely known?"

"To the best of my knowledge, it was in the news the next morning but was buried by all the ceremony of our wedding. We did not really consider it of any real importance beyond being a symbol of unity, so we let it slip into obscurity until now."

Bern Motl strode before the judges. "There you have it, your honors. The key to the prosecution's entire case rests on one point, that Ryma Rocker was not a Brin and therefore was never legally married to Maliche Rocker and had no authority to assume his position when he was murdered. On the contrary, as you have seen, Ryma is a full Brin citizen with all the rights and privileges accorded said citizenship and was completely within her rights as Maliche Rocker's legal spouse in assuming leadership of the Assembly. As is her right, the defense requests an immediate dismissal. "

Judge Haytk sat back, folding her talons in her lap. "While an immediate dismissal is permitted, it is somewhat unusual, especially in such a high-profile case. Are you certain this is what you wish?"

"Yes, Your Honor. We wish to end this farce as quickly as possible."

With a nod of her head, she enclosed the bench in a privacy field so they discussed the evidence. Only moments later, Haytk lowered the field and rapped her spherical gavel on the bench.

"It is the unanimous decision of this court that the charges laid against Ryma Rocker are without merit and therefore dismissed."

The courtroom erupted in cheers as the vidcams darted from one location to another capturing the reactions of all participants. Haytk pounded her bench with the gavel to quiet the room.

"Attorney Motl, since the charges against her have been proven false, does your client wish to address the court?"

He returned to the lectern and leaned on it with both hands. "As is the right of the falsely accused, is there anything you would like to say to the court, princess?" He waved toward a guard behind the defense table. The guard opened a doorway and in walked Nedia Rocker, carrying a small tablet of her own. She approached the clerk of the court and handed him the tablet. She turned and took a seat at the defense table.

"Yes, thank you. Your Honor, I would, at this time, having proved my innocence of the charges brought before this court, and pursuant to article two-six-nine of the First Town constitution, like to press charges against all those named in the documents we have just presented to this court. The information before you gives proof of a vast conspiracy to not only discredit me but the entire Rocker clan, and overthrow the Assembly and the guilds for themselves. This evidence is presented in written documents produced by those guilty parties and holo-vid recordings of events detailing their efforts in their own words."

She stepped to center stage, turning to face all members of the audience as she continued to speak. "This trial, the attempt to complete this plot, I allowed to happen so their lies and dishonorable nature would be open for all to see. When my evidence, the evidence of these conspirator's own words, becomes public, my humiliation will be as nothing, for justice will be served and all people, Brin and Kolandi together, will be protected from such evil."

***

As Ryma predicted, all charges against her were dropped, public support for her soared to new heights, and the courts reinstated her as the rightful heir to the head of the Assembly until a suitable quorum could be gathered. She returned to her quarters and her first order of business was to imprison six of the guards at the prison for cruelty and abuse of the prisoners. New regulations were put in place to train and monitor all the guards.

Five weeks later, the final verdict in the Trial of Conspirators, as it became known, was announced. All the former heads of guilds and families of those involved were stripped of their titles and properties. Of greatest note was the passing of Brachspark and all the Honj interests into sole control of Nedia Rocker, in recognition of her heroic efforts to gather evidence against all the guilty, particularly her own family. Nedia took her two children and moved them to Brachspark, which she promptly renamed The Citadel, after a reference she found during her spying days to an ancient holding of the Rockers, now lost in time. She retired from public service and took up a quiet rural life. Any other family members or descendants of the convicted were required to take oaths of loyalty and only then were permitted limited and supervised participation in decisions regarding their holdings for a period of no less than twenty years.

"I certainly hope this puts an end to all that nonsense. We have some serious threats to deal with. Any word from Maliche and the others?" Ryma sat in private council with Tival Rocker, a Kolbri second cousin to Jontar. She sat in her favorite cushioned chair, exuding calm except for her tapping left foot.

"Not since they arrived at Seriph. Our mind link went blank yesterday and has not been reestablished. It could be an effect of the Cosmic String density near the planet. We've never tried to communicate through such interference as that before."

Tival, being another Rocker, was nearly as powerful in his Kolbri abilities as Jontar and served as an intermediary to prevent any possibility of communications between Maliche and Ryma being intercepted. He sat across from Ryma, leaning forward and speaking in hushed tones, tried to be as diplomatic in his report as possible.

"Are you certain they aren't in any danger?"

"They gave no indication of any difficulties prior to going dark. I wouldn't worry. They are well equipped to deal with any problems the Skae can throw at them."

"I still don't have to like it. Their report about what the Skae were up to was cause for alarm, but there's nothing we can do about it until Jontar communicates again. Let me know as soon as that happens. For now, I need to get some air. If anyone needs me, I'm taking Rilo and Danet on a hunt in the mountains."

Chapter Seventeen

Nalot leaned against the wall as he faced his companions. "How are we going to contact the Gorvin before they blow us out of the sky? In case any of you have forgotten, in this time Brin and Kolandi are allies of the Skae. I don't think we would be welcomed with open arms into their space."

Thyka replied without looking up from her console. "The Gorvin don't blast anyone. Their weapons are usually non-lethal."

"Yeah," Duval contributed. "They would most likely disable us and maroon us on a distant planet, or imprison us and try interrogating us to learn how we got this far undetected."

"In any case," interrupted Jontar, "we may have a plan to deal with that. During our trip to Lethnon and Shyfar, we picked up a few Gorvin codes which may help us get through their security."

Nalot shook his head and leaned on Jontar's console. "Those codes are ancient history. Not only would they have been changed thousands of times over the centuries, but modern technology might not even recognize the signal at all. They would be worse than useless."

"The Modiri system we hijacked can help us there. They've been monitoring Gorvin communications. We can adapt the signal with today's tech signatures, but the core would still be Gorvin. It might give us the chance to convince them we are here to help."

Head cocked, he stared at Jontar's console, and then tapped the panel with his palm. "It's risky, but it might give us the window we need to talk with them. Unless anyone else has a better idea..." He looked around the bridge for any comments.

Maliche shifted in his seat and took a deep breath. "Since there's nothing more, Jontar and Nalot, you two are in charge of getting us into Gorvin space, hopefully to Kluton, without getting us killed or imprisoned. The rest of you, don't hold back anything. If you have any thoughts or suggestions, speak up." He scanned the bridge and grinned as he noticed everyone thinking and nodding. "Yalmut, set course for Kluton. Duvar, keep us invisible to everyone out there. We can't afford to run into any fights now. Get ready, everyone, only six days until we reach the Gorvin home world. Engage all systems, Yalmut. Let's get going."

**

"What the kak!" The blast of an energy beam shook the small ship, knocking Duvar out of his bunk and landing him hard on the metal floor of his cabin. Gathering himself together, he pulled on a shirt and ran down the corridor amid the blare of emergency sirens and flashing lights. He collided with Seykel and Nalot as he rounded a corner near the bridge.

"What's happening? Are we being attacked?" Seykel, hair disheveled and still buttoning her blouse, grabbed Duvar's arm to regain her balance.

"I don't know. We were still cloaked when I went off duty. I'm guessing somebody found us."

The entry to the bridge stood open as the three arrived. Charging in, each one took their stations, examining their consoles as they engaged the field restraints to keep them firmly seated. A quick glance at the main viewport showed a large Gorvin warship holding steady directly in their path, its heavy energy cannons aimed squarely at them.

Thyka, having relieved Duvar at the communications station, spoke with a strained calm. "… I'm trying to explain. We are here to help you against the Skae. We have information of vital importance to your leaders. Our broadcast contained some of that information to prove our intent in coming here…"

A gravelly voice boomed over the speakers. "You will hold your position and prepare to be boarded. Skae vessels, and their allies, are forbidden in this sector." They watched as a small vessel separated from the main ship and flew toward them.

With a clank, the boarding vessel attached to the air lock. Maliche watched the control panel turn violet and, with a press of his talon, the door slid open with a whoosh of air as the pressures between ships equalized. Built like cement blocks, garbed in heavy grey armor, laser rifles at the ready, three Gorvin soldiers marched in.

Maliche raised his hands. "We will not resist you. We are not Skae allies. My crew is assembled in the galley. I will assist you in any way I can."

The boarding party marched past Maliche toward the bridge. A thorough search of all cabins and cargo containers ensued, including a full body scan of each crew member. When completed, it looked as if some severe storm had whipped through the vessel.

"Your crew will remain here, under guard. You will come with me." The soldier in charge waved his weapon at Maliche signaling him to fall in. Glancing over his shoulder, Maliche saw the two remaining soldiers take up positions on either side of the galley hatch as the door panel slid shut.

At the air lock, Maliche hesitated and swung around to face the soldier. "Before I go with you, I want assurances my crew will be unharmed."

"You are in no position to ask for anything, but it is not Gorvin policy to harm unarmed prisoners. Your crew will be safe so long as they do not attempt to escape or deceive my guards." With another wave of his weapon, the soldier escorted Maliche onto the Gorvin boarding vessel. Taking off his helmet and setting it aside, the soldier sat at the controls and soon the two were headed to the Gorvin warship.

***

"I've tried explaining our mission to you a dozen times already. I don't know what else you want to hear." Maliche, exhausted and frustrated from the endless interrogation, slumped in his chair. Built for Gorvin physiology, the chair itself nearly served as a torture device. Maliche's back and legs ached from the unnatural fit.

"What you tell us makes no sense. Time travel? We have heard tall tales of the Skae using the strings for such a purpose, but if they could do this, why haven't they gone back in time to change the outcome of battles they have lost? And how could any but the Skae gain this power? The Kolandi were defeated many millennia ago. You could not possibly have Kolandi with you."

"I don't understand the technical aspects of Skae time travel. I only know they cannot use it for mass transit of large numbers of vessels, and even if they could, their control is arbitrary at best. It is not something they ever pursued as a war strategy. I don't know why. And you examined my companions. They are not full Kolandi, except one. I am a Brin. The Skae brought us to the Kolandi planet centuries ago. Our mutual offspring developed immunity to your virus and are free to leave the planet again. We have reverse-engineered a cure and a few Kolandi, as evidenced by my crewmate, have been successfully inoculated. You need to trust us. We are here to help. We believe we can put an end to your war with the Skae once and for all."

Tufa, sub-commander of the Gorvin ship Tulop, sat impassively; of course, the Gorvin always seemed impassive with their stony features. "The possibility of your statements being true is the only thing keeping you and your crew alive for now. But before we can trust you, we need more evidence this is not some clever Skae plot to infiltrate behind our defenses."

This is getting nowhere. Let me try something. Maliche felt his body freeze up as he felt his mind being shoved aside.

Maliche's mouth moved, but it was Tol's voice which spoke. "Sub-Commander Tufa, my name is Tol. Do not be alarmed, I am a sentient biocomputer, originally of ancient Skae design, but I have surpassed my original programming and have allied myself with these beings. I want to show you some proof of what my host says, but I need to utilize your computer system to do this. I will in no way interfere with any of your systems. I only wish to show you some holo-vids collected by my companions during their travels through time. Perhaps they will help convince you of the truth of their words."

Before Tufa could object, Tol projected data he had downloaded from Jontar's voyage to Lethnon and Shyfar. He selected specific clips showing their interactions with Clugat and Eisoph. Images flashed across the screen until Tufa reached out and stopped the play, reset the time frame, and watched a brief clip several times.

"Where did you get the image of this woman? What do you know of her? How can you know of her?"

Peering over Tufa's shoulder to see what he was referring to, Tol returned Maliche to his chair. "That is Eisoph. She was an assistant to a researcher named Clugat. According to my companions, she was the first of your people to raise an alarm about the Skae plans to create their gravitational wave generator and the disastrous potential of its completion."

Sub-Commander Tufa gripped both arms of Maliche's chair with white knuckles and loomed over him. Otherwise, he gave no outward appearance of his emotional state. "Our history is not in the open records, except in the most general form; certainly no images of our most revered ancestors are available. How did you obtain this?"

Tol kept a calm voice while controlling Maliche's reactions. "We have told you, Sub-Commander Tufa. Our companions traveled into the past and..."

Tufa threw his arms in the air and stormed back to his console. "And I have told you I do not believe your fanciful tale. I will show you proof of your lies and then we will see what you have to say."

With a few stabs of thick fingers, Tufa found the file he searched for and punched for it to project above the panel. There was the Shyfar conference room in all of its glory, with the Skae governing panel and presenters on the dais.

"You claim your companions were at this conference with Eisoph, and you have even been clever enough to manipulate your holo-vids with their likenesses alongside her and the others. Here are the Gorvin records of the event." He manipulated the controls to swivel the view around to see the audience. He zoomed in to Eisoph as she stood to argue her discovery. Tufa watched and listened as her voice rang clearly through the interrogation room. As she finished and took her seat, Sub-Commander Tufa gasped. There, directly behind the heroine of the Gorvin, sat Jontar, Yalmut, and Duvar.

"This is not possible."

"I assure you it is. If you have your superiors do a search through the old records, I think you will find Eisoph and Clugat referring to a trio of Kolandi researchers collaborating with them and verifying their findings."

"We will see about that. In the meantime, you will be returned to your vessel. Do not attempt to escape or communicate with anyone. If we detect the slightest irregularity, you and your crew will be placed in cryostasis and imprisoned."

With a wave of his hand, the guard signaled for Maliche to follow him.

Tol returned control of Maliche's body to him and retreated to wherever he normally lived in Maliche's mind. *I think that went well.*

Did you know those three would show up on the commander's holo-vid? That was an awful risk.

A calculated risk, but the odds were definitely in our favor. Jontar's files were the ones he captured from the Skae records of the conference. They should have been identical to the Gorvin copies.

***

The next day, Sub-Commander Tufa sent a command to Maliche Rocker. His stern visage loomed large on the main view screen. "My superiors have confirmed your claims. I am to escort you to Kluton where you will be permitted to speak with representatives of our Supreme Congress and top scientists. Stay on this course. Any deviation will result in the direst of consequences." His image vanished, replaced by the view of the Tulop.

"Course heading coming in now, Father." Jontar flicked his talons over his panel, sending the instructions to Yalmut's station.

Maliche touched the controls to open his communication with Commander Tufa. "We have the coordinates laid in, commander. Lead on."

Two days later the planet Kluton, home world of the Gorvin, filled the view screen. A signal came again from Commander Tufa. "I am sending one of my pilots to bring your vessel in to port. You and your crew will provide him access to your controls and then vacate your bridge. No outworlders are permitted to know our approach codes or procedures. I am sure you can appreciate our need for such high security protocols."

"Of course, subcommander. We will respect all of your regulations." Maliche signaled for everyone except for Jontar and Yalmut to go to their quarters and remain there until the Gorvin permitted them to have access to the bridge again.

***

"Where are the buildings? I can barely see anything through this dust." Seykel shielded her eyes from the stinging dust storm howling across the landing port.

Kluton's environment was harsh on its best days. Orbiting at the innermost limits of the system's habitable zone, the heat was oppressive. What little water existed on the surface could only be found in the permanent shade of deep canyons in the high mountains or at either pole. The remaining landscape, scoured by intense sandstorms on a regular basis, was a nightmarish scene of weirdly-shaped rock towers and vast plains of flowing dunes.

"I thought you were raised in a desert. Doesn't this remind you of home?" Duvar covered his mouth with a portion of his sleeve as he laughed at his own joke.

"The deserts on Kodut are nothing like this. How can anyone survive here?" She took shelter in Nalot's leeward side, grabbing his shirt to help stabilize her in the strong wind.

"The Gorvin live underground. That's where the water is, and temperatures are much cooler. You'll be amazed at the beauty of their cavern cities. Only a few rise above the surface. There's a couple over there." Jontar pointed in the direction of a pair of only slightly more regular-shaped rock spires off to their left.

A hazy structure rose in the shadows before them and, as they arrived, a panel slid open to reveal a square, well-lit opening. As soon as everyone entered, the panel slid shut and the silence became deafening. The air stirred as vacuum pumps activated, pulling the dust out of the air and off their clothes.

"This way to your holding center." The soldier who piloted their ship to the Gorvin port led the way down a tunnel carved in the rock.

A squat, brick-like individual came running up the passage toward them. At least he was running in the odd Gorvin way of swinging from side-to-side as his short, thick legs carried him as fast as he could travel. Dressed in a dark brown wrap-around robe with at least eight pockets of various sizes, he actually smiled as he came to a halt in front of the group and presented his credentials to the soldier.

Without a word, the uniformed man turned, stepped his way back through his charges and vanished around a curve in the tunnel.

"Greetings. I am Gnobis. I have been assigned to escort you during your visit to our city." Holding up his left hand with three fingers extended, he offered the traditional Gorvin greeting.

Jontar stepped forward, holding his left hand up with two fingers extended. "Greetings, Gnobis. We appreciate your guidance. And, might I add, without meaning any offence, you display much more expression than most of the Gorvin we have encountered so far."

"Ahh, yes, I have been cautioned against my expressive tendencies many times." The man frowned, slightly, but for a Gorvin it was considered an almost vulgar display. "You see, I was raised by outworlders after I was orphaned during a battle where my parents were stationed. I learned to express myself in a most un-Gorvin-like manner. As a result, most of my fellows consider me quite the oddity, although they find me particularly useful as a liaison to visiting dignitaries. But do not let their stark exterior deceive you. We are a passionate race on the inside. Our physiology simply does not allow an outward expression of our emotions, at least not that others can easily detect. To us, what you might see as only the meerest twitch of an eye is a grand display of sentiment. Experience will help you discern the signs. Of course, the soldiers are, understandably, more gruff and confrontational."

"It certainly took us a long time to begin recognizing emotional cues the last time we had extended contact with some of your people." Jontar glanced at Duvar and Yalmut, smiling at their new host's exuberance.

Gnobis's head cocked, his eyes wide at Jontar's statement. "You've had contact with Gorvin before? I wouldn't think that possible, considering our people are on opposite sides of this war and have been forever."

Maliche shot a stern gaze at his son and the others. "It's a long story, Gnobis. One best saved for when we know each other better. For now, could you take us to our quarters? We desperately need some rest."

"Of course, of course. Follow me. We are not far at all." The squat Gorvin led the way out of the corridor and into the vast cavern containing Zenotime, the Gorvin capitol city. Maliche and the others stopped in their tracks, gaping at the incredible visage unfolding before them.

"This is incredible. I've heard tales of Gorvin architecture, but I never imagined such magnificence." Maliche stood open-jawed as he examined the view.

Bioluminescent algae coating every centimeter of the cavern ceiling and walls provided illumination for its inhabitants, and levitating spheres of the same algae floated above nearly every intersection. Most of the structures seemed to be carved out of the natural stalagmites, some dozens of meters in diameter, and a hundred or more meters tall. Others appeared to be built in imitation of the natural features. The multi-colored glittering of tiny gems and reflective minerals imbedded in the stone flickered with every turn of the head, giving the city a beauty unlike any other. Mismatched windows in the buildings, constructed in every conceivable geometric shape, glowed with the soft yellow-green light of the algae lighting the rest of the city. Echoes of voices, running vehicles and other sources blended together as they reverberated off the cavern walls into a hum of activity.

"It's beautiful. Our caverns back home were nothing like this. I must learn how you accomplished all of this." Seykel practically drooled as she gaped at the city. "If we could learn how to build cities like this, we could move back into the cave and avoid all the discomforts of above-ground dwellings in the desert. It's a bit dark, but that can be fixed."

Gnobis let out a deep rumble, the Gorvin equivalent of laughter. "Dark? I was about to put on my visor, it is so bright in here. I am used to being indoors in my lab. You must remember we Gorvin have evolved as cavern dwellers. Our senses, particularly our eyes, are much more sensitive to low light levels than yours. Come now, we must get you settled."

Occasionally stumbling as they let their eyes feast on the city's unique features, Maliche and the others followed their host and in a few minutes, found themselves in front of one of the hollowed-out stalagmites. Gnobis stood in front of the doorway and a thin red beam skimmed over his body. "Gnobis, research assistant viral nanobot division, sector eight." A light above the door turned blue and a nearly-seamless panel slid open, spilling a shaft of yellow-green light onto the ground.

"I apologize, but for security purposes, you will not have access to the locks. Either I or one of my associates will escort you whenever you are permitted outside of these quarters. Welcome to the visiting dignitary facility. Please forgive the dust; we do not have many visitors these days. The war has taken a terrible toll on actual physical visits from our colleagues." They stepped into the main lobby and took one of the pneumatic lifts to the thirty-sixth level.

When the lift door swished open, Jontar and his two friends recognized the layout of a Gorvin dwelling. The large central gathering room contained six tunnels leading off to the kitchen and sleeping rooms. The room itself contained a large central table with seating specifically chosen to suit humanoids with physiology most similar to the Brin and Kolandi. Cushioned sofas formed a nook in one part while two separate desks with computer terminals occupied the opposite side. Holographic three-dimensional images of various star systems hung on each highly-polished stone wall.

"This will do nicely," Maliche stated as he surveyed the area. "What about our personal belongings? Will we be able to retrieve them from our ship?"

"That is being arranged. Someone will be here soon with your possessions. For now, I will let you get some rest. We will meet again tomorrow morning. It will be a very busy day. I hope you convince my superiors that you really are here to help end this war. I must warn you, though. They are very skeptical that you can provide anything so momentous after all this time."

Jontar held his hand up with three fingers extended, and Gnobis joined him with the two-fingered response. "There has never, in the history of this galaxy, been any like us. We can deliver on our promise."

Gnobis grinned and looked hard into Jontar's eyes. "Time will tell, young one."

Chapter Eighteen

Dravite, Master of the nano-virus technology unit, crossed his thick arms across a barrel chest. "I'm not convinced you three are the same individuals in the archive footage. Before I allow you access to our files, I'm afraid you need to make me believe your time travel story. I don't care what your calculations say about getting our tech through the Skae barriers. Until I am certain of who you are and what you can do, my facility is closed to you."

The tech lab conference room glowed with the same dim light as the rest of the city. The polished walls sparkled with the reflections of mirror-like minerals laced throughout the marbled pattern of stone. Three Gorvin scientists, in addition to Dravite and Gnobis and the one military escort, sat opposite Maliche and his companions at the large oval table which seemed to grow from the stone floor. Four hours of talk, examinations and demonstrations using network-blocked devices had little effect on the tech master. Hope began to fade in Maliche's heart. "The only way we might truly convince you of our ability to time travel is to take you on a trip. I doubt your superiors or the military will allow us anywhere near our ship, much less fly off into history. Isn't there anything else we can do?"

Dravite, with typical Gorvin impassive features, uncrossed his massive arms and leaned on the table. "Make me trust you and I can arrange for you to do exactly that."

You won't like this, but I think I've worked out enough of the Gorvin cerebral structure to help us out. Maliche's brain tingled with Tol's building energy.

Wait! What are you going to do?

Remember what I did to Ryma when you first met?

No, Tol. It's too…

The Gorvin half of the room filled with a bright blue glow, surrounding each of them and holding them immobile as Tol entered their minds and shared Maliche's history with them all.

"Tol, what are you doing?" Jontar sent out his thoughts as the glow grew in intensity.

"Something I did to help your mother and father out a long time ago. Be quiet now, this takes a lot of concentration, connecting to so many alien minds at once. Tell the others not to interfere or try anything stupid."

Jontar broke contact and instructed the others to sit still and let Tol complete whatever he was doing to the Gorvin.

"But this is our chance to gain some leverage." Nalot half-rose from his seat before Seykel took hold of his arm and pulled him back.

"Wait, Husband. Have faith in our friend. I have seen this before and so have you, back in the caves."

"I think it's working. I feel their anxiety fading." Thyka studied the faces of the Gorvin scientists, reaching out with her mind to test their emotional state.

Five minutes later, the blue glow faded and the Gorvin gasped, holding on to the table to prevent themselves from falling. The guard, standing against a far wall, collapsed to his knees.

"What in the name of Sacred Anatase happened? What did you do to us?" Dravite struggled to keep his composure as his senses flooded back.

Tol, still in control of Maliche's body, spoke reassuringly to the scientists as they sat staring at Maliche. "No harm has come to any of you. I simply did as you asked and shared this Brin's history with you. You asked to be convinced of our desire to help and our power to do so. This was the only way I know of to accomplish the task in less than decades of working together. We don't have that kind of time. Did I succeed?"

Gaping in amazement, at least what served as amazement on Gorvin facial features, Dravite nodded his head slowly. "I think so. Unless this is some sort of trick... no, I do not believe that. Yes, I believe we can trust your intentions. I still need to see this time traveling ability of yours in person, but I think now more for my own scientific curiosity than any doubt of your talents. Will this afternoon be too soon?"

***

After their meeting broke up, Dravite and the other scientists contacted the authorities and used their influence to gain a special permit to allow the alien 'guests' access to their vessel, to leave the planet and, with the scientists and the usual guard along for the ride, attempt a scientific demonstration. Within hours, everyone met at the ship, boarded and blasted off into space in search of a nearby cosmic string.

"There's some sort of problem connecting with the string, Father. I don't know what is wrong." Jontar hovered over Yalmut's shoulder as they tried several times to match their ship to the resonant frequencies of the string. "These frequencies keep shifting before we can make a connection. I've never seen anything like it."

Thyka joined them at the console and studied the readings. Reaching out with her mind, she tried to read the string itself. "The string doesn't like the Gorvin. The Skae have somehow convinced the strings that only they and their allies can be trusted."

Dravite stiffened, his hand resting on the hilt of the weapon at his belt, as he turned to address Maliche. "What is she talking about? The cosmic strings are an astronomical phenomenon, a state of energy. She makes them sound like something alive."

Maliche shrugged his shoulders and smiled as he stood next to the Gorvin tech master in front of the main view screen. Filters allowed the string to become visible as they watched. "Thyka has a unique perspective on the strings none of the rest of us have. I don't know if the strings are alive or not, but she treats them as if they were and has gotten some unusual and favorable results. We just go along with her with open minds."

Thyka continued her efforts to meld with the string when she suddenly stiffened and screamed. Collapsing to her knees, Thyka held her head.

"What happened? Are you alright?" Jontar dropped beside Thyka, holding her with both arms wrapped around her tiny frame.

"I think they got angry with me and kicked me out. I've never felt such pain. It was like a lightning bolt split my skull wide open… It's better now." She took in a few deep breaths and, with Jontar's help, sat in Yalmut's chair.

Seykel shoved Jontar aside and took her daughter's face in both hands, examining her closely. "What did you think you were doing? I don't ever want you to try that again. You could have been killed."

Brushing her hands away, Thyka attempted a weak smile. "No, Mother, they would not kill me. They're not like that at all. It was just a warning. I have to go back in and try again."

"I thought I just told you …"

"No, Mother. This is my job. We need my abilities if our mission is to succeed. I have to do this. None of the others understand the strings like I do."

Folding her arms across her chest, Seykel lowered her head but kept eye contact with Thyka. "Promise me you will be more careful."

"I will, Mother. I may have been a bit too demanding last time. The strings are very formal and easily offended. I will try a more diplomatic approach this time."

Setting her face and taking another deep breath to prepare for another contact, Thyka closed her eyes and stretched out her mind again. Several minutes passed as beads of sweat formed on her forehead and her small talons dug deep into her palms with the effort.

Exhaling with a blast, she shook her head and frowned. "It's no good. It won't believe me. I think we need to take a bit more drastic approach."

Jontar peered over his shoulder at Thyka. "What do you mean, 'a more drastic approach'?"

She scanned the room, looking each of her companions in the eye. "The four of us need to link together and connect to the string. Possibly Tol as well, considering what he did with our Gorvin friends and your parents, Jontar. Only a combined effort to show the full spectrum of this war has any hope of altering the string's view."

***

Sitting on the floor of Thyka's cabin, lights dimmed low and the scent of sweet herbs from a small scent-pot filling their nostrils, the four Kolbri and Maliche formed a circle. Seykel stood ready in case they needed help. Nalot remained on the bridge with the Gorvins.

Thyka took a deep calming breath and reached out her hands. "Join hands now. Tol, we need you to join us. Everyone close your eyes and focus your thoughts on each other. Let me take the lead on this."

Inside her mind, Thyka heard the thoughts of her friends growing louder against the sparks and colors of the rest of her thoughts. As she saw their auras grow in intensity, the rest of her mind faded into a dim background greyness. As each one became part of the whole, a band of golden light appeared to join them together.

The mental connection solidified and she extended her thoughts out to the others. "Good. I can feel each of you as if we were one now. When I call the string, you must remain quiet until I call on you. Do only as I ask and nothing more or less. The strings have a very strict protocol of etiquette and will only listen to those they consider to be polite and considerate. Don't snicker, Duvar. That will end all of this quicker than anything. Is everyone ready?"

As the others watched, she began a song, which became visible as an abstract blending of light, color, and sound. A beautiful melody lifted above them and out into the darkness. Almost at once, the melody was joined by a much larger, more complex harmony of the same song. The small circle of crewmates became surrounded by flowing currents of intense colors, some that they could not identify, intertwined with the sound of such intricate and vibrant qualities that they sat in awe for a long moment before Thyka jolted them out of their daze.

"They have agreed to listen to us, but remember your manners. I will call on each of you in turn to speak with them. Open your minds, and allow them every access they require. No harm will come to you unless you try to fight them."

"Is this how you see the strings, Thyka? I never imagined in my wildest dreams they could be like this. We see them as pure energy, never anything even approaching this." Jontar, his mental voice hushed, touched her almost hesitantly.

She laughed. "Boys. You only see what you want to see or expect to see. You need to learn to be more open to the world around you. Be prepared now. Jontar, you're first."

One by one, the strings filled the minds of each of the group, absorbing not only the details of each of their lives and experiences, but their very essence. Their personalities... their souls were laid bare before the cosmic strings. They lingered longest with Tol. Slowly, after what seemed a lifetime in the timeless presence of the strings, the connection faded away. At last only the auras of the companions remained, still connected by the shimmering band of silver and gold energy amid the grey background of Thyka's mind.

"You may find yourselves drained for a while when we return to consciousness. The strings can be overwhelming until you get used to them."

The connecting flow of energy pulled away one by one from each individual, allowing them to return to their own minds and bodies.

Jontar's eyes fluttered as he woke up from the joining. He leaned forward, elbows to knees as he sat cross-legged in the circle and held his head. "Is everyone all right?"

Duvar chuckled quietly as the room came back into focus for him. "Yeah. What a trip. I feel like my entire life, everything I've ever known, has just been reduced to a dust particle. Compared to us, the strings are almost gods."

"No, not gods," Maliche joined in. "They're just ancient beyond belief with experiences encompassing all of space and time as we know it."

"Isn't that the definition of a god?" Yalmut added.

Thyka stretched her legs forward and bent at the waist, grabbing her toes with her fingers. "Maliche is right. They're not gods, simply something beyond our experience. All of you did very well. We have given them a lot to think about."

Maliche leaned back on one elbow, uncrossing his legs to stretch out. "Will they let us connect and travel with the Gorvins aboard?"

"Oh, yes. We satisfied them about the Gorvin's having no hostile intentions, so they will allow us to demonstrate what we can do with the strings. For now, at least.

"For now?"

"I'm not sure, but I got the impression we are on probation at the moment. They didn't tell me anything specific, but I think they are going to investigate the Skae and try to verify what we have shown them. They never really questioned the Skae before."

Duvar sat upright, tossing one hand in the air. "Why the phalk not? They started this whole mess in the first place."

"The Skae were using the cosmic strings for transportation long before they ever devised their scheme to build the gravity wave generators, and the strings did not actually pay any attention to them. Sort of the way we ignore the bacteria living inside us."

Maliche scowled as he preened his crest. "If they ignored the Skae, then why are they so angry at the Gorvin? Why pay attention to them?"

Thyka laid back, eyes closed in thought. "I believe the Skae filled the communication networks with so much propaganda against the Gorvin, often while traveling connected to the strings, that the strings picked up on the Skae's attitudes. Without any contradictory information in such close connection to them, the strings simply adopted the Skae point of view."

The group remained silent for a while, each one reflecting on their experience. Yalmut broke the stillness. "I was wondering why they spent so much more time with Tol than the rest of us."

Maliche turned over to face Yalmut, switching elbows to lean on. "It was because he was originally a Skae creation. They built him, so the strings wanted to learn his thoughts on the Gorvin and the Skae as well."

Yalmut nodded, then laid back and closed his eyes.

"I think all of us should rest for a while before continuing." She stood up, walked over to the nearest wall panel and turned the lights down to their lowest setting. Returning to her place in the circle, she, too, lay back and fell asleep.

***

A burst of light in the main viewscreen and the return of communication chatter over the speakers signaled the ship's return to current time. Their brief excursion into the past completed, the Gorvin scientists and crew members gathered in the cafeteria.

"That was the most surreal experience I have ever encountered. Absolutely marvelous. You must share this technology with us." Gnobis paced around the table in the mess hall, hands tapping as he clasped them behind his back. "Wouldn't you agree, Master Dravite? Surely there can be no question regarding their intentions now."

The master nanovirus engineer sat drinking tea at the table next to Maliche. "Yes, it was an incredible experience to be sure. I have to admit I had my doubts, but no longer. How do you manage it?"

Jontar swallowed a bite of his stew and reached for a handful of sweet tam berries. "We, I and some of my Kolbri brethren, have certain abilities which allow us to connect with technology in ways no others can. Part of this skill also gives us the ability to connect with the cosmic strings with great precision, far greater than the Skae can. We used this ability to secretly learn more about them as they thought they were training us. It is not something we can teach others, but once this war is over, we would be happy to serve as pilots. Of course we would maintain strict regulations over who can time travel and to when. None of us would want to mistakenly undo some vital piece of history."

Gnobis nodded vigorously as he strode about the room. "Of course. Nobody wants that. It is a great responsibility to bear, protecting time. There must be prohibitions on its use…"

"Something we can agree to discuss at a later time." Dravite cut in, his voice carrying a note of warning. "We have much more immediate concerns before us now. We need to return to my office and contact the authorities. A strategy needs to be devised to help our friends here with their plan to finally end this war."

Maliche grinned and pressed the communication icon on a control panel on the wall. "Yalmut, take us back to Kluton. We have business to attend to."

Chapter Nineteen

Calomel, Grand Director of the Gorvin government, sat in judgement before Maliche and his crew, with Gnobis and Dravite as spokespersons before the Congress. The sonorous qualities of her double vocal chords carried undertones of dissonance, warning the petitioners to tread carefully.

"Let me get this straight, Maliche Rocker. You want us to commit our entire fleet to one final, massive assault on Seriph while you and your crew sneak in and try to convince these cosmic strings to allow our nanovirus weapons to penetrate them, something that has proven impossible for thousands of years. You want us to believe this because of your magical ability to talk with those energy strands. My apologies, Master Dravite, but you must see how, even with your endorsement and testimony, it all seems too mystical for us to blindly trust the future of our entire race on these friends of yours."

The high-vaulted room of carved and polished stone, emphasized the tortured and intricate patterns and colors of the many layers built up over millions of centuries. The reflections of dozens of the algae lamps danced off the walls, giving it an almost life-like appearance. Statuary built into the walls depicted scenes from Gorvin history, but Gnobis did not have time to explain their significance before the audience began. The Congress, each member robed in somber greys and browns with only a metallic badge of honor depicting their station, sat behind a solid rectangular bench that seamlessly rose out of the cavern floor. A small algae lamp illuminated each of the members of the congress at the bench.

"Grand Director, esteemed Congress members, I realize how incredible all of this must seem, but I believe this represents our opportunity to finally end the war with the Skae." Dravite paced in front of the stone bench, clasping his hands respectfully at his waist. "I do not pretend to understand the abilities or the motives behind these Kolandi and Brin representatives, but I know beyond all doubt what they claim is within their power. You have seen my holo-vid report. You know my reputation. I implore you to trust these new allies as you trust me and allow them to help us defeat our enemy."

Calomel let her gaze cast over the group assembled before her, finally settling on Maliche Rocker. "Tell me, Brin, why should we trust you as Dravite says we must?"

Maliche stood, imitating the respectful hand clasp as he rose. At first, only the faintest hint of a blue glow surrounded him, but as he spoke, the aura's intensity grew. "Your honors, I have spent my life fighting injustice. I went to war against members of my own family when I learned they had committed an atrocity against the Kolandi. It is simply my nature to abhor injustice of any kind. We always trusted the Skae. They rescued us from our dying world and brought us to Kodut. We knew nothing of this great war between you. As our knowledge of the Skae increased over time, so did our skepticism. When my son and his companions learned the reality behind the atrocities committed by the Skae, despite all of their efforts to conceal the truth from us, we vowed to fight against them. Everything we have done since has been dedicated to that sole purpose. We have abilities not even the Skae know about, and we will use these talents to help you and your allies defeat them once and for all."

Several of the Congress members leaned together, whispering their thoughts. Calomel stood. "We will consider your offer, Maliche Rocker. We shall inform Master Dravite when we have reached a decision." With that, the entire Congress followed Calomel out of the room through a back tunnel. The main doors opened and Dravite led the group out, returning to their quarters in the city.

Feeling the need to stretch their legs some, the companions decided to walk back to their rooms.

Seykel strolled beside Gnobis as they walked. "This place is so beautiful. You must teach us how to do this in our own poor caverns back on Kodut. So many of our youth have abandoned our ancestral homes in favor of Brin cities, but if we could provide such wonders as these, our homes would be preserved and made so much more comfortable."

Gnobis's face beamed. "If we can end this war, I believe you will have no shortage of architects and engineers to help you learn our techniques. It would be the least we could do for those who brought us peace after so many centuries of war."

She squinted, tilting her head as if noticing something for the first time. "Is the light dimmer than when we first arrived?"

"Yes, of course. Night is closing in." Gnobis studied her like a parent wondering if his child were sick.

"But you live underground. Why would it matter about night and day?"

He laughed a deep rumbling avalanche of a laugh. "All creatures have wake-sleep cycles. We did not begin our evolution underground. Conditions above ground were not always so harsh. Millions of years ago certainly, but life once flourished on the surface and thus depended on the cycles of day and night. We only delved this deep underground around twenty thousand years ago or so. Until then, our species lived close enough to the surface to still witness the sun's rising and setting. Our biology is still connected to those cycles, so we must recreate them here."

Maliche spoke with Dravite as they walked together. "How long do you think they will take to make their decision?"

Dravite's unreadable features remained frozen. "The Congress normally is very careful and deliberate in its decisions." He rubbed a broad chin with thick fingers. "This one, though, is unprecedented. No telling how long it could take. Maybe months."

Maliche lurched to a halt. Jontar, Yalmut, and Duvar nearly ran into him as they were close behind and caught up in their own conversation. "Months? We don't have months to wait. Once those Modiri learned about us and what we could do, they are sure to increase security around Seriph. They may even be hunting for us as we speak."

"The Congress understands the situation, Maliche. Our testimony included this very information. It may be the urgency of the situation that forces them to move more rapidly than they would normally like. We will have to be patient."

"I hope they know what they are doing. Every day counts. We must get to work as quickly as possible." Maliche regained his stride, shaking his head as he went.

***

The congress deliberated for three days before a message arrived over Dravite's holo-vid. "Great news, everyone," Dravite announced as he burst through the doors into the main living area of their apartments. "It would appear the congress was acutely aware of the press of time in our case, and also due to the undeniable proof of your capabilities during our testimony, they have agreed to join forces and attack Seriph."

An hour later, everyone was sitting around a table in Dravite's research facility. Schematics of viral structures and nanobot engineering hung in the air over the table, projecting the lab's latest innovations. Reaching out to point a stubby talon at a particular location on the virus, Jontar pinched his fingers, then opened them rapidly to enlarge the view. "This is the section which specifically targets the Skae biology?"

Gnobis responded with a quick manipulation of a few controls when portions of the sequences changed colors. "Yes. As you can see, we have had this available, with modifications, since the early days of the war. We simply cannot penetrate the cosmic string barrier surrounding Seriph."

"What about the Modiri? Being all female must have some effect on the virus."

Another press of the controls and a new viral sequence appeared next to the first. "Of course, but the blood sample you brought us allowed us to develop an additional viral component designed to attack Modiri biology. It was remarkable how their isolation on that moon allowed for so much variation. We are in your debt."

Thyka startled at Gnobis's mention of blood. She narrowed her eyes dangerously as she studied Jontar. "And just how did you happen to obtain Modiri blood? You promised you would not harm any of them."

Jontar lowered his gaze from her face. "Don't worry, Thyka. I only took a small sample from a tiny incision while Zephyl was under my control. I know I promised, but I thought it might come in handy if we ever got this far. She wasn't actually harmed."

She simply sniffed at him and returned to her study of the strings they had gathered during their most recent encounter.

Jontar returned his attention to the pair of viral sequences. "Yes. If we can send both of these viruses though the barrier, it should do the trick. Do you have enough of the nanobots to deliver the quantities we will need?"

Dravite scanned his screens for the data and projected it. "It'll be close, but if we speed up production another twenty percent, we should have enough to infect both the planet and the moon simultaneously."

"Thyka, have you learned anything new about the strings? We don't want to run into any surprises in the middle of a battle."

Thyka glanced up from her tablet. "I think we startled them with our news about the Skae. If they have had enough time to examine Skae communications and ships since we spoke, there should not be any trouble. If they took the time to study them anyway."

"We can't go to war with the Skae on a maybe, Thyka. Can we rely on the strings?"

Her fingers patterned their way through a few pages on her tablet as she frowned in thought. "I think we can, Jontar, but the strings are difficult to understand. They don't normally pay attention to anyone but themselves. They don't like the feelings wars and hatred provoke in them, so I believe they will take steps to help us... That's the best I can offer for now."

Duvar threw up his hands and laughed. "Oh, great. So if the strings decide all of us are beneath them and not worth the trouble, we'll find ourselves sitting out there in Skae space with our talons up our..."

"I told you what I know, Duvar." Thyka leaped down from her chair and began thumping Duvar in the chest with two small talons. "Next time, *you* try figuring out how to understand the gods."

Leaning as far back in his chair as he could, Duvar tried without success to defend himself from Thyka's assault. "What do you mean, gods? You think the strings are the gods?"

Closing her eyes and shaking her head as if trying to explain complex physics to an infant, Thyka stopped her attack and faced Duvar with hands on hips. "No, I don't think they're gods, you phalking schutek, but that's what it feels like sometimes. The complexity of their minds and emotions are far beyond anything biological creatures like us are capable of." She glared at him a moment longer, as if daring him to say anything, then stormed back to hop up into her chair.

Jontar cut them both off, using his commander tone. "Alright, Duvar, knock it off. You know what she means. You felt their power. I have to agree with Thyka. It's like we're some sort of bacteria trying to convince the sun to shine in our favor."

"This is starting to sound like a much greater risk than we had previously thought." Dravite stared at the group stone-faced, but a hint of concern tinged his voice. "I hope you have not led us into something we cannot hope to win."

Maliche glared at the others before focusing his attention on Dravite and Gnobis. "No, my friends, things are not as dire as these children make it sound. This is merely how they work things out between themselves. The strings will cooperate and we will deliver your viruses. The question is, are your forces strong enough to defeat the Skae fleet?"

Dravite studied Maliche's group, sighed, and swiped his tablet to project images of a wide range of military vessels. "We have defeated the Skae battle fleets on many occasions. It was only our inability to isolate their planet that prevented our ending this war long ago. They have a vast military complex capable of rearming themselves rapidly."

Showing more concern than Dravite, Gnobis cut in. "Without the ability to coordinate command structures and manufacturing facilities on distant planets, their ability to wage war would end. Your intelligence has shown us the Skae's fatal flaw. Only the Modiri make decisions and order commands. If the rest of the Skae cannot communicate with their Modiri, none of them can operate in any capacity worth mentioning."

Maliche surveyed the room. "Everyone knows their responsibilities. Let's not waste any more time arguing and get down to putting together a strategy against the Skae. I want detailed plans and analysis in two days. We need to have time to coordinate and adjust before presenting our final thoughts to the grand director. Any questions?" He nodded and signaled that the meeting was over.

***

Five days later, the collaborators sat in the ornate chamber in front of Calomel and the rest of the committee from the Gorvin congress. Maliche's crest was disheveled and had gone unpreened for days, and his clothes were rumpled from his brief catnaps on the office lounger, but he presented their strategy to the Congress. "... so, esteemed Congresspersons, as you have seen, our plan carries significant risks, but, if successful, the final defeat of the Skae is well worth the effort. We believe the time for ending this conflict once and for all is at hand. Will you commit your fleet to support us?"

Silence permeated the chamber. Maliche remained standing, exhausted and bleary-eyed, before the bench. The robed leaders bent their heads in quiet whispers, nodding occasionally as one or another made a comment, or pointed to a vital component of the strategy, still projected in front of them. Calomel, with a guttural grunt full of discordant resonance, called for a decision. Each individual nodded, giving their own deep throaty response.

"It is agreed." Calomel thumped her broad fist on the bench. "Notify the fleet commanders to gather tomorrow for a briefing on the congressional emergency frequency. All ships are to be battle-ready in one week. May the everlasting Anatase protect us and grant us victory."

Maliche leaned heavily on the carved stone table in front of his companions as the congress members filed out of a doorway behind their dais. Rubbing his eyes, he barely noticed the congratulatory slaps on his back or words coming from the others. Even the tingle in his mind seemed remote as Tol talked to him. *Well done, my friend. I'll keep you on your feet long enough to get back to the apartment and into bed. You need to sleep. I can only keep you going for so long. Time to let Jontar and the others do their jobs.*

***

Nalot pounded on the wall inches above Maliche's head. "Time to get up, you lazy drunge. We need to go over some final checks before joining the fleet."

"What the phalk!" Maliche lurched upright in his bunk, throwing the blanket onto the floor.

"Seykel tried to wake you earlier, but you were sleeping like a rock, so she asked me to try. You've been asleep for two days. We need you and Tol for some last-minute alterations to our strategy before we launch. Get dressed and meet us in the briefing room."

Maliche preened his crest as his eyes came into focus. "Give me five minutes." He stretched, swinging his legs out of the bed as Nalot exited through the sliding doorway.

"... and your modifications to our nanobots was brilliant, Yalmut. Reinforcing the structural integrity to withstand the acceleration of the rail guns will give us a decided advantage."

Maliche entered the briefing room in the middle of a discussion between Dravite and Yalmut. "What modifications? You found a way to improve the nanobots?"

The others turned and smiled as Maliche joined them. Yalmut stood to give Maliche his chair in front of the holo-vid display. "Yes. I always wondered why the Gorvin used the light sails only to deliver their weapons and only against entire planets. They would make excellent weapons in ship-to-ship battles..."

"But our designs could never overcome the extreme forces of acceleration required to deliver the bots using the weapons our battleships use. Light sails take a long time to build up speed and must be launched from great distances. We can target a planet from those distances, but enemy ships are too small. And in the close quarters of a battle, the light sails are too slow and easily destroyed before reaching their target."

"Exactly. It took me a while to figure out the precise design flaw, but I found it, and, with a few modifications, I was able to give the bots enough strength to handle railgun accelerations. With these devices added to the beam weapons of the fleet, we might have enough of an advantage to overcome our disadvantage in numbers."

Maliche looked up at Yalmut, his stomach clenched. "What disadvantage in numbers? I thought our surveys showed the Skae fleet only slightly larger than ours."

With a deep, raspy cough, High Commander Rutile, officer in charge of the Gorvin fleet, announced his presence. "We received communications yesterday from our advanced scouts of a massive buildup of the Skae fleet around Seriph. It appears they have recalled nearly their entire force to protect their home world." He projected the latest figures for Maliche to see.

Clicking his talons rapidly, Yalmut added the new weapon's capabilities into the battle assessment projections. "As you can see, without the nanobot weapons, the size of the Skae fleet was bad news for us, but, with the new armament, we are every bit a match for them."

Maliche studied the data and preened his crest again. Looking at Thyka, he took in a deep breath and expelled it forcefully. "Are you certain the strings will help us?"

Thyka paused before replying. "I can't say they will help us, exactly, but I believe they will not stop us. Jontar took me out to a nearby cluster yesterday, and they are definitely becoming increasingly angry with the Skae the more they learn from their investigations."

"They can't be too angry if they still allow the Skae to use them for travelling."

"I know. It's complicated. The strings need more reassurance we do not intend to commit genocide against the Skae. They will not allow that. I've tried telling them our nanobot weapons are intended to kill technology, not living beings, but they are still nervous. Whatever they may be, life in any form is sacred to the strings."

"We need their cooperation, Thyka. If we can't penetrate the strings to get the nanobots to Seriph and its moon, everything will fail."

"I know, Maliche. I have faith in the strings. They won't let us down. But I will stay in contact with them once we're out there and continue trying to allay their fears."

Maliche nodded and surveyed the room. "What else is going on? Launch day is getting terribly close."

A flurry of discussions, projected data, and holograms gave life to the room as they made final preparations.

Chapter Twenty

Blackness filled the portal in Seykel's personal compartment as she stared into space. She wore the traditional leather outfit of a Skatak, but the empty loop at her belt where her kital once hung stabbed at her heart. She felt like she was going into battle with only one arm. She pulled Thyka into a tight embrace. "I feel so useless. My skills are not much use against a battleship in space."

Thyka returned her mother's hug, her head leaning on Seykel's shoulder. She reached under a fold in her dress and pulled out a plainly-wrapped package. "If anything goes wrong, we may need your warrior talents, so I brought this for you." She held out the package for her mother.

"What is this?" Seykel took the heavy parcel from her daughter, eyes squinting, head tilting as if searching for something.

"Open it."

As Seykel unwrapped the bundle, a glint of silver caught her eye. She gasped as the final wrapping was removed. "How...? What in the...? My kital? It was broken. How is this possible? A broken kital is beyond repair." She fingered the blade's curves with a gentle touch of two fingers, her eyes brimming with tears.

Thyka, tears now flowing down her cheeks as well, smiled at her mother's shock. "The Gorvin have worked in metal longer than any other civilization. They have forging skills far beyond ours. Once I saw their grand city, I talked with Gnobis. Forgive me, but I stole the pieces from your cabin and showed them to him. He examined it and assured me it could be repaired. I wanted to surprise you with it."

Unable to take her eyes off her beloved heirloom, Seykel's tears dropped onto its gleaming surface. A minute passed before Seykel looked up into Thyka's face, threw her arms around the girl, and pulled her into an embrace worthy of any grendel. Her voice, choked and barely audible, found itself. "Thank you."

The two women held each other for a long moment before separating. Seykel made another protracted examination of her restored kital before tossing it into the air in a series of complicated patterns, finally hanging it on its belt loop. "We need to get to the bridge. Today we go to war."

The hatch slid open and mother and daughter stepped from the brightly-lit corridor into the darkened bridge. The hum of intership communication filled the room as they took their places amid the rapidly-changing lights of data streams and holo-vids showing at every station. Dominating the room, the main portal showed an enhanced view of the Skae battle fleet surrounding the planet Seriph, shimmering in the glow of cosmic string energy.

"Light sails have launched. At present rate of acceleration, they should reach one-half light speed in two hours and only minutes more to reach the planet. We must punch a hole in those defenses before then." Yalmut relayed his information to Jontar, who sat at Maliche's left in the center of the bridge.

Duvar called out to Jontar from his station. "High Commander Rutile reports the Gorvin fleet is ready to attack. Only the Tulop and its battle group will remain behind with us. He asks if we are in position to approach the strings."

After a quick glance at Maliche, Jontar responded with a wave of his talons. "Tell the fleet commander we are in position and ready to connect with the strings once the battle is fully engaged. Tell Subcommander Tufa to stand by."

Five minutes had passed when the main view screen showed the bulk of the Gorvin fleet powering up and darting into the distance, beginning a three-pronged attack on the Skae home world. Like a swarm of bimits surrounding their hive, the Skae vessels held their defensive positions but maneuvered to face the attack.

"Ships are within range, firing beam weapons now. Skae vessels returning fire." Yalmut spun out a running commentary of the battle as it progressed. Explosions burst from the grey metallic surfaces of ships in both fleets as focused shafts of high energy beams impacted them.

"There goes the first one!" Duvar pointed a stubby talon at the screen as a Skae battleship lit up in a brilliant soundless flash and ripped in two. Nearby vessels scattered to avoid the debris but maintained their constant fire.

"The Gorvin weapons appear to be doing more damage. Are the Skae ships not as powerful as we thought?" Maliche leaned in to Jontar, trying his best to sound calm.

"No, the weapons are equal in strength, but the Skae ships are not as heavily reinforced as the Gorvin's. Remember, the Skae tend to emphasize design over function. Nobody builds for durability like the Gorvin."

Yalmut called out from his station. "Six more Skae ships down. The fleet is preparing to deploy the railgun nanobots."

"Two Gorvin battleships down." Duvar indicated the drifting and burning hulks that were part of the center prong of attack. As he watched the screen, hundreds of Gorvin cruisers let loose with their railguns. The impact of the new weapon did not result in any explosions, merely the sudden appearance of large gaping holes in the sides of the ships they hit. The holes did not appear to be lethal, but in less than a minute, those vessels ceased firing and began to drift aimlessly.

"No power reading emanating from those Skae ships. The nanobots seem to be doing their job. They just took out fifty-three of the enemy."

Without warning, ten of the Gorvin cruisers and one heavy battleship exploded. Streams of heavy fire came in from above, and below the fleet.

"New Skae attack ships closing in, Gorvin ships taking heavy damage."

Maliche bolted up from his command chair and leaped to Yalmut's side. "What happened? Where did those ships come from?"

Yalmut waved over a few controls; his holographic display changed views and showed projections of the new combatant's flight paths. Tracing the pathways with the talon of one finger, Yalmut followed them back to their origin, a single cosmic string. "They must have been waiting in another sector before joining the fight. That string allowed them to transport in. I guess they aren't fully convinced of our intentions yet."

Thyka closed her eyes, composed her mind, and allowed her thoughts to flow out to the offending cosmic string. "This one is not like the others. It is angrier. It's almost as if it feels betrayal. I think this one has decided to work against the wishes of the others and fully aid the Skae."

Maliche turned to face Thyka, leaning on the back of Yalmut's chair. "Isn't there anything you can do? Can't you convince it to stop helping the Skae?"

"No, I can't. It's made its choice. But maybe I can try something else." She let her mind roam free again.

Jontar shifted in his chair, pointing to the main view screen. "What are those two strings doing? I've never seen strings move like that before."

As the bridge crew watched, the enhanced view screen showed two cosmic strings leaving the edges of the planet and surrounding the rogue string, cutting it off from the space around it.

Thyka sighed as she regained her composure. "The other strings were not happy with that string or with my request, but they agreed to prevent any further interference. We should be safe now from any more surprises."

Duvar pointed his chin at the screen. "Those new ships are making a mess of things. They just took out twenty more cruisers and two light battleships before the Gorvin were able to make adjustments. They sacrificed half of their group and appear to be retreating to join the planetary defenses."

Yalmut pulled up a new data batch on his panels. "Yes, but they wiped out one-third of the ships equipped with the nanobots in the process. I hope we have enough left to do the job."

Maliche stared at the view screen, now a mass of flaming vessels, some in pieces. The battle continued in a fierce exchange of energy weapons, but more difficult to follow now with the debris field growing by the minute. A crackle of the intercom broke the silence. Subcommander Tufa's voice boomed over the speakers.

"Twenty minutes until light sails arrive. Our fleet has opened up significant holes in the Skae defenses. It is time to move in and open up the string's energy field. Stay inside our protective cover." He hesitated a moment before continuing. "Are you certain you can shield all of us from their sensors?"

Jontar gave a quick nod to Maliche while holding up two talons held close. Maliche waved a finger pattern over the communication panel on the arm of his chair to respond. "Yes, we can maintain the shield, but only for a short while. And once we are in contact with the strings, we will become visible to the Skae. If you can bring us in with a string between us and the Skae, maybe we can stay hidden longer."

"Roger that. Subcommander Tufa to battle group, stay in close. Keep the pattern tight, no strays. Set for heading theta-nine-six, half thrusters... engage now."

The view screen showed the Tulop settling into position directly in front of Maliche's ship, the remainder of the battle group taking positions, completely surrounding them.

"Thrusters at half, maintaining position. Shield is holding," Yalmut reported as he studied his panel and simultaneously linked minds with Jontar and Duvar to build the sensory shield around their small pack of vessels. Any sensor sweeps from the Skae ships were absorbed by their efforts, creating a simulated hole in space as far as the Skae were concerned.

"Four hundred more Skae ships disabled, only minor casualties detected aboard those hit by the railgun nanobots. Five additional Skae vessels destroyed with massive casualties by conventional weapons. Twenty-three Gorvin ships destroyed or out of commission. Heavy losses reported. Fifteen minutes until light sails arrive." Yalmut continued his reports of the battle as they approached the glare of the string's energy field. He adjusted his controls to dim the brightness in the main view screen.

Maliche turned to face Thyka and her parents. "Time for you to do your thing, young lady. Are you up for this with only Jontar and Duvar to help?"

"I'm ready. The strings are much more receptive now." She hopped off her chair, gave her parents a long hug and headed off the bridge toward her cabin.

Seykel took Duvar's station while Nalot replaced Jontar at Maliche's side. He grinned as he watched Seykel caress her kital as she listened to the communications coming in to her station.

***

Back in her quarters, Thyka sat on a cushion on the floor and joined hands with Jontar and Duvar, linking their minds. Once again, as she slipped into her aura, she watched as the auras of her companions took form and solidified next to her. Sparks of color flashed around them as if they were made of electricity. The room was replaced by flows of color and patterns, ebbing and flowing like rivers of pure energy. In the distance, but rapidly approaching, appeared the blinding energy of the cosmic strings.

Thyka and the others remained still, allowing the strings to surround them. Her skin crawled as if armies of tiny electric bimits marched all over her. "Stay still." She cautioned Duvar as he squirmed with discomfort. "Do nothing to cause them alarm or concern. And let me do all the talking. Understand? No snarky remarks." She cast Duvar a withering glare, causing him to shrink and barely nod in agreement.

Reaching out with her aural hand, she touched the energy flow of the strings. The flows seemed to absorb her hand, joining with it, becoming one with it. "Hello. We have come to tell you it is time. Our devices are arriving soon and we need your permission to allow them to reach the Skae planet and its moon. Will you assist us?" Her voice glided like silk in a light breeze through the energy patterns.

A chorus of voices, like all the strings of an out-of-tune harfel playing at once, responded. "We are still concerned. How can we trust you will not eliminate the entire Skae race? We observe your war, and you have killed thousands."

"Have you not discovered the lies and horrors the Skae have inflicted on the rest of the galaxy? They have killed trillions and brought dozens of civilizations to extinction."

A silence followed briefly, accompanied by a deep feeling of sorrow and guilt, penetrating to their core. "We know of their atrocities and of their schemes. We agree their plans to engage the energy device they are building near the two stars must end. We will assist you to those ends, but how are we to believe you are different from them? We cannot allow genocide of even ones such as the Skae."

Thyka sat quietly, thinking when she felt a nudge at her right. She looked and Jontar sent her a mental request to speak to the strings. Studying him briefly, she nodded agreement.

Jontar's voice, while not as smooth and reassuring as Thyka's, still maintained a calming influence. "My friends. You examined us during our last visit with you. You have experienced our hearts and desires. But if you need further proof of our difference from the Skae, I offer this. Which of us has been open and transparent with you and which has hidden truth from you? Which of us has enslaved and ruled over others without concern for any but themselves and which of us is striving for freedom from oppression? You have examined us. Which do you view as the more trustworthy?"

A dissonant tone rang through the energy streams as if an argument had broken out among the strings. Then harmony returned. "Your words are powerful, but how do we know you are not hiding truth as well?"

Thyka replied before Jontar's growing irritation got the better of him. "Look at the battle we fight. Examine our weapons. Which of us is attempting to save lives and only disable the technology of the ships? While we both use weapons for killing, which of us using them only from necessity? We prefer to save as many lives as we can, even the lives of our enemy. We kill only because they leave us no alternative to reach the peace we desire."

The string energy field aura dimmed slightly, the voices quieted. Seconds later, the chorus sang out. "We understand now. Your devices will be permitted to approach the Skae planet and its moon. Be forewarned, however, if you have deceived us in any way, we will be forced to take actions we have sworn never to inflict on another since the darkness."

Thyka squeezed Jontar's hand, mentally asking him to return to silence. "Thank you, my friends. We will honor our promise. The Skae will not be destroyed, only restricted to this world, and isolated from traveling the galaxy. You will have no cause to regret assisting us."

Slowly lowering her hand, the energy flows separated and the strings receded into the distance, their chorus fading with them. The three unclasped hands and Thyka watched as Jontar and Duvar's auras faded into nothingness. She remained only briefly before allowing herself to re-inhabit her body. Darkness replaced the light, but a pale replica of the light grew behind closed eyelids.

"Thyka, are you alright?" She felt the gentle shaking of her shoulders as she regained full consciousness and opened her eyes.

"I'm fine. I always hate to leave. It's so restful there." She patted Jontar's hand on her shoulder, stretched her legs and arms, and allowed her friends to help her to her feet. "We need to get back to the bridge. I hope we were in time."

***

A minute later, the three stepped across the threshold of the bridge. A scene of horror greeted them on the view screen. The Tulop, spouting flames from dozens of breeches in her sides, hung in space before them. Only three of the battle group remained active, circling protectively around the flagship. The rest floated helplessly as a debris field around them, along with the remains of several Skae ships, all destroyed or disabled.

"It's about time. The light sails are only three minutes away. Will the strings allow them through? Maliche looked up from bandaging Nalot's leg. A red circle showed through the grey fabric of the wrap.

"What happened? Father, you're injured." Thyka rushed to Nalot's side, examining his face and body with her eyes and hands. "Where's Mother?"

Nalot winced as she touched his leg. "It's nothing; I caught a piece of shrapnel. I've had worse, believe me. Your mother is fine. She's back in our cabin letting Yalmut stitch her up. She hit her head on one of the panels during the attack, but she took out those four first." He shook a taloned hand toward the view screen. "Did you convince the strings to let the light sails through?" He held her arm, grip tightening with each word.

It was only then she noticed the bodies, seven in all, stretched out on the floor beneath the screen. Skae bodies. "Yes... yes we convinced them. The light sails will get through.

How did Skae get in here? What happened? Are you sure Mother is alright?"

"We're both fine. Help me into a chair." He grimaced as Thyka and Jontar helped him up, gently depositing him into the closest seat.

"One minute until light sail arrival." Maliche called out after returning to his command station.

"The Skae sent a small attack force against us. The Gorvins fought them off, but a boarding vessel escaped our attention and docked with us. Tol warned us at the last second, so we were ready when they stormed the bridge."

"Here they come." Maliche switched the view screen to show the planet. Thousands of streaks crossed the field of view instantly, continued for thirty seconds, and then the view returned to normal. Except for the few pockets of ships still fighting, nothing appeared amiss.

The bridge speakers crackled to life. "Subcommander Tufa here. We are intercepting communications from Seriph to the Skae vessels. It appears our nanobots are knocking out their technology at a rapid pace. Distress signals are arriving from every city. Even the moon is sending distress signals. They've never revealed themselves before. Things must be pretty desperate down there."

"How long before they take full effect?" Maliche asked. "Will anyone be able to leave the surface in time to avoid contamination?"

"Not a chance. The virus will take some time to work, but the nanobots will eliminate anything capable of escaping the planet before they can fire up the engines."

Duvar clapped his hands together and laughed. "Look at them! The Skae ships are all turning tail and heading to Seriph. Looks like they want to try rescuing their precious Modiri."

The crew sat transfixed before the view screen as they watched the remaining Skae fleet vanish through the cosmic string barrier. The speakers popped to life again.

"This is Commander Rutile to battle group seven. Commence rescue operations for all disabled Skae vessels. Provide oxygen and other supplies as needed. Do not... repeat, do not board ships or approach the planet without specific permission from me personally. Send drone ships with required supplies. All other able ships assist our people in your area. Report casualties and specific requests on beta frequency."

"Is that it? Is the war over?" Thyka gaped in amazement from Nalot to Maliche and back again.

"That's it, dear one. The war is over. You have done incredibly. You cannot imagine how proud I am of you." He hugged his daughter, feeling her tension relax as she pulled herself deeper into his chest.

Chapter Twenty-One

Four days later, after ensuring the Gorvins added protections to their ship against the tech nanobots, Maliche and his crew followed a reconnaissance team down to the Modiris' moon. As the vessels approached the landing pad, nothing appeared different except the lack of traffic and communication signals. A few Skae personnel could be seen in the vicinity, but they barely reacted to the arrival of the Gorvin spacecraft.

"They appear to be in a state of shock. Look at their faces." Seykel watched out a portal in her cabin with Thyka at her side. As the dust rose by their landing thrusters settled, she could make out greater details. "They look lost, like a child realizing its mother is gone."

"The Modiri can no longer tell them what to do. All communication is cut off, aside from direct word of mouth." Jontar's voice startled the two women as he spoke from their open doorway. "Imagine a hive of bimits suddenly cut off from their queen. Without someone telling them what to do, the Skae are incapable of making any but the most basic decisions. It will be much worse on the planet."

Thyka shook her head. "It didn't have to be like this. If they had only listened."

"They paid the price for their arrogance. They're lucky to escape with their lives after the millennia of destruction they caused. Nobody but the Gorvin would be so forgiving."

"Forgiving? This is horrible." Seykel hung her head and slid down from the portal. She turned on Jontar, a powerful rage rising in her. "Have you forgotten your ancestors... my people? We Kolandi suffered the effects of this weapon we just loosed on the Skae. Once we were a thriving, valued member of the intergalactic community. Hundreds of millions died of starvation and disease before our population leveled off at a level sustainable at a hunter-gatherer level of existence. The Skae now face that same fate."

Taking Seykel by the shoulders and gazing into her eyes, Jontar tilted his head and smiled. "No, I have not forgotten. This is why we are here. I convinced Rutile to allow us one shot at offering the Modiri our help in avoiding the fate of the Kolandi and other civilizations destroyed by the nanobots in the past. We are heading to meet them now. You are welcome to join us, if you wish."

★★★

"I'm not so sure I like this trip to meet the Modiri any better than our first visit. I don't miss the guards and interrogations, but this emptiness is eerie." Duvar shivered as a chill ran up his spine. "Where is everyone?"

The faint hum of their mag-lev cars was the only sound in along the streets of Alasar, the Modiri capitol city. The throngs of Skae citizens were now gone, replaced by the few individuals wandering aimlessly in rumpled and dirty clothes, obviously not washed in days, their faces blank and the palest shade of blue ever seen on a Skae. The soaring abstract structures still shone brilliantly in the morning light, seemingly mocking the gloom of its inhabitants.

"Time bring our offer to the Modiri." Jontar parked their mag-lev behind their Gorvin escort at the foot of the stairway leading up to the palace. Only the sound of a slight breeze rustling the nearby trees could be heard. Halfway up the stairway, he noticed a Modiri prelate stop suddenly, her face shocked into sudden awareness at the arrival of a working piece of technology. She turned and ran up the stairs two at a time, disappearing inside the large doors at the top.

"Do you think they'll listen?" Thyka nearly whispered her question, wary of disturbing the stillness.

"My bet is on that Tiphan schuteka refusing to even see us. These Modiri make the Skae look like saints." Duvar chuckled as he ascended the steps alongside Yalmut at the rear of the group.

Entering the palace, the companions walked to the throne room, their steps echoing in the empty hall. The door stood ajar, creaking slightly as Maliche pushed it open enough for them to pass through.

"So now you come to gloat and dictate terms." Tiphan, high priestess of the Modiri, all-powerful ruler of the Skae, sat alone on her throne. A shaft of light, dust motes dancing in its path, illuminated the transparent magnesium work of art. Intricate threads wove their patterns, reminiscent of the wind as they intertwined with each other in forms that escaped description but created beauty nonetheless. Tiphan's gown sparkled in the light, even though it was slightly wrinkled. Her dark curls swooped magnificently on top of her head, only a few stray strands escaping the restraints of her golden crown. "Very well. Say your piece. We are in no position to prevent you. But then be gone from our sight. You have nothing to offer us, and we have nothing of value remaining for you."

"Yep, gracious to the last. This ought to be interesting." Duvar whispered under his breath to Thyka, who kicked him in the ankle in response.

Maliche took a few steps forward, and bowed respectfully. "High Priestess, we want nothing from you. We do, however, offer a way to save your people from the horrors they face in the near future. We can help you prevent your people from suffering as all of you adjust to your new reality. Will you allow us to help you?"

Her laughter resounded through the throne room. "You offer us your help? The Brin, the Kolandi, their half-breed offspring, and let us not forget, the Gorvin, offer us help? The Modiri and The Skae ruled the galaxy... and you offer us your pity?" She spat on the floor and glared at Maliche.

"Tiphan, do not let your arrogance doom your people. You can still prevent the tragedies ahead. Swallow your pride and think of your people."

Tossing her hands in the air as if dismissing them, Tiphan leaned back almost casually. "Fools, we do not require your help. We will soon be rid of this plague. While your fleet was busy trying to destroy us, I gave the signal to activate the keugelblitzes. Soon our singularity generators will become operational and we will have a source of unlimited energy to undo your nanobots' destruction. Go now, before I have you arrested and executed, as I should have the first time we met."

"Your Skae subjects are helpless without your direction. You cannot communicate with the ships protecting the device, so they will be defenseless. Don't do this."

Another round of maniacal laughter erupted from her. "You pitiful little things. Do you think we did not anticipate your weapon's small chance of success? After our escape, several of my priestesses and prelates were dispatched to the Telphar System. Our fleet will be well prepared for you."

Maliche shook his head. "You are truly mad, Tiphan. That device will destroy half the galaxy. There is nothing, not even your precious singularity generator, to bring back your rule over the rest of the universe. I offered you a way to at least save your own planet. The destruction is now on your head." He turned and signaled for the others to follow him as he strode out of the hall. Tiphan's laughter and taunts followed them, growing dim as they left the palace.

"We have to stop that device. Why didn't we send ships there in the first place?" Maliche faced Jontar as they followed the Gorvin escort back to their ship.

"Gorvin fleet resources were stretched dangerously thin as it was. They couldn't afford to risk the assault with anything less. We didn't think they were this close to having the kak thing working yet. It was a risk we thought worth taking."

"One we have to take care of now. Get in touch with Dravite and let him know what has happened. He needs to inform Commander Rutile as soon as possible. How long before the device turns critical?"

Jontar looked up at the mag-lev's roof for a moment before responding. "A week, maybe ten days. After that, nobody can stop it. We have to get the nanobots there before it reaches critical mass."

Chapter Twenty-Two

"Two hours before we reach the device. Long range scouts report only a minimal Skae fleet. Only two cruisers, one battleship and a dozen assorted small ships." Subcommander Tufa reported the intelligence via holo-vid to Maliche and his crew as they sat in the conference room behind the bridge of their ship.

"How can they possibly hope to defend their device with so few ships? It's suicide." Nalot clicked his talons, now showing the wear and tear of abuse.

"Unless the scouts missed something. Maybe the Skae have more ships than we thought. Could they be hiding somewhere?" Jontar drummed his stubby talons on his leg as he studied the attack plans on his tablet.

Yalmut sighed heavily, swiveling in his chair. "Not unless the combined intelligence of generations of surveillance on the Skae has been wrong. They only had so many ships at the start. We have accounted for all of them."

"Tiphan seemed confident she could still win. Maybe she knows something we missed."

"There is always something the enemy knows which we do not. That is the nature of war. We prepare for what we can and adapt as the situation changes. Make your preparations." Tufa saluted with a closed fist to his shoulder and flickered out as the transmission ended.

"I hate surprises." Nalot grumbled under his breath. "They always bite you in the tail when you least expect it."

At the appointed time, Jontar released the controls connecting them to the cosmic string. The small fleet of Gorvin ships he brought with them on the string spread out into a defensive pattern surrounding the small Brin vessel. Ahead of them loomed the double star of the Telphar System. The stars' light ebbed and flowed as the thousands of asteroid-sized keugelblitzes orbited the stars collecting their energy, transmitting it to a massive central collector, which combined the small sources into a single massive beam of pure energy. The yellow-white beam vanished into the distance where, as Yalmut's sensors indicated, the gravitational wave generator absorbed it all, powering up in preparation of creating the massive singularity. It was this singularity the Skae hoped would ensure their complete dominance of the universe. They were too sure of themselves to admit the truth of the Gorvin data foretelling the destruction of half this galaxy. Once the device reached full power, four days from now, the Skae would have the supremacy to control all of the known civilized worlds.

"Engage all defensive shields. Enemy ships approaching on vector alpha nine-four-two." Sub Commander Tufa's gravel voice boomed over the bridge speakers. "Arm all energy pulse and nano-rail cannons. Prepare to open fire on my command."

"This shouldn't take long. Those Skae ships are—" The main view screen blazed so bright Jontar had to shield his eyes before finishing his sentence. Alarms blared and warning lights flashed on every station panel.

"What happened? What was that?" Maliche held a death grip on the arms of his command chair as Jontar sprang from one location to the next, helping regain control of the ship.

"Some sort of energy weapon fired from the largest of those collectors around the stars." Duvar frantically worked his controls, reading the information as fast as it appeared in front of him. "Both battleships took heavy damage but are still functional. Six of the ten cruisers are out of commission and we lost all but twenty-five of the smaller fighters. I don't know if any of the reserve fighters can be launched. Communications are still out."

"What's our status?"

"Long range sensors are dead. Engines only have one-third power. Surge circuits tripped everywhere, but our hull is intact and we should be able to maneuver... if we don't push it too hard."

"Is our stealth cloak still working?"

Duvar punched a few more controls. "Yes, our shield only took a minor hit. We were close enough to the Tulop that it took the brunt of the hit for us."

Through the view screen, Maliche watched as the Skae vessels closed and opened fire on the virtually helpless Gorvins.

Those ships still able to fight closed quickly with the enemy and laser fire erupted in a fierce battle.

"Can we contact Tufa?" Maliche scratched his crest feathers with his talons as he tried to think through the alternate strategies they had prepared. None of them considered anything like this.

Jontar returned to his station next to Maliche as the others brought their vessel back to life. "No, Father. We're on our own, at least for now."

"If we can get to that central collector, can you get inside and shut it down?" Maliche pointed to the focal point of the energy beams from all the smaller collectors.

Nalot and Jontar conferred and came to a quick conclusion. "No guarantees, but it appears to have at least two access points for maintenance personnel. If Yalmut and I can get inside, we should be able to connect with it and shut it down. The problem is getting there."

"I'll worry about getting us to the thing. You figure out how to turn it off permanently."

"They'll need protection in case the thing is protected by any Skae soldiers. Those Modiri probably know enough to protect such a vital key to their operation."

"In that case, I'm going with you." Seykel jumped down from her controls to stand in front of Nalot, hands on hips and daring him to disagree with her.

Nalot's mouth opened as if to object but shut immediately. His face contorted as at least four different arguments appeared to cross his mind, each one rejected before escaping his lips. He gave up and turned to Maliche, eyes begging for help.

"Don't ask me to try to stop her. I like all my parts right where they are." He held his hands palm up in resignation.

Nalot sagged in defeat and let out a mighty sigh. "The four of us, then. Let's make this quick."

Thyka ran up to her parents and enveloped them in a hug, or at least as far as her tiny arms could manage them both together. "Stay safe. I love you." Releasing them, she returned to her station, wiping tears from her eyes.

Fighting the urge to add his own cautions, Maliche gave the orders. "You four head to the airlock and get ready. Duvar, take the controls and get us to the nearest docking port on that satellite. Don't attract any attention if you can help it." He spared a long look over his shoulders, as Nalot was the last to leave. "Make sure everyone comes back alive. I'm counting on you."

Nalot simply grinned and waved a cavalier salute as he left the bridge. Maliche returned his attention to the main view screen as the small ship maneuvered through the wreckage of the ongoing struggle between the remaining Skae and Gorvin vessels.

"Those Skae ships are fast. The few nano-rail guns still functioning are having trouble getting a fix on them. Looks like this one will be decided by the fighters." Duvar kept a running commentary on the battle as they flew passed it. "There goes one of the Skae cruisers. The Gorvin are gaining the advantage."

"Not for long if that thing powers up and lets loose with another blast. How long before we can dock with it?"

"Another thirty seconds and we'll be there."

Back in the airlock, Jontar, Yalmut, Nalot, and Seykel donned breathing masks and armored pressure suits. Each picked up a laser pistol except for Seykel who attached her newly remade kital to a loop at her waist, stroking the blades with her fingers as she waited. A hard jolt and loud thunk announced their successful docking.

"Opening airlock door in three…two…one." Duvar's voice crackled in the speaker and the door slid up to allow them entry into the moon-sized collector.

"Keep your eyes on a swivel. Don't hesitate to fire at any Skae or Modiri you see. Don't give them a chance to shoot at you first." Nalot took the lead, stepping lightly on the metallic grid, which comprised the floor of this passageway. Dimly lit, the tunnel was lined with power cables and conduits, all labeled with warnings of high voltage, pressure, or temperature precautions, depending on their purpose. This facility displayed none of the artistic architecture typical of Skae designs. Pure functionality exuded every centimeter of the place.

"Take the next passage to the left. I'm sensing a small control room there. Not too far, probably some sort of remote auxiliary control center." Jontar removed his hand from one of the cable bundles and joined Nalot in the lead, his weapon at the ready.

"Everybody down!" Nalot shoved Jontar aside as an orange energy beam split the air where his head had been. "They must have vidcams watching the tunnels." Everyone dove for cover behind whatever protruding panels or bulkheads they could squeeze into.

"How many?" Jontar lifted his head only far enough to get a brief glimpse inside the control room.

"I counted three, but there may be more. You can be certain more are circling around to cut us off."

"Then we better act fast." Jontar raised his pistol and fired into the control room. Bursts of orange energy burned past him as the others joined in.

Shouts from both sides filled the air as the smell of ozone and burning circuits filled their nostrils. The return fire from the Skae diminished until only one soldier remained. Before anyone could react, Seykel's tiny figure flashed over them and into the room, her kital raised and flashing in the hazy light.

"Gentlemen, they're all dead. You can come in now." Seykel stood in the hatchway, smiling. Jontar stepped over the threshold, averting his eyes as Seykel yanked the kital from the last Skae soldier's forehead and wiped the blood off on his uniform.

"Make this fast, you two. We don't have much time." Nalot took up a position at the hatch they came through while Seykel guarded the hatch on the opposite side of the room.

"Yalmut, you take those controls while I work over here. You know what to do." Both Kolbri worked the controls as they sent their minds into the computers running the collector. Following the intricate pathways of circuitry, they gained control of the system, one system at a time, until their minds joined in the central processor.

"We need to burn out the controls allowing this thing to release the energy it collects. I found the files controlling that, but it will take both of us together to manage it." Yalmut's mind-voice showed Jontar the path to follow.

"Yes, I see it. Together then, but don't shut it down completely. We need it to overload slowly so we have time to get out of here with the others."

"Agreed. On my mark..."

Jontar and Yalmut leaned on the panels as they came back to their bodies. "It's done. We have ten minutes to get back to the ship and get away before it explodes."

"Follow me, then. Let's move." Nalot waved for the others to follow him, with Seykel bringing up the rear. As Jontar stepped through the hatch into the tunnel, he heard a thunk, like the sound of a heavy metal tool dropping into a metal bucket.

A flash of silver spun past Jontar's head and embedded itself in the neck of a Skae soldier a few yards down the passageway. "Get down! Fragger!" Seykel's scream, as she shoved Jontar to the ground, was drowned out by the ear-splitting explosion of a fragmentation bomb.

His head spun in dizzying whirls from the concussion. Jontar felt the trickle of something wet running down his face and slowly became aware of orange flashes of light above him. His lungs struggled to take in air as if a grendel were sitting on him. He distantly felt the pull on his arms as Yalmut dragged him down the passage and around a corner.

"Get him out of here. I'm going back to get Seykel." Nalot helped Yalmut lift Jontar to his feet, wrapping one arm around Jontar's waist and pulling one of his arms around his neck to support his barely-conscious friend.

"It's too late. She couldn't have survived that blast. You'll die if you go back." Yalmut adjusted Jontar's weight for better balance as he shouted at Nalot over the weapon fire.

"She's my wife. I'm not leaving without her. Get him out of here and get the ship to safety. I'll be right behind you." Nalot pulled Seykel's kital from the neck of the dead soldier and handed it to Yalmut. "You might need this. Now go!" With one last shove, Nalot let out a war cry and fired both pistols he carried while charging back into the control room.

Daring to look, Yalmut peered around the corner and nearly collapsed at seeing Nalot, holding Seykel's bloody and limp form in his lap, firing wildly, keeping the Skae soldiers at bay.

Tearing his eyes away, he pulled Jontar down the tunnel. "Come on, try to run. We don't have much time." He sent a desperate mind link to Jontar. *"Wake up! Run!"*

The effect was immediate, like a shot of adrenaline. Jontar, startled awake and needing only minor support, ran with Yalmut back to their vessel. Diving into the airlock, Yalmut took one last look down the passage before hitting the controls to shut the door. He yelled into the speaker. "Detach and get out of here as fast as you can." A lurch to the left and sudden acceleration sent the two crashing to the floor. Outside, shrinking into the distance, the collector satellite exploded in a massive burst of energy. The shock wave tossed the small Brin vessel like a cork in the ocean, but it held together and soon settled itself on a steady course back to the Gorvin fleet, or at least what remained of it.

A whoosh of air and the smell of fried circuits jarred Jontar's senses as the shock of Yalmut's mind link faded away. Strong arms, a pair on each side, escorted him to his cabin and helped him lay down on his padded cot. The room swam with his disorientation, but not as bad as a few minutes ago. Was it a few minutes? Or a few days? Hard to remember. He heard voices nearby, but they, too, faded as he drifted into a dreamless sleep.

He awoke to the touch of a cool, wet cloth on his face, and the sound of soft singing. A sad tune, but beautiful. He tried to move, but his muscles ached and decided it wasn't worth the trouble.

"So you've decided to rejoin the living. It's about time. Our friends weren't going to wait forever to celebrate their great victory. One less hero in the festivities wouldn't make too big a difference."

"Thyka? What are you..." The memory jumped back into him with both feet and landed hard. He reached out to take her hand.

"Thyka, I'm so sorry. I tried to... I mean, there was nothing I could..."

"It's alright, Jontar. Yalmut explained everything after we got you into bed. That was four days ago. There was nothing you could have done. The collector had to be destroyed." She sighed as her eyes drifted skyward. "At least they're still together. I don't think either one would have wanted to live without the other." She let out a tiny giggle. "And they died as two of the greatest heroes in the history of the galaxy. Mother would have enjoyed that one. She was always a little jealous of your father's stories of his ancestors." She wiped away more tears as they fell. "Oh, kupt. Here I go again. Not very Tolavarian of me."

Jontar grunted as he sat up and pulled Thyka into his arms. The two Kolbri clung together, each releasing their sorrow at the loss of their family and friends. Eventually sleep took them both as they lay together, comforted in their embrace and minds linked in silent, simple togetherness.

Chapter Twenty-Three

"Are you sure we have to do this again? I don't think I can handle another state dinner on another planet with another horde of adoring public figures showering us with titles and gifts." Duvar tugged at his neck, trying to loosen the tight collar of his ceremonial cloak. The past two months had been filled with an unending stream of parades and ceremonies celebrating the end of the war against the Skae. Untold numbers of interviewers on endless planets across Gorvin space and those from distant worlds once allied to the Skae, all wanted to honor the brave heroes from their own ranks. Tufa, greatest of the Gorvin heroes and much in demand, still limped from his injuries received during the final battle.

"You love every minute of it and you know it, Duvar." Jontar punched his friend on the shoulder and then put the last medal in place on his own cloak, grimacing at their reflections in the holographic mirror image. "This is the last of them, so we can go home in a day or two."

"How do you think a bunch of 'risen from the grave' galactic heroes will be received back home? They couldn't wait to send you and your father off to be incinerated in the sun."

Maliche stood in the doorway behind them, unannounced until his answer made them jump. "Ryma has been taking care of that little matter for us. She's made some significant changes to the Assembly since our departure. A few trusted allies were eventually let in on our ruse, and they helped gradually leak a few rumors about our survival. The traitor's trial helped expose the treachery they committed against our family and the people, swinging sympathy in our direction... and the broadcasts of all these celebrations touting us as the champions of this war haven't hurt, either."

"So you've been in touch with mother recently? How is she holding up?" Jontar tugged at his sleeves and collar, adjusting the fit of his ceremonial garb.

"Last night. She's well but is anxious for our return. The loss of our friends weighs heavily on her." Maliche shrugged and hung his head. A soft violet glow surrounded him.

Jontar approached his father in silence and laid a gentle hand on his shoulder. Yalmut and Duvar joined them, forming a mourning circle, heads bowed with arms outstretched on each other's backs. They held this circle for several minutes, each one lost in the memories of their departed companions, until Maliche broke the spell. "Time to go. We have a full day ahead of us."

Exiting their room, Jontar spied Thyka sitting alone on a small bench in the hallway. Her flaming red hair hung in long curls, intertwined with ribbons of gold and silver. She wore a long gown of deep green and displayed a heavy necklace of garnet, typical of the Tolavar. In her lap, she held a plain leather pouch containing her mother's kital. Her face was lowered with closed eyes. As Maliche and the others approached her, she gave a weak smile and rose to meet them. Jontar stepped forward and took her small hand in his. Together, they joined in their procession to the final celebration of their victory.

Chapter Twenty-Four

The farewell dinner, a private affair between friends, proved to be the perfect mix of somber reflection, and joyous celebration. The Grand Director of the Gorvin Congress had wished for a more formal reception, but discussions with Rutile, Tufa, and Dravite convinced him of the need for a smaller affair. He did, however, insist on holding the farewell celebration in his private quarters. No expense was spared. One of the finest symphonic orchestras on Kluton provided the music. Some of the finest artists and craftsmen donated pieces of their work as gifts to the departing heroes and all were on display. The table, finely carved stonework rising seamlessly from the floor and covered by a plain but beautifully woven cloth, held foods from all regions in the Gorvin territory.

"You do realize," said Calomel as she took another bite of something he called blutak, a sort of red meat dripping in orange gravy, "That with the Skae out of commission, your young Kolbri are the only ones who have the ability to navigate the cosmic strings. Your world is about to become the new center of the galaxy. Are you ready to become the leaders of the new reality?"

Maliche preened his crest and swallowed a mouthful of a slightly sour brew called suth. "Yes, your honor, we have had some talks about this turn of events. Jontar and the others have already begun communicating with the other Kolbri, those who were being trained by the Skae and others back home, and they are developing a plan to take control over intergalactic transportation requiring strings." He hesitated before continuing, shoving a piece of something greenish-yellow around his plate. "I would hope we can count on your help in setting up a type of central governing body for all the planets, Gorvin controlled, independent, even former Skae allies. We are not comfortable setting up another aristocratic system and hoped to move toward a more parliamentary central body where all planets are represented equally and all have a role in keeping the peace. An Empyrean, if you will."

Calomel sat back, rubbing her broad chin as she examined Maliche with a piercing gaze in an unreadable stony face. "There will be opposition. Those who already rule over some of the systems may need to be convinced of the wisdom of such a move. You will have no trouble from us. We have always maintained a rather light touch on our systems and work closely with them to provide for everyone under our influence."

"Do you think there will be more wars?"

Calomel let out a rumbling, harmonic chuckle. "Nothing like with the Skae, to be sure. And, if you use your authority over cosmic string transportation wisely... as a prize rather than a punishment, you may be able to gain support without actual bloodshed."

Maliche tilted his head and raised a goblet toward Calomel. "You have much more experience with matters of this magnitude than I do. I would deem it a great favor if I could have your support and guidance as we move forward."

Returning the gesture with her own goblet raised, Calomel's harmonic voice took on a much deeper, richer quality. "I would be happy to be of assistance in anything you require. Our fees and compensation for such services can be discussed later." The corners of her mouth raised ever so slightly, a beaming smile for a Gorvin. "Nothing too extravagant, I assure you, but with politicians, nothing comes free of charge."

Maliche laughed in reply. "That I am familiar with. It seems to be a standard across the universe."

The party lasted well into the night with everyone sharing stories of battles, family histories, lost friends, and a good bit of politics and commerce filling the time. Long after the bioluminescent lamps had dimmed for the evening, Maliche and his companions said their farewells and returned to their ship to prepare for an early departure. Full stomachs and time spent in good company led to deep and, thankfully, dreamless sleep for all.

***

In the morning, cargo bay loaded to overflowing with gifts from dignitaries and average citizens across the galaxy, natural sunlight filtered through the skylights in the above-ground hangar holding the now-battered ship Maliche and his crew had commandeered so long ago. Jontar fought his way back to consciousness as a sliver of sunlight penetrated his cabin's portal and struck his eyes. A shifting of weight next to him and a small arm across his chest brought a smile to his face. Since his awakening after his injuries, Thyka had moved in to his cabin. At first, she claimed he needed round-the-clock care and this made her job easier. She simply never left after he healed and he did not object. She smelled good, and her touch stirred him in ways he never imagined. Though nothing was ever said to the others, at least not by him, they all smiled when the two of them appeared together.

He sent a gentle thought to Thyka as she slept. *"Time to get up. We're going home today."*

"I'm awake, just enjoying your warmth before we head off into the cold of space."

"The ship still maintains a constant temperature. It's not cold inside."

She dug a knuckle into his ribs before snuggling in closer. *"It's the principle of the thing. Just thinking about all that cold space makes me cold."*

Jontar broke the connection and patted her on the hip. "We still need to get up." He pulled the thin heat-reflective blanket off and lifted himself to his feet.

"Five more minutes." Thyka mumbled as she gathered the blanket around her and turned her face to the wall.

An hour later, Thyka waltzed into the ship's cafeteria, her face, hair, and outfit set to perfection. The leather pouch holding Seykel's kital hung from her belt. She leaned in, gave Jontar a peck on the cheek, and ruffled his meager crest. "Thank you. I feel much better today." She emptied one of the meal packets into a bowl, added water and sat at the table next to him as steam rose from the mixture and a fruit meal breakfast loaf prepared itself.

"I thought you said five minutes. It's been an hour. We lift off in twenty minutes." Halfway through this comment, Jontar regretted opening his mouth but could not stop once he began.

Thyka's narrow-eyed glare would have cut him in half if it were an actual blade. "Bring me some strong tea, my love. I can't deal properly with ill-mannered buffoons without my morning tea."

Without another word, Jontar filled a mug and backed out of the cafeteria. From halfway down the passage he called back to her, "Love you too!" and sped toward the bridge.

***

"Prepare for string separation in ten seconds." Yalmut called out from his post. "Kodut orbit in one hour at cruising speed."

A flash of light, followed by the black of space filled the main view screen as the ship pulled away from the cosmic string that had transported them home in record time.

Thyka sent out her mind link to the string in farewell. *"Thank you for everything. I promise we will be more considerate in the future. Those like me will be trained in proper etiquette before linking with you."*

A massive, nearly overpowering presence filled her mind as the string replied. *"The gesture is not required but appreciated. Be forewarned, however. Now that we have been awakened to the abuse of our inattention, we will be more aware of those who join with us in the future. We will not tolerate using us with harmful intent."*

"Rest assured we are of the same mind on this matter. We, too, will not tolerate a repeat of the Skae's abuses in so far as our abilities allow."

"And therein lies the difficulty we perceive. Our study of your kind has revealed a basic nature, which desires good but often results in succumbing to your baser instincts. The Skae fell to their pride and arrogance. How long before others fall as well? You mean well, but you have not the power to prevent the abuse of others. We will take steps to illustrate the wisdom of listening to your better nature."

A chill ran down Thyka's spine. *"What steps?"*

A burst of images filled her mind, and then the string simply vanished from her thoughts.

Seconds later, Duvar bolted upright in his chair. "I'm getting a frantic message from the Gorvin. Something about Seriph."

He listened with one hand holding his earpiece steady, his eyes growing wider by the second. "They say it's gone."

Maliche turned to face Duvar's station. "What's gone? What are you talking about?"

"The planet Seriph. The Gorvin say it just vanished."

"That's ridiculous. An entire planet can't..."

"Yes, it can." Thyka interrupted, her face pale and in shock. "The strings took it away."

All heads turned to watch her as she slowly took her seat. "I was thanking them for their help when they gave me a warning. They said they would give us all something to think about before ever misusing them again. Apparently they shipped Seriph, all the Skae, and Modiri, off to the most remote part of the galaxy, and left them there at some distant time in the past."

Maliche felt the pit of his stomach lurch. "But they'll all die if we can't reach them. Surely they maintained a route for us to supply them as they adjust to their new zero technology status."

"No. The strings deactivated the nanobots and the viruses, don't ask me how, and removed themselves from that region of space. No strings are within a hundred light-years of the planet now. We couldn't reach them even if we wanted to. They are far removed from us in time as well as space."

"How can they move an entire planet so far so fast? And into the past? I sensed they were powerful beyond belief, but this is beyond anything I could have imagined." Jontar fell back in his chair as he thought about the potentials the strings possessed.

Yalmut shook his head slowly. "They are completely isolated. Even with an ability to regain their technology, the Skae are no longer a threat to anyone."

Maliche preened his crest and resettled himself. "Inform the Gorvin of the situation and tell them to spread the word of the strings' warning. I pray to The Eternal it will be enough to keep everyone from doing anything stupid. For now, let's get home."

With the touch of a few controls, Yalmut brought the ship around until Kodut sat in the center of the view screen. It hung in space, blue, green, and brown like an oasis in a vast desert, growing rapidly as they approached.

Maliche touched the controls to open his microphone. "First Town space port, this is the Amaethon on approach vector delta four. Do you acknowledge?" A few anxious seconds of static filled the bridge as they waited for a reply.

"Amaethon, this is First Town space port. We read you and welcome you home. We've been anticipating your arrival. Synchronize ship computer settings to planet standard and set coordinates for landing pad one A. There's quite a reception waiting for you there."

Maliche watched as his crew collectively relaxed and began to smile. "Copy that, First Town. We're happy to be home."

Forty-five minutes later Yalmut glided the ship to a soft touchdown in the center of the landing pad. "All thrusters off, commencing shutdown. Releasing locks on outer hatches."

Nobody moved. Each member of the crew was lost in their own thoughts and feelings, coming to terms with everything they had been through.

"Come on, you bunch of stiffs. Let's go breathe some real home-grown air again." Duvar clapped his hands together and jumped to his feet, pulling at Yalmut's arm and grinning from ear to ear.

Roused from their thoughts, they hugged and slapped each other on the back. Duvar lifted Thyka above his head and spun in a circle. A look of fright on his face, realizing the risk he had just taken with the fiery young woman was quickly extinguished when he saw her lit up with laughter and aglow with joy. With a quick hug, he placed her on the ground before she could change her mind and rejoined Yalmut as he left the bridge.

At the hatch, they stood aside and allowed Maliche to lead them. Light from a bright blue sky blinded them briefly as it flooded the hatchway. Maliche led the way down the ramp, filling his lungs with the brisk, fresh air of home, followed by Duvar and Yalmut, arm in arm, and Jontar and Thyka, holding hands. Waves of shouts and applause mixed with a blaring horn band greeted them.

Maliche inhaled deeply all the familiar scents of home and reveled in the feel of the breezes against his face. He broke into a run when he saw Ryma waiting at the bottom of the ramp. He collided with her, gathering her into an embrace neither was willing to break. He took in the scent of her skin and hair and listened with near-rapture to the sound of her voice. It didn't matter that what she said was beyond his comprehension. He was home and with Ryma.

The throng continued to shout and cheer as the others stepped off the ramp. The crowd kept a respectful distance from the loving reunion until they could resist the urge to join the heroes no longer. Soon Ryma and Maliche found themselves the center of a crushing embrace.

Composing herself, Ryma addressed her family and friends. "We can continue this display in private later. For now, the public is eager to greet our returning heroes... the saviors of the galaxy." She gave Maliche a quick elbow to the ribs as she said the last part, and leaned in close to whisper in his auricle. "And that is the *last* time you will hear such nonsense from my lips. I knew you when you were a simple archaeologist, my husband. Don't think I will ever see you as more than you are."

She led them up a staircase to a temporary platform erected so the gathering throngs could witness the ceremony. Holo-vid cameras zoomed around them by the dozens. Their images, at least three stories tall, appeared on the walls of nearby buildings for the distant late arrivals to see. Dignitaries from all the guilds and cities around the globe sat on chairs attached to risers built into the platform. All of them were standing and cheering.

"Wave at the people. You're all great heroes now, so you need to play the part." Ryma, with Rilo and Neri close behind, signaled for the group to gather on the stage and greet the crowd, some of which had been gathering for days once their arrival date was announced. Stunned by the enormity and enthusiasm of the reception, none of them moved at first, until a gentle nudge by Ryma set Maliche in motion.

"Weren't these the same ones clamoring for your head the last time we were here?" Duvar said in Jontar's ear.

After everyone took their seats and a few brief introductions were made, each of the twelve guild masters took their turn at the podium to give their grand speeches, carefully edited and approved in advance by Ryma herself. Each one, while full of praise and admiration for Maliche and the others, included a well-crafted apology, of sorts, usually phrased in terms of being duped by the treasonous lies, and fabricated so-called evidence perpetated by Nissend Honj and his family. Each one concluded with a declaration of fealty to the Rocker family and the Assembly.

The sun crossed well past its zenith before all were done. Then Ryma strode to the stand. Her long dark hair draped perfectly over one shoulder, the small tiara of her station as Princess to the Kolandi sat sparkling on her head. The simple but elegant white gown flowed regally around her. Interwoven threads of silver caught the sun and seemed to glow. She stood for a moment before raising one hand to bring the crowd to silence.

"My people, Brin and Kolandi alike, for we are all now one people, we are indeed here to celebrate the return of our loved ones and to celebrate not only the end of a long and cruel war," she gave the slightest of glances toward the guild masters, "but also to usher in a new prosperity. We have lost some of our dearest and most trusted friends." Holographic images of Seykel and Nalot appeared above and behind the stage. The two appeared to hold hands and gaze out over the gathering. "Their sacrifice is a symbol of the unity which should be in all of our hearts and minds. They died for each other and for all of us, Brin and Kolandi alike, so we could face the future together in their memory. Today, we celebrate. In ten days, we will mourn our loss. A new and bright future awaits us. Let us welcome it together and prove to all the inhabitants of this universe who fought and suffered on our behalf that we are worthy of their sacrifice."

Signaling for the others to join her, they rose and joined hands, held high. The crowd went mad with cheers and shouts. In the midst of the mayhem, those gathered on the stage witnessed Brin and Kolandi citizens embracing each other, and celebrating together as equals.

Maliche bent over to speak in Ryma's ear. "I hope this is not a passing fancy, soon to be forgotten in the resurgence of old prejudices."

"We will make sure it is not. The eyes of the galaxy are on us now. We have no choice."

Chapter Twenty-Five

As promised, ten days later, the funeral preparations were carried out. Of course the coffins were ceremonial; Seykel and Nalot's remains now rested among the stars. Representatives from not only the guilds but hundreds of planets attended. Calomel, Dravite, Rutile and Gnobis represented the Gorvin and offered Tufa's apologies. Despite his insistence of health, the doctors prevented his traveling in space due to his injuries and continued rehabilitation requirements.

The day reflected everyone's mood as thick grey clouds hung low in the sky, threatening to unleash the rains common in this season. A chill breeze blew, pushing fallen leaves across the ground. The kilometers-long procession wound its way through every sector of First Town. Throngs gathered on every sidewalk and hung from every window along the way. Banners, both manufactured and homemade, hung everywhere, displaying the image of Seykel and Nalot as they had appeared in holographic form above the crowd ten days earlier.

Leading the somber and nearly silent procession was the caisson carrying both empty coffins. Alongside them stood all those who, in life, had been closest to Seykel and Nalot. Brin, Kolandi, and Kolbri alike rode in the open air for all to witness. At the front, Thyka, only child of the two being escorted to their final resting place, stood gravely between them, one hand on each simple but elegantly-carved wooden sarcophagus. To her left and right stood Ryma and Maliche Rocker. Behind them stood Opet, and Tola Shatal, now The Elected One among the Tolavar, Danet, and Jontar, with Yalmut, Duvar, Rilo, and Neri at the rear. As they passed by, individuals in the crowds of mourners tossed brightly colored pieces of ribbon and white flower petals on the road before them in honor of both Brin and Kolandi rituals. The route took them to a prepared gravesite in Founder's Park, near the memorial built to honor Karm, Maripa, and the first Jontar Rocker. It was considered a fitting location so all who came to visit could be reminded of not only the struggle to survive on this world but the ongoing sacrifice required of all who want to thrive in a civilization built for them by those brave souls who came before them.

Tola Shatal and Haytk, high judge of the Assembly, acted as co-celebrants of the burial ceremony. The caskets sat on a catafalque standing in front of a marble mausoleum, carved with images of the two fallen heroes and scenes of significance from their past, including their final act of bravery. Each said a few words and performed funereal rituals of each race. At the end, Thyka rose, with Jontar at her side and her arm draped over his for support, and approached the coffins. She did not speak, but only said a silent final prayer of farewell, sending her thoughts into the empty boxes.

"Mother... Father, I don't know how I will ever go on without you and your guidance. I miss you more than you will ever know. Thank you for everything. Thank you for your strength and your love, even when I least deserved it. Your bravery has brought our two people together at last. I will use my abilities and my status as Tolavar to serve as a constant reminder so no one ever forgets." She paused, giving a brief glance toward Jontar under her lashes. *"I also ask for your blessings on Jontar and me. I pray we are as strong and as full of love as the two of you."*

She nodded silently to Jontar, turned, and walked arm-in-arm with him back to their seats. Maliche Rocker, newly reinstated as Head of the Assembly, rose and addressed the gathering.

"As we lay our brave and selfless friends to rest, here in this place of honor," he turned to look up at Karm's obelisk, "We remember hard times and good times. Today is a day for forgiveness and consolation. It is a day to celebrate a new beginning. We are about to embark on a journey unlike any other. The galaxy now looks to us. We must be prepared to answer. I will not mar this day with political speeches; our friends deserve better. I only wish to thank you for your heartfelt outpouring of sorrow, and to promise brighter days to come. I know we will embrace this brave new Empyrean we have been called upon to lead as one people, together and unbreakable, from within and without." He turned and stretched out a hand toward the two coffins. "May we prove ourselves to be their equals."

Chapter Twenty-Six

"**F**ive years and we've only begun to fill a fraction of the need for string pilots." Jontar paced his office floor, adding to the worn path already showing in the floor.

"It's a good thing we had so many Kolbri already in training with the Skae before we uncovered their secret. At least there are enough to cover most of the basic needs in every sector... for now." Duvar, surprisingly efficient and capable as an administrator, especially since his marriage to Thyka's Kolandi cousin, or third sister, or whatever she was — the intricacies of Kolandi family relationships still confounded him — sat with his tablet displaying holographic charts and tables of the recent training efforts. "We're still on track for meeting the growing needs, so long as all those Brin and Kolandi 'patriots' continue their enthusiasm for making new little Kolbri string pilots. Most of the little ones are showing plenty of ability for piloting. Your two are among the strongest, as expected for Rockers."

A sudden thought interrupted Duvar's chain of thought. "Speaking of which, how is Thyka doing? She must be ready to burst soon with your third, if my calculations are right. I heard she's still traveling to the Eastern Continent in her duties as Tolavar to her tribesmen. Shouldn't she consider settling down and stopping all her ocean hopping, at least until after the birth?"

Jontar halted in his tracks and raised his eye feathers. "You want to tell her that? Be my guest. I can always ask father if you can be buried next to Nalot and Seykel."

"She takes her work to keep us all united very seriously, doesn't she?"

"Yes, but she still finds the time and energy to be with us or bring us with her. Don't worry about us, Duvar. We're very happy and the children are young enough to still think of this as a grand adventure. We'll settle down someday, but there's too much still to be done."

"Tell me about it. Syla wants me to step down at some point and quit gallivanting around the sector inspecting the training camps. I can't do that until I've trained a decent replacement. That won't happen for a few years to come yet."

"Someday, my friend, some day."

***

Maliche, showing the grey crest and deep wrinkles of time, took his place at Ryma's side for the swearing-in ceremony. His knee creaked as he lowered himself into the comfortably-padded chair. The entire membership of the Assembly, now a fully-integrated compilation of Brin and Kolandi, with one or two of the oldest of the Kolbri, gathered for transfer of authority. Ryma, now chief judge after Haytk's retirement seven years earlier and due to retire herself in a few months, rapped for attention. Still regal, even in the plain robes of the judiciary, her silver hair shone in the spotlight, setting off her brown face, now also showing signs of age.

"In the ten years since the end of the war and the return of peace to our world, we have proved ourselves worthy of the duty placed on us by those who have departed and now rest in honor. It has not been easy and there have been struggles, but we have overcome them as one and earned their legacy and the respect of uncounted worlds who have contributed to our prosperity." She waited as a wave of applause washed over the gathering. "But all things change. It is time to honor the past and look forward with eagerness to a new leadership. Will the honorees step forward?"

Maliche and Jontar rose from their places on opposite sides of the long bench of judges and stepped forward until they stood together in front of Ryma. The dignitaries all stood with a thunderous ovation for the father and son who had worked so tirelessly for so long and righted so many wrongs of their civilization.

After a few minutes, embarrassing minutes as Maliche would later recall, everyone took their seats.

"Hi, Daddy! That's Daddy!" A loud, high-pitched voice cried out from the first row. Jontar's youngest daughter, Eisoph, named after the Gorvin scientist who helped raise the first alarm to the Skae's nefarious scheme, sat squirming in Thyka's lap, trying to escape so she could run to her father. Laughter broke out among the crowd as they witnessed mother and daughter struggling. Jontar jogged the few steps to his daughter, swooping her up into his arms. Returning to his place beside Maliche, he jostled Eisoph on his side until he had a firm hold on her. The girl, all smiles, looked around the room until her eyes settled on Ryma. "Hi, Gramma! Can I have a cookie?"

After the dignitaries regained their composure once more and Thyka uncovered her scarlet face, Ryma called for attention and continued the ceremony. "It is with great honor and a full sense of personal pride that I now pronounce Jontar Rocker, having been duly elected and accepted by all those present, Head of the Assembly."

At her nod, Maliche passed the short carved stone staff, inlaid with copper and amethyst, symbol of leadership, to his son. Once more, the assembled body rose and cheered. Ryma stepped down to join her husband and son. Thyka, carrying one child and hanging on to the wrist of another, completed the reunion. Tugging on his shirt to pull him lower for a kiss, she held him level with her sparkling eyes. "Well, I hope this at least means you'll be staying on this planet now. There's a lot of work to be done around the house and I've got your list waiting for you." She winked and released him.

"I love you too." He laughed as he raised up, returning her wink, and lifted Eisoph high above his head, laughing louder than he had in years.

Epilogue

Deep in space, on a lonely world at the far end of the galaxy, a small group gathered to celebrate.

"One-hundred-twenty-three years and we are finally ready to complete our destiny." Tiphan, high priestess of the Modiri, raised a glass of torshill scent crystals and sniffed deeply.

"Our destiny!" The rest of the Assembly raised their glasses in return and also breathed in the nourishing vapors rising from the crystals. They were all gathered in Tiphan's reception hall. Lyrith and Zephyl, now raised to Tiphan's seconds, as well as Lek, former ambassador to the hated Brin, and Molk, commander of the former Skae battle fleet, now relegated to head of scientific development and coordination of efforts to rebuild their gravity well generator in this new region of space.

"Is everything ready for activation tomorrow?"

Molk seemed to stand at attention, even while seated. "Yes, high priestess. Everything is in place and ready for your command to make the facility operational."

Tiphan's smile would have reminded any Brin or Kolandi of one of the viperous lepti on Kodut. "Very well, then. With the power we will generate from our new generators we will take our fleet back across space, and with the invincible weapons powered by the devices, we will have our revenge on our enemies. To victory over those who oppress us!"

"To victory!"

***

As the new sun rose on Seriph, dimmed by the swarm of keugelblitz collectors surrounding it, Tiphan stood on her balcony naked to fully breathe in the morning air, reveling in the thought of the dawn of their revenge finally arriving. Her skin felt charged with the excitement.

"Would you care for first meal on the terrace, high priestess?" Zephyl strode through the diaphanous curtains hanging in the frame separating Tiphan's private quarters from the balcony, already dressed in her finest, a sheer light green wrap that left her midriff and long legs exposed and only barely providing cover for the rest of her slim form.

"No, the morning breeze has been nourishing enough. I will partake of the vapors when we celebrate the activation of the collectors. You may dress me now."

Three hours later, Tiphan strode into the main hall of the research facility responsible for completion and start-up of the collectors and gravity well generator. Lyrith and Zephyl followed close behind. The gathered Skae scientists bowed at the waist and lowered their eyes to the floor, except for Molk. She lowered herself into the travelling throne she used whenever visiting the planet and waited as her seconds adjusted her gown to perfection. With a clap of her hand, the scientists sprang into action, busying themselves at a wide array of panels, each providing updates and values of the collectors as everything was brought on line.

"We are ready for your word, High Priestess." Molk lowered his eyes, his version of a bow.

Tiphan surveyed the Skae around her and smiled her viperous smile. "You may activate the device."

A hum rose in volume as all displays indicated the collectors coming to life. On a large view screen, holographic images of their sun and the devices hung in space. Slowly one, then another, shot a beam of energy toward the moon-sized wave generators. As more collectors activated, a growing number of beams started the wave generators to show signs of building up their energy levels.

"Full capacity in three minutes." One of the scientists reported to Molk.

"Fire the generators when ready. Prepare for singularity formation."

With a flash of blue-white light, all seven gravity wave generators fired their streams of pure energy to a central point. Tiphan shielded her eyes from the brilliance. After a few seconds, the focal point of the rays seemed to collapse, replaced by a sphere of total blackness, surrounded by a film of swirling distortions.

"Singularity achieved and holding stable."

Tiphan nearly burst from her throne in excitement. "Prepare to energize fleet engines and weaponry. The fleet will depart before this day is over. General, are the directional reflectors in position? We will need —"

Alarms sounded at every station.

"What is happening, Molk?" Tiphan's excitement turned to terror.

***

In a distant region of space, a research vessel from Shyfar, once a Skae world but now assimilated into the new Empyrean, recorded data from distant stars in the hopes of finding new worlds to settle. In a region of space only sparsely populated by a few stars, so remote and not accessible by cosmic strings, that their light took a thousand years to cross the distance, a supernova burst into view.

"There goes a new one, sir. How do you want to catalog it?"

Peering at the view screen only half-heartedly, the captain shrugged and returned to his duty list. "Let the stellar astronomers deal with it. Make a note in the log and pass it along."

***

Thyka Rocker, revered Tolavar and mother, wife and reluctant heroine, sat in her cabin during one of her rare visits to space on a diplomatic mission to help celebrate the opening of a new Kolbri training facility. As was her habit on space voyages, she sent out her thoughts to the string, which transported them on their journey. With a start, and a catch in her breath, she sat up and looked out the hexagonal portal into space. There in the distance, in the midst of a vast black expanse, a single bright star, one which had not been there an hour ago, burst into view. A tear ran down her face.

"We gave them their chance. If only they had listened."

About Jim Cronin

I was born in Kansas City, Missouri and lived in Arlington, Virginia before moving to Denver where I attended High School and eventually college at Colorado State University, graduating with a degree in Zoology and a teacher certification. I currently live near Denver in the small town of Parker.

My career as a middle school science teacher lasted for thirty-five years, but I am now semi-retired, working part-time as an educator/performer at the Denver Museum of Nature and Science. I have been married for thirty-nine years to the love of my life. Together, we raised two incredible sons, and now have three incredible grandchildren to spoil rotten.

Social Media Links

Website: http://jimcroninscienceedutainer.weebly.com/

Twitter: https://twitter.com/authorjimcronin

Facebook:
https://www.facebook.com/JimCroninScienceEdutainer/

Goodreads:
https://www.goodreads.com/author/show/14203201.Jim_Cronin

Acknowledgements

This has been an incredible journey. Along the way, I have had the assistance and guidance of many wonderful individuals. I would like to take this time to thank all of you who helped me become the author I am today.

First of all, to my wife, Diane, thank you for your understanding and patience with me and all the times I spent hidden away in my office working on these stories. You are the love of my life and an incredible friend and partner.

To my brother Mike, who started me on this journey with his challenge to me to try writing a book, and all the brainstorming sessions we spent developing the characters and storylines. I may not have always agreed with, or used your thoughts, but you opened my eyes to a new world of exciting adventures and learning.

To all of my editors: Meredith, who bravely took on my very first attempt, as horrible as it was, thank you for treating my work with the same patience and understanding you give your students. Arsen, as much as it hurt to see the total dismantling and shredding of my first book, the time you spent teaching me why each change was necessary and opened my eyes to how a story is built from the ground up. Susan and Cat, your insights and suggestions proved to be invaluable improvements to my efforts and continued my education in the world of writing. Fred, your contributions added the final professional touches I needed to make the stories ready for the public. Each of you provided me with the skills and knowledge to produce these books and I appreciate all of your efforts. I hope my stories have proved to be a source of pride in your accomplishments and effort to teach me the English language and hoe to put words together appropriately.

To all of you at Solstice Publishing, thank you for your faith in me and all of your encouragement and assistance in teaching me the business of being an author. This has been, and continues to be a great adventure.

Finally, to all my readers, especially to those who have left such wonderful reviews, Thank you. I am always amazed when I read how much total strangers enjoy my novels. You continue to provide me with the fortitude to continue writing. I have more works in mind and in process, so even though I am leaving the universe of the Brin behind, I look forward to sharing more adventures with all of you.

Awards and Reviews for The Brin Archives

Hegira:
Readers Favorite Award
Pinnacle Award For Excellence
New Apple Award
Literary Titan Award

Recusant:
Readers Favorite Award
Pinnacle Award For Excellence
Literary Titan Award

Reviews:
"Hegira is a very well-written story that combines so many complex layers that I was thinking about it for days after I finished reading it."

"I was really impressed with Hegira - the breadth of areas within scifi that is covers is mind-blowing! Fantastically well written - Book 2 of the series is on my wish list!"

"Mr. Cronin has created a reality with this series which will captivate and enthrall readers, young and old, for many years to come. I highly recommend *Recusant*, and the entire *Brin Archives* series."

"A superb sequel to Hegira with Cronin at the top of his game, Recusant sees an intelligent and compelling Science Fiction series go from strength to strength. It is highly recommended."

"Empyrean is must read for science fiction fans. It is the third book in The Brin Chronicles and I was excited to read this after reading the first two. It kept me engaged from the beginning and I couldn't stop turning the pages! The story was crafted well and it keeps you guessing as Mr. Cronin throws you surprise after surprise. You grow emotionally attached to the characters and it has all of the components of a great sci-fi book. I will be recommending this book, as well as the whole series, to everyone I know!"

"Cronin has given us a fantastic quest story that expands already upon his established universe. For any long time reader of the series, Empyrean will not be a disappointment and should be a satisfying way to send off the series. Cronin writes in a way that brings to mind some of the classics of the science fiction genre, but also with a slight flair all his own. His prose bespeaks of Bradbury and Heinlein, though there is enough of a bend that his prose can speak for itself."

Media and Purchase Links:

Amazon (Hegira): https://bookgoodies.com/a/B010E3EKC6/

Amazon (Recusant): https://bookgoodies.com/a/B01KTVTMNK

Amazon (Empyrean):
https://bookgoodies.com/a/B077ZBQWDT

Project 9 Vol. 2:
https://www.amazon.com/Project-9-2-Arthur-Butt/dp/1625264372/ref=sr_1_2?s=books&ie=UTF8&qid=1494
881996&sr=1-2&keywords=project+9+vol+2

Project 9 Vol. 3:
https://www.amazon.com/Project-9-Vol-Debbie-Louise/dp/1625266545/ref=sr_1_1?s=books&ie=UTF8&qi
d=1521392084&sr=1-1&keywords=Project+9+vol+3